Praise for *Nobody's Dream*

Have you ever read a book that touched you, not just in a weepy, that's so sweet kind of way…no, I'm talking about one that reaches into your soul, finds all the broken bits, pulls them out and puts it all back together again better than it was before. This is the kind of book that requires an entire box of tissues, a bottle of wine and a few cold showers! …As a survivor of abuse, I thought my demons were behind me. I thought I was healed. I thought I'd forgotten. But in these 700+ pages, I found that burying the past isn't healing, I learned that only in facing down those demons could I find true healing.

~ **LovingAngel1231, a review**

~ ~ ~

What stood out, first and foremost, was that this book is bursting with pain. Lots of pain for both Cassie and Luke, and his horses too. And the second thing, is hope. Once Cassie sees, really sees Luke, it's beautiful, truly beautiful.

~ **Debbie, a review at Archaeolibrarian—I Dig Good Books!**

~ ~ ~

I'm not even sure I could pick out a favourite moment because there just simply are too many to choose from. There are so many aspects to the book. It's not just one of the best love stories ever. It's a story of healing, learning to trust again, renewing of the soul, and acceptance.

~ **Carrie, a review at Bears Read, Too!**

~ ~ ~

A beautiful story, A sensual kiss of hope rather than the sexual intensity portrayed in the rest of the Saga and that's how this story should have been written. For those of you who are interested in Kally but don't really go for BDSM…then this is your book! …What Kally does probably better than almost every other writer I enjoy is to bring out my emotions in depth. I am invested in these characters, in a very special way they are real.

~ **Shauni, a review at Tea and Book**

~ ~ ~

I wish I could give this book a "10"!!! …I have been trying to find the words to describe this amazing book, but I come up short! Magnificent, incredible, outstanding, soul-searching, and so many other adjectives! I'm not one to re-hash the storyline in my review, so I will merely

~ **GIGIreadsalot, a review**

Rescue Me Saga
Reading Order

For the most part, the books in this series are not stand-alone novels. Please read in order.

However, *Nobody's Lost* could be read as a new entry point to the series.

In a saga, of course, characters recur to continue working on real-life problems in later books, so Megan and Ryder, the main couple in this book, will return in *Nobody's Dream* and subsequent books.

For the most part, the books in this series are not stand-alone novels. Please read in order.

However, *Nobody's Lost* could be read as a new entry point to the series.

In a saga, of course, characters recur to continue working on real-life problems in later books, so those starting with this book, I hope, will go back and read through the entire series if they enjoy it!

The first six Rescue Me Saga titles are available in e-book and print formats:

Masters at Arms & Nobody's Angel (Combined Volume)

Nobody's Hero

Nobody's Perfect

Somebody's Angel

Nobody's Lost

Nobody's Dream

kallypsomasters.com/books

Kallypso Masters will be working on more books that will include characters from the Rescue Me Saga, but some will be in spin-off series (including a trilogy with three romances featuring Mistress V. Grant, Gunnar Larson, and Patrick Gallagher). As much as she loves engaging with her readers, Kally writes by inspiration and follows the dictates of her characters, so she cannot write to deadlines or predict whose story will come next. Be sure to subscribe to her newsletter so you can be sure not to miss any release announcements!

At this point in time (May 2015), next up seems to be a story about Kristoffer Larson and Pamela Jeffery. You met Pamela very briefly in Chapter 18 of *Somebody's Angel*, but have yet to meet Gunnar's relative, Kristoffer. Stay tuned!

Nobody's Dream

(Sixth in the Rescue Me Saga)

Kallypso Masters

Nobody's Dream
Sixth in the Rescue Me Saga
Kallypso Masters

To discover more about the books in this series, see the *Rescue Me Saga* section at the end of
this book. For more about Kallypso Masters, please go to the About the Author section.

Dedication

To my husband, affectionately known by my fans as Mr. Ray or Hubby. You've put up with me all these years and are truly *my* Luke. Patient, consistent, honest, and loving. I'm looking forward to many more years with you and promise not to hide out in my office so much (well, unless I'm on deadline). Love to you from the depths of my soul. And now enjoy Cassie's story. I know she's been your favorite character in the Saga so far and hope my telling of her story exceeds your expectations!

To Toymaker, who has been a long-time source for me on my BDSM scenes, please continue to improve and listen to your brat!

Acknowledgements

Bringing this book to you—the longest book I will ever write—has been a monumental effort. I have so many people to thank for helping me publish the best book I can, including:

My editorial team for this book includes Meredith Bowery, Fiona Campbell, Rebecca Cartee, Jacy Mackin, Ekatarina Sayanova, and Jeri Smith. We began the editing process in June 2014, but my bout with cancer and need to have major surgery derailed plans to release it in the fall. Most of them came back this year after I finished the story. They put up with my promising them a 170,000-word book (that is now at just under 230,000 words), with my missing deadlines and having meltdowns— and always had my back. Rebecca is the newest member of the team. She came on at the last minute to proofread and did such an amazing job of editing, I plan to make her a member of the team moving forward. Saya helped me make sure my lifestyle references are impeccable not to mention my grammar! Meredith knows the characters in this saga like members of her family and when I am off on someone's motivations or actions, she let's me know about it. Fiona provides her expertise on medical matters and, along with Rebecca, tries to get me to embrace the semi-colon. Well, I did accept a few of them! Jeri was my first paid editor way back with *Masters at Arms*. She is a strong developmental/content editor who makes me think about the actions and consequences of the actions my characters take, thus helping me to make the story so much more realistic. And Jacy, well, not only is she my comma Nazi, but she catches my inconsistencies and foibles—even when they are eight chapters apart—and let's me know in no uncertain terms when I can do better. I love them all!

My awesome beta readers (some working last fall, some this year, and most both sessions) are Margie Dees, Cori DB, Iliana GK, Melanie Grossi, Kristin Harris, Kathy Holtsclaw, Kellie Hunter, Kelly Mueller, Jennifer P., Ruth Reid, Gilda Mary Sacca, and Lisa Simo-Kinzer—all of whom have read through the entire book (sometimes more than once!) and helped me fix both major and minor (but important!) problems. Sometimes they ask "what happened to" questions or indicate they just aren't clear on something and I went off on a tangent to find a photo or something to respond only to find it lead me to add a new element to the story. (I love these layers! I call them the "magic" of the story!)

I also had six amazing proofreaders who found typos and errors galore (usually not the same ones): Barb Jack, Alison K., Angelique Luzader, Eva Meyers, Christine Sullivan Mulcair, and Lynde Shaw.

Of course, I'm always changing something *after* my editorial team and subject experts sign off on a book and that invariably leads to new errors. This is why I delay the print version a couple of months in order to find them. My thanks to all of the readers who so graciously took the time this spring to point these out because you caught some that I still missed on my read-through for print.

As always, all new and remaining typos and errors are solely *my* responsibility.

I also have a number of subject experts who help expand my knowledge base so that you can immerse yourself in the book and not be pulled out because a crucial detail was wrong. For this book, my thanks to:

Kim Bollinger, a labor-and-delivery nurse, who helped deliver Adam and Karla's babies in a realistic way (after I am sure she guffawed at my fantasy version!).

Mr. Sayanova (Saya's Sir) for reading over a crucial chapter and confirming that our "Baby Dom" is nothing short of a Dom. With permission, Saya also consults with him whenever she wants to make sure the Dom's or male's perspective is spot-on.

Author KB Gardener for tracking down some last-minute information about a photo with a rope design I wanted to replicate in one of the last scenes I wrote in the book.

Top Griz for his expertise on weapons, military, and Marine Corps references—and, as always provides a new Adam-ism for me. In this book, it's "Whose turn in the barrel?" when he's looking for volunteers.

Ruth Reid, Ekatarina Sayanova, and Fiona Campbell for their feedback on the psychological aspects of PTSD and surviving a gang rape.

Jennifer Bosworth whose expertise on firefighting helped make Luke look better in the situation.

To the members of the Rescue Me Saga Discussion Group on Facebook who kept me writing by answering questions about past books that might have sent me researching for an hour or more. Usually, they had my answers within half an hour. They also are my sounding board for some ideas or even phrases (like, "Have you heard of "quaking aspens?") I want to use but have discovered aren't as common as I think. (That's what the glossary is for! With betas and proofreaders on four continents, I think I have identified a lot of phrases and words that are a stumbling block!)

To Charlotte Oliver, my amazing personal assistant, whose help compiling multiple files from betas, editors, and proofreaders into a single document was so much more efficient for me! And for the day in and day out calming presence she is in my life!

The Kallypso's Street Brats who always entertain me with their pimping exploits. And to my Masters Brats (fans) around the world. Without *all* of you telling your family and friends about my books, I never would have reached so many readers with these incredibly healing stories.

Leagh Christensen and Lisa Simo-Kinzer for taking care of my online groups and presence, and sometimes just reminding me to breathe.

Author's Note

For those of you who want to read a book focused on only one couple, well, my apologies. While I could have separated this into two books and pulled the many chapters about Adam and Karla into a short novel, I couldn't segregate them away from Cassie and Luke. They are a family. The story does flow seamlessly, though, because the babies just happened to come at a time when Luke and Cassie needed some time to sort out where they would be going in their journey.

Another couple you will meet in this book (or see again, if you read *Nobody's Lost*, my surprise December release) is Megan and Ryder Wilson. If you missed the announcements about this book last fall and winter, I would highly recommend that you read it before you continue. You know how my books build upon each other. You can find an excerpt and buy link to *Nobody's Lost* (Rescue Me Saga #5) by clicking this link.

I know some of you have been waiting for Luke and Cassie's story since they first met in *Nobody's Angel*, too. These characters and this journey dictate the order that their stories will be told. I am but the channel they use to share their stories. So, I hope there are no hard feelings that it took so long. I have poured my heart into this book and hope that you will find it healing, entertaining, and the perfect addition to the Saga.

Will this be the last? Oh, no! I'll be publishing some short novels in the next year or two as I try to get some of the voices out of my head and onto your e-reader screen or paperback books. But the pressure of setting preorders and deadlines are a thing of the past. So, please sign up for my newsletter so you don't miss future announcements about what's in store, both in the main Rescue Me Saga, the black-ops trilogy and other spin-offs, and even books not at all related to the Masters at Arms Club community.

To all who have been with me these past six months during my health problems, thank you! I am cancer free and grateful to everyone who prayed, lit candles, sent cards or gifts, or lifted me up in any way.

My surgeon left me with the instructions to eat healthy, don't gain weight, and to keep writing. Well, I definitely accomplished that last part! And I will continue to work on the other two!

CONTENT WARNING: This book tells the story of a rape-survivor's healing. I have kept the details of the rape to a minimum, but through flashbacks some details are revealed that may cause triggers. I had several rape survivors on my team assure me that the overall message is one of hope and healing, so I hope that you will surround yourself with supportive people you can talk with if issues arise while you read. And please use these first two resources or a rape crisis center or hotline in your nation if you are unable to find someone to talk with. You survived. It was not your fault. Be kind to yourself and seek the support and love of those around you.

Here are some web sites that can help if you need to talk with someone.

Rape, Abuse, and Incest National Network (RAINN):
https://www.rainn.org

Crisis and Suicide Prevention Services (United States):
www.suicidepreventionlifeline.org

And while Luke and Cassie are not veterans, there are some issues in this book dealing with Adam and Ryder and their PTSD symptoms. If you want to speak with someone about military PTSD issues, please contact the Veterans Administration or any veterans group.

In addition, I'm very impressed with and appreciative of the work done by these organizations for veterans and their families:

Hope for the Warriors:
http://www.hopeforthewarriors.org/

Save a Warrior:
http://www.saveawarrior.org/

Snowball Express (for the children of the fallen):
https://snowballexpress.org/

Cast of Characters for
Nobody's Dream

(Warning: Spoilers if you have not yet read the five books before this one, including *Nobody's Lost*, Megan and Ryder's story released in December 2014)

Cassatt—one of Luke's rescued mustangs

Marc D'Alessio—Navy corpsman ("Doc") and Luke's search-and-rescue (SAR) partner. Dating Angelina Giardano.

Luke Denton—Marc's search-and-rescue (SAR) partner who adopts rescued, abused mustangs; he is an artisan who makes furniture, including pieces for the kink community

Emily—a friend of Marisol's from her school in Denver

Fontana—one of Luke's rescued mustangs

Mrs. Gallagher—mother to Adam Montague, Patrick Gallagher, and Megan Gallagher

Patrick Gallagher—Megan Gallagher's brother and Adam Montague's half-brother

Savannah Gentry Orlando—a social worker on the run; in a relationship with Damián Orlando, the man who rescued her from a brutal scene in *Masters at Arms*. (Also see **Savannah Orlando**)

Angelina Giardano—Marc's fiancée; a chef by trade; nicknamed Angie by Karla and Angel by Luke

Matteo (Matt) Giardano—Angelina's brother; a fire fighter; likes to go skijoring

Rafe Giardano—Angelina's oldest brother; a fire fighter

Graciela—one of Cassie's alpacas; name means "grace" in Spanish

V. Grant—a Lance Corporal communications specialist who was briefly attached to Ryder's recon Marine unit in Fallujah

Killa—one of Cassie's alpacas; name means "moon" in Quechua

Kitty—Nickname for Karla Paxton Montague

Gunnar Larson—a sadist whip master who trained Damián, Grant, and others; retired Army Delta Force

Cassie López—Karla's friend from college who now lives in Colorado, a reclusive artist who hasn't dealt with the aftermath of a gang rape in her homeland of Peru while on a break from college

Eduardo López—Cassie's brother; married to Susana

Lalo López—Cassie's nephew; Lalo is a nickname for Eduardo

Mamá López—Cassie's mother, of Quechua descent

Papá López—Cassie's father, of Spanish descent

Susana López—Cassie's sister-in-law; married to Eduardo

Adam Montague (pronounced MON-tag)—retired Marine Corps Master Sergeant; married to Karla; "adopted" father of Damian Orlando; patriarch to the Masters at Arms Club "family"

Karla Paxton Montague—wife to Adam Montague; singer in the Masters at Arms Club; nicknamed Kitty by Cassie and Kitten by Adam

O'Keeffe—one of Luke's more severely abused rescued mustangs

Damián Orlando—Marine wounded in Fallujah; rides a Harley and is a Patriot Guard Rider; husband to Savannah Gentry Orlando; and father to Marisol Orlando.

Marisol "Mari" Orlando—Savannah and Damián's daughter

Savannah Orlando—see **Savannah Gentry**

Doctor Palmer—Karla's obstetrician

Jerry Patterson—a Vietnam veteran who runs a BDSM club in Los Angeles frequented by several characters in the Rescue Me Saga

Picasso—a neglected palomino rescued by Luke; being trained for SAR work

Mr. Proctor—Luke's high school shop teacher who encouraged him to work with wood

Qhawa—one of Cassie's alpacas; name means one who watches or monitors in Quechua

Quenti—newborn son to Eduardo and Susana López

***Padre* Rojas**—Priest at the church in Peru where the López family are members

***Tía* Sofia**—Cassie's aunt and her mother's sister

Tika—one of Cassie's alpacas; name means "flower"

Megan Gallagher Wilson—half-sister to Adam Montague and sister to Patrick Gallagher; recent graduate with an MFA in photography.

Ryder Wilson—served in the recon Marines with Adam Montague in Kosovo, Kandahar (Afghanistan), and Fallujah (Iraq). Appeared briefly in *Masters at Arms* where he was known as Wilson. Works odd jobs and hates cities. In a relationship with **Megan Gallagher**.

Playlist for the Rescue Me Saga

Here are some of the songs that inspired Kally as she wrote the books to date in the series. Because each book isn't only about one couple's journey, she has grouped the music by couple, except for the first one. **Warning**: Possible spoilers if you haven't read the entire series yet!

Relevant to Multiple Rescue Me Saga Couples

Darryl Worley – *Just Got Home From a War*

Angie Johnson – *Sing for You*

Nickelback – *I'd Come for You*

Evanescence – *Bring Me To Life*

Daughtry – *I'll Fight*

Dan Hill – *Sometimes When We Touch*

Trace Adkins – *Semper Fi*

The David Crowder Band – *Never Let Go*

Adam and the late Joni
(backstory in *Masters at Arms* & *Nobody's Angel* and *Nobody's Hero*):

Ed Sheeran – *Photograph*

Sarah McLachlan – *Wintersong*

Rascal Flatts – *Here Comes Goodbye*

Aerosmith – *I Don't Wanna Miss A Thing*

Marc and Angelina
(*Masters at Arms* & *Nobody's Angel, Somebody's Angel,* and *Nobody's Dream*):

Andrea Bocelli – *Por Amor* (and others on *Romanza* CD)

Sarah Jane Morris – *Arms Of An Angel*

Dean Martin – *Volare*

Dean Martin – *You Belong To Me*

Fleetwood Mac – *Landslide*

Mary Chapin Carpenter – *The King of Love*

Usher – *Scream*

Air Supply – *The One That You Love*

Air Supply – *Goodbye*

Lacuna Coil – *Spellbound*

Air Supply – *Making Love Out of Nothing at All*

Styx – *Man In The Wilderness*

Keith Urban – *Tonight I Wanna Cry*

Paul Brandt – *My Heart Has a History*

Michael Bublé – *Home*

Daughtry – *Used To*

Leighton Meester – *Words I Couldn't Say*

Halestorm – *Private Parts*

And a "medley" of heavy-metal music cited in the acknowledgements of *Somebody's Angel*

Adam and Karla

(*Masters at Arms & Nobody's Angel, Nobody's Hero, Somebody's Angel, Nobody's Lost, and Nobody's Dream*):

Tarja Turunen – *I Walk Alone*

Madonna – *Justify My Love*

Sinead O'Connor – *Song to the Siren*

Rascal Flatts – *What Hurts The Most*

Marc Anthony – *I Sang to You*

Simon & Garfunkel – *I Am A Rock*

Alison Krauss & Union Station – *I'm Gone*

The Rolling Stones – *Wild Horses*

Pat Benatar – *Love Is A Battlefield*

The Rolling Stones – *Under My Thumb*

Gary Puckett and the Union Gap – *This Girl is a Woman Now*

Lifehouse – *Hanging By A Moment*

Leighton Meester – *Words I Couldn't Say*

Air Supply – *Lonely Is The Night*

Beyoncé – *Poison*

Randy Vanwarmer – *Just When I Needed You Most*

The Red Jumpsuit Apparatus – *Your Guardian Angel*

Oum Kalthoum – *Enta Omri* (Egyptian belly dance music)

Harem – *La Pasion Turca* (Turkish belly dance music)

Barry Manilow – *Ready To Take A Chance Again*

Paul Dinletir – *Transcendance*

Creed – *Arms Wide Open*

Aerosmith – *I Don't Wanna Miss A Thing*

Damián and Savannah
(*Masters at Arms & Nobody's Angel, Nobody's Perfect, Somebody's Angel, and Nobody's Dream*):

Sarah McLachlan – *Fumbling Towards Ecstasy* (entire CD of same title)

Johnny Cash – *The Beast In Me*

John Mayer – *The Heart Of Life*

Marc Anthony – *When I Dream At Night*

Ingrid Michaelson – *Masochist*

Three Days Grace – *Never Too Late*

Three Days Grace – *Pain*

Drowning Pool – *Let The Bodies Hit the Floor!*

Goo Goo Dolls – *Iris*

John Mayer – *Heartbreak Warfare*

Three Days Grace – *Animal I Have Become*

Ed Sheeran – *Thinking Out Loud*

The Avett Brothers – *If It's the Beaches*

Leonard Cohen – *I'm Your Man*

A Perfect Circle – *Pet*

Pink – *Fuckin' Perfect*

Edwin McCain – *I'll Be*

Ryder and Megan
(*Masters at Arms & Nobody's Angel, Nobody's Hero, Nobody's Lost, and Nobody's Dream*):

Hard Corps – *The Warrior Song*

Kenny Chesney – *You Had Me From Hello*

Chase Rice – *Ride*

Christine Perri – *Arms*

Adele – *One and Only*

Breaking Benjamin – *I Will Not Bow*

Imagine Dragons – *Demons*

The Goo Goo Dolls – *Notbroken*

Five Finger Death Punch – *Wrong Side of Heaven*

Skillet – *Falling Inside the Black*

Sugarland – *Tonight*

Adele – *Make You Feel My Love*

Adele – *Hiding My Heart*

Deepest Blue – *Give It Away*

Inner Voices – *Baby Girl*

Kenny Chesney – *You Save Me*

Train – *Marry Me*

Blake Sheldon – *God Gave Me You*

Phillip Phillips – *Unpack Your Heart*

John Legend – *All of Me*

Phillip Phillips – *Raging Fire*

Rascal Flatts – *I'm Movin' On*

Luke and Cassie

(*Masters at Arms & Nobody's Angel, Nobody's Perfect, Somebody's Angel, and Nobody's Dream*):

Paul Brandt – *I Do*

Keith Urban – *I Want to Love Somebody Like You*

Amanda Wilkinson – *Hearts Open Slowly*

Jamie O'Neal – *Like a Woman*

Ty Herndon – *I Have to Surrender*

Leighton Meester and Garrett Hedlund – *Give In to Me*

Jason Aldean and Kelly Clarkson – *Don't You Wanna Stay Here a Little*

While?

Shannon Noll – *Don't Fight It*

Ty Herndon – *I Know How the River Feels*

Tracy Byrd – *Keeper of the Stars*

Brad Paisley – *I Want to Check You for Ticks*

Paul Brandt – *When You Call My Name*

Kip Moore – *Hey, Pretty Girl*

Dustin Lynch – *Cowboys and Angels*

Josh Turner – *Your Man*

Paul Brandt – *Take it Off*

Jason Mraz – *I Won't Give Up*

Rascal Flatts – *God Bless the Broken Road*

John Michael Montgomery – *Hold On to Me*

Dixie Chicks – *Cowboy, Take Me Away*

Keith Urban – *Making Memories of Us*

Bryan Adams – *Between Now and Forever*

Luke Bryan – *In Love with the Girl*

Billy Currington – *Must Be Doing Something Right*

Natasha Bedingfield – *Wild Horses*

Demi Lovato – *Nightingale*

Crowder – *Come As You Are*

Rihanna – *Stay*

Prologue

October 2007, Columbia University, New York City

H *is hard body pressed against the length of her back, hands reaching around to paw at her breasts. His height told her it was Diego, not Pedro. Cassie clawed his hands away as someone reached out and pinched her nipple.*

"You have quite a handful in this one, Pedro. She will need more than one man to tame her."

She elbowed him and turned to slap his face.

"Ow! Cassie, wake up. You're having another nightmare."

Kitty? Gasping for breath and batting at the air, Cassie opened her eyes to find herself crouching against the wall on her dorm-room bed. She blinked several times. The darkness prevented her from seeing her friend's face, but she recognized the voice and stopped fighting. Apparently, Kitty's sleep had been disturbed by Cassie once again in their tiny dorm room.

"I am so sorry I woke you again." Would the night terrors ever go away? She had barely slept in the weeks since she had returned to uni for her senior year. Every time she closed her eyes, she found herself catapulted back three months to that cantina in Lima.

"Are you okay now?"

Her eyes adjusted enough for her to see Kitty's worried expression as she knelt on the floor beside Cassie's bed. Cassie nodded, but had come to realize she would never be able to rid herself of the guilt and shame.

Kitty stood up and took several steps to her desk. Stretching out on the mattress, Cassie tried to convey to her friend everything was okay, but as soon as she closed her eyes the nightmarish scene returned. Exhaustion dragged her spirit down, but the vivid images allowed her no peace. Kitty padded back in her slippers and wiped the sweat and tears away from Cassie's face with a towelette.

"It's all over now. Just a dream." As reality and memories poured in, her body began shaking uncontrollably. Cassie's stomach twisted in knots. "Shhh, Cassie. You're safe now. Everything's going to be all right. Are you worrying about midterms?"

Cassie nodded as she silently asked Kitty and the Universe to forgive her for the half-truth. Of course, her grades *had* fallen drastically. She would let her friend believe that was the reason for her anxiety, because she could not tell Kitty what happened over summer break.

She resented the fact that she had not been able to climb out of this dungeon of fear and depression even months after the rape. This week, she had missed turning in two important assignments, and the midterm project due Friday was far from complete.

If she flunked out, she would be deported and forced to return to Peru. Her parents had no idea what had happened, but her fear and shame would never allow her to go back home.

"Kitty, I am scared." The words escaped before she realized.

"There's nothing to be afraid of. Your grades will be fine. You're a four-point-oh student."

Cassie shook her head, but flunking out this semester was one more thing she had been trying to hide.

Cassie wished that those monsters had killed her during the attack. Why had she stopped them when Diego threatened her with his knife? Instead, she had talked him out of it, promising not to tell her family or to press charges. As if pressing charges would have resulted in prosecution or justice in Peru anyway.

Damn her for being so naïve as to think death was a fate worse than the hell they had condemned her to live day in and day out until she took her final breath! Did she have the courage to end this life and start over, knowing the repercussions to her soul?

Everything terrified her now. Pedro and his accomplices had ripped all security from her. Why pretend she would ever be safe, whole, or in charge of her life or body again?

"I cannot go on, Kitty. I am—" *Silence, Casandra!* She drew in a deep but shaky breath to regain her composure. Still, she could not confide in Kitty how close she was to ending her life. "I am going to drop out."

She let her roommate presume she meant from school, not from life. All hope of returning to normalcy was gone. She had nothing left. For days, she had contemplated how she might put a suicide plan into action. Death appealed to her more than the thought of living in this hollow, haunted shell.

But she had to make certain Kitty would not be the one to find her body. She would never put her dearest friend in the world through that. Her only hope was that Kitty would not blame herself for failing to see the signs.

No one could have seen them because Cassie had kept everything locked inside in fear of being judged or blamed.

Kneeling on the bed, Cassie sat back on her feet. "You have always been so kind to me, Kitty."

"That's what friends are for."

"You mean even more than that to me. And what about *your* grades? My constant nightmares have been a distraction this entire term. When was the last time you were able to sleep straight through the night? You must regret choosing me as your roommate."

Kitty stood and placed her hands on her hips, glaring at Cassie, who leaned back against the wall to place more distance between them. "You listen to me, Cassie López. We've been together for over two years. You're not a burden. You're my best friend. Besides that, God, you should have met my freshman-year roomie. No way do I want to find another roommate." She shuddered theatrically—Kitty was being overly dramatic, to lighten her mood probably.

Her friend's brief smile faded when Cassie was unable to return one. Kitty sat on the edge of the bed, reaching out to stroke Cassie's leg before Cassie pulled the sheet over her lower body to break the skin-to-skin contact.

"Cassie, seriously, nothing would cause me to abandon you when I know you need me." Kitty placed her hand over her abdomen. "I feel sick that you'd even think I would!"

You do not know who I really am anymore, Kitty.

Cassie reached toward Kitty, who grabbed her hand. "Your heart is going to be broken one day if you keep wearing it on your sleeve and seeing the best in everyone, especially in the ones who are toxic to you."

Like me.

"Stop talking like that." Kitty glanced toward the picture of the uniformed Marine on her desk. When she met Cassie's gaze again, a mixture

3

of regret and determination was evident. Cassie wondered why. "Listen, I spoke with my psych professor about this situation after class."

"What situation?" Could Kitty see what Cassie had become?

"I didn't give your name or anything! Anyway, he suggested I encourage you to talk to someone in the counseling center on campus. They might be able to help you get to the bottom of whatever is causing you these horrific nightmares."

"I am not going into thera—"

"Why not? Sometimes you need to talk with someone who is better able to deal with things like this. You know I'd listen to anything you said, but I can't necessarily provide you with solutions or understanding for whatever is haunting you."

Tears blurred Cassie's vision again. Having someone who cared enough to seek help for her tore at her heartstrings. Not that it would help. How Kitty could not see the futility of aiding someone so degraded and dirty was beyond Cassie's understanding.

But she does not know.

"It is no use."

Undeterred, Kitty pressed on. "Hear me out. I called the center today, and they said they accept walk-ins right here in our dorm most evenings, including tonight. I'll go with you and wait until you're finished. How about we go to the room right after our last classes of the day?"

Cassie blinked away the tears. "You would go with me?"

Kitty narrowed the space between them, wrapping her arms around her. For the first time in a long while, Cassie did not push her away. Just for this moment, she needed nurturing human contact again. She missed *Mamá* so much.

But *Mamá* could never know. To say nothing of *Papá's* reaction if he found out.

Too often in her country, parents blamed the girl for her own rape. She had heard of an instance where the parents even forced a girl to marry the rapist. Bile rose in her throat at the thought of seeing her former fiancé, Pedro, again. *Papá* would insist she honor the agreement he had made with Pedro's family.

Better to keep this from her family.

"Cassie, you need to talk with someone who can do more than hold your hand and wipe away your tears. I'm afraid you're going to—" Again, her friend glanced away, this time staring at the floor.

How could Kitty be so perceptive about her innermost thoughts?

"Why don't we go clubbing tonight? There's a new one—"

"No!" Cassie closed her eyes and forced down the vomit that rose in her throat. *Breathe in. Breathe out.* Her hands and arms trembled violently as control slipped away—again.

Kitty squeezed her hand. "Please tell me what's wrong, Cassie. You're scaring me."

Cassie tried to fabricate a story to appease Kitty, but her mind went blank. The silence lengthened, making her increasingly uncomfortable.

"They raped me." The whispered words came out before she even knew they were on the tip of her tongue.

"Oh, God, no, Cassie." Cassie could not meet her gaze for fear of seeing condemnation for allowing such a thing to happen to her. Kitty scooted closer on the bed and raised Cassie's chin, forcing her to meet her gaze. *"They?"* Kitty's rage impacted Cassie as if it were a tangible thing. "Who did this to you, Cassie?"

"Pedro and two of his friends."

Kitty's fingers squeezed her chin, and Cassie pulled away. *"Pedro?"* That goddamned bastard! If he ever comes anywhere near you again—"

Cassie's anger boiled up before she could tamp it down. "You will do nothing because he will *never* come anywhere near me again. I will never return to Peru." The thought of Kitty going after him made her shake again. "And I do not want him anywhere near you, either." Cassie tried to stave off her tears. To feel rage or sorrow all these months later would mean she had not put the attack behind her despite trying so hard to forget.

"What about your family?"

"They can visit me here in the States."

"No, what did they say about what happened?"

She turned away. "I did not tell them."

Kitty reached out and unnecessarily brushed a lock of close-cropped hair off her forehead, causing Cassie to turn back toward her friend. "I'm sure you'll be able to talk to them about this in time, and they will support you. I know they love you."

Cassie succumbed to the weakness of tears.

"Until then, I'll be your family. You're already the sister I never had."

Kitty's lower lip trembled. "No one should have to face this alone. I should have trusted my instincts when you came back from Peru with your beautiful hair cut off. And after these nightmares started coming almost every night."

"I am sorry I shut you out, but I could not…" Unable to finish, she closed her eyes.

"I feel so helpless. I *hate* that feeling."

As do I.

"Cassie, this is bigger than you and I can handle. Neither of us has ever faced something so life-changing. But remember freshman orientation? Columbia offers counseling for things like this, and I'm sure they've dealt with lots of cases of sexual assault."

Cassie despised the politically correct terminology. She was *raped*. Why not say the word with all its negative connotations? Rape was vile. An evil thing. Nothing like the sanitized, legal term "sexual assault." She had been *raped. Violated.*

Hold on. Kitty is only trying to make me feel better, even if she has no clue what it is like to be in my shoes right now.

Kitty squeezed Cassie's hand. "No matter what happened, you're still the same beautiful, loving person you were before. Don't let those men continue to rape your soul. It's time to let out some of the rage and let go of the shame."

When Cassie remained silent, Kitty took a deep breath and continued. "Listen, I'm registered for a refresher workshop with the self-defense instructor I had freshman year. Adam…" She glanced at the portrait of the older man in uniform sitting on her desk and smiled. "Adam insisted that I learn to protect myself when I came to the city." She turned back to Cassie. "Anyway, it's Saturday afternoon at the Y. Come with me. If there's no room, you can take my place."

"It is too late to prevent what happened to me, Kitty."

She shook her head vehemently. "Maybe for what happened in the past, but learning to defend yourself can empower you to feel less victimized and fearful all the time."

Cassie had fought hard during her attack, perhaps making her injuries worse than they might have been otherwise. While there had been no broken bones, she bled for days and suffered bruises in places her family, thankfully, had been unable to see.

She should be grateful none of the men had punched her in the face, which would have been impossible to hide. No, they had used her face for other atrocities, using some kind of metal and leather yoke over her mouth that kept her from biting their penises off, as much as she had wanted to. Still wished she had been able to do so.

Regardless of her attempts to protect herself, she had been raped by three men multiple times and in heinous ways for hours. "Nothing I could have done would have stopped them."

"Well then, you can take out some of the rage and frustration you're feeling on the instructor. He'll be well-padded. You can even knee him in the groin while picturing one of your rapists. Kick all *three*, if it makes you feel better."

The visual of the description brought a tremulous smile to Cassie's face, and Kitty grinned as well, visibly relaxing for the first time since Cassie had told her.

If only I had been able to knee them during the attack.

Too soon, fear won out again, and she sobered. "Do you think there is any hope I can move beyond this, Kitty?"

"Oh, there's always hope!"

Perhaps suicide was not the answer. Her mother and grandmother, both Quechua shamans, had taught Cassie as a child that those who committed suicide were doomed to hover between this world and the next until their spirits were freed by either reincarnation or a special ceremony. She shuddered, never wanting to experience anything like that in a future life.

She needed to process what had happened and move on with her life, if possible. Cassie pulled away and met Kitty's gaze. "Do they have female counselors at the center? I will not talk with a man about this."

"I'm sure they understand that and will have women counselors. If not, we'll keep looking until we find one."

Unable to come up with any other arguments against going, Cassie decided to try the two actions her friend proposed. At least she would not have to do either one alone.

"Let us sleep some, Kitty. My first class is at ten." Kitty looked disappointed and worried before Cassie continued, "Then we can talk with the counselor this evening."

Kitty grinned and hugged her, but Cassie was so numb she did not even feel it. When Kitty's arms squeezed tighter, though, Cassie felt smothered and pushed her away, drawing in a deep breath.

Kitty seemed hurt at first, but put a smile on her face. "I'm proud of you, Cassie. You're so strong. You're going to survive this."

Cassie stretched out on the mattress, and Kitty started crooning a song Cassie found comforting, yet unfamiliar. Her friend stroked her hair, and Cassie closed her eyes.

She did not want to disappoint Kitty and keep dragging her friend down into this hellish hole with her. Logic told her that returning her head and heart to her true center would be key, but she had lost all sense of being. She had not even been able to meditate since the rape. Instead, Cassie had floated through her days like a ghost—invisible to all except Kitty. Perhaps she hoped to continue to drift away from life until she ceased to exist at all, just as her former self, Casandra, had virtually disappeared that night in the cantina.

No! I do not wish to lose this part of myself as well. Cassie wanted to reclaim her place in the Universe. She wanted to listen, once again, to that small, still voice that would guide her toward her future and her destiny. Surely she would not be doomed to hide away inside this broken body for the rest of her life.

With Kitty's help, there might still be hope for Cassie, even if Casandra no longer existed.

For her friend Kitty, Cassie would try one more time.

Chapter One

Late April 2012, Iron Horse Peak, Colorado, continued from Somebody's Angel

The nearly naked man pressed against her bare skin convulsed in another fit of shivers that rattled her jaw. After lying against Luke Denton for the past four hours with only their underwear as a thin barrier, she wondered if her body had any warmth left to give. His body felt warmer, though. Why was he still shivering? Perhaps she should go to the kitchen and warm up a hot-water bottle to aid in raising his core temperature.

Luke had crashed into her safe, quiet life with a vengeance when the snow shelf gave way and nearly killed him. What on earth made him think she needed some white knight to follow her home? She had spent the afternoon hanging out with her dearest friend Kitty at the bar in Aspen Corners, and the next thing she knew, Kitty was calling to ask if she had seen Luke.

Cassie had managed to find her way home alone for years without needing a man. Besides, she had only imbibed a near-virgin margarita. She had learned her lesson the hard way about drinking too much in bars.

Clearly, she was not the one in need of rescuing. This fool had nearly been killed when the avalanche knocked his truck off the road to her cabin. Regardless of why he was here—whether a stalker or a rescuer—she needed to keep him alive. Dragging the half-conscious man into her cabin had been the easy part. Waking him every couple of hours to make sure he was not suffering a concussion had not been much of a challenge. But pressing her body against his like this frazzled her nerves.

She was an artist, not a nurse. However, with the blizzard raging outside, no medical assistance would be arriving anytime soon. No sense calling Kitty or Marc D'Alessio again. During Marc's last call asking for an update on Luke's condition, he had conveyed what the next steps would be. Clearly, her body no longer provided him with much warmth. She crawled out from under the pile of woolen blankets and wrapped her robe around herself before running into the kitchen to put on a kettle of water.

After warming the water a couple of minutes, she removed it from the burner and filled the rubber bottle. Carrying it by the neck, she grabbed a dishtowel and went back to the bedroom. The room was at least twenty degrees warmer than she normally kept it. Still, her gaze rested on the covers quivering as the man's body suffered through another bout of shivers.

Marc said to warm his trunk, neck, and—groin. She would place the bottle close to *that* area and then focus her efforts on his chest and neck. Cassie wrapped the towel around the bottle and slipped it under the pile of blankets, laying it low on his belly and being careful not to touch him. She hoped the bottle wasn't too hot, but it would help circulate his blood and warm his extremities.

Get well, Luke Denton—and go back to where you belong.

This cabin had been her escape from the world for the past several years—more specifically from the males of the human species. No more.

She stared down at Luke a moment before fisting her hands and preparing herself to join him in the bed again.

Relax, or he will sense your fear.

With even more reluctance than earlier, she shucked her robe and climbed onto the twin mattress, pressing her full length against him.

Friction might help. She rubbed her legs against his and her hands on his chest and neck, creating more heat under the woolen blankets. Not used to so much warmth in her bed, she began to sweat. When his shivering stopped, Cassie sighed. At least she had done the right thing. Despite her discomfort, she had rescued him and was trying to nurse him back to health.

Thank you, Goddess.

The sooner Luke recovered—and they cleared the road to the highway—the sooner he could leave her mountain. Only then would she be able to breathe freely in her sanctuary once more.

While she did not own this place, her landlady, a patron of the arts and fellow Columbia graduate, had made a very attractive, affordable offer for a new artist starting out. The elderly benefactress practically let her live here rent-free, primarily wanting someone to live in the isolated cabin and studio she and her late husband had inhabited.

Without warning, Luke grunted in pain and rolled on top of her. Bile burned the back of her throat, threatening to choke her as she flashed back to the horrific scene in the cantina five years ago.

Sweat. Bodies. Three drunk, aggressive men. She pummeled the man on top of her, but could not shove him off.

Cassie clawed her mind back to the present and shoved the delirious man off her chest. Despite his weakened state, Luke wrapped his arm around her waist and pulled her with him. Even though she was on top now, she could not shake the feeling of being smothered.

"Easy, girl." She pulled away and looked down at his face. He appeared to be sleeping, but was he? "...not gonna hurt ya." She cowered from his touch, preparing to run, but his eyes remained closed. He reached up to stroke the side of her head. "That's my girl."

Was he dreaming about his dead wife? When the puma had injured Kitty's husband, Adam, Luke's dead wife had used Cassie as a channel. While friends and family gathered in the waiting room, Cassie had sketched an image of his wife and their unborn baby as if they were in heaven, letting him know they were okay.

Sympathy for him weakened the urge to swat his hand away. His gentle touch did not appear to be a threat or hurtful in any way, unlike... She shuddered. *Do not go there.* Gentle or not, the last thing Cassie wanted was to be touched by this man, by *any* man. So why did she stay here in this bed with him?

His hand made her feel something different from what the other men had. Not frightened. Just strange. Something she could not identify. Safe, maybe?

Do not fool yourself, Cassie.

She would never feel safe in the presence of a man again. Up here on this mountain, she surrounded herself with her artwork. More recently, her precious alpacas had brought her pleasure—and peace. After years of trying to reconnect with the Universe—even beginning to see some success this past year—now her sense of security had been ripped away. Perhaps unintentionally, but that tenuous connection had been shattered just the same. She wanted to meditate, but could not leave him to spend time at her altar in her studio.

Luke grew restless again, thrashing on the bed until his arm wrapped around her back, trapping her once more. Cassie's body shook, but not from the cold.

Deep breaths.

No! I am suffocating!

Cassie jerked his heavy arm off her and let it drop onto the mattress as she scooted out of the bed again. She needed to put space between herself and this man. With him no longer shivering, she could leave him with the hot-water bottle while she started a pot of soup as well as a broth for his first attempts at eating again. When he came to, the soups would help warm and nourish his body. She stocked lots of staples in her pantry, but it would take a while to turn them into a meal.

Thank you, Goddess. This would give her time to collect herself.

Grabbing her robe, she ran from the room to escape the monsters lurking in the shadows that waited for any sign of weakness before they pounced.

*　　*　　*

Luke pulled his hand back, giving O'Keeffe the space she needed as he took a few steps away from her in the round pen. The mare was more skittish tonight than she'd been since the rescued mustang had come to his ranch months ago. What had spooked her? He'd been working with the battered horse daily and had expected her to trust him more than this by now.

But he'd learned with the others that sometimes you took two steps forward only to take three more back.

What the hell had those bastards done to try and break her spirit? How could anyone treat an animal like that? O'Keeffe retreated across the pen, and her image faded away as if he'd only been dreaming…

Exhausted, Luke tried to lift his arm to stroke the horse. Dead weight. Would he ever be able to break through to this one?

Suddenly, Maggie lay next to him. Confused at the change from being with O'Keeffe what seemed only a moment ago, Luke rolled onto his stomach, groaning when his muscles protested. His wife's body had been warm beside his a moment ago, but without warning, she also disappeared. Something didn't feel right, but he couldn't analyze it now.

I need to find her.

But he was so damned weak…

A wave of shivers convulsed him. *The wall of ice and debris roared down the mountainside. Seeing his wife's crumpled body half a football field length down the mountainside tore at his gut. "Don't move, Maggie! I'll be back as fast as I can."*

Wait. Hadn't Maggie been in bed next to him a moment ago? Was he dreaming now? But what if he wasn't and this was real—again?

Maggie needs me!

Luke ran as if her life depended on him, because it did. Helpless. Lately, she'd become more independent, and he'd begun to wonder if she'd ever need him again. She'd grown so strong and confident since that first time he'd met her when she was just beginning to free herself from her overbearing family. While he'd encouraged her every way he could to gain her autonomy, he had to admit he sometimes missed having her depend on him emotionally the way she once had.

One thing was certain—at this moment, he had to find help. The temperatures tonight would drop like a rock. He still had a good six hours of daylight to bring the emergency crews back to her, but it had taken the two of them hours, albeit at a slower pace, to hike up here from the parking lot.

Run, damn it. Just run!

"God, please stay with her." He whispered his prayer as he ran. "Hang on, dar- lin'."

"I am not your darling."

Maggie? No, his wife didn't have a Hispanic accent. Besides, she loved when he called her darlin'.

Then whose warm body was pressed against his? Reality slammed into him. Of course it couldn't be his wife. She had died in the avalanche almost eight years ago.

Didn't she? He couldn't have made that up—not in a million years— unless he'd just awoken from the worst damned nightmare imaginable. He thought he'd come to terms with Maggie's death during the past year, so why the nightmares now?

He flashed to the crushing sound of a wall of snow and debris slam- ming against his truck. What the hell? He and Maggie didn't own a truck. Besides, the Land Rover her parents had given her when she went off to college had been parked miles away when the avalanche killed Maggie and the rescue worker—Angel Giardano's father—at the bottom of that scree slope.

So why did the crush of the snow pack feel so real to him now?

The body pressed against his moved, bringing him back to the present. He was in a warm bed. Next to a soft, warm body. Luke opened one eye.

Dark, straight hair. Definitely not Maggie's red curls.

She was built smaller than his wife, too. *Who the—?*

"You are awake?"

This time, the accent clued him in. Cassie López, not Maggie. His head still fuzzy, he glanced around the darkened room, but couldn't make out many details. One thing *was* certain. He lay cozied up with the girl in a cramped twin bed. Must be dreaming still.

Nice imagination, Denton.

If this was a fantasy, why was he dreaming about her in a bed this size? Then again, being cuddled up with her in the small bed's tight confines sure worked for him.

She moved against him. Soft skin warm against his body. Sure seemed real. Not a dream.

Whoa! How on earth could he have wound up in bed with Cassie? Confusion returned, compounded by the throbbing in his head. He recalled setting out from daVinci's bar to follow her home after some of them had met for pizza and drinks, including Adam and Karla, Marc and Angel. There had been some kind of threat that made him worry about her ability to get home safely. But if he'd put the moves on her, he'd remember—wouldn't he? He hadn't had *that* much to drink.

Had she invited him into her bed? No. Any woman who slept in a twin bed didn't invite men to join her. Hell, this skittish filly would have kicked him in the nuts before she'd allow him into her cabin, much less her bedroom. She didn't like him much—well, *any* man from what he'd observed the few times he'd been around her. Adam practically set her jaws on edge, too, and that man wouldn't hurt her for anything, either.

When he moved to face her, a splitting pain seared between his temples, worse than any hangover he remembered. He closed his eyes and waited for the pain and nausea to pass. How much did he drink at daVinci's?

Keeping his voice to a whisper, he asked, "What the hell happened?"

"You do not remember?"

He started shaking his head, but the motion made matters worse. "Not a thing."

"Not even the avalanche?"

So there *had* been another avalanche. He hadn't imagined or dreamed it.

"You probably totaled your truck." She glared at him. "You could have been killed. What were you doing up here?" Now she sounded pissed—and more like the Cassie he remembered.

He grinned. "I wanted to see you make it home safely."

Her body grew even more rigid. "Obviously, *I* can take care of myself. You, I am not so sure about."

The girl had a point. But he'd had the best of intentions. "Living up here all alone, well, it's good to make sure someone checks in on you regularly."

"I have lived here since soon after graduating from university four years ago. I do not need anyone checking up on me."

Her breathing became shallow, agitated. Better drop the subject. "How long have I slept?"

"Since the night before last."

"What time is it now?"

"Early evening. It has been almost forty-eight hours since the avalanche, although you have had a few moments when you spoke lucidly."

What the hell had he said? He had no memory of any conversations—hell, no memory of anything but some wild dreams about horses, avalanches, and Maggie.

Ironic that an avalanche had taken Maggie away and another had brought him into Cassie's arms. Okay, enough trying to make sense out of this screwed-up mess. He wouldn't be in this girl's arms for long. She didn't trust him. Detested him, most likely.

So damned tired. Too exhausted to do anything about the exotic, contrary beauty in bed beside him, for sure, Luke's eyelids began to droop.

"Good. Sleep now. You *need* to regain your strength." Her words filtered through his fuzzy brain briefly before they faded away, but he heard her stress the word need as if there was an unspoken *soon*.

The next time he opened his eyes, the room was still dark. He lay pressed against a soft body again, nice and warm. Maggie. His cock stirred. His favorite times were waking up slowly together on their rare lazy days.

He was naked except for his boxers. She wore a bra and panties.

"I see you are awake again."

Cassie? Coming out of his fog, Luke remembered where he was and what had happened. Avalanche. Cassie's cabin. Hell, Cassie's *bed!* Having her close like this—the closest he'd ever managed to come to the girl—

made him grin. "How'd a little thing like you drag me in here?"

"You regained consciousness long enough for me to help you out of the truck, and I had you inside before the chills hit and you lost consciousness again."

"Oh, so that's why you undressed me."

Her body grew stiff. "You had hypothermia. There would be no other reason for me to do so."

Shit. No wonder he'd been out for so long and was so confused now. He wondered if he didn't have a concussion, too. Luke suffered enough of those during his football days in college to remember the confusion they brought. He might even be dealing with some altitude sickness. Her place was barely three thousand feet above his, but the effects could be exponential.

"Luke, are you still cold?"

"Not much anymore." Being too cold definitely wasn't his problem now. His cock grew stiffer with her breasts pressed against his side. Cassie was going to be embarrassed as hell whenever they decided to move out of this bed.

Not that he planned on moving anywhere at the moment.

"Good." She yanked the top blanket off him and held it up to her chest. "Because I need to check on my soup. Now, turn your head away."

Why'd Momma raise me to be such a gentleman?

Luke sighed and turned away with deliberate caution to avoid any sudden movement that might set off the jackhammer in his head again. She hurried to cover herself and get out of bed. He regretted the loss of her body heat the moment she left his side.

"I will be right back with a bowl of soup. It will help warm you even more. Would you like some coffee, too?"

"Both sound good. Black would be great."

As her footsteps retreated and the door opened and closed, he rolled onto his back again with a groan, laying his forearm over his eyes. Damn, he hadn't felt this weak since O'Keeffe kicked him in the thigh.

Aw, hell. If his body hurt this bad, what did his new truck look like? Cassie said it was probably totaled. He'd only had the damned thing about five months. Bought it for hauling the—

Shit! Luke tossed the remaining blankets off and struggled to sit up. The room swayed, his head pounded, and his vision blurred at the sudden change in position. He held on to the bedpost until he could see straight again. He needed to find his phone and send someone out to his ranch to tend to his horses.

Luke stood and scanned the room, but it was too dark to see if his pants or coat were here. Where had he left his cell phone? He stumbled toward the living room and scanned it from the bedroom doorway. No phone in sight. Most people didn't bother with landlines these days, but alone up here on the mountain, Cassie should have a backup.

"Lucas Denton! I want you back in bed!" She stood in a doorway across the room, a steaming mug of what he assumed was coffee in her hand. At some point since she'd left the bedroom, she'd donned a poncho to cover herself.

Cassie wanted him in bed? He grinned. "How'd you know my given name was Lucas?"

"Just a guess."

No doubt she used his formal name hoping to place more distance between them. Still, he didn't mind hearing her call him that. Not as long as she let him call her whatever he wanted to.

Cassie came through the doorway from what must be the kitchen. The smell of strong coffee reached him. Damn, he needed that—but not yet.

"I need to use your phone." He reached for the doorjamb with both hands when his legs began to wobble.

"You *need* to be in bed before you pass out." She walked toward him and placed the mug on the coffee table. "Who do you want to call?"

Cassie glanced down at his boxers, and he realized that's all he wore. She'd probably taken his pants to dry them out. As if realizing where her gaze was focused, she averted her eyes quickly. Knowing she stripped him out of his clothes, well, most of them, told him the woman didn't mess around when dealing with hypothermia, despite clearly being uncomfortable in the presence of a nearly naked man.

The chill in the room made him cold again, his abs aching from many prior bouts of shivers that must have assaulted his muscles. This whole cabin was awfully damned cold. No wonder she had to wear a woolen poncho in here. He glanced over to find a fire burning in the fireplace insert, but heard no motor running the fan to put out heat. How did she survive the winter up here? Either the fire wasn't burning hot enough or the blower was broken. He'd investigate later.

His focus returned to Cassie. "Listen, I need to check on my horses and find someone to go to my ranch to take care of them."

"They are fine. Adam and Kitty spent the night there after the aval—"

"Kitty?"

"Sorry, Karla. I knew her as Kitty in college and the name stuck, although she did not let anyone call her that but me. Anyway, I called her a little while ago to let her know you were conscious and doing better. She said one of Angelina's brothers—I forget which one, Matteo maybe—moved in at the ranch until you can return home."

Luke hadn't relied on anyone to take care of his commitments since the day he'd lost Maggie. Those horses were *his* responsibility. Sure, Angel's brothers, Matt and Rafe, knew a lot about horses, but his animals had special needs.

"They won't take too kindly to strangers. I still need to check in on them." He realized it sounded like he planned to put a call through to the horses. He leaned his shoulder against the doorway and ran his hand through his hair, hating the feelings of helplessness overtaking him again. "Look, I need to talk with someone down there." His raspy voice sounded barely above a whisper to his ears. He'd never felt so weak.

Trying to take command of the situation while fighting to remain upright, he held out his free hand palm upward. "I need to use your phone." She stared him down, silent and unrelenting. "Please. What would you do if it was your alpacas in the hands of a stranger?"

Her features softened. She sighed and pulled a cell from the pouch in the front of her poncho. "But I insist that you sit down before you fall over."

He walked up to the fireplace instead. Maybe being closer to the flames would stop his body's incessant shaking. As he leaned his shoulder against the mantel, he accepted her phone and then stared blankly at the buttons. He had no clue how to reach any of the Giardano brothers. Glancing back at Cassie, who stood with her arms folded over her chest, he asked, "Do you think Adam's still at my place?"

"No. Adam took Kitty home yesterday. She's been having some back pain, and he wanted her in their own bed last night."

Not that he could remember Adam's number, either, but his or Karla's contact info would be on Cassie's speed dial. *Dammit.* Luke couldn't think straight. He sat up, took a few steps toward the coffee table, and reached down to pick up the steaming mug, but must have tripped over something and lost his balance. He pictured himself about to be sprawled out on top of the table.

"Luke!" Before he landed, Cassie ran around the table and grabbed him around the chest, surprisingly quick and strong for such a little thing. She helped set him upright again.

The room continued to spin. "Sorry, darlin'. Got a little dizzy." When he patted her shoulder to convey that he was okay, she stepped away from him abruptly, forcing him to steady himself on the arm of the couch. He drew in a deep breath.

Fear. He saw genuine fear in her eyes, much like he saw in his horses. Why would she fear him?

"You should be in bed. *Please*, Lucas, cooperate with me. Make the call from there." The plea in her voice caught him by surprise, too. Almost sounded like she cared. Well, if she didn't, she'd have left his ass to freeze out in that newly formed snow mound. The woman was a mass of contradictions.

"Let me just call Angel before going back to bed. She'll know how to reach her brother." He heard her sigh as he stared at the phone a minute longer. Hell, he didn't have a clue what Angel's or Marc's numbers were, either. He always used the programmed contacts. Even if he did recall, the blow to his head had probably scrambled his memory.

Cassie came to his rescue, taking the cell from him. "I do not wish to bother Kitty, but Marc's number is in the recent calls. He was with Angel the night of the avalanche and called to check on you. Maybe they are still together. If not, I am sure he will know how to contact her."

"Good thinking." Luke sat down hard on the small sofa, too late realizing the jarring movement would set off more jackhammers between his temples. He held his head in his hands, hoping the throbbing would go away before he had to speak to anyone.

Cassie hit the callback button and handed it to him again. When it went to voicemail, he left a brief message.

Let go. There's nothing you can do now.

No doubt Marc had taken care of everything after hearing about the accident. The man was good at taking care of everyone's needs but his own.

He ended the call and handed the phone back to Cassie. "Thanks.

Guess I'm going to have to trust that they have things under control down there. How long do you think it'll be before I can head home?"

Cassie shrugged and pocketed the cell again. "The road is covered with twenty feet of snow, ice, and debris from fallen trees and rocks. I would guess a couple of weeks. But it is late April, so the snow will melt in the coming month."

"Damn. That's a long time."

"Look, I did not ask for this, either."

He shouldn't be so ungrateful for putting her out like this. "I'm sorry. It's just that I'm not used to lying around doing nothing."

"But that is just what you are going to do for the next few days. Plowing snow can wait. Now, back to bed."

He stood and swayed on his feet. Cassie placed an arm around his waist and led him back to the bedroom, piling up pillows and blankets so he was sitting up. "I will return in a few minutes with your lunch."

With it being so dark in here, he would have expected it to be time for breakfast or supper. Much as he hated to admit it, being back in bed was just what he needed. The shaking had finally stopped, and he leaned into the pillow. He needed to regain his strength.

Cassie returned a minute later and handed him the mug of coffee. "Drink this while I prepare a bowl of soup for you."

"Why don't you join me?"

"It will be easier for me to eat in the kitchen."

She probably preferred to keep her distance from him. He sat up and took a sip of the black brew. It was stronger than he made it at home, but damned good. Maybe it would clear some of the cobwebs from his brain and give him a boost of energy. Not that there was anything he needed to be doing or that she would allow him to do for a while.

Except maybe checking the blower on her fireplace insert. He made a lousy patient, but thankfully, stayed pretty healthy most of the time. Too bad Cassie would be subjected to his frustration until he was well enough to go home.

When she returned, he didn't waste any time trying to set a different tone. "Cassie, darlin', I'm not blaming you for my being stuck up here. It's my own fault, but I have a lot of obligations right now. I can't be away from my horses too long. It's a crucial time in their recovery and training. I don't even know what the weather's like down in the valley. O'Keeffe doesn't like being shut up in the barn, but I can't leave her out in a blizzard, either."

She sat down on the bed as far away from him as practical and traded him his mug for another filled with soup. "The storm was mostly up here in the mountains. Kitty said they only had a few inches at your place that first night." She cocked her head. "How many horses do you have?"

He grinned. "Four at the moment. All rescued mustangs that had been abused or neglected. I'm training them for SAR work." He didn't want to think about the day coming when he had to turn them over to someone else, for the same reason foster parents found it hard to let the kids they cared for go.

"SAR?"

"Search and Rescue. I just transferred to the squad out of Fairchance. When these horses go to new owners, I'll take on three more. My mustang sanctuary is small potatoes compared to some, but I can't afford to hire a lot of hands to help right now, so three's my limit."

"But you said you have four."

Luke smiled. "The fourth is Picasso, a gelding I plan on keeping. He was my first one and a damned good SAR-trained horse already. When Pic's ready, he'll be valuable in mountain rescues, but we'll remain a team."

Thinking about how he'd recently been rescued himself, Luke shivered and took a sip from the mug of soup—well, more like broth. Still, it tasted better than what he would have served himself from a can. The heat from the liquid warmed his insides, and he finished it off, handing her the mug when he didn't see a nightstand nearby.

"Thanks. That hit the spot."

She held out her empty hand, and their fingers brushed. Luke had a feeling that's what caused her to pull away so quickly. Why so spooked? Didn't she know he'd never hurt a flea? Even if he were so inclined, he most definitely wasn't going to hurt anyone in his current condition.

His eyelids grew heavy.

She set both mugs on the floor. "Lean forward." Pulling the blankets out from behind his back, she left only the pillows. "Lie down. Sleep."

"Yes, ma'am."

All fight gone, he let sleep claim him.

* * *

Cassie watched his eyelids droop as his body relaxed into the mattress and pillows. He looked like a little boy, but that vulnerability was only temporary because of his weakened state. When he recovered, she would need to be on her guard every moment until she could send him home.

How long would that be?

As she spread the blankets over him, her smartphone buzzed. She returned to the living room before answering quietly.

"Hi, Cassie." Angelina's voice conveyed worry, but not as much as she had heard the first night. "How's he doing?"

"He is sleeping again, but he did manage to drink some coffee and a weak soup."

He no longer needs my body heat. Thank you, Goddess.

Angelina sighed. "That sounds great."

Cassie filled her in on Lucas's physical condition as best she could.

"Sounds like you're taking good care of him. I hope he's not giving you any...problems."

Her hesitation reminded her that Angelina had been part of the cleansing ceremony around Adam's hot tub that night. She understood why this situation was so difficult for Cassie.

"For the most part. It seems that I am the problem more than he is. When do you think Marc and the others can start digging out from the other side?"

The pause set her on alert. "I can't speak for Marc.... He's...not..." Angelina's sniffle made Cassie wonder what had happened.

"Is everything okay?"

A longer pause punctuated with more sniffles followed. "I don't know. He's..." Angelina's breathing sounded shaky. "We just haven't been able to work things out. I don't know if we ever will, but I'm sure my brothers and their rescue squad teams will help as soon as the blizzard is over up there."

"Angelina, what happened? You two seemed to have a lot to talk about at daVinci's the other night."

"I can't talk about it right now."

"Okay. I understand." Cassie would never pry. There had been many times she did not wish to share her feelings, either. "Thank your brothers for me." Normally, being snowbound made her feel safer, but with Lucas in her bed, she no longer enjoyed that sense of security.

"Listen, Cassie, tell Luke not to worry about his horses. Matt's loving every minute of this. He'd love to have a place like Luke's. He'll stay at the ranch until Luke returns home and is back on his feet. Beats his tiny apartment in Leadville."

"How can Lucas contact him to check on the horses? I know he is going to worry no matter how much we try to reassure him." Like Lucas, she would have worried if she had been on the other side of the avalanche and cut off from her alpacas, especially with Graciela in her condition. She walked over to her desk and jotted down the number on a slip of paper.

Angelina's voice came through the phone, stronger now. "Lucas? Surely he hasn't forgotten his name!"

"No! It is just that…Luke seemed so…familiar. I was not comfortable calling him that."

"How are *you* doing, Cassie?"

I am trying to keep myself emotionally distant despite our being thrown together like this.

Cassie cleared her throat. "I am fine, thank you. Just tired." She had not slept much while in bed with Lucas the past two nights. Blankets and the space heater were enough to keep him warm now. She could sleep on the floor by the fire or on the nearby loveseat, which was plenty long enough for her. While the cot in her studio was much more comfortable, she should remain closer to Lucas in case he had a relapse or needed something.

"We love you for taking care of our friend. I know this isn't easy for you."

"I am only doing what anyone would do."

Even if it kills me.

Something told her she would never be the same.

After saying goodbye and disconnecting the call, she stared at the open bedroom door a moment before pivoting around and heading to the kitchen. Certain he would sleep for a while, she would add more ingredients to the heartier soup to nourish his body later—which should speed up his healing.

The tactile memory of her body pressed against his sent an uncharacteristic wave of heat into her face before her stomach churned. She thought she might be sick. Even in his weakened state, the muscles under his skin spoke of strength she would be hard-pressed to overcome if she had to fight him off.

Being alone in this isolated cabin with any man other than her brother scared her beyond reason, but Lucas Denton had a charm about him that most likely weakened the resolve of many women.

Not Cassie. No man could charm her. Never again.

Lucas. Somehow calling him by his formal name made her feel less intimate with him, despite the fact they had spent two nights together in her small bed. She threw a handful of amaranth into the pot and stirred absently as she tried to shake off the memory of his body on top of hers. The smothered sensation dragged her back to the pool room at the Lima cantina. Feelings she thought she had long ago buried erupted to the surface. Raw. Exposed. Thankfully, Lucas had not taken advantage of the situation.

Drawing a ragged breath, she pulled back the curtain in the pantry and searched for the quinoa. Perhaps she would make a healthy salad for herself so Lucas could have more of the hot food. She doubted his taste went to the South American grains and delicacies in her pantry. No matter what, she needed to keep him from becoming feverish or chilled again, which would result in her returning to the bed with him.

"Maggie, no!"

The anguish in Lucas's voice brought her hand to a standstill. She set the canister down and ran into the bedroom. Lucas thrashed on the mattress, sweat dotting his forehead as his powerful hands clenched the sheet.

"God, no! Can't reach you!"

For a few seconds, Cassie weighed whether she should try to wake him or let him fight whatever monsters invaded his sleep until they passed. The suffering on his face made her cross the room and touch his shoulder, hoping to pull him back to the conscious world.

He grabbed onto her arm. "I have you! Don't let go!" He yanked her arm, and she lost her balance, tumbling into the bed on top of him.

A scream reverberated in her mind. Lucas opened his eyes, and she realized the scream had not been a silent one. Breathing hard, she pushed off him, but he stared at her with unseeing eyes and placed his hands on either side of her head, pulling her toward his face as if he intended to kiss her.

She fought to escape him. "Let me go! I am not your Maggie. I am

Cassie." She pried at his hand, attempting to loosen his grip as bile rose in her throat. Her mind flashed back. The way they sneered their words in her native language and the sounds of their voices made her lose the love that she had for Spanish.

Cassie beat against Diego's chest. She refused to open her eyes to see the look of triumph on his face. "Get off me, you pig."

"She wants to fight. Que bueno. I like a chica with some fight in her."

Her fear mounted as he undid his belt, and she pounded her fists against him again and again until her wrists ached and her hands grew numb.

"Whoa, darlin'. Wake up. You're dreaming. Not sure what all you said, but you were screaming in Spanish."

Her hands stilled. Even without opening her eyes, she knew that Texas drawl did not come from Pedro or his friends. She blinked several times and stared into Lucas Denton's eyes, a mix of blue and green that looked like gray to her. What was he doing on top of her—again? Cassie shoved him away, a feat made easier when he simply rolled off her.

"Sorry if I scared you, Lucas. I am fine now." How long had she become lost in the flashback? The two of them were a mess. She had probably bruised his chest if the throbbing in her hands was any indication of the impact of the blows delivered. She pushed herself upright and darted to the foot of the bed, gasping as she attempted to draw a deep breath. Her upper arm ached from some unknown reason.

Still not certain how she had gone from trying to ease Lucas awake from his nightmare to being submerged in her own, she contemplated how to explain her reaction to him without revealing more than he needed to know.

"You were dreaming about Maggie." She gasped for a full breath, not realizing she had been breathing so shallowly until she tried to get a sentence out. "I heard you scream for her. I came in to check on you." *Breathe, Cassie.* "When I tried to wake you, you grabbed my arm." *And my head.* That had been the real cause for the flashback. She rubbed the skin on her arm where it had grown tender from his grip, but more disturbing was the lingering tingle she felt from his holding her head.

No, not tingle. Memories of the touch of those other men so long ago made her stomach churn.

"I don't remember anything, darlin', until you called me *el puerco* and screamed at me to get off you. I'm real sorry. I was asleep. I wouldn't hurt you for anything. You sure you're okay?"

She nodded. In reality, she had to admit his touch was nothing compared to… She swallowed the bile before it erupted. "I am fine."

And I will be much better when you are off my mountain.

*   *   *

Luke fought the urge to pound his fist into the wall, but any kind of violence would only add to the fear he'd put in Cassie's eyes. Sure, he'd been beyond sound asleep at the time, but he was solely to blame for scaring her, even if he had no memory of what he'd done. She continued to rub her arm where he'd grabbed her. The thought of causing her physical pain burned his gut as well.

But the momentary terror he'd seen in her eyes shook him to the core. He would never hurt her—or hell, any living thing—not intentionally, anyway. Clearly, he couldn't be trusted around her if he could lose control of himself like that. What if he hurt her again? Judging from her responses, someone had already wounded or abused her before.

Luke sat up and leaned toward her. "Let me see that arm."

She shook her head fiercely and leaned away from him. Hell, he couldn't blame her. Luke ran his hand through his sweat-matted hair.

"I just want to be sure I didn't injure you."

Cassie crawled off the bed and made a beeline for the door. "It is nothing to worry about. I am going to finish preparing dinner."

Luke knew sleep would be elusive and didn't want her to avoid him, even if she had a reason to run. Perhaps he could prove to her he was safe to be around by just, well, being around her. Time and proximity had a way of breaking down barriers. Sure had been working with O'Keeffe.

"Let me help."

She pivoted sharply. "No!"

Fear again. No, *still*. She'd been showing signs of fear since he'd met her. Knowing someone had hurt her so badly pissed him off.

The girl had intrigued him from the moment he first met her. Seeing her nurturing side when Karla was beside herself after Adam's cougar attack. Attending her art gallery showing last winter and witnessing her amazing talent. Heck, even thinking at one point Cassie was the angel Maggie said she was sending him. He'd wanted to get to know her better for a while, but not like this. Still, they were stuck together, so he might as well make the most of the opportunity—if only he could get her to stop constantly shoving him away.

"I told you to stay in bed. You…" Her gaze darted sideways. "You need your rest." Not waiting for a response, she turned and bolted from the room.

Luke pressed his back against the wall that ran the length of the bed. Damn it all, how was he going to fix this?

Remnants of the nightmare that had led to this mess played at the edges of his mind, but he didn't want to think about Maggie right now. She was gone. Clearly, his own brush with an avalanche was stirring up memories he'd buried long ago. He couldn't help Maggie then, and he sure as hell couldn't do anything for her now.

He needed to do something to fix this situation with Cassie. He scooted off the bed and stood, but the room lurched so badly he plopped back onto the mattress, leaned forward, and held his head in his hands until he could see straight again.

He sure as hell wasn't going anywhere for a while. He had no experience with being incapacitated. Maybe having something more substantial to eat would rebuild his strength. With Cassie, timing would be everything, and his instincts told him she needed time to reach a place where she would trust him. He didn't know if they'd be together long enough for that to happen, but in the meantime, he'd try to keep from hurting her again.

That meant he needed to find another place to sleep.

When he thought he would be able to stand upright, he rose again more deliberately and grabbed the bedpost. His stomach churned, but he took a deep breath and put one foot in front of the other until he reached the doorjamb. Holding on, he steadied himself and waited for the room to stop swimming before his eyes.

It didn't. *Aw, hell.* Who was he kidding? He gave up and went back to bed. Clearly, this ordeal had taken more out of him than he realized. Right now, the best thing he could do was rest. He'd have time to fix things later.

The next time he awakened, the room was still dark. Had he slept through another day? Glancing around, he realized the room had no window. It felt like a cave in here. Swinging his legs over the edge of the mattress, he sat up, happy the walls didn't rush him this time.

Progress.

He stood and made his way slowly to the doorway. A fire roared in the fireplace, but after correctly guessing which door led to the john and heeding nature's call, he propelled himself into the living room. Compared to the bedroom, the temperature dropped at least ten degrees. The space heater made a huge difference in that small, confined room, but wouldn't do squat in a room this large. His gaze zeroed in on the fireplace, and he staggered somewhat as he made his way across the room. He searched for and found the blower switch and clicked it into the "on" position. Nothing. He checked the cord. Plugged in. No sign of fraying.

"The blower broke a month ago, but the flames still put out more than enough heat." He turned to find Cassie setting two mugs on the coffee table.

"Not if you're more than a foot away. Do you have any auxiliary heat source?"

"Of course. I would be foolish to rely on only one up here."

Okay, he'd pissed her off—again. Touchy woman, but he'd cut her some slack after what he'd done to her in the bedroom earlier.

"I have two back-up sources—propane and the fireplace in the main house and a wood/coal-burning stove in my studio."

"Why don't we turn on the propane to take the chill off?"

She cast her gaze to the floor. "I only have enough left this season for cooking."

If that was one of her backup fuels, how could she let it nearly run out?

As if she heard the accusation in his thoughts, she put her hands on her hips and glared at him. "I *like* it cold. This is *my* house, and I was not expecting to have company. *You* are the one complaining about the lack of heat, not me."

True enough. He ran his hand through his hair. "Listen, I'd like to see if I can fix this blower. I'll probably need to pull the insert out. Can't do that until the fire dies down. Mind if we just let it die out tonight and clear out the ash and coals in the morning so I can have a look?"

She stared at the hearth and then back at him. It wasn't like he'd just asked if she wanted to go back to bed to have some rough, raw sex. He was talking survival here. His, anyway.

"You are not here to repair things. You need to stay in bed where you belong."

"Darlin', I grew up in West Texas. One, real men earn their keep.

Two, I don't intend to freeze my ass off if I don't have to."

She raised her chin and looked cute as hell when she was all riled up. "As long as you are my guest, you will not be working."

Luke sighed. He'd never spoken to a woman like that. "Sorry. Listen, my head's splitting, and I'm cold."

"Then why not put some clothes on?" She glanced at his crotch, and he could have sworn she blushed before averting her gaze with haste. "I washed and dried your jeans and shirt. They are folded on the chair next to the bed." She bit the inside of her lower lip, and his cock jolted to life. He'd better move before he embarrassed himself—or her. "While you dress, I will find you something for that headache." She walked toward the bathroom.

After dressing in the bedroom, he returned to the living room to find her staring into the flames.

She turned toward him. "Lucas, if you want to repair the blower fan in a few days, fine, but until then, all you are going to do is rest and eat. Nothing more. Do you understand?"

Maybe she wouldn't be sharing her warmth with him in the bed any longer, but damned if he would keep her out of her own bed. "I'm not taking your bed and blankets away anymore."

"I am fine sleeping in here. When you are feeling better and I do not need to be as close, I can sleep in my studio. If you stay in the bedroom, you should stay plenty warm. I can keep the space heater on."

He'd prefer to curl up with Cassie again, despite her mood at the moment, but knew that wouldn't be happening anytime soon.

"Fine." *For the time being.* He walked over to the table in front of the couch and picked up one of the mugs she'd set down. Coffee smelled as strong as before. He took a sip and thought he'd died and gone to heaven. "Just the way I like it. And something smells awfully good in the kitchen."

"Black bean soup. Sit down." She pointed to a glass of water on the table and two white capsules beside it "Take those Tylenol for your headache. Excuse me while I prepare you a bowl of soup."

"Grab yourself one, too. We can eat together."

She turned away and started for the kitchen. "No, thank you. I am not hungry."

Like hell. Luke followed her into the kitchen. No way was she going to skip dinner on his watch. She barely weighed anything as far as he could tell under that baggy poncho she wore constantly. A strong wind coming down off the mountain would have blown her away.

He smiled as he remembered the feel of her naked body against his, though. Soft in all the right places.

Small and functional, her kitchen was as spartan as the rest of the cabin. A rustic wooden table for four stood butted against the wall in the corner, with only two chairs. Books were piled on one end. She probably read while she ate. Living alone, he did that, too. The small gas stove had two burners, and the large stockpot occupied half the range's top.

"Smells good."

She turned toward him, and sparks blazed from her eyes. "I thought I told you to wait in the living room."

He'd invaded her territory. "Never been much good at following orders." He grinned, finding perverse pleasure in teasing her. At least being pissed at him was a response. More emotion than he'd receive otherwise. He glanced in the direction of her covered arm. Well, except when he'd hurt her a short while ago. He hated that.

She sighed and resumed stirring the pot. "It is a simple soup. Marc said to go easy at first."

"You talked with Marc again?"

"No. He gave me instructions the night of your accident, though."

He grinned at the image of the expression on her face when Marc delivered the news about how to avoid any worsening of his hypothermia.

"Oh, Angelina called while you were asleep. Matteo is staying at your ranch. I wrote down his number for you."

"Thanks. I'll give him a call in a little bit."

Cassie crossed the tiny space to the cutting board on the table where a loaf of home-baked bread awaited. "I hope you like brown bread. *Mi mamá's* recipe."

"Looks wonderful. I appreciate you for going to all that trouble."

She shook her head. "No trouble. I make it several times a week." She cut several thick slices before placing a dish of softened butter in the center of the table. "Please, sit. You should not be on your feet."

Bossy little thing.

From the cupboard, she pulled out a hand-thrown earthenware bowl with a deep green and rust-colored pattern and ladled out his bowl of soup. When she turned to place the bowl on the table, she saw he hadn't sat down yet and scowled at him.

"You take that bowl," he said, motioning to the other chair. He might be weak as a kitten, but he wouldn't forget his manners. "I'll grab my own." Call him stubborn, but he'd been taking care of himself for a long time and wasn't about to start letting her or anyone else wait on him.

"It is my duty to take care of you."

Whether she wanted to or not. The unspoken words hung in the air between them.

"I'm fine. You've worked hard enough preparing this meal. I think I can manage to fill my own bowl." Without awaiting a response, he pulled out a chair for her. She hesitated and finally took her seat. He helped scoot it in, filled a bowl with the savory soup, and took his own seat on the exposed side of the table to her left.

Head bowed, she reminded him to offer a silent blessing over his meal before she picked up a slice of bread and extended the tray to him. She left the heel, which was his favorite, so he took and slathered it with the creamy butter.

"Is this butter homemade?"

She nodded, placed a spoonful of soup in her mouth, and swallowed before speaking. "Not by me, though. I purchase it from a local farmer."

After taking a healthy bite, he decided he'd have to find out who sold it. Glancing down at his soup again, he noticed some little balls floating in it that reminded him of pictures he'd seen of caviar. He took a spoonful, minding his manners and trying not to slurp. The balls tasted more nutty than fishy. "Soup's excellent. What's in it?"

"Just a hodgepodge of things I had on hand."

She wasn't going to enlighten him, so he might as well ask. "What are these little balls?"

"Amaranth. I used amaranth flour in the bread, too. I am sorry if you do not like it, but it is a Peruvian staple."

"No, it tastes great! Don't ever apologize for your cooking, darlin'. I didn't experiment with a lot of exotic foods growing up. Mostly meat and potatoes at my house because my dad wouldn't try anything else. Angel exposed me to some new things when she was staying out at my place last month, but I'm a functional cook at best. Anything you make, I'm sure I'll love."

"Potatoes are a staple in my native country, but we have so many more cultivated varieties than you have here. The Quechua, *Mamá's* people, have a potato to cure every illness, I believe." Cassie smiled then averted her gaze. "Sorry."

"About what? I love hearing about other cultures and places."

She didn't continue to share, though. They ate in silence for a few moments. He didn't feel a need to fill the silence between them as he might have with someone else. Still, after a few minutes, he spoke anyway.

"My wife wasn't into cooking any more than I was, so we ate out when we could afford it or kept it simple and quick when we ate at home." She nodded, remaining focused on her soup. She was a quiet one. Normally, so was he, but he felt like talking today. "Growing up, I usually ate whatever I could rustle up from a can or a box. My parents worked long hours on the pipeline projects. I had to fend for myself a lot as a teen, too, even though we'd settled down in El Paso by the time I hit high-school age. Guess I became used to taking the easy route with cooking." He stopped, wondering what had made him share all that useless information. Maybe the silence between them grated on his nerves after all.

"That is unfortunate. *Mamá* was very traditional and stayed home to care for me and my brother."

Luke took another bite and swallowed. "I envy you having a sibling." His childhood had been a lonely one. They'd lived in half a dozen places from when he was born in Wyoming to when Momma declared they were settling down in El Paso—mainly so Luke could attend high school in one place. Lots of friends came and went, but nothing more than surface level until he met Maggie. Later, Marc had become the closest friend Luke had since Maggie.

"My wife was one of five kids. Very different dynamic."

"I imagine so. Are they in Texas?"

Luke shrugged. "I suppose they still are. They don't have a lot to do with me." Her family blamed him for what had happened eight years ago—maybe not unjustly. Hell, they blamed him for taking her away from them, even though they were a dysfunctional mess from what she told him and other things he figured out on his own about how they'd treated her.

Recently, though, he'd come to realize Maggie was the one who had put the two of them in the dangerous predicament that killed her. She had been on yet another quest to find the next rare plant, hoping that doing a scientific paper on its properties might give her a leg up before the tenure board. Honestly, she probably sought the approval of the department chair. She never really lost her insecurities and the desire to please men of authority.

But neither of them knew anything about the mountains when they went to Colorado that spring, assuming winter was over due to the warm temperatures.

The rescue workers forced him away from the ledge.

Don't think about that. Nothing he could do to change things now.

Luke's head continued to throb as he finished the bowl of soup, and he leaned forward to place his forehead in his left hand as his stomach started to churn. He might be revisiting the john soon. Damned if he'd make her think he didn't love her cooking, though, so he'd try to fight off the nausea.

Nope. Not working.

Luke stood too abruptly, and the room spun. He grabbed at the air to steady himself and found Cassie's arm around his waist, holding him upright.

"Are you all right?"

"Sure." *Well, no, not exactly.*

"We need to put you back in bed. You are still very weak from that blow to the head."

"I had a few concussions during my college football days." Even when he was a decade younger, Luke never wasted the day away sleeping, though.

"Perhaps that is causing this one to hit you harder, Lucas. It has only been a couple of days."

While he didn't want to start letting his body rule him, he had no fight left. "You might be right." Now his only thought was reaching the bed, not the bathroom.

"Let me help you."

Dammit, he would make it to the bed under his own steam. "I'm fine." *I'd be better if the floor would stop moving.*

"Do not argue with me, Lucas. I do not want you to fall and suffer another injury under my care." Next thing he knew, Cassie placed a hand on his chest and an arm around his back to steady him before steering him into the living room.

Unable to resist even if he'd wanted to, Luke let her guide him one step at a time until he was back in her small, dark bedroom being tucked into bed like a sick kid. He didn't like being seen by her in that light—no way, no how.

But his stomach stopped churning now that he was flat on his back. Exhaustion made him too damned tired to argue. His body sagged into the tiny bed, and he closed his eyes. He'd rest a few minutes and be good as new.

Seconds later, he heard the click of the door and let the world fade away.

Chapter Two

C assie knelt on *Abuela's* folded green and black woven blanket that served as her meditation pallet in front of her altar in the far corner of her studio. Candlelight flickered, making the shadow of the potted bay tree dance against the wall and appear to grow before her eyes. The plant provided protection and helped invoke her psychic powers. A statue of her deity, *Mama Quilla*, also stood on the altar with arms outstretched and welcoming. While her alpaca had the Quechua spelling for moon, Cassie chose to use the Spanish spelling when referring to Goddess, perhaps because her spirituality was tied up in both Quechua and Catholic traditions, among others she learned about at uni.

She had strayed away from the Catholic traditions when she explored her own truth in college. She had begun to embrace a goddess deity over a male one even before she had been attacked. But the rape had only strengthened her faith in *Mama Quilla*. Praying to a male deity with so much power frightened her at that point in her life.

Even though her goddess had not spoken to her in years, she continued to try to connect during her meditation time. Usually, the exercise gave her moments of peace and quieted her mind, at least.

Not this morning, though. Cassie's body trembled from touching Lucas familiarly so often these past few days. The contact might not be considered intimate to anyone other than her, but touching any man went far beyond her comfort zone. Of course, not so long ago, their bodies had been pressed against each other as she tried to keep him warm.

She lit her white meditation candle to bring her inner peace and comfort. Breathing in its pure light, she invited *Mama Quilla* into her sacred space, hoping She would remove this sense of…fear? That was the only word to describe what she felt. Her stomach had churned every minute since Lucas crashed into her sanctuary. Her heart beat erratically any time he drew near.

Similar feelings of fear around men had plagued her for five years, and yet it had evolved to be different somehow now.

Cassie closed her eyes and let her mind float to a place of beauty and peace, an Andean meadow where mountain flowers bobbed on the spring breeze, against a backdrop of steep, snow-covered peaks. Soon her body stopped shaking, allowing her to begin her meditation.

Confounding thoughts of Luke—*no, call him* Lucas—continued to keep her earthbound and unable to reach the deep meditative state she sought.

Lucas smiling.

Leave me alone.

Lucas bare-chested.

Leave me alone!

Lucas lying on top of her.

Leave. Me. Alone!

She could not rid her mind of the intrusive images. Her body trembled uncontrollably. She sighed and leaned forward to pinch out the candle flame with her finger and thumb. Perhaps she should go to the shed to check on the animals and make sure they were okay. Were her babies aware that an unwanted male had invaded their once safe, peaceful sanctuary? Did they care? Life was so simple for them. They had each other for company and Cassie to see to their needs.

Lucas would sleep for hours most likely. His body remained weak from his accident—although, when her hand pressed against his chest, she had not detected any sign of such weakness. The man was solid sinew and muscle. He must be very active at something besides carpentry and art. She had no interest in finding out how he stayed in shape.

None whatsoever. In fact, she had no interest in the man at all. She just wanted him off her mountain!

When she entered the shed, Graciela came to her side immediately, distressed about something. "What is the matter, girl? Having a hard time sleeping with that swollen belly of yours?" The alpaca hummed, expressing her misery, and Cassie sympathized with the poor dear. This cria would be a first for both of them. So far, everything seemed to be going well with the pregnancy. According to Cassie's sources, alpacas tended not to need a lot of help birthing their babies. Still, Cassie sensed this would not be an easy delivery—perhaps because neither of them had been through the experience before. And she had learned the hard way to trust her instincts.

Or was she projecting her own jitters about being a first-time *mamina* onto the creature? The four alpacas had only been here about six months, and she still had much to learn.

"What shall we do about him, Graciela?" The alpaca gave her a blank stare before humming again. Of course, she did not know the person Cassie mentioned. The alpacas had not yet met Lucas.

Cassie gave her a pat on the neck before setting to work filling the feed bins and heated water trough. Leaving the warm, dry shed, she fought to find her way back to the house using the rope lines strung between the buildings. The wind had whipped up, and torrents of snow lashed at her face. The snowstorm had brewed slowly the first two days at blizzard strength, but now the winds had decreased somewhat. She wished they would blow away the snow blocking Lucas's exit, but knew from experience strong winds only meant even higher drifts to deal with, lengthening the amount of time he might be stuck up here.

When would she be rid of the man sleeping inside her cabin?

She entered the mudroom and removed her boots and wet poncho, hanging the latter on two hooks to dry. Her socks grew wet from the melting snow on the floor so she stripped those off, too, and started toward the fireplace to warm up.

An anguished shout from the bedroom stopped her dead in her tracks. "Noooo!"

Not again. Her heart pounded at the fear and horror in his voice. She could not stand to let him remain lost in the dark world of his nightmare, knowing that place quite well herself. She inched toward the bedroom door with dread. He had overpowered her before, triggering her flashback. Light from the living room shone on Lucas as he lay in her bed. His feet thrashed, apparently trying to kick off the blankets. Still, Cassie hesitated, afraid he might lash out at her again if she came too close.

But she remembered her training. If she could not fight off a man in Lucas's weakened state, her self-defense training had been for nothing. That assurance did not make this situation any easier.

"Lucas, wake up! You are dreaming!"

His arm thrust outward, extending over the edge of the bed. But he remained asleep. She banged on the headboard, hoping to awaken him, but nothing.

Goddess, why me?

Climbing onto the bed, she straddled him, grabbing his hand as he swung it toward her face. She pressed it into the pillow above his head. "Lucas, you are only dreaming."

"Oh, God. Take me, not them!" The gravelly sound of his voice broke her heart.

Perhaps he would answer to his nickname. "Luke, wake up. Now!"

He blinked his eyes open and squinted in the dim light spilling in from the living room. She had kept the light off so he could sleep. His body needed rest more than anything else, but he would not recover quickly enough if his sleep continued to be plagued with nightmares. Did he dream like this all the time? If so, how could he function on so little sleep? Her nightmares had lessened over the years, but when they came, they were just as fierce as if she were back in that cantina.

He furrowed his brows as he searched her face. Did he recognize her? She released his hands and sat up to break contact with him.

"Do you remember where you are?"

He nodded. "In your cabin, Cassie. There was another avalanche."

"Well, only the one this year."

He nodded. "Right. I was following you home to make sure you were safe."

At least the delirium had not returned.

He reached up and tucked her hair behind her left ear before stroking her cheek as if uncertain she was real. "Last year, I dreamed of an angel. Got confused about who it was at first until you…"

Clearly, he was still confused. "What are you talking about?" *I am in nobody's dreams, much less as an angel.* Maybe the delirium had returned after all.

"I dreamed you were…well, it's a little complicated. First, Maggie said she was sending me an angel. In my sleep, I saw you in a meadow working on a painting of quaking aspens. It was autumn." He reached up and ran a strand of her hair between the side of his index finger and his thumb, setting her stomach on edge. "You had long dark hair…" His knuckle brushed against her breast and robbed her of her next breath. "…and soft, olive skin."

Dreaming about an angel, though? Had his wife reached out from the other side to deliver some kind of prophetic message from the Universe? As if Cassie could be any man's angel. Then it dawned on her.

"Your wife must have been predicting that I would be the one to rescue you from your truck after the avalanche." Yes, of course. That was it. She relaxed and pulled farther away so that her hair was no longer being touched, and he rested his hand on the mattress. She could see how he might have misinterpreted the dreamed message to mean she was his angel.

Lucas seemed to mull over her explanation, and the light left his eyes. He nodded. "Yeah, I reckon you're right. I didn't put two and two together, but that makes more sense than…"

He trailed off, but they both knew what the alternative interpretation to that vision might be. She shuddered. Her spiritual obligation must end the moment she nursed him back to health and took him home.

Realizing she still straddled his waist, Cassie swung her leg off him and stood beside the bed as he sat up. She thanked the Goddess she had not been pressed against his hips because if he had become sexually excited, she would have hauled him out to the shed to sleep with the alpacas. He did not appear to be coming on to her—just momentarily dazed and confused.

"What were you dreaming when I came in here just now?"

He winced as the memory came back. "About my wife. How she…died."

"You miss her very much, do you not?" The question popped out before she could stop it. She did not want to delve into his past.

Lucas looked down at the blanket covering him. "She's been gone eight years. I don't think about her every waking moment the way I used to."

No, but she still invades your dreams.

Perhaps the avalanche churned up unresolved feelings he was unaware of harboring. Regrets? No, worse than that. "You blame yourself for not saving her."

He scrutinized her a moment, and then his words came out in a hoarse whisper. "Some, I reckon. Mostly, I'm pissed that I didn't know more about the nature of these mountains and didn't stop her from that fool mission to photograph one of her rare plants."

Against her better judgment, Cassie sat at the foot of the bed, ensuring she was far enough away from him to escape if she needed a head start. Perhaps talking about his living nightmare might help him find some much-needed healing and peace. "Tell me about that day."

Again, he stared long and hard at her. She doubted he would be forthcoming. Then, as if the floodgates had opened, he began to tell the story.

"It was spring, early May. She was on a break at UT. Should have been grading final papers, but she heard about this plant in a remote area of Mount Evans that only bloomed for a short time, so she insisted we take a long weekend and drive up here."

He pulled his knees up and propped his wrists on them, letting his large, tanned hands dangle between them. Non-threatening.

"We hiked quite a ways from the parking lot before she spotted a clump of them on an outcropping of rock, tucked into a crevice." He closed his eyes, lost in the memory. "She asked me to photograph it. I did a lot of nature photography then, mostly for her."

The silence spread out between them, making her feel as though she might tumble into the same abyss that stored his memories.

Just let him tell his story, Cassie. Do not make yourself a part of it.

"I wasn't paying attention to where she was—just wanted to take the best photo I could. All of a sudden, she screamed."

He made a fist with his right hand, and she fought the urge to reach out and comfort him. Realizing that would only pull him out of the story, not to mention bring the two of them too close together, she remained still. He needed to relive it until he could release himself from the misplaced blame and guilt.

"God, sometimes that scream wakes me out of a dead sleep to this day."

"I know."

He opened his eyes and looked at her. "Is that what brought you in here? Did I scream out in my sleep again?"

She nodded. "I know what it feels like to be in the grip of nightmares." *And flashbacks.* "I did not want you to suffer. These memories have too much power over us when we are asleep."

Sometimes during the daytime, too.

"Thanks for understanding. I appreciate that. It's been a long time since I've dreamt about that day. Now, every time I close my eyes…"

"The avalanche probably stirred up old memories."

He nodded. "Probably."

She waited for him to continue, but when he remained silent, she prompted him. "What happened next?"

"When she screamed, I turned in time to watch her body come to a sudden stop at the bottom of a scree slope. When the dust cleared, I saw that the sharp rocks had cut up her face. She banged her head on a rock ledge where she landed." He closed his eyes again and then opened them quickly, as if the image had only grown sharper in his mind's eye.

"Was she conscious?"

"She didn't respond at first, but a minute or two later—seemed like hours—she moaned. I called to her, and she spoke with me a bit. Confused, for sure, but she recognized me and knew where we were. I figured I'd better go get help because it wouldn't do her any good if I went down to her and got stuck, too. We didn't bring ropes or rappelling equipment."

He reached for the worn leather band on his wrist and twisted it. "I've only felt that helpless one time since."

She did not ask but wondered what other event could have left him any more helpless than watching his injured wife and not being able to save her from certain doom. Had he lost—or nearly lost—someone else close to him?

Her heart tugged, but she refused to allow herself to pity him. She could not let her guard down. No doubt, many women would find him attractive with his classic features—high cheekbones, strong chin, and affable smile. Not Cassie.

Would he continue to share the story about his wife? Should she encourage him to or just let him keep those sad memories buried deep inside? She would not have wanted him to prod her about her own past. So why did she ask, "What happened when you returned to her with help?"

He refocused on her face. "The EMTs, rescue workers, and I came back within an hour of the fall since we weren't wandering around on a wild-goose chase the way Maggie and I had been. She was lucid, but in a lot of pain. Probably broke her arm or wrist in the fall." He paused, blinking several times. No doubt he would have traded places with her, if only he could. "They wouldn't let me go down to her. God, I just wanted to hold her. Let her know she wasn't alone." His voice broke, and Cassie wanted to hold and comfort him, but kept her distance out of fear. He might misinterpret her intentions. "There wouldn't have been much I could have done to help. I hadn't been trained for SAR back then."

Perhaps she could help ease some of his pain by sharing her experience when channeling his dead wife. "I know it does not bring her back, but when she came to me to create that sketch of her and your unborn baby, she was at peace. She held no anger or resentment toward you or anyone else."

Tears swam in his eyes before he turned away. "I look at that picture every morning when I get out of bed. It's given me peace of mind, especially knowing she's together with our baby. Thank you for sharing it with me."

"I am not a medium or anything. Perhaps she came to me because you and I were in the same room. She guided me to sketch that image. I just conveyed what she showed me onto the paper."

Lucas grinned and met her gaze again. "Yeah, she could be forceful like that. Lord knows I never could tell her no." His smile faded, and she saw regret in his eyes. He blamed himself still. She hoped he would one day let go of that useless emotion. Regret never solved anything.

Perhaps someday I will take my own advice to heart.

"May I get you anything?"

"No, I'm fine. Too tired to get up. I'll just try to go back to sleep now. I appreciate you checking on me. Sorry to be such a pain."

His gratitude warmed her heart, even though she felt guilty accepting it given how much she wished she had not been forced to take care of him at all. "Just get well. I am sure you wish to return home as soon as possible."

Not as much as I wish for you to go home.

"I'll do my best."

She nodded and stood. "Only pleasant dreams this time."

Cassie realized she truly hoped he would sleep peacefully. Something about this man made her want him to heal from his unbearable loss.

*   *   *

Luke ached from head to calves when he sat up in the tiny bed and swung his legs over the side of the mattress. How long had he slept this time? He had no concept of time in his windowless prison room. Last he remembered, he was spilling his guts to Cassie about Maggie. What had prompted that much revelation? He rarely talked about that day to anyone.

Sitting up was a chore, harder than training a horse to saddle and rider. Hell, much as he hated calling that process breaking a horse, *he* felt like the one who had been broken this time. A shiver made him aware he was half-naked. He'd been the one to strip off his clothes after that nightmare. He had finally warmed up, but being out from under the covers reminded him that he was at twelve thousand feet, near a mountain pass, in a cold-ass cabin.

Damn, but Cassie kept this place glacial, despite the space heater she'd left running for him in here. No wonder she wore so many layers of clothes. He needed to work on that fireplace blower today. He hoped it wouldn't require any parts he couldn't fashion himself out of whatever she had laying around.

What day was it? His internal clock had been broken, too. Noticing a floor lamp for the first time, Luke flipped the switch, but didn't see a clock in the room. He glanced around the seriously utilitarian bedroom. He thought his house was bare of ornamentation, but at least his mom had helped him set up his condo and put some of her soft touches here and there, which he'd brought with him to the ranch—chenille bedspread, fake flowers in pots in the kitchen, even the bowl of seashells in his bathroom that he'd collected at Galveston Beach on a rare vacation when he was nine. Momma was sentimental about things like that and had kept them all those years.

Cassie's bedroom was small and dark and had no mementos whatsoever to hint at her past. Kind of reminded him of how a monk or nun lived in the olden days. Hell, even they probably had more personal touches in their rooms than he saw in this one. The only splashes of color came from the Indian blankets on her bed. The geometric patterns in vibrant greens and reds on one blanket counterbalanced the somber blacks and whites of another. He wondered if she'd made them herself. No, probably not. They looked like heirlooms. And at daVinci's bar, she'd said fiber art was new to her.

Then again, she might have used a loom back where she came from—Bolivia? No, Peru. Many people made a distinction between creating functional items like blankets as opposed to artwork only to be displayed on a wall but never used. He didn't agree with that thinking. He preferred creating pieces of art that would be useful items as well, like the furniture he made for his and other people's homes, or even play equipment for the Masters at Arms kink club. Somehow, he could see Cassie feeling the same way about functional art—even if she only enjoyed the art herself.

But she had done that gallery exhibition of her paintings months ago, so clearly she wanted to share her art. Come to think of it, he hadn't seen many decorations on her walls anywhere in the cabin, so maybe her art was only created to be shared with or sold to others. Not for her to enjoy.

In this room, the cabin's chinking and logs provided the only wall adornment. Hell, who slept in a room without a window? Did she enjoy living in a cave? More like a tomb. How could someone living on a gorgeous mountain peak want to be so closed off from all that beauty? If he'd built this place, he'd not only have a window but a skylight above the bed so he could watch the stars come out at night and make their trek across the sky.

He shook his head to clear it of his fanciful notions. How Cassie chose to live was none of his business.

Luke grabbed his shirt from the ladder-back chair beside the bed, again showing she had an appreciation for functional art, before he pushed his feet and legs into his jeans. With a grunt, he rose and waited for the expected dizziness to hit. When it didn't, he figured maybe the worst of the concussion was behind him. He tucked his shirt into his jeans before zipping and buttoning them closed.

Luke's stomach growled, taking his attention away from the chill in the room. His appetite had returned full force. Steak and eggs sure would hit the spot this morning.

Luke entered the frigid living room and glanced around. No Cassie. He didn't hear any sounds from the kitchen, either. She must be in the shed with her alpacas, or maybe she'd gone to her studio. He'd like to see where she worked, but wouldn't invade that space the way he had the rest of her house. An artist's place of work was sacred, deeply personal, and no one should enter without an explicit invitation.

Somehow, he didn't expect that invite to be forthcoming anytime soon. She was one private person. Hell, so was he. The only time anyone had been in his studio was when he needed help moving a covered piece to his truck for delivery.

The fire had died down—whether because he'd asked or from neglect, he didn't know. Had she slept in her studio? She sure as hell hadn't shared that bed with him. He hoped she'd been warm wherever she had bedded down. Tonight, he'd take the floor in here and let her have her bed back.

But his first order of business was rustling up some breakfast—or whatever meal it was time for. Then he'd take the insert apart and see what the problem was with the blower. Maybe he could have some decent heat blazing in this cabin soon.

Although, Cassie sure seemed to prefer the cold. Must be from growing up in the Andes. Or maybe his body had softened in the comparatively warmer climes of West Texas? His stomach growled again, and he decided he'd eat before trying to find—or decipher—the woman who was Cassie López. A thorough survey of the contents of the fridge told him eggs wouldn't be on the menu, and he wasn't going to invade her freezer hunting for a steak without permission, so he ladled out a bowl of the delicious soup she'd served at his last meal. While it microwaved to a scalding hot temperature, he sliced off a thick slab of her amaranth bread. Soon, he sat down at the table and dug in, blowing on the spoonful of soup to cool it down. He took a tentative bite and closed his eyes.

Damn, but the girl could cook.

He'd been living out of cans and prepared boxed dinners for so long he appreciated every flavorful bite. After having his fill of a second bowl, he still had not seen or heard any sign of Cassie, so he decided now was the time to tackle that fireplace repair before his energy failed him again. He noticed the circuit-breaker box on the wall in the corner. She'd clearly labeled the circuits, and he cut the juice to the fireplace.

Thirty minutes later, he had the insert pulled away from the fireplace and quickly figured out what the problem was. Luckily, it was fixable using the tools he'd found in her kitchen drawer—exactly where his momma kept hers, too. Good thing. A run to the hardware store wasn't going to happen anytime soon.

"What are you doing up?"

Luke glanced across the room to where Cassie stood covered shoulder to knees in her ever-present woolen poncho. She'd come from outside. Her studio must not be inside the cabin. Or maybe she'd been taking care of the alpacas.

"Fixing the insert's fan."

"You should not be doing that so soon."

"Sorry, but I'm tired of freezing my ass off." He heard how cranky he sounded and gave her a smile to soften his rant. "It was an easy fix. Besides, I'm almost good as new thanks to your wonderful care, darlin'."

He expected her to bite his head off, but she merely took a deep breath. Maybe she was warming up to him and his endearments. He wiped the grin off his face before he pissed her off—again.

"You should be in bed."

"Spent enough time in bed already. I need to do something useful."

He stood from his kneeling position and shoved the stove insert back into the fireplace with both hands and his shoulder as if shoving a blocking sled down a football field. His upper body strength was pitiful at the moment, but it slammed home, and he stood, working out a kink in his shoulder. Man, he was seriously out of shape.

"Now, I'll turn the circuit back on, and we'll build a fire we can enjoy together this afternoon."

"I do not have time to sit by the fire."

"Then why don't you let me help with your chores to free up some time?"

"I can handle my responsibilities, Lucas."

"Call me Luke."

"I prefer Lucas."

Probably because she wanted an air of formality between them, even though they were sharing the same house. Hell, they'd even shared the same bed a couple of nights. He grinned at the memory. Luke was all about tearing down the barriers between them. She might come across as a prickly-pear cactus, but Luke sensed it was all a façade. Why was she trying to hide her true nature? If Karla thought so much of her, there must be more to her than she allowed the rest of the world to see.

"Darlin', we're going to be together here for at least a week or two. Might as well get it through your head that I'm not going to just lie around here and mooch off you. Put me to work."

The sparks that flew from her gaze told him he had his work cut out for him on that front, too. "You are supposed to be recuperating. Marc said no strenuous exercise for at least a week."

He'd deal with Marc later.

"Where's your woodpile?" He pointed to the four remaining pieces of split wood on the hearth. "These aren't going to last more than a couple of hours."

He didn't expect her to back down, but after a tense moment, she pointed toward the front door. "There is some split dry wood in the mudroom. I will chop some more later if we need it."

Like hell you will. "Splittin' wood's a man's job."

She placed her hands on her hips. "If I had waited for a man, I would have frozen to death a long time ago."

The girl had a point. "But now you have me to help out."

"Lucas, you need to understand something. You are only here until you are well enough to go home. If you can split wood and make repairs, then you can hike out of here and call someone to pick you up along the highway at the pass."

Luke wasn't sure if it was the image of making that daunting hike in his current condition or the thought of leaving Cassie so soon that hurt the worst. He'd better cool it with the "he-man provider" shit if he didn't want her to kick him out on his ass. Apparently, she wasn't in need of being taken care of, probably because she'd had to rely on herself for a long time. Too bad for him. He liked being able to take care of a woman's needs.

Maybe there were other needs she did need a man's help with.

She started toward the kitchen before facing him again. "What would you like for breakfast?"

"Nothin', darlin'." Her hackles must have risen when he used the endearment again, judging by the stiffness in her shoulders. Half the time, the word was out before he even realized he'd said it. Hell, he'd been using words like that on girls since college—maybe high school. She sure was cute when riled up, though. "I helped myself to your delicious soup and bread already. You go ahead, though. I'll start a fire."

He watched her body as she walked away, wishing he could see the sway of her hips in those thigh-hugging jeans, but the long poncho/sweater-like thing she wore hid most of her backside from view. Front side, too, for that matter. The design on the back was an abstract of falling leaves.

Obviously, she wore so many layers around here because it was so cold. Once these flames caught and started putting out heat, would he manage to get her to peel off any?

Luke sighed. *Yeah, right.* No woman sent out more "don't come near me" vibes than this one. She clearly wasn't putting out any signals that indicated an interest in him sexually or any way other than as her patient, despite his efforts to engage her in conversation. Although he'd been drawn to her since the first time he saw her in that hospital waiting room, the only reason he was here with her was because he'd gotten himself stuck up here against her wishes. Sure, the gentle grace and slight vulnerability she exuded brought out every male instinct he possessed, but she was capable of taking care of herself and had no interest in male companionship, much less anything more carnal. It was best to keep his physical distance and just focus on getting well.

But while he was here, he intended to do his share of the work. At the very least, he wanted to show his appreciation for all she'd done for him. Jeezus, she'd saved his damned ass. He owed this girl—big time.

As he arranged the kindling and cardboard on the grate, he thought he heard muttering in the kitchen. No doubt Cassie was chewing his ass up one side and down the other. How appealing was it that she talked to herself? He guessed living alone did that to a person. He was guilty of the same thing, although he waited until he was inside the barn with the horses so at least the horses heard his ramblings.

Luke opened the dampers, struck a match, and the fire soon roared to life. He waited a few minutes as the heat built up, mesmerized by the flames, before he closed the doors. Fire always fascinated him when it was controlled like this. He'd been involved in a number of rescue missions where wildfires had taken a toll on life and property.

When the blower kicked on, he smiled and adjusted the dampers. Score. At least he had earned some of his room and board. Suddenly worn out, he crossed the room and stretched out on the loveseat, his legs sticking over the armrest from the calves down. He leaned his head against the top of the opposite armrest and closed his eyes, planning to rest his eyes for just a few minutes.

"I am sorry I snapped at you earlier, Lu—"

Luke blinked his eyes open to glance up and find Cassie standing across the room from him.

"Oh! I did not know you were sleeping."

How long had he dozed? She didn't have any food with her, so she must have already eaten in the kitchen. He swung his legs to the floor and stood up. "No worries." His head throbbed at the sudden change in position.

"I am not used to having anyone taking care of things I should be

48

doing myself."

Sounded like Maggie. She never wanted his help much, either. "You're a busy girl. I have nothing but time on my hands."

"Would you at least give yourself a couple more days to heal? And stop thinking you have to repay me for anything. I would take care of any injured person or animal without expecting anything in return."

"Darlin', I wasn't raised to freeload. I've made my own way in life since college, and I'm not going to start mooching off you or anyone else now." He pointed to the fireplace. "I have a knack for fixing stuff like this. Might as well put me to work while I'm here. Otherwise I'm just going to follow you around and wind up in your hair." He glanced at her long, thick tresses, wondering what it would feel like to run his hands through them.

She blinked at him a few times as she processed his speech. "If I asked again, would you stop calling me 'darling'?"

He grinned. "Shoot, where I come from everyone uses darlin', sugar, or sweetie. Would you prefer one of those instead?"

"I'd prefer Cassie."

"If I call you Cassie instead of Casandra or whatever it's short for, will you call me Luke?"

"I am Cassie. Only Cassie." Fire smoldered in her eyes. "But Lucas is *your* given name."

"Same difference then. I'd rather you call me Luke."

She stared a long moment and then sighed deeply. "Fine, then." Touchdown pass. "You may call me whatever nickname you like, *Lucas.*"

Or maybe another fumble. While he was happy to hear that he could still use the endearments that came so naturally to him, he wished she'd stop calling him Lucas. His momma used his full name—Stephen Lucas Denton—when he was in trouble, but everyone else had called him Luke since second grade. On the other hand, Lucas was probably a sight better than what she probably called him in her head when she was ticked off at him.

Like now.

"I do appreciate you fixing the fireplace. I am not mechanically in-clined."

He grinned. "No worries…Sweet Pea." He wasn't sure what prompted him to choose that unique pet name just for Cassie, but it fit. On the surface, she was beautiful, just like the purple flowers. But underneath, the girl was one tangled up mess. He hoped he'd be able to sort her out someday.

She blinked a couple of times at his words and then sighed. "I am going back to the studio." She walked away from him and then tossed over her shoulder, "You should rest."

Clearly, she wasn't allowing him inside her private sanctuary any time soon.

He grunted noncommittally and, after she left the cabin, searched for something to do. Everything seemed to be in its place, even though, like the bedroom, this one had very little clutter. No knickknacks to make the place personal. Resembled a mountain vacation rental rather than the place someone had called home for years.

Earth tones dominated the living room, except for a rare splash of color in an Indian blanket draped over the loveseat. This one was primarily red and showed terraced triangles and arrows in black.

Restless and once again feeling the effects of diminished stamina, Luke returned to the fireplace to poke at the flaming logs and added the last ones. The room already felt warmer than the bedroom ever would, but the loveseat wasn't long enough for him to sleep comfortably. He pulled a couple of cushions off the couch and retrieved a couple blankets and some pillows from the bedroom. He went to the bathroom where he shucked off his clothes, including his boxers. After washing them out in the sink, he hung them to dry in front of the fire and stretched out on the floor, a blanket around his waist.

Memories flooded him of the time when he was a kid pretending to camp out by the fireplace in that rundown farmhouse in South Carolina. Even though that one had been boarded up, he had used his imagination. He'd done that a lot as a kid. Didn't have a lot of friends since they moved around so much.

Thinking about his childhood reminded him he needed to call Momma in a day or two or she'd worry. She only called once a week now, so she wouldn't think anything out of the ordinary unless he went beyond Sunday. She'd be heading north to visit him at the ranch. For years now, she'd been spending July with him in Colorado. This would be her first time seeing the ranch.

His dad had never visited him in Colorado, period, not even when Luke lived in the townhouse in Denver. Surprised the hell out of him that

Dad said he might join her this year. Said he looked forward to seeing Luke's mustang rescue operation, but more than likely, he'd back out.

Luke hoped so, anyway. The thought of passing Dad's inspection made Luke as nervous as a long-tailed cat in a room full of rocking chairs. When he was younger, he'd dreamed about gaining the old man's approval, but now he didn't really care. Much. He was proud of what he was doing and hoped his dad would be, too. If not, well, status quo.

The flames licked at the air above the fire, and Luke's eyes drooped. He needed to bring in more wood, but he was so damned tired…

The smell of an unfamiliar spice awakened him, and he glanced around the living room. Alone. The scraping of a pot alerted him that Cassie must be back in the kitchen, so he pulled on his boxers, which had dried thanks to the blower, and his jeans. He stood to fasten the fly. Too hot now for the shirt. For the first time since he came to in Cassie's cabin—except maybe when she was pressed against him in her bed—he felt warm.

Cassie's back was turned as she stirred a pot on the stove.

"Something smells good." Her shoulders tensed when she heard his voice, but she recovered quickly and stirred the pot some more.

"*Puca picante* with rice."

He approached and glanced over her shoulder into the pan. "Wow, that sure is red!"

Cassie giggled, the cutest sound he'd ever heard. "That is what *puca* means in my native language."

"And *picante* means it has a helluva kick to it."

"Oh, yes. I hope you do not mi…" She turned and her eyes opened wide.

*   *   *

Cassie found herself staring at Lucas's bare chest. A slight tan line on his arms showed he did not always go shirtless outdoors. So why was he not wearing his shirt now? His nipples stood out ruddy brown against a light sprinkling of sandy-colored hair around his pecs. Blond. Not like…

The tight confines of her kitchen became even more restrictive. Her face grew warm as her heartbeats fluttered erratically, stealing her breath away. Confused, she did not know if he had triggered her fight-or-flight response or if she was merely embarrassed at his state of undress. He did not send out a danger vibe at all, so it must be the latter.

I am safe. He is not one of them.

Swallowing past the lump in her throat, "Um, this might be a little too spicy. I sometimes forget how hot my cooking is for those not used to it." Her words came out in a rush. Lucas's half-naked body set off too many alarm bells for her to process. She turned back to the stove.

"Don't mind a little spice at all. I grew up in West Texas. I even came out the victor in a serrano pepper eating contest at an Austin Tex-Mex cantina once during college."

"The *aji panca* peppers in here are much milder than serrano. You should be fine." *But I am not.* He was much less threatening when naked and delirious. Cassie's face grew as hot as if she had bitten into a serrano herself—or perhaps a habanero. "Excuse me."

Needing to put some space between herself and the heat pouring off this man's naked chest, she scooted around him and lifted the curtain over the pantry to scoop out some rice from the bin.

When she turned around, he had not budged from near the stove. "You should go rest until I finish making dinner. I will call you when it is ready."

"I've slept long enough. Tell me what I can do to help."

Remove your half-naked body from my kitchen.

Be nice, Cassie. He probably was unaware of the effect his nearness had on her. "Would you please set the table?" At least that would move him away from her stove—where she needed to be if they were going to eat tonight. He went about doing as she had requested, lifting several curtains at the cupboards before finding plates. She poured the rice into the boiling water. With surprise, she noted that seeing Lucas's naked chest had not triggered an actual flashback, only discomfort of some unknown origin. A man had not aroused her in more than five years. So it could not be that.

As she stirred the rice, she wondered if he would put on a shirt anytime soon. She did not intend to sit beside him at the table if he remained half-dressed. At least he had put his pants on. When she had come in from the studio to find him sleeping by the fire, his white underwear hanging like a flag of surrender from the fireplace tool set, she wondered if he had fixed the fireplace so he could strut around her cabin nude.

If so, he had better think again.

"What are you working on in your studio?"

Cassie refused to face him. "I just finished a portrait of my parents, but have not gone on to a new piece yet."

"Ah. Planning a trip home soon?"

Now that made her turn to stare at him—but at his face, not his chest—wondering how he had come to that conclusion. "No." It was none of his business, so why did she feel compelled to tell him anything about her plans? "My brother will be visiting soon and can take it to them. I cannot…leave my animals."

"If you ever need someone to take care of them so you can go home for a visit, I'm just down the highway."

How to respond without seeming ungrateful? She turned back toward the stove. "I appreciate that. I will keep your offer in mind." Even though she would never take him up on it. She could never return home, no matter how much she missed her family. Missing occasions like her parents' upcoming anniversary and renewal of vows tore at her heart, but there was no way she could make that journey to her former home.

Cassie stirred the potato and beet dish and blinked away the stinging in her eyes. Maybe she had used hotter *aji panca* paste than intended.

She hoped Lucas would like what she had prepared but had not planned on having him or anyone else up here as a guest, so her pantry was filled with comfort foods and staples more familiar to a Peruvian kitchen than an American one.

"Excuse me. I'd better check on the fire." Lucas left the room, and she took several deep breaths while she could. She wished he would let the blasted fire go out so he would become cold again and put on his clothes. Fortunately, when he returned a few minutes later, he wore his shirt.

Thank you, Goddess.

After filling their plates at the stove, they sat at the table and ate in silence for a few moments.

"Can't believe I'm eating beets. You sure make them taste better than the ones my momma boiled and slathered with butter."

"It is *mi mamá's* recipe." She was surprised he ate them without balking if he did not care for beets, but his second bite had been as big as his first. Apparently, he was an adventurous eater.

"So your brother will be coming for a visit?"

"Yes. In a couple of weeks."

"I'm an only child. Must be nice having a sibling."

She shrugged. "Sometimes it can also be exasperating. Eduardo is very…protective of me. Smothering almost. Bossy. He is the older one. I love him, but we do not see eye to eye on many things, including how often I should return home for visits." Hoping to change the subject, she asked, "Why did you start rescuing horses? I thought Kitty told me you were a carpenter and artist."

"Just fell into it, kinda like most of the things I've done in my life. Heard about Picasso, a SAR-trained horse whose owner became too old and sick to care for him properly." He paused a moment and took a deep breath. "Maggie and I used to dream about one day owning a small ranch in Texas, but…well, we didn't…" He took another hearty bite and chewed slowly, perhaps to gather his thoughts before continuing. After swallowing, he went on, "But I had some money from the insurance policy she had at the university and decided it would be a nice legacy for her if I started a little horse sanctuary up here. It's almost as easy to take care of four horses as it is one."

"Why did your other horses need rescuing?"

Lucas clenched his jaw, exuding anger. She sat back to put more distance between them and glanced toward the door, certain she could escape if need be. But somehow she understood his anger was not directed toward her.

"O'Keeffe, Cassatt, and Fontana had been abused and neglected." He fisted his left hand as if wanting to punch something—or someone. "All three mustangs were rescued from a ranch downstate where they'd been through hell."

Tears shimmered in her eyes. "How can anyone hurt a defenseless animal?"

"Search me." He set his fork down and leaned toward her, stealing the air from the room and her lungs. "We work on establishing routine activities. I haven't even started introducing them to other people yet. That's why I need to go home as soon as I can." He ran his hand through his hair. "I hope they're learning with Matt that there are other people around who aren't going to hurt them. I worry about how they're handling my absence, although when I spoke to Matt earlier, it sounded like he had everything under control."

She reached out and touched the top of his hand. "You are a good man for taking in those poor horses, Lucas."

"Anybody with half a heart would have done the same." His words reminded her of how she had explained her reason for rescuing him.

Suddenly seeing that her hand covered his, she yanked hers back. "But you gave up your house in Denver to move into a new place just so they could have a safe haven. That is more than most would do."

Lucas shrugged and then grinned. "Always was a sucker for someone who needed rescuing. Even Maggie…" His smile faded, and he shook his head. "Sorry. Still miss her."

She wondered what he had been about to say, but did not pry. "I cannot imagine what her death must have done to you. You are a very strong man to go on."

"Not much choice."

"But I hope you will never be afraid to do what is right, especially if the well-being of a person or an animal is at stake. 'We can judge the heart of a man by his treatment of animals.'"

Lucas met her gaze. "That's one of my favorite quotes from Kant."

She smiled, surprised to find he'd read the philosopher. "Mine, too." There was more to Lucas Denton than met the eye, but his love of animals told her he was a gentle, caring man.

The silence drew out a moment, but she did not feel discomfort in the quietude. Perhaps Lucas would find some of the usefulness he sought by spending time with her alpacas. Might make him feel less frustrated, too. He seemed to be someone who needed to be doing something to keep from going stark-raving mad.

"How would you like to help me prepare my babies for bed?"

He quirked a brow and then nodded. "I'd like that a lot. I'll grab my coat."

Chapter Three

Luke didn't know what had changed the mood between them, but he welcomed this relaxed Cassie over the one with her defenses on high alert.

Like him, she had a soft spot for any living creature in need. They also had art in common.

While cooking supper, she'd taken off her poncho. He'd tried not to stare and make her uncomfortable, but the girl had curves in all the right places. She shouldn't hide her body so much.

After the dishes had been scraped and stacked in the sink to soak for washing later, he followed her outside to the shed. The sun was setting, its softer rays gleaming off the drifts of snow. When had the blizzard ended?

A quick survey of the compound revealed a shed to the left, a lean-to nearby half-sheltering her Tahoe, and a more modern but smaller structure down a winding path from the cabin's front door. Her studio? He hoped she'd allow him inside before he had to leave. But he'd wait for an invitation.

Cassie had donned a wool poncho that came to her knees. At least this time there was reason for being bundled up. Man, it was frigid up here, and the wind blew like a banshee.

She slid the bolt back and opened the door to the shed. He grabbed for it, and held it against the battering winds until she entered then followed her inside, letting the door slam shut. The shed smelled of straw and alfalfa. Warmth from the animals and what looked like a heating system over each of four stalls took the chill away.

"Nice and cozy in here."

He didn't remind her that these creatures were used to being outdoors in the mountain climes of South America. "Does all the heat affect how thick their fleece is?"

She ran her hand down the flank of one very pregnant alpaca. "If it does, then so be it. I want them to be comfortable."

Cassie had a good heart. He came up on the other side of the pregnant one. "When's she due?"

"Any time really, but the vet says two weeks."

He'd probably miss out on seeing the birth, which bothered him for some reason. He would have liked to experience that with Cassie.

He stroked the animal's long neck. "Man, that's soft."

"Nothing softer. Graciela is the only one pregnant now. I wanted to start slowly this first year until I know what I am doing."

"Good thinking." To the alpaca, he said, "Did you know you have one smart momma, Gracie?"

The animal made a humming noise as if agreeing with him.

He glanced across the animal's back to where Cassie retrieved two empty buckets and a scoop for the bags of feed. The woman didn't acknowledge his words of praise. Perhaps she didn't take compliments too well. He'd have to make sure she heard them often and fix that problem.

As he filled the buckets, she instructed him on how much feed to place in each of the stalls. When she walked away and then nearly filled two large buckets with water, he set the scoop down. Sure enough, she lifted them without asking for help.

"Here, I'll carry the water. You dish out the feed."

She refused to set the buckets down. "No, I do this all the time." The words were forced out between tight lips.

Not while I'm around, you don't.

Cassie glared at him when he reached for one of the buckets she held, but she relented and set it down before carrying the other to the opposite end of the shed. *Stubborn girl.* He picked it up and poured it into Gracie's water trough.

As they worked together, he learned the names of the other three—Tika, Killa, and Qhawa—all girls, Cassie said. "Unusual names."

"They are Quechua girl names. *Mi mamá* is Quechua, a major native population in Peru, descendants of the Incas. Tika means 'flower.' I chose it because of her orange-colored fleece. Killa for 'moon'." He noticed that one was snow-white. "And Qhawa stands for 'one who watches or monitors'." She wrapped her arms around the neck of the last one—a mix of white and tan. "She is very curious, but timid. Is that not right, Qhawa?"

Luke looked into Qhawa's big brown eyes and sensed the alpaca never missed a thing. She'd been watching him since he'd come inside the shed.

"You're good at giving your animals meaningful names. When I adopted Picasso, he already had his name. For most of the others, I just named them after some of Maggie's favorite women painters." *Except for O'Keeffe.*

He lifted the bucket and dumped it into Tika's water trough as he glanced back at the pregnant one. "Why doesn't Gracie have a Quechua name?"

"I gave her a Latin name to honor that part of my heritage." She left the feed scoop in Qhawa's bin and walked toward the white and tan, very pregnant alpaca. Cassie buried her face in Gracie's neck while wrapping her arms around the alpaca. "Graciela means blessing or favor, because she is a gift from the Goddess to help me heal."

Cassie ended the embrace abruptly without further explanation and returned to the feed bins. Was Cassie sick? She didn't appear to be. So did she mean another type of healing? Any fool could see she had a chip on her shoulder when it came to men.

God, he hoped some asshole hadn't taken advantage of her innocence. Or maybe she was recovering from a traumatic loss. With the anniversary of Maggie's death coming up in days, he certainly could relate there.

Luke filled two more buckets with water for the last two stalls, trying not to think about this gentle soul from Peru suffering pain of any kind. But he couldn't shake the feeling that she'd been hurt and hurt badly by some jerk.

Would he ever be able to convince her to confide in him?

"That should take care of them for now." Cassie clapped the alpaca hair off her hands and waited while he stowed the buckets upside down for tomorrow's use. He pushed the door open against the ever-present wind and let her precede him into the cold.

As they drew near the cabin door, he pointed to the building down the path to the left. "Is that your studio?"

She only nodded and continued toward the cabin door. Having Cassie let him anywhere near her studio didn't seem likely in the near future.

*   *   *

Six nights later, no closer to going home, Luke found himself beside

Cassie in the shed again, only this time watching Gracie struggle through another contraction. He placed his hand on her swollen belly, but had no freaking clue what signs to watch for. His SAR training covered the basics of delivering human babies, but nothing about alpacas. He patted the soon-to-be momma's belly, hoping to reassure and comfort her, to let her know she wasn't alone in her maiden birth.

"I read up on birthing crias and watched some online videos." At the sound of Cassie's voice, Luke turned to the woman who had spoken to him only rarely these past few days. They had shared meals, but the rest of the time she'd escaped to the privacy of her studio, leaving him to fend for himself. He'd managed to split some wood when he didn't think she'd jump down his throat. Felt good to do something active and try to rebuild his strength after his bout with hypothermia and a possible concussion had left him weaker than a newborn foal.

Cassie stroked the alpaca's neck, her fingers combing through the soft fleece. Cassie hadn't let her guard down many times since he came to, but watching her touch the animal with such tenderness broke open a longing inside he'd thought had been buried too deep to surface again.

Not that Cassie would ever touch him that way. More likely he'd receive a kick in the butt to send him on his way down the mountain. She'd been sleeping in the studio the last few days. When she'd come running to tell him about Gracie's labor, he'd been thrilled to be able to do something for her.

Now he wished she'd ask him to help her with something he could actually do well. If he screwed this up, she'd never forgive him.

"Anything I should be doing on this end, darlin'?"

Cassie's hand stilled, and he realized she still hadn't warmed up to his use of one of his favorite endearments. She met his gaze, the wariness blatant in her expression. "They are not like horses or cows." *Damn—she'd gone on the defensive again.* "Alpacas need very little assistance when birthing their babies. Most owners just sit back and watch."

That sounded good to him, especially because he found himself positioned closer to the business end of things than he liked. So why had she come running to him in a panic? Who was she trying to convince this would be a breeze—him or her? Luckily, the mother-to-be seemed calmer than either Luke or Cassie, merely standing and waiting, with an occasional glance behind her when she had a contraction.

Luke wished he had his camera to record the first photos of the baby. The lighting in here would have made for some beautiful shots. Okay, maybe the thought of making some kind of lasting and positive impression on Cassie was part of it, too.

But he hadn't planned on being stranded up here in an avalanche, so he hadn't packed anything when he went to Aspen Corners to hang out with friends over a week ago. While he'd finally located his phone in the crashed truck, the charger was stuck in the mangled dash. At least he'd been able to use Cassie's phone to call his momma, check on his horses regularly with Matt, and try and figure out what the hell was going on with Marc. The man hadn't answered his phone for days. Rafe and Matt said Angel told them Marc was doing some deep soul searching. Luke hoped to hell the man found the answers he needed to turn his life around before he lost Angel for good.

But right now, Luke had his own worries.

The small shed was warm and cozy, even though the early May winds continued to howl outside. Luke moved to the spot behind Graciela and saw the bulging sac beginning to emerge. Shouldn't be long now—at least he hoped not. His gaze wandered to Cassie's face as she focused on her beloved alpaca. The girl had a sweet spot for Gracie. Didn't she say this one had been sent to heal her?

Jeezus, don't let me screw this up.

The soon-to-be momma gave a moan. "Shhh. You are doing fine, Graciela. I will not leave you alone." The alpaca calmed under Cassie's gentle touch. The two had some kind of silent connection. When she was near this one, a sense of peace seemed to come over Cassie more so than with the other three. He wished he could have put that expression on her face, but for some reason, he only put this lady on edge.

Another attempt to push left Graciela pacing in the stall. What he thought might be a snout stuck out a tiny hole in the sac, but she had a long way to go before the cria would be on the ground. He walked closer to Cassie, hating it when her hand clenched into a fist. What the hell did she expect him to do to her?

"Any idea how this works?" He left off any endearment, not wanting to push his luck.

"The feet should come out first then the baby's head. Sometimes the head is first, but that can make for a more difficult birth. Once the head comes out, Graciela will walk around while any amniotic fluids drain from the cria's mouth."

Sounded simple enough—a damned sight easier than horses. They moved behind the animal again and watched as the cria's head crowned.

"Oh, no."

Luke cast a glance at Cassie, who had a death grip on the towel she'd used to wipe the sweat off Gracie's neck and belly. He returned his gaze to the alpaca. Where the hell were the cria's legs? He wished he knew more about what to do. He wondered if the anatomy was all that different from a horse's. He'd helped deliver a horse once while in 4-H.

Luke stepped closer to the animal and stroked her side, feeling another contraction hit her as she pushed once more, moaning when her effort didn't seem to progress the birth any. Luke took off his coat and rolled up his sleeves.

"What are you going to do?" Cassie came toward him as if to keep him away from Gracie until she knew of his intentions.

"I'm thinking she might need a little help, this being Gracie's first baby and all. I'm going to see if I can find the legs and help this delivery along a bit."

Cassie remained silent a moment and then nodded. "Do not hurt her."

"You know I won't, darl…"

Quit while you're behind, Denton.

One thing he'd learned from his SAR work—and even his Dominant training with Adam—was to do no harm, so Luke waited for Gracie to work through one more contraction before intervening. No progress. Clearly, she wasn't going to deliver this cria until the baby was in the right position. Not sure if an alpaca momma's contraction could crush bones the way a horse's could, he decided it was now or never and reached into the opening of the birth canal, feeling around until he found what felt like two skinny sticks. He sure hoped he was doing the right thing as he pulled the legs forward until they popped outside the sac. They dangled there a moment before another contraction came, and the baby's head pushed the rest of the way out.

"Thank you, Goddess. It worked!"

Luke opened the cria's small mouth and let its head hang as fluid seeped out. Gracie took to pacing again, and after several more contractions, the cria's legs were practically touching the ground. He'd never watched an animal give birth standing up before. Horses and alpacas were very different creatures.

"The baby is not moving."

Luke's gaze returned to the cria. Shouldn't it show some effort to be born? He wondered if there might be a problem. Should he help pull the baby out or let nature take its course? He pressed his fingers against the neck, trying to find a pulse. Where the hell were a cria's pulse points, anyway?

Luke positioned himself at Gracie's hind legs and watched the miracle of birth unfold before him.

When the cria slid gently onto the shed's floor, Luke pulled away the remnants of the sac and glanced up at Cassie feeling like a proud new daddy. Her gaze never left the baby, though. When Cassie's expression of wonder became one of horror, she turned to Luke, her dark-chocolate eyes pleading as if waiting for him to do something.

His attention returned to the cria. Motionless. Not breathing. Foals usually struggled to their feet within minutes. Was it normal for a baby alpaca to just lie there?

He felt clueless—and helpless.

Cassie handed him a soft cloth and hunkered down beside him, her body warm and trembling.

He took the cloth, opened the cria's mouth, and cleaned out any fluid, hoping to help it breathe on its own, but still saw no sign of life.

"*Por favor*, Lucas."

Dear God, don't let me fail this girl.

Hearing the desperation in Cassie's voice—begging for the first thing she'd ever asked of him—he couldn't let her down if he could help it. But why did she have to ask for the near impossible? Still, his training kicked in. He opened the baby's mouth and stuck his finger in to check for any remaining mucous. Clear.

"Bring me that flashlight."

Cassie brought it over and cast its beam down the cria's gullet. He didn't see any other obstruction. "Thanks." Lowering the head to the ground, lining up the spine with the back, he cupped his hands over the cria's snout and blew as hard as he could. The small chest expanded. He repeated with three more breaths.

He waited for some response. Nothing. "Cassie, compress the cria's abdomen, alternating with when I breathe. I'll be doing two breaths. Then you do ten compressions after each set of breaths."

"Okay." She moved beside him and placed her hands on the baby's belly, interlocking her hands. Apparently, she had learned CPR.

Good girl.

They worked together until the cria's front leg kicked. "Did you see that?"

"Yes! Oh, Lucas!"

He hoped it wasn't some kind of involuntary response. This baby had to live. Cassie would be devastated if they lost her.

They repeated another round. Another kick—definitely a kick this time—and soon all four legs were in motion. Luke let out a whoop and reached out to hug Cassie, who hugged him back. At first, anyway, before she grew stiff. Knowing to let go, he stood, walked around the cria, and helped the little thing to its feet. Luke glanced over the wobbly critter's back to see tears streaming down Cassie's face. Her lips trembled with emotion. He wanted to reach out and wrap his arms around her again, to offer her some comfort and support, but didn't want to push his luck.

"*Muchas gracias*, Lucas."

Their gazes met, and she smiled. His name never sounded so good as when he heard it from her lips.

"I think we had some divine intervention."

"Grace."

"You got that right." She'd sure given the momma alpaca the right name.

They both stood staring at the baby for a few minutes. "Have you picked out a name yet?"

Cassie started toward him, but she knelt beside the baby cria, which was now curled in the straw near its momma, and stroked its back. Tears continued to stream unheeded down her cheeks.

Such a gentle soul. Anyone who loved animals as much as she did couldn't hide behind her gruff façade forever. One of these days, he hoped to see her show that kind of affection toward him. Even though he knew next to nothing about her, he felt a connection with her he hadn't felt since...well, not in a long time.

"Her name will be Milagrosa."

"What does it mean?"

Cassie's gaze returned to Luke's. "Miracle."

"Fitting. Perfect."

Out of the blue, he realized today was the anniversary of Maggie's death. *Sorry, Maggie.* He used to mourn for days before and after this anniversary, but with all that had been going on up here, he'd forgotten.

Somehow, though, he looked on this as progress. He didn't feel as depressed as he had last year at this time. That sketch Cassie had done had allowed him to move on.

Luke hoped God would pull off another miracle and help Cassie to open up to him one of these days. Something told him the two of them would be good together, helping each other heal.

*   *   *

Cassie stroked Graciela's neck, hoping to still the shaking inside her stomach that threatened to overwhelm her while Milagrosa nursed on the rich colostrum that would help her fend off disease and grow strong in her first months of life.

When Lucas had wrapped his arms around her, she had been so lost in her exhilaration she hugged him back before coming to her senses. The man brought her cria back to life. Her emotions were jumbled, stretched so thin she had to blink away the tears.

Movement out of the corner of her eye shifted her focus to the man in question, and she watched him lay down on the straw and place his hand protectively on top of Milagrosa's belly.

Cassie gave him a sidelong glance, the urge to reach out to him even stronger.

No, Cassie. You've trusted the wrong men before.

Pedro had fooled her. He had always been solicitous, especially around her parents, and seemed to care about her, as well. Lucas might be gentle, kind, and almost like another brother, but he was not her brother. She needed to guard herself against becoming too comfortable around him.

Still, he had saved Milagrosa's life.

"How did you know what to do?"

He glanced at her. "About what?" He didn't seem to be on the same wavelength as she. What had he been thinking about?

"How to breathe life back into Milagrosa."

He grinned. "I figured the basic principles of CPR were the same for alpacas as for humans."

"I would not have been able to think clearly enough to know what to do in that situation. I panicked, but you stayed so calm."

"Only on the outside, darlin'. I didn't want you to lose your first cria." He turned his gaze to the still-nursing baby. "But my SAR training does help me to keep my cool, I reckon."

"I cannot thank you enough."

He smiled at her. "You already have."

Cassie didn't know what he meant, but thought he referred to something more than her words of gratitude.

Hungry herself, Graciela moved to her feed bin. Milagrosa seemed at loose ends and stood on wobbly feet. Cassie and Lucas moved away quickly and stood side by side as they watched the baby cross the stall and seek out her mother's teat and another meal.

Cassie had never thought much about being a mother, but seeing the two of them warmed something inside her she'd never expected to feel. Not that she'd ever have more than furbabies. Having them would provide her all the maternal satisfaction in her destiny. Well, except when doting on Kitty's baby.

Two mornings later, her thoughts remained confused. She had not been able to sleep for days and had worked through the night again last night to finish something. She sipped her coffee and stared nervously across the table as Lucas devoured his breakfast. With his appetite so strong again, he would be well enough in no time to head back down the mountain to his ranch.

That was what she wanted, but the thought of him leaving so soon left her feeling…strange. Not the jubilance she once thought she would feel at his leaving. Perhaps the memory of the moment in the shed as she watched him revive her precious Milagrosa clouded her thinking now. Had *Mama Quilla* brought him into her life at this time so that he could be here to save her cria? She'd found herself less resentful of his presence since then.

But when he left, chances are she would rarely see him. Their relationship would end. *No, relationship was too strong a word. Interlude, maybe? No, that sounded too romantic. Their brief time together. Yes, better.*

Cassie set her empty mug on the table. "There's something I would like to show you in my studio sometime today when you have a few minutes."

He wiped his mouth with his napkin and grinned in her direction. Her stomach flip-flopped. She hoped she was not coming down with something. No time for being sick. She still had to finish a piece for the exhibition next month.

"I'd love to see your studio. Nothing but snow plowing on the agenda today, and I'll need some breaks."

He had been doing all kinds of fix-it projects around her cabin and shed, thinking she was not aware of his activities. She could not quite allow herself to smile and hoped she had not made a mistake by inviting him inside such a private place.

But she truly wanted to share with him the piece she had been working on the past few nights and days.

*   *   *

Luke approached the studio and saw that the door was ajar. No sense actually knocking.

"Knock, knock, darlin'."

Cassie stood facing an easel, surveying an oil painting of an older couple. Luke hated seeing the stiffness return to her shoulders and back at the sound of his voice, as if steeling herself for an attack. What would make her think he would ever hurt her? He thought they had moved beyond that level of discomfort and distrust after Millie was born.

Give her time.

She had relaxed a lot more than when he'd first come to in the cabin. Cassie had invited him to her studio—finally. That alone spoke volumes in his favor.

Maybe she was in the middle of something and didn't want to be disturbed. "Sorry, darlin'. I'll come back la—"

"No, Lucas, stay!" She turned to face him. Her dusky cheeks hinted at a blush. Hard to tell with her skin coloring, but he liked to think he could make the girl blush, whatever the reason. "I...did not hear you come in."

Oh, yes, you did. He hung his coat and hat and walked toward her. "What are you working on?"

"Actually, I finished it earlier—a portrait of my parents. Just want to make sure it is right before..." She trailed off, and he turned his focus to the piece.

She'd mentioned this piece before. Said it was something she planned to have delivered to Peru. The colorful oil depicted her mother's bright red headwear suggesting Native origins, but the man was dressed in a black embroidered shirt with a bolo tie, definitely more of a Spanish influence. Something about the man's green eyes seemed familiar.

The couple's gnarled hands clasped before them suggested a hard life. They stared out with little emotion.

He didn't know why, but a sense of sadness in the painting made his eyes sting. His parents had never been particularly demonstrative with each other—with him, either, for that matter—but they loved one another and him, too.

"It's beautiful." He cleared his throat of its raspy sound.

She nodded and turned away from him and the easel. With their advanced age in this portrait, surely Cassie wouldn't refuse to return home to see them every chance she could. Then again, some families became estranged for varied reasons. She seemed adamant about having no desire to return to Peru.

If she wants you to know, she'll tell you.

Having her allow him to visit her in her studio was enough for now. He glanced around the room while she crossed the room to a cloth-covered canvas.

Clearly, she spent most of her time in here. The cabin was merely functional—cook, eat, sleep, and not much else—but this room had a homey feel to it. The wall of windows likely allowed for natural light much of the day, but it was cold as hell in here. A freestanding, black woodstove occupied the corner opposite the bed, although no fire burned in it now, despite the chill in the room. The girl preferred the cold, although he spotted a space heater near her workspace. She'd need to keep her oils warm enough to work with, for sure. A stained coffeemaker sat on the counter next to the sink.

A futon waited in the corner for those nights when she didn't want to abandon her work for too long. He sometimes slept in his work-shop/studio, too tired to make it back to the house. Lying there next to whatever he was working on often gave him further inspiration.

They were two peas in a pod in that way.

In a corner to his right, he saw what looked like a prayer mat on the floor in front of a low table or stool decorated with plants—bay leaf and fennel, for sure—as well as stones and some type of pagan statue. Probably Peruvian. He smiled at the sense of joy and abandon in the figure.

But the art pieces covering the three walls soon captured his attention, especially one of a native woman with arms upstretched to the moon that hung just beyond the altar area. The vibrancy absent from her house and studio, except in her Indian blankets, reminded him of the underlying passion in the woman he had first noticed at her gallery opening in Denver several months ago. At that exhibition, her work reminded him of Georgia O'Keeffe, but this one had a Lee Bogle feel in some ways, perhaps because the subject appeared to be Native American.

He pointed to what looked to be a depiction of a moon goddess near an altar in the corner. "Did you paint that early in your career?"

She nodded. "I am sure it shows, but she has been with me such a long time that I cannot bear to part with her. Not that anyone would buy that one."

"Oh, I wasn't knocking the skill. Just thought perhaps you were emulating someone else's style on your way to developing your own. I did that a lot, too."

His gaze strayed once more to the oil painting of her parents. "You've matured as an artist with this one."

She followed his gaze before glancing away. "Thank you."

Her style had changed with this one, though. He felt a tension not obvious in the others.

Dutiful.

The word rattled around his mind, and he wondered about it a moment before he realized that word described the feeling the picture exuded perfectly. Had she created the portrait out of a sense of duty rather than because her artistic heart had been moved to do so? Had she done it more to please and honor her parents than from inspiration?

Guarded.

The painting didn't express the exuberant emotion he felt in some of her other art such as her moon goddess. True, most of her other pieces showed glimpses of nature, rarely human subjects. Yet the emotion in her flowers and trees was much more evident than in the faces of her parents in this one.

Closed off.

Was it their personalities—or Cassie's distancing herself from them?

"When's the last time you visited Peru?"

"Five years ago."

"Do you miss it?"

"No. This is my home now."

He understood what she meant. "I like it much more here in Colorado, too, than at my old home in Texas. If not for my parents, I'd probably never go back there, either." But wouldn't she suffer through a visit to Peru again to see her parents? What kept her away from them?

"So you came to the States to study art at Columbia. Bet there was a great deal of culture shock between Peru and New York City."

Cassie shrugged. "I enjoyed my time in the city. That is where I met Kitty. I felt…safe there."

Luke didn't think he'd ever heard New York described as being safe before, but she didn't elaborate.

"I invited you here to show you this." She removed the cloth from the canvas, and Luke positioned himself so he could see what she wanted to reveal.

Wow.

"Me and Millie?"

She nodded and cleared her throat. "I was moved very much by your actions and inspired to create this piece to remember what you did."

Luke drew closer to the pastel of the newborn cria cradled in his arms. He'd never seen himself depicted in a painting before. The muted pastels cast him in the shadows while a beam of sunlight bathed Millie in brighter, warmer colors.

"It is not much, but I want you to have it, along with my eternal gratitude."

Luke's eyes burned. He turned toward her. "You sure you don't want to keep it? I know I regretted not having a camera to take photos for you to have."

"No. The image will never leave my mind. I just thought…you might like to see…I mean, well…" She turned away.

"It's the nicest thing anyone's ever given me. Thank you, Cassie."

"*No es nada.*" She started toward the door, dismissing him. "I should check on Milagrosa and Graciela before I start supper."

Not so fast, baby girl.

Luke placed his hand on her shoulder, but didn't grab or force her to stop and turn toward him. When she halted her retreat, he spoke. "Thank you, Cassie. I'll cherish this forever, just as I will the memory of our delivering our first cria together."

Cassie stared at him a moment and blinked before she retrieved her poncho from a hook by the door. She turned to him again, quirking a brow but not smiling. "Would you like to join me in the shed?"

Luke grinned. "Love to. I feel like a proud godparent. I want to check on Millie, too, and make sure she hasn't had any setbacks."

Cassie nodded curtly, covering her head with a wool hat and opening the door to a blast of wind. He pulled his coat closed and turned the collar up to cover his ears as he followed. They ran down the path to the shed, and he helped her close the door behind them, fighting another strong gust.

The alpacas began clicking and bleating as soon as they heard Cassie enter. He smiled, watching the pure joy erupt on her face as she nuzzled Gracie and accepted her adoration.

Surprising him, Gracie broke away from her mistress and moseyed toward him, baby Millie in her wake. The new momma met his gaze, and he could have sworn she conveyed her appreciation to him. If he hadn't been around his horses so much and seen similar looks in their eyes after months of working hard to give them a sense of peace and security, he might have scoffed at his musings. Instead, he reached out and patted her slim neck.

"'Tweren't nothin', little momma. All in a day's work. Gotta earn my keep with the boss lady."

"I am not your boss."

Luke raised his head and met Cassie's gaze over the backs of the two alpacas. He'd hit a nerve, but she needed to understand his boundaries, too. "Listen, I know it's hard for you to have me around, but while I'm here, I need to feel useful. Think of me as a temporary hired hand until someone can clear the road and get me off the mountain. It might decrease some of the tension."

"I am sorry. I will try."

Gracie nudged his hand, reminding him he was in the middle of petting her. After a few minutes of appeasing the momma alpaca, he returned his gaze to Cassie, who had started the nighttime ritual they'd shared the past few nights. As if she hadn't had it wrested from her hand every night, she lifted the huge bucket to fill it with fresh water.

"Here, let me do that!"

He rushed over to take the heavy bucket from her, but she glared at him, daring him to try. "I can do this, Lucas Denton. I have been taking care of my animals alone for months. Go back inside before you have a relapse."

Back off, Denton.

Something else was going on with her tonight. Was it sharing the drawing and her studio with him? Did that make her feel vulnerable and exposed? One thing's for sure, he wouldn't endear himself to her by charging in like a stallion. This girl had a serious problem with men. Hell, she didn't even have any male alpacas.

He let go, and she hefted the bucket until the contents had been emptied into the trough.

"I didn't say you couldn't handle it, darlin'. Just that I want to pull my weight around here. After all, you saved my life."

She didn't make eye contact, but took the rake and tossed some more straw bedding into Killa's stall. "You do not owe me anything, Lucas. You saved Milagrosa's life. We are even. Why do men always think they have to take care of women, as if we cannot survive without them?"

Clearly, she wasn't too keen on any member of his gender. He'd seen her response to Adam at daVinci's and at Adam's house while he was recovering, too. That man raised Cassie's hackles every time. Was it just resentment toward him for taking her friend away? He didn't think so.

Suddenly, he realized where he'd seen her father's eyes before—in Adam Montague's.

"What's your father like?" Was he the reason she couldn't stand men? The man's eyes in the portrait of her parents were much colder than her momma's. Some despicable men abused their daughters horribly. Luke always suspected Maggie's father had molested her, but she never wanted to talk about it.

She spun around to face him. "What?"

"Your father. Did he… Did you get along with him?"

Her eyes shimmered with unshed tears before she glanced away and began petting Killa. Damn. If the man had hurt her, Luke would—

"He was hard working, but is retired now. Honest. Fair. A man of integrity. He is much older than my mother. He does not understand the way the world has changed. He did not understand me. We…became estranged while I was in college."

It didn't sound like she was angry at him for abusing her. Was it the age difference between Karla and Adam that set her off around the Marine?

But she wasn't too fond of men in general. Take Luke. He'd never done anything to hurt her. He'd been extremely careful not to come on too strong, either. After nearly two weeks here, Luke had seen only a few moments when she'd let down her guard and become, well, civil.

Sharing the birth and rescue of the cria should have softened her more. Tonight, though, he was clearly wearing on her nerves. Again. Her mood swings left him dizzy.

Even so, the lady hadn't taken her Tahoe's plow blade to the snow mass yet in an effort to try and clear the road faster. Maybe she wasn't as sick of him as she pretended to be.

He grinned. Could he be wearing down her defenses a little?

After Cassie said goodnight to her alpacas—just short of tucking them into their straw beds—Luke followed her out of the shed, and they hightailed it back to the cabin as the wind bombarded them. How'd she stand living on a mountain pass like this? Luke couldn't wait to return to his cozy, warm house in the basin below.

He might as well admit he would have nothing more than friendship with Cassie. Even that might be a long shot. The woman preferred isolation. Solitude. Why was it he always chose the ones who didn't want to admit they needed him?

Luke sighed. He longed for some time with his horses. They loved him unconditionally, needed him to see to their needs, and were learning to trust him. At least he had made some progress with some of them. Unlike Cassie, they liked spending time with him.

God, he hoped his horses wouldn't fall too far behind in their training and rehabilitation. He'd worked with them day in and day out for months, beginning as soon as each one had arrived at his place. He had no clue what Matt was doing other than meeting their physical needs, but what about their emotional ones?

He needed to go home.

Chapter Four

Luke came out of the alpaca shed late the next morning after hearing the sound of wood being split. *Stubborn girl.* He charged across the yard and around the side of the cabin to find Cassie with an ax raised with both hands over her head before she brought it down on the wood to split it.

"Why didn't you tell me we needed more wood?" Hell, why hadn't he noticed himself? Wait, he'd checked yesterday, and there was plenty in the mudroom.

Cassie stacked the two new pieces on the sizeable pile. Had she been at this all morning while he mucked out stalls? "I thought we decided that I'd chop the firewood."

She didn't make eye contact with him, simply placed another piece of wood on the block and set her chopping stance. She didn't appear to be in a good mood, so he approached her cautiously—after all, she was armed with an ax. Her eyes were hidden behind her safety glasses.

"Here, you've done enough. My turn." He held out his hand for the ax. She lifted the glasses to the top of her head but only stepped away, glaring at him.

He stood his ground. After a few rapid breaths, she turned it over to him along with the glasses and went to work picking up the wood she'd already chopped, placing it in a cart. The woman didn't seem to know how to let anyone help. But at least that job was less strenuous. Now that he was feeling stronger, he wanted to step up to the plate and do more around here.

They worked side by side for a while. He wouldn't admit how exhausted this chore left him, not after making such a big deal that it was man's work. He'd worked up a good sweat, his arms and back screaming from overexertion when Cassie screamed, "Milagrosa! What are you doing out here?"

Luke turned to see the baby cria slipping in the snow near the Tahoe. *Damn it.* Hadn't he shut the door? A moment later, Gracie came into view in search of her little one. Luke buried the ax in the wood he'd been about to split, grabbed Gracie's halter, and ran to the shed to stem the flow of alpacas before any more escaped. Cassie led the baby inside right behind him and Gracie.

He breathed a sigh of relief until he heard the worried tone in Cassie's voice. "Where is Tika?"

Luke glanced around counting heads and saw only three adults and Millie. *Sonuva…* "I'll find her."

He headed outside the shed, checking to make sure he had his flashlight in his coat pocket, when a blast of frigid air hit him in the face. He followed one set of larger hooves, but quickly realized those were Gracie's. Going back to the doorway, he spotted another set of tracks heading to the left and followed them around the shed where they disappeared into a stand of aspens. No Tika in sight. How far could an alpaca go? Hell, they were pack animals that loved the mountains. *Shit.*

He increased his pace, slipping a few times but managing to stay upright as he made his way through the trees. When the wind picked up again, he buttoned his sheepskin collar around his neck. How long ago had Tika left the outbuilding? They'd been splitting and stacking wood for at least half an hour. He'd never seen her alpacas outside once. Maybe Cassie should have given them some time to wander around outdoors so they wouldn't bolt at the first opportunity. Did she have a pen for them? He could build her one while he was here if she had any supplies. If not, he could come back and do so this summer.

Right now, though, he needed to find her missing baby.

"Tika!" Did they know their names enough to come when he called? He continued to follow the tracks down the steep mountain, sliding onto his ass on the cold, wet ground at one point. The sun was about to set. He didn't think the animal had wandered that far away when he started off, but she must have bolted the minute he went outside. Or she was managing to stay upright a lot better than he was.

He began shivering from his wet jeans. Would the animal be able to handle nighttime temperatures out here if he couldn't follow the tracks with his flashlight? Cassie hadn't shorn the animals yet, so the fleece should be thick enough to keep Tika warm. But how pampered were her alpacas? Heated shed and water troughs. He had no clue if their instincts for survival were still intact.

He switched on the flashlight and kept going another half hour. Almost impossible to follow the tracks now. Just when he was ready to turn back, he heard a familiar humming. "Tika!" He muttered under his breath at first then yelled louder. He couldn't make her out in the twilight, but followed the sound until he rounded a stand of spruce trees. There she stood, tangled in some briars. He expelled a pent-up breath and ran over to her.

He set down the light and, with his suede-gloved hands, worked to clear away the brambles from the animal's now-matted fleece. It was hard to see anything because the moon hadn't risen yet. He wasn't even sure there would be enough of a moon tonight to provide any light.

"Hang on, baby girl. I'll have you out of here in no time."

The animal's cries tore at his heart. She'd need some first-aid to salve her cuts once they made it back to the outbuilding. Another bout of shivers tore through him. Damn, it was cold. Finally, he managed to free her, grabbed her rope halter, and started to lead her back home to her worried momma.

At least he'd found her before a bear, puma, or some other predator had. He'd never forgive himself if…

Luke lost his footing on another icy patch in the dark. In no time flat, his feet went out from under him, and he hit the ground with a grunt, banging the back of his head as he knocked his Stetson over his face. Dazed, he climbed to all fours and tried to shake off a wave of dizziness, but the movement only made him feel worse. His stomach roiled and convulsed in dry heaves.

Damn it all. Fighting the shivers even worse, he struggled to his feet. Holding onto the alpaca's halter again, he leaned over to pick up his hat. He idly wondered if the alpaca could carry him on her back, but couldn't trust Tika to go straight home without being led. She hadn't seemed able to find her way back earlier.

The ground dipped and swayed as he tried to remain upright. Maybe if he hadn't been showing off his he-man skills for half an hour chopping wood, he wouldn't be so damned weak right now.

What choice did he have? He'd never ridden an alpaca before, but he didn't have the strength to make it back up this mountain under his own steam.

Luke searched for a rock or boulder to act as a mounting stool. He clicked his tongue, led the alpaca to one nearby, and stood on it while lining up Tika. *Almost there.* He swung his leg over the animal's back, but apparently, Cassie's alpacas weren't used to being ridden. The skittish beast bolted, and Luke lost his balance. Once more, the ground rushed him, and he impacted it with a grunt.

The night grew blacker as he closed his eyes.

*   *   *

Cassie settled the rest of the alpacas into their stalls as best she could, but they were agitated and knew something was wrong. What was taking Lucas so long? How far could Tika have strayed?

Sensing he was in trouble, she made her way back to the cabin to gather supplies. She would have to take a lantern to be able to follow their tracks. She did not think he had a flashlight with him. How would he be able to see in the new moon's darkness? What if he was injured? He was barely recovered from the avalanche. Why had she not gone with him? But he had taken off so quickly. She had been trying to get Graciela and Milagrosa back into their stall when she turned and watched him sprint out the door of the shed.

In the mudroom, she grabbed rope, a wool blanket, and her purse and stuffed them into a backpack. The last rays of sunlight had long since faded by the time she started across the yard and around the shed, the glow from the lantern showing her the direction in which the hooves and boots were headed. She saw a spot where the man's boots had slipped, but he didn't seem to have fallen.

Thirty minutes later and still no sign of either of them. Were they together or was Lucas still tracking her wayward baby?

Her legs ached, and weariness set in as she trudged through the snow. She hadn't been sleeping more than a couple of hours a night out in her studio. Why she let Lucas's presence affect her like this, she did not know. Just having him on her mountain had left her feeling…unsettled.

Frustration set in. "Tika! Lucas! Where are you?"

The wind whistled through the spruce trees, but she heard no response. What if she could not find them or became lost herself? No, she knew these mountains like the back of her hand. All she had to do was continue to follow their tracks in the snow.

Rounding the curve of the mountain, a large shape loomed. Her heart stopped a moment until she saw the animal's long neck, and she relaxed. "Tika! You are okay, you naughty girl!"

She nearly giggled as she ran toward the alpaca, surprised when the animal did not come to meet her. As Cassie grew closer, she saw another dark form, this one lying in the snow at the alpaca's hooves.

"Lucas!" Her heart jumped into her throat as she bent down to his still form.

Please don't let him be dead.

She felt for a pulse in his neck and was relieved to feel a steady, but weak, one. His head must have hit that rock when he fell. His Stetson was lying upturned nearby on the ground. How long had he been exposed to the elements here?

"Lucas, look at me. Please, open your eyes."

No response. She did not know if she should move him, but letting him lie here in the snow was not going to keep hypothermia—or death— at bay. Pulling the blanket from her backpack, she lifted his head and placed it between the back of his head and the ground. How was she going to carry him up the mountain? He was dead weight.

His body began shivering.

Not again.

She had her cell phone with her, but waiting for help, assuming anyone could find them, would only increase the chance of him dying on the mountainside. Taking the rope, she worked a lasso around his chest, under his armpits, and faced Tika.

"Girl, you need to help me. Down on your belly."

The alpaca stared blankly at her until she tapped the backs of the animal's knees. Tika lowered herself to the ground, tucking her front legs underneath her, awaiting her precious cargo. Despite a burst of adrenaline, Cassie tugged at the rope, but he still didn't budge.

Tears of frustration wet her eyes. "Lucas, you have to help me. I cannot do this alone."

She tugged again, and he grunted. The shivering grew worse, but he seemed to become semi-conscious. "I want you to crawl onto Tika's back. Please, Lucas. Help me here."

"…throw…me."

"Come. Tika is waiting for you." She placed the blanket that had been under his head over the alpaca's matted coat and then wrapped her arms underneath Lucas's chest and pulled upward, surprised that he seemed to help by crawling partway onto Tika's back. She shoved his backside, and he plopped belly side down onto the alpaca with a grunt. Tika stood and waited for further instructions. Between the blanket and Tika's body, he should warm up quickly.

"Good girl." Cassie snatched the ends of the rope from around him and tied them under the patient animal's belly. Satisfied that he was secured, she tugged at the halter. Soon they were headed back toward the cabin.

"Please let him be okay, Goddess." She hoped the Universe would hear and answer her plea.

Earlier, she had been so angry at his carelessness for leaving the shed door open, but that he would sacrifice himself to save one of her alpacas warmed a cold place in her heart. The man had done nothing but try to help her as soon as he was strong enough, but she had shown very little gratitude for all he had tried to do.

Guilt over snapping at him the night she had shown him the painting of him washed over her. She had painted the picture from the depths of her soul, gratitude for a man—a *man*—who had saved her cria's life when Cassie would have failed Gracie.

She owed him, but he was still a man. Dangerous. Why was he making her feel something for him, knocking her off kilter?

What might he ask for in return? All men expected to be repaid, after all. Could she afford his price?

Then again, they had reciprocity. She had saved him, and he had saved Milagrosa. They were even.

"Lucas, you had better not die on me. I do not need that karma and…" *Be gracious. This isn't about you.* The man had been injured trying to save one of her babies. The least she could do was be—honest. "I like having you here, Lucas." *Please do not die.* "We will soon be back at the cabin."

Cassie kept up a steady conversation as she continued up the mountain, one hand on the lantern held high above her head to illuminate as much of the surrounding area as possible. Her other hand remained tightly wrapped around the alpaca's halter. She glanced back often to make sure Lucas was not slipping off Tika's back.

"Hang on."

The hillside grew steep just before they reached the aspen grove.

"Please, Goddess, keep my feet steady and sure," she chanted over and over.

She increased their pace at the top of the hill. "Almost home, Lucas." She doubted he heard her, but talking to him made her feel less alone. As they entered the yard, she breathed a sigh of relief. She led Tika inside the warm shed, out of the wind and elements. Cassie stood beside Lucas's head, touching his face and crouching to see if he would make eye contact. No response.

"Lucas, can you hear me?"

Unlike the time she had pulled him from the truck after the avalanche, she received no response at all, just more shivers. If he did not come to, she would never be able to haul him inside the cabin. Seeing the fresh straw he had placed in Tika's stall earlier, she made a decision.

"You redeemed yourself by bringing him home, Tika, but you are going to have to double up in Killa's stall tonight, because Lucas will be sleeping in yours."

Leading the animal to the stall, she loosened the ropes that held Lucas onto the animal's back. She tapped the backs of Tika's front knees again and held out Lucas's legs while the alpaca lowered her front half to the ground. She kept Tika's hind end up until Cassie could slide Lucas onto the straw without crushing his hands underneath the animal. Free of her burden, Tika stood, and Cassie removed the blanket from the alpaca's back to spread it out on the straw.

After leading Tika to Killa's stall, Cassie ran to the house for more blankets and some pillows. Apparently, she would be sharing a bed of sorts with Lucas again. She would also need the hot-water bottle because the shed did not have enough heat. Then again, perhaps she could have some of the alpacas provide warmth around them if she brought them close enough in the stall.

By now, Cassie knew the drill for treating hypothermia. Did he have a concussion again? The road was no closer to being passable. She'd heard Angelina's brothers working on it from the other side the past two days, but it could take another week to clear it. If not, she would have to let

Eduardo know not to come for his visit.

Her mind wandered as she avoided the thought of having to strip both Lucas and herself again to provide skin-to-skin warmth as she had done before. This was going to be another long, sleepless night.

Piled high with her first load of supplies, she entered the shed and dumped them beside Lucas's shivering body. She needed to return to the cabin for more, but first, she layered several blankets over him. She would not remove any of his clothing until she had everything in place.

In the kitchen, she filled the rubber bottle with hot tap water, put in the stopper, and ran back to the shed. She should have everything necessary now.

Kneeling beside Lucas, she tucked the hot-water bottle between the layers of blankets low on his chest. Turning away, she removed her poncho before unbuttoning her shirt and taking it off. Sitting on a nearby stool, she took off her boots. Her jeans followed. Stripped to her bra and panties, she surveyed the unconscious man and reached for his boots. As soon as he was out of his wet clothes, she could begin warming his body. After two bouts of hypothermia and head wounds so close to one another, she wondered if she needed to do something more this time, but there was no time to call anyone. What could they do? He had been unconscious for an unknown amount of time, and she did not want him to sink any deeper.

At least he was still shivering. Did that mean he was not in a coma? She peeled off his jeans, leaving his boxers, and unbuttoned his shirt. She rolled him from side to side until she removed it then moved the hot-water bottle to a spot lower on his trunk. Sweating from the exertion, when she lay down beside him, the chill from his body sent her into a rare fit of tremors, too. Not wanting to deprive him of even an inch of body heat, she unhooked her bra and tossed it aside, followed by her panties. Feeling his damp boxers against her skin, soaking wet from melted snow, she realized she would have to remove them, as well.

Kneeling beside him, she hooked her fingers inside his waistband and pulled down, closing her eyes to avoid seeing his privates. Surprisingly, she was more embarrassed than repulsed at the thought. Of course, the man was unconscious and posed no physical threat to her. Not at the moment, anyway.

Laying beside him again, skin to skin, she pulled the blankets over them both and formed a cocoon of warmth with their bodies and the water bottle.

He groaned and pulled her closer. Unlike the first time they had been this close, she did not worry that he might hurt her. Lucas Denton was a gentle soul. He had risked his life for a defenseless animal. How could she fear someone with a kind heart like that? He would never do anything to hurt her or her animals.

She blinked in wonder. How had he wiggled his way into her life so quickly?

Suddenly, he became agitated and pulled away, shouting, "Tika!"

"Shhh, Lucas." Tika responded with a hum from the other end of the shed. Cassie stroked his bare chest, her finger rubbing over his hard nipple inadvertently before she pulled her hand back to the center of his chest, which seemed safer. "She is okay. You found her in time. Everyone is safe at home now."

He said nothing more, simply relaxed against the blanket-covered straw while pulling her closer to his body. His heartbeat increased a bit before he relaxed and fell asleep. At least he had tried to fight his way back to the present. She felt more confident he would recover as soon as his body temperature rose. She would try to wake him periodically as she had been instructed after the avalanche.

Tucking her head into the crook of his arm, Cassie pressed her face against his chest. So exhausted, or perhaps the adrenaline rush had subsided. Maybe she would rest a bit, too. There was nothing she could do now other than stay close to his body and keep him warm. She would need her strength and stamina for when he came out of this stage of hypothermia. Once he woke, they could go inside where she might better be able to keep him warm. Perhaps by the fireplace, now that the blower worked.

"Thank you for fixing my fireplace. And for all the other things you have been doing around here. I know I do not always show it, but sometimes it is nice to have someone around to help."

He grunted as if in agreement. Her hand paused, and she lifted her head to look at his face to see if he had heard the thoughts she probably should have kept to herself. But his steady breathing convinced her he slept soundly. That was not right, though. Tomorrow, she would acknowledge all he had done and how much she appreciated him.

Cassie settled back into his arms.

Sleep now. I can worry about all these things tomorrow.

*   *   *

The throbbing in his temples nagged him without any let up. He tried to roll onto his side, but a weight on his chest made movement nearly impossible. He opened his eyes and blinked several times to adjust to the low lighting. Silky, black hair.

Cassie? He was in bed with Cassie again?

Hot damn. This was a habit he could get used to fast.

His grin faded with a stab of pain to his temple. *Jeezus.* What the hell had hit him?

Something stirred beside him, and he turned to find a hairy beast curled up on his other side. One of Cassie's alpacas. He couldn't tell which one in this lighting, but clearly, they were in the shed, not Cassie's bed.

What the hell?

Still, Cassie was in his arms for some reason. Moving his hand down her back—her very bare back—he became even more confused. While waking a few moments ago to find her on top of him was any man's dream, what had prompted Cassie to strip down and curl up with him like this? A shiver wracked his body, and the image of Tika in the snow flashed through his head. He had no memory of making it back to Cassie's, though.

He felt as weak as a newborn kitten. Hell, some rescuer he was. Couldn't even bring a stray alpaca home safely. Even if he wanted to, he wouldn't be able to muster the strength to sit up.

Cassie. Stretched out on top of him, she had sandwiched one of her legs between his. Thankfully, his cock behaved. Right now, he simply wanted to hold her this way, before she awoke and hightailed it away from him again.

Luke adjusted the blanket over her and wrapped both arms around her to keep her warm—and close. Exhaustion won out even with that minimal amount of movement, and soon he drifted off to sleep again...

"Why, Pedro?"

Luke awoke to Cassie pushing away from him and onto her side, but her eyes remained closed. Pre-dawn light filtered through the window.

Who the hell was Pedro? He didn't particularly like the idea of her lying next to him while dreaming about another man, although he'd have been surprised as hell if those dreams were about him.

"It's Luke, darlin'." He stroked her hair, figuring that would freak her out less than if he touched her bare back. Having just had her breasts brushing up against his chest as she scooted off him stirred his cock to life.

"Hold me, *por favor.*"

With pleasure, darlin'.

Even if dreaming about another guy, she was in *his* arms now. Cassie calmed down as soon as he wrapped his arms around her and promptly fell back to sleep. He held on to her like that so long his hands fell asleep, too. Despite wanting to treasure this moment forever, after a while he couldn't keep his eyelids from drooping...

"Nooooo! Get off me!"

Cassie's screams and her fists pounding against his chest woke him again. Daylight streamed through the only window in the shed. Her eyes were closed still. She must have been exhausted, too, to have slept this long. Maybe she hadn't been sleeping out in the studio, but staying up at night working instead.

Somehow in his sleep he'd rolled onto her, and now she fought and clawed at him.

Luke attempted to kneel, but his arms and legs wouldn't cooperate. What was wrong with him? A sound behind him made him try to turn, but before he could maneuver around to see what it was, two hands grabbed him by the ears and pulled him off Cassie.

Fuck! He needed to protect her from whoever was trying to get to her but could barely stand upright. So damned weak.

The man—definitely a man—grunted when Luke tried to grind the heel of his foot into his groin, but that only made the attacker angrier. He locked Luke's elbows and yanked them back with a pop, nearly dislocating his shoulders.

"Cassie, run to the cabin and lock the door!"

She opened her eyes and stared up at the man somewhere behind Luke.

"No! Stop! It is not what you think!"

He had no clue if she was yelling at him or the attacker. "Run, damn it!" Why didn't she just do as he said? He couldn't fight this bastard off to protect her. If anything happened to Cassie...

Fearing for her safety, he pulled from some reserve deep within and elbowed the man in the gut. The resounding grunt told him he'd found his mark. But when he tried to take a backward swing at the intruder, Luke lost his balance and fell over. *Damn*. On all fours, he gasped for breath and the strength to attack. Could he take advantage of his position and charge at the man to knock him over? His head swam, but he prepared to do that when Cassie's shout stopped him cold.

"Stop! Lucas, he is my brother!"

What? Luke peered at the man and saw the familiar Latino features. *Shit*. He'd tried to take down her brother. Having no strength left once the adrenaline rush left him, Luke collapsed to the ground. Cassie took the end of the blanket he was lying on and tossed it over his naked ass.

Some first impression he'd made on her family.

Cassie rushed to hide her nakedness in her poncho before she came over and knelt next to her brother. The man didn't seem too worse for wear, just winded. Good thing he wasn't trying to do Cassie harm, because Luke wouldn't have been able to protect her in his current physical state.

The thought of someone hurting her twisted Luke's gut.

"Wait for me in the cabin, Eduardo."

"You are coming with me."

"I need to see to Lucas."

Luke stood, his fist holding the blanket around his lower half, and tried to show he didn't need her taking care of him. He squared his shoulders and stared at her brother for a long, tense moment. Eduardo glared back.

"Men!" Cassie growled and swung around, her hair flying, before leaving the two men to their pissing match in the shed.

Yeah, it was kind of funny now that he thought about it. Luke grinned and held his hand out to her brother. "I'm Lucas…Luke Denton. Nice to meet you."

When her brother didn't shake hands, Luke shook his head and reached for his denim shirt on a bail of straw near where he and Cassie had spent the night. Better not press his luck.

Not that his luck had been all that great lately.

Hell, he was just trying to help. First to rescue Tika—and now Cassie when he thought the man was a threat. Obviously, she didn't need rescuing from her own brother.

Epic fumble, Denton.

*   *   *

Cassie sped along the slippery path to the cabin to escape the explosion of testosterone in the shed. What was Eduardo doing here so early? He had said he would not arrive for at least another week, after the last of his conferences. How did he make it past the snowpack covering her road?

Eduardo caught up with her halfway to the cabin and reverted to Spanish. "I thought he was attacking you. You screamed for him to get off you."

Cassie had no memory of screaming anything or even that Lucas had been on top of her. Her face grew warm with embarrassment. She'd gone from the throes of one of her night terrors to finding Eduardo attacking Lucas.

Please, Goddess, save me from macho men.

"I was having a nightmare."

Strange, however, because at one point in her dream, she thought she watched as Lucas fought Pedro off her. She'd never deviated from the actual rape memories before. And then Lucas had held her so tenderly. Even in the fog lingering from the dream, Lucas's hands had been different from any other man's. Gentle, loving, protective.

Giving, not taking. For the first time since the rape, she had felt safe with a man—until Diego's face entered the nightmare.

She blinked away that man's evil visage, her head no longer fuzzy from her deep sleep and confusing dreams. Thankfully, Lucas had stayed behind in the shed until she could clarify this situation to Eduardo without distractions.

Cassie could well imagine what Eduardo thought about finding the two of them entangled in each other's naked bodies.

Eduardo continued to struggle for composure. "Who is this man—Luke Denton?"

Lucas must have introduced himself. Such a gentleman. This would all be comical if she did not know how her brother's *machismo* could make things very uncomfortable during this visit. So how to explain the man who invaded her cabin nearly two weeks ago?

"He became stranded here in the avalanche." She narrowed her gaze at him.

"What was he doing up here with you—alone?"

"No, it wasn't like that. He actually was nearly killed by the avalanche when he followed me home to make sure I arrived safely. I have been nursing him back to health."

Eduardo touched his side where Lucas had elbowed him. "He does not seem all that weak to me. And what were you doing naked with him?"

She shared what had happened when he had gone after Tika, but her brother seemed skeptical. Perhaps if she changed the subject. "How did you get through? It will take at least another week to clear my road."

"I hiked my way around the mountain." Pointing in the direction of the shed, he added, "*He* could have left...*if* he had wanted to." Eduardo's intense stare made her uneasy enough to turn away. She and Lucas really hadn't made clearing the road a high priority. The slightest exertions seemed to wipe out what little strength he had mustered, even before this latest setback. Of course, he served on the mountain rescue squad in their village and had been here to see her several times over the years. Still, she felt compelled to defend Lucas.

"He did not grow up in the Andes at these altitudes and temperatures. But he also has suffered two possible concussions and hypothermia since he has been here."

Eduardo rubbed his abdomen. Cassie marveled that Lucas would even attempt to protect her in his weakened condition. No one had ever come to her defense at potential risk to himself. His actions created feelings in her that...she did not wish to explore at the moment.

Opening the front door to the mudroom, she gestured for him to enter, but he insisted she go first. Eduardo's backpack sat next to the door, so he must have come inside before he went in search of her in the shed.

In the living room, she gestured toward the loveseat. "Please sit down. Would you like some coffee?"

"*Sí.*" He went to the fireplace to start a fire instead. His thick hair and dark brown skin showed off his Quechua roots. She wished she had taken more after their mother, too. She loved her Spanish heritage and olive coloring, but Eduardo's features were much more...classic.

She escaped to the kitchen, hoping to postpone the inevitable interrogation to follow. Eduardo could be worse than having to face her *papá*, perhaps because he knew enough about American ways to think the worst of her.

She had never told her family what really had happened the night she had come home in the wee hours and had avoided her family for days while nursing her wounds in her room. Even though Eduardo had a wife and son at the time, *Papá* and *Mamá* had told him about her being out all night with Pedro. They blamed Eduardo for her newfound American morals because he had been the one to talk his parents into allowing her to go to uni.

Eduardo had shown up in her bedroom demanding that she marry Pedro sooner rather than later so as not to shame the family with her "New York" behavior. He chastised her for not respecting her parents enough to leave her lewd behavior behind when she visited Peru. Clearly, he assumed she had slept with Pedro—willingly.

Yet she had remained silent. Two days later, she announced that the engagement was off and she would be returning to New York early. Even without a place to stay until she could move back onto campus, all that mattered was being as far from Pedro, Luis, and most especially Diego, as possible.

Papá had been so upset he had not even said goodbye. However, Eduardo's accusations had driven a wedge between the once-close siblings.

Sometimes she wished she had called Diego's bluff and told her parents what had truly happened that night, but she had not been thinking clearly at the time. She only knew she needed to escape the hurt and pain. The shame of having put herself in such a situation as to be raped.

Only, the hurt and pain had hounded her every day since.

Cassie returned to the living room a few minutes later with a mug of coffee and placed it on the coffee table. "I need to go check on Lucas."

"Who *is* he to you, Casandra?"

Here we go again. "Lucas is an acquaintance. A fellow artist. I ran into him recently in Aspen Corners while visiting a mutual friend." *Do* not *mention you were in a bar.* "He followed me home to make sure I arrived safely. That is all there is to it."

Eduardo made a fist at his side before reaching for the mug. "I found you naked with him lying on top of you. Let me ask another way. What kind of relationship do you have with him? Tell me truthfully."

"I am being truthful! I hardly know him." The censure in his eyes told her he did not believe her to be telling the truth. She could not blame him on the face of things. Before this spiraled out of control, as it could with Eduardo, she explained further. "His truck was hit by the avalanche that closed my road. He was injured and needed my help. Why are you not listening to me?"

"Why would you let a stranger follow you home?"

"I did not even know he followed me until our mutual friend called asking about him after the avalanche. I guess he was worried about me living alone up here. Maybe he has some of your *machismo*." *Goddess, I hope not.* Eduardo and *Papá* were bad enough.

"Or perhaps he had something else on his mind."

Cassie found herself wanting to defend Lucas who had never done anything to so much as suggest ulterior motives. "I swear to you, he has been recuperating ever since the accident. As soon as we clear the road, he plans to return to his ranch and horses."

Eduardo scrutinized her. "I thought you said he was an artist."

She sighed. "He is an artist by trade but also adopts and rehabilitates abused wild horses at his ranch sanctuary."

Eduardo took a tentative sip, apparently mulling over what she had told him. After a moment, he set the mug on the table again. "Did he touch you, other than what I saw for myself?"

Not before I touched him.

Her face grew warm thinking about how her fingers had caressed his pecs and nipple last night while he was unconscious. Perhaps that's what had sparked the sensory memory of having his arms around her when she woke. The reason her nipples had responded without physical contact of any kind to his close proximity. No, best not to mention that part.

Too late. Eduardo began breathing in short bursts. He was psychic, even if he chose not to hone his skills. Had he tuned in on her thoughts? She hoped not. Perhaps he'd only jumped to conclusions again.

Ignoring his agitation, she continued the story the way *she* wanted it told. The truth. Reality. Not the distorted happenings from her dream state. "Yesterday, one of my alpacas ran away from the shed. Lucas was injured again trying to find her. I was trying to warm his body. He blacked out. Too heavy to carry to the cabin, I chose to stay with him in the shed where it was warm."

"That does not explain what you were doing lying naked with him today. Did you have sex with him?"

"No! It is not like that, Eduardo." Frustrated with his one-track mind, she stood, but tried once more to explain things to her brother. "He had hypothermia again. I was just trying to raise his body temperature. You know I would never be with a man in that way unless we were married."

Let him think she was honoring her upbringing and not that she had an aversion to men. She never gave them what they wanted. They took it by force.

He narrowed his gaze. "Why have you put yourself in a situation where a man—a stranger you hardly know—can misinterpret your intentions, *pequeña?*"

Shame poured over her like a bucket of ice-cold water. No! She had no reason to be ashamed. Nothing had happened between her and Lucas. How could she, a grown woman who had lived on her own for many years, let her brother and his code of *machismo* reduce her to childhood guilt again?

"I am not under your protection, Eduardo. We are not in Peru."

Still, the censure in his words told her he would never understand what had happened between her and Lucas, much less what the men in the Lima cantina had done to her. Not that he would ever know. Good girls did not go to cantinas with men, not even their fiancés.

Eduardo searched her face until shame once again forced her to cast her gaze away. The memory of so many hands touching her, forcing her, made her skin crawl. She closed her eyes and swallowed hard.

"Excuse me." She needed to check on Lucas—and escape her brother. How long would Eduardo stay? She hoped it would not be long. Despite anticipating his visit for months, craving news of their family, and hoping to rekindle what she and her brother had once had as children, his presence brought back too many sad memories.

Before she reached the mudroom, the outside door opened. The concern on Lucas's face when he homed in on her made her feel...cherished.

No. The heat rising in her face and the way her heart pounded made her feel decidedly *uncomfortable.*

She didn't want Eduardo to read anything into Lucas's worried expression, but cringed when he walked up to her. "You okay, Sweet Pea?" His words were barely a whisper, but she feared Eduardo would hear them and jump to the wrong conclusion again.

Nodding, she ignored her brother and did not make eye contact with Lucas. "I am fine. I need to prepare dinner." She walked toward the kitchen and away from both men.

*   *   *

Luke had sensed the tension between Cassie and her brother the moment he entered the cabin. Maybe they weren't all that close to start with. Luke had no experience with being a sibling, although he had two friends—Marc and Angel—who were what he imagined having a sister or brother would be like.

But Cassie? Well, his hormones fired on all cylinders whenever he was around her—or pressed against her. Luke wondered if he could settle with just being friends with her. Friends. No benefits. Sure he could.

He hated seeing Cassie hurting—and she was downright miserable right now. Strain around her mouth told him she probably wished both of them were out of her home at the moment.

Fighting a headache and extreme lethargy from the events since he'd set out after Tika yesterday, Luke went into the bathroom to clean up. He didn't have anything but the clothes he'd worn the day of the accident. While damp from his trek in the snow yesterday, they were drying fast enough against his skin. No way would he take them off. Last thing Cassie needed was for him to be running around here in his underwear again while she tried to convince her brother they didn't have an intimate relationship.

Half an hour later, after he'd warmed himself some more by the fire and wondered if he'd ever stop shivering, the three sat down at her small kitchen table. Cassie had added a third chair and sat on the long side between the two men. He noticed she'd found a pair of pants at some point after she'd come back inside. Must be awkward to have your brother see you naked. He bet she'd had to do some explaining. He hoped the man hadn't been too hard on her but figured he might feel a little overprotective if he'd just found his little sister in a bed of sorts with a man.

Maybe they could find something to talk about besides what did or didn't happen between him and Cassie. "Eduardo, what is it you do back home?"

"I'm a seismic geoscientist." His terse response didn't make Luke particularly want to know more, but he needed to cut the tension in here.

"So you study earthquakes?"

"Mostly the faults that lead to earthquakes, but also volcanic activity." Something must have broken loose in the man because he then spent the next fifteen minutes discussing the likelihood of earthquakes hitting Peru and California. He'd just come from one conference in Seattle where he'd presented on volcanic seismic activity along the Ring of Fire. To hear him talk, the whole Pacific Rim was about to blow. Good thing Luke lived here in Colorado just in case he was right.

Next week, Eduardo said he would be speaking at a university conference in California. He must be some kind of international expert. *Impressive.*

"When I heard there had been an avalanche on Cassie's mountain, I decided to check on her between my two conferences rather than after the last one as planned."

"You could have called." Cassie hadn't said much until now, but her mood hadn't improved.

"I tried, but there was no answer."

She furrowed her brow at first. "Oh! I received a couple of missed calls with an area code I didn't recognize, but there was no message so I assumed they were telemarketers."

Eduardo shrugged and went back to eating, but Cassie had barely touched her meal. Luke removed the spoon from her hand and scooped up some soup. "Open wide."

"I do not need you to feed me, Lucas."

"I won't if you feed yourself." He placed the spoon back in her bowl and stared pointedly at her until she picked it up and began eating. She was way too thin from what he'd seen after she'd removed that damned bulky poncho and gone skin to skin with him in the shed.

Satisfied she would continue to eat, Luke turned his attention back to her brother, who scrutinized him more closely for some reason.

After she'd taken a few bites, he asked her, "So it was just the two of you as siblings?" Eduardo nodded. "I was an only child, but my wife was one of five. They drifted apart when she left home after college." Okay, Luke was rambling, but he didn't know what else to talk about. Obviously, the two of them weren't going to talk to each other, and he only knew so much about earthquakes and volcanoes.

Cassie kept her gaze on her bowl and whispered, "That happens sometimes between siblings." She glanced at her brother with longing before focusing on her soup again.

Clearly, something had caused the two to drift apart even before Eduardo had arrived on her doorstep. Why was her brother giving her a hard time for helping him recover from hypothermia? Hell, she'd rescued him—twice. While their sibling relationship problems were none of his concern, he hated seeing the yearning for acceptance and love just now in Cassie's eyes. Apparently, she hoped in vain for something her brother couldn't—or wouldn't—give her.

Was he the reason Cassie didn't want to visit her homeland again?

Luke kept Eduardo talking while surreptitiously watching Cassie empty her bowl.

Good girl.

The two siblings maintained their silence, but after a few more minutes, Luke's curiosity took over. To no one in particular, he said, "Tell me what it was like growing up in Peru. Sounds exotic."

*   *   *

Cassie smiled at Lucas. "Peru and the Andes in particular are very beautiful. The mountains are higher than here. That is probably the only thing exotic about the place. Where we lived, there were mostly miners— all men—and the women were domestics who worked for the mine owners, or wives and mothers taking care of their own households." She shrugged. "Not very exotic, I am afraid. Our father owned one of the smaller mines, but he is retired now. *Mamá,* who is Quechua—a member of a native tribe—kept house for our family. She also performed shaman-istic ceremonies for anyone interested in the old ways."

"Shaman like the Native American healers?" Luke asked. Cassie nod-ded. "Perhaps you have some of your mother's healing ways about you."

Before she could negate his words, Eduardo interrupted. For a mo-ment, she had forgotten he was here. "Casandra was raised Roman Catholic, the same as I." Eduardo did not embrace his Quechua back-ground.

But then Eduardo surprised her. "Cassie is a healer. She saved my life during her last winter at home." Eduardo had never acknowledged her helping him overcome the unexplained fever the month before the rape.

Lucas smiled at her. "I couldn't agree more. She's sure healed me a couple of times now."

Embarrassed by their praise, she focused on her empty bowl without saying anything more. At least the conversation had turned to subjects other than—

"What are your intentions toward my sister?"

She sighed. *Intentions? Really, Eduardo?* The man refused to let it go. He was worse than a wolf feeding on a fresh carcass.

Rather than become defensive, Lucas smiled and turned to Cassie. "We have a lot in common. I think we're becoming good friends."

Oh, Lucas. I cannot be friends with you.

"I found you naked and asleep with her."

Enough! Cassie slammed her spoon onto the table. "Eduardo, stop it! I explained to you why we were together that way."

Eduardo glared at her. "I have seen how familiar he is with you—enticing you to eat, causing you to blush when he looks at you, calling you pet names." Eduardo paused, and she hoped he would stop. But no. "There is something you are not telling me."

He turned his focus on Lucas. "Have you taken advantage of my sister's innocence?"

Well, that was a loaded question. Eduardo had found them naked in each other's arms. Of course, nothing had happened, but Lucas paused too long, whether from shock or trying to find the right words, which only fueled Eduardo's suspicions. Guilt and something she could not read were evident on Lucas's face.

"I knew it." Eduardo's breathing grew shallow and rapid as he fisted his hand.

Would he attack Lucas? He would have to go through her to do so. Why did Lucas not simply reassure him that nothing had happened? Cassie set her lips in a straight line. She was not sure now if she wanted to deck her brother or Lucas before running to hide from both of them. Her chest rose and fell several times as her own breathing became more agitated.

In Spanish, Eduardo directed his next words at her. "As your brother and guardian, it is my place to make sure that your honor is upheld and that you are protected."

Cassie glanced at Lucas, but he resumed eating without making eye contact. Did he understand Spanish and know what Eduardo had said? Was his lip twitching as if he fought bursting into laughter? Perhaps this was funny to him, but certainly not to her.

She decided to respond in Spanish, as well, just in case. "I am no longer under your protection. I have lived alone now for five years. The only way anything about me will be learned by our parents is if you take your lies back to them. I suggest you keep your conclusions to yourself and let me live my life as I see fit."

Could this conversation make her any more uncomfortable—or angry? If only Eduardo knew he was too late to preserve something that no longer existed. Her innocence, honor, and reputation had been destroyed long ago—the night she snuck out of the house to go out with Pedro, looking for a little excitement after having so much fun clubbing with Kitty in New York City.

But she had no intention of enlightening him. Even if Pedro's and Diego's threats against her and her parents were idle ones, she would not take the chance of shaming her family with the knowledge of what she had allowed to happen by her own stupidity. Too much time had passed for her to prove she had been anything but a willing participant.

Cassie did not want to relive those memories by having to tell the story anyway. She had left that behind in Peru. Her honor could never be avenged, but she had no desire to have the filth smeared in her face again.

No man. No sex. No marriage.

She shuddered, speaking under her breath in Spanish, as rude as it was to Lucas. She feared her brother would say something about what he thought had happened that night with Pedro, only to embarrass her further. "Eduardo, if you say another word, I will kick you out of my house and never permit you to return. Do I make myself clear?"

Her words reverberated in her head as if through a megaphone. Had she really just stood up to her brother? Her hand shook from the enormity of it.

Lucas set his spoon down and took a deep breath before glaring at Eduardo. She had never seen him angry, but something seethed beneath the surface. "Cassie's a grown woman, and what she chooses to do is up to her."

No! Now he made it sound as though they *had* been doing something they shouldn't. "Lucas, tell him what happened. We have not been alone to corroborate our stories. As long as you tell the truth, he can see that I have not been lying to him."

He grinned at her. "I'm coming to that part, darlin'."

Stop calling me that, especially in front of Eduardo!

"Listen, your sister has done nothing to dishonor herself since the day we met last year. She—"

Instead of responding to him, Eduardo addressed her with steely eyes. "You have known him for a year? I thought you said you just met with some friends a couple of weeks ago."

Cassie slammed her fist on the table, rattling the spoons in the bowls. "Eduardo, stop this immediately! Nothing happened! We hardly know each other!"

"But I found you in bed together. There is something you are not telling me."

There were a lot of things she had not told Eduardo, but when it came to Lucas, she had been completely honest.

Now he twisted her words, attempting to trip her up. She glared at him before venturing one more time to prove her innocence. Through gritted teeth, she explained again. "We first met last September through my friend and college roommate Kitty. You remember her from your visits to me at Columbia?"

"The Goth singer?"

"Yes, but she is not as Goth anymore. She will soon become a mother and sings at her husband's um…private club in Denver now."

Best not to mention what kind of club.

"Anyway, some friends of hers were hanging out near here recently, and Kitty asked me to join them. We do not see each other very much anymore. I told you about this gathering already. Lucas happened to be among them. He and I had not seen each other since last October. No, I mean, December." He flustered her to the point she had completely forgotten about their brief encounter at her first gallery opening.

Eduardo opened his mouth to pounce at her slip of the tongue. Why was he being so accusatory? Why assume she was being anything but honest with him?

Did he know she had lied to her family about the rape?

Her soup refluxed into her throat.

"Stop badgering your sister." Lucas's hand reached out to hers, but she pulled away. This was no time for him to display what Eduardo would interpret as Lucas being her solicitous lover.

Cassie glanced at Lucas, imploring him not to make matters worse, but he was not finished with Eduardo yet and ignored her. "She's told you what happened. Why do you refuse to listen to what she's saying?"

Eduardo stood and stared down at him. "If you were any kind of man, you would protect her reputation by doing the right thing."

Lucas also stood, more slowly, his chair scraping on the linoleum floor. Her brother was several inches shorter than Lucas, but drew himself up to his full height in an attempt to intimidate Lucas anyway.

Without success. "I think you owe your sister an apology."

Goddess, they are going to come to blows.

"Please, Lucas. Sit down. I can handle this." Not that she was making any headway with her stubborn brother, either. The two men's demeanors infested her home with negative energy. Well, not Lucas's so much as Eduardo's.

After a long, tense moment, Lucas complied and sat. She faced her brother and smiled, hoping to diffuse his anger. "I realize you think you saw something inappropriate this morning, but it was not what you think. I have explained what happened. If you choose not to believe me…"

Eduardo narrowed his gaze at Cassie and addressed her in rapid Spanish. "If *Papá* had seen what I saw this morning, he would demand that you marry this man immediately to save your honor and reputation."

Cassie stood so quickly her chair tumbled backward. *No one* would coerce her into marrying against her will. She had avoided one such arranged marriage already. Thank the Goddess she had never told Eduardo or her family about the rape. A friend who found herself in a similar position had been forced to marry her rapist.

Her family would not control her actions any longer. Of course, her parents' generous monetary gifts helped pay her living expenses. Because it was still early in her career, Cassie needed time to build up her savings. She had hoped last year's gallery exhibition would be more successful than it had been, but she had been forced to schedule another one next month. Peddling her artwork was a necessary evil. She found much more joy in her studio creating the works than smiling at people as they scrutinized her art and decided whether they would pay to take something home.

What if the upcoming gallery showing was unsuccessful? And her parents cut her off because she refused to return home or to marry Lucas?

The walls closed in around her. Her hands grew damp, and she fisted them at her sides. In Spanish, albeit with false bravado, she spoke through her clenched teeth, "Lucas will not be forced to marry me. And I will not be returning to Peru."

She hoped to keep Eduardo from further intimidation tactics. Lucas struck her as the kind of man who would defend a woman's honor if he thought he had been responsible for damaging it.

But nothing immoral had happened between them! What man would allow himself to be coerced into marriage without anything in it for him? Eduardo would never be able to shackle Lucas with a defective, unwilling, frigid wife.

No, marriage was out of the question. End of discussion.

Memories of being held in Lucas's arms last night—touching him even—left her confused. What if...

No. Out of the question.

She had no interest in marrying—ever.

Chapter Five

M *arry her?*

Luke's Spanish might be rusty, and she had spoken in rapid-fire Spanish, but Luke caught a couple words, including his name and *casarse.*

Marry me.

Judging by the expression on her face and the anger in her voice, she just told her brother she wouldn't marry me if I were the last man on earth.

Hold on here. It's not like he'd even asked her. He didn't know how things were done in Peru, but weren't shotgun weddings a thing of the past?

No wonder Cassie had been pissed at Eduardo since he'd arrived. Hell, Luke barely knew the girl and had done nothing inappropriate with her. He wouldn't let her brother force them into a farce of a marriage just because the man was a century—maybe two—behind the times.

Then something else the man said earlier sunk in. It pleased the hell out of him to hear that those *were* blushes on Cassie's face just as he'd suspected a few times. If Luke wasn't so pissed at the way her brother was treating her right now, he'd have grinned in triumph.

The silent showdown between the siblings continued until Eduardo waved a hand in frustration and marched out of the kitchen. Instead of relishing her victory, Cassie began shaking. *Aw, hell.* Luke automatically reached out to hold her, but she held up her hands to ward him off.

"I am fine!"

Was she trying to convince him or herself? "Mind telling me what that was all about?" He might as well play dumb because he had only caught a little of what they said after they lapsed into their native language.

"A difference of opinion."

I'll say.

Surprising him, she elaborated. "My brother thinks I am still sixteen and in need of his protection." She took her and her brother's near-empty bowls to the sink and rinsed them out. He carried his own over to set it down but tried not to invade her personal space. Cassie needed a wider berth today. Too bad, because they had been making progress over the past twelve days.

"Want me to have a talk with him? Maybe I can set him straight about how things are done in this country." Hell, in this *century*.

She dropped her sponge and pivoted around. "No! If he will not listen to me, he will not believe you, either. Just let him be. He needs to learn that I am grown and live by American social standards now. What I do with my life is my choice. If I choose to have a lover, it would not be any of his business."

Do not *think about her choosing* you *as her lover, Denton.*

"I don't want him thinking things about you that aren't true. You and I both know nothing happened out in the shed."

A shadow clouded her eyes, and she looked down. "There are things you do not know about me. Eduardo will always feel he needs to—"

He tucked his index finger under her chin and forced her to meet his gaze. "I know all I need to know about you, darlin'. Don't let him or anyone else tell you different. You are one special lady." Well, when she wasn't all prickly, but maybe she had her reasons for being wary of men and putting up a front. All Luke needed to know to judge her character was that she'd risked her own safety and peace of mind to see to his needs. She'd nursed him back to health—twice. Cooked amazing meals for him. Even let him share in the experience of bringing Gracie's baby into the world. And her alpacas loved and trusted her. Animals were good judges of people.

So was he. Despite the façade she showed the world, deep down, she was kind, compassionate, and loving. She just didn't seem to know how to deal with those emotions and tried to shut them off.

"Any man would be proud to have you as his wife."

She narrowed her gaze. "You understood what I said to Eduardo?"

Luke recognized the spreading ruddiness in her cheeks as a blush this time and forced himself not to grin. "Just bits and pieces. Stick to your guns. Don't let him force you into doing something you don't want to do." He lowered his hand to his side. "But if the day ever comes that *you* want to get hitched, you could do a lot worse than me, darlin'."

Damn. Where had that come from? Maybe his ego had been a little bruised by the way she'd made him feel like shit on her boots when she'd told her brother she wouldn't marry him. Still, she'd pretty much been yanking at his heartstrings since that day last fall in the waiting room when she sketched the picture of Maggie and his baby.

Realizing how cocky he sounded, he grinned. "Sorry, darlin'. My mouth has a mind of its own sometimes."

"You will make some lucky woman very happy someday, Lucas. I am just not that woman. Too much has…" Her voice drifted off, and she turned back to the sink. "Thank you for not taking offense at my brother's words. He was raised in a strict, patriarchal society in which girls and young women are seen as innocent beings who need to be wrapped in woolen blankets until their wedding night. It is a matter of honor for Peruvian men that their daughters and sisters remain pure and untouched until marriage." She sighed and muttered under her breath, but just loudly enough he caught the words. "It is too late for me."

So she'd had a boyfriend back home, and it sounded as though they'd had a serious relationship if she thought she was no longer pure by her culture's standards.

"Pedro?" The name slipped out before he had time to apply a filter.

She spun around and blinked at him a couple of times. "How do you know about Pedro?" What was it he saw in her eyes—fear? Hatred? Certainly not love and affection.

"You spoke his name in your sleep this morning."

She closed her eyes and swallowed hard. Again, he wanted to reach out and hold her, comfort her, but knew she wouldn't let him. After a moment, she glanced up again, her gaze empty of emotion.

"Pedro was my fiancé. We were to be married after I graduated from uni." Her hand shook first, and then the tremors moved up to her shoulders. Poor girl wasn't holding in her emotions as well as she wanted.

Aw, hell. Luke closed the gap. Her rigid stance told him not to put his arms around her, so he stroked her arm gently instead. "Shhh." If anyone needed a hug right about now, it was Cassie. However, something told him baby steps would work better with her. She didn't pull away from his gentle, nonthreatening touch on her arm, at least. He wished he could give her more, but didn't want to send her running again.

So if she'd willingly had sex with him before marriage, something must have happened to Pedro to break off their engagement. Some kind of accident or something? Was he dead? "I'm so sorry, Sweet Pea."

He'd suffered the loss of his first love, too. Still, he might be jumping to conclusions. Cassie hadn't really said what had happened to her fiancé. Maybe he'd betrayed her. Cheated on her. Left her.

He'd definitely left her hurting.

"Wanna tell me about him? Maybe it will help."

She took a step back until she was pressed against the wall. Her glance darted toward the doorway as if planning her escape. "No. I never want to talk about him again. He is dead to me."

That didn't sound as though he was literally dead, just that she'd ended things with him. But she still dreamt about him, so some part of her hadn't resolved the end of the relationship.

"Then he wasn't worthy of you in the first place. You'll find the right man someday."

A man like me.

Whoa!

After his initial shock, though, he wondered why *not* him? Dammit, he could love, cherish, and protect her better than most.

"I will never let any man that close again."

So much for that idea, Denton.

Sounded like Pedro was the bastard who sent her up here to hide away. "I'm sorry he hurt you, Cassie. But not every man you meet will be like him."

She drew in a ragged breath. "You don't understand."

"Then help me understand."

Her breathing stilled, and he thought she might actually confide in him. But the walls came up again quickly. "I do not wish to speak of it."

Luke ran his hand through his hair. He wasn't going to get anywhere in lowering her defenses with a battering ram. Eduardo's ultimatum sure hadn't helped. Things had been going so well before he turned up. With the two of them left alone up here long enough, maybe passions could have flared and landed them back in the sack.

Instead, I got sacked by her brother.

This might be a good time to go inspect the road and see what the chances were of putting that plow onto the front of her Tahoe and digging his way out. He needed to expend a little frustration right now, too.

"I've got some work to do." He walked into the living room with Cassie following and found her brother staring sullenly into the flames. Maybe he could ease some of the tension with him by finding a common purpose. If nothing else, asking him to help him clear the road could prove Luke didn't intend to live in perceived pseudo-sin with the man's little sister forever.

"Eduardo, why don't you give me a hand outside with the snow-blade?"

"No, Lucas! You just had another blow to the head. You should be resting."

He turned and glared at her, hoping he silently communicated his response. The last thing he wanted to admit in front of her brother—or her—was that he couldn't pull his own weight.

She shook her head and muttered something in Spanish about men that didn't sound too nice. "I need to check on Milagrosa." Cassie rushed from the room, and the front door slammed seconds later.

For the next half hour, the two men worked in near silence hooking the plow blade onto her Tahoe. So much for getting-to-know-you conversation, but Luke realized he was afraid to say anything for fear of misinterpretation—again. The man had a one-track mind. Instead, he spoke only when he needed a tool or help lifting the blade.

Once the plow was in place, Luke waved Eduardo away and sat behind the wheel. He needed time to think. The next few hours he managed to make a small dent in the snowpack but didn't clear more than six feet of snow from the road. It would take weeks at this pace to break through. He hoped the Giardano brothers were having more luck on the other side.

Maybe he should ask Eduardo for directions for hiking out of here. But the thought of leaving Cassie and going back down the mountain opened a gaping hole in his heart.

He barely knew her, but his instincts told him she was hurting and lonely. Damned if he didn't want to try and make it better.

Luke understood the loneliness he saw in her eyes. He'd experienced that himself, worse than ever since Angel had left his place. Just having a companion around made the days so much fuller.

Before he left here, he intended to propose a no-strings-attached friendship between Cassie and him. Karla had her life in Denver, but with a baby on the way, she wasn't going to have much time for friends. Cassie said earlier that she'd begun feeling the loss when Karla married Adam.

So why shouldn't these two lonely people forge something together? They both could use some company every now and again. What would she say to being friends with him after he left here? Hell, they didn't have to date or do anything serious. Maybe just meet at daVinci's once in a while for a game of pool and a beer. Or a margarita, in her case. Wait, she said she didn't play pool.

Luke grinned. He'd love to teach her the finer points of the game and show her how much fun it could be. The thought of her body pressed between his and the table…

Okay, don't go there, Denton. Safer to focus on having her join him for a nice steak dinner once in a while in Breckenridge. No, she wouldn't be having steak. Maybe one of the many health-food restaurants then. He could eat that stuff every now and then if it meant spending time alone with Cassie again.

Luke shifted the Tahoe into park and stared down the mountain. He couldn't see his ranch from here, but he'd looked up at her mountain pass often enough this winter and spring, even though he'd never been able to see her place, either. Just knowing the girl of his dreams—well, one dream at least—was up here gave him a sense of peace for some reason whenever a case of the lonelies came over him.

Did his feelings for her have anything to do with the dream where Maggie had come to him last fall? The one where Maggie told him she was sending him an angel. He'd misinterpreted that dream ten ways from Sunday since then. Maybe now he finally understood what Maggie meant. Cassie was an angel with broken wings. She needed someone who would love and nurture her. He'd like to place his bid on a job like that.

Maybe Luke had been put in Cassie's life to help her grow a pair of strong, new wings. Surely that was it. "Maggie, I think I understand now."

He hadn't heard from Maggie in half a year at least, but he still talked to her.

Luke had always been a nurturer. First with Maggie, whose family had beaten her down, too. Despite being successful and happy at what she chose to do, she'd never gained their love and acceptance. It had bothered Maggie that they'd cut her off emotionally, but in some ways she seemed relieved not to have to spend time with them.

And then it was too late.

Luke had only wanted his wife to be happy doing what she loved most. Yeah, and doing what she loved wound up killing her, their unborn baby, and Angel's dad.

He scrubbed his hand down his face. He didn't like thinking about that day and all the mistakes he'd made.

Bottom line, he needed to be needed. His caregiving tendencies had come out again this spring with Angel when she left Marc and needed a place to lick her wounds. If Cassie needed a friend, then couldn't she see he was standing right in front of her?

Because she seemed content to live up here alone. This refuge enabled her to shut out the world. No wonder he'd upset her when he crashed into her life. Now she had to deal with her brother's invasion, too.

Whatever Cassie was running away from only made him want to know her better. What if it was something he could help her overcome?

Why did he have such a strong compulsion to rescue wounded creatures?

Casarse.

Her brother pushing her toward marrying him wasn't the way to breach Cassie's walls. Perhaps Luke could assure her that, if it would make peace with her brother, he'd agree to some kind of temporary arrangement. Both could keep their own places and their separate lives but still form a legal bond that would appease Eduardo and her parents. Who knows? Affections might grow into something more—or she could change her mind and ask for an annulment or divorce.

Could he forego sex if that was what she disliked most about the thought of marrying? She sure didn't like being touched, but since he'd been up here, there had been a few times where she had tolerated him. Maybe he was growing on her. Hell, he'd gone without intercourse for eight years. When he missed Maggie, it wasn't sex he missed most, but all the little things like time spent together, fleeting touches, and being tangled up in bed.

Of course, he and his wife did have sex. Being around Cassie and not being able to touch her would be frustrating in the extreme.

But look at all they had in common. Art and their animals, for sure, but loneliness was at the top of his list. As friends, they could help each other out when needed and just give each other someone to talk to or have dinner with now and then.

Hell, draw up a companionship contract, Denton. That's not what marriage is about.

Yeah, what was he thinking? People didn't get forced into shotgun weddings nowadays. Hell, most didn't marry at all. They just lived together. In that thinking, he and Eduardo had something in common. Luke was old school when it came to making a commitment to a woman.

If he spoke vows to Cassie, he would damned well mean every single word.

He opened the door of the Tahoe and stepped down, nearly buckling under his own weight. Hell, he was still too damned weak to think or walk straight anymore.

He'd best keep working on finding a way off this mountain and back to his horses. At least he understood them a little better.

The only way he could make Cassie López happy was to vamoose out of her life.

*   *   *

After spending time with Milagrosa and Graciela, Cassie's nerves calmed somewhat, but soon fear encroached again. Her psyche had been battered and bruised. Tonight, she would escape into her art, just as she had hidden there all afternoon preparing to work on a piece that called to her. She should be working on the final piece for the gallery exhibition, but this one needed to be done first. It would not be for sale, though.

Immersing herself in the creative zone helped to ground her, but the sound of her Tahoe's snowblade scraping against the ice kept distracting her and pulling her focus away. Someone was attacking the snowpack with a vengeance. Most likely, Lucas was trying to dig himself out of this prison. However, it was only a prison to him. She preferred her solitary confinement here. Only now, too much of the world was on the wrong side of the perimeter wall she had erected.

Her hand shook, and she pulled the brush away to stare at the watercolor. Muddy, gray colors. A single aspen leaf swirled against a bombarding wind. Startled blackbirds flew away to seek shelter as a thunderhead loomed over the scene. She had not permitted such darkness into one of her paintings since coming to her mountain.

Her mountain?

No, she held no claim on any part of this mountain. Not even squatters' rights.

Her gaze moved to the flock of birds. Wings. Freedom. They could seek new shelter and safety without worry.

But the leaf had no choice. No control. It could only drift on the wind until falling to the earth to lie in the mud…perhaps trampled upon by careless or uncaring footsteps. Worse yet, to decompose unnoticed back into the earth.

I am the leaf.

Cassie blinked away the sting in her eyes. Her mountain home had given her so much peace and solace—until now. Perhaps her art would be her legacy, rather than having children. All the more reason to suffer through gallery showings. Hiding away, she would never make a difference in anyone else's life, but through her art, she could provide others with a new way to interpret their own world.

Finished with as much as she could do today, she cleaned the brushes and moved toward her altar in the corner of the studio. Let her brother say what he wanted about her. Let him plan her future until he was blue in the face. Cassie dashed the tears from her cheeks. She stared at the meditation blanket, but refused to kneel. Now more than ever she needed to find her center, but she would not enter her sacred space filled with such foul and negative thoughts.

Restless, she walked over to the oil painting she had completed in anticipation of Eduardo's visit. An anniversary gift for her parents. She flipped on the track lighting and lifted the gauzy dust cloth that had kept it clean while the oils hardened.

Her parents' eyes stared out at her. Did they forgive her for never returning home? For leaving them without explanation? Every time they spoke via Skype or e-mail, *Mamá* begged her to return home, even for a visit.

Papá just stared out from the painting with those intense eyes, blaming her for making *Mamá* so sad. Her vision blurred as her chest tightened.

But she refused to go anywhere near the three men who had raped her ever again. She might be able to avoid Diego and Luis by staying in her village, but *Mamá* had told her Pedro had taken over managing his father's mines, so he would still be living near her parents.

A knock at the door interrupted her thoughts, but she did not respond. She glanced away from the painting and tried to find something that could help ease the pain and shame she felt, but nothing here offered her any comfort. Or hope.

"Cassie, you okay?"

She shook her head. Dead. She felt dead.

"Open the door, darlin'. I won't invade your space. I just need to make sure you're all right." He paused a moment. "Your brother, hell, he's just trying to intimidate us, but *we* know nothing happened. Don't let him upset you."

Cassie fought a sudden and irrational longing to feel Lucas's arms around her the way he had held her in her dream. She yearned to rest her forehead on his solid chest and feel the steady, strong beat of his heart.

No! She could not allow him to come that close again. Not only would Eduardo interpret such a scene as damning evidence, but it would give Lucas the wrong idea, as well.

She sought comfort, not intimacy.

Men did not understand a woman's needs and desires. They thought only of their base carnal drives. Better not to put herself in a position for him to misinterpret what she wanted.

"I am fine. Please, Lucas, go back to the cabin. I need to be alone. I will sleep here tonight."

Her words met silence. After several minutes, she decided he had done as she asked.

Good.

He had not forced himself into her personal space or disregarded her need for solitude. Since the rape, she had tried to keep her distance from people. Sometimes even being with Kitty was too painful, especially now that she had found love and happiness with Adam Montague. She had been mourning the loss of her closest friend since Kitty became serious about him. The loss of Kitty's brother last year had changed her. When she had invited her friend to leave New York City and come to Colorado to grieve, Cassie never imagined Kitty would inadvertently reunite with the Marine who had rescued her when she was sixteen and trying to run away from home.

In some ways, Cassie was jealous of her friend's good fortune in life and love. Kitty had only ever been with Adam. Cassie's virginity, on the other hand, had been stripped away from her, leaving her empty inside and too damaged for any honorable man to want her.

Not that she sought to have that kind of relationship with a man. Throughout her teens, she had been warned that boys could not be platonic friends. Hormones, *machismo*, and seeing women as good for only one thing came into play. Every innocent touch, word, and gesture was misconstrued to mean something vile. Something *sexual*. As they grew older, it worsened. No, men did not know how to simply be friends with women.

Better to send Lucas away and resume her life the way it was intended to be—alone. Perhaps there were lessons to be learned in living this way.

Yet Lucas had far exceeded her low expectations of men. They had been thrown into situations where he easily could have taken advantage of her, but he had not. He was the first man in five years she wanted to spend time with. How had he breached the wall so easily?

She shook her head. What was the matter with her? She did not want a husband, but a friend. A companion. Talking about their shared love of animals and art was not what marriage was based on. Given time, though, he would interpret familiarity and affection to mean something more and would encroach on her personal space.

Would she never learn that men's personalities could change at the drop of a hat? She would not allow herself to be duped again.

Cassie crossed the studio to the sleeping area near a wall of windows. The sun had long since dipped behind the mountains forcing her to turn on more lights so she could see without bumping into anything. Outside the French doors was her hot tub. The oval tub was only big enough for two—nothing like the one she, Kitty, and Angelina had used at Adam's place last fall—but she only needed enough space for one as she performed some of her spiritual ceremonies, most often her cleansing one.

No way did she intend to use the tub with Lucas and her brother around even though they would have to work awfully hard to see her in it, because it was on the far side of her studio.

She crossed the room to the dresser and pulled out a nightgown before stepping behind the privacy screen in the corner. No one could see inside the window, but at night, she imagined dozens of eyes peering in at her just the same.

Lucas and Eduardo could fend for themselves in the house. The fridge was filled with leftovers if they were hungry. It wasn't until she turned down the covers on the bed that she stopped short.

"My babies!" She had never forgotten her alpacas before and quickly donned socks and boots again. She put on her poncho covering most of her because she did not have time to dress again. She was hours late for their evening meal. This would only take fifteen minutes at most. She picked up her flashlight.

Opening the door to the studio, she admitted feeling relief that the path to the shed was empty in the beam cast from her flashlight. Lucas had not lurked outside her studio on the chance she might answer the door eventually.

The wind whipped at her bare legs as she ran as quickly as possible, catching herself as she slipped a couple of times. Light showed around the cracks of the shed's door. Had she left it on?

The sound of a deep voice singing reached her ears at the same moment she yanked open the door. Her gaze met Lucas's as he stopped singing and turned away from filling Graciela's feed bin. He sang to her girls?

His eyes lit up before he gave her a slow once-over and smiled.

"Good to see you're okay, darlin'."

"I, um, told you I was fine." She folded her arms, trying to shield herself from his scrutiny, even though she wore a heavy poncho.

"Yeah, but I'd rather see for myself." He lowered the feed bucket to his side. "Better close that door before you let out all the heat."

Lucas did not like being cold. Why he chose to live in the Rocky Mountains puzzled her. She contemplated whether she should run back to the studio or stay and help. Obviously, *he* had not forgotten her animals. But they were her responsibility. While deciding what to do, she pulled the door closed.

Surprisingly, no sense of fear arose at being alone with him. Lucas had torn down some of her self-preservation barriers. She reminded herself she had not known him long enough to trust him, though.

Cassie kept a safe distance from him and crossed the shed to the water faucets. "Who still needs water?"

"They all do, but why don't you take care of this while I fill the water buckets?"

He closed the gap between them, and the air seemed to disappear from the shed. He simply handed her the feed bucket, still half full. Their fingers brushed on the handle, and a jolt of electricity ran up her arm. Not like the discharge of static. More potent. She pulled away, taking the bucket with her.

"Which ones have been fed?" Her voice sounded husky.

"Gracie and Tika. I also brushed Tika down. She was a mess from her little adventure last night."

Mortified that she had neglected her babies today, she skirted him, leaving plenty of space between them while ignoring the way her stomach clenched at his scent.

Musky.

Soapy.

All man.

Her heartbeat accelerated.

Dangerous. Stay away from him.

They worked together in silence with as much distance between them as the small shed allowed. Cassie finished filling the other bins and came over to visit with Graciela a minute before Lucas entered the small space to fill the trough with fresh water.

The air sizzled with energy, and her breathing became labored. When she moved to escape, Graciela side butted her without warning, and she yelped as she hurtled toward the wall.

"Whoa, darlin'!"

Water sloshed from his bucket as Lucas reached out to steady her, dousing her poncho with frigid water. "Oh, Goddess! So cold!" The trough would have warmed it some, but this water had come straight from the tap.

"Here, let's get that wet thing off you."

Before she could escape, his hands lifted the lower edge of the garment and yanked it over her head. While happy to be rid of the cold, wet covering, she soon realized her nightgown was not substantial enough to shield her body from his gaze.

Cassie crossed her hands over her breasts, but not before Lucas zeroed in on the swelling of her nipples. To his credit, he quickly looked away, but fear coursed down her spine. She took a step away, running into Gracie's side.

Trapped.

His gaze met hers, concern in his eyes. "You okay, Sweet Pea?"

She was nearly hyperventilating. No, she was far from okay. She needed to escape before he touched her. Putting one foot out to the right, she sidled along the length of Graciela's body. Just a few more steps.

Lucas came toward her. Her mind flashed back to the cantina.

Panicked, Cassie backed into Milagrosa who had come around her mother, perhaps to see what was going on or to see Lucas with whom she had formed a solid bond. Lucas's hands grabbed her.

She batted his hand away and screamed. Fight back!

She lifted her knee in an attempt to connect with his groin, but he was too fast and deflected her movement with his own knee before spinning her around and pulling her against his body, his arm below her breasts like a vise.

She fought him. "I...cannot...breathe."

"Take it easy, darlin'! You're safe. I'm just trying to keep you from falling over Millie."

Lucas?

He held her as if to show he only wanted to steady her. She breathed in and out rapidly, her heart pounding, before rational thought began to filter into her consciousness.

This is Lucas. He will not harm me.

How could she be sure? She had ignored her instincts once before with disastrous results.

He lowered his mouth to her ear. "Trust me, Sweet Pea. I wouldn't hurt you for anything."

Cassie wanted to believe him. She had no reason not to, other than history with other men who were not as honorable. As the adrenaline rush subsided, her body shook. Lucas turned her around to face him and pulled her against his hard chest before tucking her head under his chin.

His hands stroked her back. He wasn't holding her prisoner. Instead, his hands and body almost seemed to shelter her. He gave her a safe harbor until able to stand on her own again. "Shhh. Just relax. You're safe with me."

Cassie replayed several self-defense training moves in her mind to help her prepare in case she needed them. Against her better judgment, she rested her forehead against his chest and felt the steady beat of his heart. The rhythm calmed her for some reason.

"'Atta girl." He stroked her hair, and she relaxed a little more.

A creaking sound preceded the rush of wind through the door.

"In his arms again, Casandra?"

Cassie broke free and spun around to find her brother staring at her with condemnation. His gaze took in her lack of clothing, and he narrowed his gaze.

"Eduardo, it is not what you are thinking. I almost fell. Lucas caught me."

"What would our parents say if they knew what was going on up here? No, I do not intend to tell them what I found you doing—twice now. It would kill them. But is that the reason you do not visit them? Are you too ashamed to face them? If I had known you would forget your upbringing, I never would have convinced them to let you take that scholarship."

Anger boiled up inside her.

She pushed away from Lucas. "I have done nothing to bring shame on our family." *Except to trust the wrong man, someone my family chose for me.* "But even if Lucas and I were involved with each other, this is the twenty-first century. No one cares about my reputation."

"I care."

Lucas's words forced her to face him again. What was he saying?

"Call me old-fashioned, darlin', but I don't want your parents thinking badly about you because of me."

"Lucas, you are not helping the situation any."

"Hear me out, Sweet Pea."

Please stop calling me by your silly endearments in front of my brother!

She clenched her hands until the nails dug into the palms.

"I don't want your brother thinking the wrong thing about us. We both know how far off base he is." Lucas met Eduardo's gaze and addressed her brother in a stern voice. "You need to respect your sister enough to know she's telling you the truth when she says nothing inappropriate happened."

"I trust what I see with my own eyes."

"Maybe you need to pull your eyes and mind out of the gutter then. I've never met a woman with more integrity or a bigger heart than your sister. I'm still waiting to hear you apologize to her."

Cassie shook her head, wishing the floor would open up and swallow her. She hated confrontation and did not want the two men to come to blows if Eduardo refused the challenge thrown down by Lucas.

Feeling like a pawn in this game of *machismo*, Cassie had reached her limit. "When is someone going to listen to what *I* think? What *I* want?" She vowed long ago never to be in the position again where other people controlled her life, her future. "I am going back to bed." She grabbed her poncho and fled from the shed, heading to her only remaining sanctuary.

Cassie hung the wet poncho on the hook by the door and removed her boots and socks. She stretched out on the bed, but after staring at the ceiling for what had seemed like an hour or two, she decided she needed something to help rid her of the day's negativity. Perhaps immersing herself in her hot tub, regardless of who might invade her privacy, would help. Shucking the gown, she ran from the warm studio into the frigid night. Her body soon prickled with goose bumps.

She immersed her lower body into the tepid water but had to reset the temperature to warm the water—closer to ninety than eighty. As the water heated—or her body adjusted to its temperature—she closed her eyes and imagined herself deep within the womb of *Pachamama*.

Safe.

Clean.

Innocent.

She began her ritual chanting, standing with arms outstretched as she let the cold air wash over her from head to knees. The moon shone over her view—*Mama Quilla* watching over her as well. When she began to shiver, she immersed herself again in the warm waters. Three times, she did this as she attempted to restore peace, light, and harmony to her life once more.

When finished, she climbed out of the tub and reentered the studio. Wrapped in a silk robe, she went to her altar where she knelt. She burned desert sage leaves to rid her mountain and her heart of negativity.

After lighting her spirit candle, she surrounded herself in the white light and entered into a deep meditation.

Confusing images floated across her third eye. Riding a horse with Lucas's arms wrapped around her. Another image was with Lucas beside a stream, mountains looming behind them. Her panties hung on a nearby bush. Heat infused her face. A final image was of Lucas, his hand shaking as he placed a wedding ring on her finger and vowed to cherish and protect her forever.

Cassie's eyes shot open, pulling her abruptly out of the meditation.

Fantasy or prophecy?

Mama Quilla might be showing her the future, but how could Lucas play such an important part in her destiny? Then again, it was equally preposterous to fantasize about the man. He needed to return to his life and leave her alone.

What if he was the man chosen by *Mama Quilla* for her? She questioned the Goddess seeking answers, but as She had been for years, She remained silent.

Giving up, Cassie dressed in her gown again and crawled into the futon bed. Sleep did not come for many hours that night.

In the morning, she went to the cabin to start breakfast. Eduardo sat in an armchair by the fire reading what looked like a voluminous report given the number of pages. She greeted him, but his grunt told her he was not paying attention. He was probably engrossed in something about volcanoes or earthquakes.

Lucas was nowhere to be seen. A plate and mug sat rinsed in the sink. One of them must have eaten already.

"He ate before heading out to work on the road." She glanced toward the doorway where Eduardo stood leaning against the jamb.

With Eduardo's constant badgering about Lucas since the moment he arrived, she really did not care to have any further conversations with him.

So breakfast needed to be something quick. She prepared two bowls of oatmeal and set them on the table with two glasses of juice. Eduardo poured each of them a mug of black coffee that he must have brewed earlier, and they sat together eating in blessed silence for a while.

"Pedro asks about you."

Cassie's stomach threatened to heave the contents of her meal. "Did you tell him where I am?"

He narrowed his gaze. "No. I honored your request. I still do not understand why you broke up with him. He could have provided you with a fine home and many children."

She clenched the spoon. Thankfully, the rape had not resulted in a pregnancy. She would not have known which man was the father. Cassie swallowed against the acid burning her throat and set her spoon down.

The thought of facing Pedro again made her even more ill. Perhaps she should tell Eduardo what happened, but what good would it do now?

"Did he do something the night you went out unchaperoned that we should know about?"

Change the subject. "You thanked me last night for saving your life. Well, you saved mine as well."

He quirked his brows.

"Without you paving the way for me to go to uni, I might not have found my true path. It definitely did not lie in our village." She smiled at him. "You opened doors for me and gave me the chance to earn my degree. *Papá* never would have agreed to let me go without you, so thank you."

"If given the chance, though, I am not sure I would do it over again knowing that the experience took you away from us. But I have always understood how important your career is. Your talent should be shared with the world."

She drew in a deep breath. "Eduardo, I am happy in this place and plan to stay here."

"Human beings are not meant to live in such isolation. Why would you shut yourself off like this?"

Lucas's image flashed across her mind. She wondered if Eduardo was projecting that image to her, whether intentionally or not, to make her think about what it might be like having someone to share her life with up here. Then she remembered her meditation last night and shuddered.

Was Lucas part of her destiny? How could that be?

"Never mind, Casandra. I am sorry if I have been unbearable during this visit." Overbearing was a more accurate term. He reached out and squeezed her hand. "I miss you. My logical mind tells me you are an adult who can make her own decisions. But my heart sees you as my little sister and probably always will. When I found you in the shed—struggling to get away from a man I thought was taking advantage of you—well, that image is hard to eradicate."

"You know now that he was doing no such thing." Hearing him admit he thought she was being attacked and then how quickly he tried to coerce her into marrying the very person he thought was attacking her made her grateful she had kept her mouth shut in Peru. Countless women there had been forced into such marriages, a deplorable fate.

Machismo. The men in her country lived under its archaic influence. But Eduardo had seen enough of the world to know they did not have to follow the dictates of the generations who had come before them. Why was he so adamant about marrying her off? Was he tired of having to be her protector from so far away?

"Is Denton successful at what he does?"

She glanced at Eduardo and blinked a few times as she attempted to follow the shift in the conversation. "I suppose so. He is a Renaissance man with a number of talents and stays quite busy."

"Would he be able to support you?"

Ah. This again. "Eduardo, I can support myself. I do not need a man for that or anything else."

"He said himself he would marry you."

"*If* he had damaged my reputation, which you know he has not done." Why is it men only heard what they wanted to hear?

She still had no clue why Lucas had said that, making them both sound guilty. She sighed. "I think he is just traditional, like you." Maybe he was not as bad as Eduardo, but bad enough. "Lucas does not understand our culture, and I am certain he had no idea you insinuated that he should marry me because you think he slept with me." She could not bring herself to say, "have sex."

He paused a moment, perhaps weighing whether he should say more, but then he went ahead anyway.

"Casandra, I came here to remind you that our parents are growing older. *Papá* had a health scare a few months ago."

"What do you mean?" *Papá* had been sick? Why had no one told her?

"A precancerous growth on his face was removed."

Her mind flashed to the painting of their parents sitting in her studio. She had astral projected while painting it—letting her spirit leave her body and travel to them in another dimension. This was the only way to see what *Papá* looked like now. Then, as often happened when she created a piece of art, she zoned out and let her hands and subconscious create the work without interference from her mind.

Now she remembered what had appeared to be a burn mark just above his lip. While it had puzzled her, she painted it in thinking perhaps he had burnt himself with one of the cigars he loved so much. "Why did no one say anything?"

He shrugged matter-of-factly. "They removed the spot, but he did not want to worry you."

Cassie tamped down her anger at being left out. *Papá* had a brush with what might eventually be cancer and no one had bothered to tell her? Was he afraid to find out if she would have ignored him at such a time?

Would she have? She did not know. Tears stung her eyes. Still, she could have tried to speak with him by phone at least.

"They miss you very much, Casandra. Why do you not come back home? Just for a visit at least."

She glanced down and shook her head. "It breaks my heart not to see *Mamá y Papá* again and to know they are hurting because of me, but this I cannot change. If only we could meet somewhere outside of the village or Lima."

"*Papá* is too old to travel, and *Mamá* will not go without him."

"I know. So I will have to content myself to Skype with *Mamá* and…" Of course, he did not understand her spiritual abilities, so she did not mention astral projection, the only means she had of seeing *Papá* again.

"I am sorry, Eduardo." She stood. "All I want is to be left alone."

"Someone has hurt you. I have to guess it was Pedro."

She did not intend to tell him the extent to which Pedro had hurt her, but wanted to remove the shame she had carried all this time. Pedro would never again have any power over her. "Pedro is not the man *Papá* thought he was."

He made a fist. "You know I would keep him away from you if you do not wish to see him."

She held up her hand. "Thank you, but I still cannot go back there."

He leaned forward. "Tell me what he did."

She retreated and pressed her back against the chair. "It is in the past. I have let it go." Or tried to.

"Are you sure? Did he hurt you so badly that you will shut out every other man who might want to love and cherish you?"

Yes, Pedro had hurt her, betrayed her in the vilest way, but she could not reveal to Eduardo the details for fear her brother would attempt to avenge her innocence, her honor. When Cassie began shaking uncontrollably, Eduardo stood and came toward her. He hunkered down beside her and wrapped his arms around her, pulling her closer.

She tamped down the feeling of being smothered.

This is my brother.

"I do not wish to speak of him ever again."

"I understand, but do not let him keep you estranged from your family. Your place is there, not here in this lonely cabin."

"I am not lonely." *Not anymore. Wait!* Clarify that thought. "I have my alpacas to keep me company now." *And Lucas Denton.* The unbidden thought wheedled its way into her brain anyway, despite efforts to block it. "This is my home now."

Thankfully, Lucas would be leaving soon. Her heart was growing too attached to having him around. She hated to become dependent upon anyone, especially a man.

They always want more than I am willing to give.

Her meditation visions from last night came back to haunt her. What did they mean? She had no future with Lucas or any man.

The walls were closing in on her. She needed to escape right now. She tore herself away from his arms and stood. "I will see you later. Please do not harass Lucas anymore. He is a kind and gentle man who does not deserve to be treated that way."

"If he is so wonderful, why would you not want to marry him?"

"Because he deserves someone who can love him back. I am not that woman."

"Nonsense. You have much love to give. Besides, if you marry him, we will not have to worry about you alone in this foreign land anymore."

She rolled her eyes. "I am twenty-six years old. Consider me a lost cause, and let me live my life as I see fit."

"Susana and I both enjoy our time alone, too, but there is nothing more special than coming home and being greeted by someone who loves you unconditionally and gives your body, mind, and spirit a restful peace."

She sighed. "I am glad you have found that, Eduardo. But I could obtain that from having a dog—or alpacas. Same outcome."

"Oh, Casandra, how can you have such a low expectation of marriage when you see how our parents love each other so?"

Once more, thoughts of her parents and how she had hurt them put her on the verge of tears. Before responding or allowing him to say anything to make her feel more guilt, she excused herself and walked quickly toward the mudroom. Shrugging into her poncho, she left the cabin and made her way to the studio.

She heard the sound of the ax as Lucas split yet more wood. The man was obsessed with laying in enough wood to last her through the entire next year.

She did not veer off the path, but once inside the studio could not keep herself from going to the window to stare out at him. He had removed his coat, and sweat soaked his denim shirt. While not built like a narcissistic bodybuilder, his muscles were strong and well-chiseled. She remembered the time she had spent in his arms, lying against his chest. Fortunately, he did not like the cold or he might have removed—

As if he heard her unformed thought, he set the ax on the woodpile and began unbuttoning his shirt.

Oh, no! He wouldn't!

Despite knowing what he looked like naked, she could not tear her gaze away. She should go back to work but convinced herself she was only watching him for research, in case she ever wanted to sketch a man.

Not that she had ever had a desire to do so before.

He picked up the ax and went back to work. Sweat glistened on his chest. His pecs rippled with each steady movement. The man's abdominals were distinctive and well-formed. A six-pack as Kitty would call it.

Her forehead grew damp from the temperature in here, despite the fact there was no heat on.

Be honest with yourself, Cassie.

All right, she knew exactly why she was becoming overheated. She supposed she should thank the Goddess for having such good taste in men, if indeed She had sent him to wear away her defenses. But what on earth was *Mama Quilla* thinking?

Chapter Six

Luke hadn't slept well on the floor in front of the fire, but he'd given Eduardo use of Cassie's bed last night, hoping a good night's sleep would make the man less ornery.

His thoughts had turned to Cassie throughout the night. In fact, he'd taken a walk to blow off some frustration and heard an unusual chanting. Curious, he rounded the studio to find a very naked Cassie rising from the water of an oval hot tub. He didn't think he stared long, but the image of her with her arms outstretched to the heavens, her already high breasts even higher, and her delightful curves had been seared onto his brain forever.

What was with her insane obsession with the cold? Not only was she naked with air temperatures in the teens, but she was soaking wet. The steam rising from the pool of water told him the tub probably warmed her instantly when she sat back down, but in the interim…

Hell, the last thing he expected was to find an uptight woman like Cassie skinny-dipping in her hot tub.

When he'd returned to the cabin to try and sleep by the fire, he found himself hotter than a firecracker. Every time he closed his eyes, he saw Cassie naked and standing in that hot tub. No sleep to be had last night.

In an effort to expend some pent-up energy, he'd risen long before dawn and spent a few hours mucking out the stalls. Four o'clock wasn't all that much earlier than when he went to work on his ranch. He spent some time with the alpacas, surprisingly intelligent, affectionate animals. He'd never really thought about alpacas before, having not been around them. After brushing out the girls, he gave Millie a little extra attention. Nothing like newborn babies to make everything seem possible.

Man, as much as he missed his horses, he hated to think about leaving here. He had bonded with Cassie forever over the birth of Millie whether the woman liked it or not. Being there to bring her back from the brink of death made him feel on top of the world, too.

Back at the cabin by dawn, he grabbed a quick breakfast and had a civil chat with her brother, who seemed more intent on a report he was reading than making small talk. With energy to burn, Luke went outside again to chop firewood, hoping the exertion would help him sleep tonight. Unfortunately, he hadn't been able to rid his mind of Cassie's image from last night, which only served to work him up even more. He'd never painted water nymphs, but had studied John William Waterhouse. The artist's innocent, yet sensual, creatures had nothing on his vision of Cassie López in that hot tub.

I'm going to miss that girl something fierce when I go home.

He'd miss this place, too. And the alpacas.

A rapid movement out of the corner of his eye caused him to glance up and catch Cassie running across the yard from either the cabin or shed, heading back to her studio. The distress on her face upset him. Another run-in with her brother?

They needed to discuss why her brother kept trying to strong-arm them into admitting wrongdoing they hadn't done. Should he go to her now? No. Cassie was a proud woman and didn't like to show any sign of weakness.

He wielded the ax a few more times, and once again, his thoughts strayed to the way she'd looked in the moonlight last night. The more he thought about the beauty, the hotter he became. He removed his shirt. The air took the place of a cold shower until he could take one tonight.

Later, he would stack the wood neatly near the alpaca shed and restock the bin in the mudroom. Cassie could enjoy fires as late as she wanted this spring. Hell, it was probably chilly enough in the summer at twelve thousand feet to have the fireplace burning every night. If he lived up here, he would.

By midday, the temperatures had reached the upper thirties. His next job would be to attack the snowpack while the sun made it nice and slushy. When the temps fell overnight, it would be hard ice again.

Worn out from chopping wood, at least he'd be able to sit in the Tahoe's cab. Setting down the ax, he picked up his shirt and put it on. While he buttoned it, he glanced over at the studio and saw a blur in one of the windows. Cassie? Had she been watching him?

He grinned. While he was only half-naked, he didn't feel as bad for happening upon her last night. She must have been embarrassed being caught spying if she ducked out of the window so fast. What thoughts simmered beneath the surface with her?

He'd probably never find out. He climbed into the SUV and tackled the slowly melting snowpack. He figured a couple more days, and he'd meet up with where the Giardanos were working on the other side.

After an hour or so, he put the plow in park and looked out at the mountain range. The views up here were spectacular. The avalanche had cleared out a number of spruce trees, opening up an even greater vista he supposed than what had been here before.

No wonder Cassie loved it up here. He wondered what the view from that hot tub must be like and grinned. The V in the mountains would be directly in front of her. She also enjoyed that spectacular view from her studio.

Speaking of which, he needed to check on her. Seeing how upset she'd been earlier, he decided it was better to reach out to her in her studio without Eduardo around.

Hoping he wouldn't catch her in the middle of something, he made his way down the path to her studio. At the door, he knocked, but there was no response.

"Cassie, darlin', do you have a minute?"

Another pause. She surprised him eventually, though. Good thing he had patience. "Coming."

Even through the door, her voice sounded thick, as if she'd been crying. Why did Eduardo keep badgering her? He and Cassie hadn't done anything he had accused them of doing. The woman wouldn't let Luke anywhere near her, although she didn't give Eduardo that look of fear she sometimes gave him.

Give her time. Someone had hurt the girl badly.

Look how much her guard had come down in the past two weeks. Not that he had that much more time with her. The thought of not being able to see her day in and day out left him with a crushing weight on his chest. Once the road was cleared, she'd send him on his way.

Luke did look forward to reconnecting with his world when he left here. No word from Marc, but Angel said he'd been through some kind of ordeal last week. He'd check on him first thing by cell phone. Then the horses.

The door creaked open, and Cassie stood there with red, puffy eyes and her eyelashes clumped together, wet from tears. She waved him in and backed away so he wouldn't come too close.

"What's wrong, darlin'?"

She shook her head. "Nothing. I am fine. Just overly emotional."

He wanted to take her in his arms and provide her some comfort, but she'd probably kick him out. Maybe he could help by just being here and distracting her.

Give her space.

His gaze lighted on a watercolor in the center of her work area. Close by was the portrait of her parents. Were they weighing heavily on her conscience and emotions today? What had Eduardo said earlier to upset her?

"Painting something new?"

She shook her head. "Well, I tried to work on that watercolor some more but am having a hard time concentrating."

Big surprise with all the intruders at her mountain hideaway. "Mind if I take a look?"

She shrugged. "No, not at all."

He walked across the studio to examine the piece. The canvas was a wash of browns, blacks, and grays, but a single, bright-yellow aspen leaf drifted on the air currents. It provided a splash of light and color amidst one very depressing background. "I feel a real sense of motion with the leaf."

"Thank you."

The dark emotion on the canvas tugged at his heart. Did she see herself as the leaf, buffeted by the winds, no control in her life? Or was he projecting his own feelings onto the painting? Artists rarely intended what others interpreted in their pieces. Each work of art spoke differently to each person viewing it. "Will this be shown at the gallery?"

"I am uncertain. It is not quite finished and was not planned for the show, but I need to finish a couple of others first. I have an idea for a fiber-art design but have not had time to work on it."

"Sorry, I've taken up so much of your time lately. You'd have been able to get more work done if not chained to my bedside after the avalanche."

Don't think about restraining her to a bed, Denton.

She shook her head and smiled. "No, I needed you here to save Milagrosa's life. I will always be indebted to you. Besides, I still have plenty of time. The exhibition is not for seven weeks. As long as I deliver the bulk of the pieces in a few weeks, I am sure she will accept a couple of late ones shortly before the opening. The owner is easy to work with."

Her gaze drifted to the oil of her parents, and he saw her chin start to quiver. A fat tear rolled down her cheek before she took a ragged breath and turned away. Again, he fought the urge to wrap her in his arms, but she didn't like to be touched.

"Missing your home?"

She tried to dash away her tears surreptitiously before turning toward him. "This is my home."

He nodded in the direction of the oil painting. "I mean your folks. I reckon having Eduardo here stirs up feelings of missing those you love."

He wondered if there was some man in Peru she ached for as well.

She cleared her throat, and her eyes filled with tears again. In a husky whisper, she said, "I have disappointed and worried my parents."

"I doubt that, darlin'. I'm sure they're proud of your talent and that you followed your dream. Not enough people are brave enough to venture out and pursue their passion in life."

"No, my avocation does not bring them joy. I should have married after graduating from college and settled down. Presented them with two point five grandchildren by now. Instead, I have caused them to worry about my safety and grieve over my absence." A sob tore from her.

Aw, damn. He closed the gap between them and wrapped his arms lightly around her, surprised as hell when she didn't push him away. Instead, she laid her forehead over his heart and gave in to the tears.

"Shhh." He reached up and stroked her hair, trying not to mess up her braids. "It's probably not as bad as you think."

She shook her head vehemently and continued to cry. "*Papá* has been ill. And you can see he is old. I may never see him again."

"Why don't you plan a trip down there this summer? I'll take care of things for you here."

"No!" She shoved him away and stared at him before continuing. "I cannot face them. I just wish there was some way to please them, but nothing short of moving back home or marrying will achieve that, and I can do neither."

Not much he could do to help there other than buy her a round-trip ticket. Or marry her. The discussion yesterday had him thinking what it would be like to have her as his wife. But that was obviously out of the question. She didn't want a man around at all.

"Well, you may be rid of me in a couple days. I'm close to clearing the road."

Did he detect a mixture of relief and sadness churning across her features? "You are not the problem, Lucas. I have enjoyed having you here—most of the time."

He chuckled. "Given how we started out, I'll take that as a sign of progress."

"Eduardo does not understand a woman wanting to live without a man. He is very traditional and has been conditioned by the customs in my country. I have explained what really happened. He understands now."

"What Eduardo believes shouldn't matter. You're an adult now. We know the truth."

"Then why do I feel like a child when I think about pleasing my parents?"

He chuckled. "I think we all do that. The ones who are lucky enough to have loving parents worthy of pleasing, anyway. I doubt I've ever made my dad happy in my life, especially not since I pursued an artisan's life."

She broke away and wiped her tears. "I am sorry." She touched the wet spots on his chest. "You must think me a mess."

He framed her face and tilted her head to meet his gaze. Jeezus, he could get lost in those big brown eyes. "Darlin', you can't keep everything locked up inside and not expect the dam to burst every now and then. That's what friends are for—to lean on when you need someone."

"I used to have Kitty for that." The sadness returned, but she broke away.

Give her time to regroup.

He glanced at the wall of paintings behind the easel and zeroed in on a winter scene showing an ice climber. Luke pointed to it. "That one reminds me of Marc. Almost got himself killed when he fell while ice climbing on Iron Horse Falls in March. The man's a loner—and a risk-taker. Not a healthy combination."

"It is a popular place to climb but dangerous in winter. I have seen a number of reckless stunts on those falls, but that painting was inspired by a trip I made down the mountain in February. The ice was more stable then." Cassie paused while staring at the painting, seeming to have regained her composure. "You and Marc seem to be good friends."

"They don't come any better."

She continued more quietly, "I miss Kitty since she married. I know I will continue to see her now and then, and I will help when the baby arrives, but he will not allow her to visit me here after her accident last year. We do not have as much time alone together. I know that is selfish of me and that she is happy, but sometimes I wish we could be close the way we once were."

The sadness in her voice tugged at his heart a bit. "I don't see as much of Marc either since I moved to the ranch." He was more than two hours away from Denver now, and Marc was too busy building—or rebuilding—his relationship with Angel to spend time down here. Luke's horses and work filled his days, but he still got lonely.

He turned toward her. "Karla will always be your friend. Once she has the baby, she'll need you more than ever."

"I hope you are right."

Great as it was having friends, they did have their own lives. No one would begrudge them that, but maybe two lonely people like him and Cassie needed to stick together. "You know, I'm just down the road. Gets a little lonely down there. I'd love for you to stop by anytime."

Cassie stared at him, blinking a couple of times without responding to his blatant invitation to continue to see each other after he left here.

Maybe he ought to plead his case. "We have common interests in our artwork and animals. No reason why we can't become good friends."

He waited as she formulated a response. "I like you, Lucas…"

Wait for it…

"…but there are many reasons it would not be a good idea. The main one being I do not let people get too close. I have been hurt before by someone I thought I could trust."

Luke wished he could take away that hurt, but all he could do was try to convince her over time to trust again.

"Well, the offer stays on the table. If you need a reference, Angel will vouch that I'm safe and trustworthy." He shrugged. "I'm not going anywhere, either. Planning to build my operation over time and put down roots." What else? "Hey, if you ever need help up here with the alpacas or making some repair, you have my number. Or you will before I leave. I'm pretty handy with a hammer and a screwdriver."

She smiled, and her face lit up. "I have noticed. Thank you."

With Cassie, friendship was all he'd ever have probably, but that might be enough. He didn't know many people down this way and was too busy with the horses and many projects to seek new friendships. Aside from Marc and Angel, the Giardano brothers were acquaintances thanks to the horses and their search-and-rescue work, but few others understood him the way Cassie did.

He wondered if she had any casual friends, either. They truly were better friends than he was with almost anyone else. Both he and Cassie enjoyed their solitude, but Luke still needed to connect with people at least once in a while.

He grinned at Cassie. "We'll just take it slowly. Friends. I'd like to visit Millie and the girls, hang out from time to time, help, if needed. When times are rough, call me. We can have dinner and talk anytime. You can even come down to the ranch and ride horses with me if you'd like." He sounded like he was begging her to throw him a bone. Man, he really was lonely.

"What I'm trying to say is just remember you'll always have a soft place to land with me."

*   *   *

Cassie blinked. Nothing about Lucas looked soft, except maybe his heart. He truly seemed to be a kind and gentle soul. If any man in this world could be trusted, it would be him. In their short time together, she knew more about him than she had ever known about Pedro. About any person other than Kitty, really.

Lucas seemed lonely, too.

He walked over to the bank of windows and looked down the mountainside. "Beautiful up here. Great spot for that hot tub." He pointed to it just outside the windows.

Her face flushed as she imagined what he would think if he knew how she used it. Joining him, but standing a few feet away, she glanced out over the mountain peaks that went on as far as the eye could see. More rounded than the peaks back home, but no less majestic.

Tears formed in her eyes. Why was she so tearful today? Eduardo probably was right. She must be lonely. Until Lucas, she had no idea just how isolated she was here.

Cassie needed her space, and Lucas seemed aware of that. He had become a good sounding board. She missed talking with him since her brother's arrival.

Would she see Lucas again after he left? Did she want to remain friends with him in some way? She had never found more in common with any other man and genuinely enjoyed being with him. He had stood up for her when her brother tried to make her feel guilty. Lucas always encouraged her. He had even shared in Milagrosa's birth—and saved her life. He was handsome, too, with his high cheekbones and smoky-grey eyes.

Wait. What did looks have to do with being a good friend?

When he cast her a sidelong glance, Cassie's cheeks grew warm making her heart flutter erratically. Dear Goddess, earlier today she had even ogled him half-naked while he chopped wood. Why was she suddenly behaving like a young, innocent girl again?

It was as if he had cast a spell over her.

All she wanted or needed was a new friend. But what guarantees were there that a friend would be around when you needed them? Look at Kitty. She had found love and was starting her own family. They would drift apart as they had less in common. Cassie would know nothing of marriage or children.

Unfortunately, friendships did not come with contracts binding people together as did marriage vows.

The vision of Lucas placing a ring on her finger during her meditation last night flitted before her eyes. Was *Mama Quilla* telling Cassie that she was destined to be this man's wife?

Marry Lucas? No matter what Cassie wanted or needed, what earthly reason would possess him to want to marry *her*? At every turn, she had been trying to show him how miserable he would be staying up here any longer than necessary.

What would marriage to Lucas look like? She would have someone to talk with, share common interests with, have a ready friend when lonely. In those aspects, marriage might work, as long as it did not include a physical relationship, and they did not have to live together. She could retain control of her life and calm her parents' worries.

Oh, what was she thinking? Men married for one reason—sex. Did they not?

Sorry, Mama Quilla. *Not even You, with all Your power, can make this happen.* She looked down at his scuffed boots.

Of course, he asked to be her friend, not her husband. Why the flight of fancy? When she would have changed the subject, something compelled her to ask the next question. "Would you ever marry someone who could not love you, Lucas?"

He turned toward her, and she met his gaze as he quirked his eyebrows. "Depends."

"On what?"

"On how much I loved her. On whether the arrangement benefited us in other ways. On what we'd hope to accomplish from being married in the first place. Companionship? Meeting each other's needs? Hot sex?"

Her heart skipped a beat. "Let's say it's something more along the lines of companionship. Without…benefits."

He chuckled. He had been teasing her with that last part, no doubt, but quickly became serious. "While it might be hard to love someone that much and not have their love returned, her reasons for wanting to get married to me would be important."

"But what if there was *no* love from one party?" She needed him to understand this above all else.

"There are all kinds of love. However, if that happened, then I'd loved her enough for the both of us. Given time and patience, I would hope she'd learn to trust and care more for me instead of merely closing the door to any possibilities." He smiled at her, as if knowing he lacked the words to respond to such a hypothetical question.

His expectations might be overly optimistic.

Perhaps loneliness was a cross each of them must bear.

"How about you, Sweet Pea? Could you marry someone who didn't love you?"

"I could never have a traditional marriage, so I think so."

"Darlin', you can make your own rules when it comes to marrying. Just be sure that the man you do marry treats you with nothing short of love and respect. That he treats you with great reverence. Worships and honors you as the center of his world. Sees you as his greatest treasure. Knows that he is the wealthiest man on earth because he has you by his side."

His romantic words swirled around her, catching her up in the fantasy until she realized he made her out to be some great prize. If he only knew she was nothing more than a tarnished bauble.

No, Lucas Denton deserved someone who could love him whole-heartedly and give herself completely. Not someone like her.

Yet he painted such a beautiful picture of what life with the right man could be like. She did not wish to be a possession or placed on a pedestal, but if a man existed who would enjoy her company, share her interests, and respect her boundaries…that would be a dream come true.

Stop, Cassie. You're nobody's dream.

"But I see nothing wrong with marrying for companionship. Meeting people is a problem when you're as busy as we are. That night at daVinci's was the first time I'd been out with friends for drinks in months. Let's face it, you aren't the type to hang out in bars, either."

Her stomach clenched, and she shook her head, unable to form the words.

"God works in mysterious ways. I think He brought two lonely people together that night."

Oh, Mama Quilla, *you even have Lucas thinking divine intervention is at work with us.*

"If you had stayed home and worked that day, you would not have been stranded all this time away from your horses."

He stared at her until she met his gaze. "I love my horses, but, darlin', if I hadn't followed you home that night, I never would have gotten to know you the way I have. Besides, when I would have heard about the avalanche, I'd have been worried sick about you being stranded up here all alone and been the first one on the other side of the snowpack digging you out."

She drew a deep breath, exhaling slowly through her mouth. "I can take care of myself."

"I know, but sometimes allowing yourself to be vulnerable to someone else can be freeing, too."

He did not understand her at all. "I can never allow myself to be vulnerable again."

"Trust is hard to come by once it's been shattered."

Oh, Lucas, you have no idea.

She wondered what his first marriage had been like. "You must have loved your wife very much."

Pain flashed across his face, but was quickly quashed. "Maggie was a great woman. We only had a couple years together as husband and wife. It's been eight years since…" He paused a moment and cleared his throat. "Eight years on May the third to be exact since she died."

Mere days ago? She had no idea. She reached out and stroked his arm without thinking until her fingertips felt the warmth of his skin through the sleeve of his shirt. She could not pull away, though. The wound was still so raw for him. The need to comfort him was greater than her fear. "I am so sorry. If I had known, I could have helped you honor her in a remembrance ceremony."

He shook his head. "I have no problem remembering. It's the forgetting that's the hard part." He shrugged. "But you did help me move on to a better place that day."

"I did?"

"Yeah. It was the day Millie was born." His voice broke off, and his eyes shone bright with unshed tears.

Every bone in her body screamed at her to hug him. A friend would offer comfort at such a moment. Like steel to a magnet, she moved toward him and wrapped her arms around him. "Maggie was a lucky woman."

He remained silent, but after a moment, his arms encircled her, and they just held on to each other for a while. "No, I was the lucky one. We had two beautiful years together." Lucas let her go, and she took a step back into her comfort zone.

As though this embrace had not happened, he continued to respond to her earlier question, thankfully not mentioning the fact she had been referring to herself. "There are a lot of different reasons to marry. Maggie and I started out with the lust and hormones kind of marriage. If given enough years, it might have grown into the deep and abiding love we all hope for."

He shrugged. "On the other hand, I think a marriage based on shared interests or common goals can be just as rewarding. Might even last longer. Passion burns out, but if you have nothing else in common, well, that can make for disappointment and loneliness, too."

Should she continue to speak in general terms? His words a moment ago almost charmed her into believing that he knew she was speaking about them and that such an arrangement might succeed in breaking down her walls.

She scoffed on the inside. She gave up long ago on being rescued by a prince on a white steed. What had brought on those ridiculous romantic notions during her meditation last night of the two of them marrying?

Cassie did not want or need a hero. No husband, either. Especially not one with a romantic heart.

'Passion burns out.'

His words echoed in her mind. Did that mean sex wasn't a requirement for him to marry someone? "What if there was never any sex?" The words rang in her ears before she knew she had spoken them aloud. Heat suffused her face.

He grinned. "*Never?* Or just not as often as some experts say there should be?"

"Never *ever* in my case." *Oh, no!* She had not intended to let him know she was asking her questions in connection to herself—and him. What was wrong with her self-control?

"That's an awfully long time, darlin'. You're still young. What, twenty-five or so?"

She held her head higher. "Twenty-six in July. In Peru, that is an 'old maid,' as you call it in America."

"Maybe you just haven't met the right man. Hard to find him tucked away up here—well, unless one happens to be dumped on your doorstep in an avalanche."

She avoided his gaze. *Had* the Universe brought him to her mountain for a reason other than to save Milagrosa? Was *Mama Quilla*—who not only served as a protector to all women but was also the deity who watched over marriages—casting a spell over her to entertain these preposterous thoughts of marrying Lucas?

After all, what kind of man would stop at companionship in a marriage? At sharing a love of art and animals—nothing more…physical?

Ha. Men always expected sex, later if not right away.

Following her long silence, Lucas turned to stare out the window again. "Having someone around to talk with when I'm lonely or to share my day with, well, I didn't realize how much I sorely missed that until spending time up here with you. I have no time right now to meet girls or date between the horses, SAR work, and my orders for furniture and carpentry jobs. Hell, I rarely leave the ranch."

Was he burying himself in those activities to keep from making such a commitment again? "I understand." She had no time to commit to a husband, either. Lucas would be the perfect husband/companion. Marrying him, she would be able to calm her parents' worries but remain independent at the same time.

Goddess, what is the matter with me? Lucas was not going to marry her, even if she did agree to have sex. He still loved and grieved for his wife. "Have you ever thought about remarrying?" Once again, the words spilled out unintentionally, as if her mouth was no longer under her mind's control.

Lucas had never forced his intentions on her at all. He was actually very sweet. Helpful. Nurturing. Protective.

But only my parents and brother think I need a protector!

He raised his brows. "A powerful thundercloud just passed over your face, Sweet Pea. You thinking about doing an end run on Eduardo?"

She met his gaze again. "A what?"

"End run. A football term for when the ball carrier attempts to circumvent the defense."

"Oh. Sorry, I do not understand your American football."

He grinned and shrugged. "Only kind I know. I played quarterback in college." She did not picture him on an athletic team. He seemed almost as much a loner as she was. Well, she had not been that way before…

"My football scholarship to UT—the University of Texas—made it possible for me to continue my education. Wouldn't have been able to go to college without it, but I didn't really plan to make football my life or legacy. It was just a means to an end. I wanted to study industrial arts, but UT didn't offer that program, so I majored in studio art instead. Surprised the hell out of my dad. I don't think he's recovered yet."

The muscles in his jaw tightened, despite his grin. Something else they had in common—being a disappointment to their fathers.

"You planning to tell me what's running through that mind of yours, darlin'?" Lucas's lips twitched as though he was stifling a grin. She turned away again.

A sharp pain made her realize she had been picking at the skin around the cuticle of her ring finger. She clasped her hands together to hide them from him and refused to make eye contact again.

"Eduardo said my parents are worried sick about my virtue and my safety. I do not wish to burden them any longer." She swallowed hard and took a deep breath. "I need a husband." Before she lost her nerve, she blurted out, "Would you consider marrying me, Lucas?" Slowly, she met his gaze, surprised to see he was not horrified—or choked with laughter—at her unexpected question. If anything, there was a twinkle in his eye.

"Any other reasons you'd like to marry, darlin'?"

He had not said no outright. She took a deep breath. "Like you, I would like to have companionship. I enjoy spending time with you. Perhaps we could visit each other's places, help with the animals, things like that. Have dinner occasionally." She would leave *Mama Quilla's* machinations out of this, even though She was a large part of the reason for this about-face when it came to Lucas, in case he put extra stock in divine intervention.

Needing to clarify further what she was proposing, she added, "I would retain my maiden name and tell my family I chose to do so for professional reasons. We would not live together, of course. You would be under no financial obligation whatsoever. And, if at any time you wished to end the arrangement for any reason, we could quietly annul the marriage."

Was that disappointment she saw in his eyes? The silence stretched out until she prepared herself for a rejection.

"Sounds as though you have it all figured out, Cassie." The slight tremor in his voice was at odds with his calm exterior. Why was he not relieved this might be a brief marriage with no strings attached?

He closed the gap between them, reached out, and stroked her cheek. She fought down her fears and did not turn away. She would need to be this close to him if they were married, especially when others who knew were around watching them.

"If I marry you, it's 'til death do us part, Sweet Pea. There will be no annulment. If you can commit to that stipulation, then we can continue to discuss this arrangement."

Goddess, what am I thinking? I am no actress. And deceit was one of the worst sins imaginable in her spiritual belief systems. Her hand shook. "A real marriage? But I told you…there can be no sex."

"I didn't say 'real.' I said 'lasting.' Sex isn't a requirement for me, but there *will* be intimacy."

"What is the difference?"

"Intimacy is about knowing someone on a deeper level. Being comfortable in our own skin around each other. It's more important and lasts longer than passion if you ask me." He paused a moment. "Sex gives a quick physical release. Don't get me wrong—it's nice. But intimacy goes further. It involves touching, holding, cuddling, and being vulnerable with one another."

He almost made it sound as if intimacy would make her more exposed to him than giving in sexually. A physical response could be blocked out if need be, but regular intimacy? What if she let him break down her barriers?

Dread clawed at her throat. No, she could not allow him to see the ugliness inside her. "You understand that I am not in love with you."

"I do. As long as you promise to let me touch you—again, I don't mean sexually—I'll be satisfied. Hand holding. Maybe a foot massage. Hugs when either of us needs them."

Touching. *Non-sexual* touching. Well, it might take some adjustment, but the benefits of pleasing her parents and forming a lifelong friendship with someone she cared about made the idea of a platonic marriage palatable.

So far, Lucas had kept every promise, not that she had known him all that long. But he did have friends who thought the world of him. Even Kitty trusted him.

Cassie nodded. "Then I can agree to that."

"We'll arrange for dates at least once a week. And maybe once a month you can come and stay longer at my place. Your girls might enjoy a visit down the mountain every now and again. I have plenty of grazing space."

She had not thought about how such a merger would affect her alpacas. "I think they would like that." Her heart pounded with excitement at the possibilities, but also trepidation for the next question that had to be asked. "What about sleeping arrangements?"

He grinned. "Sorry, darlin'. Your girls will have to be content with sleeping with the horses in the barn."

She laughed and punched him playfully. "You know what I mean." She sobered. "Us."

"I have a double bed in the house and a twin in the studio. You're welcome to either one."

"But I would sleep alone, correct?" This needed to be specified.

He shrugged. "Unless you invite me to join you."

She shook her head. "That will never happen."

"Never say never, darlin'. You know, we can share a bed and not have sex. Cuddling is one of the best ways to be intimate with your partner."

"No. That would be *too* intimate."

"Well, keep an open mind. You can trust me not to go beyond your boundaries. You'll be more comfortable in the house, though, so you'll take the bedroom when you visit."

"I do not wish to put you out."

"No trouble. I've spent a lot of nights either in my studio or the barn." He turned and took a few steps toward the window. "I'd enjoy visiting you up here, too. Probably couldn't stay more than overnight, although I have friends willing to help me out with the horses. Maybe I can eventually hire some part-time hands to help so I can be here to help you whenever you need something."

He turned to face her, and his gaze swept over her from head to toe and back. "I'll enjoy every minute visiting you here."

Somehow, she did not think he was referring to the mountain scenery. Her face grew warm.

"That would be nice. In fact, it would be helpful to me if you checked on the alpacas when I am away for the gallery opening and when Kitty and her baby come home from the hospital." Perhaps if she arranged his visits for the times she would be away, this arrangement could work even better.

He nodded, and she relaxed. "But I'll want to spend time with *you* up here, too." How did he know her thoughts? "I like being with you. We have a lot in common. Who knows? Maybe we'll—"

She held up her hand to stop him. "No, Lucas. Do not expect anything more than friendship to come of this arrangement. If you delude yourself into thinking I will one day succumb to your charms and fall passionately in love, this marriage agreement will not work. There can be no underlying motives or unrealistic expectations."

The more they negotiated, the more it sounded like a business proposition.

He grinned. "Make no mistake that I plan to treat you as my wife in every way *except* sexually. What's mine is yours. Ain't much, but it's still yours." She did not want his money. He grew more serious. When he reached out to her, Cassie took a step back. "I hope you'll wake up someday and realize you can trust me to never hurt or disappoint you."

Her heart pounded at the image of them entangled in each other's arms in bed. "I will *not* be sharing a bed with you, Lucas."

He nodded. "We already covered that. But we can cuddle together on a couch, the floor, under a tree. Cuddling is not off the table."

What am I getting myself into?

"We might also want to establish a word you can say if something I'm doing goes beyond your limits or boundaries. What might seem like a simple touch to me may not be interpreted that way by you. In that case, just say 'pickle,' and I'll back off."

"Pickle?"

He grinned. "I figure this negotiation isn't far from what Doms and subs at the Masters at Arms Club enter into."

What did he say? Wait a minute! "You are a Dom? Like Adam?" The thought of him telling her what to do and expecting her to follow his orders the way Kitty sometimes bowed to Adam's dictates scared her more than having him touch her intimately.

"Every Dom is different. I'm pretty subtle and laid-back if that's what has that pulse in your neck beating triple time." She raised her trembling hand to hide the telltale sign from him, but he only grinned wider. "I've been learning some rope tricks from Adam, and Damián taught me how to place butterfly kisses on a woman's back with a bullwhip."

Kissed with a whip? She shuddered and squared her shoulders. "Let me make something clear. We are not entering into *that* kind of arrangement, Lucas Denton. I will maintain my independence and freedom. No man will smother me like that."

"I know a number of submissives, Karla included, who would argue about that common misconception. Besides, there are plenty of people in non-sexual BDSM relationships."

BDSM without sex? Was sex not the point?

"No matter, darlin'. We're not entering into a power-exchange but our own unique brand of marriage."

She did not wish to know anything more about bondage and deviant behaviors. "I am not into that and never will be."

His smoldering gaze sent a shiver up her spine. Her face grew warm, and her heart did that fluttery thing again. Too much stress, no doubt.

"You might as well know, though, that some aspects of being a Dom are innate in me."

Cassie's heart skipped a beat. "Like what?"

"First and foremost, the need to be needed. But other traits like honesty, consistency, protectiveness, chivalry." He grinned. "And maybe this makes me a chauvinist, but I enjoy the hell out of having a girl take care of me on occasion, too."

In sickness and in health.

Of course, she would have affection and concern for him as her husband. Had she not already nursed him while sick and injured? *Twice, actually.* Her compassion would extend to any person or animal in need, vows or no vows.

She could even see to *some* of his physical needs.

Not the sexual ones, though.

She loved to cook and share meals—as long as he did not ask her to grill a steak or touch dead meat.

If what Luke sought most was a companion, well, they enjoyed doing many things together. He also would be a helpmate if, Goddess forbid, she ever became too sick to care for her alpacas. No doubt in her mind he would make sure they had a home with him or someone else who would care for them.

But one issue still made her uncomfortable. She might as well just come out and ask. "Will you continue to go to the club if we marry?"

"Not without you."

Then 'No,' in other words. "You could give up that part of your life completely, even though you enjoyed it in the past?" Why would he give it up?

He shrugged but did not wipe the grin off his face. "The few times I've ventured into the club in Denver were primarily for social reasons. Of course, we've both visited with friends in non-club areas of the house. But we can see Adam and Karla at their new place, and Marc and I will have regular SAR training sessions required by the state. I'm sure I'll run into Damián at Adam's. I don't need to visit the club to remain friends."

Cassie relaxed, not realizing how stiffly she had held her body during this phase of their negotiation.

"Seriously, though, most of the time I go to the club because I like hanging out with those guys. I respect the hell out of Adam, Damián, Marc—Grant, too. They're all heroes in my book."

Cassie nodded in agreement with his last statement. "They have sacrificed a lot to serve their country. Very courageous."

They seemed to have come to the end of their negotiations. She wondered if she should write this into a contract, not so much to hold him to his promises, but to remember what they had agreed on up to this point.

"So pickle will be our safeword, darlin'. Either of us feels things are more intense than we want, we just say that word, and then we can discuss it or just drop it."

Dear Goddess, what was she setting herself up for?

"So we are in agreement to marry?"

$*$ $*$ $*$

Luke suppressed a grin. The poor girl looked like she had taken a bite of the sourest pickle out of the barrel—or was ready to take on the most despicable arrangement known to man.

He doubted any Dom/sub went through more strenuous negotiations in setting their boundaries, but in many ways, this was a similar agreement. Sure, he was optimistic enough—call it cocky, even—to think he could win over her heart in time.

Still, she had floored him, to say the least. He tried to keep his cool, but after his initial shock, the more she started listing her stipulations, the more he wanted to marry her. That she would be a challenge was a given, but he also saw in her a vulnerability that brought out every Dom instinct he had.

He'd blown his chance with Maggie by not being the man she needed. By not having the strength of conviction to keep her out of harm's way. As much as he hated to admit it, not wanting to disrespect the memory of his wife, his connection to Cassie felt stronger than the one he'd had with Maggie. He wasn't that young man anymore, going into marriage all full of lust and clueless about long-term commitment. Not that he wouldn't have learned how to be a good husband and father over time, but it looked like he was going to get another chance after all.

Well, husband, at least. The only kids he was going to have would be their furbabies, but that was okay. Hell, they'd delivered one themselves. Didn't get any better than that.

Maybe it was that Maggie didn't need him as much. Cassie may not admit she needed him, either, but something kept her hiding away up here. Maybe he could help ease her back into the world.

"Looks like we're headed to the altar, darlin'."

Her eyes opened wide. "I do not want a church wedding!"

"It's just an expression, but what's wrong with marrying in a church?"

She suddenly became interested in his boots. "I…think marrying in a church makes it so much more…real. Perhaps we can find a judge or whoever marries people to perform our ceremony."

"Consider it done. Priest, minister, rabbi, or judge, though, when I speak my vows, they will be heard in the ears of God."

She looked ready to bolt and call the whole thing off before taking a deep breath. "We must each do what is right for us."

"Sounds good. Now, I need to clear the road so we can get hitched."

*   *   *

Two days later, true to his word—because with Cassie he would need to do his best to be consistent and not disappoint her—the road had been cleared.

Cassie stayed behind at the cabin while he and Eduardo drove down to the ranch to check on things and to pick up a change of clothing before they headed to Breckenridge for the ceremony later today. Luke invited Eduardo along so he could set the man's mind at ease over who would be looking after Cassie's needs from here on out. The man's rental car had been towed after he'd abandoned it on the shoulder of the highway, so they'd need to return him to the airport after the ceremony.

"You do not intend to desert her as soon as I leave?"

"I'm not doing this for you or anyone other than Cassie. When I speak my vows this afternoon, I'll mean every single word of them because I wrote them myself."

Luke drove on in silence until he reached the county road leading to his ranch.

"Casandra has been hurt by someone before. If I ever find out you have hurt her, too, you will regret it."

He didn't expect her brother to like him right off the bat, but if he thought so little of him, why had he been so gung-ho to marry his sister off to him a few days ago?

Luke was confident that, over time, they would grow to love each other more deeply than she could ever imagine.

"If I ever do anything to hurt her, I'd expect you to do just that. Don't worry, though. I intend to treat her like the delicate, but hardy, flower that she is."

My Peruvian lily.

Damn. He needed to get her a bouquet. This might be a JP wedding, but he wanted her to know how special she was to him. He turned into the lane, kicking up a little dust in his haste to finish and get back to Cassie before she got cold feet.

"We should hurry. Casandra is waiting." Eduardo must be thinking the same thing.

"Be right back." Unable to check on the horses, Luke took the stairs two at a time and went inside the house. He changed into his newest western dress shirt and black jeans and wrapped a bolo tie around his neck. Sitting on the edge of the bed, he put on his square-toed leather boots. In a few hours, he'd be standing before a judge and saying "I do."

Married. Again. On his way to the closet to grab his suit coat, he glanced at the framed picture Cassie had sketched of Maggie and their baby. He hoped he and Cassie would have many more years together. If anything ever happened to her…

Stepping outside again to head back to the Tahoe where Eduardo awaited him, he heard a familiar voice.

"Welcome home, Luke!"

He turned as Matt Giardano left the barn and walked toward him. They shook hands. "I'm afraid I need you to keep an eye on things a little longer, but I should be back home by tomorrow at the latest. Thanks for everything, Matt."

"Loved helping. I envy you having this place." Matt spent a lot of time doing equestrian activities, but had to board his two horses. A third-year firefighter's salary didn't afford him the luxury of a spread like this, but Matt was young. Luke had saved many years to be able to afford this place.

"Your horses are welcome here any time if you want to change where you board them. Free board if you don't mind helping out here when I have to be away." This might make it possible for him to spend more time with Cassie.

"Damn sight better than the place in Leadville. I might take you up on it, even if it's an hour farther for me to come to see them. Then I can help you out here, too. O'Keeffe and I have kind of taken a liking to each other—after we straightened out a few things." Matt grinned.

141

What the hell? "How is she?"

"Come see for yourself."

Turning toward the Tahoe, he yelled, "Eduardo, come stretch your legs if you want. I need to do one more thing before we head back up."

Luke waited for his future brother-in-law and introduced him only as Cassie's brother before following Matt into the barn. Luke whistled, and three of his horses came to their stall doors. What a sight for sore eyes. First stop, Picasso. He wished he'd had time to grab some carrots from the house as a treat, but Matt reached out to hand him a few small apples.

Apparently, Matt had more than taken care of their basic needs. "Man, I owe you."

Matt shrugged. "It was a group effort. We all took turns—Rafe, Frank, and Tony. Luckily, our shifts at the two fire stations weren't usually the same, so it worked out."

Luke didn't want to get dirty so he reached through the bars in the stall door to feed the apple to Pic, who nickered as Luke stroked his neck. A peace came over him he hadn't experienced since the avalanche. He'd spent a lifetime searching for a place to call his own, but on this ranch, he found a sense of belonging.

Home.

"'Atta boy."

He'd forgotten about Matt until he spoke up. "O'Keeffe is still out in the corral. She's not too fond of tight spaces."

"Never has been. I had her in here a while, but she just wasn't making any progress. Turned out, she just felt cooped up. She's happier outside."

So am I.

He decided to wait until he had more time with O'Keeffe and fed the remaining apples to Fontana and Cassatt at the windows of their stalls.

"How many horses do you have?" Eduardo asked.

"Four." He hated that there were so many abused and neglected horses in need of rescuing, but there was only so much he could do. "How are Marc and Angel doing?"

"Saw them the other day. Marc looks like he's been put through the wringer, but neither one would talk about what happened."

Damn. He needed to get to Denver and see what was going on if no one would tell him over the phone. But he had something even more important to do first. Not wanting to share the news prematurely and without Cassie's permission, though, he kept his mouth shut.

"Now, Matt, if you'll excuse me, I have an important date with a beautiful woman."

"Lucky you!"

Damned right he was lucky. Assuming they tied the knot before his bride chickened out.

*   *   *

After obtaining their license, they were led into the judge's chambers. Lucas placed his hand low on Cassie's back and guided her ahead of him. Eduardo and the judge's clerk followed.

Lucas held his Stetson in his left hand near his waist. She held the small bouquet of pink Peruvian lilies Lucas had given to her when he returned from his ranch earlier.

The flower native to South America signified friendship and devotion. Did Lucas choose them for their meaning or because they carried the name of her homeland? Either way, she had not expected to carry a bouquet like a true bride in this unique wedding. Nor to have him choose such expensive wedding bands at the jeweler's shop.

Lucas continued to surprise her. They had negotiated to where they could both find benefits in this arrangement, even if not for any of the typical reasons people wed.

She had chosen to wear a single-layered skirt, a simple white blouse, but at the last minute, picked up *Abuela's lliclla*. Wrapping the colorful cloth in her village's design around her shoulders, she felt as if her grandmother's arms surrounded her once again. Around her neck, she wore the silver locket her parents had given her on her sixteenth birthday, with their photos inside. It almost felt as if they were at the wedding, too, in spirit at least.

They placed the license before the gray-haired woman who had her glasses perched on the tip of her nose as she read some official-looking document. She shook her head and glanced up. Smiling, she removed her reading glasses and stood, picking up the paper as she rounded her desk.

"So nice to meet you..." She glanced down at their license. "Stephen and Casandra."

"I prefer Luke or Lucas, ma'am."

"Very well. And whom do we have here?" She focused on Eduardo.

Cassie cleared her throat and spoke up. "Eduardo López, my brother…from Peru. And I am called Cassie now." Casandra ceased to exist long ago, although her family still called her by that name. Apparently, there were no problems with her being an international bride when they filled out the paperwork. She had shown her green card and driver's license, and they had granted the license immediately.

The clerk agreed to be a second witness and offered each of them a sheet of popular vows to choose from. Cassie had never attended a wedding outside of a Catholic church where everyone spoke the same vows. Even so, the ones on the sheet did not fit their unique situation.

Even though Lucas said he would never want to end their marriage arrangement, he would likely change his mind when he realized she never intended for this union to be consummated. What if one day he met someone with whom he wanted a physical, sexual relationship? She would gladly grant him his freedom when that day came. In Colorado, from what she had read in the clerk's office, there was no limit on when an annulment could be granted.

The judge picked up a black portfolio and opened it. "Have you had a chance to select your vows?"

Cassie stared at the options in her hand again and shook her head in the negative just as Lucas said, "Yes, ma'am." He surprised her again by reaching into the pocket of the western-cut suit jacket. He filled out the suit well.

Do not notice how handsome and well-built he is, Cassie.

"You brought your own vows?"

He winked at her and grinned, leaving her a little nonplussed. "Wrote 'em myself. But be warned, I'm no poet."

He had *written* his own vows? She assumed they would both mimic whatever standard vows were appropriate. When had he had time to write his own?

"With Mr. Denton's permission, perhaps you both could repeat the vows he prepared."

Before she could respond, Lucas said to the judge, "That would be fine by me." Then he glanced down at Cassie. "Would you like to read them over first?"

Why are you trying to make this like a real wedding, Lucas? She had expected them to repeat vows by rote that held little meaning. Impersonal and detached.

"Why don't you read them over before you decide, Sweet Pea?" He handed her the folded slip of paper. Her heart thudded erratically as she unfolded it. After blinking several times, the words came into focus. In his very neat printing, he had written words even she could abide by. Tears blurred her focus before she gazed into his eyes.

"They are beautiful. And perfect. Yes, I would be honored to share these vows with you, Lucas."

The judge held out her hand for the paper, and Cassie extended it to her. She read it over quickly and turned her attention to them once more, smiling. "Now, please face each other holding hands, and repeat after me, inserting your name after 'I' and your partner's name after 'you.'"

Thankfully, the judge's routine instructions helped Cassie regain some emotional distance. They took their places. Cassie stared up into Lucas's gray eyes and slipped her hands into his much larger ones. He brushed his thumbs over her knuckles, sending a strange tingling sensation up both of her arms. She wondered, not for the first time, why Lucas had agreed to make such a commitment. What did he truly expect from this arrangement? How quickly would he come to regret this decision?

And yet he did not seem the least bit hesitant about anything at the moment. He actually seemed happier than she had ever seen him.

Everyone else faded away as she stared into Lucas's gentle eyes and repeated her vows after the judge's prompts, despite the lump in her throat.

I, Cassie Beatriz López,
receive you, Stephen Lucas Denton,
as my partner, my friend, my…love,

Okay, the hardest part was over. But there were all forms of love, and she did love many things about Lucas that she had observed during their weeks together at her cabin.

The judge continued.

Focus!

Cassie repeated:

I promise to be your best friend.
Beside me and apart from me,

> *in laughter and in tears,*
> *in sickness and in health,*
> *in conflict and serenity,*
> *asking that you be no other than yourself.*

Cassie paused. *He accepts me as I am.*

> *Loving what I know of you and*
> *trusting what I do not yet know,*
> *I bind my life to yours*
> *until death parts us.*

Lucas smiled and squeezed her hands. She held on to him for dear life as he repeated the same vows. A hoarseness in Lucas's voice conveyed how affected he was by the beautiful vows he had written from the heart.

When he had finished, the judge continued. "In all that life may bring, you have vowed your love to each other. Are you now ready to confirm that love by accepting the responsibilities of marriage? If so, answer 'I am.'"

Lucas spoke the words loudly and surely. These vows had been so nonthreatening, words she could commit to without feeling a fraud. All eyes were on her as she tried to form the two words that would make her Lucas Denton's partner in life.

Lucas's smile never wavered. His hands remained steadfast as he infused strength into her shaking ones. She opened her trembling mouth and took a deep breath, still not knowing what would come out of her lips. "I…I am."

She felt Lucas slip the simple ring, warm from his hand, onto her finger, and blindly, she did the same with the matching silver band they had purchased at the jeweler's a block from the courthouse. The bands against their brown hands looked beautiful and solid, but again, she had to wonder what kind of union she and Lucas had just entered into.

"Mr. Denton, you may kiss your bride."

Cassie took a step backward, but Lucas remained in his place, still holding onto her hands. Her heart pounded, and she fought the urge to flee. She could not let him kiss her. If that was part of the deal, she needed to call this sham of a wedding off. Why had she not thought about this eventuality before and mentioned it as a limit?

Just when she thought she would turn and run, he lifted her left hand to his lips and kissed the ring he had placed there moments ago.

Something melted inside her heart.

Tears stung her eyes as she met his gaze. She would need to be very careful of this man. He could break through her defenses with only a smile—and a kiss.

*   *   *

Luke glanced over at his bride. They had dropped Eduardo off at the Vail/Eagle airport, and she insisted on driving her Tahoe back to Breckenridge where they had married, what, four hours ago? Her brother was probably in Denver by now and soon would make his connection to continue on to California.

Too bad Cassie hadn't relaxed one bit since her brother departed.

"Why don't we stop for dinner, darlin', before you drop me off at the ranch?" There would be no wedding night for them, but they could at least have a romantic dinner.

"I am not really hungry."

"Seems a waste to marry and then go our separate ways. Especially since we're already dressed up."

Her hands gripped the steering wheel until her knuckles turned white. "This is what we agreed to."

He ran his hand through his hair before a grin broke out on his face. "Just thought perhaps we could have one of those occasional dates tonight."

"We have been together for the last two weeks. Consider that one long date."

"Sure has been a whirlwind romance." He grinned at her, but she didn't seem amused.

"Are you not anxious to return to your horses?"

His wife wanted to be rid of him, no doubt about it. He'd known going into this that they would go their separate ways, but tonight, he just didn't want to. Would he see her again anytime soon? What were the chances? *Somewhere between slim and none.*

"You're right. Matt probably has things to do back in Leadville." They drove on for a few more miles, and she relaxed some. "How about dinner next Saturday? I can pick up a rental until the insurance company settles on my truck."

"Perhaps."

"You need to do better than that, Sweet Pea. Your place is right on the way to Breckenridge. How about I pick you up at six next Wednesday and we can celebrate our one-week anniversary?"

She took her plump lower lip between her teeth and thought a bit before responding. "I suppose. Just dinner."

He grinned. "No worries." *Slow and easy does it.*

Maybe on their next date they could go dancing at a western bar. If she'd let him that close. But on their first date, he wanted candlelight and lots of time to talk. He'd make reservations for a private room at his favorite steakhouse.

He felt like a teenager planning his first date.

Take it slow, Denton. This girl's a skittish one.

*   *   *

A week passed by. Cassie's first date with Lucas—she still found it strange to call him her husband—went well. He had taken her to a Mongolian grill as a second choice after she was less than enthusiastic about going to a steakhouse. They knew so little about each other that her food preferences weren't even known to him yet. Over dinner, he shared some humorous stories about situations he had dealt with while working with the horses this week. She described the progress on the last piece for her art exhibition. They both seemed to enjoy their time together.

Returning home later that night, the cabin had never felt so lonely. Everywhere she turned were reminders of Lucas. During the past week, how many times had Cassie wanted to run inside the cabin to tell him about something Milagrosa had done, only to remember Lucas was gone?

Cassie went to bed early. Sometime in the wee hours, she tossed the blankets off as she came awake with a start. She willed her breathing to slow as the remnants of a night terror threatened to encroach upon her yet again. Tears burned her eyes, only adding to the frustration at her inability to keep these persistent monsters away.

Longing filled her—a yearning for something she could not name. She had been content with her life here on the mountain for years. Suddenly, she did not wish to be here alone any longer.

Lucas.

How had he invaded her sanctuary—and her heart—in such a short time? No, not her heart! She was not destined to love any man. What man deserved a woman who could not return his love?

The wind howled, rattling the windows. She wondered what Lucas might be doing tonight.

Sleeping, of course. It's three o'clock.

Thoughts of watching him sleep in this very bed set her heart to fluttering in a strange way. Cassie breathed deeply, surrounding herself with white light. The desire to visit Lucas made her heart ache, even though they had been together mere hours ago at dinner. She willed her mind and body to separate. She took two more deep breaths and forced her mind to become uncluttered. Soon she floated above herself, taking a moment to adjust to the weightlessness. She didn't linger long, hating to see the loneliness in her eyes as she looked down upon her earthly body.

Free.

For so long, her body had been weighing down her spirit. She enjoyed being able to soar and to leave her cares and sorrows behind.

Fly.

Anxious to be on her way, she projected her spirit into the astral plane, through the doorway, and out the picture window in the living room. The wind continued to howl, but she did not feel the coldness of its kiss. Down the mountainside, her metaphysical spirit floated. She had not astral projected since *Mamá's* birthday. At least she did not have as far to travel this time. Drifts of snow dotted the mountain, heavier in some places than others. She followed the state highway down from the pass before veering off to float over trees and fields in a shortcut to her destination. She had never been to his place before, but her heart knew exactly where to go.

The ranch-style farmhouse sat dark and lonely beneath the waning moon. Of course, there were no lights on inside. He would be asleep, which was just the way she wished to find him. Cassie's spirit drifted down toward ground level, and she found an open window, not that she needed it to be open in order to enter the house. She slipped inside and saw her golden-haired husband tangled in the sheets, his chest bare.

Lucas.

Her heart ached to reach out and touch him, to brush the lock of hair off his forehead. Her ethereal hand extended toward him until he grimaced and rolled over. The sheet rode low on his hips, showing her he was naked below the waist, too. Cassie turned away ready to flee, but his cry of anguish drew her back to him.

"Stay, Cassie!"

How did he know she was here? Her mother usually sensed her presence when she visited, but *Papá* and Eduardo never had a clue. Lucas was not a shaman and did not seem particularly spiritual. So how had he detected her?

She turned back in his direction, but saw his eyes remained closed. He stretched his hand out beside him and then grabbed the pillow in his fist. "Can't have you, can I?"

Why would he be dreaming about her? Well, they *had* married recently.

Fearful that he would become fully awake and possibly see her, she pulled away from him into a far corner of the ceiling. Soon, his breathing became steady again, and she watched him as he slept. The alarm clock on the nightstand showed it was nearing four o'clock. Lucas was an early riser, so she could not linger much longer. She glanced around the sparsely decorated room, but had no interest in the furnishings or décor.

A loud noise pierced the air, and she recoiled. Lucas groaned, and his hand slapped blindly at the clock on the nightstand. He rolled onto his back and covered his eyes with his forearm. Cassie's gaze strayed to his erection tenting the sheet.

Leave. Now!

Even more quickly than she had projected here, she returned to her mountain and reintegrated with her body lying in a bed so much tinier than Lucas's. However, it did not seem enormous like the king-sized ones Adam and other American men liked to sleep in.

Images flashed across her mind's eye of sharing her twin bed with Lucas those first few nights while she had tried to combat his hypothermia, but she forced them away. Their bodies had filled the small space, forcing them to spoon against each other.

Her face grew heated at the memory.

Tamping it back down, she wondered why Lucas set his alarm so early. He did not wake naturally at this hour given how groggy he appeared to be. Perhaps the man had many responsibilities to attend to and needed to start the day early in order to keep up.

Cassie lay with eyes open wide for a long time, wondering if there was anything she could help him with. She knew nothing of horses, but knew how to cook. Perhaps she could prepare him some meals and store them in his freezer so he wouldn't have to waste time in the kitchen. He didn't seem fond of cooking.

After a while, her eyelids became heavy. She had no reason to be up this early. Time to sleep and figure out how she was she going to rid herself of this growing fixation on Lucas Denton.

* * *

The alarm blared again, and Luke turned it off this time. He'd spent another restless few hours in bed. Another night filled with dreams of Cassie. Her essence had permeated the room so strongly moments ago he thought she'd been lying beside him when he reached out for her.

How could he be so obsessed with a girl who wanted to have nothing to do with him? She'd sworn off all men in general, not just Luke Denton in particular.

What had happened to make her so distrustful of men? Could he change her opinion of his gender with time and patience?

Hell, he didn't care what she thought of other men. He wanted her to want to spend time with *him*. Only him.

Not likely he'd see much of her again, married or not. He needed to quit obsessing about her and head to the barn. "Make hay while the sun shines," Momma often said. Well, the sun wouldn't be shining over the mountain peaks for hours, but he tossed the bedspread off and stumbled toward the bathroom. A cool shower would revive him a bit. He had a lot on his agenda today, including some grueling training sessions with O'Keeffe and SAR exercises with Picasso.

Coming out of the bathroom and back into the bedroom fifteen minutes later, he couldn't shake the strong presence of Cassie.

He needed coffee. Black and hot.

In the barn half an hour later, he no longer sensed Cassie's presence. *Good.* He immersed himself in his chores instead.

Clicking his tongue, he waited to see which mustang would respond. Picasso—Pic—came to his stall door first, as usual. Luke smiled. The gelding had shown great strides in learning to trust him over the past six months. But many long months of neglect had undermined the years of training that had once put this horse at the top of his game nationally.

Luke intended to see the horse back on missions doing what he did best soon—saving lives.

Focus on those you can save.

But a voice in the back of his head told him not to give up on Cassie, either.

Chapter Seven

Denver, early evening, 1 June 2012

"I think it's time, Adam." Karla had been surreptitiously timing contractions for the last two hours. At first, she thought it couldn't possibly be time. She wasn't due until July the eleventh and today was only June the first. Despite a bolster pillow against her lower back in the glider chair, the area had been killing her all day.

He glanced away from the latest baby book and the notebook in which he had been scribbling further plans of attack for how to manage life with twins. "I'm going to stay up a little while. You go on to bed, Kitten. I'll go downstairs and work on this some more."

They had been sitting in their new bedroom for the past two hours. Doctor Palmer had warned them to expect the babies anytime. Should they be heading to the hospital? But what if it was a false alarm?

Good grief! What if the babies had wanted to come while they were driving to or from San Diego last week for Damián and Savannah's wedding! No wonder Doctor Palmer had not been happy about them making the trip.

Karla didn't want to worry him unnecessarily. He had enough concerns now. At least they no longer had to worry about where they would raise their family. She still couldn't believe they now owned this amazing place. Closing on Marc's house this morning with the very jet-lagged Marc and Angelina had been a dream come true.

Even though this was too much house for Marc, it would be a wonderful place to raise their twins. If these babies really were about to be born, she needed to give Marc an extra kiss for making it possible to move from the cramped quarters above the Masters at Arms Club into a real home. While she loved the club—after all, it had brought Adam back into her life almost eleven months ago—a kink club was no place to raise children.

Adam stood and picked up his cell phone, checking for messages again.

"Stop worrying." As if he could. Adam had so many family members leaning on him now, both blood-related, adopted, and those he'd brought into the Masters at Arms Club. Their kink community was strong and supportive of each other.

"I'm sure Megan's fine now that your Marine is there to take care of her." Apparently, someone had broken into his brother Patrick's condo night before last where Megan had been staying since graduation early last month. Thank God she hadn't been home at the time of the burglary. Grant and Adam had located one of the Marines they served with who was living nearby, and he had sent him to check on his little sister immediately. Both of them had reported in yesterday that everything was fine.

Karla had never heard Adam mention this Marine before. Most of the ones he had been close to had attended their wedding, but not Ryder Wilson.

She once mistook the creases at the corners of Adam's eyes as laugh lines, but accompanied by those dark circles, they were a sad testament to how he took on the troubles of his loved ones.

But he obviously didn't understand what she'd meant by her earlier comment. One more contraction, and she would grab his attention. These babies seemed anxious to meet their parents—much sooner than expected.

As her enormous belly hardened with the next one, Karla timed it at almost exactly five minutes since the previous one. "Adam, I mean I think it's time for the babies!"

He turned from his path toward the door. Eyes opening wider, his stare remained blank. "What did you say?"

"I thought I'd just been having more Braxton-Hicks practice contractions, but they've gotten progressively..." *Don't tell him how much it hurts.* "...stronger... And closer together." Doctor Palmer said one sign would be the inability to talk or smile through a contraction. "I have no clue what going into labor is supposed to feel like, but I think this is the real deal."

She'd had to use every bit of the discipline Adam had taught her to hide from him the fact she was in so much pain. Mainly because of the expression on his face right now. Fear bordering on terror. She hoped he would make it through the delivery with her. She didn't want to be alone for this.

He shook his head with firm resolve. "It can't be time, hon. You're not due for another six weeks. We still need to set up the bassinet, choose the right bottles for breastfeeding multiples…" He paused to glance down at his notes. "Hell, lots of things aren't ready."

Karla sighed as he ticked off all the reasons she couldn't possibly be in labor before she reminded him of the facts. "We're having twins, Adam. Doctor Palmer said they can come weeks early."

He met her gaze. "But not six fucking *weeks* early!"

She'd rarely heard Adam shout before, much less drop the F-bomb around her. Hearing the anxiety in his voice only increased her nervousness. She blinked away the waterworks that threatened to spill. God, she hoped her hormones returned to normal quickly after birth.

Suddenly, a look of steely determination came over his face, and he stood. He squared his shoulders like a man on a mission—Operation Delivery perhaps—and crossed the room to slide his arm around her back.

He tossed the notebook onto the bed. "Here, let me help you up, Kitten. We probably should get you checked out. Better safe than sorry."

She leaned into him, wanting his comfort as much as to have him lift her enormous body out of this chair. She hoped that the next time she sat here she'd be holding both of her babies.

Her *healthy* babies. Doctor Palmer said at her last checkup the babies each weighed over four pounds. Big, healthy babies for multiples this early. That must be a good sign.

Please, God, don't let me lose either of them. Adam had already had one baby stillborn with Joni. The thought of losing a baby after carrying him or her all these months…

Don't go there, Kitty.

Adam steered her toward the door. "I'll call Doc Palmer's service on the way to let them know we're heading to the hospital."

Any control she had over her emotions went out the window. She was about to start a whole new chapter with Adam. He held on to her arm as they navigated the winding staircase. When another contraction hit, she stopped on the landing.

Adam turned toward her. "Eyes on me."

Her body responded in typical fashion to those words, only this time, her heart dropped into her stomach with a solid Ka-thunk! A mild contraction followed, and she placed one hand over her enormous belly and the other on Adam's shoulder for balance.

He didn't miss a beat. "Don't fight it, Kitten. Breathe. We Marines have a saying—pain is weakness leaving the body. Inhale."

She shook with the effort but managed to take a deep breath and to exhale slowly on his command. "I…just want…these precious *babies*…to leave my body."

*   *   *

Two hours later, Karla had been admitted to the maternity department with steady contractions, although the IV in her hand was supposed to stop them, if possible. Her blood pressure was good, but the contractions continued to come closer together and stronger. While they waited for a nurse to check her again and for Doc Palmer to show up, it couldn't hurt to do some relaxation techniques.

"Eyes on me, Kitten." She grimaced before locking gazes with him. "Breathe in. Slow, deep breath." He ought to take the same advice, but couldn't if he wanted to. If anything happened to Karla or the babies…

Don't go there.

They did several repetitions, and Karla seemed to relax before another contraction hit. Adam stared at the monitor showing the babies' heartbeats. They seemed strong and steady, but what did he know? He tried to keep his focus on Karla through the next two contractions as they continued to breathe together while he stroked her belly, happy to have something to do besides sit and watch the monitors.

When her abdomen grew hard under his hand, he met her gaze. "Did you feel that?"

"Are you kidding me?"

"Is it normal?"

"How should I know what's normal?"

She's in labor. Cut her some slack.

A nurse came in, checked the screens, and then did yet another pelvic exam. "Doesn't look like these babies plan to wait. You've gone from two centimeters on admission to four now. We're in active labor. Radiology should be here soon to do your admission ultrasound."

"Is something wrong?"

"No, it's totally routine with multiples."

True to her word, activity picked up in the room as a male technician wheeled in a machine that looked more elaborate than the one in Doc Palmer's office. Adam held his breath, waiting to see that both their babies were moving, had healthy heartbeats, and were okay. He'd dreaded every scan they'd undergone up to now, always expecting the next one to be abnormal.

Don't think about Joni facing the birth of their stillborn baby all alone. He'd been deployed when she needed him the most.

Adam leaned closer to Karla and pressed his fingertips against her temple. "I'm here, Kitten. I'm going to be with you through it all. You're the strongest woman I know. You've got this." His throat nearly closed at the thought of what she would have to face to bring his babies into the world. "Just remember there's purpose in this pain."

"Like a good impact session, Sir?"

The technician chuckled until Adam's glare sobered him. Let him think what he wanted. But if *his* submissive wanted to compare childbirth to kink, so be it.

"Even better, Kitten. Soon you'll be holding our babies." He continued to stroke her temple and felt her body relax. For good measure, Adam pressed his lips against her forehead. "I love you, Kitten."

"Love you, too, Sir."

With the ultrasound monitors hooked up, the tech pointed out the two heads. Everything seemed routine until the man made a sound that put Adam on full alert. While he quickly recovered his stone-face demeanor when Adam glanced over at him, Adam's heartbeat ramped up double time. He hoped Karla hadn't noticed.

"Is…is everything all right?" The fear in Karla's voice told him she hadn't missed a thing.

"Your OB will be in shortly to speak with you." He left the machine and started toward the door. "Be right back."

As soon as they were alone again, Karla turned to him. "Something's wrong, Adam. What aren't they telling us?"

"Don't jump to conclusions." *As if.* He'd long ago jumped to a few of his own. "Doc Palmer will be here soon to talk with us. Why don't you close your eyes and rest? You need to conserve your energy."

She closed her eyes, and he alternated between stroking her belly and forehead, watching her calm down for him. He forced himself to take some slow breaths of his own and was doing fine until the door opened and Karla's eyes shot open. They both watched a worried-looking Doc Palmer enter the room.

Adam zeroed in on Doc Palmer's face. His heart pounded in earnest as he reached for Karla's hand. Something *was* wrong. "What is it, Doc?"

"Adam, let go. You're hurting me."

He realized he had a death grip on her hand. "Sorry, Kitten."

Adam turned back to the obstetrician who was running the wand through the goop on Karla's belly. Hell, he had to ask. "Karla and the babies aren't in any danger, are they?"

"Don't worry." The rote words did nothing to reassure him as the doctor stared intently at the monitor. That made one person in the room who wasn't worried.

"Karla, Adam, I don't know how to tell you this. How we could have missed it on the earlier ultrasounds confounds me, but you aren't having twins."

Fuck! One of the babies must have died because he had definitely seen two heads on the ultrasound pictures. Karla glanced over at him, her face blanched. This couldn't be happening. He'd already lost one baby. How could God allow—

"No, there's definitely a third baby."

What? He and Karla swung their focus back to the doctor. "What did you say?" they asked simultaneously.

"It's clear that there is a third baby in a third amniotic sac. The other two must have been hiding it all this time. I thought your labs were high, but the two we could see were bigger than most, so I attributed it to that."

"Another baby, Doc? *Three?*" Adam's throat had grown so tight he could barely get the words out.

"Clear as day." Doc Palmer turned to Karla. "I know you wanted to try for a vaginal birth, but triplets mean an automatic C-section." After a quick exam, she stood. "Four and a half centimeters. I'm surprised you haven't complained about these strong contractions, Karla. You must be able to tolerate pain better than most."

Her lips quivered as she attempted to keep from grinning, but failed miserably. "My coach is helping me stay focused on my breathing."

"Well, Adam, just keep taking care of her. I'm going to pull the teams together, and we'll take you into the OR shortly."

Left alone again, Karla's silence worried him after a few minutes. "You okay, Kitten?" She nodded and turned tear-filled eyes toward him, twisting his gut. "Don't cry. You heard the doctor. Everything's fine. Just not what we were expecting." He hoped his words sounded more reassuring to her than they felt when he spoke them.

"I wanted to have a vaginal delivery."

That's what she was crying about? "Hey, let's not worry about *how* these babies arrive. Only that they come into the world healthy. If that means a C-section, then bring it." Okay, easy for him to say. He wouldn't have his gut cut wide open. God, if they intended for him to watch... The thought of Karla going under the knife made him sick, but he wouldn't risk their lives if it was the only way.

The full impact of the doctor's words hit him. They were taking Karla to the operating room *now*. Those babies could be born in the next couple of hours.

This shit just got real. Am I fucking ready for triplets?

Hell, he wasn't even ready for twins, and he'd known about them since February. How many times would he have to say the word triplets before reality set in?

He just prayed there would be three healthy babies when this was over.

*   *   *

Karla cast a worried glance at Adam. The expression on his face made her wonder if he would make it through a C-section delivery. She truly didn't want one, but would do whatever it took to give Adam three healthy babies.

Three babies! She couldn't believe it. Wait until she told Mom and Daddy and all their friends. Of course, she had told her mom they were expecting twins to allow her to make plans to take vacation from work as soon as the babies arrived. Now she would need her help more than ever. At Adam's insistence, though, no one else knew—not even Cassie. Everyone would be floored.

Karla had expected her only surprise to be finding out the sexes of the twins, not that a third baby would be added to the Montague household. They weren't identical, either, so that meant there could be babies of both sexes. Picturing Adam with a baby in each arm and a third in his lap made her giggle.

"That's it. Just think happy thoughts."

Dear Lord, just let them be healthy!

Regaining her focus, she decided June was perfect. Adam's birthday was on the fourth and Marisol's on the twenty-fourth. Now three more family members would have a June birthday.

One thing was certain, she'd be happy to have the pregnancy part over. Some women might love being pregnant, but it had been one long period of frustration for her—not just sexual deprivation, but her ever-changing body. No wonder she looked like a whale.

Three babies!

"Why some women choose to have a second pregnancy is beyond me."

"What, Kitten?" Adam tore his gaze away from the baby monitor screen. He'd been giving the monitor the Dom stare as if he could will it to obey him. She giggled. "What's so funny?"

"Nothing." She sighed, wishing he'd give her that stare again—and mean business.

Karla tried to move to adjust her position to a more comfortable one, but there was none. The monitors limited her to lying on her back or sides. "I just don't think I ever want to be pregnant again."

"I hear you."

What did he mean? The relief in his voice surpassed hers. Tears sprang to her eyes. "You mean you don't want to have any more kids?"

Adam stroked her belly. "I didn't say that. I'm your labor coach, not to mention your Dom. I'm just trying to be supportive. But don't worry. I think you women have some kind of hormonal mechanism that makes you forget the pain and aggravation. We fathers don't have that luxury."

"Oh, please." She rolled her eyes before glaring at him. "Don't even go there telling me how hard this is on you, Adam."

Adam laughed. "Point taken. If childbirth was up to men, well, there wouldn't be any overpopulation problem to worry about."

Karla stared long and hard at him. "Just so you know, though, we aren't going to remain celibate any longer than necessary after the babies arrive, Adam. I've waited long enough." She hoped her warning tone made that perfectly clear.

He chuckled. "Don't you worry; I've been planning our first time again for months."

"Don't tell me that now! You know Doctor Palmer isn't going to give the go-ahead for sex for at least eight weeks after this C-section."

"There are lots of things we can do short of having sex."

Well, why didn't he do any of those things these past few months? Okay, they had enjoyed that one night in April at the hotel's honeymoon suite, the same room in which they'd spent their wedding night. She blushed, thinking of the many ways he'd brought her body so much pleasure that night.

"Anticipation is good for you, Kitten."

He'd also become more cuddly lately, holding her close in bed. Her smile faded. Unfortunately, as soon as she fell asleep, he left to sleep elsewhere in the house for fear of hurting her if he had another night terror like the one apparently triggered by Marc's interrogation scene. That incident could have been so much worse if he'd jumped like that and landed on her belly instead of flying over her and winding up crouched on the floor.

Adam's phone buzzed, and he checked the screen. He furrowed his brows. "It's my mom."

"You'd better take it."

He nodded and answered. "Mom, is everything okay?"

Karla could hear the woman's voice from the cell phone. "I'm fine. I thought I would see how Karla's doing."

Adam met her gaze and raised his eyebrows in question.

"Go ahead," Karla whispered. "She'll know soon enough."

Adam had been afraid to jinx the chances of both babies surviving to birth by announcing they were having twins. Apparently, he was more confident now even with the third, perhaps because it was almost over and so far, so good.

"Mom, we're actually at the hospital now." Mrs. Gallagher's next question was about how things were going, to which he added, "Everything's fine. She's in the early stages of labor, but they're going to need to do a C-section."

"It's so early! Is there a problem?"

"Yeah, well, it turns out we're having triplets."

"Whaaaattttt?" The scream of the usually calm, collected woman made Karla smile. Adam's blunt way of delivering the news made Karla grin, too. As Adam filled his mother in on the news about the imminent arrivals, Karla felt her cervix twinge again. She looked up at the ceiling to find her focal point and took a deep breath.

"Mom, Karla needs me, but I'll call you back as soon as I can after the babies are born."

"Wonderful, Adam. I'll be down as soon as I can arrange for Megan or Patrick to bring me." Being older and a paraplegic made it difficult for her to travel alone.

"Listen, Mom, let me tell Megan the news myself." No doubt, he didn't want Megan to say anything to worry their mom about the break-in. "But go ahead and tell Patrick. He just flew back from Italy yesterday. He might be a little jet-lagged, though."

Adam ended the call abruptly, and the worry on his face grew stronger. He set down the phone and began rubbing his hand in circles around her humongous belly. His touch was magic, helping relieve her tension. Karla closed her eyes.

"Let's think about something else, Kitten. What else do we still need to do to get Marc's house ready for the babies?"

Their house. Good thing Marc had encouraged them to move in while he and Angelina were in Italy. Now, with the prospect of raising *three* children all at once, she welcomed all the space. Would there someday be even more children? Adam said once that he wanted six. She was fairly certain he was joking. Now she was about to fulfill half his order. She giggled.

"What's so funny?"

"Nothing. Just thinking that we're incredibly blessed."

"No doubt about that."

Despite all the room, she wanted her babies in one bedroom for their first few years. She and Ian had only had the Jack-and-Jill bathroom in between separate rooms. She regretted having no memories of nights lying awake and talking things over with him. Or having him comfort her if she became afraid. Angie said she and her four brothers once shared a single bedroom when they were little. No wonder they were all so close.

Karla sniffled.

Adam stiffened. "What's wrong? Are you in pain?"

She shook her head and cleared her throat. "I was just thinking about Ian." She'd miss him until the day she died.

"It's hard not to think of those we've loved and lost, especially when we're about to bring new lives into the world." He idly moved a strand of hair from her forehead. "I'm sure he's watching over you right now."

She nodded. "I hope so." Some people felt the presence of their loved ones who had passed. She had felt nothing from Ian. No signs. No dreams. Nothing.

"I want the babies to share a bedroom until they go to school at least."

"We have plenty of room for them to spread out now."

"I know. But children form unbreakable bonds during those dark moments alone with siblings in their bedrooms at night. I want my kids to experience that."

"Sounds nice. But multiples already have a bond that defies explanation or distance."

She'd never even been around multiples before. Adam said his mother's family had a history of twins.

"We'll figure out what's best for them later. For the next few months, I want them as close to us as possible. In our bedroom. But they'll soon outgrow a shared bassinet. I wonder if they make bassinets for three."

"Let me talk to Luke. I'm sure he can custom build something for us."

Karla grinned. The man making BDSM furniture for their playroom would now be working on furniture for their babies. Something seemed strange about that—but she knew the quality of his work and couldn't wait to see—

"Oh!" A gush of liquid ran between her legs. "My water broke!"

Adam jumped up and ran for the door, yelling for a nurse before she could remind him this was normal. Hadn't he been the one who read a thousand books about what to expect? She shook her head when a worried-looking Adam returned to her side with a nurse in tow.

"Are you in pain?"

"No. I didn't really feel anything but the gush of water."

Doctor Palmer soon returned. "Let's not keep these babies waiting any longer to meet their parents." The obstetrician grew serious. "The anesthesiologist is waiting to insert the spinal we talked about. I'll join you there soon."

Karla reached for Adam's hand and squeezed it. His was cold for a change. He must be a nervous wreck, even more than she was. They'd be giving her drugs, after all.

Please don't let this be too early for them to be born healthy.

The third baby must be much smaller than the other two to have gone undetected so long. Even though she'd only known about this one a few hours, the thought of losing any of…

Stop it, Kitty!

Adam helped her into a dry gown with the assistance of two nurses who then covered and wheeled her to the OR. Karla nibbled her lower lip.

"No more worrying, Kitten. Everything's going to be fine. Doc Palmer does this every day."

"That's not what I'm worried about." She paused then decided to say it anyway. "What if I'm a horrible mother?"

Adam laughed. "Nonsense. You'll be the best mother these babies will ever know."

She grinned at his silly-assed remark. "That's not saying much. I'll be their *only* mother."

"Eyes."

Her heart dropped into her stomach with a solid Ka-thunk! Only this time a harder contraction followed, and she placed one hand over her enormous belly.

"Breathe, Kitten." The contraction soon waned, and she nodded to let him know she was okay. When they paused in a little nook outside the OR, Adam cupped her chin, and she met his gaze. "We're going to love them and do the best we can. Lots of kids have it a whole lot worse in life than these three will."

Adam certainly hadn't had any kind of healthy upbringing. But Karla had, and she could draw on what Mom and Daddy had done with her and Ian to make their childhood such a positive experience. She'd also seen how Adam was with the young people he mentored. He treated Damián as his own son, and he made a wonderful grandpa to Marisol. No doubt in Karla's mind he would be an awesome daddy.

Together, they could do anything. "Yes, Sir. No more insecure thoughts—for *either* of us, Adam. We're going to rock this, because no one could love them more than we do."

"Absolutely right. Keep your head up and your powder dry, Kitten."

Karla giggled. "Yes, Sir. I'm ready."

"That's my girl." He leaned over to kiss her, and her heart jumped in her chest. Or was it one of the babies kicking her ribcage? She giggled, and he broke the kiss. "Glad you're feeling calmer. Now let's go meet these little people who have controlled our entire married life."

"And probably will continue to do so for the rest of our lives."

Adam chuckled and held her hand as the nurses wheeled her toward the operating room. He was stopped at the entrance by a nurse. "Sir, if you want to take this opportunity to go to the little boys' room, things are going to be happening fast once we get inside. But most husbands don't like watching the spinal being inserted."

Karla wasn't sure she wanted to stay for it, either, but encouraged Adam to escape while he could. She'd need him at her side more than ever soon.

"Just be sure you put on a sterile gown, mask, and gloves from over there before you join us," the nurse added, pointing to shelves of supplies.

Within minutes, Karla was ensconced in the sterile, overly bright operating room. Before she could prepare for it, the next contraction hit—the strongest so far. These babies meant business. Couldn't the pain let up now that the decision had been made that she wouldn't be giving birth to them vaginally?

Hurry back, Sir.

*   *   *

Adam hated leaving her, but took the opportunity to hit the head—*'little boys' room,' my ass*—and checked his phone for missed calls and text messages. Nothing from Wilson or Megan. He'd assume that meant they were okay. Jenny had texted. He'd let Karla know her parents' travel status when he joined her in the OR. And Damián called less than an hour ago. Said to call anytime, so Adam did.

Karla wouldn't need visitors until after she had some time to recoup and be with the babies, so he told Damián to spread the word to family members not to come to the hospital until morning.

Adam promised to text again when there was news and disconnected the call.

Inside the OR again, in fresh scrubs, Karla appeared more relaxed than he'd seen her since she told him it was time to go to the hospital. The meds must be working already. He decided not to touch her and disturb her rest, so he simply watched over her as she dozed. God, he loved this woman more than life itself. What did he ever do to deserve her? Nothing.

It was grace, pure and simple.

When Doc Palmer walked in, activity increased. The anesthesiologist introduced himself as did a man and two women who told him they were the neonatologists here to look after the babies. Each would have its own doctor. Karla's obstetrician had left nothing to chance. Good.

"Karla, Adam, are we ready?"

Karla opened her eyes. "Hmmm?" She focused on the doctor and smiled. "I am."

The visual of Karla being cut open flashed across his mind. Did they make fathers stay in the room? How could he watch that? Adam's own gut contracted as if the knife had sliced him open.

"Now, I want you to prepare yourselves. You'll need to wait a little while before you can hold the babies. We're going to have to take them straight to the NICU for evaluation and observation."

One glance at Karla and he saw tears welling in her eyes. He reached down to stroke her arm, stretched out on an arm attached to the gurney.

"The two we've been monitoring on the ultrasounds are close to the desired five-pound minimum weight we like to see, but we just don't know the size of the one that's been hidden. Most likely, he or she will be smaller. Regardless of birth weight, though, they are premature and need to be monitored closely until we can be assured they will be okay." She turned to Adam. "You can visit with them immediately in the NICU while we're finishing up with Karla in here."

See the babies without Karla? He didn't like the thought of any of his loved ones being out of his sight, his wife included. But before he had time to worry further, everyone moved into action. Seven or eight more gowned personnel entered the room.

The anesthesiologist injected something into her IV. "This is going to help you relax overall." Hell, she seemed pretty relaxed already. Had that been under her own steam or because of the drugs? Whatever, his woman's discipline was amazing. "The spinal will take care of the incision site, though."

Karla met his gaze, a mix of fear and excitement in her eyes. "Any word from Mom or Daddy, yet?"

"Jenny texted that they plan to leave Chicago on the first flight they can catch in the morning. I'm sure your dad has them on standby for every Denver flight the airline he works for has scheduled."

Karla nodded and closed her eyes. A tear rolled from the corner of her eye and into her hair. She'd wanted her mom to be here for the birth. Hell, so did Adam. Jenny was a nurse. She'd know better than Adam how to help Karla get through this.

Jenny had arranged time off work to be with Karla when the babies arrived and to help her daughter after she went home from the hospital. No one had guessed the babies would barely wait until June to make their appearance. June the first, to be exact.

Fuck, in three days, Adam would turn fifty-one. At least he could say his babies were born when he was fifty. That was old enough to father newborns.

Three nurses wheeled in three clear-plastic isolettes. Karla focused her gaze on the doctor, but her eyelids drooped as the drugs took effect.

Before he missed the chance, Adam texted a group message to Marc, Damián, Cassie, Megan, and Jenny letting them know what was going on.

Karla's moan cut through Adam, and he pocketed the phone. He stroked her sweat-soaked forehead. "Are you still in pain, Kitten?"

"No. I just can't feel or move my legs."

He grinned and leaned close to her ear. "Pretend I have you in ropes, suspended from the ceiling."

Karla glared at him. Okay, maybe reminding her how little playtime they'd had these past few months wasn't the way to go here. Be a coach, not a Dom. "Won't be long now, Kitten. You're doing great."

She relaxed even more. "I'm not doing much of anything. I feel a little loopy."

Thank God she wasn't in any pain. Watching her going through such intense pain earlier made it much harder for him to maintain his dignity than if he'd been the one enduring that kind of torture. Thank God that suffering was over for them both.

He needed to be calm and strong for Karla. Adam picked up the washcloth, dipped it in the basin of water, and wiped the sweat off her forehead.

The nurses draped a sheet over her chest so that he and Karla wouldn't be able to watch them making the incision. *Thank God.* He relaxed a little.

Surely the babies would be born soon.

Adam wiped her forehead with a cool, wet washcloth. Karla pulled at the collar of his gown until his face was close to hers, lowered his mask, and gave him a quick kiss. Apparently exhausted by the maneuver, she slumped back against the pillows. "I'm so glad you're here with me. You make the impossible so much less daunting."

"We're in this together, Kitten. We'll help each other every step of the way."

Doc Palmer stepped up onto a platform. "All right, folks. Here we go."

Adam's heart thudded to a stop before adrenaline pushed the blood through his bloodstream. Activity stilled as the nurses and newborn pediatricians took their places. Doc Palmer said something to Karla, but he couldn't hear for the blood rushing through his ears. Adam reminded *himself* to breathe now. He tamped down his own anxiety.

"You're going to feel some pressure now." Doc Palmer bent over Karla's belly.

Adam felt his stomach lurch as he imagined the scalpel—

"Adam! Eyes on me!" The command in Karla's voice captured his attention. When he met her gaze, she smiled. "Breathe, Sir."

He grinned and did as she'd ordered. "I'm trying to, Kitten."

Please, God, let her and the babies be okay.

He needed to stop thinking about something bad happening. What God would be so cruel as to take another of his children from him?

"Let's see who's on the top of the baby heap."

Karla let out a laugh of sorts, more like a stress-relief giggle than anything.

"Okay, it's a…girl!"

Adam faced the doctor who held up the bloodied, crying baby. Looked like it had white paste smeared all over it. *Her*, not it, Marine.

My daughter.

The doctor handed the squalling baby to the nurse to her right and clamped off and cut the cord. In the doctor's office, they'd discussed having Adam cut them, but that was when this was expected to be a vaginal birth. With three babies needing to be born in rapid succession, there was no mention of him cutting the cords. Secretly, he had to admit his relief. He'd only agreed to do it because it seemed important to Karla.

Adam squeezed Karla's shoulder. "Congratulations, Baby Tiger."

"You, too, Sir."

Karla winced and shifted her gaze to the doctor. Was she in pain?

"Here's the one who was hiding from us all this time. Let me see—oh, another girl!"

Two girls. What did he know about girls?

Aw, who cared? *Un-fucking-believable!* He'd just become the daddy to two little girls. Wetness dampened his mask, but he didn't give a rat's ass who saw him crying. This one had hair as black as the first, but he wasn't sure if that was because she was wet.

Unlike the first, she didn't make a sound. "Is she…okay?" Didn't doctors hold babies up and whack them on the butt anymore to clear their lungs or whatever?

Adam held his breath, waiting for the doctor to finish clamping and cutting the cord.

"Sometimes the smaller babies aren't as vocal, but she's moving her arms and legs. We'll check her out right away, but I think she's just not ready to test out her lungs yet."

He turned to Karla, who had tears streaming from her eyes as well, as she tried to catch a glimpse of the babies before they were placed on the tables near their isolettes. She bit her lower lip and gazed up at him. Her eyelashes spiked together from her tears. "I hope I can give you a son, too."

What was the matter with her? She glanced away. "Now hear this, Kitten. I don't care if the next one's another girl. I won't hear any mention of regrets. You've just given me two beautiful daughters, and they both appear to be healthy. That's all that matters. Hell, I like girls."

Even if I don't understand a fucking thing about them.

Wasting no time, the doctor went to work again. Soon the third Montague baby was lifted above Karla's belly. Adam grinned. He didn't need to hear the announcement. This one was all boy.

Adam's vision blurred, blinding him until he blinked his eyes clear.

I have another son. A second chance.

At Karla's sob, he grabbed her shoulder tightly, avoiding her arm with the IV line. She held on as they half-consoled and half-congratulated each other.

A boy? And this one was crying as loudly as the first.

Doc Palmer turned to him. "Adam, since he's the last one, would you like to cut this cord? I didn't want to delay in the delivery of the others, but don't want to deprive you of the experience you had wanted."

There wasn't much he could do in here to be a part of this birthing experience—not the way Karla was—but he wasn't sure he could do this. When the nurse held a drape over Karla's incision, some of his concerns drifted away. He stood and walked toward the doctor and his son—his *son*.

Don't fuck this up, Marine.

Adam took a deep breath, and the doctor handed him a pair of surgical scissors like the ones Marc used in Fallujah. He willed his hand to stop shaking as he took them between his finger and thumb. She placed two clamps on the cord and pointed to where he should cut between them. The cord still seemed to be beating to Karla's heartbeat. He swayed on his feet, and the room grew fuzzy. A strong odor brought him back, stinging his nose and eyes.

"Sit."

Adam followed the nurse's command and plopped onto the stool she indicated before he keeled over and embarrassed himself. He stared blankly at the cord.

"Don't worry," said the nurse holding the smelling-salts capsule under his nose. "You wouldn't be the first one to pass out in the delivery room."

I'm not going to fucking pass out.

Doc Palmer pointed to the cord again. "Cut right here, Adam."

He stood once more and closed the scissors around the inch-thick cord. Surprisingly, it felt like cutting through thick nylon rope. After three attempts he made it completely through, separating their baby—their *son*—from Karla's body.

I'm his daddy.

Mine.

Okay, he'd gladly share him with Karla.

Another nurse whisked the crying boy away to a table several feet away, and Adam zoned out for a moment watching the activity going on with his three babies until Karla asked, "Is he okay? Did you see him?"

Fuck, he'd been so focused on the cord he hadn't really looked at the baby. He glanced over at the boy, but could barely see his tiny feet now. Starting to speak, he couldn't get the words out. After clearing his throat, he met her gaze. Adam had no clue what a perfect newborn baby looked like, but said, "He's perfect, Kitten."

One of the babies let out an indignant wail that curled his toes. Soon another chimed in, and his attention turned once more to the babies. The nurses and pediatricians evaluated the three—weighing, measuring, and checking whatever else they did. The middle baby continued to sleep through all the excitement, but did complain a second or two when her foot was stuck with a needle for one of their tests. Good. Nothing ranked higher than the sound of a newborn baby's cry.

New life.

The other two hadn't let up much. Eyes open, they didn't seem to miss a thing.

All three babies had Karla's black hair—and lots of it. He didn't have to see them cleaned up to know his girls would be as beautiful as their mother, his son handsome and strong.

Holy fuck.

How could he and Karla handle three babies? They were outnumbered. All his tactical plans just flew out the window. Hell, everything he'd learned from the baby books had barely prepared him for two. Now there were three of them.

Adam shook off this feeling of pure terror—and it could be described as nothing else. Somehow, they would manage this, too. Together they could do anything they set their minds, hearts, and bodies to do.

He returned to Karla and leaned over, kissing her cheek through his mask, not wanting any germs to touch his babies. "Thank you," he whispered. "I know that's a fucking lame thing to say at a time like this, but I don't have the words…"

He stroked her face, and they huddled together in the afterglow.

"Here's your firstborn. Have a quick peek before we head to the NICU."

Adam moved to let the nurse place the baby, wearing a yellow knit hat and wrapped tightly in a blanket, near Karla's face. A fresh stream of tears blurred his vision. He blinked, not wanting to miss a thing. The baby opened her gray-blue eyes and stared at Karla as if communicating on some level he couldn't be a part of. Even though the baby books said a newborn's eyesight was limited to blurry shapes and shadows, his daughter seemed so aware of everything. Pride swelled his chest. No big surprise their baby would be above average in her early skill sets. Smart and beautiful, like her mommy.

Mine.

Karla's hand reached out to stroke the baby's cheek. "Hi, precious."

All too quickly, they had to say their temporary goodbyes. Next, their sleeping beauty was brought over only to be whisked away even faster. He hoped her lungs were okay. Lastly, their son paid them a quick visit.

"Aren't they beautiful, Adam?" Karla asked after their boy had gone to join his sisters.

He still couldn't believe he had a baby boy and two daughters. He'd once teased Karla that they'd have six babies, and he'd love and care for any baby Karla delivered, even if there were a dozen. But right now, three was the perfect number.

A new spate of tears streamed down her cheeks. "Oh, Adam, I feel like a piece of us is missing."

He cleared his throat. "I know, hon. Me, too."

Doc Palmer finished stitching up the incision and turned to them. "You'll be able to see them again anytime, Adam. And, Karla, I just want you to lie flat for a while. The nurse will be checking frequently for the next couple of hours to make sure everything is okay. We'll move you to your room soon. With the weight of the first and third babies, I anticipate they will join you there by this evening."

A nurse handed the doctor a slip of paper. She smiled. "For triplets, you have amazingly big babies, Karla. The first girl was five pounds even, the next four-ten, and the boy is five-two." She rattled off the lengths. Each was nineteen inches, give or take.

Three healthy, perfect babies as far as he was concerned.

Thank you, God.

Chapter Eight

Adam let Karla doze while being transferred to their new room and just followed along. They had asked for a family room so the babies could be with them. When they entered their home away from home, he was surprised to find a full-sized bed dominating the room.

"Here we are!" The nurse helped Karla from the smaller bed into the large one.

Fuck. Was he going to be able to stay awake if he joined her in there? What if he couldn't and hurt Karla while she slept? The night terror he'd suffered not a month ago—probably triggered by something during the interrogation scene from hell with Marc—had left him worried about whether he could keep the past at bay when he let his guard down.

Karla slept off the anesthesia the rest of the night, interrupted almost every hour by someone needing to check on something or press on her belly some. Man, that had to hurt. Not wanting to disturb her much-needed sleep, he used the time to catch up on texts. Jenny and Carl were in flight and should be here in a few hours. He answered Megan's text from last night and let her know the news. Since their mom knew, he might as well let her in on it, but those were the only four who had been informed about multiples of any number. Maybe he was crazy to keep it quiet, but if, God forbid, the unthinkable happened and he lost another baby, it might be easier if he didn't have everyone around him blaming him for the loss. Not that he would ever do anything remotely close to causing intentional harm.

Anyway, sounded like Wilson had things under control with Megan.

One less person to worry about today.

When he received a text that several members of his chosen family were assembled in the waiting room at about zero-eight-thirty, he went out to let everyone know about the C-section and that she was sleeping.

Without spoiling the news Karla wanted to share about the triplets, he accepted their back slaps and hugs before asking them to come back later to visit.

Marc and Angelina looked dead on their feet anyway, but at least they were holding hands and smiling at each other again.

Cassie steered clear of him, as usual, but asked him to give Karla a hug for her. He walked over to her anyway and reached into his pocket to retrieve his keys. Taking one off the ring, he handed it to her. "This is the key to our new house. I don't want you running back and forth if you don't have to. Anytime you need to, just bunk down there. We have lots of room, although the guest rooms aren't completely set up yet. But I'll be sleeping here with Karla for a few days, so feel free to take the master bedroom."

Her hand shook when she reached out to take the key. What the fuck did she expect him to do to her?

"Thank you." She put the key into her purse. "I don't mind going back and forth now. I have to take care of my alpacas. But I'll make arrangements for someone to help there when Kitty comes home."

"Damián can give you the address to the house so you can GPS it."

"No need. I remember how to get there from your wedding."

"Oh, yeah. I forgot." He was surprised he'd even thought about how far she'd come to be here today.

Adam said his goodbyes to them. Before returning to Karla's room, he checked on the babies in the NICU. Sleeping, all three of them. He was told two of them would be taken to the room in a couple of hours unless any complications arose. The other baby had no serious health problems, just needed to be on oxygen and watched more closely to be sure she could regulate her body temperature and a few other things they were measuring.

When he reentered their room, Karla opened her eyes and smiled groggily. They must have really doped her up on some powerful drugs. Good thing because he didn't want her feeling any pain. He wondered how long it would take her incision to heal. He didn't want to think how big it was if they could pull three good-sized babies from her.

She patted the mattress of the bed.

"You sure? I don't want to hurt you jostling around on the mattress."

"Just what kind of jostling do you have in mind, Sir?"

"Don't get any ideas. If I join you, I'm going to be afraid to touch you because of that C-section incision."

Karla sighed. "I'm getting used to that."

He felt like a heel now, but had only put them on a sexual hiatus to protect her and the babies. Maybe it hadn't been necessary in retrospect—but having these three babies arrive in good health was the prime objective for both of them. Sometimes a man had to make decisions that weren't popular but were best to achieve the goal.

Adam removed his shoes, crawled onto the bed, and stretched out next to her. He'd been surprised at the accommodations in here, but figured it helped couples reconnect and start to bond with their new babies.

Only they were baby-less at the moment.

"Are you in any pain?"

"The drugs wore off, but I'm okay."

He reached out to stroke her arm, loving the rise of gooseflesh in the wake of his touch. "I'm so proud of you, Kitten. You took such good care of yourself so our babies could grow as big as possible inside you."

She giggled, and damned if his dick didn't respond the way it always did. "I think you had a lot to do with making sure I did everything I was supposed to, including eating right."

"God, I was so worried. I don't think I can handle another pregnancy for another decade or so—and by then, I'll be too old."

Karla took his chin and raised it until their gazes met. "Adam Montague, if I hear you mention another pregnancy again before these babies are at least out of diapers, I'll…"

"You'll what?" He grinned.

"I don't know what I'll do, but let's not talk about any more babies. I think we're going to have our hands full."

No fucking way will she be pregnant again anytime soon. He'd triple up on contraceptive measures if he had to. He wanted time to enjoy his bride's body again, well, when his three kids weren't making their own demands on her.

"Kitten, I'll never be happier than I am at this moment. I don't need any more children. I don't want to see you go through that again."

"I hear my hormones are supposed to kick in to where I don't re-member much of the delivery. But as of this moment, I agree. Three's the perfect number."

"We're so blessed. Some couples can never have one, and here we are with three."

Karla stroked his arm. "I can't wait to get my hands on them."

"The nurses in the NICU said we'd have the two bigger ones soon. Rest while you can. Oh, and your mom and dad are in flight. Could be here in an hour or so."

She nodded, but remained silent, and soon, he heard her shallow, steady breathing. He decided to take advantage of a little shut-eye himself, but pulled away to the other side of the mattress. He didn't want to accidentally strike her while sleeping. One of his Marines told him he'd broken his wife's nose twice before he gave up on sleeping with her. Adam couldn't imagine the remorse of putting a loved one through such pain when there was something he could do to avoid the problem.

A soft knock woke him, and he sprang up to place himself between Karla and whoever opened the door. He soon realized it was the nurse and she rolled in one of the bassinets.

"Adam! They're here!" Karla was awake in an instant, trying to sit up.

"You just stay put." He left her in the bed and wondered if only one of the babies would be able to stay with them. Then the door opened again, and a second bassinet was wheeled in. That meant two of them were healthy enough to leave the NICU. One to go.

The nurse scanned her wristband and the baby's. "Now, Mrs. Montague, your OB indicated you wanted to have skin-to-skin contact with your babies as early as possible. If you'll loosen the top of your gown, we can get started." He helped Karla with the gown while the nurse unwrapped the baby in the blue cap—their son, he supposed. They'd better stick to color coding their clothing until they could tell them apart. At least none were identical twins. But all their faces looked alike to him right now.

Hell, they hadn't discussed names yet. They'd better come up with something more than son and daughters soon, though. Adam hadn't wanted to jinx anything, so they'd kept talk of baby names to themselves. Yeah, as if he hadn't bonded with these babies the moment he saw two of them on the ultrasound monitor. He'd only been playing mind games with himself to pretend otherwise.

Moments later, Adam watched as Karla cupped the heads of their son and older daughter skin to skin except for their tiny diapers. Karla had never looked more beautiful than now, holding two of their babies.

He lifted the blanket to cover their bare backs. When their son began to squirm on Karla's chest, rooting for food probably, Adam blinked away tears and bent over to kiss the baby's cheek. Softest skin he'd ever felt.

His son promptly let out a scream followed by a steady bawling. Adam jerked away. "What did I do? Did I hurt him?"

Karla laughed. "Don't be silly. Mom says babies are tougher than you think. He could be crying for any number of reasons, but maybe your whiskers surprised him."

Damn. He'd better shave before he kissed the babies in the future.

"Don't you dare stop touching and kissing them, though. They need to be close to their daddy, too. Join us in bed."

She'd barely picked up any of the books he'd encouraged her to study in preparation for this moment, and yet, despite all the reading he'd done, Adam seemed to be the clueless one. Maternal instinct must be pretty damned powerful. Why didn't dads have something similar built in? He was screwed unless he kept reading—or listening to Karla for pointers. Being a dad to a grown man like Damián was a whole lot easier than taking on that role with someone who'd only been around a few hours.

Adam went around to his side of the bed and scooted closer to where Karla and the babies were. The nurses left after reminding them of the call button if they needed anything. Alone, he rolled onto his side, cupped his head in his palm, and just stared down at Karla and the babies.

Hoping to soothe the boy's distress, he reached out to rub slow circles on his back. "Hey, Ian, Daddy's here."

A sniffle from Karla distracted him, and Adam glanced over at her. Tears brimmed in her eyes. "How'd you know I wanted to name him that?"

He hadn't really thought about any other possibility for a boy. But to her, he said, "After seeing his eyes and that same black hair as yours and Ian's, what else could we name him? Glad you're okay with it."

She nodded, and two tears trailed down her cheeks. "How about his middle name?"

"What do you think about Paxton?" Her maiden name could be carried on through their son, in a way, since her brother's death would keep him from doing so.

"Ian Paxton Montague." She smiled through her tears. "Perfect. But let's call him Pax or Paxton to differentiate him and…" She didn't have to finish. He leaned closer and kissed her.

After clearing her throat, she smiled and asked, "What about the girls' names? I only had one girl and one boy name picked out. I was so sure there would only be one of each."

"Your turn to name this one." He'd more or less named their son without consulting Karla, so he ought to let her decide on the first girl's name at least. "What name did you come up with?"

"Kate."

Adam swallowed past a lump in his throat. Adam had hoped to name one Kathleen, after his great-great-grandmother Montague. Kate. Without saying a word, they were on the same wavelength naming two of their children.

"I've felt a kinship with your ancestor ever since our honeymoon at her and Johnny's cabin. Staring down from her portrait over the mantle, I felt she was letting me know everything was going to be okay."

He'd been drawn to that portrait since he was a kid. His great-great-grandmother had ventured from Ireland to South Dakota once upon a time. "Kate, it is. Well, for a nickname. Her given name will be Kathleen after Kathleen Gannon Montague."

"A fine Irish name."

"Well, except that Montague is French."

"We're Americans. You have a mix of cultures from Lakota, Irish, and French. I have Irish and quite a bit of German on Mom's side, too."

He stared down at Kate, who had been alert and inquisitive since she'd been placed on Karla's chest. Her hand stuck out from the blanket and rested protectively on her brother's shoulder. "Kate's a guardian."

Karla nodded. "Like you, Sir."

Lord knew he tried, but with so much happening lately that he couldn't predict or control, he wasn't sure how successful he was anymore. Now, he not only had Karla and his extended family to worry about, but their *three* babies.

Karla pulled him back to the present. "Why don't we make Gannon our Kate's middle name?"

"Fine by me. We'll be carrying on two more family names now."

She nodded. "That just leaves our little princess in the NICU."

* * *

Karla's heart ached for her missing baby. Even though she had two here with her, knowing she'd carried the three of them for almost eight months inside her body only to have them separated now physically hurt.

She stroked Paxton's cheek as Adam lifted the blanket higher over the babies. She was the mother of three children. Reality probably wouldn't set in for a long time to come.

Dear Lord, keep my babies safe and healthy.

Karla hoped everything was okay with their other daughter. She wished Mom were here. She worked as a nurse for a pediatrician and could calm Karla's fears. Perhaps she could even glean more information about the baby's condition. Karla looked up from the two babies.

"What's wrong, Kitten?"

She blinked away the tears. "I miss her. Not knowing how she's doing is going to drive me crazy."

Adam cleared his throat and squeezed her arm. "I know, hon. I'll run down and check on her again in a minute."

"That would make me feel better."

Paxton let out another wail for no apparent reason, bringing her focus back to the two beautiful babies on her chest.

"Hey, son, what's all the fuss? You don't know how good you've got it there on your mommy's breast." She grinned as she listened to Adam trying to reason with him about why he really had nothing to cry about.

Tears stung her eyes again. Would the waterworks never end?

Ian had been on her mind so much lately. Was it because she had hoped for a namesake to carry on in his absence? No one would ever replace her own big brother, but having him remembered in his nephew's name would keep his memory alive. She couldn't wait to tell her parents.

"Any word from Mom or Daddy?"

"Damián texted me that he would pick them up and bring them here first thing. They should be here any time."

"Is there anyone in the waiting room?"

"No, I told them to go home and come back later today. I wanted to keep the babies to ourselves a little longer—and give you time to rest."

She smiled. Always so protective. Paxton finally stopped crying and blinked at his daddy, taking his measure. "Pax, your daddy is the best daddy ever, so you go easy on him."

Adam placed a kiss on her lips again before pulling away to whisper to the baby, "Your mommy isn't so bad, either, if you ask me. Don't you give her as much trouble as I did my own mom." He sobered. "What are we going to do, Kitten?"

"Do about what?"

"We have *three* babies? I still can't believe it."

"We can do anything we set our minds to, Adam." But she blinked as the enormity set in once more for her as well. She let out a laugh but only to keep from screaming in panic at the daunting thought. "And, no, I can't believe it, either."

A whimper from Kate drew her attention, and she watched the little one squirm and start rooting for her breast. *Oh, no!*

"Adam, how will I be able to feed all three of them?"

The door swung open, and a nurse entered. "Oh, don't you worry about that, sweetie. Your body will provide what those babies need. We'll keep an eye on their weight gain, and you can always supplement as needed. Our bodies are really an amazingly efficient system. Their demand results in the right supply once it gets regulated."

After pressing hard on her abdomen until Karla wanted to scream, the nurse said she was doing fine. "We can return the babies to the NICU tonight if you would like to get some rest, but anytime you want to visit with one or both or need anything else, just press that call button."

Karla placed a protective hand over each baby's back. "No, we'd like to keep them here."

The nurse nodded. "Just letting you know your options. We're here for you and the babies and will help however we can."

The nurse moved Kate up to Karla's bare breast. When she latched onto her nipple and started to suck, Karla felt her womb contract. "Let's put your son to work over here, too. The sucking sensations of nursing will help get your uterus back in shape naturally."

"I felt it contract. But are they getting anything?"

"Your milk won't come in for a couple more days, but we want them to enjoy the benefits of that good colostrum. Antibodies and all kinds of healthy things are in there to ward off some of the nasties in the coming year."

After the nurse left, Karla glanced over and witnessed the awe in Adam's eyes as they experienced this latest miracle of life. They both watched as Paxton's lips worked feverishly to extract whatever he could from her. When she returned her gaze to Adam, tears traced down his face that only led her waterworks to start again.

"Isn't this totally unbelievable, Adam? To think that last evening we were sitting in our new home relaxing, and now our household has grown from two to five."

He nodded, but didn't speak. "I'll be right back."

Karla wasn't sure where he was headed, but assumed he needed time to compose himself. He didn't like to show tears in front of her or anyone else. But she knew he shed them when deeply moved. How could he not cry on this, the happiest day of their lives so far?

She cupped the back of Kate's head. Both wore tiny knit caps to keep in their body heat, but they also drew heat from direct contact with her skin. Mom said breastfeeding made her feel like an earth mother or something. Karla hadn't expected motherhood to be so primal for her this quickly, but now understood what her mother meant.

Paxton's insistent sucking grabbed her attention again. A voracious little man. Could she really feed all three of them this way?

Fifteen minutes later, Adam walked back into the room smiling. "We still need to name our Sleeping Beauty in the NICU. She didn't seem too worried about her nickname when I told her."

God, she loved this man. "Thanks for checking on her. So she's still sleeping?"

"Far as I can tell. They have her eyes covered because of the bright light."

Worry clawed at her chest. "Are they worried about jaundice?"

"The NICU nurse said it's just a precaution. That it's normal for the tinier ones to need more sleep, but that all babies sleep most of the time their first few weeks. She did let me stroke the baby's feet. She squirmed around a little. Maybe she's ticklish."

Karla hoped they would let her out of bed soon to go check on the baby herself. Being separated was like having a piece of her heart ripped out. Her third baby was so far away.

Kate let out a wail of discontent before latching on again, and Adam chuckled. "I guess Sleeping Beauty applies to only one of the two girls."

"Don't get too attached to that nickname, Adam. It won't go over very well when she goes to kindergarten. Well, maybe *in* kindergarten it would make her the cool kid, but definitely not in the board room or wherever she wants to be when she grows up."

"What about Aurora then?"

She turned to Adam and quirked a brow. "You want to name her after Aurora, Colorado?" Where on earth had that come from?

"No, not the suburb. The movie. I watched *Sleeping Beauty* the other day with Marisol for like the fifth time." He shrugged and grinned. "It sort of stuck in my head. Means 'dawn.' Anyway, would that be a good name?"

She smiled. He was going to be such a good daddy, watching endless kids' videos and spending time with his children just the way he did with his granddaughter, Marisol. Karla had been watching the movie with them, too, but had been too preoccupied making lists—of things they needed to add to the nursery, buy at the grocery, and accomplish before she went into labor—to pay attention to the video. Of course, she'd seen the movie as a child.

"I think Aurora would be perfect. Marisol will have a special connection with her auntie when she finds out. But it's a mouthful. Maybe Rori for short?"

"Sounds good."

"Any ideas for her middle name?"

"I'll leave that to you, Kitten."

"What do you think about Casandra?"

"After Cassie?"

She nodded. "She only uses one 'S' in her formal name, well, when she used it. But she's as close as any sister could be to me." If only she would warm up to Adam. The two of them had clashed from the beginning, due more to Cassie's hesitance around men than Adam's doing anything to upset her intentionally.

He seemed to mull it over a moment then smiled. "Aurora Casandra Montague is beautiful—in name and in person."

"They're all named! That wasn't so hard. Maybe we're going to handle this parenting thing just fine." *Wait!* Karla's smile faded. Which girl had been born first? Everything had happened so quickly, already the memory of the delivery was fading. What kind of mother forgot something like that? Tears stung her eyes.

"What's wrong, Kitten?"

She sniffled. How could she admit to something that horrible? "Nothing."

"Kitten."

Ka-thunk!

His stern tone of voice and Dom stare told her she needed to 'fess up. "I can't...I can't remember the birth order of the girls, only that Paxton was third." She sniffled again.

"Kate was first then Aurora."

"You noticed."

"I didn't have as much work to do as you did. I thought I was handling everything pretty well until Paxton showed up." His smile lit up his eyes. "Yeah, I noticed."

A tech wheeled in her equipment. "Time to check your vitals."

Karla winced as Paxton suckled with more persistence on her sensitive nipple. "When one finishes, just place your pinky finger in the corner of the baby's mouth, and you'll break the suction." Karla followed the tech's instructions and moved Paxton higher on her chest to give her sensitive nipple a rest.

"They're going to become sore fast with three tenacious mouths to feed, even using the pump to help keep up with demand. But they'll toughen up soon enough. We'll bring you something to help, though."

Karla couldn't keep from grinning and glanced over at Adam, who had a rather sadistic grin on his face. *Hmmm. Planning some nipple torture to aid in the process, Sir?* Now that she could handle.

When the tech left after checking her vitals, Karla's doubts assailed her once again. "What if I don't do it right or can't provide enough milk?"

"They're Montagues. Finding a source of food that works for them won't be a problem." His words didn't give her the assurance she needed. "Stop worrying, Kitten. You need to pace yourself. You're catching on quickly. If there are problems, we ask for help and, if necessary, go on to plan B." He smiled and leaned closer. "You're the best mommy ever." Adam kissed her until Kate squirmed and tried to push him away.

Adam jumped back as if burned. "Did I hurt her?"

Oh, dear Lord. And he thought Karla had it bad. They were quite the basket case of jittery parents. She hoped they would be able to adapt to parenthood without a hitch once they got the hang of it.

A light faded in his eyes, and he looked back down at Paxton, now fast asleep on her chest. She wondered if he was thinking about his boy growing up and going off to war to defend his country. Adam had sacrificed so much in his twenty-five years as a Marine. Karla didn't want her son to choose that, after seeing how it had affected his father, but wouldn't stand in his way if that's what he wanted to do.

Karla shuddered. Nowadays, women were warriors, too, so her daughters might even be the ones wanting to protect and defend their country. Little Kate already displayed signs of being a guardian and protector of her brother the way her little hand stretched out over his shoulders.

They'd just brought three innocent, defenseless babies into such a scary, unsafe world. How were they going to be able to keep evil away? Suddenly, the thought of what they'd undertaken hit home.

*   *   *

Adam stared at his sleeping son lying on Karla's chest. Would Adam's mother have worried about him if she'd known he joined the Marines a couple years after running away? His father had been to hell and back in Vietnam. Adam didn't truly appreciate his father's sacrifices until going through it himself. Hearing the 'Nam stories from his friend Jerry Patterson on Adam's many visits to the crusty veteran's kink club in LA brought home a lot of understanding, too. Jerry had served in 'Nam during the same time and probably under similar conditions as Adam's father, although the club owner was a Navy man.

Would he want a military career for his own son? Adam had seen the bowels of hell himself on more than one occasion. His mom's family had a long history of serving in the Marines, back to the Civil War. When Adam had run away at sixteen, he'd changed his name to her maiden name because he respected the hell out of that tradition. But would he be able to send this little fella off in eighteen or nineteen years if Paxton wanted to serve as badly as Adam had? Hell, what about his girls? They could join the Marines or any other branch, as well, and be sent into combat zones.

Fuck that. His girls probably wouldn't want to do anything like that, although Marisol sure asked him a lot of questions about what it was like when her daddy was in Iraq.

Adam and Damián had served willingly, but would future generations have the luxury to choose?

Why the fuck are you going down this path right now? This kid didn't even know how to wipe his ass yet. Hell, didn't even know he *had* an ass. Adam would make sure his kids grew up strong with a deep pride in the country of their birth. If they chose to serve in the military, fine. If not, they'd give back by serving in other ways.

When the nurse came back again to press on Karla's belly, she asked if they wanted to put the babies back in the bassinet now.

Karla's eyelids drooped. "Sure. I think I need a little nap, too."

The nurse asked Adam if he would like a lesson in swaddling Paxton. Adam left the bed with more than a little trepidation and stood beside the nurse, staring down at the tiny boy. He froze, unable to pick him up. What if he dropped him or did it wrong?

After she spread a baby blanket over the bassinet, she stepped aside. "Go on. You won't break him." When he remained motionless, she shook her head, lifted Paxton, and placed him in his little bed. After changing his diaper, she had him swaddled again within seconds. Next was Kate's turn. When the kid wouldn't let go of the nipple, Karla broke the suction as she had been taught a little while ago.

Alligator clamps had nothing on what his kids could do to Karla's nipples.

The nurse changed Kate's diaper on the bed and placed her beside Paxton on their backs. Despite being bundled up in blankets, they snuggled against each other in the bassinet. He blinked away the sting in his eyes.

The nurse gave Karla some cream for her sore nipples. Now, toughening up tits was something he *could* help with. Sounded sexy as hell, too. He'd missed one of their favorite kinks. He was a bit of an expert in that area, too.

He just didn't know a thing about babies despite all the reading he had done.

"Your lactation nurse will give you all kinds of advice on how to make the most of your breastfeeding experience." The nurse prepared to leave after asking if Karla wanted anything else. She was almost asleep already.

The babies barely filled the tiny bed. Two would definitely fit in the larger one at home. Aurora might not be home for weeks, so they would be fine sharing until they could arrange for something bigger. He'd talk with Luke.

Kate opened her eyes and seemed surprised to find Adam leaning over her. He stroked her downy-soft cheek, but she looked like she was expecting his finger to be her mommy's tit the way her little mouth opened up and started rooting around. Finding nothing of substance, she scrunched her face up to protest. Not wanting to wake Karla or Paxton, he wheeled the bassinet to the other side of the bed. She seemed to enjoy the movement because she calmed down. Paxton slept through it all as Adam wheeled them around in circles in the free area of the room. "You like going for a ride, baby girl?"

He continued to move her around and to speak softly to her. She calmed down surprisingly fast. Was it the motion or his voice? He hoped she remembered him talking to her all those nights and mornings while still in Karla's belly. He'd made that a ritual the past six months or so, hoping what he thought at the time was one baby would recognize his voice when they finally met. Ever since they found out there were twins, though, he pictured two little ones listening to their daddy's voice. Who knew there actually were three all this time?

Soon she was fast asleep again.

A sense of accomplishment washed over him. "I can do something right at least when it comes to the babies."

His phone buzzed, and he pulled it from his pocket to answer Jenny's call as quietly as possible. They were at the airport. "Great. Damián Orlando will be giving you a ride to the hospital. Karla and the babies are sleeping right now." They still didn't know about the triplets, but were expecting to meet twins.

One of the babies began crying, and he said goodbye. Adam checked and found that this time it was Paxton. He tried wheeling them around the room again, but his son wasn't as easy to console as his big sister was.

"Bring him to me." Adam wheeled the bassinet toward Karla, dreading the moment when she'd ask him to pick him up. Luckily, the nurse came in and returned the boy to the place he liked best—Karla's breast.

"Would you bring Kate to me, too?"

Even though Karla had asked him, Adam turned to the nurse in a panic. The woman shook her head with a tsk-tsk, but smiled her understanding and placed Kate in Karla's outstretched arms. Soon she was rooting around on her other breast until she latched onto her swollen nipple. The sight of Karla with two of their babies at her breasts nearly made him come undone.

So beautiful. So perfect.

God, he would never have her all to himself again. He regretted all the time he'd lost with her during the pregnancy. He could have had his bride's undivided attention all this time.

Man, did you ever blow it.

Whoa! If he didn't know better, he'd think he was jealous of his own kids' time with their mommy.

Kate began to fuss as if frustrated she wasn't getting whatever she expected. Adam reached under the blanket to stroke her soft skin.

The nurse poked Karla's belly again, and Karla gasped this time. "Can she have something for the pain?" The nurse promised to bring whatever the doctor ordered.

He wished they would go easier on his kitten. Hell, she'd just delivered three babies through a gaping hole in her belly. But his reading prep told him it was important for her uterus to shrink back to normal size to avoid hemorrhaging. She'd been stretched far beyond what most women would have been for a single baby.

Fuck, we aren't out of the woods yet for weeks on that score.

So he let them do their job. He reached down to squeeze Karla's shoulder, pinching her to try to direct her focus away from the pain in her belly. Karla glanced up and smiled.

"Thank you, Sir. You always know just what to do."

I wish, Kitten.

Right now, he was free-falling without a parachute. Adam turned toward the window, his back to the door as he fought to regain his equilibrium. As if that would ever be possible again.

Time passed until a knock on the door gave him something to do, and he crossed the room to find Jenny and Carl had arrived. No Damián with them, but Adam figured he wanted to give the new grandparents time alone first. Or maybe he'd headed home to pick up Savannah and Marisol.

His in-laws barely said hello to him as they rushed into the room and toward Karla and the babies.

"Do the pink and blue caps mean we have a girl *and* a boy!" Karla nodded and started to speak, but Jenny interrupted. "They're so little. How much did they weigh, Karla?"

"Kate's the oldest. Five pounds exactly."

"That's big for a twin at thirty-four weeks. Good for you, Karla! I'm so glad they're healthy. And her brother?"

"Ian Paxton's the biggest at five-two."

"Oh, Carl." Her husband placed his arm around Jenny before she hugged and kissed her daughter. "Thank you for that." Carl turned to Adam, looking lost. Adam swore the man had gone misty-eyed.

Join the club. The babies had that effect on him, too.

A loud sniffle from Jenny told Adam he needed to ward off sad thoughts at a time like this. Adam cleared his throat. "And Aurora was four-ten."

Adam watched Jenny's gaze go from one baby to the other in confusion. "I thought Karla said she was five pounds."

"*Kate's* five. But our second daughter is down the hall in the NICU. I can take you in there one at a time to meet her in a little bit." The new grandparents stared blankly at him and then Karla before their eyes grew wider as realization dawned. Carl reached out to grab the bassinet before he fell over.

"Triplets?" Jenny's incredulous tone made Adam smile. The woman didn't lose her composure often, but she seemed at a loss for words. Only for a moment, though, before she glared at Karla. "How could you keep something like that a secret?"

Karla just laughed. "I assure you, it was as much a surprise for us as it is for you. Even the doctor hadn't detected the third one. Apparently, during the ultrasounds she only saw one boy and one girl. Aurora was hiding behind them."

Tears flowed down Jenny's cheeks. She stroked Paxton's forehead. "May I?"

Karla nodded, tears overflowing from her eyes, too.

A visibly shaking Jenny took the little boy and bundled her first grandson before holding him in her arms. Carl comforted his wife as they huddled around Paxton.

Adam's thoughts strayed once more to the son he'd lost at birth. So much for keeping sad thoughts out of the room. Losing him without ever knowing him had been hard enough, but to have had a son for more than twenty-eight years, like the Paxtons had known Ian, and then lose him would have been unbearable.

But maybe Doc Palmer had been right all along, and his son's death had just been a very cruel accident that couldn't have been prevented regardless of what he and Joni had done in the months before his delivery. Guilt would plague him the rest of his life, though.

He glanced down at Kate, asleep on Karla's chest, and watched her tiny back rise and fall as she breathed. His vision blurred.

I'm so fucking blessed.

A squeeze on his shoulder brought his attention to the man standing beside him. "Thank you, Adam. You and Karla and these babies are going to make it possible for Jenny and me to return to the living again."

Seeing Carl crying, too, Adam refused to do a damned thing to hide the wetness on his own face.

"Your daughter did all the work. I'm so proud of her." Adam choked up, and his gaze shifted to Karla, who teared up as well. At least the babies hadn't joined in the bawl-fest yet.

A tentative knock on the door broke the awkward moment. He opened it to find Cassie. "You're back. Come on in."

She entered the room, and her gaze flew to Karla first then the babies.

"Cassie, come meet two of my babies."

"Two?"

"The third is in the NICU."

Cassie's hand flew to her mouth. "Then there *are* three?"

How did Cassie suspect three? They hadn't even told her about the twins.

Karla seemed a little puzzled, too, but didn't question her friend. "She's the smallest of the three. They're worried about her lungs."

"Do not worry about her, Kitty. I have seen you together with all three, and they were much older than newborns."

"You saw this and didn't warn me?"

"I thought perhaps you were going to have your pregnancies really close together, not that all three would be born at once."

After introducing Cassie to these two babies, Karla added, "I should have known keeping the news from you about our having twins was pointless, Cassie. You always know everything before I do."

No sooner had Jenny and Carl excused themselves to grab a bite of lunch when another knock had Adam waving Damián and his family inside. If the nurses found out they'd exceeded their four-guest limit, they may have a fit. *Ask forgiveness, not permission.*

Damián and Savannah walked over to the bassinet and took a peek.

"Madre de Dios! Dos!"

He met Adam's gaze, shock on his face. "We didn't stop there. There's another girl in the NICU. She just needed a little extra looking after. These two are Kate and Paxton, and the third one's Aurora, but we'll probably call her—"

Marisol squealed when she heard the name. "My own Princess Aurora! Wait 'til Emily finds out." He was happy she'd made friends easily, making her move to Denver a smoother transition.

Damián grinned. "I guess I don't have to ask where that name came from."

Adam cocked his head to one side. "Marisol had you watching the video, too, apparently."

His adopted son nodded. "A few times."

"*Maman*, may I hold one of the babies? Please?"

"No, dear, not just yet. Let's wait until they're a little bigger."

Marisol stuck out her lower lip, but quickly forgot about her request when she reached out to stroke Kate's cheek.

Karla said, "Savannah, I'm okay with her holding one if she's sitting down. She'll probably be babysitting them in a few years."

"If you're sure."

"Absolutely. Mom says babies are tougher than you think, so I don't want to coddle them."

Marisol jumped into the chair, her short legs bouncing in midair over the edge in anticipation. Adam brought over some pillows to stuff around her. Savannah placed Kate on her lap. Hell, a seven-year-old kid could hold one, but he still hadn't. What was his problem?

"She's all wrinkly," Marisol observed.

"Well, she's been in water for a long time, dear." Savannah smiled apologetically at Karla.

Knowing Damián hadn't met his daughter until she was seven years old, Adam asked him, "Why don't you pick up Paxton? You'll probably need the practice soon."

Damián's gaze went between Savannah's and then Adam's faces. "You know something I don't, Dad?"

"No, but I have no doubt you'll have more kids. You two are naturals at parenting. Now, meet your new little brother."

Unlike Adam, Damián had no qualms about picking up the baby. Must have been his practice as an uncle to Rosa's kids. Why couldn't Adam pick him up? What was he so fucking afraid of?

Adam placed his finger under the rim of the knit cap and lifted it. "Check out all this hair."

"Wow. And black as…Marisol's." The younger man had to clear his throat. Another tough Marine just hit his knees, figuratively speaking, felled by a tiny baby. Damián held the baby a little tighter and didn't take his eyes off Paxton's face. Adam let him bask in the moment, experiencing a small bit of what he'd missed.

"With his grip, he'll be playing baseball in no time. But I won't unbundle him to prove it."

"Takes after Kitty." Adam turned to Cassie, a wistful expression on her face as she gazed at Karla. "She also holds on and does not let you go."

Adam knew that feeling.

Karla smiled. "Cassie, why don't you head down to the NICU with Adam to meet Aurora *Casandra* Montague?"

Cassie stared first at Adam, probably not too keen about having to go through him to meet the remaining baby. Then she turned to Karla.

"Casandra?" Cassie swallowed hard, visibly moved. "Truly? She shares part of my name?"

"Just as you will always share a part of my heart, Cassie. Sorry I've been so busy lately, but I wanted you to know how much you mean to me. You're my sister from another mother."

Seeing Cassie blinking away tears surprised Adam. She really did love Karla and had been a loyal friend all these years. Everyone should be so lucky to have a friend like her.

"Kitty, I don't know what to say."

"You don't have to say anything. Just go see her for me. They won't let me out of bed until later today."

"Ready when you are, Cassie," Adam said. "I haven't been to see her in more than an hour. I'm anxious to see how she's doing." Adam crossed the room and held the door for her. She gave him a wide berth.

Damn it, he was going to win this woman over if it killed him. Cassie loved Karla almost as much as he did. Karla loved her, too. Cassie had to be worth the effort to get to know better. Time to figure out a way to do it. Maybe the babies could be the bridge.

Chapter Nine

C assie tried to tamp down her irrational fear, but the man strolling down the hallway beside her set off warning bells she had learned not to ignore again. Adam had never done anything to hurt her. However, she needed to be cautious.

"I appreciate you coming up here today. Means a lot to Karla."

She would suffer being with Adam because of Kitty. If this was the way she could get in to meet her namesake, then so be it. But she sensed that Adam wanted her to go with him, as well. He seemed a bit insecure when it came to the babies. Somehow, that made him less threatening.

"I would not have missed this for the world."

Aurora Casandra.

Tears pricked the backs of her eyelids. Nothing could have surprised her more than hearing they had chosen to honor her in such a way. And triplets! What a shock that must have been for the new parents.

"I will talk with Kitty's friends and family and make sure someone is with her and the babies at all times during these first few weeks."

"That would help a lot. Karla's been through so much, and I want to be sure she's getting as much rest as possible."

She would decide what to do later. Now, she needed to meet the third baby and help however she could until Kitty and all of the babies were home. Apparently, this tiny one could be here for weeks, though. The separation would be difficult for her friend.

Adam showed the nurse his wristband, and she scanned it before allowing them both inside the NICU. They scrubbed their hands and forearms before suiting up in gowns, gloves, and masks. The nurse led them to the isolette where the tiny baby slept with patches covering her eyes to keep out the bright light. Seeing the baby naked except for a diaper, Cassie wondered why she wasn't tucked in a blanket.

Her skin was red and wrinkled. Cassie's heart constricted at the sight of the beautiful little girl. She reached in and stroked the baby's forehead.

"Keep fighting, little one. Life is worth it."

The nurse said, "She'll be fine. The lights are to prevent jaundice, but her lab work and vital signs are all good so far. We're rotating her to a new position every two hours."

Adam reached out tentatively and stroked the baby's foot. The infant jerked away from his finger.

"I think she's ticklish," Adam remarked.

The isolette was warm inside, so Cassie worried less about her being cold. "So soft."

When Adam did not respond, she gave him a sidelong glance and saw tears in his eyes. Something melted in her heart to see the usually brusque, no-nonsense man reduced to tears at the sight of one of his newborn daughters.

Without thought, she reached up to touch his arm. When realization came, she forced herself not to pull away. Adam needed reassurance. "She will be joining her siblings in no time."

He nodded. "I hope you're right."

"All will be fine." Cassie sensed Adam was one to worry about every-one in his life. He certainly was overprotective when it came to Kitty.

Everything had to be okay. Kitty said Adam had lost a baby before.

Mama Quilla, please protect this and all of their little ones as they journey through this earthly plane.

Adam was a watchful guardian and protector, so like *Papá* and Edu-ardo. Cassie had always seen *Papá* in Adam's green eyes. After lying to her parents by not telling them what happened with Pedro and his cronies, and then returning to New York City earlier than planned, she had been riddled with shame and guilt whenever she glanced at Adam's censuring scrutiny in the photo on Kitty's desk. Of course, he was not looking at Cassie, but those stern eyes had made her uncomfortable anyway, reminding her of how she had failed her parents.

Perhaps she should have been honest with *Papá*, but telling him about that night would have forced him to either seek revenge, or worse, to keep Cassie under wraps at home. There was always the real possibility she might have been blamed for going to the cantina with Pedro. Her stomach clenched. If she had been unable to escape to New York, she could not have survived in her Peruvian village without shriveling up and dying. She shuddered.

"Cold?"

She brought herself back to the moment. "Just felt a little draft," she lied. "At least Aurora Casandra is warm."

Staring into Adam's eyes confirmed her suspicions. In the past, every time she had come face to face with the man or his photo, she had not been able to shake the feeling of being scrutinized—and found lacking. But it was her *papá's* disdain she had sensed, not Adam's. She hadn't realized the resemblance between the two men and their skin tone and green eyes until she painted the portrait of her parents and saw that his eyes were so similar to Adam's.

The new *papá* beside her moved his hand and tapped Aurora's closed fist with his pinky finger. She opened her tiny, wrinkled hand to latch onto him. "Definitely as strong as the other two."

Adam said, "Like Karla," at the same moment Cassie said, "Like Kitty."

He cleared his throat and continued in a whisper. "I think you're right. Rori's going to be just fine."

Rori. She liked the nickname. She would still remember the baby's full name.

But the pride and love in his voice melted any remaining irrational resistance she had to Adam. The time had come for her to open her heart to the man who made Kitty happy and fulfilled. "You are going to be a wonderful father, Adam. Just as you have been a good husband to Kitty."

Adam's gaze sent her back to the past, leaving her longing for *Papá* before she centered herself once again in the present.

"Thank you, Cassie. I'd give up my life for any one of my family members, and that includes you because you're a sister to my Karla."

Cassie blinked away the tears, but they spilled anyway. A crushing weight lifted off her shoulders. Perhaps the time had come for her to stop painting all men with the same brush of evil she used for Pedro, Luis, and Diego.

There *were* good men in the world—Adam Montague was one of them.

And Lucas Denton, another.

* * *

"How are Gracie and Millie doin'?"

Cassie looked up from her pressed-paper cup of coffee to find Lucas towering over her. Her heartbeat ramped up before she reminded herself he was not a threat, even at his imposing height. She had chosen this table in the corner, facing into the cafeteria, so she would notice anyone approaching but had been too absorbed in her thoughts about Kitty's babies to pay attention to her surroundings. Not wise. Although with Lucas, she felt more safe than scared.

"Milagrosa's doing fine. Graciela's a wonderful mom." Cassie's throat grew tight. Seeing Kitty's three precious babies churned up feelings she did not know she had inside her. Motherhood was something she would never experience herself.

"Mind if I join you?"

"No, of course not!" She picked up her purse and hooked the strap over the back of her chair. "I am sorry."

Lucas took the only other seat at the table, at a ninety-degree angle to her, and sipped from his cup as they sat in silence for a few moments.

"They sure have their work cut out for them. Triplets. Damn."

The words came out before she thought. "Have you ever thought about having kids of your own, Lucas?" A fraction of a second later, Cassie realized that she had given him a life sentence with a woman who did not want to have his children. "I am sorry. I forgot about—"

He waved his hand in the air. "Don't apologize. Tell you the truth, back then the thought of being a dad scared the piss out of me."

She wanted to crawl under the table with embarrassment twice over now. She had not been referring to the loss of his unborn baby, either. If she had been sleeping better, perhaps she would not be so careless.

"I plan to be one of several doting uncles to Adam's three—and to Marisol, too."

Cassie nodded, thankful he did not put any pressure on her to be a true wife, as if pressure from him would change the situation any. "I am going to be the best aunt I can be to those babies. I so miss seeing my own niece and nephews grow up. Eduardo's wife is due this month with their fourth."

"So Eduardo made it home okay?"

Cassie nodded.

"What did your parents think of the portrait?"

"They have not seen it yet. It is for their anniversary next month. I feel a little guilty that I am not presenting it to them in person." Until now, she had no desire to be at the celebration, but strange feelings were stirring within her. She missed her family.

"You'll visit when the time is right. I assume they know we're married. How'd they take the news?"

"*Mamá* cried. She told *Papá* for me. He does not like to Skype. But in later conversations, she told me he hoped to meet you someday."

She furrowed her brow, unable to imagine that time ever coming. She still did not wish to return to Peru, with or without Lucas. Heat rose in her face, and she avoided making eye contact with him.

Shame.

At least only Kitty and Angelina knew about her past. Neither would share that information with Lucas.

"Why don't we have supper together again when things settle down here?" She felt ashamed of herself, too, for shirking her promise to have dinner with him occasionally. So far, she had only met with him once for dinner two weeks ago.

"I am not sure when that will be, but I will let you know soon."

Lucas nodded, as if he trusted her to follow through. She would this time. Once she settled back into her routine.

Lucas drained his cup. "After I visit upstairs, I'm going to head back down to the ranch. Need to get in the workshop and make a special bed for the babies to share. I'll check on the alpacas on the way so you can have more time here."

She gazed at Lucas's face. Why did he always have to be so nice? "Actually, I cannot do much while Kitty and the babies are in the hospital, but I could definitely use your help when she and the babies go home. She is going to need all of us pitching in to help, I am sure."

"Just to make sure I don't put my foot in it upstairs, have you told anyone about our marriage?"

How could he call it a marriage? She glanced down at her bare left ring finger. She had removed the ring soon after the wedding, although for some reason she carried it in her purse. She glanced at Luke's finger and saw he still wore his.

Cassie shook her head. "No. Our arrangement would be too complicated for them to understand and so much has been going on with everyone." She reached across the table to tap his ring. "Would you mind terribly not wearing this around them? I fear someone will notice and remark on it."

He shrugged, but did not move to take the ring off. "I meant my vows, Cassie. If anyone notices and asks, I'll say something about my wife, and they can draw their own conclusions. Most will probably think I'm referring to Maggie."

Cassie pulled her hand back to a safer distance. Was she wrong in refusing to acknowledge this man as her husband by law?

No.

"It is not right that I am tying you down to something you only agreed to in order to please my parents."

"Don't be puttin' words into my mouth, darlin'. I very much want you as my wife."

He wanted her? *Why?* She sighed. "I can never be a wife other than on that piece of paper we signed."

"I'm a patient man."

More like a saint.

"Lucas, you deserve much better."

He grinned. "You don't hear me complaining, do you? I'm also optimistic. Have dinner with me this week before Karla goes home."

She nibbled her lower lip, unsure why she did not turn him down immediately. "You also are a *good* man."

"Tryin' my best. I was a Boy Scout, after all." His grin disarmed her. "Besides that, I had a momma who'd kick my ass if I was anything but a gentleman."

She smiled. "Your mother must be very special."

"Oh, that she is. Come down to my place next month, and you can meet her yourself."

Cassie glanced down at her cup. "No, I do not think I should do that."

"Even with Momma as a chaperone?" he teased. "Hell, we've been alone in a much smaller place without anything happening." He paused, and his voice became more serious. "You know you can trust me, Cassie."

When she met his gaze again, she saw his grin had faded.

You ask too much of me, Lucas.

"I should head home now. I'm sure Graciela is missing me."

"Don't run yourself down, Sweet Pea. Glad you're going to get home before dark."

She saw genuine caring in his eyes. Suddenly uncomfortable, she stood and slid the chair back, letting its legs squeak along the linoleum. "Thank you again for the offer to help with the alpacas in the coming weeks. I will let you know when I need you there."

He stood and nodded. "You have my number. Use it. Anytime you need me, just call or text. I'm only ten miles away from your place and happy to help out. Not much else I can do in this whole baby thing but make baby beds and take care of *your* babies."

"That means a lot to me, and I know it will to Kitty and Adam, too." For some reason she could not put her finger on, she was reluctant to part from him. She had to admit she missed having him to talk with, not realizing how quiet and lonely it was on her mountain.

But she did not need the complication of a man in her life. "Be careful on the roads, too, Lucas." The thought of anything happening to him hurt her heart. He had been through so much already.

"You, too, darlin'."

Feeling awkward, she walked away, but Lucas fell into step beside her. Her body responded to his nearness. Heart racing, chest tightening, breath quickening. Why would being near someone as safe as Lucas trigger her fight-or-flight response?

When they reached the main lobby, he said goodbye again, and she watched him make his way to the elevators to go up and visit. She suffered a pang of regret that nothing more than a superficial friendship could ever exist between them, despite the certificate of marriage that should have promised more.

She still had the slip of paper on which Lucas had handwritten their vows. She had reread them more than once. Perhaps when things settled down, she would make an effort to try harder to live up to her end of this arrangement and have dinner with the man again.

Most certainly, Lucas Denton deserved something in return for all he had sacrificed for her.

*   *   *

Four days later, Cassie joined Kitty to help her prepare to leave the hospital.

"Kitty, let me help." Cassie hoped she was helping, at least, given how little she knew about human babies. She opened the diaper bag and pulled out two tiny diapers while Kitty unsnapped Paxton's sleeper, his feet in perpetual motion. "The nurse should be here with the wheelchair soon. I know you will be happy to go home."

"Yeah, but it's torture leaving Rori behind. We'll be torn between spending as much time as possible here in the NICU, and at home with her siblings. I hate that they will be separated so long at such a young age."

"Do not worry. Even if decades and thousands of miles separate these babies, they have an invisible, indestructible cord attaching their hearts to one another. The Universe will continue to move through their lives and keep them emotionally close, no matter what."

Kitty brushed away a tear. "This is the hardest thing I've ever done, Cass." Her voice had grown husky with her tears.

Cassie kept one hand on Kate, who patiently awaited her turn, while stroking Kitty's back with the other. "It will only be a few weeks. Just concentrate on all the happy years you have to come with your children. Giving Aurora a healthy start in life is the most important thing now."

"I know. Mom was right. Motherhood sure isn't for wimps. I worry about everything now."

Cassie could only imagine. She looked forward to experiencing the joy of motherhood vicariously through Kitty's wee babies. Such precious gifts. How one mother could care for three babies was beyond Cassie's comprehension, though.

"It is good your mom's going to stay the rest of the week to help you settle into a routine."

Kitty laughed. "You and Adam with your talk of routines. I don't know that there will ever be anything routine about life with triplets." She fastened the last of the snaps covering Paxton's legs. "Next."

Cassie changed places with Kitty and swaddled Paxton the way the nurse had taught her while the new *mamá* changed Kate's diaper. Picking up and holding Paxton pulled at heartstrings Cassie thought had been severed long ago.

"Hi, precious little boy. *Tía* Cassie is going to spoil you rotten." She had spent the night in Kitty's house last night, but slept on the sofa rather than her friend's bed. Everything was as ready as it could be for the new family.

"May I join the club?" Cassie glanced up as Angelina entered the room. She, too, had been here every one of the past four days, usually bringing delicious meals for everyone to feast on. Angelina was empty-handed today. Undoubtedly, a feast had been prepared to welcome them home.

Angelina pinched Paxton's cheek affectionately. "Ah, *bambino mio.* Here's another auntie ready to commence spoiling you."

"Hey, you two, don't forget that you'll go home eventually, and I'll have to be the mean-old-mommy who has to correct all that spoiling." Kitty wrapped Kate tightly and waved a hand toward Angelina. "Oh, heck. I guess you can spoil this one a little bit, too, while I pack the last of my toiletries. Adam is probably waiting at the door downstairs for us already."

Angelina smiled and accepted the sweet bundle. "Come to *Zia* Angie." She cooed at the baby before growing serious and turning toward Kitty. "My biological clock is going to go haywire, you know. Marc and I might have to move up next year's wedding date if we're not careful."

"Don't rush it, Angie," Kitty said. "You have plenty of time to have babies. Enjoy this time with Marc."

Cassie envied her friends and their bliss-filled lives. Did they know how blessed they were to have been granted the gift of love and family?

You could have that, too, Cassie.

Fortunately, her covetous musings were interrupted when the door swung open and a nurse pushed a wheelchair into the room. "Mrs. Montague, I believe there is one impatient Marine waiting at the hospital entrance to collect his new family...well, most of it."

Soon, they had Kitty seated with Paxton in his car seat on her lap. Cassie carried Kate in the car seat while Angelina slung the diaper bag and overnight bag over each shoulder and picked up the remaining flower arrangement. Adam had taken three other potted plants to the SUV earlier. Maybe Cassie could help plant the hardy azaleas at Kitty's new house after it finished blooming. Kitty would not have time for gardening for a while.

Thank God, they did not live at his sex club any longer. Cassie had always been afraid to venture from her guest room there for fear of seeing some man wandering the halls naked, or nearly so, a dominated woman in tow—or worse yet, on a leash.

"Dominance isn't a need of mine, although there are aspects of being a Dom that are innate in me."

She shuddered at the disturbing image of Lucas leading an oppressed woman on a leash like that. All the more reason to keep their relationship on a friendship-only basis.

But Kitty wore no collar, and she had never seen Adam treat her with anything but love and respect. Besides, Kitty would never exchange the pretty necklace made of Black Hills gold that he had given her on their honeymoon for a dog collar. Cassie had not seen Kitty without that necklace since she had returned to Denver in January.

Forty minutes later, the newborn brother and sister were snuggled together in a single bassinet in Kitty's new bedroom. This enormous house had felt rather cold and impersonal at the wedding, but even in the short time Kitty had been here before going into labor, the place already had a family vibe to it. Soon it would be filled with the squeals and laughter of three children.

You are so fortunate, Kitty.

A real marriage with children was not part of Cassie's life chart this time around.

Kitty's gaze never left her two sleeping babies. She smiled. "They'll outgrow this arrangement all too soon. Luke is coming by today with something that all three can share once Rori comes home."

Cassie moved over to stand beside her. Paxton had his arm stretched over his sister in a protective way. She remembered when she and Eduardo had been that close.

But she did not wish to think about him now. "You know what they say, Kitty. *Mamá* should sleep when her baby—or babies—do."

"I know, but I'm not tired, and there's so much to do."

"You must follow doctor's orders. Now, lie down."

Kitty sighed and moved toward the bed. "Yes, ma'am." She still moved gingerly from her incision.

Cassie pulled a coverlet over her. "You have enough baby items to last a year, and we will be adding more when we have your shower next week. Since they will not be sleeping in a crib for a while, this cozy arrangement is perfect." Their bonding with one another was so important to Kitty. If only she could see, they had already formed that bond *in utero*. "While you rest, I will go see if your *mamá* needs any help. I will bring your lunch up so you do not have to go downstairs."

"Thanks, Cassie. I don't want to leave them alone yet, even though I have monitors and receivers all over the house compliments of Grant."

Cassie nodded. "This is why I am here."

"Are they still sleeping?" Adam whispered as he entered the room and checked on the babies before removing his shoes and joining Kitty in the bed. His hand rested just below her breasts, and he placed a kiss on her cheek.

Their display of intimacy made Cassie uncomfortable. "I will return with lunch in a little while." Is that what Lucas wanted her to do? Let him cuddle her like that? Clearly, Adam had no expectation of having sex. He only wanted to be close to his wife.

"Thank you, Cassie," Kitty said, although she only had eyes for her husband.

Cassie made her exit quickly, hearing Kitty remark on the way out, "Oh, Adam, did you notice how Paxton has his arm around Kate?"

Tears stung Cassie's eyes. What a beautiful life Kitty had.

Would Cassie have been a good mother if she had been blessed with a traditional marriage? Memories of the evil on Pedro's face as he raped her assured her she had dodged a bullet, as Americans said. At least she had learned his true nature before she had been saddled to him in marriage.

Beside me and apart from me…
asking that you be no other than yourself.

Oh, Lucas.

Memories of the vows they had exchanged last month haunted her nights and now even her days. Could she ever open up to him? Would he accept her as she was if he knew of her past?

She shook her head. *No.* He must never know the truth about her. She needed to remain cold and elusive to keep him at a distance—to protect him more than herself.

*   *   *

Luke rang the doorbell. Seemed strange that this was no longer Marc's place, but his friend was right to leave here. He'd never been happy here. Adam and Karla would be able to turn it into a real home with their new babies.

The door opened, and he was surprised to find Cassie on the other side.

"Hey, darlin'. How've you been?"

The familiar wariness crossed her features. He kept hoping she'd come to accept him without being so cautious all the time, but with how little they saw each other, he didn't see how he could ever win her over.

"Fine. Please come in."

"Let me just run to the truck and get what I came to deliver."

"Do you need any help?"

"Maybe. Do you have a minute?"

She nodded and followed him. "Thank you for taking care of my babies, Lucas. How are they adjusting?"

"They love it out in my fields. Lots of room to roam around and graze. I take them into the barn at night, of course." He didn't want her to think they were at the mercy of any predators.

"I am sure they are happy there. They adapted quickly when I moved them to the mountain, too. As long as they are together, they are happy."

If only their momma could adapt as well to being around him. He lowered the tailgate and pulled the heavy blanket on the bed of the truck toward him. On it laid the unique crib he'd just finished last night covered by a tarp and bungee cords. He left the tarp over it, not wanting to reveal anything yet.

"You tell me if it's too heavy, now." He lifted the heavier end, and Cassie grabbed the other. He'd made this quickly in a primitive style, but knew they needed it sooner rather than later. Already he was working on a special rocking chair that would accommodate the new momma and all three of her babies at once. He'd try to finish working on that over the next few weeks, though.

They maneuvered the bed inside the foyer and set it down.

"Kitty is taking a nap right now. I will be taking her lunch soon, so you can show this to her then. Would you like something to eat?"

"Sounds great. I haven't had a bite since five this morning."

He followed her and sat at the bar behind the stove island. Watching Cassie move around the kitchen, pulling leftovers out of the fridge, reminded him of their time at her cabin.

Jeezus, I've missed her.

"Where's Mrs. Paxton?"

"Oh, she wanted to shop for a few more things. The early births caught us all by surprise."

"I'll bet."

They discussed the alpacas and horses and the upcoming gallery exhibit preparation before they finished eating in companionable silence.

After lunch, he helped her carry two trays up to the bedroom for Karla and Adam. They caught the two of them cuddled in bed. He hoped the couple knew how lucky they were to have each other.

Adam awoke first and motioned for them to set the trays on the dresser. When one of the babies began to cry, Cassie went over and changed the diaper, then swaddled and lifted Kate to her shoulder.

Seeing her mothering the little thing caused his chest to tighten. He'd fantasized about one day having a real marriage with her, but if something didn't break loose, that was doubtful.

She carried the baby into the hallway and turned to him. "Let us go prepare Kate a bottle. I want Kitty to sleep as long as she can."

Back in the kitchen, she indicated with a jerk of her head for him to sit. When he did, she said, "Here. Hold her while I prepare the bottle."

"Whoa, darlin'! I've never—"

"There is nothing to it." She placed the baby in his arms and molded them around the baby's head and body until he cradled her like a football.

He gazed down at the bright-eyed little girl staring up at him. *Dayum.* Adam had to be over the moon when he held one of these babies. Luckiest man alive. A beautiful wife and three adorable babies.

Luke hadn't had a chance to get to know his and Maggie's baby. His throat closed up. Cassie returned to his side. "Would you like to feed her or have me do it?"

He met her gaze and saw her through a haze of tears, but managed to reach for the bottle. "I'll do it."

Cassie narrowed her gaze. "Are you okay?"

"Sure." He placed the bottle to the little angel's lips and watched her latch on and suckle. "Kate, I'm going to take you for your first horseback ride. You come visit Uncle Luke anytime you want." He continued to carry on a conversation with her, oblivious to everything until the bottle was dry. As if he'd done it all his life, he lifted her onto his shoulder as he'd seen others do and patted her back until she let out a loud burp.

"You did that like a pro."

He grinned at Cassie. "Nothin' to it."

A few hours later, with Adam's help, he carried the special bed up to their room. "I might have gotten a little carried away."

Karla smiled from her bed where she sat propped up. "I can't wait to see it, Luke."

They set it down in the alcove near the old bassinet, and Luke removed the tarp. "Oh, my gosh! It's beautiful!"

The half-moon shaped bed, with tiny star cutouts, as well as some carved raised ones, would be plenty wide enough to hold all three babies for a while. The babies were placed inside on the store-bought mattress covered in a crib sheet that carried over the moon and stars theme.

"When the babies are older, it can be converted into a place for one or two of them to crawl into and play, read, or whatever. If they don't want to share, I can make one or two more later."

"Adam, please help me up. I want to see them inside."

Adam went to her and lifted her into his arms. He carried her over to the bed where Luke and Cassie stood and set her on her feet. "Look! They're kissing each other! Oh my gosh! Where's my phone?"

While they searched to find something to record the moment, Luke glanced inside. Sure enough, with their arms and legs bound inside the blankets, they'd found the only place of contact was their faces. Kate looked like she was sucking on the blue-blanketed Paxton's chin more than kissing him, though. Probably hungry again.

Karla turned to him and gave him a hug. "Luke, you are so amazing. Thank you so much for making this for us."

"Cassie told me how important it was for you to have them sleep together. I know I got a little carried away with the design—"

"No! It's perfect! I love the thought of them sleeping inside the crescent moon."

"I love the moon design, Lucas. Makes me think of *Mama Quilla* watching over them." He turned to Cassie who smiled at him. Well, he'd scored with her, too. *Hot damn.* "It really is beautiful."

Not nearly as beautiful as you, darlin'.

Chapter Ten

Karla felt another wave of dizziness as she placed Paxton next to Kate after nursing him. She gripped the sides of the half-moon baby bed Luke had delivered yesterday. Soon, the room stopped spinning, but she'd mention it to Mom or Adam when they brought her lunch upstairs. Perhaps she wasn't eating enough to keep up with the demands of feeding three babies. Between nursing these two and expressing milk for Rori and some to freeze, she probably needed to eat more. Already, she had to supplement with formula sometimes when she couldn't keep up with those demanding little mouths.

She stroked Paxton's hair as he slept beside Kate. Coal black like her brother's.

"Oh, Ian, I wish you could see your namesake."

Maybe he could, from the other side. *Cassie says our loved ones never really leave us. We just can't see them anymore.*

She'd never even felt his presence since he died. Maybe she just wasn't reading the signs. So much had happened since he was killed. Just in case he was listening, she'd continue to talk to him as if he were here.

With both babies sleeping, now would be a good time to catch one of those catnaps Doctor Palmer insisted she take. She'd never been so exhausted in her life as she had been since the arrival of these babies.

Tonight, the family planned to gather for dinner to celebrate Adam's fifty-first birthday. Of course, Adam hadn't wanted anyone making a big fuss over him turning a year older two days ago, so they had kept it small. Mom had ordered the cake and bought ice cream for after dinner. Angie was preparing another wonderful meal.

Karla had two gifts tucked away in her dresser drawers. She had insisted on being the one to unpack the bedroom boxes last week to make sure Adam didn't find her hiding places.

One of the gifts she could present to him after dinner tonight with the family gathered around. It was very much a family friendly gift with lots of meaning. She wished his mother could be here, but Patrick promised to fly her down for the baby shower next week. The early arrival of the triplets had upset a lot of people's plans.

However, the other gift was for them to share in a private moment. She giggled. Good thing she'd thought to have the gifts finished early. Luke had been a willing accomplice putting the finishing touches on the private present. He had been at the house on move-in day, looking into what it would take to make a soundproof studio for Karla to record her music. Adam had insisted there be a place for that in the new house, not that she was going to have time to sing much more than lullabies in the coming months.

Wanting to check to make sure the gifts were still tucked away in the back of the dresser drawers, Karla pivoted and started to walk around the king-sized bed when something warm ran down her legs. Glancing down, she saw blood pouring from her body. She reached for the bedpost when her abdomen seized up with a sharp cramp.

No! This couldn't be happening!

Her knees buckled, and she crashed down onto them, jarring her insides with a sudden jolt of searing pain. Tears burned her eyes as she wrapped her arms around her belly.

"Adam, help me!" Was the baby monitor on in the dining room downstairs where he and Mom were folding laundry? He might have turned it off, knowing she was with the babies. Her head grew light as black spots danced before her eyes. Losing her balance, she pitched forward.

"Someone hurry! Something's wrong!"

Karla's head hit the floor seconds before her world went black.

*   *   *

Adam had no clue how two tiny little human beings could generate so much laundry. Of course, they'd have more clothes to go through after the baby shower the girls had planned. The babies would be nearly two weeks old by then. In some ways, it seemed like they'd been here forever; in others, he could see the time passing by too quickly.

He couldn't blame the shortage of clothing on having triplets instead of twins, though, because Rori was still in the NICU. She wouldn't be released for at least three weeks. But she'd gained an ounce since her birth. Maybe she'd reach the five-pound mark before then. Not wanting to wait that long and disrupt everyone's plans, Karla insisted they go with the original date for the shower.

In the meantime, everyone was pitching in to make sure the babies had what they needed. Cassie had run to the store a few minutes ago to stock up on more disposable preemie diapers. The babies went through those like wildfire, too.

After Karla's nap and another feeding for Kate and Paxton, he'd drive her to the hospital to see Rori. She took to being a mother like a duck to water. He just wished he'd been doing as well on the fatherhood front.

He folded a Kelly-green undershirt. Karla didn't want them dressed in anything too pale. At least she was out of her own black phase. He preferred to see her in red. "Babies sure go through clothes fast, Jenny."

His mother-in-law gave a laugh. "I think their mommy is enjoying the novelty of dressing and undressing them, too. She did that with her stuffed kitties, too, when she was little. This phase will wear off quickly when she has to take up the laundry duties herself."

Adam didn't want Karla doing anything but taking care of the babies. Watching her feeding them turned his insides to jelly every time. When Jenny returned home to Chicago next week, he'd take on the household chores. Cassie needed to prepare for a gallery showing later this month. Surely, he could handle laundry. Angelina promised to keep them well-fed. And when Savannah wasn't busy with Marisol, she'd be a great help.

With Karla focusing solely on the babies, he'd be off the hook for having to hold them. The little things scared him to death. He'd yet to pick one of them up for fear of hurting or dropping them. He had rocked Paxton and Kate once, but only after Karla put them—one at a time—in his arms after he was already seated. Scared the piss out of him until she took them back.

Karla wanted him to man up, but what if something went wrong on his watch? Better safe than sorry.

The baby books sure made it all sound less complicated—no, make that less terrifying.

"Oh, Ian. I wish you could see your namesake."

The words coming through the baby monitor jarred Adam from his thoughts. He'd forgotten the thing was on. Jenny's hands stilled as she folded another tiny gown.

Aw, damn.

"Sorry, Jenny." He reached out and turned off the monitor, not sure what else Karla might say to her dead brother thinking she was having a private moment with two of their babies.

"I feel the same way she does." She met his gaze. "It means so much to Carl and me that you would name your son after the one we lost."

Adam gave up trying to figure out how to fold the fitted crib sheet. He stood and walked around the dining room table to where Jenny sat and wrapped his arms around her shoulders. "Ian topped our boy-names lists even before we knew we were having multiples. Good thing we didn't have three girls, though."

Jenny chuckled, which made Adam feel a little better. She focused again on folding the nightgown. "He'd have made a fantastic uncle."

Adam sat down next to her and reached for a wad of baby clothes from the basket. "No doubt. We'll make sure Paxton and the girls grow up knowing who their uncle was, especially that he was a brave American soldier who fought hard and proud for his country."

"I hope your Ian Paxton isn't the daredevil mine was. He always took so many risks." She shook her head.

Riding his motorcycle on rain-slick roads had led to Ian's death. Adam didn't want to think about all the near misses he'd had in his own life. Boys were natural daredevils. Would he want to curb Ian's natural exuberance and kill his spirit?

No, but I don't want him getting killed either.

Good thing he had two daughters. That should be easier—well, except for having to crush the balls of any teenage boy who came within a football field of one of them.

Fatherhood was a lifelong commitment. He hadn't yet grown used to the idea that he not only had a baby son but two daughters now. They'd be a part of his life for as long as he had left on this earth.

How many years did he even have left? Thirty, if he was lucky. Nothing scared Adam more than the thought of something bad happening to one of his kids—or to Karla. But what if he wasn't around for them when they needed him? Fuck, he'd just turned fifty-one.

Fucking fate had better not take anything else he loved from him.

Adam and Jenny worked on in silence a few more minutes. Adam's hand went to the back of his neck where he rubbed his scar. He froze. He hadn't done that in a long time. Maybe it was just all this talk of Ian Paxton and thoughts about his own kids growing up.

He thought he heard something fall upstairs. "Did you hear that?"

"What?"

"I don't know. Maybe Karla needs something." Adam reached for the monitor switch and turned it on again. Silence. Too bad they didn't have a two-way radio. Maybe he'd see if Grant could set up—

"Someone hurry! Something's wrong!"

Adam dropped the baby clothes and leapt from the chair running into the hallway. The pounding heartbeat in his ears drowned out the sound of his feet on the steps. Had one of the babies stopped breathing?

Not again. Please, God, you can't take another one of my babies.

No sound came from the bedroom when he entered and scanned the room. No crying babies, no Karla.

"Kitten, where are you?"

He checked the bathroom. Empty. The whimper of one of the babies sent him around the bed toward the sound only to find Karla lying on her side in a pool of blood.

"Jenny! Call 911! Karla's unconscious! And bleeding!"

He knelt beside her, afraid to touch or move her. Jenny was the nurse. She'd know what to do. "Kitten, can you hear me?"

So pale. How long had she been lying here? She'd called out no more than a couple minutes ago, so she must have been conscious then.

So much fucking blood.

A strobe-light effect superimposed the scene with the one where his father had been shot, but no way could anyone have shot her. The discharge nurse had warned to watch for excessive bleeding, more than a pad every so many hours. Hell, this went well beyond a pad. Adam pulled the bedspread off the bed and covered her.

In combat, they would have used compression against the wound. Towels.

"Oh, my God! Karla!" Jenny soon took charge, thank God, and knelt on the other side of Karla, tilting her head to clear an airway. Why hadn't he done that? Hell, he couldn't think straight. Jenny took the pulse at Karla's carotid artery.

"Adam, I need some towels. All the clean ones you have."

He'd forgotten them already. Glad to have orders to follow, he stood and ran to the bathroom, pulling four towels from the closet. He also grabbed a box of Karla's feminine pads from under the sink, in case they might help, and brought everything back to Jenny.

"Help me turn her."

She had removed the comforter to examine Karla. Adam and Jenny gently laid her on her back, and the pool of blood continued to spread.

Stop the bleeding.

He froze once more.

Don't take her. The babies and I need her. Hell, take me. They need her more than me.

His bargaining with God was futile, but he'd gladly have taken a bullet to change places with her. He couldn't lose her.

"Hold her legs open for me."

Adam did as Jenny told him, Karla's legs limp in his hands. He tried not to look at all the blood smeared on the insides of her thighs. Instead, he focused on her face—so pale and still. Jenny worked efficiently to stanch the flow of any more blood. How could there be any more?

What if she bled out?

"If her uterus clamps down, it might stem the flow." Jenny pressed against the top of Karla's abdomen and massaged the area.

Where's the fucking ambulance?

Seconds later, the sound of sirens far in the distance gave him hope that they'd be here soon with all the modern equipment necessary to keep his wife alive.

"Hang on, Kitten. You're going to be fine."

You have to be. I can't go on without you.

He stroked her hair, but received no response.

Don't you dare die on me, Karla.

Yeah, make this about you, asshole.

One of the babies went from sound asleep to outright squalling. Did she sense the tension in the room? Adam glanced at Jenny, but she had her hands full taking care of Karla. He stood and walked over to the bassinet and jiggled it a little, hoping to calm down the baby. Hunter-green blanket—Kate.

"Shhh. You're okay. Mommy's…"

What? Going to be here in a minute? No.

If anything happened to Karla, what would he do with three mother-less babies?

Please, Kitten, don't leave us. Don't leave me.

At the moment, he was the only one who could comfort the crying baby. *Don't let me fuck this up.* He reached down and lifted the crying baby into the crook of his arm. He'd watched Karla do it a hundred times. Was he doing it right?

"That's enough."

His curt words only made Kate cry louder.

Okay, don't go master sergeant on her.

Well, how the fuck else was he supposed to act? He knew more about being a master sergeant than being Dad to a newborn. He glanced down at Karla again, feeling as though a tank had landed on his chest. He'd never been more terrified of anything in his life than losing her. He hadn't even been this scared when he lost Joni to cancer.

Don't leave us, Kitten. We all need you so much.

He rocked back and forth, finally holding Kate upright against his chest at which point she stopped crying. He pulled his cell phone from his shirt pocket and with the thumb of his free hand punched in Marc's number. No answer. He tried Damián's cell next, and Savannah answered. He must be nearby.

"Savannah, I need you or Damián to come to the house quick. Something's happened to Karla. We're waiting on the ambulance. I need someone to help with the babies."

"Oh, no! Do you want us at the house or the hospital?"

"House."

"We'll be there in twenty minutes."

"Fifteen!" he heard Damián shout in the background.

Adam ended the call and stared down at Kate again. She blinked several times and stared back as if expecting him to do something else. What did she want? He had no clue. Another bottle? Thank God they had stocked some formula for when Karla couldn't keep up with their needs.

Damn it, he hadn't expected a catastrophe like this. He'd have Jenny stay so she could let Savannah know where the formula was before joining her daughter at the hospital.

Hearing the siren cut off as the ambulance pulled into the drive, Adam had a more urgent duty. "I'll go let them in."

At least that he could do right. He walked down the grand staircase carefully, trying not to drop the baby. She seemed to like being on the move.

He reached the foyer and re-pocketed his phone to free up his hand before opening the door. Minutes later, he led two paramedics up the stairs to the bedroom. Jenny filled them in on her condition and then stood up to give them room to work. Jenny now seemed as helpless as he felt.

She stared blankly at Adam and Kate and then blinked. "Do you want me to take her?"

Adam held on to Kate a little tighter. "No, I have her."

I need her. She's a living part of my Karla.

"I'm glad you were here, Jenny." If it had been up to him, Karla might be dead already.

He needed to stop thinking about Karla dying. She was too young to die. His heart squeezed in his chest. She still might die. What the fuck had happened? She'd been fine this morning.

"I'll go grab a garbage bag for the towels," Jenny said to the paramedics.

Wanting Doc Palmer at the hospital as soon as possible, he rang her office and gave them the news. Again, he had nothing to do but watch as his unconscious, deathly pale wife was lifted onto a stretcher. Adam headed out of the bedroom and down the stairs to make sure the door was open for them. They carried her down, and his mind flashed back to when she'd been carried down on a harem litter not six months earlier. Their wedding day. His bride. Now she was being carried to him on a different kind of litter.

As they wheeled her past him, he stared down at her. They weren't doing CPR, so she wasn't dead. Was she? Or had they given up on her and just didn't want to tell him?

Jenny came up to him and took Kate from his arms. "Go with her. She needs you most. Keep talking to her. Don't let her leave us."

Let her? As if he had any control here. Adam nodded and followed the stretcher down the sidewalk to the driveway. Once Karla had been placed inside the ambulance, he climbed in and took her hand. So cold.

"Kitten. You're going to be okay."

You have to be.

"The babies and I need you. Fight your way back to us, hon."

He swayed as the ambulance took the corner out of the drive and sped toward the hospital, siren blaring. The paramedic across from him finished taking her vitals and adjusted her IV.

"Has the bleeding stopped?"

"The doctors will assess her in the labor and delivery area. Don't worry. We've alerted them to her condition and you and the woman at the house did everything you possibly could."

Jenny had kept Karla alive, no question about it.

"Keep talking to her."

Hearing Jenny's words prompting him, Adam leaned closer to Karla. "I picked up Kate all by myself. Got her to stop crying." *Eventually.* "I promise, when you come home, I'll stop being so afraid of them. I'll help out more with the babies." He smoothed her silky hair back from her face.

Had he left her to do too much too soon after giving birth? He'd tried to take on as much around the house as he could, short of hands-on care of the babies. Hell, they'd just moved into the house in the days before she'd gone into labor. Had she overdone it, secretly unpacking or lifting boxes, or something when he wasn't aware?

Please, God, don't take her away from us. We need her.

I need her.

*   *   *

Cassie located Kitty's mom in the surgery waiting room. "Mrs. Paxton, what can I do to help?"

Jenny gave Cassie a blank stare. "Nothing right now, Cassie. We'll just have to wait and see how quickly she bounces back after surgery. She's in recovery now. Adam's with her."

"What happened?"

"The obstetrician said the hemorrhage was caused by an overstretched uterus. They did a transfusion, and she's being given IV antibiotics to fight infection. Her blood pressure is almost back to normal."

Cassie had kept her distance from Adam, unable to process the intensely black energy around him now—a mix of anger and what could only be described as deep despair. This man could not suffer another loss. He'd been abandoned by the ones he loved so many times from what Kitty had told her. How would he survive if he lost Kitty?

Do not think like that.

"I'll talk with Angelina and Savannah. We will set a schedule so we can make sure the babies have someone at all times so you and Adam can focus on Kitty here." Cassie sat in the seat beside Jenny. Savannah and Damián were at the house now with Kate and Paxton.

"Thanks, sweetie. I'd like to take my turn, too. Those babies need Gramma time."

"Of course! I just know how exhausted you must be worrying about Kitty." After a pause, she asked, "What about Aurora Casandra?"

Jenny smiled, although her eyes remained sad and pain-filled. "Maybe they'll allow a couple of us to visit her in Karla's place. I'll talk with the nursing staff to see if any exception is possible. If not, we'll just ask Adam to take breaks from Karla's side and give us access to the NICU."

"When Kitty wakes, she will be pleased to hear that her babies have been well taken care of by her friends."

Jenny reached for her hand. "You know, Cassie, you're the only person Karla would allow to call her Kitty after college."

Cassie was not sure why she had changed the subject, but followed along. "Except for Adam."

Jenny laughed. Cassie hoped she was helping take her mind off things.

"Adam calls her Kitten. That's different."

"She never told me why Kitty was her nickname when we first met."

Jenny's smile turned wistful, and when Cassie saw tears in her eyes, she squeezed the older woman's hand.

"When she was little, she didn't play with dolls, but with stuffed animals instead—kittens and tigers, mostly. Her father is allergic to live cats, so we could never have one at the house. That was his concession, and he doted on her, always buying her more stuffed kittens. When her friends came to play, they soon began calling her Kitty after seeing her menagerie."

Jenny remained silent, lost in thought a moment. Then she blinked back to the present. Did Kitty remember that? She'd never mentioned it, although by sophomore year, she had rid herself of the nickname by all except Cassie. For whatever reason, she allowed her to continue to use the childhood moniker.

"Oh!" Jenny stood and reached for her phone on the coffee table. "I promised to call Carl at dinnertime and give him the update. I know he's worried sick and probably waiting by the phone."

Karla's dad had returned to work in Chicago yesterday, happy knowing his daughter and two of his grandchildren had gone home. He must be beside himself. Jenny headed out of the room in search of a private place to talk with her husband. He would probably be flying back to Denver soon. No parent could be away from his child when she was in such grave danger.

Restless, Cassie rose from the uncomfortable chair and walked down the hallway toward the nursery. She knew she wouldn't be able to see Aurora without Adam and his ID bracelet allowing her access. The NICU did not have observation windows, but seeing some of the other newborns would give her hope for Kitty and her babies.

Everyone was trying to give Aurora as much human contact as possible until she could come home. The doctor said that might be a few weeks, which frustrated Kitty immensely.

During these visits, Cassie had grown attached to Aurora Casandra. Until Kitty could be with her little ones again, Cassie would do all she could to fill in. She would call Lucas and let him know what was going on and that she might need to be here longer.

*   *   *

"Kitten, we need you. Don't leave us."

Adam. His muffled voice sounded as if he spoke through a pillow. Why would he think she would leave him and their three beautiful babies?

Distorted.

Dim.

Distant.

She wanted to reassure him he had her heart forever, but no words came from her mouth. Paralyzed, she was unable to control her own body anymore. As hard as she tried to lift her hand and seek out Adam, who must be nearby, she couldn't move.

Numb. No feeling either. Where was she? Her eyes remained closed. A blast of cold air hit her face.

"This might help her come out of the anesthesia."

Anesthesia? She'd been in surgery? For what? The babies had been born days ago, hadn't they?

An alarm sounded, and in a flash, she found herself up on the ceiling looking down at where she lay on a narrow hospital bed hooked up to tubes. Was this a dream? Why was she in the hospital again? What had happened?

"Sir, I'll need you to return to the waiting area."

"What's wrong?" Adam's voice was filled with worry. Fear.

Two men came and forced Adam to move away from her. "We need space to work on her. Wait outside. We'll call you when you can see her again."

No! Don't take Adam away! Karla screamed, but no one responded.

Adam stood there looking like a lost little boy. *Please, don't make him leave.* He'd been abandoned by everyone he ever loved. She needed to let him know she would not leave him. Not willingly.

"Sir, you can help your wife most by returning to the waiting room. We'll call when she's stable."

The anguish on Adam's face tore at her, but he relented and left. Activity increased around her bed as at least three people worked frantically on her at the same time.

Oh, God! Where are my babies? She remembered taking two of them home, so they must be there, but Rori had to stay in the hospital at least a few weeks. Cassie once told her she could ask the Universe to take her soul to another place. She'd never tried astral projection before, but had never wanted to be in two places at once more than in this moment.

"I want to see Aurora Montague. Take me to the NICU."

She waited. Nothing changed. She hovered just below the ceiling.

"Damn it! Take me to my baby!"

Did she just curse at God? Or was someone else holding the strings for her right now? Whatever, an instant later, her detached spirit floated through the wall and down the bustling hospital corridor. She soon turned down a hallway she recognized and knew the NICU was just around the corner.

"Mommy's coming, Rori."

She floated through the door and into the NICU, immediately homing in on her precious baby.

*   *   *

While waiting for an update on Kitty's condition, Cassie decided to go to the chapel rather than return to the waiting room. The place was empty and quiet at this hour, and she made do with two battery-operated candles on the altar to help her reach a meditative state.

Soon, her spirit separated from her heavy body behind and she willed herself upstairs into the NICU. This was the only way she could gain access to Aurora Casandra at the moment.

When her hand touched the baby's tiny foot, she responded with a kick. Cassie smiled. They were connected on this plane, too.

"Continue to grow, little one. Your *mamá* and *papá* love you very much." The baby's lips made sucking motions in her sleep.

"I hope you grow up in a world more accepting of your rights as a woman, *pequeña*." Cassie blinked. She didn't know what had led her to convey those words to a baby, even though she meant them. She patted Aurora's arm. "I have no doubt your *mamá* is going to make sure you are independent and strong, just like she is. You are a very lucky little girl."

But only if Kitty survived. Cassie and the others could never be more than a temporary substitute to the babies.

Oh, Kitty, come back to us.

Cassie hovered closer to the bassinet and startled when Kitty joined her. No, not Kitty. Her spirit. Or was it her soul?

"No, Kitty! It's not your time. Go back to Adam." She wanted to push her friend away, back to where her loving husband waited for her. Had she crossed over? "Adam loves you so much, and these babies need you. Go back to your body."

In a flash, Kitty disappeared.

Cassie willed herself to return to her own body. She needed to find out what had happened to Kitty.

*   *   *

Adam figured he'd be the one to go first, never imagining in his worst nightmare that Kitten would be at death's door so soon after giving life to their three children. This couldn't be happening. Not fucking again. He needed to get back in there with Karla. Needed to know what the hell was happening.

He pressed the intercom button incessantly until someone answered. It had only been minutes according to his watch, but felt like hours since they'd kicked him out of post-recovery. The person on the intercom surprisingly unlocked the door. Within a minute, he was approaching the place where he'd been with her a short time ago. A somber-faced nurse told him her blood pressure had bottomed out again, and she had to be resuscitated.

How much more could her body take?

She was strong, but she'd been through so much in the past week.

Adam took a seat beside her and brushed the hair away from her forehead.

Did she know he was here? She hadn't spoken a word since he'd found her lying on the floor in their bedroom last evening.

Jenny said to talk to her. Rather than plead with her again to not leave him, maybe he'd talk about the babies.

"I held Kate. Picked her right up when she was crying." Adam shuddered. He didn't want to think about why he'd had to pick her up. "We'll be taking Rori home soon, so you need to get out of here, too." Paxton and Kate alone overwhelmed him, especially when both started crying at once, but he wanted to have his family together again for the first time since the babies were born.

Adam had barely been able to breathe since this nightmare started. Being beside her and not feeling her vital spark of life reminded him of the time when Joni slipped away from him.

But Karla's not going to die. She can't.

Her eyelids flickered, and she opened them. But her unseeing eyes didn't focus, and she closed them again. He thought he detected more color in her cheeks in the past few minutes. Every now and then, her eyelids moved as if dreaming.

Adam breathed a little easier when they moved Karla to her room, but wished she would wake up. Sometimes she moaned, and he worried she was in pain, but still she didn't open her eyes again.

Adam took a break and let Jenny in to visit while he went to the NICU with Cassie. Like Jenny, she had been here all night.

"How is she?"

"Still sleeping." The nurse assured him she wasn't in a coma. They kept her heavily sedated to give her body time to heal from this ordeal.

"Savannah called this morning to say that everything is fine at the house and you are not to worry about the babies."

Hard not to worry with his family spread out so much. As much as he missed Kate and Paxton, he didn't want them in the hospital with all the germs. Savannah was a mom. She'd take good care of them. Angelina and Marisol were there to help, too, no doubt.

Before they reached the NICU, Cassie placed her hand on his forearm, and he halted. "Do not worry. She is not going to leave you or the babies."

Adam couldn't speak for the lump in his throat. "How can you be sure?" *He* certainly wasn't.

She shrugged. "I know. She chose to come back to you and her babies. She will fight this, but needs time for her body to heal."

Come back? From where?

"Thanks, hon. I hope you're right."

He showed his armband, and they went into the NICU to check on Aurora. God, he swore Aurora had gained weight since yesterday morning. Her skin wasn't yellow anymore, either, and when he reached out to rub his thumb on her forehead, she opened her eyes. Tears burned his eyelids. Karla's eyes.

He leaned close to the baby to whisper, "Your mommy says hi, too. Keep getting stronger so you two can be together again."

Anxious to return to Karla, he left Cassie in the NICU and returned to Karla's bedside. Jenny had her head face down on the mattress, her hand holding Karla's.

Adam rested his cheek on her forearm, one of the few places he wasn't afraid to touch her, as he stroked her upper arm.

Come back to me, Kitten.

Adam awoke with a start and looked around the room. Jenny was gone. Karla still slept. He hadn't intended to join her in sleep. A glance at his watch told him he must have been out for a couple of hours. Time to talk to her again.

"Aurora's jaundice is gone, Kitten. Betcha she'll be coming home in no time." What other news did he have? "Savannah's taking good care of Kate and Paxton, so don't you worry about them."

Doc Palmer came in and did a quick examination. She assured him Karla's body was on the mend. How could she tell? The doctor expected her to make a full recovery and said there shouldn't be any problem with her having more kids.

Fuck that shit. No more kids. Lots of people would kill to have three. He'd get a vasectomy before he'd put Karla through this hell again.

Adam willed Karla to open her eyes and talk to him again. Life without her was a lonely black hole.

Chapter Eleven

P axton squirmed in her arms and stared up at Savannah. So alert. She'd forgotten how observant—yet tiny—newborn babies were.

"Seeing you with a baby in your arms turns me on." Damián's words made her smile as he joined her.

She hoped they would know soon if her suspicions were correct, but her intuition told her she was carrying his baby. Again. When she returned to the clinic, she'd ask Dr. McKenzie to do the test. She didn't trust the over-the-counter ones.

If confirmed, that would mean perhaps another child had been conceived in the cave at Thousand Steps Beach, since they hadn't had sex again until their wedding night—gosh, only two weeks ago. So much had happened since then.

She grinned and turned to plant a kiss on Damián's cheek. No sense getting his hopes up until she knew for sure. Damián wanted to add to their family—and soon. They certainly had been making love often enough since settling into their new house. So if not now, then soon.

She turned to Damián. "Sit in the glider chair."

"I can't stay long. Heading to the shop. Just wanted to say goodbye and make sure you or the babies didn't need anything."

"I. Said. Sit."

He cocked his head. "What did you say, *Chica?*" When she didn't back down, he grinned and shrugged as he sat. "I do need to get to the shop soon. Have a new mechanic coming in for an interview."

When he was seated, Savannah walked over and placed Paxton in his arms.

"Hold Paxton for me." She placed him in her husband's arms. Seeing him hold a baby brought tears to her eyes. He was a natural, given how he hadn't hesitated at all in the hospital. When he met her gaze in Karla's hospital room, she had seen he'd been affected in the same way.

"I missed so much with Marisol." She didn't want to think about that now. Nothing could be done to bring back the past. She hadn't been ready to be with a man then. So much had changed this year, all because of Damián's love and patient guidance.

Hoping to lighten the moment, she said, "Mari weighed three pounds more."

He gazed down again. *"Madre de Dios."* His words were spoken in a reverent tone. Seeing how profoundly moved he was, she prayed she'd soon give him a newborn of his own to hold and cherish. He was such a good father to Mari.

Fifteen minutes passed while she changed Kate's diaper and sat on the bed, alternating glances between Kate and the man she loved holding Paxton. How she had ever found him again was a miracle, but to be married to him now and—

Mari scampered into the room, still dressed in her pajamas. *"Maman!* Can I hold one of them?"

"Sit in the middle of the bed, and I'll put Kate in your arms." With Mari situated far from the edge, Savannah placed the baby in her arms. She usually played with Barbie dolls rather than babies, but seemed to know just what to do.

"I know what I want for my birthday."

Savannah smiled. Maybe this year she would ask for a baby doll instead of—

"I want you and Daddy to order us some triplets from Dr. McKenzie."

"Whoa! Not so fast." What did Mari know about where babies came from? Probably nothing, if she thought you could just place an order for them.

Savannah met Damián's gaze, expecting him to be looking on in horror at the thought, but his sappy grin told her he might not object. He mouthed the words, "I'm game." She shook her head. Of course, multiples were rare. Karla and Adam had to be over the moon with their three, but if given the choice, Savannah preferred having one at a time.

Savannah's phone buzzed, and she pulled it from her pocket. Cassie. Karla was still unconscious. She sent up a quick prayer for her friend's recovery. She needed to be here with her babies, well, two of them at least.

"Hey, Pax. Take your fist out of your mouth and say hi to *Tío* Damo."

Savannah giggled. "It's a little early for them to speak, Sir."

Damián's gaze never left Paxton. "Well, he *is* speaking to me with his eyes." The two did seem to be locked in some silent communication. She and Damián sometimes communicated that way, too. A shiver coursed down her spine.

And her heart melted. *Please let me be pregnant. If not already, then soon.* How different the experience would be with him beside her than it had been with Mari.

"Do you want me to take him so you can get to work?"

He held Paxton closer as if to ward her off. "Work can wait. Family is more important."

For Damián, family always came first.

Even so, she was so proud of how Damián was opening his own Harley Davidson customization shop. His work was exquisite, but now that he owned the shop, he could hire others to keep things running so he could be here for family when necessary.

Maman's money had been put to good use there, and allowed her to help Dr. McKenzie expand his clinic and buy much-needed equipment. Soon, she'd be working there three days a week as a therapist. Construction of her office had to take place evenings and weekends so as not to disturb the important work happening at the clinic. She'd be holding individual and group sessions helping patients deal with life crises.

Damián's sister would be working as a receptionist there after she moved to Denver next month. In the fall, Rosa planned to take two classes at the university and begin working on her bachelor's degree.

The Orlando family was so blessed.

"*Maman*, I want to go downstairs now. *Zía* Angelina promised to show me how to make crepes." The attention span of the newest Orlando—who had legally taken Damián's name soon after the wedding—maxed out quickly. Maybe she wouldn't remember her wish to have triplets or even a single baby after getting her fill of Karla and Adam's.

"Ask *Zía* Angelina to bring me two bottles first. The little ones are hungry." She took Kate and held her against her shoulder, patting her on the back. Damián met her gaze, a question in his eyes. "Yes, you get to feed one if you don't have to run off right away."

His smile warmed her heart. "I'm not going anywhere."

Minutes later, Angelina and Mari entered the room, each holding one bottle. "I have a wonderful sous chef today. We're going to be cooking up a storm and take some food to the hospital for Adam, Cassie, and Jenny."

"I'm sure they'll appreciate some real food for a change."

Angelina nodded, solemn. "Adam has barely left Karla's side. I'm worried about him as much as her."

Damián accepted the bottle from Mari. "When I leave here, I'll swing by the hospital and check on Dad."

"Let us know if there's anything we can do to help." Savannah hated that the couple's joy had turned to sorrow so quickly. The man had seen so much heartache. Adam was one of the strongest men she knew, but how much more could one person take?

*   *   *

Adam begged for fate to step in and give him his life back. "Kitten, I know you didn't leave me because you wanted to. But you need to come back. Now." Nothing he could have done would have kept her from hemorrhaging. Other forces had taken her from him.

But he wasn't going to sit back and let her drift away.

The sight of Karla lying here so helpless and frail brought an ache to his chest that stole his breath. What would he and the babies do if anything happened to her? How could he raise three babies alone?

He laid his head on the bed, covering her arm and grasping her hand. His extended family would help to make sure the babies were cared for, but they needed their mommy.

He needed her, too.

"Baby, come back to us."

A hand rested on his head, and Adam jerked his head up, wondering how he had missed hearing someone entering the room. Had he fallen asleep? Before he could search the room, he watched Karla's right hand fall to her belly. His gaze tore to her face, but her eyes remained closed.

"Kitten, eyes on me."

She blinked a few times and furrowed her brow before focusing those beautiful blue eyes on him.

"Yes, Sir?"

Ka-thunk! Thank you, God!

For the first time he understood that feeling Karla referred to all the time when her heart dropped into her stomach. Something like that anyway. He took his first full breath in days. "That's all. I just needed to see your eyes again."

Needed to know you aren't leaving me.

She smiled, and while weak, it was the most glorious ray of sunshine he'd seen in a long time.

Slowly, she took in her surroundings. She pointed to the IV pole. "What happened? Why am I back in the hospital?"

"Had a little complication, but Doc Palmer fixed you up in no time." *Like hell it was no time.* Not the doctor's fault, though. Any amount of time with Karla unconscious was too fucking long.

He stood and bent over her, capturing her lips in a searing kiss, leaving both of them gasping for breath. "I've missed you, Kitten."

"How long have I been in here?"

"Couple days." *Felt like a year to me.* He smiled for the first time since he'd found Karla hemorrhaging. God, he'd almost lost her.

She started to sit up until she grimaced in pain. He pressed her shoulder to the mattress. "Hold on. You aren't going anywhere."

"I need to go to the babies. They need me."

"Damned right, they do. But they're being taken care of. You need to take care of you first. Savannah's with Kate and Paxton, and Rori is right down the hall. You can visit her when they give you the go-ahead." Time to catch her up. "Rori's jaundice is cleared up, and she's gaining weight steadily. We may even have her home with us sooner than expected."

Karla blinked away the tears and visibly relaxed. "Oh, that's so good to hear. I just want to go home and have all my family with me."

"You and me both." He reached out and stroked her hair. "You're an amazing mother and the best wife a man could ask for."

Her chin quivered. "This is so scary. I feel as if I've missed half their lives already."

"You never left them." The babies probably knew that better than Adam did.

"I dreamt I visited Rori in the NICU." She wrinkled her brow and shook off the memory.

The door to the room opened. "Adam, Angelina has brought something for you to eat." Cassie's gaze went from Adam to Karla, and he watched the expression on her face become one of pure joy. "Kitty! You are awake!"

She set the containers on the windowsill and ran to the other side of the bed to give Karla a hug. Cassie had shown what a true friend she was to Karla—him, too, although Adam knew she wasn't doing any of this for him. Her heart belonged to Karla and the babies.

But somewhere around the second visit to the NICU, Adam had stopped getting hostile glares from Cassie. They'd reached some sort of truce. It was a good thing, because she and Karla were like sisters. Adam had never understood why Cassie disliked him from day one, but whatever it was seemed to have been forgiven in the midst of making sure Karla and the babies had all the love and attention they needed.

He'd ask the nurses if Karla could have something besides IV fluids. He reached over, pushed the call button, and summoned the nurse to check on her, too. He needed to know everything was okay now. Giving Cassie and Karla a moment—and hungry for the first time in days—Adam went to the window to see what Angelina had made.

He overheard Karla ask, "How's Rori?" She lowered her voice, but Adam still heard, "I know you have been watching over her. I saw you in the NICU the night you told me not to cross over."

What the fuck did she mean cross over?

Realization hit, and the dish in his hand shook so badly that he had to put it down.

Cassie whispered, "I could not stay away. You scared me when you came in there. I thought—"

Karla met Adam's gaze and saw he had overheard. "Adam, you know I would never have left willingly. I screamed at you when I first found myself out of my body and told you I didn't want to leave you."

Her dream of visiting Rori had been no dream at all. He *had* nearly lost her.

In a moment of clarity, Adam realized his mother, Joni, his first son—none of them had abandoned him intentionally. None really had a choice, not even his mother. Death, tragedy, it could come for anybody at any time. No one could control it and, most times, couldn't prevent it.

He needed to let go of living on the edge of panic, worrying about what might happen. He'd been given so many second chances and blessings. Time to live in the moment and appreciate what he had.

"I know, Kitten." Unable to have even a small space between them, he returned to the bed and squeezed her hand, afraid to touch her anywhere else. He kissed her and felt Cassie move away, but he didn't care who saw him. He loved this woman more than life itself.

She'd fought her way back to return to him.

"I love you, Kitten."

* * *

Two days later, Karla awoke to the sound of one of the babies crying. Being home in her own bed with two of her children nearby was the best medicine ever. She started to get up and felt the tug at her abdomen. She took the pillow and pressed it against her to support her belly with one hand while swinging her legs over the side of the bed and pushing up with her other one.

The door opened, and Adam came in, the cell phone to his ear. "Kitten, you should be in bed!"

"But the babies need me."

"I'll take care of them. Lie down." He pocketed his phone and bent over the bassinet to pick up Paxton in his blue receiving blanket.

Karla's jaw dropped as she watched him leave the room to fix the baby a bottle. Her world had shifted on its axis these past few days. Cassie was talking with Adam as if the two were good friends, and Adam was holding babies as if he had done it all his life.

Nothing made her happier. She'd been worried about Adam ever becoming comfortable with his babies. Adam returned and fed Paxton while rocking and talking with him as if this was something they did all the time. She blinked back the tears seeing his enormous hands holding the baby with such tenderness.

As he lifted the baby to his shoulder to burp him, Adam glanced over at Karla with a worried expression on his face. "Are you in any pain?"

"No. Why do you ask?"

"There are tears in your eyes."

She grinned. "Happy tears. I love seeing you caring for the babies with such ease."

Adam gazed down at the sleeping bundle he held against his chest. "Took some practice—okay and maybe having no choice in the matter." He grinned. "But you were right all along. I'm not going to break them. Not if I'm careful, anyway."

"You're always careful, Adam, with everyone you love."

Sometimes way too careful.

Oh, dear Lord, with this medical setback, she could probably kiss having sex goodbye until these three were walking and talking, if then. Honestly, though, having sex was the last thing she wanted right now. She pretty much had everything she'd ever dreamed of having—and more.

Thank you, Lord, for my family and friends.

Her complication had been more than a little setback. She could have died. Perhaps she was clinically dead at some point—when she had floated to the NICU and had seen Cassie with Rori.

Thank goodness Adam had found her, and Mom had been able to do what she could. Karla shuddered as she stretched out on the mattress again.

"Are you cold?"

"No." She blinked away the tears and cleared her throat. "I love you, Adam."

"I know, hon. I love you, too." He glanced down at Paxton, sucking away on his little bottle. Doctor Palmer said she could start breastfeeding again tonight, rather than pumping and tossing the milk while her system had been on so many drugs. But seeing Adam feeding one of the babies was a beautiful sight.

"I'm so glad to be home."

"Not as glad as I am to have you here."

Adam must have nearly lost his mind these past few days, thinking he was going to lose her. "I'm sorry I put you through that."

"You didn't do it on purpose, although you have one helluva pain threshold, woman." He did not look happy with her. "Doc Palmer said she would have expected you to be complaining about pain a lot more than you did."

"I had no idea my cramping was anything out of the ordinary." She grinned. "Just remember that the next time we play. I can take more pain than you think."

His pupils dilated in apparent excitement. Time for her to drive *him* crazy with anticipation for a while.

Oh, no! "Adam! I missed your birthday!"

"I don't give a rat's ass about a birthday. You coming back to me is the only present I could've ask for. Besides, you know I didn't want any fuss."

Karla grinned. "Well, I do have a couple gifts for you."

*   *   *

Adam had carried Karla up here only this morning after bringing her home from the hospital. Being in the room where she'd almost died was surreal. He refused to look at the place where he'd found her, even though he knew Marc had sent in his cleaning crew to remove all remnants of the horrific scene.

Karla giggled, and he grew hard. After burping Paxton, he returned him to the bassinet. Kate remained asleep, so he'd feed her later.

He turned and Karla patted the mattress. "Join me?"

"You need to sleep."

Sticking out her lower lip just made him even harder. *Damned minx.*

"I'm tired of sleeping. That's all I've done for days. I want your arms around me. We both know we can't do anything more than cuddle."

Oh, what the hell? The babies were asleep. Adam reached for his belt and unbuckled it. Karla's breath hitched, and her nipples bunched against her T-shirt even showing through the breast pads. *Great.* He presented his back to her as he slid the belt from its loops and sat on the edge of the bed to remove his shoes and jeans.

Karla's hand reached out to stroke his bare thigh.

"Kitten." He hoped the warning note in his voice kept her from tormenting him any further.

"Sorry, Sir. I've just missed touching you."

He'd missed her, too. He would be taking her back to Doc Palmer's in two weeks for a checkup, but it would be at least eight weeks from when the babies were born before they'd be having sex again. Not that they couldn't enjoy each other's bodies in less energetic ways. He glanced down at her, and the sultry smile she gave him warmed his heart.

God, I almost lost you.

"Wait! Before you come to bed, I need to give you your presents!"

Her and her damned reminders that he was another year older. "They can wait."

"No! They can't! Really!" She started to sit up.

"Lie down." She obeyed, her eyes dilating at his command. He reached out to stroke her cheek. "God, I've missed that look on your face."

"I've missed everything about you, Sir." She leaned into his hand and kissed it before glancing at the dresser beside him. "Now, I want you to find your presents. The first one's in the top drawer under my panties."

More than one? Curious, and a little surprised that she'd found time to shop before going into labor, he stood. Whatever it was, she wanted to please him with it, and he should accept her gifts with gratitude.

He opened the drawer and saw a jumbled mess of lacy panties and her equally sexy boxer briefs. The woman had never had to pass inspection, apparently. He pushed them to the side. Nothing. Then he shoved them to the other side and saw a flat red package wrapped in a black bow. He pulled it out and set it on the bed.

"The other is at the back of the bottom drawer."

He hunkered down to open the drawer. He encountered the red bustier she'd worn the first time he'd ever done Shibari on her, right upstairs in Marc's playroom.

Their playroom now, not that he had given any thought to how he would set it up. They'd be pretty darned busy in the coming months. He doubted there'd be time for much personal play, although she seemed anxious to resume singing at the club.

Still no present in sight, he pulled a latex mini-skirt out of the way and then saw it. This box, wrapped in the same paper, was bigger than the first, more square than flat. He pulled it out.

"Open the flat one first." Karla scooted slowly toward the middle of the bed to give him some room. He hadn't opened a present from her since Christmas Day while they were on their honeymoon.

Don't think about what happened after you played the song she sang to you on that CD. But this gift was too big to be a CD. She'd attached a full-blown red silk rose to the black ribbon on top as well as two unopened rosebuds.

"When I wrapped it, I didn't know about the third baby. But the open rose is supposed to be me because I've blossomed under your watch, Sir."

"You bloom more beautifully every day, Kitten." He bent over and placed a quick kiss on her lips before sitting up and tugging at the ribbon. He pulled it off and tore into the paper like a kid at Christmas. He never understood why people opened packages delicately. It wasn't like they'd ever use the paper again.

Besides, he was anxious to see what she'd given him.

He'd keep the ribbon, though. Might use it sometime when they could play again, or maybe in Kate or Rori's hair. He set it on the bed beside him so it wouldn't be tossed out with the trash.

"If you're going to save the ribbon and roses, I'll see if I can add a third rosebud for you."

"That would be great, but don't go to any trouble. One can stand for our two daughters and the other our son." '

With the paper removed, he found a flat box and opened the lid. Pushing the tissue paper aside, he found himself staring into the faces of his parents and him back in South Dakota the summer they had camped out at the cabin.

Smiles on all three faces. Everyone—including Adam. He remembered that summer as if it were yesterday. One of the best times of his childhood. Dad had stayed sober. The two of them had fished, cooked out, and swam in the lake.

"Megan and your mother helped me with it."

He glanced up, pulled back from the past. He mouthed a thank you when the words wouldn't go past the knot in his throat.

She blinked away tears. "At our wedding, I asked them if there were any photos of your childhood. When we were in California for Damián's wedding, I met with Megan."

He didn't remember her being out of his sight much and quirked an eyebrow.

"I told Savannah, and she excused me from being at the bachelorette party. But Megan floored me. She spent months working on this! I had no idea there were so many photos your mother had saved, even though I'd seen a number of them in e-mailed scans from Megan and your mother over the winter. Then Megan worked her magic on the album." Karla lifted the book out of the box. "Go on. Open it. There's more!"

He blinked back tears but didn't try to hide them. Family was everything. If he couldn't be sentimental about his family, then he'd be one sorry soul.

So much of what he remembered of his childhood had been the bad times. Now here he was confronted with some of the best days ever. He couldn't stop staring at the ones from that summer when he was eleven. His dad's face was bloated from years of heavy drinking. His mother's face weary. She'd only remembered that this trip had been a lot of work for her.

But Adam remembered that summer with his parents as the best time in his childhood. They'd been evicted from their home after Dad had been fired from another job. All Adam remembered was that, for the first time ever, Dad had taken him fishing and they'd cooked over a fire pit.

He lifted the album cover and saw photos of him as a baby being held by not only his mother, but his dad, as well. His dad's face had been thinner then. Healthier. The one of baby Adam sleeping on his dad's chest made him long to have a photo taken of each of his own babies in a similar pose. Maybe all three at the same time, only he'd better stay awake for his.

He turned page after page of photos in the scrapbook, all depicting happy occasions. Hell, who brought out the camera to record the bad times? He glanced up at Karla, who watched him with an anxious expression on her face.

Adam cleared his throat but still couldn't speak.

"Oh, Adam, I'm so glad you like it. I was worried it might stir up things from the past."

"It's only bringing up good stuff. Things I'd forgotten about."

"Megan and your mother did all the work, sorting through everything."

"Enough. If not for you, I wouldn't have found my mother or known about my siblings, Patrick and Megan. You also spearheaded this project. I doubt they'd have dug through all the boxes of photos and memories without a nudge from you. Then you helped choose which ones to include. All I can say is thank you. Just thank you."

"Adam, I'm so glad you have your family again."

"My family keeps growing. You've given me a reason to live again." She smiled, and tears trickled down her cheeks. He started to set the album on the nightstand.

"Keep going. There's more."

He flipped a few blank pages and saw photos of their wedding day, the honeymoon, and—

Holy fuck.

The last photo was one of Karla suspended in water. A red gown billowed out from her very pregnant body as her long, black hair fanned out around her head. The photo was the sexiest one he'd ever seen.

"Where? When?" The photo left him almost speechless.

"Over Easter, when your family came to Denver. Megan and I told you we were going shopping for the nursery, but instead, she had lined up a photo shoot at the local Y during their off hours. I'd been swimming there for months. It was the only place where I didn't feel the pull of gravity and the weight of what we now know were three, not two, babies. You can't imagine how good it felt to be weightless in that pool."

"I imagine." His three babies had been growing inside her. He cleared his throat before attempting to speak again. "You've never looked more beautiful—until now, maybe."

"Oh, I look like a frumpy housewife. All I need are curlers in my hair—"

"Don't go there. You've been to hell and back. And still you're gorgeous." He would have a hard-on every time he looked at that photo. Not that he wanted to see her pregnant again—ever. He couldn't risk losing her. Their family was complete.

"I owe your sister huge thanks for pulling this off. Megan's photography skills are phenomenal. She'll be the official Montague family photographer for all the babies' milestones—whenever she can be here, at least."

"Oh, yeah, Megan texted me this morning. Said she'd arrive in time for the baby shower. Has a surprise for us." He wondered what it could be, but would have to wait a couple of weeks. They'd postponed the shower after Karla had been hospitalized.

Megan had asked about coming up ever since Karla had been taken back to the hospital, but he'd had all the help he needed then. Better to wait until everyone else had to return to their lives.

Now he placed the album on the nightstand and removed his T-shirt, wanting to be pressed against Karla. "I'm going to go through these again after we get some shut-eye." He'd probably go back to the album thousands of times before he tired of it.

"You still have one more present." Adam followed her gaze to the square box on the bed beside him. What more could she possibly have gotten him? She smiled enigmatically.

"You'll see why I wanted you to open this one privately."

He lifted this much lighter present and opened it the same way he had the other. Lifting off the lid, he peeked inside at something with golden-yellow and white stripes. He reached in and pulled it out. A stuffed baby tiger? His first thought was a toy for the babies, but it had been trussed up in a red bra and panties made of paracord. Were those wooden dowels simulating a St. Andrew's cross?

Clearly, this wasn't a present for the babies. He glanced up at Karla.

"Your baby tiger just wants to make sure you know she's waiting patiently for you to continue her journey into submission whenever you're ready."

Adam grinned. "Where'd you learn to tie rope like that?"

"Nowhere. Luke did it for me. You taught him well, Sir."

Adam shook his head. That boy sure had learned fast. He hoped he found a special subbie someday to practice his rope skills on.

Chapter Twelve

Luke stowed his gear in the truck and said goodbye to his SAR team members before heading for home. The team had managed to rescue a child caught unaware by a rapidly spreading wildfire south of Breckenridge.

Too close. Cassie lived on the next mountain. If the firefighters hadn't been able to control the spread of this one, it could've reached her? Over the past two weeks, there'd been fires all over the state of Colorado. Some had been caused by lightning in the dry conditions, but too many had been started by negligent dumbasses or outright arsonists. Warnings were posted on all the highways. How could anyone claim to be unaware of the extreme fire danger?

No question about it, though, there would be more.

After parking the truck and trailer at the side of the house, he stared up at Cassie's pass, halfway between him and Breckenridge. He worried about her up there all alone. If fire broke out on her mountain, could she escape in time? He wished there was more than one access road out to her isolated cabin.

Of course, Eduardo had managed to find another way in. Not easy to reach, but do-able and might be used as another escape, but it was to the north and in the direction of the current raging fire.

Nothing would keep Luke from her if she needed him. Problem was, he hadn't seen her since he'd taken her alpacas home last week. They had dinner and talked a while, and he agreed to pick them up again in a few days before she headed to Denver for the baby shower and gallery opening. At least between helping with the alpacas and running into her at Adam's when he delivered the baby bed, he got to see her.

He'd actually seen her a couple of times in Denver and even coaxed her out for a few dates, but they both stayed so busy with everything going on that time together was minimal. The longer they were apart, the greater the chance of her rebuilding those walls that had started to come down.

When they were together, he saw glimpses of the woman she tried to hide from the world. Anyone who would open her heart up to a friend and her babies the way Cassie did wasn't the unfeeling hermit she portrayed herself to be.

Who had hurt her so badly that she would hide away from the world as she had? Clearly, she had friendships. However, as far as he could tell, he was her only male friend, although she seemed to be getting along better with Adam since the triplets were born. Maybe he should ask Adam what he'd done to get her to let her guard down around him.

Backing Pic out of the trailer and down the ramp, he led him into his stall in the barn. Cassie encouraged him to stop by anytime he wanted to see Millie. At least they shared a bond as parents to the cria. Maybe he'd stop by tomorrow and visit his family.

The other horses seemed agitated when he came near their stalls, and he realized he must smell like a smokestack. Luke promised Picasso he'd be right back and trudged inside the house where he began stripping off his clothes on the way to the bathroom. A shower would remove the day's grime and soot from his skin. Then he'd attend to Pic's needs. He'd done a great job today locating a frantic family's four-year-old boy who had strayed from the family's home in the chaos of trying to evacuate.

He removed the leather wristband and placed it on the sink.

Thank God this one had a happy ending.

Tonight, he'd work with O'Keeffe a while. She'd made a lot more progress these past weeks, but he didn't want to slack off. While Picasso was ready for some high-country SAR missions, he eventually wanted to train an elite equestrian SAR team that could access terrain too difficult to reach by vehicle or on foot.

Places like Cassie's cabin.

Funding a team like that would be a financial challenge, but he might be able to apply for grants. Marc said they could possibly do a fundraiser in Aspen at his family's resort sometime to infuse some money into the operation, if he decided to go that route. One thing he knew, while he wanted to bring in new rescues, he couldn't send O'Keeffe, Fontana, and Cassatt off to someone else's care. They were his now.

The lukewarm spray slowly made him feel human again and cooled him off. The smoky smell faded with liberal use of the deodorant bar. He shampooed his hair and removed the last remnants of the day's dirt. At least this fire had been easily contained thanks to some observant locals.

He shut off the faucet, reached for the towel on the shower rod, and rubbed himself dry. Damn, Cassie had no neighbors to report a fire early on. Maybe he'd call and check on her after he settled the horses for the night. Make sure she knew to keep a watch on the conditions up there in case she needed to evacuate fast or even in the middle of the night.

Out in the barn again, a quick check of Cassatt and Fontana told him they were fine, so he gave them their oats and water and moved on outside. O'Keeffe avoided him in the corral, and after trying to engage the skittish animal, he realized he was the problem. He just couldn't keep his focus on her. After twenty minutes or so, he called it a night and filled her feed and water containers.

Inside the barn aisle again, he went to the tack room and grabbed a currycomb. He'd spend some extra time with Pic tonight. The horse helped calm him down. After thirty minutes brushing and talking with the gelding—okay, and singing a song or two—Luke relaxed some.

Unfortunately, the palomino had no answers for him concerning his bride.

Horses taken care of, Luke went into the house and microwaved the last of the dinners Cassie had given him for his freezer. Man, he loved Cassie's home cooking. He even stocked amaranth now for his bread machine.

Thoughts of Cassie hit again when he sat at the table to glance at his latest copy of the Denver newspaper, coverage of the wildfires dominating the front page. He flipped the paper over, needing a break from bad news.

Cassie, I miss talking with you.

Luke glanced at his cell phone. Would she answer if he called her? Only one way to find out. He picked up the phone and hit her name in his contacts. He listened while it rang. And rang and rang.

No answer. Damn.

Just as he went to end the call, a breathless Cassie picked up. "Hello? Lucas? Are you all right?"

He wished she didn't think he'd only call because something was wrong. Still, he grew hard hearing the breathlessness in her voice. He grinned. "Hey, darlin'. Everything's fine here. Good to hear your voice."

Jeezus, I miss you.

"I just returned from shopping and errands."

"Just checking to see how things are going up there." *Are you working too hard?*

More loud breathing and then, "We are okay. How about you and the horses?"

"Keeping busy."

He took a bite of his dinner and closed his eyes to pretend she was sitting across from him while he ate.

"What are Millie, Gracie, and the other girls up to?"

"You will not believe what Milagrosa did today." The joy in her voice made him happy, too.

After a few minutes, a lull in the conversation followed before she filled the space. "I heard about the rescue of the lost little boy. Were you one of the SAR workers?"

Good girl for paying attention to the fires raging near you.

"Yeah. Pic helped, too."

"Pic?"

"Picasso."

"Oh, your SAR horse! I did not know his nickname." He was surprised she remembered their conversations about the horse at all, but Cassie loved animals as much as he did.

"Yeah. This was his first mission, but he picked right up where he left off, it seems." He reminded her of Pic's history of neglect.

"I am so glad you found him and have a place to raise and train him. You are a good man to work so hard with them." She spoke her last words through a yawn.

"You aren't overdoing it, are you, Sweet Pea?"

"No, not at all. Had a sleepless night, and it has been a busy day with the alpacas and errands."

Another awkward pause ensued. Luke wondered if she lay awake at night thinking about him as much as he did her.

"Oh, I will be shearing the alpacas soon."

"Takes two to do that. Let me know when, and I'll come up."

Silence.

Say 'yes,' baby girl.

"Okay, thank you. That would be good. But let me get through the gallery opening first." Asking for a man's assistance wasn't easy for Cassie, but she'd just accepted his offer to help.

Progress.

"How are the other horses?"

"All moving right along." *Faster than we are.*

"I hate to cut you off, but I need to finish unloading the Tahoe and put things away. Left my phone on the table when you called, so it took me a minute to run in and answer it."

Ah, that's why she was out of breath. "Listen, Cassie, keep an eye out for signs of fire up there. Whole damned state's going up in flames. Pack up what you can't live without and be ready to evacuate at a moment's notice. Call me and I'll be there in a flash."

"Do not worry, Lucas. I have been watching and have signed up for phone alerts from both counties." Her place straddled the borders of two counties, making response times from either department longer.

"Glad to hear that, darlin'." He just hoped it was enough.

Silence again.

"Was there anything else you wanted, Lucas?"

"Why don't we have dinner this week and really catch up?" *Not just dinner over the phone, either. I need to see you.*

"Let's wait until after I get back from the gallery opening."

"Actually, I'm planning to come to Denver to do some renovation work at Adam and Karla's next Tuesday and was going to stick around for your opening, too."

"Oh. Thank you. I never think anyone will show up."

"Don't know why you'd think like that. Your last exhibition was a huge success, wasn't it?"

"Yes. Much more than I ever expected, although not many buyers."

"Don't you worry. You're gonna be mobbed. I can feel it." Meaning he wouldn't have any time alone with her. "Hey, maybe I can take you to dinner before the opening."

"Oh, well, the gallery is hosting a reception that evening. Not that I will be able to eat a thing. Opening-night jitters." Her laugh sounded forced, but he could imagine how crowds like that would freak her out.

He grinned. "How about breakfast the morning after?" He'd find someone to cover things for him here. His heartbeat ramped up at the thought of spending some time alone with her again.

"Breakfast would be nice."

Hot damn! He felt like he'd just thrown a touchdown pass to the receiver in the end zone, but he tried to contain his excitement. "So are you all ready for the show?"

"One more piece to finish. I cannot wait to see what you think of it."

"Can't wait." He glanced across the table into the living room at the picture she'd painted of him and Millie. "I hung the one you gave me over the mantel."

He must have surprised her because she grew silent again for a long moment.

"Please stay safe if you are called out on any more search-and-rescue operations."

"Always am. You be safe, too."

"I will."

The silence drew out until she bridged the awkwardness. "I have enjoyed talking with you, Lucas. Thank you for calling."

"You, too, Cassie. Keep in touch."

They ended the call, and Luke felt the loss of her company more than ever. Maybe he'd spend some time in his studio tonight. He needed a creative outlet.

*   *   *

The next day, Cassie's eyes burned from lack of sleep, but the Denver gallery exhibition opened in a few days and she needed to finish this fiber-art piece. She yearned for the day she would be able to use the fleece of her own alpacas, but for now, she had to rely on fleece purchased from a local farmer.

All the preparation and planning finally came together as she immersed herself so deeply in her work the world ceased to exist. These were her favorite times as an artist, not to mention as a human being—the times when she felt alive again.

She had been preparing the fleece and spinning the wool all winter. After Lucas and Eduardo left, she had begun dyeing the fleece to perfection. She had to take a break while helping Kitty with the babies, but had returned home at Kitty's insistence this week to finish.

Watching the piece emerge from a nebulous thought in her mind months ago to almost-finished today invigorated her. She did not wish to stop working for a moment. Two nights ago, she had screwed the eyehooks in what appeared to be a random pattern on the inside of the rustic wooden picture frame she found at a flea market last summer.

She had spent the last two days using the *quipu* techniques learned at her grandmother's knee decades ago to tie cords and knots in a deliberate, timeless tradition of storytelling. Each strand, each knot, each color represented a part of her journey, from joys and sorrows to triumphs and failures—a lifetime to date of her experiences.

The predominant color was green, depicting ritual, ancestors, and her love of plants. She felt closest to *Mamá* while working with green. For *Papá*, she had chosen blue, the color of the sky and blue signified the Spanish influence on Peruvian *quipu* and art. Blue also illustrated Cassie's spiritual growth. Several strands of white fleece had been interwoven to show how *Mama Quilla* had a part in her life, as well. Red was kept to a minimum, the color of conquest and rulership.

Black also seemed in short supply. In her culture, black represented the space between the stars, reminding them of creation, the life energy, and the People's origins. But the color also embodied love and happiness. Wanting balance, she had added a strand to illustrate her marriage commitment to Lucas, even if it was not a traditional marriage.

The longest strand was of deep purple, signifying *Pachamama*. That thread eventually would embrace the others in the piece to show how the mother of all life had wrapped her in her loving arms since the beginning of time.

In addition to weaving together the threads of her life story, she also included splashes of colorful beads, as well as small, meaningful charms—angel trumpet flowers for *Abuela*, a kitten for Kitty, three sets of baby booties for the triplets, and others.

When finished, the piece would represent the interconnectedness of all things, living and inanimate, past and present, real and imaginary. Her stomach began growling and she realized she needed to eat. She took a break and walked over to the table where a bowl of fresh fruit awaited. Quick and easy, then she would return to work.

Cassie would wait and mount the piece to the mirror after going to Denver. Less chance it could be broken. She envisioned the visitors to the gallery standing side by side before the four-by-two-foot piece, their faces intermingling as part of the piece itself.

The web of life.

Feeling closer to *Abuela* than she had in a long time, she made a note to put her grandmother's most special blanket among the items to take in case of an evacuation. Fires were starting in new places every day it seemed. She did not remember so many wildfires in one season since coming to Colorado.

She took a bite of an apple. Working on this piece had helped to keep her mind off of Lucas until she picked up the cell phone yesterday. Hearing his voice for the first time in more than a week, she could not believe how quickly he had wrapped himself around her heart once again. She actually looked forward to seeing him again at the gallery in Denver. Of all the people who would be there, he was the one she most wanted to share and discuss her artwork with.

Still, true to his word, he had remained in touch and seemed solicitous of her, which surprised her. Must be loyalty to their marriage vows. Lucas was a man of his word. She, too, found herself anticipating the times he would stop by or call. She had wanted companionship from their arrangement and enjoyed it. Lucas would never be relegated to mere acquaintance again.

She had even added a crescent-moon charm to her piece to further represent Lucas's recent influence in her life.

The man did strange things to her psyche. Oddly enough, her body responded to him, as well. He invaded her dreams, pushing away the darkness and bringing only smiles, and, well, sometimes thoughts of touching him.

She had not allowed herself to astral project to him after that first time. That had been an invasion of his space and privacy. And yet, even though she was not actively going to him, he was still so often on her mind when she let her guard down.

Please let me return to my once-safe life, Lucas.

Her mind and heart had found peace in her solitude, but when she was with Lucas, the overload of conflicting, confusing emotions nearly brought her to her knees.

Moving to the sink, she washed the stickiness from her fingers. Even though she had no intention of becoming involved with him any more deeply than she was now, she did worry about him. With all the fires breaking out, she wondered if he had been called for additional search-

and-rescue missions. She hoped he always found whoever he was looking for.

Back in her workspace, before her fingers returned to the piece, she sent angels of protection to surround him now as she had done each morning since their wedding ceremony as part of her daily meditation.

Mama Quilla, please keep him safe from harm, as well. He had come to mean a lot to her during his time up here.

Sometimes, she even missed him. Not that she needed him. She had learned to need no one.

But with Lucas she had discovered companionship with a man for the first time since... She had never expected to find that again. Lucas understood her artist's mind, and even influenced her work now. The art she created came from somewhere deep inside. She almost went into a trance when creating it, but she did not always understand its meaning even after it was completed. This piece was different.

Of course, art was open to interpretation, and the best pieces spoke differently to each person who viewed them, mingling what the artist wanted to convey with the art patron's own experiences and biases.

She had enjoyed hearing Lucas describe what he saw in her work.

Yes, I miss him.

Cassie shook off the melancholy that had plagued her since she had married the man. She had never been lonely up here before, but something had changed. *She* had changed.

What had this man done to her comfortable existence?

She did not view her cabin as the sanctuary she once had. The cabin had become her prison with reminders of Lucas everywhere she looked. Nowadays, she spent most of her time in the studio or hiking on the mountainside.

The burning in her eyes stung. Cassie blinked, but could not relieve the dryness. Was she overtired? Eye strain?

She glanced away from the piece and out the window. Smoke?

Almost at once, Cassie's mind registered the smell of burning wood coming in through the open window of her studio. She dropped the crochet hook she had been using to draw the fleece through the piece and ran for the door. Flames and smoke covered the top of the next hill.

Fire!

She ran down the path toward the shed until something told her to turn around. More smoke from a different fire billowed up from the access road leading to the state highway. Cut off. She needed to leave this mountain now! Her only escape would be to head straight down the mountain and hope the two fires did not meet. Depending on which way the wind blew, the flames from either fire could be at her doorstep in no time.

Her Tahoe would be useless without a road to follow, so she would have to escape on foot. Inside the shed, she tried to calm the alpacas, which were agitated and making mournful sounds.

I know. I am frightened, too.

"We are going on an adventure, girls."

She placed harnesses on each one. When the cell phone in her pocket blared, she pulled it out to see a fire alert text message. These fires must be fairly recent—unless they had gone undetected so long because they were far away from any roads or homes.

It gave a code to text back, but she also sent a message informing them of her escape plan before putting the phone away and filling several small burlap bags with feed. This should be plenty until they reached safety and could restock. At least they were pack animals and able to carry water and supplies.

What else did she need to take with her? She ran into the house. Lucas had instructed her to be prepared, and she picked up her backpack filled with toiletries, underwear, and extra clothing.

Lucas!

Should she let him know what was going on? He would never reach them in time to help. She needed to rely on herself. But what about when they did make it to safety? She would need help with the animals. Her babies were familiar with Lucas and his barn already, so she could give them a sense of normalcy there. The poor things already were shaken to the core by the fire.

Pulling out her phone on her way to the kitchen, she pressed his number on her recent calls list, but it went to his voicemail. While gathering a loaf of amaranth bread and two gallon-sized jugs of drinking water, she left her message.

Please, Goddess, let the signal be strong enough for him to hear my words.

Just in case, she repeated the message twice. "Lucas, there is fire closing in on us from two directions. My access road is blocked. I plan to hike down the southern side of the mountain with the alpacas. If you get this message, please head toward the pass pull-off and bring your trailer. I will call again when I reach the highway." The second time, she added, "I need you, Lucas. I am sorry to have to bother you."

Cassie disconnected the call. She had practically pushed the man away for weeks, so to beg him to rescue her seemed the most selfish act of all, but she could not risk her babies being harmed.

Unsure why, she suddenly hurried back to the bedroom and over to the center drawer of her vanity. The folded slip of paper fit easily into her jeans pocket. Perhaps the vows written in Lucas's hand would be the good-luck talisman that would help them all escape this burning mountain unharmed.

She would try better to live up to the promises made to him, even if she was not the whole person he should be loved by.

On her way out the cabin door, instead of going straight to the shed, foolish though it was, she ran back to her studio. The piece she had been working on called to her. She had poured out her emotions over the birth of Kitty's babies and everyone coming together to make sure they were cared for. She could not let this piece burn if the fire destroyed the studio.

At least it was not attached to the mirror yet. She grabbed the lightweight frame and ran back to the shed. She must hurry.

Inside, she tied the feedbags and water containers onto the backs of the animals. She filled four more jugs with their drinking water, balancing all six on the backs of Tika, Qhawa, and Killa. Graciela would have her hands full keeping Milagrosa fed and calm, so the new mama would only carry Cassie's backpack.

Once she had everyone ready, she tied the animals together on the same tether so no one would stray. Standing outside the shed, she assessed the fires, but neither seemed to have come much closer.

She pocketed the phone, grabbed the rope harness with Tika in the lead, and started down the mountain following the stream flowing from where remnants of the snowpack above her cabin were melting.

Do not look back.

She did not wish to think about losing the place that had been her sanctuary for four years, but all that really mattered was right here with her. She hoped Lucas received her message. She would need him to be there when they reached the road. By then, they all would be exhausted, no doubt.

Goodness. She had never admitted needing Lucas—or any man—for anything since that night in the cantina. If she were alone, she could have escaped unaided, but she could not risk harm coming to her babies.

Still, she could not imagine asking any other man for help. With Lucas, as least she could feel safe, albeit uncomfortable.

She clicked her tongue. "Come on, girls. No time to waste!"

She had to be a disappointment to Lucas. Perhaps while staying with him, they should discuss calling off this sham of a marriage. She had never been able to follow through on her promises to spend time with him. A handsome, compassionate man like Lucas would have any number of women flocking to marry him. The kind-hearted man did not deserve to be saddled with a cold and distant woman who could not love him the way he should be loved.

She and Lucas had negotiated something they had agreed would benefit them both. She was the only one who had shirked her promises and vows.

She would try to be a better friend to Lucas, a helpmate with his animals, and a confidante. He had never demanded that she be a wife in the true sense of the word.

Lucas, please forgive me.

She did not bother to check her cell phone. Coverage was spotty away from the signal booster at the cabin.

Thoughts of living with him again until she could return to her cabin—*if* she could go back—left her with a knot in the pit of her stomach. Heat warmed her cheeks. The exertion from guiding the alpacas down the hillside must be leaving her overheated, but she needed to make haste. She smelled smoke and, at this point, had no clue where the fire was located. She could stop for a drink later.

If only she had been able to speak directly with Lucas. Was he on his way? He would have contacts with the fire department who could give him the safest path to follow, knowing where the fires were burning.

At least one of the fires had been reported. Perhaps other rescue workers were on their way, too.

Cassie continued to follow the stream. Despite the dry conditions, it still had water flowing, and if she needed to wet her alpacas down or give them fresh water, that would be an easy source rather than pouring water down their throats from the jugs they hauled.

She suddenly realized she hadn't remembered to take *Abuela's* blanket from her altar area. Nor her *lliclla*, or shoulder cloth, that had been worn on both *Abuela's* wedding day as well as her own. Tears stung her eyes. She had been focused on saving other possessions—her wedding vows and latest artwork—not to mention caring for her babies. How could she have forgotten the treasures of her happy childhood? Her cheeks grew wet.

Graciela nudged her shoulder, and she stopped a moment to bury her face in the alpaca's soft hair. But she soon squared her shoulders. "Thank you." Now she must trudge on and think about the living, not the dead. Her foot slipped on the muddy bank of the stream, but she grabbed for Tika, who kept her from falling.

Lucas, please be waiting for us at the highway.

Smoke became thicker. It was blowing from the direction she was headed. Now what? She would have to change her plans.

She clicked her tongue. "Come on, girls. We need to move faster!"

Would Lucas worry when she was not waiting at the road as she had said she would be? Would he come in search of them? She hoped so. She would greet him with a hug and a kiss if only he could help them reach safety.

*   *   *

"Rafe, Luke Denton here. I'm seeing smoke up near Iron Horse Pass. Any reports?"

"Yeah. Looks like two separate fires."

"Cassie López called. She evacuated about an hour ago. I missed the call, and the message was a little garbled, but sounded like she's headed south from her place." The fear in her voice burned his gut. If only he hadn't left his phone on the kitchen counter. He tried to call her back, but could only leave a message on voicemail. "I'm going to load up Pic and try and see if I can meet up with her, but watch for them to come out along the state highway south of the pass. That's most likely where she'll head."

"Got it. Listen, we have teams there now. If you don't see anything on your way up the hill, meet us at the staging area at the pass's parking lot, and we can assess the situation better to make sure we cover as much ground as possible."

"On my way."

He disconnected the call and ran for the door, grabbing his Stetson and gear by the doorway.

"I'm coming, Sweet Pea. Just hang on."

Inside the barn, he went straight to Pic's stall. "Sorry, boy. No rest for the weary. Cassie needs us."

The horse pricked his ears and pranced. His saddle and bridle were already inside the trailer. Luke kept them there to be prepared in case of another SAR call. He hadn't expected the next one to be for Cassie.

Ten minutes after talking to Rafe Giardano, he was tearing up the state highway to the pass. The smoke grew heavier the closer he drew to the source of the fire. He wasn't sure exactly where her cabin was in relation to the highway, but thought she was on the opposite side of the mountain. That meant one of the fires was between her and escape.

Damn.

He floored the new Chevy Silverado 2500 until he remembered he was hauling Pic and forced himself to take it easy. Wouldn't do to injure his horse. That horse might be the only thing enabling him to find Cassie.

Hang on, darlin'.

Luke reached a roadblock turning drivers back at the last county road turnoff. He showed his SAR credentials to the police officer, who waved him ahead. Good thing. No one was going to keep him from reaching his wife this time.

No one.

Maybe she assumed she was his wife in name only, but he meant every word he'd spoken in front of that justice of the peace. He had no intention of breaking those vows as long as he lived.

No sign of her on the way to the top of the mountain. At the fire department's staging area, he turned into the parking area normally for tourists and pulled out again on the side of the road with the front of the truck facing toward home. Somehow, he didn't think Cassie would still be at this elevation if she'd started out nearly an hour ago. Most likely, she'd already started her descent. But it would be easier to follow her trail than to try and guess where she might come out of the woods. He'd try to ride Pic to her point of origin—the cabin—unless fire blocked his way.

After parking and easing Pic out of the trailer, he saddled and bridled him quickly. Mounting, Luke rode back up to the staging area. A scan of the lot, and he zeroed in on Angel's oldest brother, Rafe. The fire squad leader out of Aspen Corners studied his aerial maps and discussed strategies with two other firefighters. One looked like Angel's youngest brother, Tony.

Drawing near, Luke dismounted and led Pic by the reins as he approached the men. "Any word from Cassie?"

Rafe, a rugged Italian with weariness in his eyes that belied his years, shook his head. "We've attempted phone contact, but there's no connection. Any idea which way she might've gone down the mountain?"

Luke shook his head. "Is the road to her place blocked?"

Rafe nodded.

"I know another way around to her cabin. My SAR horse and I will make it through okay. Once I make sure she's escaped, I'll let you know which way she's headed.

Rafe glanced at the horse standing almost at attention and awaiting orders. "Have your sat phone?"

"Yeah." He could kick himself for missing her call. She'd had a signal then. He could have at least discussed her evacuation plan.

"Rafe, Cassie's very special to me."

He scrutinized him. "You know we aren't going to leave anyone in danger. I don't care if they're the governor's wife or a homeless person."

"You might as well know that Cassie's my wife. I'm not coming off this mountain until I find her."

Rafe narrowed his eyelids. "Don't do anything stupid, Denton. If you can't keep your head on straight and follow protocols, you aren't leaving this staging area."

"My head's never been straighter." *Nothing is going to stand between my wife and me.*

After scrutinizing him a few seconds more, Rafe searching Luke's eyes for something, the man seemed satisfied and nodded. "Show me on this map which quadrants you'll be covering and then move out. Wish I had another man on horseback to go with you. Report when you know something."

"Yes, sir."

Chapter Thirteen

"Cassie!" he called out again, but heard no response. *Damn!* Which way did she go? Her place had clearly been deserted. She couldn't drive them off the mountain with fire blocking the only access road. At least the fire on the next mountain wasn't a threat to her place.

He'd learned that you didn't assume someone had left an area without a thorough search, but seeing the alpacas gone, he was pretty damned sure they had left together. Absently, he rubbed the black leather wristband. When he realized what he was doing, he reminded himself that Cassie wasn't a scared little girl. She would know to find a safe route down the mountain, away from these wooden structures that would go up like matchsticks if the fire reached here.

The fire he had skirted raged less than half a mile away. Thank God she evacuated when she had. But her message said she was heading toward the highway, which would put her in a direct path with the fire.

"Trust your instincts, baby girl."

She hadn't left any note or map inside the cabin. On his way out again, he grabbed the poncho hanging in the mudroom. She'd worn it enough that her essence would be strong on it, enough for Picasso to zero in on her trail. After giving Pic a good whiff of the woolen cloth, he folded it and placed it inside a plastic bag to try and preserve as much of her scent as possible if Pic needed to refresh. The smell of smoke would obliterate all other scents.

Wait. She had the animals with her. He went inside the shed and saw that their food bins had been left nearly empty. He took the discarded feed scoop and gathered some dried manure pellets. He carried that to Picasso, too. The pungent manure would be even easier to track. "Sniff, boy."

Picasso did so and nodded, fully aware now of his mission. Luke remounted. "Find Cassie. Help me find my girl." Swirls of smoke drifted up the mountain. What if she had headed down that way and come face to face with the newest outbreak of flames?

Luke pressed his thighs against Picasso's flanks and set off. Going downhill slowed him, but he saw visible signs of tracks near the seasonal stream. The water would find the fastest and easiest path to the foot of the mountain.

Good thinking, Sweet Pea.

A half-mile down the mountainside, Pic alerted on a ragged trail that must have been used by deer. Maybe even bear. The horse veered off the path they'd followed near the stream, snorting to let Luke know he was on to something. The smoke was thicker here. Luke coughed as he tied his bandana around his nose and mouth to act as a filter.

Luke reported his coordinates to Rafe then gave his horse free rein to follow his keen sense of smell. The ground became less steep, and Pic was able to work up to a lope. Smoke billowed around them, and he prayed Picasso really was onto their scent and not some false lead. Luke scanned the mountainside and determined where the fire was burning. He'd have to stay alert and in touch with the command center or he'd get all of them killed today. His need to reach Cassie was clouding his judgment and messing with his training.

The tracks were less obvious here where the ground was packed dry. He'd seen some occasional droppings from what he hoped were the alpacas, but they had to slow down when the undergrowth grew thicker.

Had the sight and smell of smoke scared Cassie or her animals? They seemed to be heading toward Iron Horse Falls now. The terrain quickly became steeper and rockier. Thoughts of Picasso slipping made him slow the horse down, but the horse soon alerted again with a flicking forward of his ears. "What do you hear, boy?" He whinnied and took off through the trees and brush. Luke ducked to avoid being thrown off the horse by a stray limb, but trusted him. Pic knew something was wrong and that they needed to get there fast.

When the horse's hooves came to an abrupt stop, Luke had to grab onto Pic's mane to keep from flying over its neck and head.

Luke sat up and scanned the area, but his eyes burned from the thick smoke, blurring his vision. A soft clicking noise caught his ear at the same time Picasso snorted. Sounded like one of the alpacas.

"Cassie! Where are you?"

Please, God, let her be okay.

Silence.

A rustling of leaves caught his attention, and he turned to his left. He still saw no source of flames, only thick smoke. The rustling sound grew louder until he saw a long black neck poking up over the side of a hillock.

Millie! *Damn.* What was she doing here without Cassie or her momma?

"Come here, baby girl!"

He dismounted and ran toward the cria as she scrambled through the brush to reach him. She rubbed her face against his chest, body shaking and emitting noises that sounded like she was crying.

"Where's my Cassie? And your momma?" The baby nuzzled him some more, leaving Luke even more worried. Pulling a rope from the saddle horn, he tied it to the cria's halter. She must have strayed away from the group, but Cassie wouldn't have allowed any of the alpacas to wander far—unless she'd been injured.

His heart jumped into his throat. He remounted and, using pressure from his knees, sent Picasso in the direction from which Millie had come. They traveled another eighth of a mile down the mountainside before Picasso alerted again.

"What is it, boy?"

Before he could figure out what the horse had seen or heard, Graciela raised her head from a resting place a couple hundred yards away. She let out a distressed cry, and Luke dismounted again. Why didn't the alpaca stand up? Had she been injured? Still no sign of Cassie. As he drew closer, though, he saw a familiar turquoise jacket on the ground. No, not just the jacket.

"Cassie!" *God, no.* She sat hunched over a rock, coughing. He knelt beside her, and she looked up, squinting as if she didn't believe he was really here.

"Lucas?" Good. Her voice didn't sound too raspy. She coughed and tried to draw a deep breath, but only coughed some more.

"You okay, darlin'?"

She nodded. "Just resting."

Luke pulled out his satellite phone and called the station. She seemed disoriented. He wanted to have the EMTs standing by to check her out when they reached the highway.

Cassie coughed again and struggled to stand up, but swayed.

"Whoa! Sit down until we're ready to hit the trail."

"Trail? Where are we going?"

"I'm going to get you and your alpacas off this mountain."

Her eyes opened wider, and she looked around. "Millie! I started to go after her, but became short of breath and had to sit down."

"Don't worry. Millie's fine. She found me a little while ago and led me over here. She's tied to Pic." Luke pointed to her, and Cassie visibly relaxed when she saw the cria was safe. "Let me do a quick assessment before we move out."

"Please, I am fine." She tried to push herself to her feet, but his hand on her shoulder stopped her.

"Did you fall?"

She seemed confused. "No. At least I do not remember doing so."

"Tell me today's date."

"I do not remember."

Damn. Maybe she *had* hit her head or the carbon monoxide from the smoke had messed with her ability to reason.

She blinked and stared at him, annoyed. "I do not pay much attention to the calendar unless I have an appointment. If I had to guess, I would say it is the twentieth. I think."

He shook his head and grinned. Cassie lived in her own little world up here, cut off from everything and everyone.

"Tell me where you were born."

"Lima, Peru."

"Who's the president?"

"Humala."

"Who?"

"Oh, sorry. He *is* the president of Peru. You were asking questions about my homeland. May I sit up now or are you going to keep playing twenty questions?" She glanced around. "We need to get off this mountain."

Okay, she was back to her old feisty self. He relaxed a little. "Before you move, tell me where you're feeling any pain."

"Really. I am fine."

Cassie craned her neck and scanned the hillside, and his gaze followed. For the first time, he noticed the other three alpacas were laden down with bags of feed, jugs of water, and a rectangle of some kind covered in a tarp.

The smell of wood burning reminded him they weren't safe to remain here much longer. He called the fire crew's dispatcher and obtained the coordinates for the fire after reporting his own. Too close.

Cassie sniffed the air, and he instructed her to cover her nose and mouth with her blouse. Before complying, she asked, "Do you think it will reach my cabin?"

Fire tended to rise, moving quickly upslope, so chances were likely this one could unless the fire crews sent smoke jumpers in before it was too late. But he needed to keep her calm. "Everything that's irreplaceable is right here. I know the fire crews will do all they can." She'd done the right thing to try to remove her and the alpacas from the path of the approaching fire.

"Let me help you up."

He took her hand and pulled her slowly to her feet. When she began to sway again, he wrapped his arms around her waist to steady her. Damn, how many times these past weeks had he dreamt of having his arms around her again?

Too soon, she pushed him away, averting her gaze. "Let us gather up the alpacas."

"You stay here. Hold onto Pic. He'll steady you. I'll round them up."

He roped the animals together so he could lead them out of here without worrying about any of them straying or becoming spooked if they came too close to the fire. When he came back to her, he saw a wary look in her eyes he hadn't seen since those early days when he'd been stranded at her cabin after the avalanche.

Damn.

Then something changed. Without warning, she placed her hands on his biceps and planted a kiss on his cheek. "Thank you for rescuing us." Just as abruptly, she pulled away.

He had no clue what had prompted her, other than gratitude, but he didn't even try to hide his grin as he attached the guide rope to his saddlebag before picking up Picasso's reins.

"Okay, darlin', let's get you mounted." He reached for her foot while holding the stirrup steady. She grabbed onto the pommel and swung her right leg over the horse's back.

"Now, scoot as far forward as you can."

She glanced at him a moment before her eyes widened. "We will both ride Picasso?"

"Your alpacas already have enough weight to carry. Having either of us on foot will just slow us down and be more dangerous. Pic is very sure on his feet."

"I do not think we both will fit."

He removed her foot from the stirrup. "Trust me. Sit forward." Without waiting for her to follow his command, he swung himself up onto the horse, as well and she scooted as far forward as she could without sitting on the pommel.

Luke grinned. "See? We fit just fine."

Feeling her ass against his crotch set off all kinds of feelings he needed to suppress—for the moment, at least. No sense spooking her. The last thing he wanted was for her to jump off the horse in an effort to put distance between them.

This could be yet another way he showed her she could trust him. Even if it killed him to try and curb his erection. He allowed graphic images of what might happen to them all if they didn't reach safety to put a damper on his libido. Their main order of business now was to find the highway and the EMTs.

He'd programmed the GPS for the coordinates for where he'd left his vehicle, so at the push of a button, he'd know which way to head once they had skirted the fire area completely.

Cassie sat rigidly upright, trying not to let her back touch his chest. He grinned.

"You're going to be awfully sore tomorrow if you don't relax. You know you're safe with me, darlin'."

*   *   *

Cassie refused to give in to the weariness in her body. Yes, she trusted Lucas—as far as she could trust any man. He could have taken advantage of her anytime during their weeks together at her cabin, but he had always been a gentleman.

He sighed and whispered so close to her ear he sent a shiver coursing down her back, "Lean against me, Cassie." His words wrapped around her and lured her in to do as he said. She was so tired, but had to fight the temptation to give in. "Darlin', you're making my muscles ache just watching you. Don't you worry about falling. I have you."

The way his arms braced her as he held the reins, that was not what worried her. Falling for this kind, gentle man who had somehow wheedled his way under her once-ironclad shield of protection scared her much more. All her adult life, she had stayed strong and handled what life threw at her without having to lean on a man. So why did she have to fight the desire to melt into this man's strong, secure arms. Doing so would give him the wrong impression… Sometimes men read a woman's intentions all wrong.

"How're you feeling?"

"Fine. I am more worried about the alpacas. I hope they did not breathe in too much smoke."

She had to admit she was a little worried about surviving such close contact with Lucas, as well. His hands remained together and still, for the most part. They held the reins as his arms wrapped around her to keep her from falling off.

Her seat was sandwiched between the saddle's bump in front, stimulating a long-dormant part of her anatomy in uncomfortable ways with Lucas's crotch pressed firmly and intimately against her. If she tried to tilt her pelvis forward to break that contact, she only increased pressure on the other. The sporadic zings to her sex with the sway of the horse's steady gait wreaked havoc on her nerves.

Arousal. She remembered experiencing that before…

The lack of food and sleep over the last few days were messing with her mind. She could not be aroused. That part of her was dead.

All she wanted was to rest her back against Lucas's chest, but such contact would overload her senses and send him the wrong message.

Cassie drew in a breath. So hot. She reached up to unbutton her jacket. "The fire must be increasing the temperature up here."

Lucas reined in the horse, as he scouted the best path to continue to move toward safety. "No, darlin'. We're far enough away from the fire now that it wouldn't have any effect on the air temperature. Must be something else heating you up." She thought she detected a smile in his voice. Was he teasing her?

Did he know the effect the saddle had on her? She removed her jacket and wedged it between their bodies, hoping to break some of the contact. But when she leaned back against him, he wrapped his arms around her and set the horse in motion again.

Smothered.

She bolted upright, pulling away from him. "Shhh, darlin'. Lie back. Nobody's going to hurt you."

"Stop calling me darling."

"I thought we'd been through that already." Lucas's gloved hand stroked her bare arm. "Who shattered your trust, Sweet Pea?"

Sweet Pea was even more intimate than darling! She had never heard him use that term on anyone but her. "Why do you have so many silly nicknames for women?"

She felt his shoulder shrug. "Maybe it's a Texas thing. Or plain old country. My dad always used little endearments like that for my mom, especially ones with flower names like Rose and Petunia."

"Thank the Goddess you do not call me Petunia."

He chuckled, and the rumble transferred from his chest to her back.

That he used the endearments because of his parents surprised her. He was not patronizing her at all by using the silly words. It was a cultural thing.

Still, she wished he would not use anything but ones he might use with a server at a restaurant. Impersonal ones. Not "Sweet Pea." And definitely not "baby girl." She was nobody's baby girl.

The smoke all but disappeared as they continued to navigate the side of the mountain.

Cassie relaxed a bit. "I think you are right. We have evaded the fire."

"Hope so. GPS says we still have another three-fourths of a mile to reach the highway."

As they continued to cut across the slope of the mountain, Cassie found her body relaxing even further. The horse's steady, rhythmic gait lulled her into a state of calm she rarely experienced when not immersed in her art. She had never ridden a horse before, but found it to be...harmonious. She was almost one with the animal, although her body seemed to be responding as much to the man sitting astride the horse with her as to the four-legged animal itself.

As her eyelids drooped and her head relaxed against his shoulder, Lucas's arms wrapped around her more tightly. Rather than feeling smothered this time, though, she knew he only wanted to make sure she would not fall. Just for a moment, she would relish the strength of this man's arms around her. She would have trusted no one else, but Lucas was a good and gentle man. She was safe with him…

The sound of a fire engine's air horn caused her to jump. Cassie glanced around, seeing flashing lights and several red trucks on the highway ahead of them. She had nodded off! How had she let her guard down enough to—

"You must have been exhausted."

Between working on her woven *quipu* piece almost nonstop for days followed by the adrenaline rush, stressing over packing what she needed, and leading her animals to safety, she had not been sure she could find a way off the mountain.

Cassie shuddered, remembering how disoriented she had become. "My girls and I might have died if you had not found us."

"Your voicemail scared the hell out of me, Sweet Pea. I could only hear every other word in your message, but when I heard you say you were evacuating… Just didn't know where you'd go, so I had to start where the trail began at your place."

"You could have been killed coming through the fire like that."

"I used Eduardo's shortcut. Avoided the worst of it."

Her skin felt warm against her back. "You're very good at tracking."

"Only so-so. Picasso did most of the work." He reached in front of her to stroke the horse's neck.

"Did you train him or is it instinct?"

"A bit of both. Working one-on-one with the same animal, you learn their signals, alerts, habits, and such." The horse picked up the pace a little as they neared the side of the road, and they began the climb up the highway to where Lucas had parked his truck.

"I've been thinking lately about training some of the other horses I'm working with for SAR missions, too, rather than give them up for adoption. I can pair them up with some of my squad members, eventually. Situations like today's prove the value in finding other ways to reach the lost and injured."

He continued toward the trailer. "Pic and I have been training a while, but this is only the second rescue mission we've done. He answered the call today and then some. Didn't you, Pic?"

Lucas patted the horse's neck, and the animal nickered his acknowledgement. Horses seemed to be very intelligent creatures, not unlike her alpacas.

He made another phone call to a dispatcher to let them know they had reached safety. "Let's settle the animals near the trailer and go to the ambulance and have you checked out."

"I am fine."

"Better safe than sorry. Probably won't take but a few minutes if your eyes, throat, and lungs all look and sound good."

Knowing the man did not back down on such things, she nodded. Realizing how close she had come to being lost out there, Cassie began to shake. Lucas reached for something in his saddlebag and soon placed her poncho over her head. She had left without it. The poncho had been a gift from *Abuela* the last Christmas before she passed over.

"I am so happy you rescued this. It holds much meaning for me, but in the rush to leave I did not have time to take everything I should have."

"It helped Pic to understand who we were searching for."

She reached up and stroked the nose of the tall horse. "Thank you, too, Picasso."

After tethering the horse and alpacas to the trailer, she grabbed her jacket from the saddle, and they walked to the parking lot at the pass. The area was teeming with activity, but someone called out to him.

"Hey, Rafe! Found her!" Lucas pointed to her and gave the man a thumb's up. "That's Angel's oldest brother. He'd have had my hide if I didn't make it back with you."

After an EMT pronounced her no worse for the experience, they started toward the trailer.

She turned toward her mountain, seeing smoke billowing at the peak. Flames shot upward in very close proximity to her place. It seemed the entire mountain was about to go up in flames. Tears sprang to her eyes. Nothing could survive.

Chapter Fourteen

Nearly an hour later, Cassie preceded Lucas into his ranch-style house. They had settled the alpacas into one of the empty horse stalls in the barn, and the poor, exhausted animals had promptly curled up and fallen asleep.

Exhaustion was doing a number on her, as well. She thought about what she had left behind, but there really were only a few things up there she had grown an earthly attachment to that could not be replaced—*Abuela's* blankets and shoulder cloth. All her artwork had been delivered to the gallery in Denver for the exhibition, except for the one she had taken with her. The portrait of her parents had been transported safely to Peru when Eduardo went home last month. But she had not remembered *Abuela's* things.

Tears stung her eyes. One of the most important remnants of her time in Peru with someone who loved her unconditionally and helped her form the foundation of her faith, and they had most likely been destroyed. Everything else could be replaced.

She pushed her regrets aside and began thinking more about the present. What would the sleeping arrangements be for her while she was here? The house was not very large. He had mentioned his double bed when they were negotiating the terms of their marriage arrangement, but she wondered now if there might not be another bedroom, too. If she was going to be here any length of time, she could order another bed and mattress set so as not to put him out.

Close quarters. Of course, they had managed fine in her even smaller cabin—well, once they had stopped sharing her twin bed. She would not be sharing a bed of any size with him.

"Let me take your poncho."

She shrugged out of it again, having experienced a bout of shivers after sitting in his truck, either from the air conditioning or the aftermath of the adrenaline drop. She handed it to Lucas who hung it on a hook near the door while she continued to survey the room.

Cozy room. Brighter and airier than her place. A Buck Stove dominated the room, with a red and black braided rug filling the open space between the stove and the couch.

Lucas offered her something to drink, and while he was in the kitchen, she wandered around. Above the mantle, he had displayed the pastel painting of him and Milagrosa, sending warmth through her heart as she remembered that special moment with Lucas. On the mantle itself sat a photo of an older couple smiling down at her. The man wore a Stetson, and there was no mistaking his resemblance to Lucas. The woman's eyes looked tired, but her smile seemed genuine.

"That was taken on their fiftieth anniversary two years ago."

Cassie wondered how his parents could be married so long. How old were they when they had Luke? She had not intended to ask, but Lucas must have anticipated her question. "They were married close to twenty years before they had me. I think I more than wore them out before they were done raising me."

"Oh, I am sure you were as easygoing then as you are now."

He grinned enigmatically, but did not respond.

Cassie's focus returned to the photo. Imagine trying for almost twenty years before finally becoming pregnant. Not that pregnancy was something she had ever thought about for herself, but the thought of wanting a child and having to wait so long seemed…torturous.

"Momma thinks I hung the moon. She was the one most involved in my upbringing. They worked the pipelines, so we were on the road a lot. She wanted to quit her job to stay home with me, but it just wasn't feasible until I was in high school."

"What kind of pipeline?"

He motioned for her to sit down and handed her a glass of iced tea. "Crude oil. I forget everyone doesn't live where pipelines are an everyday part of life."

"Did you always live in Texas?"

"Not in the beginning. We lived in Wyoming for a few years, I'm told. Then one summer they were transferred to Alaska. Maybe that's where I fell in love with the mountains and snow, but I was only nine and didn't learn about the power of the mountains." A cloud descended over his eyes, no doubt remembering his wife, but he smiled ruefully. "Before and after Alaska, most of Dad's jobs were in Texas or South Carolina." He took a sip of tea. "Until high school, when Momma put her foot down and insisted they settle down so I could make friends and prepare for college in a good school district. So they retired and bought a place in El Paso."

"I have never been to Texas. What is it like?"

"Big." He grinned. "And brown. Not a lot of trees. But damn, the spring is nice, with the Indian paintbrush and cacti flowering, not to mention all the bluebonnets. Still, I don't think I could live there again. Colorado has been home for a long time, since soon after I lost Maggie." He looked away and took a long drink of his tea. "This is home now. How about you?"

"You know already that I grew up in Peru. Went to uni—Columbia— in New York City on an art scholarship and moved out here after graduation thanks to a generous alumna."

"Why didn't you go home to Peru?"

She took several sips of the iced tea as she contemplated how to answer his probing question, but decided less would be more in this case. "My heart was no longer there. But the mountains here remind me of what I loved most about Peru. I can work from anywhere."

"You ever feel lonely up on that mountain?" Cassie wondered why he wanted to know, but before she answered, he elaborated. "I used to think I was okay being alone until Angel moved in here a few months back. Only stayed a couple weeks, but the place sure felt lonely after she'd gone." He grinned. "I sure miss her cooking, too."

The thought of Angelina coming here when she was clearly in love with Marc seemed odd, too. Did she not worry that Lucas would make advances—or that Marc would go into a jealous rage like...?

Don't think about Pedro.

The silence dragged out a little too long, and Cassie cleared her throat. Wanting to make sure she understood what he meant about sleeping arrangements, she asked, "So you have a spare bedroom?"

"Nope. Just the one."

Her hand trembled until she willed it to remain still by gripping her glass harder.

"When I bought this place, I just needed a functional house fast. Since it was just me, I figured one was enough. Wasn't expecting all this drop-in company." His teasing grin did nothing to calm her nerves.

She patted the cushion between them. "I will sleep here on the couch then."

"Like hell. You'll sleep in my bed."

Her hand shook in earnest now. When Lucas reached toward her, she flinched and pulled away, sloshing her drink, but he only took the glass away and placed it on the coffee table.

"You need to stop thinking I'm going to break our agreement every chance I can, Cassie. Angel had my room to herself. There wasn't anything sexual about it. I told you before that I have no problems being friends with a girl. If friendship is all you want out of our marriage, I can live with that decision, whatever your reasons. You've marked our boundaries clearly. I'll honor them. But you need to stop expecting the worst from me at every turn. Have I ever done anything to break your trust?"

He had never been anything but respectful of her boundaries. "No. But wh-where will you be sleeping?"

"Plenty of options. Weather's warmer now. I can bed down in the barn or in my studio."

"No! I do not want to put you out of your own house."

"No matter how you see it, you're not only my friend—you're my wife." He reached up and brushed his thumb over her cheekbone before she placed more distance between them by sitting back. "There's also this couch, which I've spent a few nights on when the bed was just too big." He glanced away. "Stop worrying so much, Sweet Pea. Consider this place your home until you can return to your cabin."

Tears pricked her eyes, and she blinked them away. "What if the fire…" She couldn't complete the sentence.

"Don't think like that. Lots of these fires just burn themselves out on trees and don't come near structures. Crews are working night and day. Human lives, pets, and homes are their highest priorities."

"But it seems like there are much bigger fires burning all over the state. My mountain is not very populated, so it will not be high on anyone's list of priorities."

"The local fire companies will make it their priority. Important thing is that you and the animals are safe. Possessions can be replaced. Your alpacas and you…"

Lucas broke off and turned away. He must be thinking about Maggie again. "You did all you could to save her."

When he met her gaze, he seemed confused. "You know about her?"

"Your wife?" How could he think she didn't know?

"No." He fingered the worn wristband she'd never seen him without. "I've pretty much let go of the blame for that. But there was a rescue I botched up where we lost an eight-year-old girl..."

"Oh, Lucas." She reached out and squeezed his hand, covering the warm leather.

He stared at her hand before he continued. "It was my first year doing SAR work. I got into it after meeting Marc while doing some work at the club they were about to open. I thought it might help me unload some of the guilt I carried over losing not only my wife but a rescue worker who tried to save her."

Lucas took a deep breath and turned his arm over to where the wristband showed. "This was her necklace. We found it...on the trail. Apparently, she used to make beaded necklaces, and this thong was one she wore that night. It must have gotten snagged on something. The beads were scattered nearby, so I think she must have been running." He continued to twist the braided leather and finished on a husky note. "Her parents didn't want any reminders, but I couldn't just toss it away." A tear splashed onto her hand. She moved closer to him and wrapped an arm around his back.

He cleared his throat. "She'd wandered off from her family's campsite one evening. Temperatures went below freezing that night. We did what we could, but by the time we found her..."

"I am so sorry. I know how much you care about every living creature, but to be unable to rescue her... Still, you have rescued so many others."

"Those aren't the ones that haunt you. I became more determined than ever not to quit after that. Haven't lost anyone since then. Maggie used to help guide me to the lost ones, especially children. But I don't feel her presence anymore. I think she's moved on."

Cassie had not sensed her around him, but did not know for certain.

He met her gaze. "When I went in search of you, I begged her to help me." Seeing the tears in his eyes and tearstains on his face broke her heart.

"But you found me."

"Thanks to Pic."

"No, you deserve much more credit than that. Picasso would not have been on that mountain if not for you. You trained him to find the lost."

He shrugged. "His former owner did a lot of the training. I just gave him a refresher."

"I will not hear another word about this. You saved us with help from Picasso. That is all I will ever believe. You have saved many others in your years as a rescue worker. Do not ever doubt that."

"I took the wrong path." He looked at the wristband again. "When I found this, I thought I must be close. But I came to a fork and took the wrong path."

"You are human. How can you be expected to find a lost child in the dark?"

"It was my job."

"Were you the only person out searching that night?"

"Of course not. We had every available person looking for her."

"Lucas, you did your best with what you knew at the time. Now with Picasso, you will do even better in the future."

He nodded. "That's one of the reasons I'm so passionate about training horses for SAR work. He'd have been able to track her even in rough terrain like that. He could have covered more ground than the search dogs, too."

"May I ask why you torture yourself by wearing that band every day?"

He shrugged. "I can't let myself forget her death. By wearing this, I not only remember her and what she taught me, but I think her parents wanted me to keep it so I would never let down another family like that again."

"I do not think they would be that cruel. I think they just did not want the reminder. They were in shock. No parent would blame you for trying."

"I was the one who eventually... I had been within feet of her at one point during the night, but she didn't answer when I called her name."

Cassie could stand it no longer. She wrapped both arms around him and held on tightly. He returned the hug, squeezing the breath from her lungs.

"Lucas, she was probably terrified and taught not to speak to strangers. Perhaps she was already unconscious and succumbed to hypothermia without being aware what was happening."

He ran his hand through his hair. "I'll never know. But I'll never forget, either."

Her cabin had been her sanctuary for years, but since Lucas left, it had seemed more like a prison. However, she dreaded the thought of having to start over. What if her landlady would not rebuild the only home Cassie had known for the past four years? The woman was up in years and might not want to undertake such a daunting task just to have a rental property.

If forced to move, Cassie would miss the spirit of the place she had found in the mountains of her adopted state.

Please, Goddess, do not take my home away. Not again.

*   *   *

Luke decided Cassie needed her space. She seemed a little fragile. No surprise given what she'd been through today.

"Why don't I show you around before I go out to the barn to settle Picasso down for the night?"

"That would be nice." She stood.

Luke showed her the kitchen first, in case she was hungry. "I have some ready-to-eat stuff in the pantry. Simple fare, but we won't starve. Just choose what looks good to you, and I'll fix supper when I come back in."

"I can fix us something."

"No way. You've been through a lot today. Just relax."

The wariness never left her expression. Luke sighed. This girl had some serious trust issues. Pissed him off that after all this time she still didn't trust him as far as she could throw him, even though he'd never done anything to disrespect her boundaries.

Her wounds must be bone-deep. If he ever got his hands on the asshole who hurt her…

After explaining the idiosyncrasies of the old appliances he'd inherited with the place, he guided her toward the bedroom door. Knowing she'd probably freak out if he was with her in there, he opened the door and pointed. "Bed's all yours." Good thing he'd made it this morning. "Bathroom's over there. I have plenty of western shirts in the closet and T-shirts in the dresser if you want to change into something clean. Just leave your clothes in the laundry basket, and I'll put in a load of wash before we go to bed."

At the mention of them going to bed, she glanced at the only bed in sight, nibbling her lower lip. Damn it, how was he going to make her see she had nothing to worry about?

Show her. Don't tell her.

Trust building took time. He'd continue to be patient. *God, don't ever give her a reason to doubt his trustworthiness.*

Cassie walked into the room and turned, her hand on the knob. "Thank you for everything, Lucas." Without waiting for him to say anything, she closed the door.

Well, now...

Luke shook his head as he carried their empty glasses into the kitchen and set them by the sink before heading for the front door. Grabbing his Stetson, he left the house and glanced up at Cassie's mountain. Smoke covered half the west side of the mountain, just where they'd been a couple of hours ago. A shudder passed through him as he thought what could have happened if Pic hadn't tracked her down. That horse was in for a bonus scoop of oats tonight and an extra-long rubdown.

He'd try to keep Cassie busy in the house so she wouldn't watch the progression of the fire toward her cabin, but Luke knew the chances of her place being spared were slim now. When he was eight, their rental house had burned to the ground. Luke had learned then not to become too attached to material things. Had Cassie taken everything of sentimental value with her?

More than likely, the studio held the most sentimental value for her. Maybe it would survive. There wasn't much in *his* studio Cassie could use. Her artistic talents took a different form than his. Maybe they could get through to Breckenridge tomorrow. She could stock up on new art supplies. Best medicine for her would be to get back to creating art.

Of course, she'd be headed to Karla's again in a few days for the baby shower. Then came her gallery opening. Still, he would have at least a few days with her.

Inside the barn, he heard the cria clicking. Funny how he recognized Millie from the others. They had a special bond, though. He poked his head inside and found the youngest alpaca poking at Gracie's teat for some milk. Did alpaca moms have milk production problems when stressed? Luke let himself inside and walked over to the two. He stroked Gracie's long neck.

"There now, girl. You're safe now. No one's gonna hurt you here as long as I have anything to say about it." The soulful eyes of the new *mamá* searched his, and then she nodded almost imperceptibly. Smart animals. It was as if she understood as much as his horses did.

"She's never handled change very well."

Luke turned to watch Cassie let herself inside the stall and lock it behind her. The girl didn't follow instructions well. She should be resting. He noticed she wore one of his plaid shirts and a pair of his jeans, rolled several times. He wondered what she used to hold them up around her tiny waist, but didn't ask. She let the shirt cover her down to her thighs.

They needed to go shopping for clothes, too.

Gracie moseyed over to her. Almost sounded like she was crying. Cassie wrapped her arms around her neck, nuzzling her cheek against the animal's soft fleece.

"*Todo va a estar bien, estamos seguros aqui.*"

Luke smiled. He'd been around enough Spanish speakers in Texas to translate her "*Everything's gonna be okay. We're safe here.*" Would she have admitted that she felt that way to him? Probably not. He ought to 'fess up about his limited Spanish skills, but it might be interesting to see—and hear—what he'd learn about her.

"I'll just leave you to take care of these girls while I check on Pic."

Cassie glanced in his direction and nodded. He waited to see if she'd say anything, disappointed when she didn't.

As he turned away, he heard her whisper, "Lucas is our hero, girls."

Pride swelled in his chest. He was glad he'd heard those words. He wanted to be a hero in her eyes. Luke wore a sappy grin the entire time he took care of Picasso. The horse barely flinched when he came into his stall now. "You were amazing today and a great sidekick. I'm so proud of you." He stroked the horse's neck. "Thank you for finding Cassie and her girls. They needed us, and you were there for them."

The horse nickered and dipped his muzzle into his feed bucket. Luke picked up the comb and grooming spray and began to work the brambles out of his tail. He'd worked his way almost halfway up the tail when he heard the stall door hinges squeak.

"May I help? I owe Picasso a lot."

"Sure. Why don't you grab the currycomb and start on his mane? He picked up a lot of dirt and debris out there today." Out of the corner of his eye, he watched Cassie eye the assortment of combs and brushes on the table. "It's the blue rubber one."

She nodded and picked it up, going to work with a persistent but gentle hand. "Here, spray on some of this. Makes it easier to remove the tangles and will keep them away a few days. We may get called out again."

She nodded and accepted the bottle from him. Their fingers touched, and he felt electricity spark between them. Damn, he'd gone too long without a woman if the mere touch of their fingertips turned him on.

Not that it was any surprise he found her attractive. He'd been aware of her in that way since they met last fall at the hospital. Hell, even before Karla had shown him the sketch Cassie had drawn, he'd been watching her for hours as her hand flew over the sketchpad, never realizing she was sketching an image of Maggie and their unborn baby.

He and Cassie worked side-by-side on Picasso's grooming in silence. He instructed her in how to make the small, circular motions, and she curried the right side of his neck working her way toward his tail. Cassie reached out a few times with a comforting pat to Picasso's neck if the horse became agitated. She understood animals and had a natural connection with them.

She softly crooned in some language he wasn't familiar with. He felt left out. "What's that song you're singing?"

"*Punulla Waway.*" She avoided making eye contact. "It is something *mi mamá* used to sing to me. A traditional lullaby from the Peruvian Andes."

"I like it. Very soothing. I think Pic liked it, too."

After finishing with Picasso's tail, Luke grabbed another currycomb and began to work on the horse's loins, bumping against Cassie's arm accidentally before she retreated. He didn't apologize, but tried to keep a little more distance between them so as not to spook her. Working beside her like this was too enjoyable to screw up.

"You came when I called you today."

Luke's hand slowed to a standstill. He gave her a puzzled sidelong glance. Something was being sorted out in that beautiful mind of hers. Maybe she'd come to realize not all men were unworthy of her trust. "Nothing could have kept me away. You needed me. I'd been worried sick for days already with all these fires."

She met his gaze. "I have not been so frightened in…well, a very long time."

He hated the thought that she'd been through worse at some point, but someone as skittish as Cassie must have been in the bowels of hell at least once.

The lady didn't talk much about her past. Everyone faced some kind of adversity in their lives. Part of the reason they were here on earth, he supposed, was to learn from those trials. Some spent their lives running from their fears. Others faced them head on. Hell, when he heard what Marc had done while Luke was stranded up at Cassie's place, he'd been floored. The man was impulsive and a risk-taker, but no way in hell would he have risked his sanity in such a hardcore interrogation scene like that for anyone, not even Cassie.

Of course, maybe he shouldn't say never until he was in a situation where he felt he had no other choice, the way Marc had been. He hadn't thought about his own safety today when he went after her, after all.

"Thank you for making that call, Sweet Pea." Asking for help was not something Cassie was comfortable with doing.

After they had worked the dandy brush and body brush through on both sides and Luke had taken care of Pic's legs and hooves, he cleaned out the brushes with the metal currycomb.

Cassie moved to stand beside Pic's head and began whispering to the horse. "There you go, Picasso. All done." Luke walked cautiously around the back of the gelding watching for any sign he might kick him and tried to look busy while surreptitiously watching the two of them. She made eye contact with the horse and began to speak in another language. He tried to decipher what she was saying. Not Spanish. Sounded more like Native American. Then she became silent and seemed to "speak" to the animal through her eyes and the touch of her fingers and palms.

Suddenly, Pic leaned forward and nuzzled Cassie's cheek. Luke smiled. He didn't know what communication had passed between the two, but clearly they had made a heartfelt connection.

Luke tamped down an unexplainable sense of jealousy. Where had that come from? He was thrilled Pic was able to connect with Cassie—and Cassie with the horse, as well. Maybe he envied the horse's ability to break through her defenses so quickly. Luke had barely been able to touch her without sending her into a retreat.

Sack the pity party, Denton.

Maybe Cassie would find peace here like Luke had found when he first started taking in the abused horses. He sensed the same vulnerability in Cassie that he'd seen in his horses. He wished he could heal her wounds, but she wouldn't let him that close.

As if coming out of a trance, Cassie blinked and shifted her gaze to Luke. He rubbed his hand over Pic's shiny coat, trying not to appear as though he'd been eavesdropping, as if he could understand anyway.

"Picasso told me how much he loves you."

Luke furrowed his brow. "Beg your pardon?" Pic communicated with her? "You're a horse whisperer?" Cassie smiled. He wasn't sure if she was teasing or dead serious.

She continued. "He said you're much more caring than his last owner. You give him space when he needs it, but you also provide a sense of security when he wants to venture beyond the safety of his stall."

His chest practically swelled to hear Pic felt that way. "I thought you said you hadn't been around horses before."

Cassie shrugged and returned her attention to Picasso. "I have a tele-pathic connection with most animals. I am sure Picasso has never heard my Quechua language before, but he understood my words on the heart level."

Dayum. The girl was full of surprises.

Luke could meet the needs of these animals, keep them safe, help them heal, train them for a new or renewed purpose, but he'd never communicated with them like that. Now he had an opportunity to change his relationship with them, with Cassie's help.

"Would you tell him something for me?"

Cassie gazed at him and nodded.

"Tell him…" Luke cleared his throat but spoke in an almost reverent whisper. He felt like he was back in church. This was a very spiritual moment for him. "Tell him I won't let anything bad happen to him ever again, if I can help it. That I'll protect him and give him shelter for as long as he needs. Just tell him he'll always be safe with me."

Cassie closed her eyes and drew in a deep breath, making Luke realize she might just have taken the words to heart as if meant for her, as well. He hoped so, because they applied to her, too.

Picasso would be a good surrogate, though. His words would be less personal or intimidating when he spoke to the horse. Cassie would be uncomfortable with declarations like that from Luke to her, but maybe she'd see she shared a bond with the horses and could heal alongside them.

Surely she could see that Luke would never hurt her, either.

She opened her eyes again and stroked Picasso's cheek as she stared into his eye, apparently passing along the message in a mixture of her native tongue and mental telepathy. When a tear trickled down Cassie's cheek, he figured he'd broken through to her, too.

Maybe there's hope yet.

Cassie stroked Picasso's neck, and once again, Luke couldn't help but feel a little jealous that her gentle hand wasn't touching him. Before he let himself become too sappy or flat out embarrassed himself, he figured he'd better hightail it inside. "I should be startin' supper. I'm sure you're hungry by now."

"Let me do that. I am sure I can find something, and you still have your other horses to take care of."

He watched her leave the stall and turned his focus back to his horse. "Well, Pic, I think you've made a new friend." The horse nickered and nodded. Luke smiled and patted his rump. "Good thing. She could use a few more friends."

Chapter Fifteen

Cassie entered Luke's bedroom again, carrying the backpack and poncho she had left in the truck earlier. She scanned the room more slowly this time. The double bed covered in an off-white chenille coverlet dominated the room. The bedspread looked well-worn. Vintage, no doubt. She wondered who it had belonged to before. She marveled again that the bed had been made. What single man made his bed when he could not possibly have been expecting company?

Heavy woven blankets served as room-darkening drapes over the two windows. Opening the drapes to let in the waning sunlight, something about the bed caught her eye. She walked closer and noticed the carvings in the pine post on the footboard.

The hummingbird captured her attention, flitting at the mouth of the trumpet-shaped flower that reminded her of the angel trumpet vines back home. So lifelike she almost thought she caught the fluttering of the tiny bird's wings. On the other post, she found vined sweet peas being visited by bumble bees. She had never seen detailed carvings like these on a bed before—or possibly anywhere else—and wondered if this was some of Lucas's work.

But he seemed to work on much more functional pieces, not chiseling whimsical figures on his bed. Artists rarely indulged in creating art for themselves. If he did carve such things, he most likely would have done them for a client.

Turning around, the dresser drew her closer, and she saw carvings of flowers, butterflies, and other insects. Her gaze rose to the top of the dresser, and she stopped breathing for a moment. In a hand-carved frame was the sketch Cassie had drawn at the hospital following Adam's attack by the puma. She still did not know where the inspiration had come from, but assumed her spirit guide had led the woman to her in that moment to be able to deliver a message of comfort to Lucas from the other side.

Lucas had told her he saw the sketch every morning when he awoke, but she did not realize he had taken such steps to enshrine it. Embedded in the wood were matching wedding rings, no doubt his and his wife's. His *first* wife's. She blinked away the sting in her eyes. He must have loved her very much. How sad to have lost her and their unborn child so tragically.

"I can't thank you enough for sharing that sketch with me."

Cassie jumped and pivoted to find Luke standing in the doorway, leaning on the jamb. The joy she had seen earlier in his gaze had been replaced by profound sadness. Her heart and soul felt a piercing ache, absorbing his grief before she shook it off, not wanting to take on this man's pain.

He entered the room, and her breath caught. As he drew near, the scent of soap and leather assailed her. Heat rose in her cheeks, probably from the rapid beat of her heart. She did not fear Lucas, so why was her body responding in such a way? Why did he affect her so? He did not scare her exactly, but her body went on high alert whenever he drew near.

Cassie forced herself to take a slow, deep breath. Allowing herself more room, she took a step back and came up against the dresser.

He turned toward Cassie and smiled, but his eyes did not let go of their sadness. "I found peace for the first time with knowing she was okay in heaven or wherever it is we go after we…"

Cassie did not know what to say so she merely nodded. Then she found her voice. "She wanted to convey that message to you very badly."

"I think she'd been trying to get it through my thick skull a while by that point, but I wasn't receiving the message. She'd come to me in a couple dreams. Sometimes even helped me out on search-and-rescue missions. She always seemed happy and content, but I just figured it was wishful thinking on my part."

"Some people are so afraid of death for themselves that they do not realize the only part of us that dies is our physical self. Our souls never die. We can even communicate with those on the other side if we tune into them."

Luke glanced at his wife's image for a long moment and, without turning back to Cassie, said, "For me, I think it's best I leave her to continue her journey over there. It's enough to know she's happy and they're together. I'm finally at peace with their loss."

Cassie was not sure if that was true but could understand his need to move on. Hanging on to those who were no longer here could make his own life's journey more difficult and less fulfilling.

Cassie thought about her parents. She had cut herself off from them except by infrequent video chats when Eduardo arranged them. Tears pricked her eyes, blurring Luke's image before her. She missed them both and knew they would not be alive forever. But she had shamed them and could never face them again.

I miss them.

She supposed this sudden longing to go home to Peru was a product of not knowing if she had a home to return to here in Colorado. Of course, she could never return to the way Peru was when she was a little girl or even as it was during her teen years. Life had been good then, although she supposed the same *machismo* attitudes existed. She just had not been affected by society's rules and expectations of her gender then.

"Hey, no tears." Lucas's thumb brushed away a tear from her cheek, and Cassie took a step back, dashing away the remaining tears herself. "They're okay on the other side, remember?"

She nodded, letting him think her tears were for his wife and baby. Perhaps they were the lucky ones. Their difficult journey was over, at least for this lifetime. Hers stretched out forever in front of her, a long, lonely road.

"Sorry. I will go fix dinner now. I just wanted to put my things away. Are you sure about having me stay in your bedroom? You know I am not used to anything as enormous as this. I can sleep on a cot or on the floor if need be."

"We already settled that. I'll meet you in the kitchen, and we'll see what we can rustle up."

Cassie nodded and watched him leave the room. She breathed deeply, not realizing she had been taking only shallow breaths while standing next to Lucas. Her body responded to him as if afraid, although she knew there was nothing to be afraid of with him. Why was the feeling the same but different?

She placed her bag on the blanket chest at the foot of the bed, went to the bathroom to wash her face and hands, and then headed toward the kitchen. Unpacking would not take long. She could deal with that later. For now, she wanted to feel useful and show her appreciation to Lucas for giving her and her alpacas a safe place to live.

For saving her life.

Apparently, *Mama Quilla* was not finished with her yet.

*   *   *

Luke opened the door to the walk-in pantry. "Let me know what's workable. There's onions and potatoes in that bin over there." When she hesitated, he realized she wasn't going to go inside as long as he was standing at the door. "I'll check the fridge and see what's still edible. Haven't been grocery shopping all week."

As soon as he moved away from the door, she stepped inside, and he heard her moving things around on the shelves. In the fridge, he found carrots, tomatoes, and lettuce in the crisper and pulled out a couple of steaks from the freezer. Perfect. She didn't seem to have meat in her budget. This would be a real treat.

"How about a cookout, Cassie? I can fire up the grill in no time."

She stepped out of the pantry with several cans of vegetables in her arms and stared at the butcher-paper wrapped packages he held before glancing up at him.

"I'm vegetarian, but you go ahead if you want to eat that."

Damn, he just figured she didn't have any meat at her place, not that she had sworn off meat altogether. Then he remembered their first real date and the face she'd given him when he'd suggested a steakhouse—as if he'd asked her to eat road kill. Why didn't she just come out and tell him before?

How could she stay strong and healthy without any meat protein? He checked out the cans she'd chosen and saw broth, whole-kernel corn, and black beans. He supposed beans were where her protein came from and remembered her serving a lot of them while he was at the cabin.

"Maybe I'd better leave the cooking to you tonight. I'm so hungry I could eat a…" Okay, better not finish that sentence with any of the usual clichés. "Anything you make will be perfect. What do you want me to do?" For starters, he put the steaks back in the freezer.

"Baked potatoes would be good."

Yeah, with his appetite, that just might help. But he'd had no problem eating his fill on the wholesome meals she prepared at the cabin.

This woman sure can cook up a storm.

He walked around her, hating the way she stiffened as he came near her, and entered the pantry to grab some spuds. He wished she wouldn't be so skittish around him, but maybe with time, she'd come to realize he wasn't going to hurt her. He'd worked with enough abused horses to know time and patience were the only way to cure that.

Luke oiled and wrapped the potatoes and placed them on the center rack in the oven. Cassie was busy filling a Dutch oven with the ingredients for what he guessed would be a soup or stew. "Hey, I just remembered that there are some scallions ready out in the garden. Let me yank up a few. They should be good in that soup."

She smiled at him. "You have a garden?"

"Well, it's pitiful compared to the ones my mom tended, but I try to enjoy a few of the basics in the summer." He went outside the back door and came back a few minutes later with a handful of scallions. After washing them off, he took them over to the island and laid them on the cutting board. Once again, Cassie's body went on the alert with his close proximity, and he stepped away from her.

"Might be too many cooks in this kitchen. I'll leave you to finish up in here while I go make up the bed in the studio."

"Lucas, you are certain you do not mind?"

He grinned. "I'm enjoying the company. Don't mind at all."

She nibbled on her lower lip, and he figured he needed to leave—fast. Damn, but her innocent sensuality would tempt a monk. Luke might have lived almost like a monk since Maggie died, but that didn't mean he planned to be one forever.

He needed to face it. His marriage to Cassie might never include anything more than companionship. She reminded him of his early days with O'Keeffe. She had some serious issues concerning men. Lord knows someone had hurt her bad. Would pushing her limits help or hurt?

Tonight, he'd just enjoy their time to sit down and talk over dinner. A second chance. He hoped to get closer to her. Maybe being on his own turf would give him an advantage. Just spending time with her every day was a big improvement. That was enough for right now. If anything came of this relationship, so be it, but he'd learned a long time ago not to let his hopes rise too high.

"Be back in a bit." He left the kitchen by the back door again and crossed the yard to the simple structure he'd built as his studio and woodworking shop. The smell of pine and cedar assailed him as he walked into the cluttered space. He had a number of projects going at once, as always. He should have built a bigger space, but he had been on a tight budget after buying this spread in foreclosure and paying the back taxes, to say nothing of the expenses for the mustangs.

Besides, he'd been so busy with the horses and the baby furniture lately that he'd fallen behind on his work here. The headboard he needed to repair for Damián and Savannah sat against the wall, and he'd been working for the past two months on an intricate piece of suspension equipment for Gunnar's dungeon in Breckenridge. Of course, everyone understood how his accident had put him behind. No one was being hard on him but himself.

He'd always been harder on himself than anyone else had been. Well, except maybe his dad.

The cot was covered with tools and hardware, so he cleared them off and went to the cabinet in the bathroom for fresh linens. The cot was stripped and made up in no time. He wondered if he should give Cassie more time to adjust to his place before returning to the house. No. She would spend too much time in her head imagining the worst from him and only make matters, well, worse.

He headed back to the house and entered through the kitchen door. Cassie's face and hands were covered in flour as she kneaded a loaf of bread. *Damn.*

"You don't have to go to all that trouble for me, Cassie."

She blew a puff out of the corner of her mouth to get the hair out of her eyes. "No trouble. I like being useful. I needed something to do while the soup simmered."

He couldn't very well tell her to stop when she was almost finished. "Did you see I had your amaranth flour here?"

She nodded and smiled. "I brought a loaf with me, but this one's for tomorrow."

"Soup smells great." How did she and Angel do it? He'd never made those canned goods and staples come out like a gourmet meal. He walked over and lifted the lid.

"No peeking! You will let the flavor escape!"

He smiled as he replaced the lid. "Yes, ma'am. I'll put in a load of laundry and set the table."

After returning from the bathroom with the basket in hand, he went straight to the laundry room near the back entrance. He poured a cup of detergent into the bottom and began pulling her clothing out. Something hard in her pocket made him check. Probably some money she'd forgotten about.

He pulled the folded paper out. Tossing the jeans into the washer, he didn't have to unfold the paper to know what it said. He'd written the words himself—the night before their wedding.

Luke grinned. She'd fled her home with very few possessions. That she had brought their wedding vows with her told him he might have made some kind of connection with her.

He put the paper in his pocket. He'd leave it on her nightstand before dinner. After starting the washer, he returned to the kitchen. She covered the dough with a dishtowel to let it rise. He didn't say anything, but rinsed his hands off at the sink nearby. He then set two placemats at a ninety-degree angle to each other on one corner of the table. When she brought in the bowls of soup, she eyed the proximity of the placemats a moment. He'd let her contemplate that while he went into the kitchen for a pitcher of iced tea and two glasses of ice.

Back in the dining area, he saw she'd moved her place setting across the table from his. Luke sighed. Okay, he'd give her some space tonight. She'd been through a lot today.

Now, what would be a non-threatening topic of conversation?

"So did you deliver everything to the gallery for the showing?"

"Yes, thank the Goddess. I would never have been able to save the pieces when I fled." She ate without making eye contact with him.

Her religion might be a topic to explore, but didn't society always say not to talk about politics and religion? Better stick to art and animals for now, although someday he wanted to explore her thoughts about spirituality and the afterlife. He'd read a lot, but had never been around anyone who seemed to live what he'd only studied intellectually.

"Is there a particular theme with this show?"

"No. Mixed media. A progression of my work over the years. I will be doing a watercolor workshop for gifted students in one of the Denver high schools."

"How's the work with the alpaca fleece coming?"

Her face became more animated as she spoke, and she set her spoon down inside the bowl. "It takes so much time to prepare the fiber, but I am loving working with it. Very earthy, vital. It will take a while before my alpacas produce enough fleece to include in my artwork, but I enjoy having the animals for companionship mostly. Fortunately, there are ranchers in the area I can purchase fleece from while I continue to experiment."

A shadow crossed her face. No doubt she was thinking about the fate of her mountain sanctuary now.

"After dinner, I'll call the fire station and see if there is any report on damage up your way."

"Would you? The not knowing..."

"Sure. The dispatcher may not have an answer right away, but she'll relay a message. I saw a couple of Angel's brothers up there working the fire."

"Why are you not out with them?"

"I'm not trained for firefighting, but I'm on call in case there's a need for search and rescue. My beeper hasn't made a sound. That's a good thing, because it means no one else is in danger."

She cast her gaze down and picked up her spoon again. "You did have a mission today. You saved our lives." She met his gaze. "Thank you."

"Now we're even. What do you call it? Karma?"

She smiled. "Something like that. It does not normally happen that fast, though. Sometimes not between the same people or even in the same lifetime."

"I don't want to think about living any other lifetimes. It's enough for me to make it through this one."

Would he be punished for the things he'd done wrong in this life and have to live through similar shit again until he learned his lessons?

Lord, I hope not.

Time to change the subject. "Soup's delicious. My compliments to the chef."

"I do not do anything fancy in the kitchen."

"Oh, but what you did was just what I needed tonight. Worked up an appetite." Damn. He didn't mean to remind her about what they'd been through today. Seeing that they were finished, he stood and picked up his bowl. "Since you cooked, I'll do dishes."

"I will carry mine to the sink." He followed her, watching the sway of her hips under his shirt before he came to stand beside her at the sink.

"Before I turn in, I am going to check on my girls. They might be frightened after today's experience."

"Sure thing. They've been in that stall before, though. I'm sure they'll adjust in no time. I'll be out in a little bit."

She nearly ran from the room, and he figured she was the one who was frightened. How could he make her feel at home here? Feel safe?

Trust him?

After he finished the dishes, stacking them in the dishwasher he rarely ran, he went into the bedroom and pulled the vows from his pocket. He set them on the nightstand and walked out of the room.

*   *   *

Cassie rounded the house and glanced up at the mountain. The fire had spread. She wasn't sure exactly where her cabin was located and whether the fire had come close—or already destroyed it. Not knowing was the hardest.

She hurried inside the barn and took refuge in the stall with her alpacas. They all came to her, whether seeking food or just some reassurance, she did not know, but she touched and spoke to each one to make sure they knew she had not abandoned them.

Lucas seemed to be trying really hard to make Cassie feel at home, too. Why was it so difficult to accept his hospitality—or his nearness?

A heavy weariness overcame her. She should go back inside the house and prepare for bed, but she was not ready to engage in further conversation with Lucas. Seeing Milagrosa curled up asleep in the straw, she went to her and lay down beside her, burying her fingers in the cria's soft fur.

Safe. The animal's soft breathing comforted Cassie. If only she could stay out here tonight rather than sleep in Lucas's bed.

Had he even changed the sheets this morning? Would his scent be on the pillow? He smelled of leather, a once-pleasant scent reminding her of her homeland, but she no longer wanted to be reminded of that place.

And yet she missed her parents and Eduardo and his family so much. "I envy you, Millie." Now Lucas had her calling the cria by the nickname he had given her. "You still have your *mamá*. I miss mine so much." Cassie heard the latch on the stall door and quickly dashed the tears from her eyes. She batted them quickly, hoping to remove any wetness that might be a sign of weakness.

Never let a man sense your weakness.

"Everything okay?"

Lucas's caring voice made her feel even more homesick, this time for her cabin on the mountain. She struggled to her knees, keeping her back toward him. "Milagrosa is feeling a little homesick tonight."

"Know the feeling. One trick I used to help keep homesickness at bay was to take something familiar from my old house to bed with me at night."

Curiosity won out, and she turned toward him. "What kinds of things?"

"All kinds of things. Might be a rock I'd found in the yard. One of those tiny classmate portraits of a friend from picture day at my last school. The string I had left from flying a favorite kite before it wound up in a telephone line."

His childhood sounded intensely lonely. "My childhood was so different. I grew up in the Andean village where my ancestors lived for centuries." She closed her eyes and pictured her house with *Mamá* working in the garden, tending to her medicinal plants. She'd been the healer everyone in the village came to when sick or needing spiritual guidance when the church did not have the answers.

There had been many times Cassie had wanted to consult with her *mamá* about something these past five years since her return to the States following the rape. But whenever she tried, *Mamá* usually wound up crying and begging her to come home. She could not do that. Never again.

"Sure you don't miss it?"

Cassie opened her eyes and stared at Lucas. "No. I miss my family, but not the culture of that place." He did not say anything, and Cassie felt the need to put more distance between them. "If you will excuse me, I am going to bed early." She paused and glanced away before adding, "You are a good man, Lucas Denton."

The words surprised her, but she believed in speaking the truth. Hopefully, he would not interpret her words in the wrong way.

She started toward the stall door where Lucas stood and breathed a sigh of relief when he opened it and stood back to let her pass. He seemed to sense how to keep from frightening her. He never invaded her personal space unless he had to, like today when they had to ride Picasso together to reach safety.

Cassie did not want to think about the feelings that horseback ride had stirred up, though. In some ways, Lucas was even more dangerous than the strangers she could simply ignore. He had found ways to connect with her soul that no man had done since before Pedro had shattered her trust.

For that reason, Lucas frightened her, even though she knew he did so without malice or intention to trick her into something she did not want.

She did not want to feel afraid ever again.

* * *

Luke watched Cassie practically run toward the house—or, more likely, run away from him. He sighed. Would he ever break down her barriers?

Speaking of which, O'Keeffe hadn't been worked today because of the emergency SAR mission. Luke sauntered down the barn aisle past the stalls and out into the corral. He'd had this rescue since February, but a short stay in the barn had convinced Luke she was more content out here. She didn't like being confined in tight places. She might just have been the most abused of all his horses.

Luke knew one thing she enjoyed, though. He picked up the worn football, set it on the ground, and then kicked it in O'Keeffe's direction, careful not to let it hit her. She needed to engage with the ball under her own terms. The mane covering her withers shook as she prepared to make her move. At the same moment, he edged closer. Her front hoof struck at the ball and sent it rolling back toward Luke.

"That's my good girl."

The bay-colored paint tolerated him more each time he worked with her. He continued to play with her for half an hour, coming closer to the horse with each kick of the ball. Sometimes she retreated backward a few steps, but not as far as she had when he started working with her late this winter. Discovering her love of football sure had surprised him.

Hell, with her, he liked playing football again. He would never have expected that. Good thing the former owners of this place had left the ball behind in the barn.

When O'Keeffe didn't kick the ball back this last time, he reached into his pocket. "All done for the night, girl? How about a treat?"

She eyed the carrots lying in his flat, outstretched hand. He waited for her to snatch them, but O'Keeffe whinnied her displeasure with him for forcing her to make contact with him. She continued to eye the treats with longing. Eventually, she stepped forward, closing the gap a bit more, and Luke took a step forward as well. They sized each other up again, and O'Keeffe took another tiny step in his direction.

He'd reached her previous limit. Would she take one more step? Luke waited. Patience was the key. He could outwait her, but wouldn't coddle her by giving her the treat without some work on her part.

Come on, girl. Come to ol' Luke.

She snorted her frustration, and just when he thought perhaps they were finished for the evening, she took one last step, closer to him than she ever had been to this point. Score! She gobbled up the three baby carrots in his flattened palm, and Luke scooped up the football and carried it back to the barn in the crook of his arm.

His mind flashed back to a Friday night game with his high-school team where he'd been the quarterback. He was heading off the field after a rare interception.

"You should have evaluated the coverage better."

"Sorry, Dad. I'll do better next time."

"You'll have to. Recruiters from UT could show up at any game. Hell, maybe they were in the stands tonight. They'll move on if they see you playing like that."

"Yes, sir." He didn't know what he could promise other than to do better, so he left it at that. Maybe he'd go over to Mr. Proctor's workshop tonight and work on that cabinet. He always found the troubles of the day drifted away when he was working on a project there.

Luke shook off the memory and wandered back inside the barn. As he approached Picasso's stall, he heard the horse whinny his greeting. He opened the stall door and crept inside, careful not to approach him too quickly, but Pic came over to him willingly. Luke wrapped his arms around the horse's neck and pressed his head against his shoulder, absorbing his energy and spirit and filling the void left by that memory.

"Love you, boy."

He snorted a reply of sorts, and Luke smiled as if Pic had returned the affection. The moment of sadness passed. Luke released the horse and pulled the remaining carrots from his pocket, feeding the whole bunch to him even though he knew Picasso hadn't come to him only for a treat. This one had come to love him unconditionally, of that Luke was even more certain after what Cassie had told him earlier.

"We rescued each other, didn't we, Pic?"

The bond he had with this horse was stronger than he had established yet with any of the other horses. Hell, with anyone, actually. They'd started out on shaky ground, but after months of work had reached a point where they knew they could trust each other.

"Thanks again, boy, for finding Cassie today." Luke's tracking skills were rudimentary, but this horse, once neglected by an aging owner, remembered his training when Luke and Cassie had needed him. Luke would have to work more on those skills now that he knew the horse was up to the task.

Eventually, he hoped all his horses could be trained for SAR work. But for now, he'd rely on Picasso. The wounded horse gave Luke hope he'd someday be able to reach O'Keeffe, too. That one had suffered more abuse than neglect in her past. She'd take longer to reach, but the reward would be that much sweeter.

Maybe someday he'd reach Cassie's wounded spirit, too. Somehow he couldn't think of O'Keeffe without also thinking of Cassie.

Chapter Sixteen

C assie tossed fitfully in the enormous bed for more than an hour after awakening in the wee hours of the morning, but sleep would not return. If she had been at her cabin, she could have gone to her studio and worked on something, as she often did on sleepless nights like this. As long as the animals were fed on time, she could keep any hours she liked, especially in winter when the daylight hours were shortened.

A glance at the clock told her it was not quite three o'clock. She wished she had a book or something to read, but there had been no time to pack the heavy things when she was forced to flee her home. Would her art books survive the fire if it reached her cabin? She had been amassing her own personal art library since college. While there were few material possessions in the cabin she would miss, the loss of that collection would hurt.

She sighed and tossed the coverlet aside. Flipping on the bedside light, something on the nightstand caught her eye. She had not placed the familiar folded paper with her wedding vows there.

He had found it in her jeans!

Lucas now knew she had rescued that scrap of paper when she fled her cabin. Why had he not gloated that the vows meant more to her than she had led him to believe? Still, he had placed them here to let her know he was aware she had them.

She opened the paper and reread the words he had written:

Beside me and apart from me,
in laughter and in tears,
in sickness and in health,
in conflict and serenity,
asking that you be no other than yourself.

She could not read more. In some ways, she had grown closer to Lucas, but not as a wife. And yet he seemed intent on living these vows—until death parted them.

Why? Who was this man she had married?

Cassie scanned the room searching for answers. On the other nightstand, she saw a book called *Angel Horses* next to one on the raising of alpacas. He must have been reading about alpacas because he had had to jump into taking care of hers. So conscientious.

She walked around the bed and picked it up opening it to a chapter on how important it was for alpacas to be together. If one was isolated from all others, she might die of loneliness. Cassie had instinctively known that she wanted more than one, after seeing how close they were on the ranch from which she had adopted them.

She understood loneliness. Isolating herself on the mountain, while safe, had left her slowly dying inside. Her spirituality had been the first thing she lost, although she kept trying to reconnect, and then she had slowly drawn within herself to venture out very rarely—usually only to see Kitty. But the alpacas had accepted her among them almost as if she were one herself. She would have hated for any of them to be taken away from her.

Next, she picked up the one about horses, stories of how they had affected the lives of the wounded and disabled. The healing power of animals. Lucas believed in that as much as she did.

Under that book had been one on building furniture, which did not surprise her but also did not interest her. She had noticed a bookshelf in the living room, though. Dressed only in a T-shirt and panties, she did not worry about Lucas seeing her because he had agreed to sleep in his studio or the barn. It was funny that both of them had studios separate from their living quarters.

Well, she used to, anyway. No doubt it had been destroyed by fire as well.

In the living room, she bent down and perused the shelf. Mostly non-fiction titles about horses, photography, and woodcraft.

A number of well-worn paperbacks on a lower shelf caught her eye, all with the theme of grief and coping with the loss of a loved one. Had Lucas made peace with the tragic losses in his life? She had the feeling he still harbored some anger…and a lot of guilt.

Cassie could relate to the anger and even grief, only she mourned the loss of herself.

If only she was not so restless tonight. When would she learn about the fate of her home? Lucas said the dispatcher had no news about her section of the mountain because their crews were focused on more populated areas first and knew she had been safely evacuated. She did not blame them. Possessions and houses could be replaced.

Cassie scanned the room and found it rather sparse. No knickknacks cluttered the space. The furnishings gave it a homespun, rustic appearance. Someone had handmade the dust cloths and doilies on the backs of the sofa and chairs. The old-fashioned tatting was something rare these days, a lost art. Her grandmother had tatted, but Cassie and her mother had not shown any interest in being taught how to carry on that fine skill. Regrettable, because Cassie might have been able to use the technique in some of her fiber-art pieces, but she would just have to make do without that knowledge since her grandmother had passed over many years ago.

Surely there was something here that would occupy her mind—or help her go back to sleep. Her gaze returned to the bookshelf where a small tome with a well-worn cover nearly jumped out at her. She had not noticed it before, but lying horizontally on top of the lower shelf of books was a copy of *The Secret*. She pulled the small volume from the shelf and stared at the cover a moment. She had heard of the fairly recent book before, although the philosophy was nothing new.

Like attracts like. Positive thoughts lead to positive outcomes in your life. She did not need a book to tell her how thoughts manifested into vibrations that would come back to bite her in the backside unless she made her originating thoughts more positive.

Knowing the book would not delve too deeply, she decided to read it a while as she waited for sleep to return. Then she noticed a book about one of the techniques she had been studying in fiber arts—Shibori. Excited, she pulled the book out and opened it only to find herself staring at images of women tied in elaborate rope bondage. She closed the book and looked at the title again. *Shibari*, not *Shibori*. The two-toned cover looked like a scientific journal or textbook, not a book filled with pornographic images.

And yet something made her open the book again. In truth, the images were not obscene, but artistic. The intricate designs used in binding and sometimes suspending the women were exquisite. Was this an art form Lucas dabbled in or wanted to explore? How could something so beautiful also be used to subjugate women?

And yet the peaceful-looking women in the photos seemed more enraptured than vanquished.

A key turned in the door, and Cassie slammed the book shut and crammed it back into the bookshelf as Lucas walked into the room. She stood to face him, heat rising in her face even before his gaze zeroed in on her and roamed up and down her body. She trembled, feeling for the first time the cool air on her bare legs.

"I'm sorry, darlin'. I saw the light on and wanted to make sure you were okay. Do you need anything?"

Just to be left alone.

She'd kicked the man out of his home and bed. The least she could do is show some gratitude.

"I am fine. I woke up and am having trouble going back to sleep." She fought the urge to run to the sofa and drag the afghan off the armrest to hide her body from his scrutiny. Why did he continue to stare at her like that?

"But I am headed back to bed now. Just wanted to find something to read." She realized she held no book in her hand. At his puzzled expression, she quickly turned to the bookshelf and grabbed *The Secret*, triumphantly showing him her selection. There was nothing to be embarrassed about with this reading material.

He grinned. Had he seen the book she had been looking at when he entered the house? Mortified, she moved away from the bookcase.

"I can make you some cocoa or warm milk, darlin'. Always helps me sleep."

"No, thank you." The only thing that was going to relax her was putting distance between them. The man left her…unsettled. She put her feet in motion in the direction of the bedroom, but something drew her up short before making her escape. "It is awfully early. You should be sleeping, too."

He shrugged and averted her gaze. "Sleep doesn't come sometimes. Your past comes back to haunt you when you're at your weakest—sleeping."

You do not have to tell me.

For the first time, she noticed the haunted expression in his eyes. After all he had done for her, the least she could do was spend some time talking with him until he was ready to go back to bed in the studio or barn or wherever he slept. Her own chances of sleeping would elude her this night anyway.

"On second thought, cocoa sounds delicious."

When he smiled in her direction, she hoped she had not made a mistake. He turned toward the kitchen before she could change her mind. "I'll put the milk on."

Cassie drew in a deep breath and tried to calm her nerves before grabbing the afghan and following him. She placed the book on the table. A manual for communicating with this man might have been more beneficial at the moment.

Taking her seat, she watched him work. Lucas knew his way around a kitchen. No surprise. He had been on his own a long time, apparently. He had above-average survival skills when it came to providing for his needs—his physical ones, at least.

Do not *think about Lucas's physical needs.*

She returned her focus to the chocolate. Kitty had introduced her to instant cocoa on those cold winter nights in the dorm at Columbia. They spent many nights sipping the drink while trying to keep Cassie's monsters at bay. Poor Kitty had put up with a lot during their senior year, including nights on suicide watch debating whether she needed to take Cassie to the psych ward or if talking it out would be enough.

Do not think about those days. They are in the past.

But in Peruvian culture, cocoa was the food of the gods and even part of traditional betrothal and marriage ceremonies.

She would not think about that connotation, either, while sipping cocoa with Lucas. Here in America, it was merely a comfort drink for a restless night.

Lucas brought two mugs of steaming cocoa to the table and placed one in front of her. As far as she could tell, he did not seem to be depressed or to need anything from her other than companionship. She marveled that he seemed pretty upbeat most of the time, considering the great losses he had suffered. She glanced at the cover of *The Secret* again as she stirred the brown liquid in the mug.

"Is the bed comfortable enough, darlin'?"

She nodded as she took a sip of the overly-sweet cocoa. "How about your makeshift one?"

"It's fine. I've slept there many nights."

Silence dragged out between them for a few minutes, as they each seemed inordinately interested in the contents of their mugs. While Lucas seemed comfortable just sitting and sipping cocoa with her, she soon became uncomfortable with the silence—or was it his nearness?

Cassie pointed to the book. "I was surprised to find this on your bookshelf."

"I found it a few years after Maggie died. Helped me turn things around in my life."

Ah, so that explained how the man remained upbeat most of the time.

"What did your wife do?" She would not invite him to question her on why she suffered from insomnia, too. Perhaps talking about his wife would help bring up whatever issues were keeping him awake tonight. If he was plagued by ghosts, his wife would be front and center.

"A biology instructor at the University of Texas. Botany was her specialty. Knew everything about every plant growing in Texas." He paused a moment. "Then she wanted to learn more about mountain ones, so we ventured up here one spring." His voice grew softer. "Neither of us knew anything about the mountain climes."

After a moment of watching him stare into his near-empty mug, Cassie prompted him to continue. "You must have felt very helpless."

His chin shook almost imperceptibly before his jaw tightened. "I was her husband. I should have been able to protect her."

Before she was aware she had moved, her hand covered the one wrapped around his mug. "Lucas, each of us is responsible for ourselves. She made the choice to put herself in that position."

"I know. She never had any regard for her safety, but usually, I foresaw the dangers and kept her from being hurt. Not that time. I had no idea that shelf was unstable. Just assumed it was a solid mountain ledge. I've learned since then about the dangers of permafrost melting and weakened snow masses." He shrugged. "Back then, I was clueless about mountain conditions."

She brushed her thumb over his knuckles, trying to comfort him, but nothing she did would take away that kind of pain and regret. He needed to forgive himself. He was so much like Adam in that regard.

His gaze pierced her with his smoky-gray eyes. "Can you tell me something, Cassie?"

She hoped she would not regret this response. "I will try."

"When Maggie came to you that day at the hospital, did she have any message for me other than what you depicted in that sketch?"

"I am sorry. I am not a psychic medium. I did not hear her speak. The image was imprinted on my mind and would not let go until I had sketched and released it. I did not even know who she was at the time."

Luke quirked his mouth in regret and nodded.

"Is there something you want to hear from her?"

He shrugged again. "Nah. Just wondered."

It seemed he was being less than truthful. She pulled away. "Is Maggie the reason you could not sleep tonight?"

He closed his eyes and shook his head. "No. I don't dream about her anymore. Not since I was semi-conscious in your cabin. They came back to me then mainly because of the avalanche."

If that were true, why would he be dwelling on Maggie tonight? She wished she could remove some of his pain. He was a good man and should not allow regrets over something out of his control to keep him from living life to the fullest.

"The accident was no one's fault. Maggie's destiny in this life may have been to die on that mountain, just as yours was to survive. She was a fortunate woman."

He furrowed his brows. "What do you mean?"

"To have a man who loved her and still pines for her all these years later is a rare and special gift. Most people never find that kind of connection."

And some, herself included, avoided any chance of allowing someone like Lucas to love them for fear of being…smothered.

But something bothered her. "She should not have put you in a position to have to live with this much regret."

*   *   *

Blaming the victim?

Luke stared at her, finding no words to respond as her words sank in. He'd gone through the anger phase of grief long ago but had been overridden with guilt afterward. Accuse Maggie of causing her own accidental death? "She didn't get herself killed on purpose."

"No, but she put herself in a dangerous situation. We have to take responsibility for our actions." A pained look flashed before her eyes before she blinked and looked down at the table.

"She's dead." Why was Cassie so adamant about this? Did she blame herself for some action she took that led to disastrous consequences, too?

Cassie continued without meeting his gaze. "Her soul did not die, only her earthly body. I am sure she continues to work from the other side to make amends for making you watch her die like that. She doesn't want that karma to follow her for eternity."

Luke blinked. Karma. He believed in an afterlife. Only his was the kind where you have one go-around on earth and then go to heaven or hell. No do-overs.

"But you drew a picture of her in heaven, Cassie. Why would she have to worry about making amends for the mistakes made down here anymore? She's home."

"That was how you interpreted the sketch. I only drew her in the depiction of an afterlife she showed me. She probably knew you would be most comfortable picturing them in the clouds. Heaven, as you see it."

Luke wanted to go to the bedroom and bring her the sketch to point out other heavenly symbols in the sketch. "You made her an angel."

"Again, that is how she came to me. I just conveyed her message. You are the one who interpreted it as her being an angel. But I do not believe we humans become angels when we cross over. They are special souls who have held that designation since time began."

Luke had never been particularly spiritual and hadn't attended church a lot since he was in high school. "She…" He cleared his throat before he could continue. "She came to me in a dream once and told me she was sending me an angel who needed me." Had that been Maggie trying to make amends, as Cassie said? Cassie stared back at him without responding, so he continued. "I met Angel—Angelina—the next day."

When Cassie relaxed, he let her think the same thing he'd thought at first—that Angel was the angel Maggie was talking about.

"So that's why you call her Angel?"

Luke grinned. "Well, it started out that way." He hadn't realized until a week later that Angel, while needing his and Marc's help that night at daVinci's, wasn't sent for him at all. "Then the nickname stuck."

But at the hospital waiting for news about Adam, Luke began wondering if Cassie wasn't the angel he awaited. Her long dark hair and olive skin fit the image, but so had Angel's. After the avalanche this spring, he became more certain than ever Maggie only meant she was sending an angel to save *his* life. He'd been the one to decide to make her his wife, but maybe that wasn't what the stars had in mind for them at all. Was he trying to force something that wasn't meant to be—namely having Cassie fall in love with him?

He'd also turned around and rescued her and her alpacas. So that meant the dream's prophecy had been fulfilled. Then why was it he didn't want things to end there with Cassie? She'd tugged at his heart since the day they met. Beautiful—inside and out. Smart. Creative. Only Cassie was a lot more than the sum of her parts. She hid her light under the thickest damned bushel basket he'd ever seen, but every now and then a beam of her inner light peeked out. Like now, with her just talking to him and trying to help him sort out his feelings about the loss of his first wife.

Not wanting this connection to end, he decided to pursue the conversation further. "You believe in reincarnation, then."

"Yes."

"You've lived in other bodies in earlier times?"

She nodded. "So have you. But not all incarnations are here in earth's linear time."

This conversation was growing deeper than he had intended to take it, but he didn't want to stop talking and have both of them return to their lonely beds.

"I am certain you are an old soul, Lucas."

Their marriage license application indicated Cassie was twenty-five, making him eight years older. He just remembered that her birthday was July the thirty-first. He'd have to be sure and do something special for her.

He grinned. "Sure it's not that I'm just old...period?"

"Chronological age has nothing to do with the age of the soul. An old soul must begin each incarnation on earth as an infant just like others do."

Okay, she wasn't going to let him tease her about this, and he probably shouldn't. Her thoughts on spirituality made a lot of sense. He wondered what his old man would think hearing about this. Dad insisted Luke find a traditional church to attend back home and throughout college. He'd done so out of respect for his dad, but Luke wanted to explore this philosophy a little further. "What are the signs of an old soul?"

"Being a loner. Introspective. Not quite fitting into the role of child while growing up. Understanding the transient nature of life."

She'd nailed him on the first three, but he stopped her litany on that last one. "Who said I understood it? I just learned to accept the unpredictable nature of life for what it is."

"But what if you planned a chart before you were born in which you and your spirit guides chose which issues you would learn from?"

"Predestination?"

"Not exactly. You might have said you needed to work on handling the fleeting nature of fame, for instance, and you then gained success on the football field only to lose it after college due to an injury or waning abilities."

He wondered what made her bring up football, but he was more intrigued by this notion that he might have set the Universe in motion to have certain things happen in his lifetime just so he could learn a lesson from them.

"I don't want to be saddled with guilt that Maggie died so that I could learn some life lesson. I've always believed there's a loving God, and we aren't here randomly. All this talk of karma makes me wonder how someone with a disability came to be that way. Did they choose it, or did it just happen and then they had to learn to deal with it?"

"That is where predestination becomes interesting and nearly impossible, because you do not know what she put into her own chart or what is a response to karma and what is just, well, random. While we each prepare our own charts, we cannot exist in a vacuum. We have to engage with other souls. That makes life less predictable. You also do not know how the two of you connected in prior lifetimes together. Often we return to work on issues with souls we were with in past lives."

"I don't remember any feeling of *déjà vu* or anything with her. How would I know we had shared some other lifetime?"

"Through meditation, past-life regression…"

No chance in hell he'd be delving into hypnosis and mysticism to try and find out what he and Maggie were doing in a past life. He had both boots planted firmly on the ground and intended to keep it that way. "I'll pass."

Her eyelids narrowed. "What scares you about it?"

He leaned back in the chair and sat upright. "Nothing. Just don't see the benefit in churning up things best left alone."

Cassie stared down at her mug, and he regretted trouncing on her wholehearted beliefs. He had always been one to live and let live.

"It's fine for those who believe in such things. I just think it's better to put the past behind you and move on."

Her voice was barely above a whisper. "Sometimes it is impossible to do that until the lessons you needed to learn have been internalized."

Okay, then he wanted to learn so he could put it behind him. "By saying you set certain things in motion, aren't you blaming the victim?"

She closed her eyes. "No. Free will leaves the responsibility for heinous acts solely on those who perpetrate them."

Cassie had an answer for everything. But she had demons in her past, too. Luke reached out and stroked the back of the hand she had wrapped around the mug.

"What is it you haven't forgiven yourself for, baby girl?"

She pulled the mug closer to herself, breaking contact between them immediately. She didn't answer, but he had no doubt she'd heard him. He let the silence drag out, thinking she might fill it by answering his question.

"I think I can sleep again now." Without making eye contact with him, she took her mug to the sink, rinsed it, and started back toward his bedroom. "Good night, Lucas. Sleep peacefully."

Seconds later, the door clicked shut, and she was gone.

Luke didn't regret prodding her a bit, but wished he'd done a little more of that with Eduardo when he'd had the chance. Surely the man would know what had happened with Pedro. Somehow, Luke was sure that man was at the center of Cassie's heartache, but he might never know what happened.

Uncovering secrets from this girl was next to impossible.

*　*　*

Cassie closed the bedroom door and leaned against it. How had they gone from discussing spirituality to having Lucas pry into her past? She'd only wanted to help him deal with his survivor-guilt issues, not stir up any of her own issues.

"What is it you haven't forgiven yourself for, baby girl?"

She closed her eyes, but when the movie in her head hit the replay button and she found herself flirting with Pedro and his friends at the bar, she opened them again. Sleep would not come to her this night. She wished she had a studio where she could work on something, as she had done on nights like this many times before. If only…

First thing in the morning, she would ask Lucas to see if they could return to her place. She wanted to retrieve some of her things, if anything had survived. Maybe the fire would be under control by then.

Pushing herself away from the door, she walked across the room and climbed back into the bed. Earlier, she'd worried Lucas's scent would linger in the bed, but the fabric softener smell masked that, assuring her he'd made up the bed as recently as this morning, before setting out to rescue her and her babies.

Thank you, Goddess.

Being near Lucas in the other room, having his hand touch hers, stirred feelings she preferred to keep buried. She relaxed when she heard the front door close as Lucas made his way back to his bed in his studio, she supposed. Maybe he would have more luck than she would letting go of the past tonight.

She could never let go.

She closed her eyes, knowing sleep would continue to elude her…

"Don't go back there, Cassie!"

Cassie startled awake, her own shouted warning reverberating in her ears. She'd trusted the man her parents had chosen to be her husband. If only she had known to trust her instincts instead.

Images of the men's brutality brought bitter acid into her throat. She tossed the covers aside and ran to the bathroom, heaving the cocoa and contents of her stomach into the toilet. Tears streamed down her cheeks, and she washed her face and brushed her teeth.

Dirty. She felt so dirty. How could she ever be clean again?

She tore off the T-shirt and her panties and entered the shower stall, turning on the spray. Picking up the bar of deodorant soap, she scrubbed. A sob tore from her throat. Thankfully, the shower would mask the sound if Lucas happened to return to the house.

The scent of the bar of soap conjured up visions of Lucas. She pushed them away, not wanting to think of him. With a washcloth, she scrubbed her breasts until they burned but still could not banish the feel of Diego's hands on her during the dance that had been a prelude to her nightmare.

Or had it started there in the bar? Pedro knew both of those men. Had Pedro planned for this terrible attack to happen just the way it had? Why else had his demeanor changed so abruptly?

Cassie sobbed and sank down the wall of the shower until she huddled in a tight ball on the tiles, letting the water continue to spray over her face and body. Perhaps if she stayed in here long enough, she could begin to wash away what she had allowed to happen that night.

The filth.

The guilt.

The shame.

Lucas's face swam before her eyes. *Loving what I know of you and trusting what I do not yet know...*

Could she share her story with him? Another sob tore from her already raw throat. No. She should call the therapist Savannah had recommended to her when Cassie had opened up one day while caring for Kitty's babies.

Cassie needed to regain control of her life.

Chapter Seventeen

Luke heard the water running in the bathroom when he crossed the yard to the barn later that morning. Cassie must be up. He anticipated having breakfast with her. She'd stirred up a number of issues last night with her talk about the afterlife and reincarnation. He wanted to explore the subject further, curious about beliefs so different from the ones he'd been raised on. But he couldn't say that one belief or the other was wrong. Just different.

Nearly an hour later, after tending to the horses and alpacas, he walked into the house. The shower was still running. Even for a woman, that was an awfully long one. Momma sometimes used the shower steam to smooth wrinkles out of her clothes, but that water couldn't possibly still be warm. He did have to worry about her running the well dry, though. Colorado didn't have an endless supply of water. Besides, the water heater wouldn't keep the water warm much longer.

Luke walked over to the bedroom door and knocked. He didn't expect an answer, but didn't want to barge in on her naked, either. He called out a warning and cracked open the door. The covers had been tossed back and the bed deserted. The water continued to run. His heart began to pound. Had she fallen? He rushed across the room and knocked on the bathroom door.

"Cassie?" The silence made him worry even more. He banged harder on the door and shouted. "Cassie, you okay in there?" No response.

Luke tried the doorknob and breathed a sigh of relief when it opened. No sign of Cassie. He ran across the small room to where he saw her huddled form through the opaque glass, slumped on the stall floor. He yanked the door open to find her apparently unconscious.

Jeezus.

He reached out to turn off the water. She grunted but didn't open her eyes. She hadn't just fallen asleep in here. Something was wrong. Her skin was cold from the shower spray. "Cassie, it's Luke. *Lucas*. Look at me." Still no response. "Did you slip? Tell me what hurts?"

She covered her breasts and groaned as if in pain.

Luke scooped her into his arms. Her chilled, wet body soon soaked his clothes. On the way out of the bathroom, he reached out with the hand cradling her thighs and grabbed two clean towels off the rack.

"Talk to me, darlin'." He hurried into the bedroom and sat on the edge of the bed, rubbing the first towel over her hair and back in an effort to bring her out of whatever state she was in. "Cassie, can you hear me?"

God, answer me, Sweet Pea.

A sob tore from her chest into her throat, the sound gut-wrenchingly painful to his ears. She buried her face against his chest, her hair forming a curtain to hide her face. Luke wrapped her tightly in his arms and held on.

"Shhh, baby girl. Luke's here. Just let it all out."

She poured out her sorrow until he wondered if the tears would ever stop. After some unknown amount of time, she began hiccupping and gasping to catch a full breath. He held her tighter and laid his chin on the top of her head. "'Atta girl. You're okay."

Cassie trembled in his arms as yet another shard from his long-ago shattered heart was put back into place. She *needed* him. Maggie had been so independent, never allowing him to cuddle or console her. He needed to be needed like this.

"What happened, Cassie?"

She remained silent except for her ragged breaths and hiccups. An eternity later, she answered, "Bad dream."

He waited for her to elaborate, but she went to ground again. "I'm a good listener, if you want to talk about it."

She shook her head. "No. Thank you. I do not wish to give those thoughts that much power over me again."

Looked to him like they had a helluva lot of power over her now, but he wouldn't press her. Yet.

Cassie shivered before her body grew stiff, and she tugged the towel more tightly around her. "Do not be nice to me. I do not deserve your kindness."

"What are you talking about?" He stroked the side of her wet head. "You're one of the gentlest, most caring people I've ever met. Why wouldn't I want to be nice to you in return? Isn't that the karma you spoke of last night?"

"No, I am the way I am so I can try and build up dharma."

"What's dharma?"

"The actions and good deeds we perform intentionally hoping to erase some or all the bad things we have to atone for from our past. It sometimes helps erase the karma we've amassed. I don't want to have to go through these karmic lessons ever again, so I must be redeemed from my past mistakes."

Clearly, this reincarnation stuff was more complicated than it seemed on the surface, but it sure sounded like bullshit to him at the moment. How could someone as sweet as Cassie have anything in her past so bad to warrant such self-punishment? Even if she *had* done something bad, surely all the good she'd done in this life would have negated or erased it by now.

"This is really embarrassing, Lucas, but I need to figure out how to get off your lap so you can leave. I am not comfortable being here without my clothes on."

"Does that mean you'd sit in my lap if you *had* your clothes on?"

She pushed away, holding tightly to the terrycloth covering her breasts, and met his gaze. "No, Lucas."

He shrugged and grinned, hoping to lighten the mood. "Can't blame a guy for asking."

"Why would you want me in your lap? I am not a child."

He stroked her back, his fingers making more contact with the towel than her skin now. Frustrated, he pulled her rigid body against his. "I like having you in my arms." She stopped breathing, but he didn't remove his arms from around her. "Breathe, Sweet Pea. I'm not going to hurt you. Just stating a fact."

"Close your eyes, Lucas."

Luke did as she asked and regretted feeling her hurry off his lap. "Okay, you can open them now." She stood there with the towel wrapped around her like a suit of armor, as sexy as ever. Her sloping shoulders begged to be touched, or better yet kissed, but he'd keep that thought and his hands to himself. She'd let him hold her longer than she probably wanted to. They'd made some progress this morning.

"I am okay now, Lucas. Thank you. I apologize for worrying you. Please go back to whatever you were doing."

"Quiet." The command came out sounding harsher than he'd intended. "Stop apologizing for everything, Cassie. I'm just glad you're feeling better now." He stood and looked down at her. "It kills me to see you in pain. Whenever you're ready to tell me what prompted all this emotion this morning, I'm here."

She glanced down at the floor, and he knew that time wouldn't be now.

"I'll go fix us some breakfast."

"Thank you." Her whispered words lifted his spirits. Being useful made him feel good. He'd made inroads in breaking down her defenses. At least, he hoped so. He tipped his hat and left her to dry off and dress.

Ain't that a shame, too? She had a body too beautiful to hide. He wondered what it would be like if she ran around his house wearing nothing but her birthday suit.

Don't even go there, Denton.

*   *   *

Cassie watched Lucas exit the bedroom, and soon after, her legs began to shake so badly she had to sit on the edge of the bed—which was still warm from his body. A heated flush crept up her neck and into her face. She had never been so mortified. Well, of course she had, but not recently. Lucas had seen her naked in the shower.

Yet he had not taken advantage of her the way Pedro and his accomplices in the cantina had. He had done nothing but hold and comfort her. Tears stung her eyes. Even though she was not deserving of such tenderness, why had it felt so good to be held in his arms? Just to be held, nothing lurid or disgusting like most other men would have done if they had found her in such a vulnerable state.

When certain she could support her body on steady legs again, she stood and went into the bathroom to comb out the tangled mess that was her hair. Soon after, she was dressed and standing with her hand on the doorknob, but she could not bring herself to open the bedroom door and face Lucas again after her shower episode.

She rested her forehead against the door. The sound of water running in the kitchen was followed by that of a spoon stirring a pot. No reprieve. He was still in the house.

Goddess, give me strength.

She breathed deeply and straightened her shoulders and back before turning the knob. Forcing a fake smile, she hoped she exuded the confidence she did not feel.

"Hope you're hungry." He smiled at her and went back to stirring what was in the pot. "Since you don't eat meat, I figured oatmeal, cinnamon apples, and toast from the loaf of bread you baked last night might be just the thing." He nodded in the direction of the table. "Have a seat."

Everything smelled great. That he would go to so much trouble just to feed her warmed a long-neglected place in her soul. "Can I help with something?"

"Nope. Everything's under control."

Perhaps she could avoid having to be so close to him. "I probably should go check on the girls."

"No need. Took care of them while I was out there with the horses this morning before I came in the house to…"

To find you naked and catatonic in the shower.

He was too much a gentleman to finish the sentence, but merely went back to stirring the pot.

"If you really want to help, why don't you grab the dish in the oven I've been keeping warm?"

She picked up the potholders and did as instructed while he poured two mugs of black coffee. The smell of whatever was in the casserole dish made her a little queasy, but she could not see what was under the foil. She took it to the table and went back to the kitchen to see what else she could carry. Soon the table was laden with the feast Lucas had prepared.

"Thank you so much for going to so much trouble. Tomorrow, I promise to take care of making breakfast so you can eat promptly after you come in from the barn." Cassie was taken aback a moment at how domestic that sounded. Time to change the subject. "How were my babies?"

"Eager to explore. I put them out in the small pasture this morning."

Although fenced in, they would have more room here than at her cabin because she had had to keep them tethered so they would not stray. At Luke's, they could meander around a field of grassland and graze to their heart's content.

Would they be happy to return home after staying here once more?

"Let's dig in. After breakfast, we can check on them if you'd like."

Luke passed her a bowl of oatmeal with a dollop of brown sugar dissolving on top and the plate of buttered toast. Good thing she ate milk products, but she figured animals had not been slaughtered to provide those. When he uncovered the foil from the dish she carried in from the kitchen, though, her stomach lurched.

"What's wrong? You feeling bad again?"

"No. But I think what I already have here will fill me up." She watched him fill half his plate with the egg-casserole mixture, oblivious to her look of disgust. Knowing of the horrendous treatment of chickens in commercial egg-laying operations in this country had her swear off eggs long ago. Still, Cassie managed to eat her own breakfast and keep it down, despite the knots in her stomach.

Focus on something else. "These apples are delicious. I love the cinnamon flavor, but how did you make them red?"

"My mom's trick. Instead of sugar or cinnamon, she dumps half a bag of Red Hotz candies into the pot."

"She must be a great cook."

"The best. I just picked up a few of her tricks, but wait till she comes up for her visit. You'll think you died and went to heaven."

Cassie did not expect to be staying here beyond a few days, perhaps a week at most. Surely she could return to her mountain by then if her cabin or studio survived. She supposed she could come back for a visit to meet the woman Lucas spoke so highly of. She had done a wonderful job at raising her son, for sure.

"Any news about the fire?" Luke became intently interested in the eggs on his plate. He knew something. Cassie's anxiety rose. "Tell me."

He met her gaze, and the sorrow in his eyes slammed against her body like a fist. His words came as if through a tunnel with running water distorting the sound.

"Sorry, Cassie. Cabin's a total loss. Everything's pretty much gone."

When Lucas reached out to squeeze her hand, she pulled away and stood abruptly, letting the chair tumble backward. She needed Graciela and the other alpacas.

"Thank you for breakfast." Cassie ran from the house and across the yard to the barn. Once inside, she hurried to the stall before remembering Lucas had turned them out to pasture. Which pasture?

Goddess, what would she do with them now? They had no home, either.

Total loss. Everything's gone.

Cassie ran outside again and spotted Graciela near the fence wondering what was wrong with her mistress. She climbed over the fence and buried her face in the alpaca's neck. "What are we going to do? We have nowhere to live."

"You'll stay here as long as you need to."

Oh, Lucas. She could not turn to face him. "I cannot impose on you forever." Her mountain sanctuary had been destroyed. Nowhere was safe now.

She had no home.

"You're my wife. This is your home, too."

His strong hand stroked her back, trapping her between Lucas's body and Graciela's. Every instinct told her to run—before he stole her heart. Why did he have to be so kind to her? Nudging Graciela forward, she was able to put some space between them and distanced herself even more by coming around Graciela's head to her other side before turning to face Lucas.

"I do not think that would be wise." The hurt expression in his eyes tore at her emotions. "You did not agree to have me live with you when you married me."

"That's because I knew how much you loved your place on the mountain. But I'll cherish and protect you until the day I die, whether together or apart. I meant what I said in my vows, Cassie."

"*Gracias,*" she whispered. She had no choice but to stay. She had her alpacas to think about. What better place for them than Lucas's ranch?

He smiled. "This ranch is a refuge for my horses, but stopped being one for me when I had to leave you the day we married. I like having you around, baby girl. I'm not as much of a loner as I thought I was, and if the tables were turned, I hope you'd open your home and heart to me, too."

Cassie could not think. Between the nightmare and the destruction of her safe place, she struggled to keep from curling into a ball and zoning out again.

"It's no burden having you here." He added, only somewhat seriously, "But I can find chores for you to earn your keep if you'd like."

She gazed at him and did not detect any lecherous innuendo in his tone or on his face. "Of course. Just tell me what I can do to help."

"Follow me."

Luke walked over to the gate and unlatched it. She trailed behind him, preceding him through it, and waited for him to re-latch it before they headed back to the barn. He walked down the aisle between the stalls toward the open doors at the end. The light grew brighter as they neared the opening. She thought he might stop to greet some of the horses, but he seemed to be a man on a mission. Just before he left the barn, he picked up a football from a bin near the opening.

He wanted her to play American football with him? She did not know anything about the game. Football in her country was played with a round white ball. He placed the ball on his hip and held it in place with his right wrist. She found herself watching the sway of his butt encased in the tight jeans as he walked before averting her eyes to the ground instead. Her cheeks grew warm.

He led her to the corral and stopped, staring ahead. She peeked around him. A lone horse stood across the space, trying to appear inconspicuous. When Lucas opened the gate and walked through, Cassie followed. The brown-and-white horse's ears went back as her nostrils flared. She pawed the earth and bared her teeth at them. Anger? Fear?

Emotions poured from the animal, slamming into Cassie's psyche like a freight train. She reached out to steady herself on the open gate. Of all the horses she had met here, this one was by far the most wounded. Her very spirit had been crushed. After taking several deep breaths, Cassie closed and locked the gate behind her and pivoted in time to watch Lucas toss the football to the horse, careful not to hit her with it. The ball rolled close to the mare. Cassie sensed a lifting of the fear she felt a moment ago at the presence of a stranger.

O'Keeffe kicked out with her front hoof, and the ball tumbled back to Luke, who returned it. The mood of the horse had lifted.

"She likes playing with you."

Luke turned to her and grinned. "Thank God. I was never certain if she enjoyed it or just tolerated me."

"No. She was wary at first—possibly more because she does not know me—then she brightened up as soon as you tossed her the ball the first time."

Lucas's body relaxed. "Thanks. You're hired."

"Hired?"

"Well, in exchange for room and board, if you insist on earning your keep, this is what I need your help with. I can meet the needs of my horses, make sure they're safe and cared for, even train them to a new purpose, but I can't communicate with them the way you can." He nodded toward this horse again. "O'Keeffe here has the shadiest past. I don't know what happened to her and am afraid I've muddled through for months now trying to find the right way to reach her. I just discovered by accident that she likes to play football."

He shrugged and gave a sheepish grin. "I'm not too good at coming up with names. Pic—Picasso—had already been named. When I needed more names, I thought about the reproduction pieces in the gallery where you had your December showing."

Cassie recalled some of those pieces, including prints of a Fontana and a Cassatt, but not the other artist. "Why O'Keeffe?"

He scuffed his heel in the dirt but didn't answer right away. "Well, actually, one of your paintings reminded me of O'Keeffe's *Pink Sweet Peas*. In fact, the horse herself reminds me a lot of you."

Cassie blinked and grew sober as she focused on the horse again. Fear. Distrust. Brokenness. Which of those emotions reminded him of her—or perhaps all of them and more?

"Why are you telling me this?"

He glanced at her. "I want there to be no secrets between us, Sweet Pea."

He had called her that many times before, but she thought it just a Texan's empty endearment. Southern Americans liked to give women—even strangers—such nicknames.

She had studied O'Keeffe in college and actually loved some of her desert pieces, but knew exactly which painting Lucas referred to. Cassie had painted snapdragons in extreme close-up, to try to determine the secrets hidden within the petals of the flowers. But O'Keeffe's sweet peas often were mistaken for snapdragons.

She flushed as she remembered how erotic some of O'Keeffe's paintings of flowers had been. Surely, he hadn't seen anything sexual in her own paintings because that would have been so far from what Cassie wanted to convey. Hoping to steer clear of continuing this discussion, she teased in an effort to divert her thoughts and his.

"What, López wasn't famous enough to have a horse named after her?"

He raised his eyebrows in surprise when he faced her. "Did you just make a joke, baby girl?" She blushed. She supposed she had. He grinned. "Well, I have no doubt Cassie López will one day be as famous as Georgia O'Keeffe, but I decided if I named any of them that I'd have Karla and Angel on full-alert matchmaking mode. I didn't think you wanted that kind of pressure."

Goddess, no.

She relaxed, knowing Lucas was not planning to push her beyond friendship, despite the certificate and vows that said they were married. She liked him a lot—provided he did not ask for more than she could give. The thought of being friends with a man had not even occurred to her since the attack in the cantina, but Lucas was nothing like those men. He was gentle and kind, a deep thinker, and he provided a safe haven to broken spirits.

Spirits like hers.

She never wanted to admit to anyone she was broken. Wounded, yes, but being broken implied there would be no fixing her. Or that the *bastardos* had succeeded.

Being mended was not any goal she had, but remaining broken would hinder her spiritual growth in this lifetime. She was finding how difficult it was to become the shaman her mother was because she continued to hold onto so much of the past's negative energy.

O'Keeffe whinnied, and Cassie turned to watch as she used her front left hoof this time to kick the ball toward her. It bumped against the toe of her shoe, and she just stared at it.

"Go on. She wants to play with you. That's a good sign. Kick it back."

"I have never kicked this kind of football before."

"Nothin' to it." Lucas knelt in front of her and propped the ball up on one end, with his index finger holding the other pointy end. "Just give it a soft kick. We're not going for a field goal." Whatever that entailed. "Just try to get it across the corral to her."

Cassie stared at the ball, at Lucas, and then at O'Keeffe, judging the amount of pressure she might need to achieve *that* goal. When was the last time she had played anything? Her heart pounded, but she pulled her right leg back and brought it forward to give the ball a gentle kick. It only went a few feet before rolling to a stop. Embarrassed, she said, "Let me try that again. I did not put enough strength into it."

Lucas grinned and set the ball for her again. This time, she pulled her leg back a little farther, and when her toe impacted the ball, it sailed through the air and bounced off a slat in the corral fence before landing in front of O'Keeffe. The mare spooked, and Cassie's hand flew to her mouth. "I am so sorry!" She hadn't thought it would go so far.

Lucas laughed. "That's some leg you have there, Sweet Pea."

"It is not funny. I frightened her!"

He opened his mouth, but before Lucas could respond, the horse kicked the ball back to them. Apparently, she had not been too traumatized, after all. Cassie took a step toward O'Keeffe, but the mare snorted and began backing away.

"You'll have to give her time to become better acquainted before you get too close. I pushed too hard at first and, man, was she pissed. Nearly tore her stall apart trying to put distance between us, so I've learned to give her more space and time."

Cassie nodded, tears stinging her eyes. She met the horse's gaze and tried to project the message that she would do her no harm, but the spell had been broken. O'Keeffe retreated.

Lucas clasped her shoulder and gave her a squeeze. "We'll work with her some more later on."

Suddenly realizing Lucas was holding her, she shrugged away. He may only want to comfort her, but she did not want to invite him to touch her so freely. Innocent touches could be misconstrued.

She tipped her head back to meet his gaze. "I think I will go inside and clean the dishes."

He grinned. "Thanks, darlin'."

"It is only fair. You cooked."

"I don't mean about doing the dishes. I mean about taking on O'Keeffe for me."

Oh. She hoped she could build trust with O'Keeffe one day.

Patience and time. That's all the horse needed.

*   *   *

That evening, Luke looked back on one of the best days he'd had in a long time. He and Cassie hadn't done anything spectacular. Hell, he couldn't even say what all they'd done together throughout the day.

The key was that they'd spent much of the day together. Mucking stalls. Feeding and turning out the horses with the alpacas and watching them interact with each other. Discussing the artwork she had taken with her when she evacuated. She seemed frustrated she wasn't able to finish it in time, but with the upheaval in her life, he told her to cut herself some slack. It would be finished when the time was right.

He'd started out trying to find ways to distract Cassie from thoughts about the loss of her home, but her first session with O'Keeffe had broken down some kind of barrier inside Cassie. He had no clue what had done the trick, so he couldn't exactly write it down in the playbook to make sure he repeated it again later.

She'd even let him squeeze her shoulder earlier without bolting from him right away. Progress.

He wondered where she'd run off to the last half hour, though. He supposed he'd have to wait to see her again at supper.

Luke came out of the barn with a flake of hay for O'Keeffe and stopped in his tracks. Cassie stood in the corral just a few feet from the horse. The two simply stared at one another, locked in silent communication. He had no doubt they were communicating. O'Keeffe's mangled ear flicked forward then the other. When the mare bowed her head toward Cassie, Luke had to remind himself to breathe. Cassie reached up and stroked her neck, and O'Keeffe let her.

He'd worked for months to come that close to the horse. Cassie already had broken down barriers with O'Keeffe it might have taken him years to go beyond.

The girl literally took his breath away.

Time stood still as he continued to watch the two. Cassie's lips moved, but he couldn't make out her words. A horse whisperer was difficult to hear even when you stood right next to them, because they weren't necessarily communicating on a hearing level. Mental telepathy was a big part of it. And touch. Now that Cassie had made that physical contact, she touched O'Keeffe often with her gentle hand, reassuring the horse she was safe.

O'Keeffe drew closer, and Cassie patted her neck, broke contact, and turned. When she spotted Luke, she paused almost imperceptibly before continuing across the corral.

"That was beautiful to watch." As she came closer, Luke saw tear streaks down her cheeks. "You okay, Sweet Pea?"

She nodded, but the quiver of her lips told a different story. He opened his arms, and she surprised the hell out of him by walking into his embrace. What the hell had happened out there? Maybe O'Keeffe wasn't the only one who had barriers shattered today.

"How can people be so cruel?"

"Nietzsche nailed it. 'Man's the cruelest animal.'" He'd learned that saying back in college, and it had stuck with him as being true, even though he hadn't been on the receiving end of any of man's great cruelties, thank God. But his horses sure had seen their share. "If you don't mind sharing, what did you learn from her?"

She shuddered, and he held her tighter before realizing she might be reacting to his touch and not whatever O'Keeffe had conveyed to her. He started to release her when she spoke.

"Some say horses are not like people. That horses do not hold onto things and only live in the present."

"But?"

"But when I asked about certain injuries, she opened up. She remembered it all."

Luke stroked her back as she kept her face buried in his chest.

"They beat her with switches until she bled. Let her hooves grow without trimming them."

"Yeah, I'm still working on trimming them back to normal, but it'll take a while." Cassie gasped for air and wrapped her arms around him. "Let it go, baby girl. What else did she tell you?"

She shook her head, and he wondered what O'Keeffe had shared that had her so shaken up. They held on to each other for what seemed like hours, but it had to have been only minutes. When she grew stiff in his arms, he knew their time was over.

She pulled away, but didn't make eye contact with him. "I am going to turn in early. It has been a long day."

Luke hated to watch her walk away, but knew he'd made enough progress for one day. Like his horses, he'd have to give her the time and space to learn to trust him. But she'd shown him today that a firm, but gentle, hand at the right time might be able to help dismantle some of her walls.

Chapter Eighteen

Cassie ran toward the house, but stopped before she entered and looked up at the pass where smoke still billowed from the other side of her mountain. More sorrow washed over her as she imagined *Abuela's* belongings that she had left behind in the rustic cabin and studio. Both gone forever.

Her cell phone vibrated, and she pulled it out of her pocket. Kitty. Could she carry on a conversation right now without breaking down into tears? But if she did not answer, she would only worry her friend, who had enough on her mind right now.

She touched the screen. "Hello. How are you and the babies, Kitty?" She tried to make her voice sound more cheerful than she felt, but must have failed miserably.

"Cassie, are you okay? I saw on the news that the fire was near your cabin. Where are you now?"

In the chaos yesterday, she had completely forgotten to let Kitty know she was okay. With so many major wildfires burning, she had not expected her mountain's blaze would make Denver news channels.

Cassie drew another breath and walked inside the house and toward the bedroom. She did not want to have to face Lucas again when he came in after her meltdown at the corral. And he would be coming in soon to fix supper.

"I am fine. Staying at Lucas's."

"Luke Denton's?"

She smiled as she pictured Kitty's incredulous face. "Yes, one and the same. He rescued me."

"Cassie! What happened?"

Cassie recounted the story for her friend, but the weariness that had begun to set into her body out in the corral became even more pronounced as the magnitude of what Lucas had done hit her. Her hand shook, and she kicked off her shoes and burrowed under the covers.

"Cassie? Are you there?"

"Y-y-yes. I am in bed."

"At this hour? Are you okay?"

"It has been a long couple of days. Listen, Kitty, I am fine. Really. Let me call you tomorrow to talk. But trust me, everything is okay here."

"Did…Did the alpacas make it out?"

"Oh, yes! We are all down here with Lucas. Luke." Funny, but calling him Lucas after all they had been through seemed rather stilted. Yet she had grown used to calling him that. Using his nickname now might cause him to misinterpret her reasons.

"I love you, Cassie. And you can trust Luke. He's a good man."

Her chin shook, and her throat closed. "I know," she whispered. Why did that scare her even more?

Because he posed a threat of a different kind. She had spent most of her adult life keeping men away from her, wanting to have nothing to do with them. The memory of Lucas's arms around her caused her to shake even more. Before she completely lost it, she said goodnight to Kitty and set the phone aside.

Goddess, she had not even found out how the babies were, but surely Kitty would have told her if there had been any problems.

Cassie curled onto her side, pulling the covers up to her chin and her knees up to her chest. She hugged herself, but did not find the comfort from her own arms that she had found in Lucas's hug.

Cassie fought the desire to go to him and ask him to hold her, to make her feel safe again. But no one had that power. No one except the Goddess, but even She seemed to have abandoned her lately.

Her shivering lessened, and she soon found herself drifting off to sleep.

"Why don't we go play pool? We can leave after I finish the beer I just ordered."

"No, Cassie! Don't go back there!"

Despite the warnings reverberating in her head, Cassie followed Luis to the back room, Pedro behind her. At least he was here and would protect her. She hoped they would leave soon, though. Tonight had not been fun at all. Nothing like when she and Kitty went out to the clubs to dance.

A body pressed against her back, hands pawing at her breasts. Certain it was

Diego, Pedro shocked her when he whispered in her ear. *"We'll give you the advantage, Casandra."* He ordered the other men to remove their shirts.

"Take your hands off me." Cassie pushed them away and turned to glare at him as Pedro took a long draw from the beer bottle. His gaze never left her face.

Luis reached out and pinched her nipple. *"She's turned on, Pedro."*

She smacked his hand away, too, and narrowed her gaze at him. *"Do. Not. Touch. Me. Again."*

"The uppity chica *has forgotten her place while off studying in America."* Diego had joined them.

She spat at Diego, who backhanded her across her mouth, sending her flying into Pedro's arms. There had been a time when she would have expected to find safety here, but no longer. He grabbed her hair, yanked her head back, and wrapped his arm around her waist like a vise.

"Fine. If you wish to forget about the game, we will move on to collecting our prize."

Cassie kicked behind her at his shins and elbowed him, but the other two soon overpowered her, and the back of her head smashed into the beer-soaked felt on the pool table. Hands pulled at her skirt and blouse. The sound of a knife cutting through the material made her stop fighting for fear she would be cut as well.

"Don't stop fighting, puta,*"* Diego ground out. *"We like it better when our girls give us a challenge."*

"I am not one of your girls. Let me go now or my brother will make you regret the day you were born."

Pedro laughed nervously, but the other two did not seem to know her brother or what a formidable foe he could be. But he soon recovered his bravado. *"I have waited the longest for this bitch. I go first."*

Hearing Pedro claim her body as if she were some trophy he deserved made her even sicker than the putrid smell of the table and the two other men holding her down. She tried to kick him, but he was already between her legs, loosening his belt.

A scream tore from her body as she tried to alert someone from the cantina to come to her rescue, but a filthy rag was stuffed into her mouth, robbing her of the ability to make much noise. She tasted something salty, musky on the cloth and gagged as she realized what it had been used for.

"Please do not let them do this to me, Papá Dios.*"* Prayer was her only hope now. Father God would send her an angel.

*   *   *

Luke thought he heard a noise from the bedroom, but when there was no further sound, he went back to making some popcorn to take out to the studio. He wasn't hungry for a full meal, and neither was Cassie apparently. But he'd be hungry later on. He retrieved a bowl from the cabinet when a howl of anguish intruded on the quiet of the night.

Cassie!

He dropped the bowl on the counter and reached onto the upper shelf of the same cabinet to grab his loaded revolver before running for the bedroom. The door wasn't locked, so he threw it open wide, sweeping the room with his weapon, ready to defend her against whoever was attacking her.

In Spanish, she screamed, "Do not touch me!"

He quickly realized she was in bed. Alone. Face down, her legs struggled to untangle herself from the bedspread.

"Papá Dios!"

A nightmare.

Setting the handgun on the dresser, he crossed the room in three steps and called out to her. "Cassie, it's Luke. Turn over." He didn't want to add to her night terror by touching her—yet.

"Do not touch me!"

Luke needed for her to wake up so she could escape the nightmare. He reached out and cupped her head gently but firmly. "Wake up, Cassie."

He could make out some of the words.

"Noooooo! Stop! Why…?" A sob tore from her throat followed by a keening before she darted across the bed and turned around until she faced him. She pulled the chenille bedspread up to her chest like armor plating.

"Cassie, you're safe. It's me, Luke. You're having a bad dream."

She shook her head. Now she spoke in English. "You lied to me!"

About what? He realized her eyes were glazed. She wasn't seeing him, but still locked in the night terror. "I'd never lie to you, Sweet Pea. And no one is going to hurt you." Never again, not as long as he had anything to say or do about it.

"Too late." Tears streaked down her cheeks breaking his heart.

"It's never too late, darlin'."

Cassie blinked a few times and searched the corners of the room before meeting his gaze. "You do not understand, Lucas."

She knew who he was. Thank God.

She whimpered, and he walked around the bed to the other side. When she didn't crawl away, he sat on the edge of the mattress several feet away.

"Why don't you tell me about it?"

She shook her head. No, her entire body shook.

"Then why not let me hold you? Just hold you."

Her eyes widened, and the terror in her gaze tore at his gut. She didn't trust him. "Have I ever hurt you, Cassie?"

She shook her head again. "But sometimes men change."

"Who did that, Cassie? Who pretended to be something they weren't and then hurt you?"

She hugged herself and doubled over. He wished she'd let him comfort her, but wouldn't force her. It sounded as if someone had done that already. At least she was talking.

Cassie sat up again, arms still wrapped around her waist, and stared down at the bedspread. She plucked at one of the tufts in the chenille design. Some sense of resolve seemed to pass over her, and she squared her shoulders as she sat on her heels. "It was a long time ago. I was still in college."

Luke knew not to interrupt, even if it took her a while to continue. He wanted to brush the tears off her cheeks, to fold her into his arms, but she needed space right now.

Give her time.

"I was home on summer break. Well, it was winter in Peru."

Pluck, pluck.

He didn't care if she stripped Momma's old bedspread of every tufted thread. Her gaze was focused on the motions of her fingers, while her mind must be trying to decide what she would share with him.

Come on, darlin'.

"My fiancé took me to a cantina in the capital. I had never been to one in my country before. I only knew Pedro, my fiancé." She closed her eyes and took a breath. "I soon found I did not know him, either, even though we had been acquaintances since primary school."

Keep going.

"He…He would not dance with me. A *marinera* played—a traditional dance in my homeland—and I wanted to dance so badly. Why else would one go to a place like that? But he said he did not know how. A lie.

Everyone in Peru knows the *marinera*. Then one of his friends offered to dance with me."

Pluck, pluck.

"The music consumed me. It really did not matter who danced with me. My body came to life as the music coursed through me. But…" She shuddered, lost in the memory, and Luke wondered what had happened. "Something about him scared me, and I stopped dancing and went back to my fiancé at the table."

How long had she dated this Pedro guy? What kind of relationship did they have? Fiancé made it sound serious. She said she discovered she didn't know him as well as she thought.

"Pedro said some things that hurt me and made me uncomfortable, but I did not heed the warning signs as I should have."

He couldn't help but interject, given his own lack of foresight with Maggie. "Hindsight's always twenty-twenty. You expected him to protect you." Hell, he was her fiancé!

"But women are supposed to listen to their instincts to keep themselves from harm. I ignored mine."

"Haven't you paid enough for whatever happened? Maybe it's time you forgave yourself for being a mere mortal."

She met his gaze, scrunching her eyebrows as she considered his words. "I had not really thought about it that way." Her gaze strayed to his arms, and he held them out to her, hoping she'd come to him. Sadly, she did not move. He lowered his arms to his sides again, but was encouraged when her gaze followed.

"You *can* trust me, darlin'."

She continued to stare at his arms and lap alternately as he watched the struggle within her. She needed to be held in the worst way, but fought that need with everything she had.

He had to strain to hear her next words. "I trusted my fiancé. He shattered not only my trust, but my very soul."

"He didn't deserve your trust then. That's no fault of yours."

Cassie met his gaze, studying his face for the longest time. The yearning he saw there told him she was close to reaching out to him. So close.

Don't blow this, Denton.

New tears flowed. Damn. If she didn't come over here soon, he'd do something stupid like wrap her in his arms. But that would be a big mistake.

Wait for her.

"They hurt me so much."

They? Anger boiled up inside him. Both of them? "Tell me what they did."

She shook her head with a vehemence he hadn't witnessed in her before.

"Cassie, don't give them any more power over you. Until you release it, that secret's going to gnaw at your gut. By talking about it, you take away some of the hold it has on you. Otherwise, you're going to keep blaming yourself for what it sounds like someone else did, not you."

Again, her gaze strayed to his lap. He patted his thigh and coaxed her again. "Come, let me hold you. Just like I did this morning. You weren't even dressed then. Did I do anything to hurt you?"

She shook her head and leaned imperceptibly closer to him before catching herself.

"You really look like you could use a hug right now. If you don't want to talk about it, you don't have to. But let me hold you a while."

"I wish I could..."

"Nothing stopping you but you. Face your fear. Trust me."

She closed her eyes, took a deep breath, and then took another.

Come on, Sweet Pea. Trust me.

"I want to, but I cannot."

Luke took a chance and stood up. He hadn't planned to leave, only to scoop her up in his arms, but she halted him. "No, wait! Do not go! You are right. I need to talk about this. And I do need..."

She didn't finish the sentence, but scurried off the bed onto her feet and motioned for him to sit again. He did so. Surprising the hell out of him, she crawled onto his lap and sat so rigidly he was afraid she'd break if he touched her. But he couldn't stop himself.

He placed his hand on her back and stroked her nape in small, circular motions, hoping not to send her running. "I have you. Just let it out. Tell me what happened."

Silence.

"That's all in the past, Cassie. Whatever happened, you survived, and you're safe here with me now."

She buried her face against his chest and sobbed for ages.

Jesus, tell me they didn't do what I think they did to her.

Luke wrapped his arms around her, loosely at first. When she didn't panic, he increased the pressure and held her as she cried. Had those two men raped her? God, that would explain why she was so fearful of men. Hell, one had even been slated to be her future husband.

Fucking bastard.

No wonder trust was so hard to come by. "Tell me, Cassie. Let it out. We can deal with this together, but it would help if I knew what happened."

He wanted to say they could fix it together, but he'd learned that some hurts could never be fixed. Not every wound could be bandaged. Yet, even though some never fully healed, a person could learn to live with the wounds just the same. Over time, the flow of blood slowed to a trickle.

"They raped me."

Fuck.

He had hoped against hope they hadn't taken it that far, even though he'd expected to hear those very words. An intense pain seared his chest, infinitesimal compared to the pain she'd suffered.

He wrapped his arms more tightly around her and pressed her tear-streaked face against his chest. He rested his chin on the top of her head. She didn't pull away, and he wondered if she could feel his heart pounding.

"I should have run when I had the—"

He took her upper arms in his hands, pushed her away, and then cupped her chin with the fingers of one hand until she met his gaze.

"None of this was your fault. Those men violated you. Attacked you in the vilest way. I don't care if you walked through that cantina buck-naked. When you said 'no,' that meant they were to keep their filthy hands off you."

She hiccupped. "You believe me?"

"Why the hell wouldn't I? You've never lied to me, and you're torn up about it to this day. How long has it been?"

"Five years—oh, Goddess." Her eyes opened wider. "Five years ago, July the sixth."

Easy to see why all this stuff had come to a head now. She was two weeks away from the anniversary, not to mention all the trauma from being displaced by the fire.

"Anniversaries suck. Come here, darlin'." He tugged her against his chest again. "Let me just hold you. If you want to tell me about it, I'm listening."

"I do not want to think about it anymore. It's over."

"Is it? After that flashback, I think it's going to be as raw as the day it happened for a while." He'd like to believe that kind of pain could be erased from a person's memory, but knew better.

She drew in a ragged breath. "I guess we can never forget such events."

"No, but sounds to me like you've saddled yourself with a shitload of guilt that doesn't belong on your back. Want to try and sort that out?"

She didn't say anything for the longest time, and he figured the answer was 'no,' until she nodded.

"Whenever you're ready, tell me what happened, Sweet Pea."

Now she plucked at the button on his shirt pocket. Luke decided to give her all the time she needed without prodding. They had all night. He hoped Cassie would finally unload the misplaced guilt. She'd need to if she ever was going to be able to forgive herself.

"We have all night."

Hell, he could hold her like this the rest of his life, if necessary. She felt so good in his arms.

Chapter Nineteen

C assie struggled to keep the memories of that horrific night from overwhelming her and spilling out. She did not want to go back to that time in her life. Did not want Lucas to know what had happened. Those monsters needed to remain locked away. Yet the fear clawed at her throat as strongly as it had that night. She almost pushed herself off Lucas's lap to run.

Dear Goddess, why was she sitting on his lap in the first place? How blatant could she be? On a bed, no less! He could throw her onto the mattress and rape her more easily even than the three men in the cantina.

Why did she not run?

Because Lucas would never do that.

She felt safe here. It made no sense, but for one of the few times in the past five years, she actually believed nothing bad would come from being near a man. How had he penetrated her massive defenses?

His horses. Strange as it sounded, Picasso and O'Keeffe both told her of his patience and kindness. Of course, looking back, she had seen the same in the way he treated her. But if he could be trusted with animals that could never report or prosecute him if he hurt them, then she could trust him further as well.

She closed her eyes, but when the image of the cantina popped into her mind, she opened them again. "I went to the cantina late that evening. After dinner." The story began spilling out. She hoped by telling someone she could release some of what had been pent up inside her. "My parents thought I was in my room sleeping or studying. I snuck out to meet Pedro because I enjoyed going to clubs in New York with Kitty and thought it would be fun to dance and have a drink or two. I could tell Pedro and his two friends had been there before. Everyone knew them."

"What happened next?"

"Pedro would not dance with me so when Luis asked, I pleaded with Pedro to allow me to dance. But soon after, Diego cut in."

"There were three?"

She thought she had mentioned that already, but nodded. Lucas's body stiffened. "I never would have agreed to dance if Diego had been the one to ask. He scared me. His eyes were cruel. Filled with hatred." Lucas's heart beat faster against her cheek.

Cassie continued, wanting to get the story out as quickly as possible. "I tried to get Pedro's attention, hoping he would intervene when Diego touched me inappropriately. But Pedro just kept drinking his beer and flirting with the *camerera*—I mean, barmaid."

"What happened next?"

"I went back to the table. Pedro was not angry at Diego for pawing my breast..." Lucas tensed, and she stopped. His anger entered her, and she felt fear building up inside her. She reminded herself that Lucas's response was toward the rapists, not her.

She took a deep breath and let it out slowly. "He was upset with me for dancing, even though he had given his permission, but I was not to blame for Diego's actions. And I had not asked to dance with him."

Cassie was too mortified to tell Luke about her aroused state during the dance.

"Breathe, Sweet Pea. What are you remembering?"

"I do not wish to say."

"Okay. No pressure, darlin'."

She played with the button on his shirt, swallowing against the lump in her throat. Lucas patiently waited for her to continue, stroking her hair and giving her the space she needed. But all she could think about was her state of arousal that night. "I am too embarrassed to continue."

"Whatever you're thinking is affecting your breathing and pulse rate right now." She realized he had his thumb pressed against the pulse in her right wrist. "Why don't you take some deep breaths for me?"

She did and released the negative emotions on each exhale.

"One more." After this breath, some of the fear receded but barely enough to notice.

She continued to play with the button, feeling the heat rise from his chest under her fingertips. Her nipples started to bunch. Panic set in, and she pulled her hand down into her lap. She hoped he would not see her arousal. What was the matter with her traitorous body?

Soap and leather. Lucas's scent permeated her senses.

Safe.

"I'm here whenever you're ready."

He seemed certain she would tell him. He could wait all he wanted, but she was not sure she could. Her face grew heated, only she knew her body was not reacting to anyone but Lucas at the moment.

"Still awake, Sweet Pea?"

How could she sleep when her mind was in such turmoil? She nodded and closed her eyes, but Pedro's accusing gaze swam before them. She pounded her closed fist against her thigh. Numb. She pounded again. She wanted to feel something.

Anger erupted. How dare he think his obnoxious friend turned her on? "No, it was not like that!" She continued to pound her fist, wishing it was Pedro she was bruising and not herself.

"Who are you angry with right now?"

Lucas? She opened her eyes and realized she had been pounding her fist against his chest, not her thigh. Her wrist ached from the impacts. Had she hurt him?

She pulled away and sat up straighter. "Oh, Goddess! I am sorry, Lucas! I did not mean to—"

He chuckled. "You didn't hurt me, darlin'. Whatever helps you speak the words and let out those long-buried feelings, you just do it."

Patience. The man had the virtue in spades.

"You do not deserve to be the brunt of my anger."

"I know you aren't lashing out at me. Sounds like you pictured in your head that you were landing a few punches against those bastards."

She shook her head. "No, I thought I was hitting myself but was just too numb to feel it."

His hand stroked her cheek. "I'd rather you hurt me than yourself. Want to tell me more?"

She stroked his chest where she had pounded against him, hoping to help ease his pain. Even if he would not admit it had hurt, she knew it must have. In a quiet voice that still sounded too loud in her ears, she stared at his chest and asked, "Do you ever feel something so deeply that your body becomes aroused?" Oh, that did not come out right. She met his gaze. "I mean, is there music that excites your senses so much that—"

Oh, Goddess, she could not find the right words!

He smiled sympathetically. "It sounds like you're saying you became aroused by the music. By the dancing."

Her breath came out in a whoosh. She nodded and found understanding, not condemnation, in his eyes. "Pedro became angry, jealous. He thought I was turned on by having Diego's hands on me, but it was not that at all. I detested the man. It was the *music* that excited me. I loved to dance."

"And you don't love to dance now?"

She shook her head. "I have not danced since that night."

Lucas's hand stroked her back until she was able to breathe again. "Darlin', it doesn't surprise me that someone with as much passion as you have would feel the music to your bones. I hope you'll allow yourself to cut loose again sometime, even if it's just for yourself and no one's watching."

"But I was not just feeling it in my bones. My nipples hardened. Everyone saw my response, and Pedro misinterpreted it." *Oh, no!* What had led her to reveal her shame?

"Sounds to me like he intentionally misinterpreted it to serve his own twisted purpose. To make you think you asked for it."

She nodded. "He said that. They both did. If only I had stayed in bed where I belonged."

"You were a young girl wanting to have some fun. Didn't you say you and Karla went clubbing? How many times did you get raped while clubbing in New York?"

"Never."

"So why wouldn't you have some expectation of safety if you were out with the man who was supposed to protect you above all others? How were you to know he was a snake in the grass waiting to strike?"

His hand stopped moving, and his breathing became labored. His anger bombarded her, and she moved to stand up—to run—but his arm tightened around her waist.

"Let me go, Lucas." Her breathing became rapid, shallow.

His hand immediately relaxed at his side, essentially releasing her, but his words held her in place. "Honey, I'm not one of those animals. I'm not angry *with* you; I'm angry *for* you. But no one is going to hurt you without going through me first. You're safe here. Take some more slow, deep breaths for me."

Knowing they would help calm her, she closed her eyes and did as he instructed. He began stroking her back again, and she relaxed even further. "Good girl. Now, when you're ready, tell me anything else you want to get off your chest about that night."

Lucas was worse than a bulldog with a bone. Did he not see she was far beyond the point of being comfortable talking any more about that night? She had never even shared this level of detail with Kitty. Why was talking with Lucas different? Something about him, about his presence, made her want to seek this release by speaking the unspeakable.

Calm, controlled, composed.

And beyond patient with her.

Not only could Lucas handle more of the horrific details, but she knew he would be there to hold her and help her through the ordeal after sharing her darkest nightmare. He had proven he was strong enough to hear whatever she had to say without judging her or breaking down.

Oddly, she found that she *needed* to show him that his confidence in her ability to share was not misplaced. That she trusted him...

Suddenly, something clicked that she had not realized before. "Pedro was not in control of himself at all that night."

"No, any man who would sink so low as to rape a woman has zero self-control."

Until now, despite many counseling sessions at uni where she was told over and over it was not her fault, she had always felt that the rape had happened because of her actions. The "if I had or had not done this, then that would not have happened" messages had consumed her for the past five years. The guilt and shame had eaten her alive.

Instead, comparing the monsters to someone noble and self-assured like Lucas made it clear the rape was all about those beasts trying to brutally dominate her body and mind because they had no control over themselves.

From this night forward, she refused to surrender her own power to her fears.

"What are you feeling now?"

With Lucas's encouragement and support, she would take baby steps until she could achieve that goal instinctively without having to remind herself.

"That I no longer wish to be afraid, no longer wish to go through life holding back, always thinking the worst of every man. Look at you. I have never felt more comfortable with any other man, and yet I have continually expected the worst of you without any reason to do so."

She met his gaze, and he grinned. "You don't know how good that makes me feel to know you trust me."

"You have never done anything to shatter my trust, and we have been in much more compromising situations than I was in that night at the cantina."

His thumb stroked her cheekbone, and she fought the urge to melt into the palm of his hand. He made her feel safe and cherished. Her nipples hardened again, though, and she pulled away. But she should not tempt him or fate. The sooner she finished telling Lucas the story, the sooner he could go back to bed in his studio, and they could both sleep.

For some reason, the thought of him being so far away sent fear surging into her chest again. What if the events of that night returned in her dreams after talking about them so much?

"Will you stay in the house with me tonight, Lucas? I am afraid to be alone."

"I'm not going anywhere, Sweet Pea. I'll stay as close as you need me to be tonight."

Again, she was afraid her words sent the wrong message about what she wanted. "Is the couch comfortable?"

He chuckled. "Not too bad."

"Good. I will sleep there, and you can have your bed back."

"Cassie. Look at me." The stern tone in his voice surprised her. She met his gaze, as if she had any other choice. "We've been over this before. You're my wife. You'll sleep in this bed as long as you're staying here."

"I just hate—"

"Tell me what happened after you returned to Pedro's table. Keep your eyes on me. I think you're reliving the nightmare every time you close them. I might be able to keep you grounded in the moment and remind you that's all in the past."

Apparently, as far as he was concerned, the sleeping arrangements had been determined. End of discussion. Not that either of them would be sleeping much tonight, she surmised. Once she had opened the door to the past, there would be no putting the monsters back into the closet.

He continued to speak softly. "I'm here, baby girl. I'm not letting those men or anyone else hurt you ever again if I have anything to say or do about it."

A calm came over her as she stared at Lucas. The words tumbled out. "Pedro ordered another beer, and then they decided they wanted to play a game of pool in the back. He promised me he would take me home after the game." Her chest burned, reminding her to breathe. "They suggested some version of strip pool or something. When I refused, they…"

Cassie grabbed onto his shirt and buried her face in his chest, gasping for air. Breathe.

Soap.

Leather.

Lucas.

He took her arms and set her away from him. "Cassie, open your eyes."

She shook her head, not wanting to see blame or judgment there. "Oh, Lucas. Do not make me say the words!" Tears trickled from their corners as she fought for composure.

"Darlin', you're gonna feel a whole lot better when you say those words. But it has to be your choice. If you don't want to say anything more, then don't."

Too quickly the images flashed across her mind.

Hands.

Stench.

Pain.

She wanted to be rid of the memories. The pain. The shame.

"I'm not going anywhere. Hell, I could hold you like this all night and die a happy man. Okay, why don't you try and relax against me?" He placed his hand against the side of her head and guided her cheek into the hollow of his shoulder.

When she began trembling, Lucas's arms wrapped around her, but he could not pull her back to the present. Her stomach lurched, sending bile rising into the back of her throat. She tried to push away from him, fearing she would vomit on him if she did not tamp the evilness back down deep inside, but he continued to hold her.

"I'm here. I have you, Cassie. You're safe now."

"I am going to be sick! Let me up!"

"You sure it's not the words trying to come out?"

Oh, Goddess. Yes! How did he know? If wrong, she would have been sick all over him.

She groaned and met his gaze once more. She did not want to infect him with these evil words, but she was losing the battle to control them. "I cannot hold them back any longer, but I do not wish for you to hear them!"

"You speaking the words is going to be harder on you than hearing them will be for me. I think you need to get those words out. Now. Tonight. Don't hold back on my account. I can take anything you have to say. What I can't take is seeing how this is eating you alive, Sweet Pea." He brushed a tear from her cheek with his thumb.

She shuddered as she tried one last time to cram the ugliness back down inside.

"I'm here, Cassie." He whispered the words, but they drowned out the Spanish words screaming in her mind from that night. "It sounds like you're on the verge of letting go of something that's needed to come out for a long time."

I cannot hold them back any longer!

"Come on. You can do it."

The assurance and faith he showed in his eyes broke the dam. "Pedro went first." Her words were barely a whisper, but she would not repeat them. "He took my virginity while Luis and Diego held me down on the pool table."

"That's it, baby girl. No wonder the thought of playing pool the night of the avalanche sent you running. I'm so sorry I suggested it."

"How could you know something that depraved was in my past?"

"Remember, they were the depraved ones. Not you." He stroked the creases from her forehead. "I take it Karla knew by the way she tried to steer me off the idea of playing pool."

She nodded. "Some of it. I spared her the ugliest details. No one needs to hear those."

"Maybe you need to say them out loud anyway. If not to me, then to someone you trust enough." The calmness in his voice, despite the rage that seemed to be seething beneath the surface, made it easier for her to continue.

"Angelina knows a little bit, too, but Kitty, God, if she had not been there for me when I returned to school at Columbia that fall, I do not think I would be alive today. So many times during those months before I told her, I was on the verge of suicide."

"Thank God she was there for you."

"I think *Mama Quilla* brought her to me. Just as she brought you to me at a time when I needed a new friend."

Unable to hold herself upright any longer, she lay against him. His heart pounded against her cheek as he stroked her hair.

He said nothing for a moment and then, "I'm sorry your first time had to be with animals like that. I understand now why you feel that having sex is such a repulsive act."

Pedro and his friends were not only her first but would also be her last. She would never go through that horrific, pain-filled, degrading act again. *Never* again.

Anger and more details boiled up despite her efforts to bring an end to this discussion. "Pedro rutted me like an animal. I did not think he would ever stop, that it would ever end." Her stomach clenched again remembering. "But I soon learned he was not the worst of the three."

"All *three* attacked you?"

Her next breath rasped against her throat. How could she reveal more if he questioned her story? When she remained silent, he stroked her back.

"Jeezus, I'm so sorry, Cassie. No wonder you have such an aversion to men. Sorry I interrupted you, too. Just let it out, darlin'."

Lucas had not heard the worst of it yet, but continued to believe her. She breathed heavily and decided to spew out the words she had held back from everyone, including Kitty.

"Diego shook a bottle of beer and rammed it far inside my vagina, letting the contents erupt. I guess it was his idea of a douche to wash away Pedro's semen and my blood."

For a moment, his hold on her tightened to the point she could barely breathe. Had she said too much? But he spoke in the same calm voice, and she relaxed. "He was the douche, Cassie. No wonder you steered clear of men so long. That three of the most heinous monsters would all come together in one night to do such despicable things to you…" His hand shook, although he continued to caress her hair.

He took a deep breath himself.

I am sorry, Lucas. You asked me to tell you, and now I must keep going.

"I was raped in every opening." She swallowed, remembering how raw her body had been for weeks after. Sometimes, even today, she felt the pain as if it had happened recently. "When they finished, I could not move. I lay there on that table, broken and bleeding, hoping to die."

He rested his chin on the top of her head and gave her the courage to continue once more.

"I do not know how long it was before…the owner of the bar found me and drove me partway home." She had forgotten about his role in this until now. For years, she had remembered it as having walked the entire way home. Of course, that would have taken her days, even if she had not been raped that night. "He called me a *puta* and told me to stay away from his establishment in the future." Hot tears spilled from her eyes. The man had only added to her feelings of shame.

"Yet another man who failed to do the right thing and protect you that night."

She shivered and could no longer feel his arms around her anymore. "Hold me closer, Lucas."

Without a word, he pulled the bedspread around them and held her body in his tight embrace, resting his chin on her head again, creating a cocoon of protection around her much like the white light she surrounded herself with before meditating.

Tears continued to flow unheeded as she picked absently at the tufts on the chenille bedspread. While there were other details she could share, she chose to let him fill in the blanks. No further words waited to explode from her. She had revealed more to Lucas than anyone else. She had never been able to tell such things to Kitty, fearing the truth would scare her friend away from men for the rest of her life, too.

"I'm proud of you, baby girl."

She sat up and met his gaze. "Proud?" That was the last thing she expected him to say. "Why?"

"You not only survived that brutal attack, but you went on to make a life for yourself. A lot of people crumble under a burden half that heavy, but you didn't give up."

But she had! "I have lived in fear every day since. I would not have survived if not for Kitty. I am not brave at all. Just more afraid of killing myself than of existing in this hell. Thankfully, the fear has lessened over time."

"But you kept putting one foot in front of the other and continued to move forward. You survived. That's the main thing. But persevering, well that takes added courage."

Exhausted, she laid against him again. She had survived, not just that awful night, but all the nights since then.

Being held in his arms like this, telling him things she had never shared with anyone else, she was thankful he had not judged or rejected her.

He believed her.

For the first time in a very long time, she felt validated.

Sheltered, protected, and secure in Lucas's arms.

In his home.

In his life.

*   *   *

She'd surprised the hell out of him by revealing as much as she had so quickly. He'd expected an all-nighter until she became worn down enough she could no longer resist opening up.

Now it was time for both of them to move forward. With any luck, side by side. First, time to process some things.

"What made you trust me enough to sit on my lap tonight?"

She plucked at the bedspread a moment before answering. "I have seen how gentle you are with my alpacas. O'Keeffe and Picasso gave you very high praise, too."

He still couldn't fathom that she talked to their animals like a real-life Doctor Doolittle. Better yet, more like that Buck guy, the world-famous horse whisperer.

"Anyone who loves defenseless animals that much and can be so gentle with even the most wounded ones would never be cruel to me."

"Animal owners sometimes abuse or neglect them, too." He needed no reminders of that beyond the horses in his barn and corral.

"But that just proves they are not animal people and shouldn't have them in their lives in the first place. Lucas, you truly love every living creature. I saw that, too." She plucked at the blanket some more. "Besides, with you, I forget you are a guy."

Okay, Denton, that'll teach you not to push for more.

She sat up and met his gaze, her eyelashes matted in spikes from crying, but no more tears spilled. "I mean that in the very best way, of course."

His ego couldn't take much more of her good intentions, but she looked so hell-bent on not making him feel bad that he couldn't help but grin. She smiled back. Such a beautiful, innocent smile. He pretty much didn't care what she said about him now as long as she kept sharing her smile.

"Around most men, I am withdrawn and terrified. But you are different, well, once I came to know you better. You do not intimidate me any longer. You make people around you comfortable, often in situations where they feel anything but. You have a gift."

Wow. She'd just blown him away. "That's just about the nicest thing anyone's ever said about me." On impulse, he leaned forward and kissed her forehead. When he leaned away, her eyes opened wider, and she lifted her finger to touch the very place his lips had been. His lips tingled from the oh-so-brief contact.

"A kiss on the forehead is very intimate, more so than one to the lips."

Seriously? He'd gone for that spot because it seemed less threatening. The lips, well, he didn't even want to think about kissing her there. Maybe all these years of sensual deprivation had Cassie's circuits crossed.

What would turn her on?

Cool it, Denton.

Kissing Cassie on the lips would have made both of them uncomfortable albeit for very different reasons. Still, she wanted to talk about kissing. He could indulge her.

"Why is that, Sweet Pea?"

"It is where the Third Eye is located."

He glanced up at her forehead. "The third what?"

"Eye." She shrugged. "It is a mystical belief. When I meditate, it is the place from which I actually 'see' the images I receive. But even when my other two eyes are open, it is very much an active source of insight, just not of physical sight. Do you not feel something special there?"

"I've never really paid attention to it before." Sure, sometimes there was a tension there, but he just figured it was the onset of a headache.

"Maybe if I kiss you there you will see what I mean."

Darlin', you can kiss me anywhere you'd like.

Just don't scare her away by saying some asshole thing like that out loud, Denton.

"I reckon in the name of science, we should give it a try." He hoped he didn't sound lascivious but grinned anyway. When he saw her reluctance, he figured she planned to back away from her offer. Then she surprised him and placed her hands on his shoulders and pulled him toward her. He closed his eyes, well, the two he knew about. She kissed his forehead.

Hot damn.

His body tingled in a weird way, moving into his chest and shoulders. A memory crowded out what should have been a tender moment between him and this beautiful woman. "My mom used to kiss me there, especially when I'd had a run-in with my dad over a lost game." Sweet to remember his mother trying to make him feel better, but Momma sure killed the moment.

She smiled at him. "Exactly. She wanted you to feel secure and loved, I am sure. Do you still feel the imprint of my lips even after the kiss?"

Damn right. He nodded. "Yeah. Makes me feel all warm and fuzzy..." His grin widened. At least his focus had returned to the girl on his lap.

"When you kissed me a few minutes ago, Lucas, a sense of well-being came over me. Thank you for that, especially after..."

She closed her eyes, and he pulled her against his chest again.

"You'll always be safe with me, Sweet Pea." Sitting like this with her filled something that had been missing in him, too, even if it killed him not to try to ignite something more carnal between them. So what if they never went beyond being friends? He could share moments like this—the intimacy he'd asked for—the rest of his life and still be happy.

Okay, his cock had a mind of its own. But she didn't seem to notice. He didn't want to ruin this moment. How many men were lucky enough to have a girl who needed him, if to provide nothing more than comfort and security?

"Lucas, I think I will be okay to go back to sleep now. You should try to sleep, too. You work so hard, and having me and my alpacas here just add to your burden."

"I don't require a lot of sleep, and you're no burden at all, Sweet Pea. I like having you here. I've missed you something awful since I left your place."

Not to mention the fact that I don't want to put you down just yet.

Who knew when the walls would go back up and she'd distance herself again? "I know you have to head to Denver this weekend, but you can count on me while you're here. I'll sleep in the house to be close by until we know the anniversary memories have passed. I don't want you facing those moments alone. I'll be right outside this room on the couch."

She stayed silent so long he wondered if she'd fallen asleep. Then he heard a sniffle.

"You okay, darlin'?" he whispered

She nodded. "Why are you always so nice to me?"

"Why wouldn't I be?"

"Because..." She paused, and he waited. "No reason. I just have not..."

What had she started to say? He could push her and probably uncover some of those self-image issues she needed to work on, but he decided she'd been through enough soul-searching for one night. He didn't want to stir up anything else. She needed some sleep. They had years to sort things out, if she'd stick it out with him.

When she finally spoke again, her words were soft, her voice sleepy. "I am sorry that I have not been very nice to you."

"What do you mean? You hauled my ass out of a wrecked truck, nursed me back to health twice, and even agreed to become my wife."

"But I have also been a bitch, sometimes."

He chuckled. "I knew all along it was just a defense mechanism. I saw in the way you were with Karla and others that that wasn't the real you."

"You're an observer. Always watching, but not in a creepy way. Well, not once I came to know you better and did not think you were stalking me."

He couldn't contain his chuckle. "I earned your trust, eventually. That's the important thing."

She nodded and remained silent for a long time. When her body became heavier, he knew she was close to falling asleep. He stood, lifting her in his arms, and she startled awake. "Shhh, darlin'. I'm just going to tuck you into bed now so you can get some rest." He walked around the bed to the other side and placed her gently on the bottom sheet. Her legs were bare where the oversized T-shirt had ridden up, but she remedied that in a flash by grabbing the top sheet and bedspread and yanking them up to her chin.

"Good night, Lucas."

"Night, Sweet Pea." He bent down and, for good measure, placed another kiss on her forehead. "Sleep tight. I'll be in the next room if you need me, and I'm going to keep the door open a crack so I'll hear you if you have another bad dream. We'll deal with it before it becomes full-blown."

She nodded. "Thank you."

He wished like hell she'd trust him enough to join her in the bed so he could hold her safe in his arms all night long, but someone as skittish as Cassie needed her space. They'd made a lot of headway in a short time.

Be patient.

He picked up his revolver from the dresser and walked out of the room, pulling the door nearly closed. How lucky was it they had found each other? Or maybe it *was* fate as she believed. Cassie needed companionship as much as he did. He hadn't realized how lonely he was until after Angel spent those two weeks here. Did Cassie feel that way after he left her place last month?

No matter how, two lonely people had found each other. Funny how life worked out sometimes. He smiled as he made up his bed on the couch. He'd better grab a few winks while he could. Good thing he was a light sleeper in case Cassie needed him again tonight.

Damn, but he liked being needed.

Luke smiled as he crawled between the blanket and the sheet.

*   *   *

As tired as she was, sleep eluded Cassie after Lucas left the room. She was not afraid he would do something while she slept. In fact, that was what had the wheels turning fastest in her mind.

I am not afraid at all.

Amazing. When was the last time she had been in such close proximity to a man and not feared being raped?

Five years.

Many cancer patients touted the five-year mark as being cured if there were no further outbreaks. Survivors. Would she ever reach a point where she put those horrific days in Peru behind her and considered herself a survivor rather than a victim? She had survived with her life when some women were not as lucky.

But had she really *lived* since then?

Hardly.

She existed. She awakened each day. Sometimes, she poured what was left of her heart into a piece in the studio, losing whole days and nights before coming up for air. Well, that was before she had the alpacas. They kept her in the moment more because she had to see that they were fed and had water and companionship. Being responsible for other creatures helped keep her from suffering days of depression that used to hit so hard sometimes, especially in the winter months. Winter reminded her of the attack even more so than the actual anniversary because it had been winter that July in the Andes.

A double whammy. Not only did the anniversary of the actual date of the rape hit her, but visceral memories of that frigid July night came during the winter months here in Colorado, as well.

Lucky her.

She chuffed. Through the slit in the door, she saw Luke cross the room with an afghan and pillow. She hated that she had put him out of yet another bed and further disrupted his life. They could not continue like this for very long. This was unfair to him. She needed to decide what to do.

Where could she possibly go if she left here? Her heart was in the mountains. After the gallery opening, she should visit the real-estate office. But she knew most rentals were short-term ones for rich vacationers. She should call her landlady, see if there was any hope there.

Her eyelids drooped before she willed them open again. The threat of returning night terrors caused fear to settle into her belly again.

"I don't want you facing those moments alone."

Knowing Lucas would hear if she had another nightmare and awaken her, Cassie decided to trust him and allow herself to give in to sleep. She closed her eyes. Just for a moment…

The smell of bread baking awakened her. Sun streamed through the slits in the heavy curtains. Morning. She had slept through the night. No more terrors.

Incredible!

She smiled and tossed the covers off. After showering and dressing, she sought out Lucas in the kitchen. He sat at the table reading from what appeared to be a horse magazine.

He looked up and smiled, seeming to be gauging her mood. "Mornin', Sweet Pea. Hungry?"

"Famished." She realized she truly was hungry for the first time in days. Maybe longer. "The sourdough smells fantastic."

"Thanks. I use my momma's starter."

"Starter?"

He explained the complex process of making sourdough and how the baker had to keep feeding the base so the fermentation process did not die. The fact that the loaf of bread they were eating was somehow connected with loaves his mother made years or even decades ago fascinated Cassie.

"I would love to have a cup of your starter when I go…" She realized she had neither a place to live nor a clue when she would be able to leave, so she finished the sentence differently than she had expected. "…when I go to Kitty's shower Sunday. I will give her a bread machine, too." She shrugged at his confused expression. "Not the typical baby shower gift, but I know how much she enjoys baking for Adam. This will save her time and allow her to make something better for them, but still let her enjoy doing that while she's busy with the babies."

Cassie had never understood Kitty's need to do little things like bake for Adam until she had taken care of Lucas while he recovered from his accident. Cooking a pot of soup or making special dishes from her homeland and sharing them with him gave her great joy. He appreciated everything she did so much, even things she would have done anyway with or without him.

Lucas stood and came toward her as if to hug her. On instinct, she took a step back, and he stopped a few feet away rather than invade her personal space. Why did she regret that she had stopped him short of hugging her? It probably was wise to keep some space between them. She was not thinking clearly, but the memory of the time she had spent on his lap wrapped in his arms last night left her longing for his touch once more.

"You're welcome to the starter anytime, too."

She nodded, but the thought of leaving saddened her for some reason. Would she ever get back into the mountains? She had intended to put half of the proceeds from her gallery exhibition into a fund for those left homeless by these random, devastating wildfires but never dreamed she would be among those burned out of her home.

They prepared breakfast in silence, he making his beloved bacon and eggs and she a fruit plate, yogurt, and whole-grain cereal. Both enjoyed the fresh-baked bread, though.

After eating her fill, she set down her spoon. "Will you be working with O'Keeffe today?"

"Sure will. I usually take care of the others first and then work with her when things quiet down."

"Would you mind if I joined you?"

"Hey, you have to earn your keep, remember?" His teasing grin told her he was joking, and she returned the smile.

"It does not seem like I am repaying you for anything when I love doing it. She calls to me somehow."

He sobered. "Join the club. They all do in some way, but she's especially haunting, probably because she hasn't let her guard down yet. Speaking of which, thank you for trusting me last night. I know how scary that must have been, but I'm glad I could be there for you when you were ready."

"Me, too." She had fought those night terrors alone for so long. She glanced down, embarrassed for some reason. She was not used to asking anyone to do anything for her, but had become very beholden to this man.

My dear friend, Lucas.

And my husband.

In name alone.

He stood and picked up his dishes while she did the same with hers. "Let's head out to the barn and start, then. I'll bet they're wondering what we're up to this morning."

She realized how late this must be for him to set about doing his chores. Lucas promised to stay inside the house after her episode last night in case she had another, and he had done just that.

A man of his word. She reached out to squeeze his arm and almost pulled back before willing herself to take the chance and make this contact. "Thank you, Lucas."

"What for?"

"For being a man of integrity. Being who you are."

"Who else would I be?"

She smiled. "You are not like other men." At his puzzled expression, she wished she could convey what she meant, but words failed her.

He grinned sheepishly. "Let's go before you swell my head again."

She did not understand his reference, but he walked across the room, grabbed his Stetson from the hook by the door, and held the door open for her to walk through.

In many ways, he reminded her of *Papá*. Or Eduardo. Both had been raised to respect women, as well, but Lucas did so in a way that did not make her feel patronized or subjugated. Both her father and brother believed women had their place and those women who did not conform left themselves vulnerable to being hurt.

If they had any idea how badly...

But Cassie did not want to conform. She also did not want to be around men.

Except perhaps for one.

What was she going to do about this man she had married?

Chapter Twenty

Cassie lifted Aurora from the crescent-moon bed. "Precious one, I am so glad you are home now." Seeing the three babies curled up together in the bed Lucas made warmed her heart. She would sketch a picture of them in it for him.

Kitty would now be able to focus more on healing and less on running between the babies at home and the one in the hospital. Perfect timing with the long overdue baby shower just a few hours away.

"My wish for you is a life free of worry and strife, filled with the strength to face any challenge that comes your way."

"What a beautiful wish for her." Cassie turned to find Kitty standing in the bathroom doorway in her robe and slippers. Her face bore the strain of her recent illness and exhaustion, especially in the smudges under her eyes. She padded across the room, her hand pressed against her abdomen. Her body had been ravaged by the births and then her hemorrhage. But despite all that, she smiled.

Cassie wrapped her free hand around Kitty's back and hugged her. "You scared us all so much."

"None worse than Adam. He's still not sleeping—worse than ever before. I've had to get used to sleeping with him watching over me again."

"Adam is a natural guardian. He will probably always worry that something will happen to take another of his loved ones away. I just hope that he can find some peace inside to no longer blame himself for what happens to others."

"I hope so, too. At least he saw with my complication that sometimes it has nothing to do with what he did or didn't do. Things just happen."

Kitty's words struck a chord. How many times had Cassie blamed herself for being in that cantina the night of the rape? No matter what she had done, she had been horribly violated, and the only people to blame were those three animals. No, animal was too kind a word to describe them.

"You okay, Cassie?"

Kitty stroked her cheek, and she came back to the present and forced a smile. "I think I understand more about love after watching you and Adam in the midst of your crisis."

Kitty smiled, but Cassie detected pity in her eyes. "I hope you find that kind of love someday, Cassie. You have so much to offer someone, if only…"

Cassie sighed. She still had not told her best friend about her marriage to Lucas. Of course, it was not what Kitty would call a marriage, either—not like what she had with Adam. She would never understand.

Cassie did not understand her deepening feelings for Lucas, either. There were all kinds of love, she supposed. Her heart had strong emotions toward the man who had invaded her world and battered down so many of her defenses this spring. The love she felt was not like that of a sibling, more a deep friendship.

"I think having to take care of Lucas when he was injured made me think about someone other than myself for the first time in years."

"Oh, Cassie, that's not true. You've always cared about me."

You're not a man. Aloud she said, "You are easy to love, Kitty. Besides, you have seen me at my worst."

After the other night, so had Lucas. Having him hold her during her meltdown brought home the fact that he would not take advantage of her even at her most vulnerable. She trusted him more than she did any man outside her family.

Aurora whimpered, and they both turned their attention to her. She blinked and stared at first one then the other before pursing her lips and sucking. "I'll change her if you want to prepare to nurse."

Kitty was already removing her robe and unbuttoning what appeared to be one of Adam's flannel shirts. Once quite the fashion-conscious dresser, she had certainly toned down her look. How else had motherhood—and illness—changed her friend? She wore no makeup but was radiantly beautiful with her pale skin contrasted with her dark hair.

After a quick diaper change, Cassie waited for Kitty to sit in the glider and handed the baby to her. Aurora's tiny mouth opened, and she made hungry gasps as she sought her *mamá's* breast. Cassie blinked away the surprising sting of tears. She would paint a portrait of Kitty with her tiniest baby when she got back into her studio. Well, Lucas's studio. She let the image sear itself into her memory.

"Kitten, do you need anyth—" Adam stood in the doorway. "I see Cassie's already on it." He smiled at her, and Cassie smiled back. She no longer felt threatened by Adam, either. Had it been their nights at the hospital caring for the woman they both loved so dearly? Or had her time with Lucas softened her heart and lessened her fear of being near the man? Most likely the former, because she still did not fully trust any other men.

Cassie walked toward Adam without any sense of fear. "I will leave you two alone while I go down and finish up the dip I am making for the party."

"Thanks, hon. The gang ought to be here in a couple of hours. It'll be some party between the baby shower and Marisol's eighth birthday."

"Not to mention your birthday, Adam. We didn't get to celebrate three weeks ago because I was back in the hospital."

At the mention of that dark time, a shadow crossed Adam's face as his rekindled pain slammed into Cassie without warning. Adam had proven his worth to Cassie in the way he saw to Kitty's needs and put his family above all others. Kitty was blessed to have such a supportive, loving man in her life.

Would Cassie ever allow herself that kind of relationship? The only person keeping her from it was herself. Why was she so afraid to let Lucas closer? Perhaps the therapist she would be meeting with this week would help. She'd gone through rape counseling at Columbia, but had only focused on the trauma and how to cope with the day-to-day experiences relating to being a college student. She still harbored much hatred and anger toward her rapists—and men, in general.

Adam crossed the room to stand beside Kitty. "At my age, I'd rather forget birthdays." He reached out and stroked her cheek. Kitty closed her eyes and leaned into his hand.

So much love. And trust.

Could Cassie place that much trust in Lucas?

She turned and slipped out of the room unnoticed. Of course, what she and Lucas had was different. Not the same as Kitty and Adam's special bond.

* * *

Ryder Wilson rolled the throttle as they made the turn down the quiet residential street where Top—*remember he wants you to call him Adam now*—said he lived. At least he'd been able to skirt the downtown area, but city traffic around Denver made him jittery.

Megan's hand under his leather jacket continued to ground him as she stroked his chest through his T-shirt.

Still, his fear of cities would be nothing compared to facing his former master sergeant again. Why Megan had thought it was such a great idea to save their announcement until they met face to face with her brother confounded him. Her mother and her other brother knew.

How would the man he loved like a big brother respond?

How would you respond if your sister married a man she'd known less than two weeks?

Exactly what he was worried about. He had managed to win her brother Patrick over, though.

But Patrick isn't Top.

He swallowed hard and pulled into the driveway leading to the imposing house all too soon. One blue and two pink balloons floated on the breeze, tethered to the mailbox. The thought of Megan being around the babies worried him, even though she insisted she couldn't wait to spoil them rotten. He'd keep a close eye on her to help her process any unresolved or unexpected emotions.

While surrounded by evergreen trees, there were enough houses in proximity that the children would probably have other kids to play with. Nice place to raise a family. Looked like Adam did okay for himself after he retired from the military. That club he ran must be doing well because he doubted the man's pension would have been able to pay for something like this.

He parked the bike, and they removed their helmets before walking up the sidewalk to the front door. His nerves raw, he reached for her hand and squeezed.

"Stop worrying. Adam loves you."

Like a brother Marine, maybe. Not necessarily a brother-in-law.

The door opened before they knocked. A slightly older Master Sergeant Montague, grayer at the temples, stood there. But Ryder had grayed some himself.

Adam's gaze went first to Megan then to him. The confusion on his face was quickly masked, and he opened his arms for Megan. "Good to see you again, hon." He then extended his hand to Ryder. "Glad to have you here, too, Wilson. Heard the hog and thought Damián was stopping by early to check on things before the party." He zeroed in with familiar intensity. "I knew Megan was coming, but didn't expect you so soon after we talked."

He didn't seem upset to see Ryder. Then again, Adam didn't know in what capacity Ryder had shown up. He'd promised a visit to hang out with his Marine buddies, though.

"We've actually been on the road the past week. A little…" *Don't call it a honeymoon.* "…vacation." He and Megan had decided to visit the Four Corners, Mesa Verde, and the Black Canyon of the Gunnison in a circuitous route to Denver—definitely as a honeymoon.

He thought he detected some surprise in the older man's face, and if so, it was masked quickly. "Glad to hear you two hit it off."

Oh, we hit it off all right.

"Excuse my manners. A combat zone has nothing on three newborn babies when it comes to sleep deprivation." Adam stepped back and waved them inside.

Ryder placed his hand at the small of his wife's back and guided her ahead of him. Adam didn't miss the gesture and cast a puzzled glance in his direction. The sooner they came clean, the better.

But the moment they walked into the house, all hell broke loose. He heard at least two babies wailing from upstairs, and a woman called for Adam to hurry. The man's face blanched as he took the stairs two at a time.

"Oh, my. Let's see if we can help."

Ryder wasn't sure what he could do but followed Megan up the elaborate staircase. No sense hanging out down here alone.

They followed the sound of the crying babies and found themselves at the open door to the master bedroom, judging by the king-sized bed. Megan went in without knocking, but Ryder felt strange barging into his master sergeant's bedroom without an invitation. He hung back at the door. Looked like with three adults they'd be able to handle whatever the problem was.

Megan didn't hesitate and went straight to the moon shaped bed next to where Adam reached for one of the babies. She didn't miss a beat, just reached in, picked up a baby in a green blanket, and held it against her chest and shoulder.

God. The sight made his chest tighten. She turned to him and smiled, but he saw the tears in her eyes. *Oh, baby.* He ached for her and started toward her until Adam intercepted his path to take the other baby to his wife. The much-younger, black-haired woman sat in a glider chair, trying to comfort a third crying baby.

Holy fuck! She wasn't comforting; she was breastfeeding!

Ryder turned around and headed back into the hallway. He'd seen the bare breast of Top's wife. He wanted to go back downstairs, but needed to check to see if Megan was all right. He turned, making sure the door blocked the view of Adam and his wife before focusing on Megan.

She soon had the baby calmed down as if she'd been around babies her whole life. When she met his gaze, a tear rolled down her cheek. He motioned with his finger for her to come to him.

"Oh, Ryder! Isn't she the most precious thing?"

He placed a hand on her back and, with a finger under her chin, raised her face toward his. "How're you doing, Red?"

"I'm fine. I'm okay, really." She tried to glance away.

"Look at me, Red."

She met his gaze and blinked away another tear. "We're going to have our own babies someday, Ryder. Until then, I'm going to just live vicariously by being a doting aunt to these little ones."

"You're the most amazing woman I've ever met." He bent to kiss her and was finally able to look down at the baby. He expected her to be small, but she was tiny. Triplets. Hell, he'd be happy with one at a time.

A movement from his peripheral vision sent him on alert, and he shielded her and the baby until he turned to see a Latino woman with long dark hair carrying a lunch tray. When she met his gaze, she seemed just as wary of him and diverted her path to give him a wide berth.

Wanting to put her at ease, he said, "I'm Ryder Wilson. This is my… This is Adam's sister, Megan." Good save, but he needed to get this secret out in the open before it killed him.

At the mention of Megan, the woman smiled at her in recognition. "So glad you made it. Kitty's been expecting you. I am Cassie."

Who was Kitty?

"Oh, Karla's told me a lot about you. I bet you're excited about your opening on Tuesday."

The two chatted about art for a moment. He'd make sure Megan went to the exhibition. Maybe she could work on something with the owner to display her photographs there sometime. He knew how excited she was to be doing the exhibit at his sister's gallery in Santa Fe.

"I was just bringing Kitty some lunch." She walked into the bedroom.

"I'd better take this one back in there. Why don't you go grab something yourself?"

"I'll wait for you."

"I think the girls have things in hand now." Ryder turned to watch Adam walking toward them. "Megan, I think she's ready to feed Kate now. Ryder and I are going down to the kitchen. Hang a right at the bottom of the stairs, and you'll find us when you're ready. No rush, though. We have some things to talk about."

Here we go.

Ryder turned to whisper in Megan's ear. "I'm not saying anything about us until you get down there." When he pulled away, she nodded and smiled. He followed Adam toward the staircase. On the landing, he paused to look out over the Denver skyline in the distance. "Beautiful view."

"Sure is." Adam stopped walking and looked out, too. "Million dollar view. Doc—Marc D'Alessio—sold this place to us or we'd never have been able to afford something this nice. It had been a gift from his grandfather, but if you remember Doc, he'd rather be in the wilderness than cooped up in the city."

Ryder didn't remember that at all, but nodded. He certainly understood the feeling. Cities scared the crap out of him. He hoped they wouldn't have to venture out in that one anytime soon.

"Now, how about a beer while we wait on Megan?"

"Yeah. Sounds great." He'd never shared a beer with Top before, but maybe one or two would take the edge off his nerves.

"Follow me."

They walked into a kitchen any chef would want as his or her own. Every stainless-steel appliance known to man and lots of counter space. At the moment, the counters were filled with bowls of food that smelled out of this world and a large half-sheet-cake box.

"Coors, Birra Moretti, or a local IPA?"

"The IPA, please. Thanks." He glanced at the double oven. "Someone must love cooking in here."

Adam grabbed the IPA and closed the fridge. "Hell, I can barely boil water, and Karla isn't much better, even when she had time." He handed the beer to Ryder and chose a bottle of water for himself from a box on the floor. Damn, if he knew the man didn't want to join him, he'd have asked for water, too.

"I love to cook. Maybe I can help out by preparing some meals while Megan and I are here."

They hadn't discussed sleeping arrangements. Of course, Megan was invited to stay, but until Adam knew about the wedding, no invitation would be extended to him. Hell, he'd just put his foot in it—again.

Adam leaned his hip against the granite counter. "Mind telling me what's going on between you and my sister?"

He'd expected to be offered a place to sit and talk, but twisted the cap off his beer and took a swig before responding. "Megan and I hit it off. We just… We're in love."

Adam stood to an intimidating height and crossed his arms in front of his chest. "You just met her, what, three weeks ago? A little fast to be making declarations like that."

If he thought *that* declaration had been hasty… "Believe me, I know it's unusual. But the minute I met her, I knew Megan was something special."

"I sent you to protect her, not get…romantically involved."

By the way Adam said romantically, he knew the word "sexually" had been on the tip of the man's tongue or at the very least on his mind. Ryder should just come out and say they were already married, but Megan ought to be here, too. He was her brother, after all.

"Believe me, I fought it hard." *At first.* "I didn't want you to think I was taking advantage of…" *your baby sister.* "…the situation."

"Then why did you?"

Okay, wait a minute. Clearly, the man didn't know his sister and her powerful personality. "I think we should wait and include Megan in this conversation." *Hurry, Red. I need reinforcements.*

Adam glanced down at his left hand as Ryder raised it and took another swallow of his beer to wet his parched mouth and throat.

"Does she know you're married?"

Ryder nearly choked. He'd forgotten all about his wedding ring. It already seemed a natural part of him. He hadn't removed it since he married Megan more than two weeks ago.

Red, forgive me, but I'm not going to have my master sergeant thinking I'm married to someone else and screwing around with his baby sister.

"Yeah, she knows. She's the one who asked me, after all."

"Asked you what?"

"I asked him to marry me." Both men turned as Megan entered the room, walked over to Ryder, and snagged the bottle from his hand. She took a long swallow before turning to smile at her older brother. "And Ryder said yes, eventually."

Eventually? Hell, theirs was the fastest engagement on record.

"You're *married?* To each other?"

"Yes, Adam. Technically, we're on our honeymoon."

Adam ran a hand through his close-cropped hair and stared first at Megan then Ryder. "I love Megan more than anything. I'll never do anything to break her trust or—"

"You'd better not or you'll have me to answer to."

"You and Patrick, both."

Adam's gaze zoomed in on Megan. "Patrick knew and didn't say anything?"

"I swore him to secrecy. He was our videographer. Mom knows, too. Because she was so upset with us for rushing into it, we decided to wait and tell you face to face. Later on, we can show you the video so you can see the ceremony." She smiled up at Ryder. "It was beautiful, even if it was only at the justice of the peace's office. Ryder made it full of meaning."

The almost imperceptible glance at Megan's waistline told Ryder what Adam thought automatically, before he seemed to realize there was no way Ryder would have known if she was pregnant in such a short time. Apparently, he didn't know Megan's history.

"What did Mom say? I'll bet it killed her to miss the wedding."

Megan stiffened, and Ryder stroked her back. "I know she wanted to be there, but I was afraid Ryder would come up with a thousand more reasons why he shouldn't marry me if I gave him any time to think about it." She grinned up at him to let him know she was teasing, although she was dead right. "I wasn't going to let this one go. He's the only man I will ever love."

Adam be damned. Ryder lowered his mouth to hers and kissed her then pulled back and smiled. How'd he get so lucky?

Adam, for one, had helped bring them together. And a persistent lance corporal had a hand in their being together, too.

He turned back to Adam while holding Megan closer against his body. "I have you to thank for bringing us together. I know this outcome isn't what you intended. Hell, I sure didn't expect to ever find love again. But...your sister can be very...persuasive."

Adam crossed the room slowly, his expression somber until he stretched his hand out to Ryder, who had to pull away from his wife to shake it.

"Welcome to the family, Ryder. We're now brothers in more ways than the Marine Corps."

"Thanks, Top." He couldn't help the lapse to the man's former nickname. "I'll do everything I can to be the man she deserves."

"Oh, Ryder. You could never let me down." She moved back to his side and wrapped her arm around his waist.

"I guess you're planning to live in Albuquerque."

Ryder wasn't sure how to answer. *God, don't let him ask what I do for a living.*

"Actually, Adam, we're ready to start a new life. Right now, Ryder's renting a place north of Albuquerque, but we've fallen in love with Colorado during our honeymoon tour this week. I think we might just look around at the possibility of moving up here."

Adam took a step back. "That going to be a problem with your job, Wilson?"

Okay, back to the formalities. "Actually, I'm currently between jobs." That sounded better than telling him he'd been unemployed for years, holed up in a house in the Jemez Mountains, too afraid to venture near a workplace in the city for fear of having a panic attack, and—

"Ryder's great at maintenance, construction, project management—all kinds of things, really. Maybe you know of someone who might be hiring, Adam."

He probably wouldn't be unemployed for long with Megan as his agent.

"I might. Damián's bought a shop downtown where he repairs and customizes Harleys. And his wife, Savannah, is working at a clinic where they're about to expand. Might be some construction subcontracting needed there. I can also introduce you to Luke Denton. He subcontracts for local builders and can probably hook you up with a number of jobs, too. He has more work than he wants at the moment."

An enormous weight lifted off his shoulders at Adam's encouraging words, but something burned at his gut. He couldn't be less than completely honest with Adam. "There's something you need to know."

"Ryder, don't—"

He met Megan's worried gaze. "It's okay, Red."

She leaned closer to whisper. "There are some things I don't think my brother needs to know about our relationship."

Realization dawned at what she was worried about, and he grinned.

Jeezus. No fucking way was he about to tell him what he enjoyed doing to Adam's sister in private.

He smiled. "Don't worry, Red. I don't think your brother is going to let me walk out of here in one piece if he finds out what I do to you in the bedroom. Or the kitchen. Or—"

"Hush! He's only a few feet away and isn't deaf."

"You two need a room or something?" Adam interrupted.

He felt the heat emanating from her cheeks before pulling away. Her cheeks flamed. So fucking hot. He loved it when he made her blush. But Ryder quickly sobered. He still had something to come clean about. He met Adam's gaze, surprised to see the man stifling what appeared to be a grin.

"Adam, when you called me asking for my help, I was having a rough night. You know some of it from our later talks by phone, but before you recommend me for work, you might as well know I haven't been able to keep a job since my discharge four years ago." Ryder closed his eyes, wishing he had another beer. His mouth felt like it had been swabbed with cotton balls. "A friend gave me a place to live when I returned from Fallujah, or I'd have been homeless. But that's not all."

Megan rubbed his arm, still covered by his leather jacket. He wanted to wrap his arms around her and hang on for dear life, but needed to get this out and stand on his own two feet. This was Top. He didn't want to be found lacking in this man's eyes.

"Mostly I've been hiding out—away from everyone." He lifted the bottle to his lips before remembering it was empty. Adam handed him an unopened bottle of water and Ryder took it, downing half of it before he continued. Adam's steely gaze bore into him. He couldn't read the man's reaction, but still had more to say.

"I can't promise to have my PTSD under control at all times."

"No one can." Top's words took Ryder by surprise.

"Beg your pardon?"

"If you think anyone who's seen combat can just cram all that shit—" Adam paused and glanced at Megan. "Sorry."

Megan shook her head. "Please. I've heard—and *said*—worse."

Adam didn't seem happy to hear that, but focused on Ryder again. "Look, we have a lot of crap to deal with, and having our loved ones see the ugly side of what we've done, seen, or been through is less than ideal. But we're human, too. Cut yourself some slack, Ryder. Megan's tough, just like my Karla. She's going to be there for you no matter what."

Ryder turned to Megan, who smiled her support back at him. "She already has been. I've always tried to be up front with her about what to expect."

"You haven't scared me away, yet, Ryder." She walked into his arms.

"Yeah. I noticed."

"All right, let's head back upstairs. I'll show you where you can stow your gear. The house is going to be packed with people later today for my granddaughter's birthday party and our baby shower. Take some time to unwind. Since you're married, you can share a room."

Megan shook her head, but smiled. "Thanks, Adam, for not asking us to produce the marriage license first." Then she faced Ryder again and kissed him. He responded without thinking before hearing Adam clear his throat. His girl made him forget everything else.

"Sorry, Adam."

"Just remember you come to me or someone else who's been there when you're in over your head. I don't want to see Megan hurt because you shut yourself off again."

Ryder's throat closed up. "Neither do I. I appreciate knowing you and the other guys have my back, too." He faced his wife. "Just like my girl does."

*   *   *

Adam watched as they preceded him from the kitchen. Ryder had his arm around her back with his hand resting on the curve of her butt. They couldn't be any closer and remain decent. Megan seemed happy, though. He just hoped she hadn't taken on more than she could handle. PTSD triggers were unpredictable. He'd be sure to keep tabs on Ryder this time.

Something Ryder said bugged the crap out of him as he set down his bottle of water on the counter and followed them.

I've always tried to be up front with her about what to expect.

Why hadn't Adam been up front with Karla about what had been going on with him this spring? He'd suffered through one of his worst PTSD episodes in a long time just last month. Instead of talking with Karla about it, he'd shut her out. Hell, he'd even stopped sleeping in the same bed with her most nights for fear he'd hurt her if another episode struck.

Karla had shown him during her ordeal delivering the babies—and the nightmare afterward—that she wasn't physically or emotionally fragile. God, she was as tough as they came. If anyone ever had his back, she did—to hell and back.

He needed to talk with her when things settled down to a routine. Okay, that wasn't about to happen anytime soon. Tonight. After they were in bed. He couldn't tell her the details about the nightmare and why Marc's interrogation stirred things up. Civilians didn't need to hear the whole truth about that fucking shit.

"Hang a left at the top of the stairs," Adam said. "It's the second door on the left."

He'd almost lost her a couple weeks ago. Shutting her out of any part of his life wasn't an option. Time to talk with her. Damián was having fewer episodes now that he was with Savannah. When Adam asked what he thought made the difference, he said Savannah was doing some special breathing exercises with him. Maybe she could give him and Karla some pointers, too. Hell, he used breathing to regulate anxiety during BDSM scenes, and she used it during labor. Probably worked on the same principle.

"Thanks, Adam." Megan came to him and gave him a hug and kiss. He kissed her on the cheek. "I think we'll hang out here for a while, but you know where we are if you or Karla need anything."

"Sure thing."

As he returned to their bedroom, Adam decided he needed to find ways to relax, period. He would never stop trying to protect Karla from every damned thing coming down the pike, but he couldn't anticipate or handle everything that might happen. Knowing she could defend herself and the babies if he wasn't there might help him worry a little less. She knew hand-to-hand self-defense, but he didn't want anyone to get that close to her. Seeing her in the clutches of Julio last fall with a knife to her throat had nearly killed him. Maybe he'd take her to the firing range and train her to use a sidearm in case she needed one.

But not until she had more time to heal from her recent ordeal. He'd be here to protect her in the meantime.

Chapter Twenty-One

Cassie surveyed the room filled with people and found herself missing someone. Lucas had stayed behind to take care of the animals. She would see him Tuesday, but still wished he had come to Denver for the baby shower and Marisol's birthday.

She was acquainted with most of those present, but only knew Kitty and Angelina very well. Adam's mother, Mrs. Gallagher, held Paxton in her arms and smiled as though remembering holding her own son at that age. She wondered what had happened to the woman to put her in a wheelchair. But she seemed comfortable in it and had had no trouble navigating the first floor of the house during her visit. Her other son, Patrick, seemed to be very solicitous with her, making sure her needs were met.

Not at the moment, though. The men and Grant had escaped to the den to watch a football—soccer—match. Marc's team, Italy, was in the game. At least it was a European championship, and Damián's team wasn't competing against his friend's. Even though, someone was taking the match seriously judging by the shouts filtering into the room where the girls had gathered to watch Kitty open presents. Thankfully she was not in that atmosphere of rampant testosterone.

Adam had carried Kitty downstairs, and the babies were rarely tucked into the portable bassinet for being held by Angelina, Savannah, Cassie, Megan, Kitty's mom, except for when Kitty fed one or two. She would finish feeding one and start on the next, or sometimes nurse two at a time. How exhausted she must be, but she seemed radiantly happy today surrounded by friends and family.

Marisol, whose party with some friends from school would be held after the shower, enjoyed helping, too.

"*Maman*, may I hold Princess Aurora?"

Cassie and Savannah grinned. The eight-year-old birthday girl had taken to calling Aurora "princess" ever since the day she found out her name, but this was the first time she had been able to see the baby who had been hidden away in the NICU the past few weeks.

Savannah stroked her daughter's long black hair. "Mari, she only came home from the hospital today."

The little girl stuck her lower lip out. "But it's my birthday. Grampa said I helped him name her. I think *he* would let me hold her." *Poor Marisol.* Adam was very protective of his babies. But the tenacious girl did not give up on arguing her case. "Until I get a baby of my own, I need to practice with these."

Cassie cast a glance at Savannah, who smiled and shook her head. "No, I'm not." She leaned over and whispered to Cassie. "Not for sure anyway. But we're trying." She continued to smile in a dreamy way as she sat up straight again.

So much happiness among the young women in this room. Megan was a new bride. Kitty had all her babies home at last. Savannah was looking forward to having another child. And Angelina was engaged to Marc after a rough patch between them.

Why was Cassie so afraid to chase down her own bliss? What secret did these women know? She remembered the book at Lucas's house about claiming what you wanted in life and letting the Universe bring it to you.

I wish to have love and happiness, too.

Marisol went over to Mrs. Paxton and coaxed Kate to squeeze her finger. Cassie sighed.

"You're awfully quiet, Cassie. Everything okay?"

Cassie turned toward Savannah. "I am fine." The words rolled off her tongue automatically. She had only met this woman when Kitty came home from the hospital the first time, although they had spent a lot of time together while helping with the babies. At some point in the long hours together taking care of Kate and Paxton when Karla had been hospitalized again, Savannah had hinted at a tragic past of incest and abuse. The resilient woman now worked as a therapist for abused women and children. Cassie had admitted to having some problems of her own, and Savannah had recommended someone in Denver for her to speak with.

"I am just tired, I think. A lot has happened lately."

"I heard about the fire. It's devastating to lose all of your possessions like that. I once had to walk away from my home and leave everything my mother had left behind. If you need someone to talk with, I'm here."

"Thank you. I have not been able to go back to see what survived, but my landlady said the cabin was a total loss. I hope my studio has some things I can salvage."

They watched Kitty open more gifts, smiling. Cassie hoped the day was not too much of a strain for her.

"Thank you, also, for giving me the number for the rape counseling center. I have an appointment tomorrow with a follow-up on Thursday. She sounds very nice, although I am not sure what advice she can give."

"We don't really advise. More like try to assist you in figuring out what's best for you. We listen and offer coping strategies for triggers. Help you find ways to process differently what you experienced. She's good at hypnotherapy if you want to try that. Also something that's been very promising called EMDR—sorry, that's Eye Movement Desensitization and Reprocessing. Combat veterans, first-responder, and other PTSD survivors are finding it useful in helping them process the emotions rather than simply relive the memories."

"She did mention it, but I decided to try hypnotherapy since I'm trying to deal with a single event. When I was in counseling at Columbia after the rape, I was afraid to try that because I just wanted to block the memories. But I can see how redirecting the scene might take away the power of the nightmares."

She glanced at Kitty who held up three adorable outfits, all alike except for their different bold colors. "Kitty was a great support to me then."

"Having someone to hold your hand and guide you is a tremendous help. If you'd like me to go along, I'll see what I can do."

"No, I am sure I will be okay."

A cheer from the den caught Savannah's attention, and she smiled in the direction of the doorway from the living room. "Damián has helped me do that. His methods are …unconventional, but definitely effective." Savannah smiled, and Cassie wondered what Damián did differently, but didn't pry. The poised young woman pulled her attention back to the conversation. "Be open to suggestions. And accept a hand up or a shoulder to cry on from whoever offers. Healing won't happen overnight. At least you aren't living alone. Luke seems nice."

"He is." *Too* nice. Feeling the need to make sure Savannah did not get the wrong idea, she added, "We are just friends. He helps with my alpacas and gave me a place to stay after I evacuated."

Cassie sighed. She envied what Savannah had in Damián, although the thought of having sex terrified her. How had Savannah gone from her past to having such a relationship? "You are such a strong woman, Savannah."

Savannah's eyes opened wider. "So are you, Cassie. You survived a horrific attack. Now you just need to reclaim your right to happiness and those parts of yourself you've shut down. Then you can thrive again rather than go through the motions of existing."

The words hurt, even though they were spot on. Eat, pray, work. Until Lucas, she thought that was all she needed.

Savannah did not know about her marriage with Lucas, either. He understood her need to keep it between them, saying no one else needed to know or understand as long as the two of them did. Still, Cassie probably would tell Kitty at some point. She had never kept anything from her best friend this long.

"Oh, Cassie! I love it!" Kitty's exclamation brought her back to the present. Cassie's gaze met Kitty's as Angelina and Megan held up the box with the bread machine. "I can't wait to surprise Adam with my bread-making skills. You and Angie need to share some good recipes."

Thankfully, Kitty appreciated her unusual gift. "Lucas sent you his mother's sourdough starter. I left it in the kitchen, but the recipe is taped to the box." Kitty found it and thanked her again.

Her next gift from Cassie would be more appropriate for the occasion. When Kitty opened the pastel painting, tears glistened in her friend's eyes. Cassie felt the sting of tears herself.

The scene showed Kitty seated and holding her daughters while Adam stood beside her with Paxton in the crook of his arm. His free hand rested protectively on Kitty's shoulder.

Kitty cleared her throat and ignored the tears that rolled down her cheeks. "I can't wait to show Adam. With all you've had going on, I can't believe you took the time to paint this. And how you could show us together as a family when we haven't been able to have a scene like this yet. You're so amazing, Cassie."

The image had been so clear in her mind. When Kitty opened her arms, Cassie stood, crossed the room, and bent over to embrace her. "I am so happy you have Adam, Kitty. You two are so perfect together. And now your family is complete." Cassie tamped down what could only be described as a pang of longing. "You are so blessed."

"Just open your heart, Cassie," she whispered. "He's patient and kind and waiting for you—within your reach really."

Lucas? Did Kitty know about their relationship? Cassie pulled away and searched her eyes, but did not detect any clues.

Kitty smiled. "Trust your instincts, Cassie."

She and Lucas were merely friends. Memories of how he held her after her nightmare and watched over her so she could go back to sleep flooded her mind. She missed him terribly, something that surprised her. After he had returned home in May, there had been an emptiness inside, but since coming to Denver this weekend, the hole had grown larger. So many times she found herself wanting to share something with him, only to remember he was not around.

Perhaps after the exhibition opened, she could go on another of those dinner dates she had vowed to do. She would not be returning home again for days. Yes, perhaps on Wednesday night.

*   *   *

"You look beautiful as always, darlin'. Thanks for inviting me to dinner." Her black hair shimmered in the glow of candlelight from the centerpiece, softening her features and casting a warm glow around her face.

Luke couldn't believe it when Cassie asked him to dinner at last night's exhibition opening. The gallery had been mobbed with so many friends and art patrons demanding her attention that he'd written off having any time with her on this visit. But when he walked up to congratulate her and gave her a bouquet of Peruvian lilies—hoping they'd remind her of their wedding day—she smiled and hugged him back. She'd changed, become more relaxed around him. He didn't know what had made that happen other than time and patience, but he sure was happy about it.

She'd suggested an Indian restaurant where she had plenty of exotic vegetarian dishes to choose from and he could find the level of spice he liked. But, honestly, he couldn't even remember what he'd ordered even though half of it had been eaten already.

His lovely bride captured his full attention. Cassie filled him in on the party at Adam and Karla's and what her week in Denver had been like so far. She paused and cast her gaze down before admitting, "I have missed our times like these, Lucas."

She met his gaze once more and continued as if she hadn't spoken those words, but he'd remember them forever. "How is O'Keeffe?"

"She misses you. I can't read her mind, but am pretty sure she thinks I'm an idiot now. She'd rather work with you."

She waved her hand at him. "Oh, she loves you. She just has a stubborn streak—and too much fear. Someday she will see how good you are for her."

He wished the girl seated across the table from him at the moment would see that someday, too. At the very least notice that he tried to be good for her. "I'm a patient man." He scooped up a forkful of yellow rice. After swallowing, he grinned. "Millie's growing like a weed. Wait 'til you see her. She's been your surrogate with O'Keeffe. They play ball together in the round pen now."

"Oh, this I must see! I will be home Saturday."

Home. She just called his place home. *Hot damn!*

She glanced down as she fiddled with her cauliflower and potato dish. Something was on her mind. While he waited for her to speak, he ate in silence.

Her voice rose as the question tumbled from her lips. "Do you have to go back tonight, Lucas?"

Not if you need me, Sweet Pea. "No. Matt's at the ranch and doesn't go back on duty until Saturday." Luke needed to work on some things before his momma showed up Sunday, too, just in case Dad did come with her. The man hadn't committed yet, but always found fault with Luke and his choice of careers, so the fewer reminders lying around in the studio the better.

She settled back in the chair and took a bite, chewing slowly. When she didn't explain further, he set down his fork and reached across the table placing his right hand over her free one. She didn't pull away at least. "What do you need, darlin'? How can I help?"

Her hand trembled, and he squeezed it to pass along some encouragement. She closed her eyes and set her fork beside her plate. "I have an appointment tomorrow and do not wish to go alone." Again, the words came out in a rush as though she was afraid she'd change her mind.

"Appointment for what?" Was she sick? Dread sank into the pit of his stomach as he waited for her to continue.

When she spoke, her voice was so low he had to lean forward. "With a rape crisis counselor."

Good girl. "I'm sure they'll be able to help a lot."

She nodded. "I met with her Monday, and she wants to try a relaxation technique in this session. You would not be in the room for that, of course, but I am a little nervous about what she might stir up. You saw what happened after my night terror last week."

He reached up and stroked her cheek with his thumb. "You know I'll be there in whatever capacity you need. Why don't I pick you up so you won't have to drive afterward?"

Her lips quivering despite her smile, she met his gaze. "Thank you, Lucas. While I have a rental car, I would rather not be alone afterward."

"Makes me feel ten feet tall that you'd ask me. Thanks, Cassie." He wouldn't jinx it by mentioning the T word, but for her to trust him to be there for her at a time like this was monumental progress.

She blinked. "Normally, I would ask Kitty, but she is so busy with the babies." Okay, so he was second fiddle. "Savannah offered, but I do not know her as well as I do you." Well, maybe third fiddle. Hell, he'd take it. *He* was the one she'd asked. No one else.

Cassie reached for her purse and handed him a business card with the appointment time and address on it.

"Want to grab a bite to eat beforehand?"

She shook her head. "No. I do not think that would be wise, in case I…get sick." That she expected to have such a violent response to the session made him wonder why she wanted to do this. He couldn't imagine having to face something that traumatic again.

"Are you sure you want to go through this?"

Tears swam in her eyes. He scooted his chair back and motioned for her to come to him, but she shook her head and tears spilled from the corners of her eyes. If he couldn't get her to sit in his lap again, then he'd go to her. He set his napkin on the table, stood, and walked around the table.

Reaching for her hand, he pulled her up and toward him, wrapping his arms around her. "You're one brave lady, Cassie. Facing our fears is one of the hardest things we ever have to do in life. I'm proud of you for taking the bull by the horns like this."

Her giggle caught him off guard. He held her upper arms and placed some space between them so he could read her eyes. "Lucas, you always know how to lighten the moment."

Lighten? Hell, he was being dead serious here. *Aw, hell.* If something he said made her giggle like that, then bring it. He brushed away the wetness from her cheeks.

"You just say when you want me, and I'll be there. Any time. Any place."

*   *   *

Cassie rested her head against the curved back of the chaise lounge as the therapist prepared for the session. She had opted to try hypnotherapy for her first session, because of her familiarity with meditation techniques, but if it did not work, she would try the other option Savannah had mentioned.

"If at any time you feel distressed, raise your finger, and I will walk you through it. I like to give my clients a safeword to use if they need to call an end to the session. Do you have a word you would like to use?"

Without a beat, Cassie responded, "Pickle." She smiled, knowing Lucas was in the waiting area. His presence gave her a sense of calm. He would be there when she left, no matter what happened.

Abigail gave some reminders from their conversation the other day. "You will remain awake throughout our session. I cannot make you do anything you would not do normally."

Cassie nodded.

"Now, take a slow, deep breath and relax your body into the chaise." She breathed in through her nose and out through her mouth, slowly and deeply. "As you continue to breathe, you are going to feel your body grow heavier. More relaxed."

Abigail guided her in a creative visualization into a deeper state of relaxation. Cassie drifted peacefully as the therapist assisted her in letting go of all tension in her body. Her body faded away, but her mind remained awake. Under the woman's calm direction, Cassie felt safe and comfortable. She had a safeword. They could stop at any point if she became too distressed.

"Now, Cassie, you are back in the cantina, and the music is playing. Listen to the music and feel yourself dancing."

Abigail's voice drifted into the background as the music washed over her. *Dancing. First with Luis and then…Diego. Her fiancé's friend frightened her. His black eyes held no compassion. Cold. Hard.*

If only Pedro had danced with her when she had asked.

"Breathe in, Cassie. Then let the feelings of fear out through your mouth."

She relaxed again. *Casandra should not be here. Papá and Eduardo would be angry when they learned where she had gone with Pedro. But Pedro had been entrusted to protect her now. They were betrothed.*

Diego groped her, and she pushed him away. She left the dance floor and returned to where Pedro sat drinking a beer at their table. Angry? What did he have to be angry about? He had given her permission to dance with his friends. How was she to know one of them would have his hands all over her?

When Diego joined them and stroked her shoulder, she batted his hand away again.

Pedro's expression grew darker. "My chica *whores for American men while off studying in America, yet she finds the men at home so distasteful?"*

Why was he speaking to her in this manner?

Pedro stood, picked up his beer bottle, and led her toward the back room. "We'll play a game of pool before I take you home."

The door to the pool room opened.

Run!

"Tell me where you are, Cassie."

Her hands grew clammy. Casandra had never expected what had happened to her, but Cassie knew better—from experience. "My fiancé and two of his friends want me to go to the back room. They say they want to play pool, but truly they want to…" Her throat grew too tight to speak.

"Deep breath, and let it go. Before you go into that back room, I want you to imagine that the door to that area is closed. Your younger self, Casandra, is inside with those men. Now, Cassie, when you are ready, I want you to open that door and go inside. You are no longer that vulnerable, defenseless girl. You have learned self-defense techniques now. You may also choose to take a weapon with you. Prepare yourself now to go in and rescue Casandra from those men."

Cassie stared long and hard before moving forward and opening the door.

Stale beer. Sweaty bodies. The stench assailed her.

Casandra lay face up on the pool table. Terror. Fear. I cannot escape. Pedro stood between her legs and lifted her skirt. Luis held her face as Diego rammed some type of contraption into her mouth and strapped it around her head. Diego held a knife to her throat. "Scream and I cut your throat, puta.*"*

For the first time, she realized the rape had been planned, not spontaneous. Who would carry that apparatus around if they did not intend to use it in some foul way?

Perhaps nothing she had done—refusing to dance, hiding her breasts from their view—could have prevented them from attacking her. They had set her up. Pedro had betrayed her in the most heinous ways and then let his friends have their turns, too.

Escape, Casandra!

Cassie fought the urge to flee as well, but Casandra needed her. She could not leave her to suffer what these men intended to do.

"Leave her alone." She set her feet and faced the three of them.

Luis turned to her. His gaze swept over her body. Dirty. He made her feel dirty.

No, he was the filthy one!

He released Casandra and advanced toward Cassie. She prepared to defend herself as she had learned in self-defense classes with Kitty. He grabbed for a fistful of her hair. Cassie intercepted his arm, twisting it and throwing him off balance. She lifted her knee repeatedly into his groin. Luis doubled over and fell to the floor, writhing in much-deserved pain for what he had been about to do to Casandra.

Casandra shoved Pedro away taking advantage of his distraction. She kicked at his chin. His head snapped back, throwing him off balance.

Good for you, Casandra!

Two hands wrapped around her from behind. Diego. She dropped out of the bear-hug cage and swung swiftly to bring her knee up to strike him in the stomach and groin until he, too, fell to the floor.

Seizing Casandra's hand, she pulled her from the table. They ran from the room, screaming for help but not stopping inside the cantina.

"When you have escaped, Cassie, I want you to take a deep cleansing breath. You are safe now. No one can harm you."

Sweat chilled Cassie's forehead. She gasped for breath as if she truly had just run from danger.

Safe.

Empowered.

Coming out of her relaxed state, she remembered how they had delivered justice to her attackers and escaped to safety. She had done it, well, both her younger self and her stronger self.

Abigail asked her questions about the scene and her feelings, calming

Cassie more as she lay there. Cassie smiled when she left the therapist's office and walked down the hallway toward where Lucas waited for her.

*   *   *

Luke placed the rape-tips brochure back in the rack, overwhelmed after reading all the things he should do to support Cassie, now that she had opened up to him. He stood for the third time, running his hand through his hair. He'd paced the room several times since he started reading forty-five minutes ago. Good thing the reception area was empty, but the receptionist glanced up and smiled at him—again.

He turned to stare at the closed door through which Cassie had disappeared, as if beseeching it to open. Was she okay back there? Did she need him? Would he say or do the right things when she joined him?

Even though the attack happened years ago, it was still new to him. What had he done or said wrong these past months since meeting her at daVinci's? Some of his fumbles had been inadvertent—like asking her to join him in a game of pool. How could he have known that? Others well-intentioned but wrong, like the way he kept prompting her to tell him more of the ugly details the other night when he held her in his lap. In his mind, getting the story out would help more than hurt. But had he given her a choice as to when and how she told her story? Jeezus, he hoped so.

Despite having done and said the wrong thing many times with her, she had asked him to be here for her to provide companionship and maybe even comfort after the session. Maybe he was doing something right, after all. Right for them, anyway.

What kind of aftercare would she need? He'd trained with Adam and Damián long enough to know how important aftercare was following a cathartic and emotional BDSM scene. Whatever was going on back there had to be equally cathartic and emotional. Would she let him touch her?

Ask first. Don't surprise her.

How many times had he just gone up and touched her without asking? Clueless. He felt so damned clueless about how to help make her feel better.

Not to mention angry. So fucking angry. He'd done a good job of controlling that anger the night she told him, but ever since, he had wanted to pummel her rapists into the ground for what they did to her. If he ever came face to face with them…

No chance of that happening unless he went to Peru, and he had no intentions of doing that. The article even said not to go after the rapists because that would increase the victim's fear of being attacked again for telling.

Shit. She entrusted him to be here for her, expected him to be supportive, but he had no goddamned clue what to…

The door opened, and he spun around to find Cassie standing there. Her eyes were red-rimmed. She'd been crying. He started toward her then stopped. Rather than wrap her in a hug, he just held his arms open. Her choice whether she accepted the hug or not.

She stared at him a long moment. When she put one foot in front of the other and closed the gap between them, his heart soared. She wrapped her arms around his waist, and he pulled her against him, but not so tight that she'd feel smothered.

"Thank you for being here, Lucas."

"I wouldn't want to be anywhere else. I'll always be here for you, baby girl. Any time you want to talk, I'll listen."

Don't ask for the details.

"Just hold me."

Luke lost track of how much time passed, but he could stay like this forever. She felt so right in his arms. At some point, she sniffled and pulled away, surprising him with the radiant smile on her face.

"I am famished. We can eat, return the rental car, and I can ride back to the ranch with you. I just need to let Kitty know of my change in plans."

"Sounds good to me."

She didn't start talking about her session until a few hours later, after they had driven through the Eisenhower Tunnel. "I was able to rewrite the script of what had happened in the Lima cantina."

"What do you mean?"

"Abigail had me visualize what happened, only I was able to stay outside my body, well, the body of Casandra, my younger self." When she choked up, he reached across the bench seat and squeezed her arm. She cleared her throat. "I was able to change the scenario and outcome—and kick some ass in the process."

"Good girl."

She definitely had come out of the session less stressed. He'd never seen her smile so much. Every time he glanced over at her, she seemed to be smiling.

They pulled into his lane and parked between the house and barn. "Why don't you take it easy? I'll check in with Matt and see how the horses and alpacas are doing."

With Cassie in the house, he met Matt in the corral and listened to the rundown on how things had gone, especially with O'Keeffe. Later, he walked Matt to his Sierra.

"Luke, whenever you need me, just call. It's like a vacation when I come out here. Sometimes I need to get away from it all, especially after fighting all those wildfires for weeks."

"I appreciate the help."

"I need to find a place like this for myself, only closer to the station in Leadville."

"Do it. I wish I hadn't spent so many years cooped up in a condo in Denver. Buying this place last year was the best move I ever made."

Luke said goodbye and watched the truck stir up a cloud of dust on the way to the highway. He glanced toward the house. The light was on in his bedroom. *Her* bedroom. Even if she wanted to be alone tonight, he'd sleep on the couch in case she had anything come up after her session today.

Restless and at loose ends, he went inside the barn again. In the tack room, he unbuckled his case and pulled out the acoustic guitar. Playing it helped him process things sometimes. O'Keeffe seemed to enjoy hearing him sing, so he carried it out to the corral. She whinnied when she saw him, but kept her distance.

He sat on the hay feeder and began tuning up the instrument. He hadn't played in weeks. The song going through his head sure applied to Cassie, too. The opening strains of Paul Brandt's *I Do* sucked him in the way the song always did, but now he pictured his reluctant bride's face before his eyes. He hoped they could continue to build their relationship on a rock-solid foundation. They'd made a lot of progress today, for sure.

"'I rescued you; you rescued me.'"

"So true."

At the sound of Cassie's voice, he stood and faced her. Her gaze was on O'Keeffe, but did she realize the words related to their relationship, too?

She smiled and met his gaze. "I missed my sessions with O'Keeffe and thought I would come out to check on her. You are a musician, too."

"Well, that's a strong word. I'd say I'm more of a picker."

"I loved the deep tone in your voice. It resonated through me as if you had touched me." She glanced down at the ground, seemingly regretting having revealed that, but he couldn't help but smile. "You should sing often. I can see why O'Keeffe enjoys it. She says that is her favorite song."

"I've only sung a few to her, but that one's been our theme song."

"Understandable. The lyrics are perfect." She met his gaze once more. "I can see us in the words, as well."

"You do?"

"I do." She giggled. Sweetest sound ever. "No pun intended." The smile faded from her face, and she nibbled one side of her lower lip. "Lucas, may I ask a favor?"

"Always."

"Would you stay in the house again tonight, like you did when I had my nightmare last week?"

"I'd already planned to sleep on the couch. Was worried today might have stirred up some things for you."

She nodded and smiled tentatively. "Honestly, I feel less burdened than I have in a long time, but I do not know what will happen when my subconscious takes over. I hope I will be fine, but I just need the assurance you will be there to awaken me if there is a recurrence of the dreams and night terrors."

"I'll be right there in the next room, Sweet Pea."

"Thank you, Lucas. Not only for tonight, but for being there for me today."

Chapter Twenty-Two

Why was Lucas being such an ass this morning? The past three days had been wonderful. They had enjoyed each other's company and worked so well with O'Keeffe and the other horses. She had been blessed with three days of no nightmares and had kept so busy she barely thought about the past. Lucas had returned to sleeping in the studio last night when it seemed clear she was not going to have aftereffects of the relaxation session with Abigail.

Then at breakfast this morning, he had raised his voice for some small thing she could not even remember before announcing he needed to blow off some steam. He had been chopping away at the woodpile for nearly an hour.

The man could supply firewood to half of Colorado this coming winter.

He had never raised his voice to her or shown he was annoyed with her in any way before today. Was he growing tired of her being here?

While washing the breakfast dishes, she made a mental note to check for nearby rental places. She did not want to move too far away, but might have to. She wished she could afford a log-cabin kit and a small piece of land in the mountains, but that would be impossible. She had to find studio space at a minimum, even if that meant sleeping on a cot. She needed nothing more to pursue her passion. Unfortunately, studios probably weren't high on most clients' lists of must-have features in rental homes.

Cassie did not want to think about parting with her alpacas either, although she knew Lucas would give them a home if she could not.

Restless and having nothing else she needed to do inside, she hung up the dishtowel and decided to take her daily walk early. Lucas probably would not want to join her today anyway, but she loved exploring his place with or without him. Walking gave her time to process things, too. Today she had a lot to process. Grabbing her poncho in case of rain, as well as her camera, she only made it as far as the front porch when she saw a Jeep driving at a fast pace up the lane. Luke hadn't mentioned expecting visitors.

Oh, wait! Luke said his mother was due sometime this month. Could this be her?

She started to turn around and go back inside—mainly so she would not intrude or have to explain her presence—but the vehicle had already driven too close for her to do so without being seen. Inside was an older couple, not just a woman. They were the spitting image of the couple in the photo frame on his mantle. He had not mentioned that his father would be coming as well.

Could this be the reason for the sudden change in Lucas's demeanor this morning?

Had he told them about her? If so, what had he said? If not, Cassie might be a bit of a surprise for them, especially if they jumped to the wrong conclusions about why she was living here with their son. Judging by the puzzled expression on the woman's face as the Jeep pulled to a stop near the porch, they clearly were not expecting Cassie to greet them.

Lucas continued to split wood, so he had not heard them approach. *Lovely. How do I handle this?* Well, it's not as though Cassie had anything to be ashamed of being here alone with Lucas.

Hold your head high.

Cassie plastered a smile on her face and walked down the steps toward them as the couple exited the vehicle.

"We're looking for the Denton place."

"This is it." Cassie gave her name and then felt compelled to explain the situation before they jumped to the wrong conclusion. "I am an artist friend of Lucas's. My cabin burned to the ground last month, and he's been nice enough to give me a place to stay until I can find a new home."

The wariness on the woman's face faded, and she smiled, extending her hand. "I guess Luke told you to expect us."

Well, more or less.

Cassie cast a glance at Lucas's father, but he didn't seem as warm as his wife, and Cassie decided to let him make the first move.

"I'm Penny Denton, and this is my husband, Bill." The man had come around the front of the Jeep by now and extended his hand to her. His grip was firm and confident. She pulled her hand away sooner than he probably would have wanted to stop pumping hers.

"Pleased to meet you, Cassie." His accent was not as strong a drawl as Lucas's. Actually, neither of them had much of an accent, which made her wonder where they were from originally.

"Lucas is out back splitting wood. Would you like something to drink or help bringing in your things?"

She realized she had to be sleeping where he intended for them to stay—his bedroom. Was that why he blew up at her this morning? He was too nice to kick her out, so he hoped to drive her away instead.

"Just give me a little time to clear my things out of his bedroom." Oh, that didn't sound good. "He has been sleeping in his workshop since I arrived." *Mostly.* Did her explanation sound as if she were making excuses to cover something up? Oh, what did it matter? *She* knew nothing inappropriate had happened with Lucas. If his parents did not believe her, that was their problem, not hers.

Penny cast a worried glance toward her husband and then returned her gaze to Cassie. "Having us both under foot here might be too disruptive. We had no idea he had company already."

Lucas spoke about his mother fondly, but had made no mention of his dad that Cassie could recall. Did he not get along with his father?

If Cassie had anywhere else to go, she would pack and leave today. Feeling like a fifth wheel and wanting to escape, Cassie started toward them. "Let me take you to him, Mr. and Mrs. Denton." Once she delivered them into his hands, she planned to go on that long walk. Her mind was jumbled up with too many problems right now. She needed time. Quiet time. Perhaps even meditation time.

"Momma, you made it!" A bare-chested Luke dropped the ax and crossed the yard. "I'd give you a hug, but I'm hot and sweaty." He grew more serious when he turned to face his father. "Dad, you're looking well. Glad you could make the trip, too."

Sweat glistened off his chest, rolling down in rivulets between his pecs. Cassie realized she was staring and turned away. Whatever possessed him to chop so much wood on a hot July day?

"Stephen Lucas Denton, get over here and give me a hug. I don't mind a little sweat on a hardworking man." Cassie glanced back at him as

Lucas wrapped his arms around his mother.

"Great to have you here, Momma." His words were heartfelt, and he wrapped his strong arms around her. She stood nearly a foot shorter than Lucas.

After a moment, Lucas released her and turned to his dad. Cassie noted less enthusiasm when it came to his father—Bill, right? They merely shook hands. "How've you been, Dad?"

"Can't complain, although this retirement shit is for the birds." Bill turned to Cassie. "Pardon me, ma'am."

Cassie smiled. "You are fine."

"Bill's been driving me a little crazy, too. Be sure to put us to work while we're here."

"I can always use an extra pairs of hands, but before I do that, why don't I help you get your things inside…" His voice trailed off, and he glanced at Cassie.

"Don't move a thing," his mom said. "We aren't staying."

Rather than seeming relieved that the house wouldn't be overcrowded with two more guests, Lucas glanced first at his dad and then his mom.

His mother stared down at the ground. "We checked into the hotel near the frontier museum this morning." The gazes of mother and son met, and a silent message passed between them. "I think it will make for a better visit all around."

Luke looked at his dad and then nodded. Apparently, these two men did not have much love lost between them. Cassie could not imagine there being anyone with whom Lucas could not exist in harmony.

The older man's eyes were hidden by sunglasses, but his gravelly voice had a hard edge to it when he spoke. "We're only staying the week, son. Hard to be away from things much more than that."

Mr. Denton appeared to have been a stern father. Is that what caused the strain between the two? Lucas was so easygoing and laid back. Whatever their problems, they were between him and his father.

"Sure, Dad. I understand." The hurt in his voice made her wonder if perhaps he really had wanted them to stay longer, even though their arrival clearly had caused him some serious anxiety this morning.

Cassie wanted to go over and hug him, but that might send the wrong message to his parents. Not to mention to Lucas. She'd hug a girlfriend who was hurting. She just wasn't used to having male friends.

They all went inside, and Luke pulled out a couple of beers for himself and his dad and some of Cassie's sun tea for her and his mom. Feeling like she was intruding on a family moment, Cassie tried to steal away to take the walk their arrival had interrupted, but Lucas insisted she stay. Maybe her presence helped ease some of his tension.

"Dad, I can't wait to show you my horses. Why don't we go out to the barn?" He stood.

Penny set her glass on a coaster on the coffee table. "Don't think you're leaving me out of this tour. I've been dying to see those horses since you told me about them this past winter."

Perfect time to extricate herself. "Lucas, I am going to take a walk." To his parents, "I hope everyone will excuse me. It was great meeting you both, and I am sure we will see a lot of each other this week."

Penny stood and spoke for the both of them. "You can count on it. I love meeting Luke's friends." She looped her hand around Lucas's elbow. "Now, show me those horses."

Cassie watched as they left the house, Bill bringing up the rear. When they closed the door, their voices trailed off. She breathed a sigh, not realizing how tense she had been during the visit. Picking up her camera again, she folded the poncho over her arm and headed out the kitchen door, wanting to avoid running into them in case they were still in the yard.

The sun was warm on her face, even though the wind off the mountains had a bite to it. Today, she planned to go in a new direction. Lucas said there was a stream near a line of trees toward the mountain where she lived. She wanted to take some slow shutter speed photos of the rushing water for a possible series of paintings that had been bouncing around in her head since she'd come to Lucas's place. She also wanted to take some time to connect with three of the elements of nature—earth, air, and water.

She had had enough of the element of fire for a lifetime.

A country-music song Luke had sung to O'Keeffe yesterday played through her mind as she walked. *I Know How the River Feels.* She'd never known a man to sing love songs to his horses before. Cassie smiled. He did so love his horses. Maybe that's what made her so comfortable around him.

Cassie would miss those horses terribly when it came time to leave, whenever that would be. Now that she understood Lucas's outburst this morning, she assumed he was not yet sick of her.

She glanced back at the house and barn as she continued to walk, hoping Lucas would have a good visit with his folks. He was lucky they would take the time to make the visit. Her toe caught in some ground vines, but she righted herself without dropping her camera and decided it might be best if she kept her focus on where she was headed and not where she had been.

Good advice for living, too.

The sound of water drew her to a line of cottonwoods growing along the banks of the stream Lucas had told her about. The closer she drew to the rustling trees, the louder the bubbling sounds of water tumbling over the rocks became from the spring snowmelt off the mountains.

She had been so tense this morning, but everything faded away when she arrived at the bank of the stream.

Oh, Goddess, she wished she had brought her sketchpad instead of the camera.

*   *   *

"Picasso here was my first rescue. He's been a great SAR horse for me. Even helped me find Cassie when her mountain caught fire."

"Oh, no!" Momma's gasp of horror led him to put her mind at ease.

"She made it out just fine, along with her five alpacas that are grazing in the pasture now. Lost her cabin and belongings, though."

Momma patted his shoulder. "You're good to give her a place to stay until she's back on her feet again. She seems like a real sweet girl. Where's she from?"

"Peru originally, but she's been in the States since college."

Dad walked up to Picasso and pushed his upper lip back to inspect the horse's teeth. The man knew how to judge horseflesh, although Pic was annoyed at the invasion of his personal space and tossed his head and mane before snorting and taking a step back.

"How many horses do you have now?"

"Four."

"How many do you think you can keep up with and still meet your subcontracting obligations?"

Luke hadn't told his dad he wasn't doing a lot of cabinetry jobs these days. He actually had more orders for furniture—both household and kink—than he could keep up with, and as word of mouth spread, he was able to name his price, making it more lucrative than the work he'd done as a subcontractor on house renovations.

"Don't worry, Dad. I'm doing okay. I know my limits."

"Didn't say you didn't."

"Now, boys, let's not get our backs up first thing." Momma took Luke's elbow and led him to the next stall. "Tell me about this beauty."

"She's Fontana. And in the next stall is Cassatt."

Momma giggled. "I can see a pattern here."

"Fontana is the most gentle if you want to take a ride while you're here, Momma. Dad, you can ride Picasso, if you'd like." Pic might not appreciate being loaned out, but he'd remember his training and probably behave better than Cassatt.

"Where's the fourth horse?"

"O'Keeffe's out in the corral. She doesn't like being cooped up. I'll introduce you to her later on—from a distance."

Last thing O'Keeffe needed was for his dad to come charging up and touching her.

"Why don't I give you a tour of the house and my workshop first?"

Damn. His studio would be another bone of contention between him and his dad, but might as well get it out of the way first. As they entered the building, Luke scanned the room from a vanilla perspective, but didn't see anything too kinky that might lead to some embarrassing moments.

Then Dad walked up to the mahogany spanking bench he was finishing for Adam's playroom in their new house. There was only so much furniture he could hide from the man.

Dad ran his hand down the bench. "Smooth. Good work."

"Thanks, Dad." In an effort to steer him away, Luke tried to refocus his attention. "I'm also working on this bed." He moved away from the bench, but Dad just kept looking at it.

"Doesn't look very functional, though. Kind of low."

"Yeah, well, you have to give the customer what he wants. And those were the specs."

Dad shook his head, but finally moved on. *Jeezus.* Good thing he didn't have any St. Andrew's crosses in the works. Not sure how he would have explained those away. His dad might never understand Luke's chosen career, but as long as he thought whatever he was doing had a functional, rational purpose, he approved.

As expected, Dad wasn't too sure what to think about the headboard he was working on for Cassie, but Mom saved the day.

"Would you look at that?" Momma ran her hand over the symbols he had carved, and then she homed in on the flat part of the headboard. The scene depicted a newborn Millie standing on shaky legs, with Luke and Cassie looking on like proud parents.

Momma faced him with tears brimming in her eyes, and Luke felt a lump in his throat. "That's precious. Something tells me there's more to tell about you and Cassie than that you're simply helping out an artist friend in need." She hooked her arm in his elbow. "You can tell me all about it while I'm working on dinner."

Luke wished he could tell her Cassie was more than a friend, but even with vows spoken and a marriage certificate on the books, their relationship would be too complicated to explain. "Don't go matchmaking, Momma. I'm a grown man. I can handle this."

Momma chuckled and led him toward the door. "Well, I can't wait to get to know her better, but so far, I heartily approve. She's easier to talk to than Maggie. No disrespect to your late wife, but she never did warm up to me."

That Momma thought the usually closed-off Cassie had warmed up to her surprised him. He'd missed their initial exchange, but maybe Cassie was letting her guard down a little bit. Luke hoped so.

On their way back to the house, Luke glanced around to see if Cassie was close enough to join them. She'd been gone for hours now, but there was no sign of her bright red poncho. Maybe she wanted to give him privacy with his family, but he couldn't wait to show her off, even if he couldn't reveal their arrangement.

Still plenty of time for that. This was only the first day.

If Cassie wasn't back in a couple more hours, he'd take Picasso out to check on her.

*　　*　　*

Cassie spent the day photographing water tumbling over rocks and moss-covered stones, as well as the cottonwoods with their leaves quivering in the wind. Feeling the call to connect with the water, she removed everything but her bra and panties, and waded in.

Goddess, this water is cold!

Her nipples reacted to the temperature difference immediately, and she instinctively folded her arms over her chest to warm them. One of the things she had loved about living on her secluded mountain was that she had been able to commune with nature while in her hot tub without the barrier of clothing.

After a quick survey of the banks of the stream, she became confident no one was around. Might as well lose the underwear, too. She flung the white bra onto a bush near her other clothing. The panties, now wet from the stream, soon followed. She'd hang them to dry before putting them on again.

Later.

Centering her mind on becoming one with the flow of the water through her legs, she breathed deeply and then released the air, pausing a few seconds before repeating it several more times. She surrounded herself in the white light of protection and offered thanks for the many blessings in her life, including her temporary home with Lucas.

When she had exhausted her gratitude list, she asked the Universe for a sign as to which way she should go to rebuild her life after the fire.

Breathe in.

Breathe out.

Her breathing became more shallow as she went deeper into meditation, her hands stretched out comfortably by her sides, thumb and middle finger together to keep the flow of energy coursing through her body. She felt grounded with the earth through her feet. The wind blew over her body, particularly cold where the rushing water had left the skin on her calves wet.

Earth. Air. Water.

Floating. Her soul absorbed the pure energy and peace that had eluded her since the fire's devastation. It was as if the other three elements wanted to make amends for their destructive brother. For the first time since her home had been destroyed, she reconnected to the Universe.

Raising her arms to the heavens, she repeated the words of a song in her native Quechua she had not thought about for a very long time. *Tarukaq mosqoyning.* As if hearing and understanding the foreign words, a deer came to the bank of the stream and watched her. Her eyes remained closed, but she saw it with her third eye. She repeated her words in English:

Little deer, little deer, you have come this far.
You are sad like me, remembering the mountains of your home.

Confused, Cassie wrinkled her brow. She had not one but two mountain homes. "I can neither return to my mountain home here nor the one of my birth."

The deer sighed, explaining as if speaking to a young child. "When we return to the mountains, we will sing and dance with our herd."

The wind increased, raising gooseflesh on her upper body. Something brushed her ankle, perhaps a minnow or tadpole being carried by the swift current, probably not expecting to find a person in its path.

Cassie opened her eyes and blinked. The spell broken, she felt the hairs at the back of her neck stand on end and turned to survey the bank. She saw no one, but could not shake the feeling of being watched. Then she saw movement and turned to watch as the white tail of the doe swished during her retreat.

Something niggled at her, giving her the feeling that the deer portended a need for her to return to Peru, not to her mountain pass here in Colorado.

An overwhelming lethargy descended upon her. She hoped she was not sinking into depression again. Not after making progress the past few years. More than likely, her sluggishness stemmed from the lack of sleep last night. She missed having Lucas in the house and had spent most of the night reading about the fiber art techniques of Shibori in a book she purchased in Denver. The cloth-dyeing technique could also be applied to her alpaca fleece. She was anxious to begin, and the book even described how a small table could be used to prepare the fibers. She could work in Lucas's kitchen.

She sighed. Emotionally drained, perhaps she would indulge in a nap before she headed back to the house. On the bank of the stream, she hung her panties on a bush to allow them to dry. She toweled herself off with her poncho before rolling it into a pillow. Not comfortable without her bra and shirt, she put them on again before stretching out on a large flat rock near the stream. Sleep claimed her immediately.

The persistent deer visited her once more, promising to come to help her escape to her homeland. She grimaced and pushed the thought out of her mind.

The buzzing of a dragonfly awakened her sometime later, and she sat up and scanned the area. The sun was low on the horizon, and her stomach protested the lack of nourishment it had been given today. She had not eaten much for breakfast and had not thought to bring along any snacks when she made her escape. Glancing around, she did not see anything safe to forage.

"Have a good nap?"

Cassie jumped, her heart racing at the sound of the deep male voice.

Run!

"Sorry, darlin'. Didn't mean to startle you."

She turned around to see a bare-chested Lucas sitting on a nearby boulder with his forearms resting on his raised knees. How long had he been sitting there watching her sleep? How had she not heard him approach?

Rather than take advantage of her vulnerable predicament as some men would have done, he had merely watched over her.

"How long have you been sitting here?"

"Not nearly long enough."

Uncertain what he meant, Cassie stood and brushed off the dust from the bedrock. Her heart continued to beat wildly. Her fight-or-flight response to Lucas should have lessened as her trust in him deepened. Perhaps it was not fear at all, but... *No!* Of course it was fear. For her, fear when near a man had become as natural as breathing.

The cool air between her bare legs reminded her that her panties were hanging for all the world—and Lucas—to see on a bush nearby.

"Turn around, please."

Lucas grinned, his gaze flicking over the pink panties before he swiveled his body around to present her with his bare back. She quickly snatched the garment off the bush and stepped into them.

"You'd been gone nearly six hours when Pic and I came searching for you. I was worried when you didn't come back by suppertime."

"I just needed some time alone. I also did not want to intrude on your time with your parents."

"They wouldn't have minded. They want to get to know you better." He paused. "Why didn't you bring your phone with you?"

"Would it have worked out here?"

"Probably not. I need to get you a satellite phone."

"You do not need to buy me anything." She donned her jeans. "All right, you may turn around again."

He removed his white Stetson and ran his hand through his hair before nailing her with his intense gaze again. His affable expression disappeared. "Damn it, Cassie, if I want you to have a sat phone, I'll get you one. I'm your husband. It's my place to protect you and see to your needs. When you didn't come back to the house, I imagined all kinds of things might have happened, from snakebites to broken bones to a concussion from a fall."

Cassie placed her hands on her hips. "Lucas Denton, you are not financially responsible for me. That was not part of our arrangement. I need to remain independent and pay my own way if I am going to stay here."

His gaze scanned her from head to boots, making her uncomfortable. She folded her hands over her chest to conceal that part of her body from him, but short of hiding behind a boulder, most of her remained exposed to him. How could he make her feel naked even with all her clothes on? Her chin jutted out as she cocked her head. "I am capable of taking care of myself."

"When's the last time you ate?"

"Breakfast." Her stomach growled loudly enough for him to hear. He smiled as he walked toward her, reaching into what looked like a feedbag, its shoulder strap crossing his chest between his pecs. She flushed and glanced away, noticing Picasso grazing nearby for the first time. Lucas had commanded her complete attention until this moment.

He held out an apple and a banana. "Here. Eat these."

Too hungry to be stubborn, she accepted them. "Thank you. I did not think to pack a lunch. I expected to be home in a few hours."

Lucas only smiled, which infuriated her for some reason. Why she let him upset her, she did not know. She did not like being treated like a child.

"Don't make me tell you again. Eat."

His domineering, paternalistic tone rankled, but she took a bite from the apple, letting its juice dribble unheeded down her chin. She'd be a sticky mess soon, but he had not brought any napkins. The apple tasted tart and delicious, so she took another bite and then another. Soon there was nothing left but the bare core, which she tossed aside.

Picasso protested loudly, and Lucas laughed. "Pic was waiting to eat that, you know." Seeing him smile at her again did something strange to her stomach. The flip-flopping sensation caught her off guard. She really had been hungry. At least he was no longer upset with her.

Cassie cast her gaze to the ground and saw that the core had landed on the rocks so she picked it up, walked over to Picasso, and held it out on the flat of her hand. The horse soon gobbled down what was left of the apple, and Cassie peeled the banana. She glanced at Lucas moments later, indicating the peel.

"No, probably not a good idea. Besides, Pic just ate before we rode out here. He doesn't need to be stealing your snacks."

"He was not stealing. I did not want to eat the peel anyway. I just wanted to reward him for bringing them all the way out here to me."

"Well, now, how do you plan to reward me? Pic wouldn't have known to come here without me."

"But he is an excellent tracker."

Lucas nodded in concession. "Yeah, I reckon that's how we found you so fast. He made a beeline to you, probably following your exact trail."

"Sorry I was being a *little* stubborn, but I do appreciate you for coming out here. I had fallen asleep by the stream and lost track of time, but I really was getting hungry."

"You didn't sleep all that long."

She stepped back and scrutinized him. "How do you know how long I slept?"

"Uh, just a guess."

Cassie remembered the sense of being watched following the vision with the deer. She narrowed her gaze. "Just how long have you been watching me?"

He grinned. "I'd say since last fall when I first saw you in the waiting room after Adam's puma attack."

His response was not what she had expected. While some men might give off a "creep" vibe saying something like that, she did not feel that with him at all. The man had saved her life and asked for nothing in return. Still, she wanted to make it clear this could never go anywhere other than friendship.

"You have been a good friend, Lucas. Better than any I could ask for outside Kitty. You risked your life and Picasso's to go after me during the wildfire." She shuddered. "I do not want to think about what might have happened by the time anyone else found me and my babies." She stroked Picasso's mane. "And they probably would not have had your specially-trained tracking horse, either."

Before she knew what she was going to do, Cassie closed the gap between them, licking the stickiness of the apple from her lips as she walked, and planted a kiss on his cheek. Realizing in horror how that might be misinterpreted, she put some space between them again and met his gaze. "Thank you for everything."

"That's what friends are for, darlin'." Did she note disappointment in his eyes or voice? While he had agreed to companionship only, he probably wanted to be more than friends.

"Why don't we head to the house? Momma made some jalapeno cornbread and two pots of chili—I asked her to hold some out for you without the meat in it."

She smiled. "Thank you for thinking of me, Lucas."

He untied Picasso from the branch and hoisted himself onto the horse's bare back. He held his hand out to her.

"Oh, I can walk."

"I don't want you stumbling over the weeds out here and getting hurt. Besides, it would be dark by the time you walked all that way."

True. She eyed the place in front of him on the unsaddled horse and then behind him. Deciding the back might be the safest place, having been in front of him before, she held up her arm and soon found herself seated behind him, her arms around his waist to keep from falling off. At pressure from Lucas's knees, which she felt against her thighs as well, Picasso headed for the house.

Having her bottom directly against the horse differed from her saddled ride with Lucas. When she had sat in front of him that day, her lady bits made constant contact with the saddle horn. This time, instead of grinding against that spot, her breasts were rubbing against Lucas skin making her nipples hard.

Dear Goddess, do not let him feel them.

She pulled away to break contact, but at this dizzying height, she quickly became unsteady and had to draw closer again to keep from falling off.

"Hang on, darlin'."

"I am trying." They rode in silence a while, but all she could think about was her bunched nipples and now the stirrings in her lady bits that, though less blatant than on the last ride, were steadily increasing. She let go with her left hand long enough to wipe the sweat off her upper lip. She did not want him to think she was drooling down his back.

"I guess your parents have gone back to the hotel for the night."

"Yep. Left after dinner. They had a long drive today."

"Are you sure I am not putting them out? I think they would prefer to stay with you."

"No, Momma was right, as always. My dad and I need our space from each other. I've always been a disappointment to him, I think."

"How can you think that? Any father would be proud to call you his son."

"Well, my dad's just…different, I reckon. I don't think he approved of my decision to become an artist. Not the manly profession he expected me to pursue. That's probably part of the reason I chose to do carpentry on the side. Woodworking was more acceptable to my dad than carving little critters into headboards."

"You make incredibly beautiful furniture, Lucas. Do not belittle your art. Your bed is an absolute delight. Every time I look at it, I find some new creature hiding amongst the flowers."

"Thanks, Sweet Pea. I'm working on one that has more meaning for us, but those words coming from a world-class artist like you mean a lot to me."

"Oh, please. I am barely known outside of Denver and my small village in Peru."

"Well, that makes you internationally famous, doesn't it?"

She chuckled. "Okay, then, I accept the lofty designation."

After a moment, he continued in a more serious tone. "Listen, Cassie, I want to apologize for snapping at you this morning. I didn't realize how stressed I was that my dad was actually coming along with Momma. Got the text before you awoke, and it just put me in a bad mood. But I had no right to take it out on you."

She stroked his arm in an effort to relax him. "Thank you for your words of explanation. I worried I had done something to upset you, so knowing it was something—or some*one*—else makes me feel better. Do not think of it any longer. I think your dad is going to get to know you better during this visit. Perhaps some fences will be mended, as you say."

They rode on in silence, still only halfway back to the house. She must have been lost in thought on the walk to the stream, because she had no memory of most of the distance she had traversed.

Suddenly, Cassie became aware that the heat emanating from Lucas's body had increased. Making certain she wouldn't fall off but wanting to put some distance between them, she placed her hands on the sides of his hips instead of directly around his waist and on his skin. She sat up straighter, putting space between their torsos, too. Better.

She stared at the muscles in his tanned back. His arms told her he worked outside without a shirt often in the summer, but limited exposure to the sun in winter kept his tan uneven on his arms. The ripple of his muscles reminded her of this morning when she had caught him chopping wood without a shirt.

It was going to be a long, long summer.

"Dad seems to approve of my horse rescue work, though. He's always liked horses."

"Perhaps you will find common ground there. Something to build on for the future."

"I hope so. Time will tell. They'll be back in the morning. Dad's going to help me train O'Keeffe to the saddle."

Cassie hoped they didn't destroy O'Keeffe's spirit in the process. "I'm glad you refer to it as training and not breaking."

"We'll be as gentle as we can with her, but she has a future in SAR rescue work and not everyone rides bareback like I sometimes do. I need her to take to the saddle if that's what her SAR partner needs."

"I understand." In a way. Cassie didn't plan to be there to watch, though. Maybe she'd borrow the truck and go to town for supplies. Could also visit Kitty and the babies for the day. The possibilities were endless.

"I'd like to have you there."

She tensed. "Why?"

"Well, you're a horse whisperer. You can help me know when I need to try something new or just back off."

Oh, Lucas. Don't ask me to watch that.

But O'Keeffe might need her. What if they hit a trigger or the horse was in pain or frightened and the men didn't pick up on it?

She sighed. "All right, I will stay, but you have to promise me you will listen to me if I say stop."

"I will if I hear the message. We'll need to work out some kind of code word. Red for stop, yellow for slow down or pause, green for go."

"Like a traffic light."

"Yeah—among other things."

She didn't understand the chuckle that followed, but her mind was too focused on the dreaded session with O'Keeffe. Her heart hurt already at the thought.

"We're planning an early start of it. About six. Then if it takes all day, we'll have plenty of time."

She nodded.

"Gotta speak up. I can't see you from this position."

"Yes. I will be there."

Even if it kills me.

They arrived at the house soon after, and Picasso headed straight for the barn. Lucas helped her down and dismounted before leading the horse inside. The clicking of the alpacas lifted her spirits. Her babies must have sensed her presence.

"*Mamá's* home!"

Her call was followed by much movement and bleating in their stall. She smiled, happy Lucas had put them in for the night before coming to search for her. All she wanted right now was to take care of them, visit a while, and then head to her bedroom where she could be alone.

Well, after sampling his mother's chili and cornbread. She was famished, and the woman had gone to special lengths to make it for her.

Tomorrow was going to be a very long day.

"*I told you I could break you, Casandra.*"

Cassie's heart pounded to a halt before beating wildly again. Sweat dampened her upper lip. She did not want O'Keeffe to blame her for breaking her free, wild spirit.

Before she went into a full-blown panic attack, she needed to go to her babies. "I had better settle the girls for the night."

She ran into the stall wishing tomorrow would never come.

* * *

Luke brushed Picasso while Cassie took care of her alpacas. What a roller-coaster day. Between his parents' arrival and that mind-blowing horseback ride with Cassie, he was ready to hit the sack. Only thing holding him back from heading straight there—other than making sure Cassie had some supper—was that he knew the minute he closed his eyes, he'd see his Peruvian beauty naked, arms stretched up to the heavens, chanting who knows what to the gods. Or her goddess, more likely. Man, he'd about come in his jeans at the sight. Reminded him of the night he'd found her in her hot tub on her mountain.

Hot damn!

How was he supposed to view her from now on without seeing her high, firm breasts and wanting like hell to touch them? Squeeze them. Lick them. Hell, even nibble on them a bit!

Aw, hell.

He needed to pull himself together—and maybe take a cold shower— before going into the house with her.

Cassie wanted friendship from him, nothing more. The minute he'd seen her in that stream—well, maybe the minute after that—he'd hightailed it away far enough for her not to sense his presence. And, well, to stop gawking at her in such a private moment.

When he'd checked on her again by the stream, wondering why she hadn't headed home yet, she had been asleep on the rocks beside the water. Half-naked, although he hadn't seen anything. He may have looked like a perv, but he couldn't just let her lie there vulnerable to whatever animal came along.

He'd watched her for more than an hour. Her face changed when she slept. Peaceful. No edge. Her mouth and jaw relaxed. He didn't realize how tense she was all the time until then.

He wished he'd had a sketchpad, although he watched her long enough the images from today were seared into his brain. He'd put them on paper tonight when he went back to the workshop.

"All done."

He glanced over Pic's back to see her standing at the closed stall door. Thank God the horse hid his raging hard-on. He set down the brush on the ledge of the stall and patted Pic on the neck. "Let me go heat up your supper."

"No need. I can find everything, I am sure. Thank you for the…ride, Lucas."

Don't even think about riding her, Denton.

"Night, darlin'. Get a good night's rest. We have a lot of work ahead of us tomorrow."

He liked the sound of that "we." Having her with him tomorrow would make a huge difference.

He sure would miss her when she left.

Now he'd better try and catch some shut-eye himself.

* * *

The alarm blared, and Luke reached out to slap it into silence. He lay there a few minutes, surprised he'd slept until five-thirty. Usually, he was up an hour earlier, but as he'd predicted, the night had been filled with horny thoughts of the girl sleeping in his bed.

Without me.

Just the thought of her lying there gave him a hard-on. Okay, maybe this one was just because it was morning. He tossed the blanket off and headed for the bathroom. By the time he relieved himself, he remembered what he needed to be doing and decided to skip the shower and dress quickly.

Momma and Dad's Jeep was parked in the drive. As he approached the front porch, he saw three silhouettes through the window at the dining room. Hell. Dad would think he was a lazy slouch for sleeping in so long. He hoped his folks hadn't arrived too early and awakened Cassie before they needed to. No doubt Momma would have a full-on breakfast for them, but he wasn't going to eat too much knowing it would all be coming right back up after a few attempts to mount O'Keeffe.

He walked into the house to the sound of Momma's laugh. He'd missed hearing that. One thing a good ol' country boy never did was stop needing his Momma. When he entered the dining area, he saw Cassie's face with a big smile across it. Her eyes danced with humor.

God, I missed you, too, Sweet Pea.

"Mornin'!"

"Well, look what the cat dragged in." Luke's attention turned to his dad, expecting some kind of censure, but Dad just smiled. "Your girlfriend here was telling me how you gave mouth-to-snout to a baby alpaca."

A quick glance at Cassie indicated she hadn't taken any offense at being referred to as his girlfriend. *If Dad only knew.* She cast her gaze down at her plate, though.

"I couldn't sit by and let Cassie lose her first cria if I could do something."

When his stomach growled at the smell of bacon and eggs, he turned his attention to the spread Momma had placed on the table. Then his gaze went back to Cassie's plate where he saw a bowl of cereal with milk and a slice of buttered cinnamon bread. He hoped that was enough for her.

"I wasn't going to eat much before we do the deed, but Momma, how can I pass on trying some of everything at least?" He kissed her cheek and gave her a hug before pulling out a chair and sitting down. "You sit and eat, too, Momma."

"Don't worry about me. I can eat while you all are out working."

She returned to the kitchen to do Lord knew what. Momma rarely just sat down with them for an entire meal. She was always remembering to grab something else she'd made. This time she returned carrying a large bowl of fruit.

"Cassie woke up early and made a delicious salad for us."

"I thought it might set better on your stomach than some-thing…heavier." She glanced around the spread on the table, everything from biscuits to bacon. Bless her heart, she was trying to keep him from upchucking his breakfast.

"Thanks, Cassie." Luke reached out for the bowl. "This looks great. Really healthy, too."

He loaded up on fruit, but couldn't hurt his Momma's feelings, either, so grabbed two biscuits and four crispy strips of bacon. The eggs he decided to go easy on. That could be a disaster waiting to happen.

Sure didn't want to embarrass his wife by puking his guts out.

Twenty minutes later, as he and his parents exited the barn, Luke picked up the football. He tossed it over the railing before opening the gate to the corral, gesturing for his folks to enter first. Once the gate was latched again, Luke turned and kicked the ball in the direction of O'Keeffe, who was maintaining her distance at the opposite end. Soon, though, she took a few steps forward and kicked the ball back toward them.

"Well, I'll be damned." Luke glanced over and saw his dad grinning. It had been a while since he'd seen that response from the man about anything he had done.

"That's some trick. How'd you manage that?"

"Dumb luck. But it's the first thing that connected the two of us." Luke walked over to the ball and gave it another kick.

His dad shook his head. "I guess all those years of practice with the Longhorns paid off after all."

Here we go with the football career regrets.

Luke turned to his dad, who hadn't put on his sunglasses from when they were in the barn. His old man's eyes didn't appear to be nearly as disappointed as Luke remembered them being most of the time when he looked at his only son. Luke thought he saw approval there now, but that might just be overly optimistic.

O'Keeffe kicked the ball back toward them, but it bumped against Dad's shin. Luke watched in surprise as Dad took a step back and then sent the ball sailing toward O'Keeffe.

Please don't let it hit her.

The ball landed a few feet in front of the horse. The old man had always had a steady kick, probably even better than Luke's when he was at the top of his game.

"Well, Bill, I guess you haven't lost your touch, either. Maybe you should have taken that Ohio State scout up on his offer back in high school."

Dad glanced at the ball and the horse, but remained silent for the longest time. Luke didn't know his dad had ever dreamed of playing college football. Then his dad said, barely above a whisper, "My father thought football was foolishness. Better to find myself a job in the oil fields or work the pipeline, like he did." Dad faced Luke. "Maybe I lived out my dream of playing by watching you make it to the college level."

Luke had no clue what to say. This was a side of his father he never knew existed. Sure explained a lot about why performing well for recruiters while in high school was so important to him.

"Guess I pushed you where you didn't want to go."

"No worries, Dad. If not for football, I might not have been able to go to college at all. That degree helped me reach where I am today. Besides, being at that college brought Maggie into my life." He thought a minute about Cassie and her talk of karma and the interconnectedness of souls. Whoever orchestrated the Universe left him in awe. "I'm real happy with my life now, Dad."

He almost thought he saw tears in his old man's eyes before his dad turned back to O'Keeffe. Dad never cried.

"Proud of you, son." His voice was more gravelly than usual.

Momma brushed a tear from her cheek. She'd tried to play peacemaker between the two of them for as long as Luke could remember. A sense of acceptance came over Luke for the first time ever with his dad. Maybe this visit wouldn't be as bad as he'd been expecting after all.

"Day isn't getting any longer," Dad said. "Let's get to work."

Chapter Twenty-Three

Cassie joined the Dentons after leading her alpacas out to pasture. Lucas gently introduced O'Keeffe to the feel of something on her back using only the flick of the rope in his hand. The rope almost caressed the horse's back and hindquarters before slipping away. He repeated the motion over and over. O'Keeffe jumped the first few times, but she seemed to be enjoying the stroke of the rope now.

"'Atta girl."

Something tingled in the pit of Cassie's stomach at his encouraging words. He'd been working with the horse all morning, and she knew he'd performed these steps many times over the week before as he had prepared her for today. O'Keeffe didn't fight him as much as she did the first time.

Bill—he insisted she call him Bill—brought the blanket over and handed it to Lucas, who placed the folded cloth lightly against O'Keeffe's midsection. The horse danced away, trying to dislodge the foreign object from her back. But with the lunge rope in Lucas's gloved left hand and a firm command, she settled.

"Good girl."

Again, Cassie's stomach quivered. She probably shouldn't have eaten this morning. Her nerves were right on the edge. How long would it take him to train this horse to the saddle? She knew O'Keeffe was not happy with all this attention and these strangers.

Lucas stroked the mare's withers and came close to O'Keeffe's face, rewarding her with one of his endearing smiles. Without warning, he glanced over the horse's nose and shared that smile with Cassie.

She was going to lose her heart to this man if she did not take precautions.

"How's she doing?"

Cassie had nearly forgotten she had a job to do here, so wrapped up was she in the sensual dance of man and horse. She shifted her focus to O'Keeffe's right eye and stepped close enough to whisper to her.

"How are you doing, baby? You are such a good girl. Daddy is going to be gentle with you."

Lucas chuckled, bringing her up short.

"What's so funny?"

"Daddy?"

"If I'm *Mamá* to my alpacas, I just assumed you are Daddy to your horses."

"Go ahead. Sorry to intrude."

Confused, she shook her head but continued to speak softly to O'Keeffe. "Promise you will let me know if you become frightened or confused, but Daddy would never hurt you. You understand that, right?" The horse nickered and expressed her trust in Lucas.

Cassie gazed at Lucas. "She is ready now."

Lucas kissed her on the cheek for no reason and went back to work, applying the weight of the blanket to O'Keeffe's back.

What on earth was that all about?

She returned to the fence to give them the space they needed. The dance between trainer and horse continued for another hour, and O'Keeffe accepted greater and greater weights.

"Ready to break her, son?"

Cassie's vision narrowed, enveloping her in a black vortex. Her throat closed, forcing her to draw ragged breaths. *Stale beer. Sweaty bodies. Smelly breath.* Pedro's body pressed hers into the pool table, his breath moist on her neck.

"Now I will break you, puta."

Run, Casandra!

She had escaped once. She would this time, too. Cassie maneuvered him off her and followed her instincts, turning to run. Immediately, she hit a wall but reached out and searched until she found an opening to slip through. She continued to run. As she dragged air into her lungs, her vision cleared. The ground beneath her feet was brown and scrubby. She didn't recognize this place, but knew her only hope was to escape.

"Cassie, stop!"

A familiar voice with no hint of a Peruvian accent tugged at her consciousness.

Pedro's voice pierced her confused memory dragging her back down into the memory of that horrific night. *"Casandra, stop fighting me."*

No one would ever hurt her like that again.

The sound of pounding feet behind her increased her panic. There was no place to hide, only the open expanse of a field before her. She must escape them!

Run faster!

Strong arms surrounded her, pulling her against a hard body.

Diego!

No!

*   *   *

What the hell had happened? Luke had been making great progress with O'Keeffe, almost ready to apply the saddle, when Cassie tore off like a bat out of the bowels of hell. So focused on O'Keeffe, he hadn't been aware of her running away until Momma called out to him. He watched as Cassie's body slammed against the round pen fence as if blinded before she hurried through the slats. Something had to have triggered her.

Goddamned bastards.

He threw the lunge rope to Dad and took off after her, but she ran as if her life depended on it. He was having a devil of a time catching up with her, but feared she'd hurt herself running at a break-neck speed like that. The ground out here was uneven. God, he needed to catch up to her before she took a tumble.

"Cassie, stop!"

His words only made her run harder. Would she ever come to realize he would never hurt her?

Just a few more yards and he'd have her. A few seconds later, he closed the gap and wrapped his arms around her upper body and pulled her against his body. Her feet lifted off the ground and kept moving as if running, only succeeding in kicking at him. The heels of her boots dug into his shins above his own boots.

"Ow. Cassie. Stop fighting me."

"¡Nunca más!"

She spoke the words in Spanish, but he had no trouble translating. *Never again.*

"Cassie, it's Luke. Lucas. You're safe. I have you."

She continued to fight, butting him with the back of her head and nearly knocking his front teeth out. Employing some of the techniques he would use with a panicked horse, he loosened his hold enough to ease her panic, but not enough to let her hurt herself. Clearly she was lost in a traumatic memory from the past. He needed her to know he was the one holding her. Not those bastards who had hurt her.

"Shhh, Sweet Pea. I'm not going to hurt you. You know I'd never hurt you. You're too precious to me."

She continued to scream at him in Spanish, fighting against his hold, calling him a liar. She even warned him that Eduardo would kill him if he did this.

Fuck. Her head definitely was back in that bar in Peru.

His lips brushed her ear as he whispered, trying not to escalate her panic. "Baby girl, you're safe. You're with Lucas in Colorado. That's all in the past. Those men can't hurt you ever again. I won't let them near you."

Were her struggles lessening? He hoped so.

Keep whispering to her.

"'Atta girl." He kissed her temple. "You're safe. I have you now. Everything's going to be okay, baby girl."

She shook her head wildly and released an anguished sob that ripped out his guts. If he ever came across the fucking bastards who hurt her, he'd make sure they never hurt any other girl.

Without warning, Cassie's body went limp. She'd passed out or was just too worn out to fight anymore. He lifted her into his arms and stared down into her face. Eyes closed, facial muscles lax. Unconscious. He placed her gently on the ground. Streaks of tears had made a path down her dusty cheeks. He checked her respirations and pulse. Racing still. She seemed to be out of the panic attack. Wanting to take her back to the house and let her rest, he lifted her into his arms again and began walking across the field.

Momma waited for him on the lane with the Jeep and held open the passenger front door for them. Luke sat with Cassie in his lap and swung his legs inside.

Momma reached out to stroke Cassie's hair. "Is she okay?" Luke couldn't speak past the rawness in his throat and the adrenaline pumping in his veins, so he merely nodded. "Poor thing. I wonder what spooked her like that."

Luke glanced down at her as they drove back to the house. "Something bad happened in her past." He didn't elaborate, because it wasn't his place to share Cassie's story. He brushed her hair back from her face and tucked a strand behind her ear. So peaceful now. What would happen when she came to?

Oh damn. O'Keeffe. "Is O'Keeffe okay?" He'd abandoned her like a hot potato to go after Cassie. Not the way to train a horse to saddle.

"Dad's with her. I'm sure she was fine with ending the session before you got that saddle on her."

"Yeah, probably. Glad you all were here." He'd have to start over with her again tomorrow. O'Keeffe, sure, but also with Cassie. *What the hell had he said or done to send her running in terror?* She said she had made a lot of progress since her appointment with the therapist in Denver. He remembered the article he'd read, though. Rape never went away.

"Happy we can help out." Momma pulled up to the front porch. Luke opened the door, swung his legs out before easing her head past the doorframe, and stood up with Cassie. She hardly weighed anything and felt so good in his arms. Momma rushed ahead and opened the screen door for him to pass through.

"What can I do to help?"

"Maybe some herbal tea."

"I saw some chamomile in the cabinet. I'll fix her a mug." She headed toward the kitchen.

"Thanks, Momma." Luke carried Cassie to the bedroom. Not wanting to let go of her yet, he sat on the edge of the bed and held her tight. He gazed down at her now serene face.

"You're safe now, darlin'." Luke had to tamp down the rage festering below the surface. How could a man call himself a man after raping a girl like those three had done to Cassie?

At least they couldn't hurt her again. And he'd be here to pick up the pieces and help Cassie reclaim her life. With him, he hoped. But even if she chose to move on without him, he wanted her to be happy. Not hiding away from life, but embracing it fully. Her passion simmered beneath the surface just waiting to explode for the right man. He wanted to be that man.

"Come back to me, Sweet Pea. No one's going to hurt you."

"Here you go." Momma set the mug on the nightstand and stroked the top of Cassie's head. "Poor baby."

Cassie stirred at either Momma's touch or her voice. She grimaced and her left arm flailed out, clocking him in the chin again. "Let me go, Pedro!"

*   *   *

Strong arms held her tight against a hard body. Smothering. *Never again!* She fought, and the arms loosened but did not release her. Would he rape her? Or let one of his friends do so again? Diego seemed determined he would have his turn.

She pounded against the one holding her, screaming her rage at him, but could not escape. After a time, all fight left her as exhaustion set in. *"Por favor,* let me go." Had she spoken the words or only thought them? She had no strength left. This time, without a doubt, she would die at their hands. The first time, she had not known what Pedro and his friends were capable of, but this time, he had to know she would go to the authorities. And tell her family. Pedro's own father would kill him if he shamed his family's reputation in this way. She was not that same scared girl he had raped and silenced the first time.

And yet she could not totally give up. Her will to live was too great. "I will not tell. Do not do this to me again."

"Shhh, Cassie. It's Luke. You're at my ranch in Fairchance, Colorado. No one here wants to hurt you, Sweet Pea."

Her brows furrowed, and she blinked several times until his worried face came into focus above her.

"Lucas?" She struggled to sit up, and his firm arm against her back helped her. She scooted off his lap and faced him—and his mother. "What happened?"

"Some of those demons came knockin' again."

Her face burned with embarrassment that Lucas's parents had witnessed her insane behavior. "I am so sorry, Mrs. Denton."

"It's Penny, and there's nothing to apologize for." She reached for a mug on the nightstand. "Here. I made you some chamomile tea. Why don't you sit in this rocker and just relax?"

Disoriented, all fight gone, she accepted the mug first. "Thank you, Penny." She felt strange calling his mother by her first name. Seemed disrespectful. But Mrs. Denton seemed too formal. "I'm sorry I—oh, no!" She turned her gaze to Lucas. "Is O'Keeffe all right?"

"Happy as a clam that I'm not coming at her with a saddle right now."

Lucas smiled. He was not upset with her for disrupting the session.

She thought back to the last thing she remembered. She had been there to keep O'Keeffe calm and read her thoughts, and then—

"Ready to break her, son?"

The mug began to shake in Cassie's hand, sloshing its hot contents onto the floor. Penny reached out. "Here, you sit down first, and then I'll hand it to you."

Before she could sit, Lucas stood and came toward her. He wrapped her in his arms. She began to struggle to escape, instinct telling her to run to the bathroom or anywhere else to hide. But instead of revulsion at his touch, for some odd reason, he helped stop her shaking.

Safe.

She held on tightly, afraid of falling into the abyss again, and wrapped her arms around the middle of his back. Tears spilled onto his shirt.

"Did you remember something?" The deep timbre of Lucas's voice reverberated through her chest.

Penny stroked her arm. "I'll give you two some privacy. Just call if you need anything."

Cassie pulled away. "No, Penny. I do not wish to hide from this any-more. Telling Lucas, even though I had not wanted to tell him, either, released some of the shame and guilt I had buried inside all these years."

Having Penny reach out to her like a mother to a daughter made Cassie miss her own *mamá's* touch intensely. She motioned for his mother to sit in the rocker and Lucas on the bed. He indicated his lap was available, but she shook her head.

"I need to stand on my own two feet, especially after that meltdown."

"Friends lean on each other in tough times, darlin'."

She had done that for Kitty—and Goddess knew Kitty had done the same for her many, many times. But it was different being friends with a man. Even a man she thought she could trust, like Lucas.

"Thank you, Lucas, for being there. Your support means more to me than you can ever know." Knowing she had someone like Lucas by her side gave her a sense of peace and strength.

Before discussing what had happened in the corral, she filled Penny in on what Lucas already knew about the gang rape five years ago. Rather than become emotional, Cassie stated the cold, hard facts. She had already poured out her heart to Kitty, to Lucas, to Savannah, and to her new therapist. The more she talked about it, the easier it became.

"Oh, you poor child. How awful for you to have to face that at such a young age."

Not having a response to that, and in an effort to calm herself, Cassie went to the nightstand and picked up the mug again, drinking half of the lukewarm tea in several gulps. Then she turned to the man who always seemed to be there for her when the monsters came back to haunt her.

Demon was too pleasant a word for Pedro and his friends. They were monsters.

"A few days ago, I went back into therapy again. I want to reclaim my life. I have seen improvement already." She focused on Lucas. "But out in the round pen earlier, your father said something about breaking O'Keeffe. I think that is what triggered my panic attack. One of the rapists used similar words during the attack. Right now, to be honest, I do not know which man."

"You screamed Pedro's name when you were fighting me outside."

Then it probably *had* been Pedro. She thought it sounded like his voice in her head, but had spent five years trying to banish those voices from her memory. She doubted she remembered the exact words any of them had used during the attack at the bar.

"I'll talk to Bill before we go to work again with O'Keeffe. He didn't mean anything—"

"Oh, no! Do not say anything. It was not his fault."

"Still, I want to make sure he doesn't use words that are so painful to you."

Cassie hated having them make concessions on her behalf, but the thought of another meltdown held no appeal, either. "Thanks, Penny."

"Dad's old-school about working with horses."

Lucas never talked about breaking O'Keeffe, only training her. Calming her. Working with her to overcome her past. Being around horses was new to her, but his approach to his battered horses reminded her of the way he treated her.

Now something that had been nagging at her since the vision with the deer yesterday needed to be brought up. "Lucas, I have a favor to ask."

"You know I'll do anything I can."

"I need to go home."

He cocked his head. "I'll take you up the mountain anytime. We can go through the buildings to see if anything's salvageable."

She shook her head. "Not that home." Although she needed to do that, too. Her landlady said she could wait and demolish the buildings after Cassie sifted through the rubble for whatever had survived. But that place could never be her home again. She took a deep breath. "I am talking about Peru. I need to see my parents. Their thirty-fifth wedding anniversary is next week. I want to be there when they unveil the portrait I painted. I want to celebrate with them as they renew their vows. I want to be with my family once more."

I miss them.

Fear and shame had kept her away from them too long, but her stomach knotted at the thought of coming face to face with Pedro. Surely he would not be so brazen as to come near her. Eduardo would kill him if he knew what he had done—and Cassie found that telling her story became easier each time she shared it. The time was right to explain to her family what had sent her away from them.

"Lucas, I need you…" She wished she could ask him to join her but could not pull him away from his horses and responsibilities. "I need you to watch after my alpacas."

"You aren't going down there alone the first time. I'm going with you."

"I will be fine."

"Luke, you need to go with her. Bill and I can stay here and watch after the horses and alpacas."

"No, Penny, I do not want to disrupt your plans." Then why did the thought of having Lucas beside her when she went back to Peru ease the knot in her stomach?

"No disruption at all, sweetie. It will give Bill and me a chance to extend our visit up here without the expense of a hotel. You just teach us the routine to follow with your alpacas. Horses we know, but we haven't had a lot of experience with those sweet critters."

"See? That settles it. I'm going with you, Sweet Pea."

Cassie felt as if she had lost control of this conversation and her life just when she had begun to feel in control again.

"Let me think about it."

First, she needed to face something here. And for that, she did want Lucas beside her.

*   *   *

Cassie expected tears when she exited the truck and surveyed the place where her cabin had once stood. Surprisingly, she felt no reason to cry. While she had lost some treasures from her past, like her grandmother's shoulder cloth, this fire had been cathartic for her. Ironically, she'd attempted to destroy her monsters in a fire ceremony many times, only to have a wildfire sweep through her life and wipe the slate clean. If not for that—and Lucas—she might still be hiding away up here.

"You okay?"

She turned to Lucas and nodded. "Actually, better than okay."

He quirked a brow in disbelief, but she turned back to survey the charred landscape and remains of her cabin. "I wonder how long before it will be green here again."

"You'd be amazed how fast it happens. You'll come out here next spring and find a tiny seedling struggling to poke its vibrant little head out of the blackened earth. A sign of rebirth and renewal."

Now the tears did flow. Lucas wrapped his arms around her and pulled her close. "Don't cry, Sweet Pea. The important thing to remember is that you and the alpacas escaped. Things can be replaced. People and animals can't."

She couldn't explain to Lucas her gratitude to him for helping to plant that seedling of hope for rebirth inside her, but held on to him as the tears streamed down her cheeks and onto his shirt. When she no longer felt the need to cry, she pulled away.

She glanced down the path to the studio. "Funny how the studio survived while everything around it was destroyed."

"Rafe said the smoke jumpers arrived in time to save it. At least you can salvage everything from inside there."

Cassie nodded and dashed the wetness from her cheeks. "I guess we should start sifting through the rest of the place while we have daylight."

"Why don't we clean out the studio first? You'll feel better seeing what survived."

She nodded, and they spent the next hour loading up her altar area. She was not sure where she would set it up at Lucas's, but would be happy to be able to meditate at it once more.

Abuela's blanket smelled of smoke, but she would have it cleaned and smudged to replace the smell with something more pleasant. At least the last blanket her grandmother had woven had survived.

After packing up the remaining items from the studio, the sound of the ptarmigan's "sweet, sweet" call captured her attention. She glanced around until she located them, three birds pecking at the grass and rocks in search of food.

"What are they?"

"Ptarmigans. They live at high altitudes. I suppose they are resilient creatures."

"Not unlike you, darlin'." He watched a moment longer. "Be right back."

Lucas returned from the truck a few minutes later with two pairs of work gloves, and they set about the task of sifting through the charred remains of the cabin. Anything that she might be able to clean up or salvage, she placed in the cardboard box they had brought with them. The bulldozer crew would be here next week to scrape away and remove everything else.

As she entered what had once been her bedroom, the scent of angel's trumpet threatened to overwhelm her senses. *Abuela*. Her grandmother's cottage once had an enormous angel's trumpet bush. Cassie had played under its branches many summers. *Abuela* had used the narcotic parts of the plant in her ceremonial concoctions. Of course, the plant would never have survived the devastating fire, so her grandmother must be letting her know she was near.

Cassie smiled. A splash of red and green caught her eye, and she went to the corner where the nearly charred logs of the cabin walls had toppled over during the fire. Pulling on the remnant of what she hoped would be the shoulder cloth her *abuela* had woven and worn on her wedding day, only a tiny fabric perhaps two by six inches pulled loose.

Gone.

No more tears, child. You have been granted the gift of new life.

Cassie nodded as though her grandmother were speaking directly to her. *Abuela* had never been one to wallow in self-pity. Nor to hang on to the material things of this world.

She tucked the scrap of fabric into her pocket, not wanting it to get any dirtier from the things in the box. Already her mind pictured it in a place of reverence on her altar.

"Hey, Cassie, come see this!"

Cassie stood and turned around to try and locate the direction Lucas's voice was coming from. Near the burned-out alpaca shed? She hated the thought of going inside that blackened shell where so many wonderful memories had been made with her babies, including the birth of Milagrosa.

Walking in the direction of his voice, dread mounted with each step. What on earth could have survived the fire? As she drew nearer, she heard him speaking softly as he might have spoken to one of her alpacas.

She stepped over the charred foundation of the building and found Lucas hunched down, looking at something in the corner. Even more slowly, she approached, half-excited and half-dreading what she would find.

An unfamiliar noise reached her ears—a high-pitched whining that sounded like nothing she'd ever heard. Lucas looked up and smiled at her, making her less fearful of what she'd find. As she drew nearer, she saw a dog staring up at her.

"What on earth?" Cassie came closer and knelt beside Lucas. The dog was nursing five puppies! Her calm demeanor around two human strangers surprised Cassie until she saw the weariness in the canine's unique eyes. One was a pale blue, the other a mix of blue and brown.

"I'd say she's malnourished by the way these scrawny puppies are jockeying for milk. We need to get her to the vet and get them all checked out."

Cassie pulled out her phone and placed the call to her vet's office. "She said to come in any time."

All thoughts of what she had lost here went out of her mind as Lucas placed the babies in her poncho for her to carry and then scooped up the *mamá* dog and took her to the truck. The poor thing was too weak to struggle. Or perhaps she understood they were only there to help.

On the drive to the vet's, Cassie held the babies close to her body, hoping to keep them warm and give them a sense of security. Lucas reached over to pet the dog lying between them on the bench seat. She kept an eye on Cassie, but did not have the strength to raise her head. Poor thing.

"How're you doin', darlin'?" Lucas reached up to stroke her arm.

It took her a moment to understand why he was concerned about her. He was asking not because they had found the starving dogs but because she had just been to her burned-out home. "Better than I thought I would be. Thank you for coming up here with me, Lucas. And thank you for rescuing these precious dogs. I had not intended to even go inside the shed."

"No way would I let you face this alone. But when I heard the sound of those hungry babies, I knew there was a dog in there. When I was a teenager, someone dumped a pregnant dog near our place, and I can remember the sound of nursing puppies well."

"I hope we are not too late."

"The pups only look like they're a week or so old. I think the vet might be able to save them with formula. The little momma needs to build up her strength before she can give any more to them. I think they've just about nursed her dry."

Tears stung Cassie's eyes. The mother had nearly sacrificed her own life so that her puppies could live. The power of a mother was a strong one. She hoped something could be done so that they all could survive.

Mama Quilla, *please watch over this new mother and her puppies.*

After seeing Lucas with his mother and this dog caring for her babies, Cassie missed her mother more than ever. "Lucas?"

"Yeah, Sweet Pea?" He turned off the state highway and headed toward the vet's office.

"I want you to come to Peru with me next week." Somehow having him there to face whatever awaited her gave her a sense of confidence.

He smiled in her direction. "You know I'll be there with you, darlin'. I didn't like the idea of you going alone." A weight lifted off her chest as he pulled into the parking lot. "Let's get you and the puppies inside first. Then I'll bring in their momma."

The receptionist must have seen them pull in and was holding the door open for Cassie, allowing Lucas to return to fetch their *mamá*. A quick evaluation and the veterinarian said she thought all would be fine with a little tender loving care.

"I don't know who she belongs to, but she must have been in good condition when she gave birth in order to have nursed them this long. I'd say these pups are about five or six days old now."

"What kind of dog is she? Her coloring is so unusual."

"Blue merle Australian shepherd and border collie mix, I'd say."

"Is there a network or something you can check to see who might have lost her?"

"Sure. I scanned for a chip but didn't see one. I'll post her photo on Facebook and share it with other animal clinics in the area."

"You might check Breckenridge, too."

"Will do."

When the time came to say goodbye to the animals, Cassie could not hold back her tears. "I do not know what is the matter with me. I only met them a couple of hours ago."

Lucas rubbed her back to comfort her. "You care. Nothing to be ashamed of. You have a big heart."

"As do you."

Lucas turned toward the vet. "Doctor Lewis, if you can't find her owner over the next couple weeks, we'll adopt all of them. And please send me the bill for whatever they need."

Cassie smiled through her tears and pressed a kiss on his cheek. "Thank you, Lucas. You are such a good man."

He grinned. "We'd better head home and see to the rest of our babies."

Our babies.

Cassie's maternal instincts had gone haywire today, seeing this devoted mother with her babies. Kitty and her babies also were fresh in her mind. She had never thought about how difficult it was to be a mother—but knew her fate was to mother animals, not humans.

Chapter Twenty-Four

The plane landed hard on the runway, and the roar of the jet engine slammed against his chest as the brakes and flaps slowed down the plane. Luke breathed a sigh of relief as they taxied to the terminal. Never liked flying. But he wouldn't let Cassie come down here alone.

Their fellow passengers soon hurried to gather their belongings and exit the plane. Cassie preceded him down the narrow aisle and gangway. Before they reached the baggage claim area, he spotted Eduardo and let Cassie go ahead so they could have some time alone.

The two embraced and exchanged greetings. As Luke drew closer, she pulled away and gazed up at Eduardo, saying something in Spanish to the effect that she would only be here a few days. As if noticing Luke standing there for the first time, Eduardo turned and extended his hand. "Welcome to Peru."

This was going to be an interesting visit. He should at least get points for still being with Cassie. Somehow he didn't think his brother-in-law thought he was serious about his vows given the suddenness of the ceremony.

The drive to their village passed in near silence. Cassie chose to sit with him in the backseat. Luke wondered at each bend if Eduardo really knew where the road lay. Visions of them hurtling over the edge of a cliff plagued him at every hairpin turn.

Cassie giggled and squeezed his arm, catching him off guard.

"What's so funny?"

"I have never seen you so tense before. You are even more so now than on the two flights it took us to arrive here."

"I feel like my life is in his hands at each turn in the road. But this is definitely a close second to my fear of flying. I had to turn over control there, too."

She realized Luke did try to exert control over his life—mostly over himself but also in the way he made sure she was taken care of, protected. Never in a domineering way.

"Eduardo could drive this road with his eyes closed."

Luke cast a worried glance at her brother, but his eyes were very much open and focused on the road ahead. He tried to force himself to relax, not liking having so little control. Maybe he just didn't know or trust Eduardo enough to put his life in the man's hands.

The all-wheel-drive vehicle came to a sudden stop, and Luke glanced out the window beyond Cassie to see what had halted them. The early-morning light coming over the steep mountains illuminated a cement-block house. By American standards, it was simple, but was typical of others he'd seen in the rural village.

Large evergreen shrubs softened the edges, and a shrine of some sort was visible in front of a picture window.

When the engine cut, Luke knew they had arrived at her parents' house. Cassie shivered, and he pulled her closer. They wore their winter coats, but it was freezing-ass cold here. Knowing Cassie's love of frigid weather, though, he didn't think she shivered from the temperature.

Luke exited and came around the vehicle to help her out before giving her hand a reassuring squeeze. He bent down to kiss her on the cheek and whispered, "I'm here. You aren't alone."

Even though he couldn't see her face as he spoke the words, he felt her relax her hand in his. "Thank you, Lucas."

Luke helped Eduardo take their large suitcase from the trunk. He realized it gave the appearance of them being more of a couple than they actually were, but the tickets were pricy and they didn't want to turn over any more of their savings to the airline.

"I will take this inside." Eduardo took the luggage and walked inside the house.

Luke grabbed the smaller carry-on, and Cassie smiled up at him. "Are you ready to meet my parents?"

"I've been looking forward to it. Do they know about us? Being married, I mean?"

She nodded. "It was for them that I entered into our arrangement."

He must not have masked his disappointment too well because she took his hand in her trembling one. "I also found a friend for life that day." Yeah, that was the deal. Luke, her friend for life. Not that he didn't still hold out hope for something more. She seemed to be warming up to him at least.

When Cassie tried to turn toward the door, Luke halted her progress and framed her face in his hands. She held her body so tightly he feared she'd crumble. Why was she so afraid to face her parents? "Cassie, darlin', you're an amazing woman. You have an inner strength like I've never seen in anyone. I want you to go into that house with your head held high. You have nothing to be ashamed of. Everyone in there probably loves you as much as I do. If not, then we can leave and stay in Lima until our return flight leaves." Having a choice often made it easier for *him* to face things that seemed too daunting.

A tear wet his right thumb, and then another fell on his left.

Luke pulled her to his chest and wrapped his arms around her. "Baby girl, anyone who blames you for what those men did, well, they're the ones who ought to be ashamed."

"But they do not know about what happened."

"Well, you don't have to tell them about that night if you don't want to. It's your choice. And only *you* have a say in *that* decision. No one is going to force you into anything as long as I'm here." He paused.

Cassie cleared her throat. "But?"

"But I think you're going to be surprised at how much they will love and support you once you tell them. No parent wants to see their child hurt or unhappy. I know how much you love them, and I'm sure they earned that trust and love over the years. See if you can trust them on this and lift that weight off your shoulders."

"Thank you. I needed to hear those words, too."

"I'll always tell you what you need to hear. Again, if you do decide to tell them, and they can't see the truth in front of their faces, then we head to Lima. It's their loss if they can't accept you and the truth about what happened back then."

"I am grateful to have you in my life, Lucas Denton. Thank you for being here with me."

I'll take gratitude, Sweet Pea. And friendship.

For now.

*   *   *

Cassie's heart pounded as she opened the screen door and then the wooden interior one. Would her parents be waiting for her?

"*Bebé,* you have come home to us!" Tears streaming down her cheeks, *Mamá* ran across the room and wrapped her arms around Cassie. The scent of angel trumpet flowers brought tears to her eyes. She had *Abuela's* scent, probably missing her mother as much as Cassie did her grandmother.

The ice around her heart melted a little now that she was in her mother's arms again. When *Mamá* did not let go, Cassie hugged her harder and responded in Spanish. "I am happy to be back to visit, *Mamá.*" She wondered why she made the distinction between being home versus being here for a visit, but didn't want *Mamá* to come to the wrong conclusion. This was simply a quick visit to celebrate their anniversary—and to find out what *Mama Quilla* seemed to think Cassie needed to discover.

When they broke the embrace, *Mamá* dabbed at her eyes with her apron. Cassie glanced around the room. "Where is *Papá?*"

Mamá glanced down. "He is…not feeling well. Your father is not as young as you remember him."

Oddly enough, Cassie had always thought of *Papá* as being old, even as a young girl. "He is not ill, is he?" She remembered the cancer scare and wondered if Eduardo had kept anything else from her.

"He is fine. Let him rest. We will have time to catch up later." It was nine-thirty in the morning. Not characteristic of her father who usually was up at dawn and hard at work by daylight. But the man was almost eighty now.

Cassie stepped back. "*Mamá,* you have heard a lot about him already, but I would like you to meet Lucas, my husband." She had told her mother about her marriage via Skype, hoping to assuage her parents' worry over her, but Lucas had left her cabin by that time and had not been on the video monitor.

"Lucas, our new son!" *Mamá* wrapped him in an embrace that he returned wholeheartedly.

"Nice to meet you, ma'am. Thank you for opening up your home to me—and for bringing my beautiful wife into the world."

Mamá pulled away and seemed at a loss for words. Tears swam in her eyes. Cassie had made her mother happy. Despite the wrong reasons to marry someone, her decision had been the right one.

"*Mamá,* he is everything a husband should be. He takes very good care of me. A strong and fierce protector, a good provider." All true, even though he was more friend than husband.

Mamá welcomed him to the family in Spanish, then corrected herself and spoke English.

"I know a little Spanish from living in West Texas, but thank you. *Gracias.*"

"You two must be hungry. I have prepared some things for breakfast when *Papá* awakens, but I can give you something to tide you over."

"No, ma'am. Thanks, but I can wait." He glanced at Cassie so as not to speak for her, and she nodded her agreement. "I would like to put our things away and take a shower if I may. We've been traveling a very long time."

"Certainly." *Mamá* turned to Lucas. "Cassie's old room has been made up for you both."

Wait! Cassie remembered how small her room was. As a teenager, she had inherited *Abuela's* double bed, which had nearly filled the room. There would be no extra space for one of them to sleep on the floor. She would have to share the bed with Lucas.

Again.

She reached for her carry-on, but Lucas beat her to it. "Lead the way to our bedroom, darlin'."

His playful grin made her feel warm inside, but also ramped up her anxiety. Lucas would never take advantage of the situation—or of her—but this complicated their visit in ways she had not anticipated.

Cassie led the way down the tiny hallway to her bedroom. With Lucas so close behind her, the space seemed even smaller than she remembered.

She entered the room and saw Eduardo already had placed the large suitcase on the bed. "You may put my bag on the bed. There is not much room, but I will unpack my...*our* things while you shower. If you would like to visit with *mi mamá* and Eduardo while you wait for me to shower—"

"Not on your life. I'll wait here for you. If you tell me where to put our clothes, I can do the unpacking."

The thought of him touching her underwear made her face turn warm. She opened the suitcase, pulled out the clothing from her side in one big bunch, and crammed them into the second drawer of the dresser before she turned back to him.

"You can put your things in the third drawer." She kicked off her shoes, grabbed a pair of panties, a blouse, and her toiletries bag from the drawer, and nearly ran down the hallway to the bathroom. Once inside, she leaned against the door, clutching her things to her chest.

Why am I acting so virginal?

It's not as if she were going to have sex with the man. They were merely going to sleep in the same bed.

Sleep.

Nothing more.

She showered quickly, not wanting to use too much water, and took a great deal of time brushing out her long, tangled hair. To keep her hair from being plastered to her scalp, she used her fingers to fluff up it up before dressing.

Opening the bathroom door, she was happy that the coast was clear because she needed some time to prepare for the meeting with *Papá* and didn't want it to happen in the hallway. In the bedroom, she found Luke staring at her childish paintings hanging on the wall.

"I do not know why *Mamá* keeps those. I was only twelve or thirteen when I painted them."

He continued to stare at one of them, one with a blond-haired, light-skinned man riding bareback on a palomino with snow-covered mountains in the background. In the foreground was a peasant girl with long black hair, watching him. The man was shirtless and smiling at the girl as if showing off some new trick.

"You were very good even that young. What inspired you to paint this one? Reminds me of Picasso."

Was he blind? "The style is nothing like Picasso's." She suddenly realized he was talking about his horse, not her painting style. Oddly enough, her attention had been on the man riding the horse. If she did not know better, Lucas could have been the model. However, she did not meet him until more than a dozen years after she had painted it.

Cassie had not thought about the painting since then. Most of her inspiration in those days had been from books—and dreams. When she had seen Lucas in the waiting room after Adam's attack, she had been struck by how familiar he was, but had been unable to place where she had seen him before. She scrutinized the painting more closely now. Yes, the horse resembled Picasso, but palominos were not rare. The man bore a strong resemblance to Lucas, but what took her breath away was that the mountains she saw in the background very much resembled her mountain pass—as seen from Lucas's ranch.

How had she foreseen that so long ago? Perhaps she had inherited some of *Mamá's* gifts, after all.

No, her mind must be playing tricks on her. She wasn't clairvoyant. It was a mere coincidence, drawn from a young girl's fanciful mind.

"Just girlhood fantasies."

"Ah, so the girl had fantasies of my horse."

She tapped him playfully on the arm. "All girls dream of having a horse." At least he did not mention the resemblance he bore to the male subject in the scene. She was rather surprised herself, though.

"But you have alpacas instead."

"More affordable, and they can earn their keep."

"True enough." He stowed their suitcases in the closet, and she showed him to the bathroom to take his shower. When he returned, she was sitting on the edge of the bed putting her shoes on again.

"I'm ready when you are, darlin'," he announced a few minutes later, his hair still damp, but combed. He wore blue jeans and a western-cut denim shirt. Such a handsome man.

Now, am I ready to introduce him to Papá?

Of course, *Papá* would love him. Her nerves came more from facing the first, and at one time the only, man she had ever sought approval from. They had not seen each other in five years, not even on Skype. She appreciated having Lucas here for moral support.

Lucas took her hand and squeezed it reassuringly. She preceded him into the kitchen where *Papá* sat with his cup of thick, black coffee. His back was turned to her, making it impossible for her to read his expression.

She cleared her throat, which had closed off with emotion. "*Papá*." Her voice was barely a whisper, but he turned around in his seat, and she met his piercing gaze. His green eyes bore no emotion, joyful or sad. She fought the desire to rush to his side fearing he would not hug or welcome her back.

Papá's gaze turned to Lucas, equally cold and distant. He refocused on her again. "Welcome home, Casandra. It has been too long."

Even though he did not smile—*Papá* rarely smiled—he stood and opened his arms. Lucas squeezed her shoulder, and she closed the distance between herself and her father. He wrapped her in his embrace, and tears flowed down her cheeks.

"I have missed you, *Papá.*"

Do you still love me?

"I am sorry I have been away so long."

Do you forgive me?

"You are here now and with a husband. My heart is happy."

Would he have welcomed her home if he thought she was still the partying girl who had not returned home one night from a date with her fiancé? She had spent most of that night walking home, battered and broken. Yet when she arrived home, she had hidden the truth from her family. *Papá* had accused her of drinking too much after smelling beer on her clothing, but had let her disappear into her room for days. He probably thought she had been sleeping off a hangover rather than nursing her wounds and trying to decide if she wished to live or die.

Having Lucas here made her the respectable daughter he always wanted.

She squirmed out of his arms, no longer comfortable being there if his love and acceptance were based on conditions. Cassie turned to Lucas and held out her hand to him.

"*Papá*, I would like you to meet Lucas Denton."

Lucas extended his hand and shook *Papá's* firmly. "Good to meet you, sir. Cassie has told me a lot about you."

She held her breath, waiting for *Papá's* reaction, but before the two could say anything, *Mamá* carried in a platter of stew with pork and potatoes. Already on the table was her traditional *caldo de gallina*, a hearty soup with chicken and vegetables. She had prepared an elaborate breakfast meal in the tradition of the hardworking people of her homeland. Cassie debated whether to refuse to eat the meat, but would not insult *Mamá*. She could just try to avoid as much of it as possible.

"Come, let us eat."

"Will Eduardo be joining us, *Mamá?*"

"No, Susana called him home to watch the children while she and the baby nap. They will be over to visit later."

She could not wait to see her extended family, especially her new nephew, Quenti. They spent the next forty-five minutes on small talk as they ate.

"Wonderful meal, Mrs. López."

"Call me *Mamá*, my son. We are family."

Lucas smiled at her mother and warmed Cassie's heart.

Cassie surreptitiously moved an errant chunk of pork under her bread. "I have missed your cooking, *Mamá*."

"I can see your influence in some of the dishes Cassie has prepared for me, *Mamá*." Cassie smiled her gratitude to him for being so charming. "I especially love her *puca picante*."

My! She had only made the dish for him once and would have thought his concussion would have kept him from remembering the foreign name, but he had great recall. The man also knew how to charm a woman. Goddess knows she had almost succumbed to his charms many times.

"Casandra, are you still painting?"

She turned toward the older man at the table. "Yes, *Papá*."

When she did not really know what else to say, Lucas interjected again, "She had a fabulous turnout for a gallery opening in Denver last month. She sold a number of pieces to dealers and local collectors."

Her neck and cheeks flushed at his praise. "I am also doing some work with *quipu* and a Japanese fiber-art process for dyed alpaca fleece." No sense naming Shibori because they would not be familiar with the technique. "I have my own alpacas—four adults and one cria who was born in May." Cassie turned to Lucas and smiled. "Thanks to Lucas, the baby survived."

"Where did you two meet?" *Papá* asked.

Lucas grinned at her. "In a hospital waiting room, actually."

"I was staying with Kitty, my friend from college. Adam, her husband…" No sense saying they had not been married at the time. "Adam had been injured. Lucas and Adam have mutual friends, and we were all waiting there for word about his condition."

"I assume he survived."

"Oh, yes, *Papá*! And they just had triplets on June the first."

"Grandchildren are the greatest gift a child can give her parents." *Mamá's* gaze turned wistful before she cast a pointed glance at Cassie. "Our hope is to live long enough for the day you will bring your children here to see their *abuelos*."

Cassie cringed inside and cast an apologetic look at Lucas, but he only smiled. "If blessed with children, I am sure Cassie would want them to know their grandparents."

Images of a brown-skinned boy with Lucas's smile and Cassie's dark eyes flashed across her mind. Where had that come from? Cassie blinked it away.

Time to change the subject.

Cassie stood. "Let me help clear away these dishes, and then maybe we can move to the living room where we will be more comfortable?"

Not that she would be comfortable again until she returned to her cabin.

No, wait. She had no cabin. When would the loss become real to her? Lucas's ranch, while cozy, was not home. She preferred to be isolated from people. He did give her space when she needed it, though.

Unlike her parents' house. They would be on top of each other the entire time she was here. Not only she and her parents, but she and Lucas as well.

Please, Goddess, let me survive this visit.

Chapter Twenty-Five

Luke had to chuckle at the expression on Cassie's face when her mother brought up the idea of their having children, but he quickly sobered. Hell, it wasn't all that funny now that he thought about it. He'd like nothing more than for Cassie to be the mother of his children, but clearly, she had no such dreams. To her, the thought of making those babies would be a nightmare.

Still, seeing her with Karla's babies showed him what a great mother she would be. He supposed she'd settle for being a terrific aunt instead, but he wondered if she had ever thought about having kids of her own before the rape.

Luke started to follow the ladies into the living room, but Cassie's father halted him with a hand on his forearm.

"Let us talk." *Oh, man.* This sounded serious. To the ladies, the older man said, "We will join you in a while."

Cassie cast Luke a worried glance, but he tried to put up a brave front and gave her a wink. "Try not to miss me too much, Sweet Pea."

She blinked and then smiled, which surprised the hell out of him. "Hurry back." Her breathy whisper hit him below the belt. At least that's where he felt its effect. Not cool exhibiting his arousal for the man's daughter in front of him, wife or not.

She sounded as though she'd genuinely miss him. *First down.* She turned and followed her mother in the opposite direction.

"This way, Lucas."

"You can call me Luke, sir."

"Why does Casandra call you Lucas?"

To keep her emotional distance from me.

"Lucas is just her special name for me. In return, I call her Cassie, Sweet Pea, and other endearments."

He seemed puzzled at first and then nodded. "I see." The older man led him down a different darkened hallway from the one leading to the bedroom he and Cassie shared. *Their* bedroom.

Bedtime couldn't come fast enough.

Mr. López—he hadn't been invited to call the man *Papá* yet—opened a door on the left and flipped on a light before waving Luke ahead of him.

"Have a seat."

The room was small and dark, and the stench of tobacco overpowered him at first. The man offered him a cigar, but he declined and waited to see where the older man would sit before taking a seat nearby.

Memories of meeting Maggie's dad to ask for her hand flashed across his mind. He'd been a lot younger then, but this father-in-law was no less intimidating.

Waiting as the man lit his cigar, Luke glanced around. Books filled the shelves behind a desk. Some were lying horizontally on top of others. Many were leather bound with the spines he could see showing titles in Spanish. He must like to read. One thing they had in common, besides Cassie. On the desk sat an open ledger. He remembered the man had been a silver mine owner, but thought Cassie said he'd retired. Luke didn't know a lot about Peru, but images of the Bolivian silver mine in *Butch Cassidy and the Sundance Kid* came to mind. He'd have to do some reading to learn more about his wife's country of origin.

"What do you do for a living?"

His attention returned to the man seated across from him, smoke wafting around his head. Apparently, he wanted assurance his new son-in-law could provide for his daughter.

"I'm an artist, too."

To say his father-in-law was unimpressed would be an understatement. "How are you able to provide for Casandra's needs on an artist's income?"

Luke grinned, mainly to hide his concern. He wanted Cassie's father to know he would take care of his little girl. "Well, my talent is working with wood, sir. I make...specialized furniture. But I also can fall back on my carpentry skills if there's ever a cash flow problem. There's never a shortage of clients wanting to renovate or new-home builders in Colorado. Vacation homes are popular now."

The man remained silent for a bit. Had he given him the answer he needed? "Do you live in Cassie's cabin?"

"No, I…*we* have a small ranch not far from there."

Cassie's father raised his eyebrows. "I did not think she would ever leave her mountain home."

Well, she sure didn't do so willingly.

He had better stay on his toes in this conversation so he didn't trip himself up. Cassie hadn't told them about the fire. He wondered why not. Probably didn't want to worry them. She seemed to think them fragile, although they seemed pretty strong to him.

What else did he need to be careful not to reveal?

"I also volunteer in search-and-rescue and have been taking in and training some abused mustangs for my SAR work."

One of them helped me save your daughter's life.

The man's eyes lit up. "How many head?"

"Only four right now. I don't like living beyond my means, and horses require a lot of time and expense. Eventually, I hope to have an elite equestrian SAR team, but these are a good start."

The old man smiled, probably for the first time since the two had met. "I've always loved horses. My son, Eduardo, is with a search-and-rescue team here in the mountains."

Why hadn't Eduardo or Cassie mentioned that? "If you ever come to Colorado, sir, I'll show you around my spread."

The smiled faded. "I do not intend to travel to the States."

Would Cassie return here very often to visit? Hard to say. Depended on how this visit went. But this very well could be the last time she saw her father, given the man's advanced age.

Maybe he could encourage her to make the trip again at least annually. He didn't want her to have to live with any regrets.

"There was a time when I could travel, but my health is not what it once was."

Luke wondered what health issues he had, but didn't ask. If the man wanted him to know, he'd tell him.

"Will you bring my daughter to see me regularly?"

He didn't want to make promises he couldn't keep. "Our animals keep us pretty tied down."

"Who is caring for them now?"

"My parents, but they live in Texas—a day's drive away."

He nodded again, his sadness obvious. *He does love Cassie, even if he doesn't know how to show it with affection.* Something Luke and Cassie had in common with their dads.

"Tell me about your relationship with your mother."

It seemed an odd question, but he spent the next ten minutes talking about what a great momma he had and how she'd sacrificed and worked hard with Luke during high school so he would be accepted into a good college. "I owe her a lot."

"You love and respect your mother. That is good."

Apparently, he passed the test about how a man treated his mother having a correlation to the way he treated his wife. Jury was still out on whether the man believed Luke could provide for Cassie's needs. But Cassie didn't need many material things. What she needed was lots of love, encouragement, and consistency. *Those* he could provide in abundance. While her walls had been coming down in the last week or so, unless she was able to accept his love, his best efforts might not matter.

Unfortunately, Cassie saw love as a prison. Even though he had the key to free her, she might not let him.

*   *   *

"Do you love him?"

Mamá caught her off guard. How to answer truthfully? She loved Lucas as a friend. Loved his gentle soul, kind spirit, and how he treated his animals. How protective he was of her, even when he sometimes smothered her.

"Yes, I do." *In my own way.*

"I wish I had been at your wedding."

Cassie glanced away. "It was just a courthouse ceremony. Nothing fancy."

"It is not the location of the ceremony, but the words spoken to seal you to one another." Her mother narrowed her gaze, glancing briefly at Cassie's waistline. "Why such a hurried event?"

Of course, *Mamá* could not determine if she was pregnant under the baggy sweater she wore, even if there had been a baby on the way.

"No, *Mamá*. We did not *have* to marry." Well, she had felt pressured to make her parents happy by doing so, but it was still a choice. They had exchanged their unique vows, spoken from the heart. "Eduardo represented the family."

It might be a farcical marriage to some, but she considered herself tied to Lucas for life in her own way. For as long as this mutual agreement lasted. If the day came when he asked to be released from her—probably after he found the *right* woman to go through the remainder of his life with—then she would set him free.

But the type of wedding *Mamá* wanted to witness—where she would be bound to Lucas as a wife and helpmate, mother of his children, until one of them died—that was something Cassie could never imagine experiencing with Lucas or any man.

"I trust you asked God and the Goddess to bless your union."

Cassie averted her gaze. How could she? "Actually, it was a civil ceremony in a judge's chambers."

The silence that stretched out between them made Cassie uncomfortable. Then *Mamá* spoke. "You seem to care for one another. I see the love between you two."

Love of a friend, not a spouse. But knowing *Mamá* was content helped bring peace of mind to Cassie. She had done the right thing by marrying Lucas.

"I want you and Lucas to think about renewing your vows along with *Papá* and me Saturday."

She met *Mamá's* gaze. "What?" Had she heard correctly?

"If we can witness you two sharing your vows and making a commitment before the deities, your father and I will be pleased. He was not happy learning you had married without asking his blessing. Besides, his faith is strong, and he will not believe you are truly married until you marry in the eyes of his church."

How could she enter into a second phony marriage ceremony? She had more control over the words spoken in the Colorado civil ceremony, but *Mamá* wanted her to speak her vows before the Goddess—and *Papá's* God. They would have no control over the vows spoken.

"No, *Mamá*. I do not think Lucas will want to do that."

"Do what, Sweet Pea?"

Cassie turned to find Lucas and her father standing in the doorway. They reeked of cigar smoke.

Smoke. Beer.

The air closed in around her as sweat broke out on her forehead. Her hand shook uncontrollably. Out of nowhere, Lucas suddenly crouched before her, stroking her arm. "Look at me, Cassie."

She forced herself to put the past back in its box and face him, but her mind's eye was bombarded with images in strobe-like fashion.

"You're okay, darlin'," he whispered. "I'm here." He telegraphed the message, *"Nothing bad's gonna happen while I'm around."*

Lucas grounded her in the moment, until she remembered what *Mamá* had asked her to do. The smothered feeling came over her again.

She whispered, "*Mamá* wants us to renew our vows with her and *Papá* Saturday. I do not think—"

"We'll discuss it tonight after we go to bed." His firm gaze never left hers and gave her a sense of calm assurance that no one would force her into anything.

But why did he not say no outright? How could they continue to play out this farce before her parents, the deities, and the Universe?

Mamá's voice reminded her they were not alone. "Casandra, Lucas is right. You two should talk about this when you are alone. I am sure he will help you make the right choice."

Her mother turned her attention to Lucas, as though his decree would be final and that he was the one she needed to win over. *Mamá* had lived in a patriarchal society her entire life. "Lucas, it would be no trouble to make a single ceremony into a double. Everything is already set." Cassie resented *Mamá* for deferring to Lucas for such a monumental decision in her life.

"Cassie and I will decide what's right for us both." Cassie's heart grew warm that he did not intend to dismiss her feelings and input. With Lucas, she was an equal partner.

Wait! They were only friends. Why was she even considering talk of a religious marriage ceremony?

Mamá crossed the room and took *Papá's* hand, gazing at him with the love and respect she had shown him Cassie's entire life. She smiled and turned to Cassie and Lucas. "Know that *Papá* and I would be proud to share our special day with you in this way."

The walls closed in further. Choosing between pleasing her parents and doing what she wanted meant she had very little choice at all. Why did she feel like a teenager again in her parents' home?

"Darlin', let's grab our hats and coats and take a walk. You can show me around your village."

Anxious to escape, Cassie nodded. She needed time to think. She stood and told her parents they would return soon. Outside, she filled her lungs with crisp mountain air. As close to heaven on earth as she could imagine being.

"That's it, Sweet Pea. Just breathe and relax. We're going to figure out what's best for us to do. Remember, you're not a kid anymore. I know you'd do anything to please your folks, but you have to live with your decision the rest of your life. It's hard to be around our parents and not revert to wanting to obey and please them, but you're an adult now. You have to do what you know is right for you."

"Thank you, Lucas." She was not ready to discuss the pros and cons of the ceremony with him yet. "Come with me." Cassie reached for his hand and started down the street. They walked several blocks, and she shared stories about some of the places they passed, including where she had first fallen in love with alpacas. She had been permitted to help care for a neighbor's animals after school in a shed in the back of his property.

A strong wind blowing off the mountain peaks whipped at their faces, invigorating Cassie. Despite the bright sunlight, the day was frigid.

Goddess, she felt alive for the first time since the fire!

"I did not realize how much I miss high mountains. The closest place I have found to this was at my cabin." As soon as the words left her mouth, she halted and faced him. The light dimmed in his eyes, and she regretted her words immediately. When a shiver coursed through his body, she glanced around for shelter and pulled him into a recessed doorway. "I did not mean to sound ungrateful. I appreciate that you opened your home to me and my babies. But my heart belongs high in the mountains rather than in the basin between the peaks."

"I've worked hard to establish a safe place for my horses where they will not only heal but thrive. If I could do that work up in the mountains, I would find you such a home. But horses need room to run."

She pressed her gloved hand against his lips. "Oh, Lucas, I would never ask you to leave your ranch. See how impossible it would be for us to marry in the true sense?" He reached up and stroked her cheek. She did not pull away. She owed him that much trust. "Lucas, we have separate lives…different priorities." Lucas hated the bitter cold at the higher elevations. She and the alpacas thrived in it. Both of them preferred time alone, which did not make for building a strong marriage, did it? He was always so optimistic. She, more pragmatic.

Lucas always saw things from a positive standpoint. If something was not working, he tried to find ways to make it work. A fixer.

But he could not fix everything that was wrong with her.

"Don't give up on us too soon, darlin'. We'll talk more tonight, in bed where it's warm."

The mention of lying in bed beside him put a damper on her emotions. Tonight would arrive sooner than she could prepare her psyche.

*   *   *

The moment Cassie had dreaded all day came even sooner than anticipated. She could barely keep her eyes open any longer. And yet the arrival of bedtime posed a whole new set of problems.

"Let's go to bed, Sweet Pea. You look beat."

She stared blankly at Lucas, who winked at her. Why did his winks set off a fluttering of nerves in her stomach? As did his grins. Perhaps it was just the thought of sharing a bed with him again that put her stomach into turmoil. But sharing a double bed could not be as bad as when they had lain together in her twin bed after the avalanche.

They still had not made a decision about Saturday. The more she thought about it, the more certain she became that she could not stand before the Universe, the Church, *and* the parish priest and speak vows she could not live by. The law of reciprocity in her Quechua belief system would never condone deceit on her part. In their original wedding vows, she and Lucas had been open and honest about what type of relationship they were entering into. Both knew it would not be a true marriage. More a lifelong bond of friendship. But the Catholic Church's vows were much more specific and unyielding.

After saying good night to her parents, they walked hand in hand down the hallway toward her childhood bedroom. The uneasiness in the pit of her stomach weighed her down further with each step. Lucas opened the door and motioned for her to precede him.

Abuela's bed dominated the room, leaving her wanting to run to the bathroom to be sick. Lucas's hand on her shoulder and his nearness did nothing to ease her queasiness.

He bent down to her ear, his scruff tickling her, and whispered, "Trust me, darlin'."

She nodded, even though she was not at all sure she did. "I do." *More than I can trust any other man.*

But Lucas was unlike any man she had ever known. Look at how he had helped her deal with the fears and triggers, not to mention that she had wanted no one else to be there for her after the session with the therapist. She did trust him.

Cassie crossed the room and opened her drawer, gathering her night-gown, panties, and toiletries. She hated sleeping in panties, but tonight she would wear them as an added layer of protection.

Why was she thinking such things? Lucas would never force her to do anything. He was gentle, kind, and a man of his word. Integrity. He possessed that trait in spades.

"I will be back soon." She walked down the hallway to the bathroom as if in a scene from *Dead Man Walking*.

After taking as much time as she possibly could without having Lucas send out one of his search parties, she brushed her teeth one more time. When she entered the bedroom, the light was off. She knew where everything was in the room—except Lucas.

"My turn."

She jumped at the sound of his voice, closer than she'd expected. She thought he'd be waiting for her in bed. Despite the fact that Lucas spoke English and Diego's haunting threat had been in Spanish, her heart beat wildly.

"Es mi turno."

The sense of dread increased as she took a deep, calming breath. Not wanting him to see her distress, she nodded, keeping her face averted.

"You okay, darlin'?"

No, I am not. I will never be okay again.

His hand lightly touched her upper arm, but she pulled away, nodding frantically. Tears splashed from her eyes. Thank the Goddess it was dark in here.

The darkness, the triggering words, and Lucas's nearness converged on her already battered nerves, increasing her sense of dread about sharing a bed with Lucas.

She reminded herself she was with Lucas, not those men.

Stay in the moment.

Taking a deep, calming breath, she handed him a towel from the dresser. "I hope the hot water holds out for you."

She felt his gaze on her, but after a moment, he thanked her and left the room. With shaking hands, she dropped her dirty clothes into the corner before diving under the blankets. Turning onto her side, as far away from where Lucas would be as possible, she waited and attempted to ground herself with her breathing.

Do not allow yourself to be dragged back to that place and time.

The blood rushing through her ears drowned out all other thoughts and sounds. Is this what a virginal bride felt like on her wedding night? She was neither virginal nor a bride. And they were *not* going to have sex.

She closed her eyes, but images from the Lima cantina assailed her immediately, and she opened them again. Staring into the darkness was no better because her mind flashed horrific images before her. Why now?

Hands grabbed at her. Smelly breath. Clothes ripped from her body. Run!

She gasped for breath and prepared to flee when the bedroom door opened and closed quickly, engulfing her in darkness again. *Pretend to be asleep.* Maybe she could prevent having further conversation when her emotions were already raw.

The blanket slipped off her shoulder as Lucas crawled under it, but then he repositioned it. He caressed her arm, his hand warm from the shower. "I know you're hot-blooded, baby girl, but it's awfully cold in here. Is there a stash of blankets somewhere?"

She shook her head before realizing he probably could not see her. So much for feigning sleep. "No. I took the extra blankets with me to America. Most were lost in the fire."

"Mind if I scoot a little closer then so we can share body heat?"

"I…"

…cannot do this.

Her throat closed off, forcing her to clear it in order to respond. "I do not think that would be wise."

"You know you can trust me. We both have on plenty of clothes. Besides, we've slept a lot closer than this before, with a lot fewer clothes."

"That was different. You had a concussion and did not know where you were."

Lucas laughed. "Well, then, don't you think I'd be much more in control of myself now?"

But what about my control?

She wanted his arms around her. She wanted him to hold her closer.

Cherish and protect her. Comfort her. The way he had after she'd shared her story with him. Or the care he gave her after her therapy session.

"Sure you're okay? I imagine it's hard for you being back here, close to where those men who hurt you are."

Lucas understood. "I cannot stop the images from bombarding me every time I close my eyes."

"I'm so sorry, darlin'. What can I do to help?"

The sudden yearning to have him pull her against his body overwhelmed her need for self-preservation. No, she should find a quiet place to meditate, to kneel at *Mamá's* altar and find peace with *Mama Quilla*, but she did not want to have to answer more of her parents' questions.

She needed to put some distance between them in this bed. "There might be an additional blanket in the bottom drawer of the dresser." She hoped so, at least.

He chuckled, and the mattress moved as he rose to check. Being alone the next few days would not be possible. She would have to sleep with Lucas in this bed and be with him every waking moment until they returned to America.

Please, Goddess, hold me in your loving arms tonight and wrap me in a protective barrier.

She closed her eyes, trying to immerse herself in the white light and escape.

Soap.

Lucas.

She opened her eyes.

Lucas had showered away the stale scent of cigar smoke. He moved around on the bed, covering himself with the extra blanket he had found. *Thank you, Goddess.* She nearly rolled over onto her back with the bouncing springs as Lucas sought to find a comfortable position. She grabbed onto the side of the mattress and resisted making contact.

Finally, he settled down. Once more, she closed her eyes and asked that the white light surround and protect her.

"Darlin'," he whispered.

She opened her eyes again. "What?" She kept her own voice hushed, as well.

"Sorry to bother you, Sweet Pea, but aren't we supposed to be discussing something important?"

She had hoped he would have forgotten. Lucas always followed through. Some might call that dependable. Consistent. Right now, tenacious seemed a better word.

"Can we talk about it tomorrow?"

"I suppose, but there's something you need to know before you decide what you want to do about Saturday."

"What is that?"

"If I marry you in this ceremony, we would need to renegotiate our original agreement."

"How so?"

"I would be standing before a man of God and speaking vows to love, honor, and cherish you."

"Did we not already agree to those things in our first ceremony?"

"We did. But I'll admit that I wasn't sure how strongly you were committed to our vows until I found them tucked into the pocket of the jeans you wore when you escaped from the fire." He reached up to brush a strand of hair from over her eye. She should have braided her hair before coming to bed but she'd been sidetracked. "I've wondered since finding them if you had consciously decided to take them with you when you evacuated or if you just happened to have them in your pocket for some reason."

She thought a moment about what her response might reveal, but had to tell the truth. He had never disrespected her by lying, as far as she knew. She had to trust that becoming vulnerable to him in this way would not come back to hurt her.

"I had very little in my cabin of sentimental value. When I was rushing around to see what else I should take, I just happened to see them and…" *Tell him the truth, Casandra. Abuela's* voice spoke the admonishing words in her head, surprising her. Perhaps being in her bed had sparked a memory, even though this bed had belonged to a different grandmother.

Her eyes had adjusted well enough to the dark to see he was leaning on his elbow, head in his hand, and staring directly at her. She glanced away. "No, actually, it was my conscious decision to go to the drawer where I had kept them and to bring them with me." She had not thought to grab *Abuela's* blanket or shoulder cloth, but she had rescued this piece of paper. She had just left Lucas a phoned plea for help, perhaps making her think of him and the vows. She shrugged. "While I do not understand why, it was important for me to save them."

He grinned, showing his white teeth. "I can't tell you how happy it makes me to hear that." His finger tapped her on the nose. "I think maybe I'm growing on you, darlin'."

She swatted his hand away, but giggled at his teasing. "Your ego is the only thing that is growing." Had she just laughed in bed with Lucas? How did he disarm her defenses so easily?

He chuckled and lay on his back staring up at the ceiling and adjusting the covers over his lower body. "Maybe not the only thing, Sweet Pea." She flushed when his meaning became clear. "Don't worry. You'll always be safe with me. But that's one of the areas we need to renegotiate."

"We do?" Was he saying he wanted her to agree to have sex with him?

"Things have changed since we took our vows the first time. Perhaps your parents are thinking tonight, too, about how things have changed for them over a much longer period of time. It's a good thing to assess a relationship every now and then. See what's working, what's not. The first thing I'd like to discuss is you living with me."

"I am living with you."

"I mean permanently. The rest of our lives together."

"I really have nowhere else to go. But I have only thought about leaving once."

Lucas rolled onto his side once more, so close she felt the heat coming off his body in waves. "When was that?"

She heard the surprise and hurt in his voice. "The morning your parents came to visit. You yelled at me about unimportant things and were not yourself. I thought perhaps you had grown tired of having me in your house."

"Man, I'm sorry, Sweet Pea. You didn't do anything. It was just me stressing out over Dad coming. We've never really been close."

"You feel he judges you, but I think he just wanted what was best for you. His problems lie more with his own father."

"You're probably right, but I didn't know that until his recent visit. Next time I act like an ass, call me on it. You know how it is to want to please your parents, even as an adult."

She nodded. "That is partly why we married in the first place."

"Maybe for you. I married because I wanted to be there to love and protect you. Having you in my house has made me realize I don't ever want you to move away."

"It is not like being in the mountains, but my alpacas love it, and it is a beautiful place."

"How about for you?"

"I like being there, too. I would not mind staying there." As if she had any other options. But, truthfully, she wanted to stay. "Is that all you had in mind?"

"In part. I also want to introduce more intimacy into our relationship, step by step."

Her heart pounded at his words. Cassie rolled onto her back to put some distance between them. She tamped down thoughts of having him rutting inside her like... "I cannot perform for you in...that way." Her words came out in a breathless whisper.

"I said I want more intimacy."

"Sex?"

His finger traced her jaw until it came to rest on her lips. Her stomach knotted and then dropped. "Maybe eventually, if that's what you want."

"I will *never* want that!"

"Honey, I know you were brutalized by those men. My dream is for you to wake up someday, however long it takes, trusting me enough to know I'm not like them."

"I know logically you could never do that. But my body and my heart have lived in fear and revulsion so long..."

"Look how far we've come since the first time we met." She really had gone from fearing all men to lowering her guard with Lucas and even Adam. "Cassie, I'll move heaven and earth to keep you safe from anything like that *ever* happening again."

"But you already agreed to love and protect me the first time we married."

He grinned. "True. You've been under Denton Protection Services since the night I followed you home from daVinci's bar."

She could not help but point out the obvious. "And who ended up needing protection that night?" He shrugged, but her smile soon faded. "So you just want us to touch more?" The only sound for a few seconds was the pounding of her heart as she waited for his response.

"Yeah. Not just in bed, though. I want to lie on the couch with your head in my lap and read together. To take walks on the ranch, holding hands. To give you a massage to help relieve stress after a hard day." He paused. "But I want us to share a bed every night, too."

Her anxiety level increased. "I cannot have sex with you like a normal wife can. I do not understand why you would even want to. I am damaged goods."

Lucas cupped her chin and turned her face toward him. "I don't ever want to hear you call yourself damaged in any way again. You're perfect." The anger in his voice made her want to flee. "Darlin', if marriage was only for people without any hurts or wounds from the past, well, there sure wouldn't be many weddings. You've been hurt badly, but wounds can heal over time if we work at it. I'm asking you to allow me to be an intimate partner in your life. To let me help you heal by allowing me to touch you and love you in more special ways than I can as just a friend."

"Lucas, what if I can never be sexual with you?"

His finger gently grazed her lips making them tingle. "Cassie, darlin', I've been falling in love with you ever since I woke up in your bed after the avalanche. There's no one else I want to spend the rest of my life with. I want to grow old with you by my side. I want you as my life's mate, if you need another name for it than wife."

"I do not want a mate. And I definitely do not want *to* mate."

Luke shook his head. "I know sex is your biggest worry, Sweet Pea. Here's something for you to sleep on. Have I ever forced anything on you or tried to coerce you into something on your hard limits list, even when we were in bed together?"

"No. But our current agreement did not include any possibility of such a thing. We have not even told our friends we are married."

"No, only your family knows."

"But you expect to tell all of our friends about being married this time?"

"I won't hide the fact we're married if it's in the eyes of God."

"Everyone will expect us to be sleeping together. But Kitty, for one, would never believe I agreed to such a thing."

"We're going to sleep together tonight, and there's no way we're having sex. So what happens in our house will be our business and no one else's." He ran his hand through his hair. "I'm asking for increased intimacy. To be able to hold you, touch you. To lie next to you and talk over our day like we're doing now."

To be lying next to him talking about such things astounded her. Could she do this? She supposed he took her silence for a need to plead his case further.

"All I'm asking for is a commitment from you to let me become closer than we have been, both physically and emotionally. That you'll let me be a part of your life." His finger traced her lips, sending tingles throughout her body. "I'm not going to force you to have sex—ever. But I think I can help you heal, Cassie, by showing you how a real man treats his woman."

His woman.

The words created a longing inside her. Could she ever become some-one's cherished woman? She shoved her romantic notions back in her hope chest of forgotten dreams.

"I'm confident that eventually you'll come to trust that I'll never harm you. That you'll allow me to unleash the passion you keep under tight wraps. Maybe you'll even dance with me someday."

Her heart beat so loudly the blood whooshed in her ears.

"Make no mistake, though. Our love and our marriage will be defined by our terms, no one else's."

Surprisingly, she did not tell him "no" outright. How could she even think about entering into what could very well lead to a physical-love marriage with him?

"What if we try and it does not work out?"

"We may never reach the place where we make love to each other, but I already love you, Sweet Pea. Our original vows were until death parts us. We have the rest of our lives to explore and deepen this relationship."

A lifetime love, but how long would it remain a platonic one?

"But sex or no sex, we're already married. I'm just taking this oppor-tunity of renewing our vows to strengthen our commitment and take things to the next level."

He took a long strand of her hair and slowly slid his finger along her hairline until he tucked it behind her ear. Her skin tingled as if he had blazed a trail of flames. She held her breath. Was he going to kiss her? The fluttering in her stomach did not seem to be from fear, but more like…anticipation?

Was she going to *let* him kiss her?

No. She breathed deeply and tamped down the feelings. "What if you get too…frustrated waiting for me to be ready?"

He chuckled. "I haven't had intercourse in eight years. Not since Maggie. There are ways of finding physical release short of intercourse. However, if after curling up against my body one night you decide you want more, all I ask is that you're honest and tell me."

The thought of asking him to have sex made her stomach queasy.

"If asking for sex is too hard, then we can work out a signal so I'll know you're ready."

"A signal?"

"Hanging a scarf on the bedroom doorknob, for instance. Leaving a note on my pillow. Whatever. Sweetheart, bottom line, the road to deeper intimacy is honesty and communication. Don't hide yourself from me out of fear over what happened in the past."

"What if I never have...romantic feelings for you, Lucas? How is that fair to you to give up any hope of finding the right woman to spend your life with because you are saddled with me?"

He leaned closer. "I've already found her." He placed a kiss on her cheek. She was not sure if that was where he intended it to land, or just where he ended up in the dark. "Whether you agree to remain my wife or not, you've staked a claim to my heart already. I'm not looking elsewhere."

"How can you be so sure there would never be someone more special for you, someone who might even enjoy having sex?"

He sighed. "I want you to stop thinking about having sex and think more about being intimate. Animals have the ability to rut and have sex. If the intimacy between you and me heats up to that level, we'll be making love."

"Semantics."

"No. God's honest truth, I can be a lot more creative than a rutting animal." She wasn't sure if he referred to animals in general or the ones who had raped her. "If there are triggers, well, there are lots of positions and techniques we can try that won't bring up memories of what happened before. We'll explore new ones until we find the ways I can turn you on that will have you begging for more."

She huffed. "That will never happen."

He chuckled. "We can start by initiating touches without any expectation of going further." He sighed. "Cassie, there are so many things we can do that don't involve burying my cock inside you."

Her face grew warm at his bluntness, and for the longest time, no words would come. She still did not understand why he wanted to change their marriage agreement. "You have offered me companionship, protection, intimacy, a place to live, and love. I still do not see what is in it for you if I cannot love you back."

He tapped his index finger on the top of her nose. "Oh, you love me, darlin'."

What did he mean?

"You love the way I tease you. You love the way I hold you after a bad memory or nightmare. You love how I show you life doesn't have to be so damned serious and full of pain all the time."

An unexpected grin broke out on her face. "All right, I will admit I do love all those things about you, Lucas." She sobered. "But true marriage leads to something more…sexual."

"Darlin', for someone who declares no interest in it, you sure have sex on the brain a lot."

"Stop doing that."

"Doing what?"

"Making me blush."

He laughed. "How can I tell if I've made you blush? Your beautiful brown skin hides it well, even when we aren't in a dark bedroom like this."

"I know I am blushing, and that is bad enough."

"Maybe if you stop bringing up sex all the time, you wouldn't be blushing."

The heat rose in her cheeks yet again. "You have me blushing like a virgin."

"Darlin', your innocence was stripped away from you by three evil men. Deep down, you *are* a virgin. And we're going to explore your passion and sensuality as long as it takes for you to be ready to take that giant leap and consent to making love the first time."

Consent.

Control.

Communication.

"I need to sleep on this. Maybe I can sort things out in the morning."

"Take all the time you need, darlin'. We don't have to agree to 'renewing' our vows this weekend here in Peru. But what I'm proposing stands, whether you accept it now or ten years down the road. I want you in my life, Cassie López, and for us to have a binding commitment that goes beyond being friends and companions."

There would be no turning back if she agreed to take this next step. Her heart longed for the relationship he described. No man had ever made her feel anything before Lucas, even if sometimes the feelings confused her. Would she let her fears keep her alone the rest of her life?

"Good night, Lucas."

"Night, Sweet Pea."

For some strange reason, she had to fight back the urge to lean toward him and kiss him good night. Baring their souls in this way had given her a glimpse of what nights in bed with Lucas might be like. Not scary at all. Instead, she turned her back toward him.

When he stretched out behind her, he lay as close as possible without making contact with her skin. Once again, heat emanated from his body. For someone usually cold, he was not at all cold tonight. His voice reached out to her in the dark. "Why don't we try an experiment tonight?"

"What kind of experiment?" she whispered.

"To prove to you that I can sleep with you, touch you, without jumping your bones, why don't we spoon together?"

The thought of having Lucas's hard body pressed so intimately against hers all night long sent a chill down her spine.

Or was it a chill? Judging by the heat in her body, she was no longer sure her mind's interpretations of her body's responses were accurate. Lucas Denton did strange things to her psyche—and her body.

"I do not think that would be wise."

"Who said we have to bring wisdom into this? Let's focus on our hearts for a change, not our heads. If you're going to marry me—again— we *are* going to share a bed. We may not make love in it—not right away at least—but I want to be close to you tonight. I want to wrap my arm around your waist and pull you into the shelter of my body."

His words definitely ignited a smoldering fire inside her. She tossed her single blanket aside, leaving on only the sheet and her nightgown.

Why did the thought of being snuggled against Lucas tonight fill a void in her heart rather than make her want to run screaming from the room? She had never yearned to be held by a man in this way.

Why are you doing this to me, Lucas?

She sighed. A longing to have him hold her close, to cherish and protect her, became an overwhelming need. Her life had been blown apart this summer. She wanted this man's comfort.

Maybe this test also would help her decide how to respond to his proposal in the morning. "I suppose we can try."

Lucas did not hesitate for a moment, but inched closer until his body hugged her backside from shoulders to thighs. His heavy arm draped around her waist. She feared he would cup her breast, but he placed his palm against her waist instead and pulled her even tighter against his hard body.

"How're you doing, baby girl?"

"I..." Her voice sounded husky to her ears. She felt in no way like a baby girl. How could she sleep with him all over her like this? While definitely outside her comfort zone, she did not feel the need to run. "Okay, I guess. Good night, Lucas."

Chapter Twenty-Six

The sound of dishes being stacked woke Cassie. She blinked several times until she could read the bedside clock. Almost five-thirty.

Rolling onto her back, her shoulder bumped against something hard, and she remembered Lucas had shared a bed with her last night. Slow heat crept up her neck and into her cheeks. He must have turned in his sleep because he was no longer pressed against her, thank the Goddess, but heat still emanated from his body.

She had fallen asleep in Lucas's arms. How on earth had she managed to sleep with a man lying so close to her? Far from having it bother her, she had slept more soundly than she had in months.

Quietly, so as not to disturb his sleep, she removed the sheet and blankets and rose slowly from the mattress. She needed to speak with *Mamá* about the turmoil in her heart. No doubt, she was the one up at this early hour.

Cassie padded on bare feet into the kitchen, wishing she had worn socks to keep the cold of the tile floor from seeping into her skin. Usually she loved the cold, but this morning she did not, for some reason. Was she missing the warmth of Lucas's body? *Surely not.* Going back to the bedroom to grab her slippers might awaken him, though. She needed this time alone with *Mamá* before having to give him her answer.

There could be only one response to his proposal. She did not welcome the look of hurt she would see on his face, but she could not ask him to give up everything for a woman who might never be able to love him the way he deserved to be loved.

Now how to find a way to let him down gently.

"Good morning, Casandra. You seem lost in thought this morning."

After greeting and hugging *Mamá*, she poured a mug of coffee and sat across from her mother at the table. "How did you know *Papá* was the one?"

Mamá lifted her mug to take a sip of her hot tea—Cassie and *Papá* were the coffee drinkers—before answering. "I had admired him from afar during my teen years. Being so much younger and of a different social class, I had more trouble making him notice me. We were from two different worlds."

Cassie had heard the story of how *Mamá* had healed *Papá's* mother. Sadly, she died long before Cassie was born so she never knew her. But Cassie had inherited the woman's bed, and while not as close as she was to her other *abuela*, she felt a connection to her, too.

"After spending so much time at his home, eventually *Papá* noticed me. Why do you ask this question? Are you having doubts about you and Lucas?"

"Oh, I do not know..." ...*if I am capable of loving any man.* "It is not Lucas. I think he loves me—no, I *know* he does—but I am uncertain if I love him as much as he should be loved. How long did it take *Papá* to fall in love with you?"

Mamá smiled enigmatically. "Do we ever know someone is truly in love with us?"

"How can you say that? *Papá's* eyes almost twinkle when he looks at you. I have seen the two of you seek out each other's hand to hold whenever you are near."

Mamá shrugged. "Love has many levels. I know when I exchange vows with him Saturday that I will do so with greater sincerity and love than I did as a young girl. I truly do love him more today than I did the first time we shared our vows."

Cassie wished she could wait and see if love could grow to such intensity between her and Lucas, but she did not wish to be deceitful and speak vows she could not believe fully.

"What is troubling you, *pequeña?* Does it have anything to do with why you have stayed away from home so long? With your break-up with Pedro? Is he bringing a wedge into your marriage?"

Cassie blinked away the tears. *Mamá* always understood, up to a point.

"In some ways, but not what you think. I have no feelings of love for Pedro. I would rather not speak of the details, *Mamá*, but he betrayed me, hurt me badly." Hatred was an unhealthy emotion, but in her heart, she truly hated the man. "With Lucas, it is just..." She could not tell her mother she had not yet consummated her marriage.

"Why did you marry Lucas in the first place if you are unsure that you love him?"

"It is complicated."

"Why don't you spend some time at the altar this morning before Lucas or *Papá* awaken? Seek the peace you need with Goddess in order for you to find the answers you need to move forward in your life."

She and *Mamá* had shared the altar at the back of the house many times, as she learned to blend her Catholic and Quechua backgrounds into her own unique spirituality, with one foot planted in each tradition and her heart mixing in other spiritual traditions to find her place in the Universe.

Cassie nodded, although the thought of bringing her shame and guilt before the Goddess churned her stomach. Would *Mama Quilla* understand and love her no matter what? Would *Mamá*?

Mamá kissed her on the cheek. "Be at peace with yourself, *mi hija*. All else will fall into place once you achieve that state of being."

Tears pricked the backs of her eyes, and she blinked rapidly. "*Mamá*, I do not know how to find peace within myself any longer."

"You will not be able to accept the love of anyone else before you can love yourself. What is holding you back?"

"I have been unable to forgive myself for something that happened to me long ago. It has built up inside me to the point that, at times, I have hated myself so much I wanted to…" No, she would not tell *Mamá* about her suicidal thoughts, either. Those lasted only those first few months after the rape.

Mamá wrapped her arms around her, and Cassie felt hot tears flow down her cheeks. "*Hija*, you are a child of light and love, and nothing you have done or that has been done to you will ever change that. You need to go into meditation ready to forgive yourself and others for past deeds and then send love out into the ether to replace the negative energy with good."

Cassie held on to *Mamá* for a long while, until the tears ebbed, and then nodded. She pulled away, drawing a deep breath. "I will do that, *Mamá*." She did not want anything to enter her relationship with Lucas and ruin their ability to find love with each other. This man shined a light into the dark corners of her life. She wanted to keep him. If only she knew how to give him what *he* needed, too.

Mamá smiled. "By holding that resentment inside, you are closing yourself off to Lucas and anyone else who wants to love you. Release it into the hands of God and the Goddess."

"I'll try, *Mamá*."

"Go. Find your center and speak with your deities."

Cassie kissed *Mamá*'s cheek and headed for the quiet room in the back of the house. In this sacred space, *Mamá* had taught her to meditate and listen to the small, still voice inside her. As was the tradition in *Mamá*'s house, she placed a veil over her head before she entered the room. *Mamá* had adopted the Catholic religion as she, too, had to straddle two spiritual worlds after marrying *Papá*.

But *Mamá* also blended those traditions into what worked for her. With her gift of healing and shaman status in the village, she could not turn her back on the Goddess, either.

Cassie knelt on the velvet-cushioned kneeler before the altar. *Mamá*'s meditation focus was a statue of Mary, Our Lady of the Miracle, in her crown and elaborate gold and silver flared robes. Her arms were out-stretched as if inviting one into her embrace.

Perhaps no one religion could contain her beliefs. Surprisingly, Lucas did not seem to care what she believed and seemed open to discussing spirituality with her.

Cassie closed her eyes and breathed slowly and deeply. Inhale. Exhale. She allowed the white light to surround and protect her on her meditative journey.

As if the Goddess herself had instructed her, she slowed down her mind and let go of the negative thoughts.

"*Mama Quilla*, help me to forgive myself for…" She could not find the words to express the shame she felt.

"That power lies within you, dear one. You need only ask forgiveness for it to be granted. Your heart is pure. Are you ready to let go of this hurt?"

"Yes!" Goddess's words were so clear it was as if she was speaking aloud. Cassie had not really heard Her voice since the rape. "I never should have accepted their evilness into my body and heart, but now I only wish to rid myself of the hate and resentment toward them and toward myself."

"Imagine that darkness flowing away from you, into the ether."

Much like the dark swirling winds in the painting of the leaf she had started many weeks ago, she pictured the evil that the three men had spewed forth onto her body and soul blowing away from her. Her spirit became lighter, and once again, she felt like the leaf, only this time she floated on a gentle breeze against a backdrop of blue skies with white puffy clouds. The sun shone on her, warm and bright. No longer brown and muddy, the leaf was a brilliant scarlet, amber, and green mosaic representing her multi-faceted life.

Cassie no longer saw herself as one leaf struggling alone against the wind, destined only to fall to the ground and be trampled on by passersby. Instead, she felt as if she could float forever.

Suddenly, another leaf came into her vision, larger than hers, but just as beautiful and brilliant, followed by others of all sizes, shapes, and colors. Without a doubt, she knew these other leaves floating on the breeze around her represented Lucas, Kitty, *Mamá*, *Papá*, even baby Aurora and her siblings.

My family.

Cassie sighed. She had sought solitude for so long she had almost missed letting love back into her life. But the avalanche, the fire, and Kitty's needing her had all brought love and light back into her life. Lucas, most of all, had been a precious gift she might have tossed aside if not for his patience and persistence.

She knew what she needed to do.

"Thank you, Goddess, for showing me the way."

Rising from the kneeler, she stretched out the kinks in her knees a few times. How long had she been in here? Slowly she made her way back to the kitchen.

Mamá looked up from a sheet of paper, probably her list of things to do for the *fiesta*, and smiled. "I can see on your face you are more at peace already."

Cassie smiled. "I am." She wrinkled her brow. "Please do not ask me to explain, but Lucas and I intend to treat this renewal of vows on Saturday as if they are our first marriage vows. I know the marriage will not be considered legal in Peru, but with our civil ceremony in Colorado, I hope that *Padre* Rojas will grant our wish to exchange our vows in the parish here."

"We will speak with him later today. He will be less worried about making the Peruvian government happy than in seeing you fulfill the sacrament and being properly married in the Church and before the eyes of God."

Cassie had never dreamed of a church wedding, especially after her civil ceremony in May, but it appeared she was going to have one. Somehow, exchanging vows with Lucas in the church she had grown up in made marriage seem so much more real to her than the ceremony in the judge's office.

She felt like a blushing bride, but the thought of sharing a bed with Lucas no longer frightened her. Something had definitely happened last night. She had feared she would never sleep for a moment, yet secure in Lucas's arms, she had slept until the sound of *Mamá* in the kitchen awakened her.

What kind of spell had he cast over her? Was it fair of her to accept his proposal on the grounds she wanted to feel safe like that every night? Certainly not fair to Lucas, who clearly had stronger feelings for her than she could return. Would he eventually demand more than the right to merely lie down beside her at night?

No. She trusted him.

But she also would be a lifelong disappointment for him. Perhaps the day would come when she could fulfill her duties as a wife without triggers or fear when he touched her. That would be a start. Lucas was a patient man, as he had shown her time after time these past few months.

Take it one step at a time, Cassie.

"Now, please excuse me. I need to talk with Lucas." She poured two mugs of black coffee, hoping he wouldn't mind how strong *Mamá* made it for *Papá*.

*   *   *

Luke barely slept a wink all night. Between having Cassie's soft body pressed against his and worrying about what her answer would be to his less-than-romantic marriage proposal, the clock had turned slowly under his watchful eye. The last he remembered, it was four-thirty. He must have drifted off a bit because, when he opened his eyes again at six forty-five, he was in bed alone. Well, he had his answer. Of course she would run. What did he expect? He probably shouldn't have made so many demands so fast, but damned if he intended to be around her every day and not be able to give her at least a hug or a kiss when he thought she could use one. These past weeks had been a living hell.

He tossed the blankets off and swung his legs over the side of the mattress. His knees practically touched the wall. There was a little more room on her side, but this was the smallest bedroom he'd ever seen.

He glanced at the headboard. Antique. Definitely Spanish influences in the carvings on the dark wood. He reached out and touched the punched leather. Different.

The door opened, and he turned to find Cassie still dressed in her nightgown carrying two mugs of what smelled like coffee. Two nights in a row without sleep, and she had anticipated his needs perfectly. The day was looking better already.

"Thank you, darlin'." He stood and met her at the foot of the bed. "I can't tell you how much it excites me to see you standing there with hot coffee in your hand."

Oh, good move, Denton. Does she think you have a fetish for coffee now?

Her face grew ruddy as she glanced down, but he sure as hell detected a smile. *Score.* He took the cup and a few sips before making eye contact again. "Damn, that's good."

She nibbled her plump lower lip.

His morning erection throbbed. *Damn, darlin'. Show some mercy!*

Hoping to take his mind off of kissing her, he gestured with the mug toward the headboard. "Before you came in, I was admiring the craftsmanship of this bed. Like nothing I've ever seen back home."

"It belonged to my grandmother. *Papá's mamá.* Made from *mohena* wood and leather."

"*Mohena.* I'll have to look that up. Definitely different than what I use back home, but the possibilities for carving seem to be outstanding."

"I'm not sure how available it would be in the States."

"Marry me, and I can apprentice with someone down here when we come for visits."

He'd intended for his words to come off jokingly, but he needed to get past her awkward rejection and move on.

"Lucas…"

The pause indicated he wasn't going to like what followed. He took a sip of coffee to hide his disappointment, whether expected or not.

"I have given what you proposed a lot of thought."

Hell, she'd been sleeping most of the time since he proposed. How much thought had she really given it? "I told you not to rush your answer.

We don't have to decide to—"

She held up her free hand. "My answer is yes."

"—do anything this weekend. We could—What did you say?" It took him a minute to process her words and stop speaking himself.

She bit her lip again. God, he wished she'd stop doing that. Made him want to take a nibble or two himself.

"I said yes. I will make my vows with you on Saturday, and I will mean every word. I am willing to commit to marrying you and accept that you wish for us to become increasingly intimate. Just continue to be patient with me."

A mixture of joy and trepidation assailed him. She had just agreed to marry him in a much more realistic arrangement than the one they entered into in May. Could he be the man this woman needed to help her put her painful past to rest and embrace a future together with him?

She'd come so far in a short time. Hell, he'd cuddled up against her body last night in bed. There had been a time not so long ago she couldn't stand for him to touch her hand. Whether it was from her therapy session or his day in and day out whittling away at her defenses, he didn't know.

The day she shared what had been locked inside so long seemed the turning point. Luke had no doubt he possessed the patience Cassie needed. He was a man with a slow hand and gentle touch. Hell, even if the day never came that she would agree to make love with him, his journey with Cassie at his side would be incredible.

"I believe we can even convince the priest to consider this more than a renewal of vows, but the actual sacrament of marriage."

"I'm not Catholic."

"I am no longer a practicing Catholic, either, although I identify with the religion in some cultural and spiritual ways. But I talked with *Mamá* this morning, and she said they have alternate ceremonies now that would work for us. You were baptized, weren't you?"

"Sure. As a baby. Lutheran."

"That you are a baptized Christian is all that matters to the Church these days. We do not even have to agree to raise any children Catholic." She glanced down at the floor. "Not that there would be any children."

In discussing the details of the service, he'd lost sight of what they had just agreed to do. Cassie said yes to a real marriage. He set his mug on a coaster on the dresser scarf, and she did the same. Standing before her, he cupped her face and lost himself in those deep brown, need-you eyes. 'Til now, she had been totally focused on the ceremony. Time to seal the deal with a kiss.

The flash of fear on her face burned his gut, but she didn't run. "Trust me, darlin'." He leaned closer and closer still, but didn't touch her. His lips hovered but waited for her to show him she welcomed his kiss and didn't just plan to endure it.

Damned if she didn't sigh. Or was it his own? No, he definitely felt the tiny puff of her breath against his lips. *Come to Luke, baby girl.* His hands caressed her face as he buried his fingertips in her silky hair. Even though he held her lightly, and she could have broken away, she didn't.

Good girl.

Luke turned her head slightly and pressed his lips against her temple. Her pulse throbbed against his palms. Fight-or-flight response—or excitement? He trailed kisses down her cheek to her neck and heard an audible gasp when his lips sucked her skin just below her jawline. Cassie's hands reached out, but rather than push him away, she held on to his upper arms as if to steady herself.

Sa-weet!

*   *   *

Cassie's heart jackhammered as Lucas brushed light kisses down her neck to her shoulder, and he pushed her collar aside to give him better access. *I can't breathe!* She reminded herself to do so anyway, but her ragged breath signaled the state of near panic she was in. Her nipples hardened against her bra, and she fought the urge to push him away.

No! She wanted this. Why, she could not say. Maybe to show Lucas she would try to be the wife he needed. Surprisingly, her body was responding to him not in fear or disgust, but...

She steadied herself by holding more tightly onto his arms and tilted her head to give him better access. Pulse points fired up in places she did not know existed. When he gently sucked the skin over her collarbone, she gasped. He immediately moved back up the column of her neck, leaving kisses along the way until his lips hovered again just over hers. There he stopped.

Kiss him. He's waiting for you to kiss him back.

"Please, Lucas."

She could not be the aggressor, if that was the right word. Did her whispered plea not convey to him what she wanted? Did she even *know* what she wanted?

Lucas waited. Apparently, Lucas was not going to finish this kiss…so she did. Straining upward, she pressed her lips against his. Warm. Firm. Inviting. He groaned, and a surge of power rocked her to her toes. His hands at the back of her head held her as he kissed her harder.

She opened her mouth to breathe. Instead of taking that as a sign that she wanted him to invade her mouth with his tongue, Lucas's tongue brushed along her upper lip as if waiting for an invitation.

Cassie regained some sense of control and pushed at his upper arms, breaking their contact. "Lucas, I cannot breathe." She sucked air in through her nose and mouth for several seconds before disappointment with her inability to finish the kiss flooded her conscience.

"Hot damn, darlin'!"

At the same moment, she said, "I am sorry I—"

Lucas pressed the tip of his index finger over her still-tingling lips. "Don't apologize for kissing me, Cassie."

She cast her gaze down. "But I could not finish."

His finger moved down to cup her chin, and he forced her to meet his gaze as he tilted her head back. "Oh, you finished just fine, Sweet Pea. You made me forget that we're standing here kissing in your parents' house on the eve of our wedding day. I told you last night there's a passion inside you waiting to run free. You just loosened the reins when you kissed me back. That's just a taste of what's to come, darlin'."

"It is?" Cassie's breathy voice sounded sultry to her ears, so unlike her. If he kissed her like that again… *Wait! I kissed him!*

"You'd better believe it. We're going to take this slow. But just like you pleaded with me for that kiss, I'm going to stoke the fires inside you until you're screaming for more."

"I do not think I can—"

"Shhh. We have the rest of our lives to explore our passion for each other. One tantalizing day at a time." He grinned. "Now, what do we need to do to make this wedding happen?"

"Oh! I forgot! *Mamá* is waiting for me. We need to work on what I will wear tomorrow."

"Glad I'm not the only one who was lost in the moment of that kiss."

She grabbed her mug and nearly ran from the room as she smiled at him over her shoulder. "Come find me in the den when you are ready for breakfast, and we will take a break. There are clean towels in the bathroom for your shower." She turned without waiting for a response and hurried away.

But she could not run from that kiss. She had been the one to press her lips against his. He had let her control the kiss, resulting in her wanting more rather than feeling fear. How did he know to wait for her like that? Would he do the same when they touched more intimately, as she had agreed to do? Would he let her initiate touches, as well?

He left her wanting more.

Oh, dear Goddess.

Her step was light as she entered the den. *Mamá* had spread a colorful Quechua-woven *lliclla*, or shoulder cloth, open on the sofa. She inspected it, supposedly looking for loose threads or tears in the weaving.

Cassie came closer and saw some slight discoloration in the vintage garment, but the artistry remained exquisite. *"¡Eso es tan hermoso!"* And it truly was the most beautiful thing she had ever seen, except for *Abuela's* wedding *lliclla* that had been destroyed in the fire. She had not been able to tell her mother about that yet.

She and her mother conversed in Spanish while Lucas was not with them.

"I wore this the day I married *Papá*, although I had to remove it inside the church." *Mamá* turned to her with tears in her eyes. "I have been blessed to live long enough to see my daughter wear it on her wedding day."

Tears sprang to Cassie's eyes, as well. "But we are marrying in the church."

"Oh, our priest is more liberal than many. *Padre* Rojas allows couples with Quechua or other indigenous roots to express their heritage in the marriage sacrament, as long as they do not stray far from the Church's approved ceremony."

Cassie touched the woolen fabric almost reverently.

"What shall I wear under it?"

"Layers of as many *polleras* as you wish, including the one you are wearing now, and any blouse or shirt you like. This *lliclla* bears our village's design, but all Lucas will notice is the radiant smile on your face." She leaned forward and placed a kiss on Cassie's cheek. "I am so happy to see the light in your eyes again, *hija*. Lucas truly will not be able to take his eyes off you."

The image of Lucas standing at the altar watching her walk down the aisle flashed across her mind. "Thank you, *Mamá*." She had packed three skirts to wear in layers Saturday. Fortunately, clashing colors and designs were the norm rather than a fashion problem here in her homeland.

Mamá stopped inspecting the garment and sniffled. Cassie closed the gap between them and hugged her.

"I thought I had lost you forever, Casandra, but my prayers have been answered."

"I am sorry I left without explanation and caused you grief and worry, *Mamá*. It makes me happy to be home again."

"Why all these tears?"

Cassie broke away and turned toward the doorway where her father stood. She did not hesitate to share her news. "*Papá*, Lucas and I have agreed to exchange vows alongside you tomorrow."

Papá smiled. He actually *smiled!*

Mamá dabbed at her eyes. "We will see our daughter enter into the sacrament much as you and I did all those years ago. It is going to be a most glorious day of celebration for our family and friends. Oh! We need to prepare for more guests and more food."

Papá shook his head but continued to smile. "You women and your *fiestas*." But his expression sobered, and he pierced Cassie with his intense gaze. "You make your *mamá* happy by being home, *mi hija*." He paused. "And me, as well."

Some of the resentment she had harbored toward *Papá* for arranging her disastrous engagement to a man like Pedro receded. While they might never go back to the father-daughter relationship they once shared, at least she could forgive and let go of her anger.

Cassie traversed the room and walked into *Papá's* embrace. His arms closed around her. She realized she might not have been able to hug him if not for the way Lucas had hugged, comforted, and held her. Over time, Lucas had conditioned her for this moment, whether that was his intention or not.

Having *Papá* hold her this way only increased her sense of peace and well-being. She was ready to move on, forgive, and heal. The past no longer controlled her. *Mama Quilla* was already at work in her life—her *new* life with Lucas as well as with her family of origin.

*   *   *

Luke's head swam from the activities and preparations Cassie and her momma were undertaking this morning. He wished his folks could be here to see this, too, but they would be content knowing he was happy and had found someone to share his life. They seemed to love her as much as he did. After they returned to Colorado, they could celebrate with a special dinner.

Luke tried to keep up with what was going on, but all the various godmothers and godfathers befuddled him. However, he liked following tradition, and this was her culture. The customs reminded him of a wedding he'd attended in El Paso once for a Mexican-American friend who incorporated the Old World customs with the way Americans did things. That helped him understand *madrinas* and *padrinos* and their sponsorships of every aspect of the ceremony. If this hadn't been such a last-minute affair, no doubt there would be even more godparents involved.

One part of his friend's ceremony that had left a lasting impression on him had been when the couple was lassoed together by one of the godparents. He grinned, suddenly realizing there was something he could contribute to the ceremony—if he could find the right kind of rope.

Midmorning, they went to the church to meet with the priest who grilled them separately about their plans for their marriage and the future. Thankfully, they didn't have to promise to raise children by the rules of any particular religion. Last night, he thought the chances were slim they would have children, but after that kiss this morning, he wasn't so sure.

But if there were, given the discussions he and Cassie had enjoyed about spiritual matters, they would want each to be free to choose their own path. They would be sure to expose them to all kinds of faiths and let them decide. His parents had been that way with him. He wasn't a churchgoer, but followed the Golden Rule present in most faiths. Father Rojas had said one of his responsibilities in the union would be to guide his family spiritually. Cassie held stronger beliefs than he, though, so somehow he figured there would be a shift in tradition there.

Enough thinking about kids and religion. He just thanked God that this wedding was taking place at all.

Something in Cassie had broken free this morning when she met him at the door with coffee. He had no clue why, but she wasn't as nervous around him. Shy, sure, especially at any mention of intimacy. But, damn, had she ever surprised him with that kiss.

As they left the church, he held her against him to help block the wind. They hurried down the dirt streets and entered the house on a swirling blast of wind. Man, how did anyone stand the frigid temperatures here? Next time they visited, it needed to be their summertime. Maybe for Christmas or to ring in the New Year.

They'd be an old married couple of almost six months by then. Luke grinned, liking the sound of that.

The moment they entered the López house again, the smells of all kinds of food and a din of shouts and laughter in the kitchen bombarded his senses.

Cassie placed her hand over his heart and stared up at him. "I had better go see if I can help *Mamá*. She is probably a little overwhelmed now. I think half of the village is planning to be at tomorrow's *fiesta* after we exchange our vows."

He grinned. "What are the menfolk supposed to do at times like this?"

Cassie smiled. "Why don't you spend more time with *Papá*? He probably is in his office." Luke must have looked a little nervous at the suggestion. "Relax. Talk. Smoke cigars. Perhaps share a beer."

Luke wasn't sure he wanted to venture into the lion's den again, but it sounded like less stress than trying to help out in the kitchen. Cassie's *papá* intimidated the hell out of him, though. He rarely smiled, and they had little in common—except for Cassie and hard work. But the man also was his father-in-law. The least he could do was become better acquainted with him.

Luke walked down the darkened hallway and smelled the cigar smoke while still several feet from the closed door. He knocked. "Mr. López, it's Luke. I wonder if you would mind some company."

"Enter!" Luke did so and immediately had a humidor extended toward him. "Here, have one." Mr. López set the box on his desk, struck a match, and lit Luke's cigar.

While Luke had never smoked, taking a few puffs of a cigar in celebration of his upcoming wedding wouldn't kill him. He pulled one of the fat cigars from the dark container before the lid closed with a snap and was placed on the desk. Before Luke could sit down, Mr. López gestured toward the corner. "Help yourself to a beer first."

That might just do the trick to relieve these pre-wedding jitters. He wasn't worried so much about embarking on this redefined lifelong journey with Cassie. Hell, he wanted Cassie in his life more than anything.

No, what worried him most was that she would change her mind. Maybe not tomorrow, but somewhere down the line. After all, she had gone from "No way" to "I do" awfully quickly. He wasn't sure she knew *what* she wanted yet. Had she just become caught up in all the hoopla over her parents renewing their vows or did she truly want to marry and make him a major part of the rest of her life?

Mr. López drew in and exhaled a massive amount of smoke. "Any brothers or sisters?"

"No, sir. Only child." Luke inhaled and nearly choked. Better stick to the beer.

"What do your parents do?"

"They're retired now, but worked the crude oil pipeline when I was growing up."

"Hard workers."

"Absolutely. Lots of moving around, too."

"Are you a wanderer, too?"

Somehow, Luke didn't think he just meant someone who relocated a lot for a job. "I've established roots in Colorado on a one-hundred-and-sixty-two-acre spread and have no intention of going anywhere for a long time." Might as well address the underlying question. "I also am a one-woman man. I lost my first wife in an accident eight years ago and was true to her every day of our two short years together. I can assure you my eye won't stray to anyone else as long as I have Cassie."

The old man grew silent a while. "Women are mysterious creatures. I never understood why Casandra left, but thank you for bringing her back. Her *mamá* is beyond joyous."

"Cassie seems happier since coming back here, too." *Happy enough to agree to a real marriage with me.*

"She has always danced to the beat of a different drummer, *mi hija.*" He narrowed his gaze at Luke as he took a long draw on his cigar and let out another stream of smoke. "Give her a long lead, but don't be afraid to rein her in from time to time. She needs both roots and wings."

Luke certainly aimed to try to give her both. He smiled. "I'll do my best, Mr. López."

He waved the hand holding the cigar in the air dismissively. "Call me *Papá*. We are family now."

"I'm honored. Thank you." Luke took a tentative puff, but tried not to inhale too deeply. These things could kill you. "Sir, I love Cassie more than anything or anyone."

"Love is not always enough."

"No, sir, but sometimes it's the thing that's needed the most. The only thing that helps."

The door opened, and Luke turned as Eduardo entered. Luke stood to shake his hand.

"I hear congratulations are in order—again."

"Thanks. I'm a lucky man."

Papá asked, "How is my newest grandson?"

"Growing as fast as a peppertree. Keeping us up at night. Susana is going to stay home today, but we'll all be at the ceremony tomorrow."

Papá nodded and took another puff before he turned his focus to Luke. "Do you plan to have a large family like Eduardo's?"

The man had four kids. That was a lot of mouths to feed and put through college. Luke wanted nothing more than to have babies with Cassie, but the timing and size of their family was no one's business but their own. "Cassie and I will gladly raise any babies we're blessed with."

The man nodded and grinned. "We stopped at two. I'm too old, but at least I lived to see both of them through university and now married." He inhaled and exhaled another puff of smoke. "Life has been good for my family."

Not for everyone. Luke wasn't sure how to broach the subject, but didn't want Cassie to suffer any stress on their big day. Might as well come right out and ask. "Will Pedro be at the ceremony or party afterward tomorrow?"

Papá remained silent. Eduardo reached for a cigar before responding. A sense of dread curled up inside Luke's gut. Finally, his brother-in-law met his gaze. "Everyone in the village is invited. It is customary. But I do not expect him to cause any trouble. He is a quiet man. A loner. Not one to make a scene."

No, but he *was* one to fucking rape his fiancée. "If you see him, point him out to me so I can keep an eye on him." *And pummel his brains out if he comes anywhere near my girl.*

Eduardo's gaze narrowed. "Are you expecting trouble?"

Luke wished Cassie had informed her family about what had happened so they would be equally concerned about her safety. He wasn't the one who should be telling them, but he needed to protect her as best he could.

"Pedro's a low-life snake from what Cassie tells me. If he comes anywhere near her, I will make sure he never does so again. So if you know how to reach him, I'd suggest you make sure he doesn't show up at the wedding tomorrow."

Papá leaned forward and narrowed his gaze. "What did he do to my daughter?"

"That's for Cassie to tell you. But I know her safety is important to both of you, too. Take my word for it, and keep him the hell away from her."

Chapter Twenty-Seven

C assie's nerves jangled on edge all morning as she prepared for the big day. She and Lucas had been going nonstop since they agreed to exchange vows. Last night, she had fallen into bed too exhausted to say good night.

Today, Cassie's ensemble laid flat on that same bed. Her flouncy black *pollera's* horizontal strips of colorful cloth in many geometric designs were highlighted with rows and rows of rickrack. Except for patterns at the hems of the other two skirts, only this outer one would show, so she chose the most beautiful one for the top layer. The decorations on the sleeves of her red blouse matched those on the outer skirt, as well.

In less than two hours, she would stand before Lucas in this outfit wearing *Mamá's* shoulder cloth and speak her vows. Until then, she and Lucas would remain separated until they met at the altar, as was the tradition between brides and grooms. Her heart fluttered strangely at the thought, with excitement rather than anxiety. He and *Papá* had prepared for the ceremony at Eduardo's house. She and *Mamá* would dress at the church, although her cousin Evita, one of the *madrinas* for her special day, had braided her hair earlier.

She missed Lucas already. Amazing how her affections for him had deepened so quickly.

I know this is the right thing for me. Please, Mama Quilla, watch over my wedding day, my parents, Eduardo's family, and most especially my marriage to Lucas—as you have done for countless couples since time began.

Like a mantra, she repeated the words many times as she applied makeup to her eyes. Of course, when she chose a goddess figure who was the patron of marriage as well as the protector of women, little did Cassie know She could not separate one role from the other. She smiled. *Mama Quilla* knew what she needed, even if it was not what she thought she wanted.

A knock at the bedroom door pulled her from her work, and she opened it to find *Mamá* already dressed.

"*¡Mamá! ¡Te ves hermosa!*" And beautiful she was. Not many girls were fortunate enough to share the exchanging of wedding vows with their parents. She continued in Spanish. "I thought we were dressing at the church, *Mamá.*"

"You are, but the room there is too small for both of us."

"I hope I am not stealing from your special day with *Papá.*"

"No, no! This is the happiest day of my life. I have waited to see the last of my children happily married. Now I can grow old and let someone else worry about you."

Cassie smiled at her mother's half-teasing remark.

"Let me help you cover up your ensemble so we can start for the church."

Mamá placed the red wedding *lliclla* on the bed on top of the skirts and blouse. Over her arm draped a folded rectangular blanket matching her village's colors. "I want you to have this *k'eperina*, as well. I carried you on my back in this blanket when you were a baby. Perhaps one day you will carry your own infant son or daughter in it."

Tears burned her eyes. Having a child of her own would be too much to even hope for, but she reached out to accept the blanket with its vivid primary and secondary colors woven into intricate designs.

Cassie sighed and met her mother's gaze. There had been too many secrets between them. "*Mamá*, there is something I have kept from you. A few weeks ago, the cabin I have lived in since leaving New York burned in a wildfire."

Her mother gasped and placed her hand against her heart. "Were you and Lucas in danger?"

She did not wish to explain that Lucas was not living with his so-called wife. "I was able to escape in time, and Lucas came after me and my alpacas to take us to safety at his ranch. But—I lost all but one of *Abuela's* blankets in the fire, including the one in which she carried you and *Tía* Sofia as babies. I also neglected to save the shoulder cloth she wore on her wedding day."

Mamá enfolded her in her arms. "Material possessions are only of sentimental importance. We always carry the memories in our hearts, as is true for the essence of the people who once possessed those items, even if we lose the actual articles. You and your alpacas are irreplaceable. Thank God Lucas rescued you."

In more ways than one.

She remembered the song he sang to O'Keeffe about how they had rescued one another, just as Lucas and Cassie had done.

Mamá pulled away and lifted Cassie's chin until she met her gaze. "Now, explain how it is that a husband and wife were not living in the same house."

Putting anything over on *Mamá* was impossible. "We had a shaky start, mostly because of my fears and stubbornness. Pedro betrayed me, and I did not trust any man after him."

Mamá searched her eyes. "I wondered what happened between you and Pedro. He did not deserve you if he would do something to hurt you. But Lucas…" She smiled. "I think you have chosen wisely, *mi hija*. He has shown his love for you, but now I know he will also be your protector."

The two best parts of *machismo* were embodied in Lucas—love and protection—but he did so without smothering her.

"Now, we must not keep him waiting for his bride. I see why agreeing to take these vows was not an easy decision for you if you did not enter into your first wedding with true commitment. Today, the fourteenth of July, will be the date we share as our mutual anniversary."

Cassie nodded, agreeing that today's ceremony would be so much more heartfelt and real than her earlier one. That could be viewed as more of an engagement, perhaps. Cassie smiled and turned around. She spread the blanket out on Lucas's side of the bed. Then she and her mother gently laid her ensemble on top of it before rolling everything into a loose bundle. Cassie would carry this on her back to the church as many Peruvian brides had done over the centuries. The blanket would protect the clothing from any dust that might kick up from the wind, but eventually, perhaps Kitty would allow Cassie to carry one of the babies inside. To carry Aurora Casandra this traditional way would be such an honor.

Moments later, they joined the *madrinas* in the den. These godmothers who had come forward joyfully but on such short notice to make her day special and steeped in tradition would sponsor the cake and many other necessary components of the wedding and reception. At least she and Lucas already had their wedding rings. She hugged her three cousins, *Tía*

Sofia, and Cassie's friend from secondary school, Maria.

Cassie thanked each one, and soon the entourage made its way toward the church. Fortunately, the walk was not a long one. Despite the shining sun, the wind off the mountains was bitterly cold.

The nape of her neck prickled, and Cassie glanced at the windows and doorways they passed, expecting to see someone watching the procession of women. Given the frigid temperatures, few villagers joined in the procession, but a few of their younger neighbors did so. Others would be waiting for them at the church.

Would Pedro try to disrupt her special day? He must know through the village grapevine that Cassie would be married on this day. She shuddered then banished thoughts of the monster and his evil friends to the corners of her mind. She would not let him rule her life any longer.

Inside the mission-style church's vestibule, she and *Mamá* were ushered into what was indeed a small room. On a bench, Cassie set down her bundle and unrolled the *k'eperina*. The blouse would not be tucked in, so she donned the three colorful skirts before *Mamá* helped her into the blouse. Then *Mamá* placed the *lliclla* over her head and around her shoulders before pinning it with the silver antique *tupu*.

Her friend Maria brought forth the red hat with the upturned brim in the style worn by the women of her village. At the same moment Maria placed the hat on Cassie's head, *Tía* Sofia placed *Mamá's* almost identical *montera* on hers. Maria's fingers were cold as she fastened the strands of white beads to the hat and under her chin to hold it in place.

In the narthex, a whirlwind of activity ensued as *Tía* Sofia arranged the line of *madrinas* and *padrinos* for the procession, each carrying one of the symbolic objects so important in a Latino wedding. *Mamá* agreed to be their *Madrina de Velación* and walk down the aisle with Lucas. *Papá* would be the *Padrino de Las Arras*. Her parents would exchange their vows, first followed by Lucas and Cassie, but most of the activity revolved around the wedding ceremony.

The processional music began, and Maria handed Cassie the bouquet of Peruvian lilies almost the same shade of pink as the ones Lucas had given her for their first wedding. Had he chosen these this time, as well, or was it yet another sign of how perfect this ceremony would be for them?

*   *   *

Man, he wished they'd start. He couldn't wait to see his bride again but Cassie had been hidden from him in the dressing room nearby. His preparations had taken a lot less time. He wore the same clothes from their first wedding day. Given that he didn't have a lot of dress clothes in his closet, that's what he'd packed to wear at the ceremony to renew her parents' vows.

Luke took his place next to her *Mamá* about halfway down the line in the back of the church. The woman would also be serving today as the godmother whose role was to oversee their marriage. She held two lit candles.

Cassie's father would be one of the first to enter the church. He carried a bag of thirteen gold coins, a symbol of prosperity and a sharing of resources for the newlyweds.

From this day forward, Cassie agreed to be his wife. Not just his friend, but also his *wife* in every sense of the word. She trusted him to care for, protect, and nurture her.

I'm a rich man already.

Eduardo carried the white lasso Luke had spent several hours fashioning into a rosary, placing knots where beads would be. A small wooden cross had been attached to the loose end. This might be the only time he would use his rope techniques on his wife, but what better reason than this? The rope symbolized the binding of the two of them as one. Cassie was going to commit to spending the rest of her life with him.

Of course, he'd made that commitment once before, but today would be special for them both. Later, he'd let her know that he hoped this would be the day they celebrated as their true wedding anniversary.

Eduardo might have forced them into thinking about marriage sooner than they should have, but Luke couldn't fault him for being overprotective of his sister. He also seemed to have a happy wife and family. Susana could hold her own in their relationship, as shown last night when the family gathered to discuss what to expect today.

His brother-in-law's two older children, aged four and six, were near the end of the procession with flower petals and a ring-bearer's pillow, while the youngest two must have been in the care of a family member.

One of the godfathers in the front of the procession held their true wedding rings. Taking that band of silver off this morning had been difficult to do, but when Cassie placed it on his finger this time, it would be forever.

He didn't remember the names of everyone, but each seemed to have an important symbol in his or her hand. The men and women both dressed in a colorful array of Peruvian clothing.

Father Rojas and two altar boys took their places behind Eduardo's fidgety kids, and music sounded from inside the church as the doors opened. When it came time for them to enter the nave, his gaze went to the quartet of musicians standing in a boxed area on the right. The guitar, drum, tambourine, and accordion made a joyful noise all right. He grinned.

Hard not to smile on the best day of my life—well, so far, anyway.

When they reached the front of the church, he guided *Mamá* toward her husband, took his place, and turned to face the back of the sanctuary. All eyes were on the ring bearer and flower girl, who seemed to be taking their jobs very seriously and walking at a snail's pace.

The priest and altar boys followed them, and then he caught his first glimpse of his bride. So beautiful in her traditional clothing. On her head, she wore a colorful shawl under a red hat with at least eight strands of pearls holding it in place. *Mamá* had shown him a photo of a seven-year-old Cassie with a baby alpaca wearing a similar hat.

But Cassie was all grown up now. Best of all was the radiant smile on her face. No hesitation. No fear. When she met his gaze, it felt like a punch to his solar plexus.

Mine.

Her gaze never wavered from his as she walked down the aisle toward him. He'd learned last night that it was not the church's custom to have the bride given away to her husband. Luke liked that she was coming to him by choice.

At last.

When she was mere yards away, he stepped forward to meet her, crooking his elbow, and escorted her the rest of the way to stand beside her mother, with the men flanking their women.

The Mass began. Most of the words were in Spanish, so he didn't really understand much, but caught a few words during the homily about faithfulness, perseverance, and fruitfulness. Cassie tensed on that word, but he stroked her hand with his thumb.

Cassie and the priest had agreed to speak both English and Spanish during their parts of the Rite of Marriage, so that Luke would know what was going on. Not that he'd remember a thing they said. His mind was focused solely on the lady standing at his side.

Now and for the rest of their lives.

The ceremony continued, and her parents renewed their vows first, in Spanish. When he heard Cassie's sniffle, he squeezed her hand, brushing his thumb over her knuckles.

Next, in English, Father Rojas addressed Luke and Cassie. He repeated some of what he had said about marriage in his sermon before asking them a series of questions.

"Casandra Beatriz and Stephen Lucas, have you come here freely and without reservation to give yourselves to each other in marriage?"

Together, they answered, "We have."

"Will you love and honor each other as man and wife for the rest of your lives?"

"I will."

"Will you accept children lovingly from God?"

His response was spoken more quickly than Cassie's, but when she said "I will," Luke's heart soared. They were young and had plenty of time to worry about children, but that she allowed this to remain part of the ceremony was encouraging.

"Because it is your intention to enter into marriage, please join your right hands and declare your consent before God and His Church."

Father Rojas continued, reverting to their informal names as Cassie had requested. "Luke, do you take Cassie to be your wife? Do you promise to be true to her in good times and in bad, in sickness and in health, to love her and honor her all the days of your life?"

Luke smiled down at Cassie, who met his gaze. "I do."

She continued to stare into his eyes while the priest continued. "Cassie, do you take Luke to be your husband? Do you promise to be true to him in good times and in bad, in sickness and in health, to love him and honor him all the days of your life?"

She spoke in a firm voice. "I do." Cassie smiled and visibly relaxed.

"You have declared your consent before the Church. May the Lord in his goodness strengthen your consent and fill you both with His blessings. What God has joined, men must not divide."

The congregation and wedding party all said "Amen." The priest had given them permission to exchange their own profession of love, and Luke listened when it was Cassie's turn to read the words she'd spoken once before.

Beside me and apart from me,
in laughter and in tears,
in sickness and in health,
in conflict and serenity,
asking that you be no other than yourself.

Loving what I know of you and
trusting what I do not yet know,
I bind my life to yours
until death parts us.

For the first time since he'd penned those words the night she'd agreed to marry him in Colorado, he had more hope that those promises would be fulfilled than he had two months ago on their first wedding day.

I am blessed.

The rings were brought forward, blessed, and exchanged. His hand shook a little, just like the first time he placed this symbol of his love on her finger.

Her *papá* brought the bag of thirteen gold coins to Luke. He had explained to Luke earlier that he'd given these same coins to his own bride all those years ago. The older man poured them into Luke's hands slowly before returning to his wife's side and kissing her cheek. Luke took the coins and turned to meet his bride's gaze.

"Cassie," he began to drop the coins slowly into her cupped, outstretched hands, "I pledge to be a good provider, to earn your trust and confidence, and to support and care for you all the days of my life."

As the last two coins fell into her hands, Cassie teared up. She continued to hold the coins in her outstretched hands. "Lucas, I accept these coins as a representation of the trust and confidence you have in me, and I promise to return that trust and confidence thirteen-fold to you."

After the coins had been returned to their pouch and handed to one of the attendants, Eduardo and Susana came forward carrying the large white rosary fashioned from soft rope. Without his brother-in-law, their first wedding probably never would have happened. Now Eduardo would have a hand in symbolically binding the two of them together in a much more permanent way. God willing, they would be together for a very long time.

The priest indicated that Luke and Cassie should kneel once more on the pillows one of the godparents had carried in earlier. His brother- and sister-in-law formed a figure eight with the rosary rope and draped it around Luke's and Cassie's shoulders while the priest spoke in English again how the two were now bound together as one for infinity, as the sideways eight symbolized.

Luke's mind went places it shouldn't during a solemn church wedding ceremony. Would Cassie ever let down her guard enough to try a little kink? There were so many things in the lifestyle that could help her relax and enjoy her sexuality more, but she seemed to have an aversion to the topic whenever it came up.

Don't push your luck, Denton.

The ceremony continued until near the end when Eduardo and Susana were invited to remove the lasso from them and to keep it safe until they gave it to Luke and Cassie later. *Mamá* came toward them holding the lighted taper candles, her tears shimmering in their glow.

Each of them accepted one of the candles, and he placed a kiss on his mother-in-law's cheek. Luke didn't know if he was supposed to or not, but he reached for Cassie's hand as they made their way to the unity candle near the altar. Together, they lit the candle, and a single flame represented their coming together in marriage. With two puffs of breath, they extinguished the separate flames representing the end of their lonely pasts.

They'd been brought together by an avalanche and then a wildfire—ice and fire. Like this light, their marriage would burn hot and bright, no doubt. Cassie had an underlying passion just waiting to be unleashed. He couldn't wait to get home to their ranch and have her all to himself for a while.

When they returned to the priest, Luke was told he could kiss his bride. He framed her face. She seemed more serious now. Maybe the kiss would take her out of her head. He leaned down, no intention of stopping short this time, but wanted to hoot and holler when Cassie leaned toward him, impatient for their lips to meet again.

That's my girl.

My wife.

My love.

The ceremony ended, and the congregation stood. The godfathers and godmothers, led by Cassie's parents, were each handed a long-stemmed gladiolus as they took their places on opposite sides of the aisle—women on his right, men on the left, evenly spaced. Each raised one of the long-stalked flowers and formed an arch for them to pass under. It reminded him of the saber arch at Adam and Karla's wedding.

Cassie and Luke were handed one of the flowers, too. She set the pace, slower than in wedding recessionals back home, as the quartet played *Amazing Grace*. The congregation greeted them with smiles and applause.

*   *   *

Cassie walked solemnly down the aisle as they left the sanctuary, as was the custom, but there was nothing solemn about the stirrings in her heart. Elation best described her feelings. She could have floated down the aisle with her husband by her side.

My husband.

She had just turned a page in her life—no, more accurately, she had started a new book entirely.

When had she fallen for this man? For truly, this must be what love felt like. When Lucas looked at her with love in his eyes, she pictured herself as the beautiful bride he saw. Nothing would stop her from putting forth every effort to be a true bride to him this time, no matter how long it took.

Tears blurred her vision. *Mamá* and *Papá* waited near the back of the church, and she fought the urge to run into *Mamá's* arms. Emotions overwhelmed her, but her place was at Lucas's side now. When they reached the narthex at last, he turned her toward him and cupped her face once more. Kissing him was becoming her favorite activity.

She smiled up at him, but as he leaned down, she closed her eyes, already somewhat embarrassed that she had been so brazen at the altar when they shared their first kiss as a true husband and wife. This time, she would wait for him.

Hurry up and kiss me, Lucas.

When his lips did not meet hers, she opened her eyes and quirked her brow in question.

He smiled. "That's better." He closed the gap and met her lips. Rather than a chaste kiss like before, his tongue brushed across her lips, lighting a flame in the pit of her stomach warmer than the unity candle they had lit during the ceremony. Without thought, she opened her lips to him, but he broke off the kiss with a groan when everyone crowded around them to offer their congratulations.

He leaned closer to her ear. "We'll take up where we left off tonight—in bed."

The words sent shivers throughout her, but she did not think they signaled fear. Something else. Anticipation perhaps? How far would he take her tonight? He had promised to take his time. Besides, they were in her parents' house.

Yes, she had agreed to more intimacy, but how quickly did Lucas intend to move?

No time to think about such things as the wedding party moved into the hall for the celebrations. The evening passed in a blur of faces, but whenever she became overwhelmed, she sought out Lucas, and he calmed her with merely a glance.

Food and drink abounded. They toasted with the traditional *pisco*, but she did not partake of more than a sip. Their guests enjoyed the cases of beer and the *chicha morada*, a sweet, fruity punch made from purple corn.

Because there had not been time to instruct Lucas in the native dances, she asked *Mamá* and *Papá* to exclude them from that portion of the fiesta. In truth, the thought of dancing publicly again after where it had led to with Pedro and his accomplices almost made her sick.

Do not think about them now.

Lucas must be overwhelmed by how different this wedding was compared to his first one with Maggie, although he embraced each thing that came along. The monetary gift-giving ceremony made him a bit uncomfortable, but they could use the money for their animals or anything they wished. They did not live extravagantly at all.

Hours later, the crowd began to thin out, and Cassie thought it time to prepare to bring the reception to a close. "I am going to the ladies' room. Then we can go back to my parents' house."

He kissed her. "Hurry. I'm ready for bed. I'm looking forward to holding my bride in my arms all night long."

To have and to hold.

"I look forward to that, as well."

She walked down the long hallway to the restroom, her thoughts lost in what would transpire tonight while she and Lucas were in bed together.

A hand closed over her mouth, stifling her scream while a strong arm clamped around her waist. The familiar voice spoke into her ear in Spanish as his hand groped her breast.

"No screaming, *puta*. We leave now."

Diego?

She had expected Pedro to show his face, but not this man who was not even from her village. She fought against him, but her jabs and kicks were unsuccessful at hitting any vulnerable areas. Remembering her training, she let herself go limp and managed to duck from his grasp and run for the back door. She would go around to the front of the reception hall and get help, but her first thought was escaping the man who stood between her and Lucas at the moment.

A blast of cold air hit her in the face when she opened the door, temporarily blinding her. When she bolted outside, she ran into another man.

"Finally in my arms again, my betrothed."

Pedro. Before she could react, he had her in his arms, her back to his chest. Something glinted in the moonlight—a deadly-looking knife—that he placed next to the skin of her neck. Some of the beads from her chin-strap pinged to the ground as he cut through one of the strands.

"Make a sound, *puta*, and your blood will be the next thing spilling to the ground." She found herself facing Diego again. Even in the dim lighting of the alley, his black eyes bore into her soul.

Her heart hammered as bile rose in her throat. *No!* If she let them take her away from here, she would be raped again and probably would not be allowed to walk away this time. Sweat broke out on her forehead. The frigid air pierced her dampened skin as Diego came forward and squeezed the joint of her jaw until her mouth opened and he stuffed a smelly cloth inside.

Why had she not screamed when she could have? Who would come looking for her and how soon? Lucas, for certain, but he might not begin to worry for many minutes. She needed to find a way to let him know where they had taken her.

But how? The last time he had tracked her, he had Picasso. Would he be able to find her on his own?

*   *   *

Luke had asked her Aunt Sofia to check on Cassie in the ladies' room when she hadn't returned after almost ten minutes. Was she sick from the food or drink? No, she hadn't had more than that potent *pisco* toast and barely sipped that.

Worrying that something more sinister might be wrong, he had entered the hallway to the bathroom himself when Cassie's aunt came out of the bathroom clutching her hand to her chest.

"*¡Ella no está!*"

What did she mean 'she's gone'? Luke ran for the nearby exit, calling over his shoulder, "Call the police!"

Pedro, you fucking touch her, and I'll kill you with my bare hands.

How could he have let down his guard when the possibility this snake would slither into her life again was so high? He should have been standing guard outside the bathroom.

In the alleyway, he looked up and down, but saw no movement.

Sonuvabitch.

When he pivoted around to go inside to retrieve Eduardo and other men who knew this place and could aid in his search for her, his boot skidded on something. He looked down to find more than a dozen pearl-like beads—just like the ones on Cassie's hat strap.

The door opened, and Eduardo ran out. "Where is she?"

"No clue. She could have been gone for as long as ten minutes already." Luke continued to scrutinize the beads and noticed they didn't just litter the ground here, where they indicated a struggle, but the moonlight captured a trail of them. "Look! She's left us a trail to follow." Which meant she was still alive.

Luke set off down the alley.

"Where are you going?"

Luke didn't bother to glance back at her brother. "I'm going to find my wife."

Eduardo caught up and cast a beam from a small LED flashlight that helped them illuminate the darker areas and continue to follow the trail. On the street, the beads veered away from her parents' house.

Luke saw scuff marks halfway down the street, near another alley. "There are at least two of them." There had been a struggle. Had she been hurt? He didn't see any blood, but the thought of their hands on her...

How could they have taken her from under his nose? He should have protected her.

Focus. Kick yourself later, but right now, you need to find her.

Clearly, they hadn't gotten into an automobile so most likely she was still in the village. He picked up the pace, moving as fast as he could without missing clues to her whereabouts. He hoped they didn't catch on that she was leaving a trail of beads.

Inside the narrower alley, the trail ended abruptly. Eduardo shined the light on a red object near the entrance to an animal shed.

Cassie's hat. His heart hammered in earnest. Further signs of a struggle. Looking around, Luke recognized the shed from their walk the morning she agreed to marry him again. He pointed it out, down the darkened alley. "Cassie used to play with alpacas in there."

"Pedro did, too. At least I found him there with her sometimes when I came to walk her home."

Pedro had been part of her childhood? His betrayal and attack had to have been even harder if they had been friends. Luke had just assumed it had been an arranged marriage to someone she didn't really know.

"Fucking asshole."

Eduardo stared at Luke. "You are certain Pedro is the one who took her?"

Enough family secrets. This man needed to know the stakes here. "Pedro and two of his friends raped Cassie that night she went out." His voice shook with emotion. "This time, they may not want to leave a witness."

The man turned off the flashlight, hiding any emotion he might be feeling. His breathing became labored.

"Look, Eduardo, keep your head on straight. I'm only telling you this because we aren't going to let them hurt her again. She needs us."

The agitated clicking of the alpacas inside increased when he heard a muffled scream. *Cassie!* He ground his teeth, approaching the shed with as much stealth as possible. Another scream and Eduardo charged forward, but Luke stopped him.

"We need a plan of attack, or we're going to get her killed."

At least she was still alive. The thought of those bastards touching her made him sick. Under his breath, he whispered, "I'm coming for you, darlin'. Be strong for me." Of course, she couldn't hear him. Luke's hands shook as he crept slowly toward the shed. They needed to assess the situation before going in guns blazing—man, he wished he had his revolver. Upon further inspection, he found a slit in the boards. The scene before him revealed Cassie being held against one man who had a knife to her throat. Another groped her breast, knowing she wouldn't move for fear of having her throat cut. A third man moved two alpacas out of one stall into another as if readying a place to…

Get your fucking hands off my wife.

How could he rescue her when her life was hanging in the balance with that knife? One wrong move and she would bleed out.

The man holding Cassie whispered something in her ear. The terror in her eyes curled his stomach, but also gave Luke the resolve to put an end to her suffering. They couldn't wait for the police to show up. He had no clue how fast the authorities moved down here. Cassie didn't have time on her side.

He turned to Eduardo and whispered, "Is there any other entrance?"

"Not that I remember."

Luke remembered the ptarmigan whose birdcall Cassie had found so fascinating last week up at her cabin. Seemed like forever ago. Surely they didn't have them here. If she heard that sound, would it give her the comfort to know he was here so she could be ready to move when they burst inside? Might as well try.

"Sweet-sweet!" He made the sound a few times then looked inside again. The men hadn't noticed, but he saw Cassie scanning the door, hope in her eyes.

He stepped away and, in a whisper, informed Eduardo what the situation was and their plan of attack. "One has her at knifepoint. He's mine. You take the one standing in front of her. When we go in there, we need to surprise and distract them. We only have a second or two before they'll react. I'll give a rebel yell—"

"A what?"

Eduardo hadn't grown up in the American South. "Just listen and charge toward her when you hear it." Luke prepared, trying to take a deep breath and regain control of his shaking body. Rage gave him the courage to go in there. He just hoped Cassie didn't get hurt.

Remember your self-defense training, Sweet Pea.

He just needed to give her enough warning to twist away so he could take the man down. God, he hoped he could neutralize the arm with the knife quickly.

And if you even nick her pinky, I'll use that knife to cut off your goddamned dicks.

*   *   *

Diego's hand squeezed her breast harder. Bile choked the back of her throat. Was this real or another visualization with Abigail? She had been enjoying the celebration of life and love with Lucas and her family only moments ago, hadn't she? This could not be happening. Not again.

Then the blade of the knife touched her throat. Without any choice, she moved closer to Pedro, who laughed at her fear.

"*Mi chica* will not whore herself with that *gringo* on her wedding night. We will remind you what a real man feels like, Casandra."

Escape!

Cassie kicked behind her at his shins and elbowed him, but the other two soon overpowered her and the back of her head smashed into the beer-soaked felt on the pool table. Hands pulled at her skirt and blouse. The sound of a knife cutting through the material made her stop fighting, afraid she would be cut as well.

"*Don't stop fighting, puta," Diego ground out. "We like it better when our girls give us a challenge."*

"*I am not one of your girls. Let me go now or my brother will make you regret the day you were born."*

Cassie blinked. Had she just kicked at Pedro? There was no pool table here. The past and present became jumbled in her mind. *I must escape!* But how? Pedro had not loosened his hold on her since he grabbed her in the alley behind the church. She had run out of beads before they reached their destination. Had there been enough dropped for Lucas to find her? If he did not see the trail of beads, he might not realize she was in danger. Would he go to her parents' home looking for her, losing precious time?

Please, Lucas! Help me!

All three of her rapists had come back for more, with Luis waiting for them here at the shed. These men had robbed her of five years of her life, taken away her power, her family, her freedom. She was finally beginning to regain her ability to trust. She would not let them control her in that way again.

Not only were they traumatizing her, but the bewildered alpacas, too.

She despised these men for making her fearful again. She had used the imagery from the therapist's office to escape from Diego, but Pedro thwarted her escape.

She would not give up and let them do what they had done before. Lucas would be looking for her. Surely, he had seen her beads.

Lucas, I need you!

These men would not cheat her from being Lucas's wife. She loved him more than any man she had ever known. No other man had so much confidence in her. If he trusted her enough to marry her twice, she wanted to spend the rest of her life showing him how much she loved him. No one would rob her of that chance.

Especially not these three bastards.

"Hurry, Luis! We don't have all night. And I go first again. I am the one cheated out of his wedding night with this one."

Diego whispered in her ear, "I cannot wait to bury myself deep inside you again when it is my turn, *puta*."

Pedro brandished the knife at Diego, ramping up the dread that she would be cut as they fought over who would rape her first. *Do not give him the satisfaction of seeing your fear.*

Diego had been the most sadistic of the three. She would die before giving him control over her body again. But could she take him down with her if he tried to rape her this time?

If she could only succeed in hurting one, it would be Diego. He should never be allowed to hurt or terrorize another girl.

Tears of frustration burned her eyelids. She might never experience the intimacy Lucas had promised. She had wasted so much time running in fear of his touch these past weeks, no months. Now when she was finally ready to be held in his arms, sit in his lap, spoon against him in bed, the opportunity might never come.

She could knee Diego in the groin, but with the knife at her throat what chance would she have of escape? Pedro yelled at Luis again to hurry. A ptarmigan called softly outside, transporting her back to her mountain. With Lucas.

Sweet-sweet.

I want to go home. Please, Lucas, take me to our home.

If only... Diego pinched her nipple and twisted it viciously, causing her to scream against her gag. "Let me hear you scream, *puta*." He removed the gag, and she stretched her jaw back and forth to relieve the pain in her joints. Desperation rising, Cassie scanned the shed again for a weapon.

Wait! Ptarmigans were not native to Peru.

Lucas had found her!

Diego lowered his hand from her breast to his belt and began loosening it. "Remove my pants, *puta*."

When Pedro lowered the knife to permit her to follow Diego's command, he began to take off his pants as well. Knowing Lucas was near, she drew courage and opened his fly, hoping to have Diego's pants around his knees before Lucas made his move.

"I see you have missed me." The words made her sick, but she needed to distract them.

Hurry, Lucas.

Cassie raised her gaze to meet Diego's and forced a smile to her lips. "I have waited a long time for this moment." In his cockiness, let him think she truly meant those words. When he licked his already wet lips, she knew she had succeeded.

Swallowing the vomit rising into the back of her throat at his putrid stench, she pulled his jeans down leaving his boxers in place.

Stay in the moment. Lucas is near.

She prayed to *Mama Quilla* to protect Lucas from injury in the imminent struggle.

Now, Lucas!

Perhaps a verbal cue would help. "I am ready." She hoped Lucas knew she spoke the words to him, not Diego.

The door to the shed burst open, and a blood-curdling scream rent the air. Lucas? As chaos broke loose, she rammed her head into Diego's groin pushing him backward. He fell, sprawled out on a bed of filthy straw. Lucas ran past her in a blur, and she heard Pedro groan. When the knife clattered to the ground, she dove for it. Diego came to his feet, his hands fisted. She had to incapacitate him so he could not attack her or Lucas. She thrust upward with the knife and plunged it into his groin. Blood spurted between her hands, and a look of horror spread across Diego's face.

Strong arms wrapped around her and pulled her up and away. She raised the bloodied knife again to fend off this new attack.

"Whoa, darlin'. It's me." She collapsed against Lucas in relief. "Stay over there while we take care of the other two."

We? Lucas started to guide her toward a corner, but when she turned around, she saw Pedro approaching behind them.

"Lucas, watch out!"

Her husband shoved her out of harm's way as Pedro plowed toward Lucas's abdomen. Everything happened in a blur. Lucas managed to spin and avoid being tackled. Grunts in the far stall made her wonder who else had come to her rescue.

Shouts of her name from outside the shed distracted her from watching Lucas pummel Pedro's face. Her gentle husband was anything but gentle as he continued to beat Pedro long after the man was unconscious. She reached out to stop him from killing the man when movement in the back set her on alert. Eduardo stood, breathing heavily. He must have subdued Luis. The fury on his face frightened her until she reminded herself it was not directed at her.

Cassie glanced at Diego still writhing on the floor, covered in blood. The amount of blood loss told her he had been severely injured.

"Casandra!"

Papá?

She turned to the doorway to see her once frail father charge into the room ready to do battle. "No, *Papá!* You will be hurt!"

The shed filled with men from the wedding. Some held makeshift weapons, ready to protect and defend her from these monsters.

Eduardo pulled Lucas away. The way Pedro's jaw flopped, he had to have broken the man's jaw. The man who had caused her so much pain also bled profusely from a broken nose.

Her father walked over to them and kicked Pedro repeatedly in the side until Eduardo pulled him back. "*Papá*, he is not worth the energy. Be careful, or you will be hurt."

In Spanish, *Papá* said, "He hurt my little girl. He should not be allowed to live."

Tears stung her eyes. Whether he meant today's kidnapping or that he now understood what had happened in the past, he had come to her rescue.

And her brother and husband had risked their lives to save her. These three honorable men who loved her most all deemed her worthy of fighting for. They filled her with a sense of being honored, loved, and cherished.

Breathing hard, Lucas walked toward her, and she reached up to take his hand. He winced, and she let go. "Your hands!" His knuckles had to be raw from the force he had used on Pedro. She scrambled to her feet and inspected them. Red across the knuckles. "Flex your fingers." He did. Nothing seemed broken, as far as she could tell. "Oh, Lucas." She wrapped her arms around him and pulled him tightly against her.

"Are you okay, Baby? Did they…"

"No!" She did not wish to hear the word ever again. "You found me in time." When he hugged her back, everyone else ceased to exist. She trembled in his arms, partly from an adrenaline crash but more from relief. Safe. *Lucas loves me.*

And I love him.

"Shhh. I have you, darlin'. It's all over."

When her knees buckled, he scooped her into his arms, and she laid her head against his shoulder. Hearing a commotion, she pulled away long enough to watch as her attackers were dragged from the shed to the alley. Judging from the angry shouts and pain-filled groans, a few more landed kicks or punches on the monsters who had tried to violate her again. The neighborhood watch authorities did not seem interested in stopping the retribution of other husbands, brothers, and fathers wanting to keep their village safe for the women who lived here. Tears streamed down her face.

"I'm so proud of you, Sweet Pea."

A sob tore from her throat. "I was so frightened. I thought they were going to…"

"Shhh. We'll make sure that this time justice is served for what they have done."

She remembered her *montera* and saw it in *Papá's* gnarled hands. "You followed my trail."

"Smart thinking. The white beads were easy to see even at night."

She had taken so many classes and watched films to help her learn to escape, but might not have kept her wits about her if she had not just gone through the visualization with Abigail. Finally, she truly was free of these men forever. They would rot in prison; enough people from the village would testify against them.

"When I heard the call of the ptarmigan, I knew you were near. That gave me courage to put into motion what I would need to do in order to escape." She loosened her arms and glanced up at Lucas. Not even a scratch on his face.

"We should have worked out a plan for the chance that snake would come near you."

"Stop, Lucas! It is over. They could not beat us. We were smarter and stronger than they were."

"What you did to the one who had his hands all over you—"

"Diego."

"Yeah, well, remind me never to get on your bad side, Sweet Pea."

She playfully punched his chest. "Lucas, how could you even think I could ever hurt you? You would never do the despicable things that man has done to incur my wrath."

His chin rested on the top of her head. "I'll always try to watch over you, Sweet Pea. No one will ever hurt you if I can do anything to stop them."

"I trust you with my life, Lucas. And if anyone ever threatens you, I will fight just as hard to protect you. We are one now. No one can ever separate us."

"Want to try standing again?" She nodded, and he set her down. Already, she was regaining her strength from the ordeal. He tilted her face toward his as he lowered his mouth in a tender kiss that ended way too soon. "Come on, baby girl. I want to take my bride to bed." He held her hand, and they started toward the door.

His words sent a spark of longing through her, but as much as she thought herself ready to explore a physical relationship with him, she was in no condition to do more than cuddle tonight. The desire for his touch continued to build, but—

He shook his head. "Cassie, I can tell by the grip on my hand that mind of yours is going a mile a minute. I'm not going to jump your bones, darlin'. You've been through hell tonight. We're just going to hold each other close, start building that foundation of intimacy we've been talking about, and add a few more layers of trust. When we both decide the time is right for more, it's going to be in our own house away from my in-laws and an audience." He grinned, and her heart melted.

How she loved this man and stopped to turn toward him. "*Te quiero*, Luke." Were there tears in his eyes? Did he understand her words of love?

"You don't know how long I've wanted to hear you say that."

He did? How much of her Spanish conversations had he understood? Not that she cared. She needed to express her love in her native language this time. The language of her heart. "I think I knew my heart was yours during our wedding ceremony, but when I thought I might die without telling you so, well, I have learned not to hold back on expressing my feelings toward you ever again."

His eyes opened wide. "Hey, did you also just call me Luke?"

She smiled. "The first step toward intimacy is for me to stop distancing myself from you. You risked your life to protect me. The least I can do is call you by your preferred nickname." He grinned and wrapped his arm around her waist before guiding her toward the doorway.

Chapter Twenty-Eight

C assie shivered, but not from the cold in this bathroom. The roller-coaster events of the day had taken their toll. Now she prepared herself for her wedding night with Lucas… No, with *Luke*. While in some ways, her nerves made her want to avoid going to bed, she also craved Luke's gentle touch to help calm her body and mind. She no longer wished to shield her heart from him.

When they had returned home over an hour ago, *Mamá* took charge, and both of them were ushered into her meditation room. Her mother invoked the spirit of *Pachamama*, mother of *Mama Quilla* and, indeed, the World Mother, to cleanse Cassie and her new husband. Cassie heard references to bringing them good luck and fertility, but chose not to interpret the incantations for Luke. It was best not to get his hopes up in case she was unable to perform her duties as his wife.

But Luke had risked his life to rescue her. She would never give her body as a means of repayment, but her gratitude to him left her feeling selfish not to honor him in this way. Her hand shook as she brushed her wet hair. These past few months, he had shown her in so many ways what a kind, gentle, patient man he was. He did not invade her space. Did not take advantage of her in vulnerable moments. He remained positive, supportive, and protective no matter what.

She blinked away the tears that had been on the surface since she had returned to her parents' home. Plucking a tissue from the dispenser, she dabbed at her eyes and surveyed the damage in the bathroom mirror. Red and puffy. How alluring. Perhaps Luke would not even want to touch her tonight.

Cassie sighed and switched off the light as she opened the door. Luke was waiting for her. She couldn't hide in here forever. How far would she be able to allow him to go tonight? The memories of her rape remained too vivid after being mauled by those men again.

Cassie took a deep breath and held her head high as she walked down the hallway to her bedroom. *Their* bedroom.

She opened the door and saw Luke stretched out in bed, a book in his hand. He had showered earlier, and his hair was still damp against his neck. She couldn't tell which book he read, but loved that he enjoyed reading in bed, too. That was something they could do together when they returned home. Seeing him lying there, seemingly not anxious to do anything of a sexual nature, despite the fact this was their wedding night, also eased her stress.

She shed her robe and draped it over the footboard before she darted under the coverlet. She would keep her nightgown firmly in place. "Good night, Luke. Thank you again for everything today."

"How are you feeling, darlin'?" He set the book aside and reached out to stroke her cheek. "I'm worried about you after what happened tonight."

Oh, Luke. Always so in tune with her.

"I am better. The wedding was so beautiful. I am trying to focus on that, not what happened after."

His hand traced a path down her arm. His caress was light and comforting, but was he claiming what was his? Gooseflesh rose on her arm under her sleeve. Her heart pounded, robbing her of breath. She could not relax. She felt…

Anything but fear. Nothing in Luke's demeanor frightened her. She trusted him to cherish her and do no harm.

"I like how you are touching me, Luke." She should at least give him feedback on what she did enjoy. Perhaps having her clothing on made it feel safer.

His hand stilled momentarily, before resuming its exploration back up her arm and across her shoulder and collarbone. "You don't know how much I like touching you. You sure smell pretty tonight."

She grinned. "*Mamá's* angel trumpet soap."

"No, it's the essence of Cassie." He bent toward her to brush his lips against her temple. "I love you, Sweet Pea."

"I love you, too, Luke." Each time she said the words, they became easier. But fears of disappointing him if she could not show that love physically left her worried. "What if I cannot—"

His fingers against her lips silenced her. "We've spoken our vows.

Those are the only promises I needed to hear. We're going to take this relationship slowly—one moment at a time. If I go too fast, remember your safeword."

She giggled. "Pickle?"

"Well, you can choose any word you want, as long as you tell me ahead of time. That one was just to break the ice and lighten the mood."

She smiled, imagining she would need that every time they embarked on an intimacy session. "Pickle will be fine." She met his gaze, seeing the love shining in the reading light from the headboard. "You make me feel so special."

Cherished.

Honored.

Loved.

"You're the most special person in the world to me, darlin'."

She nibbled on her lower lip, unsure if she should say it. But he asked for honesty. "What if I cannot respond?"

"Let's stop worrying and just see where this goes."

"Will you be touching my private areas?"

Luke chuckled. "We'll start slowly. Arms, head and neck, legs—thighs and *below*."

"I can do that." If he stayed away from her breasts or more sexual places, what harm could be done? Cassie nodded.

"Think of this as being two teenagers exploring each other's bodies for the first time. No sex. Just touch."

The tip of his finger traced an imaginary line down her right arm and then moved slowly up again. She shivered, surprised at the catch in her breath. He had only stroked her arm, so why was she feeling so—

Her nipples peaked, and Cassie moved quickly to hide her chest from his gaze. Her cheeks flamed with embarrassment.

"Darlin', when a wife responds to the touch of her husband, it's never bad or dirty. It's just damned hot. Lower your arms. I want to see the effect my hands have on you."

Breathe, Cassie.

She lowered her arms to her sides and let him continue to caress her. Surprisingly, her body responded to his touch. He had turned her from someone totally shut down to someone who wanted…

Wanted…

More.

Her legs trembled, and suddenly nervous about being a disappointment to him, Cassie curled over on her side, away from Luke, hoping he would stop igniting her body.

Undeterred, he kept stroking her arm. Up and down in slow, tantalizing strokes. He lifted her hair, and his lips pressed against the nape of her neck above the collar of her gown. She shivered, goose bumps breaking out on her arms. She clamped her legs more tightly together. He had not come close to the area, but the juncture between her legs tingled as though he had.

Luke molded his hard body against hers. His erection pressed against her bottom, and she moved away.

"I do not think I can do this!" How could she be afraid of letting go the way he wanted her to?

His firm hand on her upper arm halted her escape. "Shhh. You don't have to do anything. I'm just going to hold you. Touch you. Just the way we agreed."

Had she agreed to respond like this? She could not remember, but having limited him to arms, legs, and non-sexual places, she had not expected his touch to be so…powerful.

Or feel so…right.

His hand moved to hers, and his thumb made featherlike circles on the inside of her wrist, sending jolts of electricity throughout her body. How could the brush of fingertips over her wrist be so…erotic? Places she had not acknowledged existing for years also sparked to life.

Cassie leaned back against him, giving Luke better access to her arm, her wrist, but Luke pulled away and knelt on the bed. Before she could guess what he had planned, he pushed the coverlet down, exposing her body. Why did she feel so naked when she was covered from neck to ankles? Without a word of explanation or warning, he crawled down the bed to her knees.

"Lie on your stomach."

She hesitated a moment, but her back felt less vulnerable than her front so she soon complied, resting her face on the pillow, turning away so he could not see her response. The material of her gown skimmed along her calves, baring them to his gaze. The exposed skin burned as if touched by his hand, but only the cloth had made contact with it.

When her knees were bare, he stopped moving the garment and she relaxed again—until he kissed the back of her left knee. Cassie jerked her knee away. "What are you doing?"

He chuckled. "Kissing my wife's body—so I can make her jump like that."

"Why would you want me to jerk away like that?"

His fingertip traced a circle on the back of the knee where he had kissed her, and gooseflesh rose there, as well. "Because having you respond to me is just about the sexiest thing I can imagine at the moment."

Sexy? "I am *not* sexy." The breathy tone in her voice made it sound as if it had come from someone else entirely. She wore a nightgown covering most of her body and yet his words made her feel desired, sensual, sexual.

Breathe, Cassie.

Luke's strokes grew firmer as he massaged her calves, moving lower. His hands eased away the tension in her left one first, then the right. Who knew she held tension in her legs? He moved lower to her foot. Bending her leg, he drew her foot closer to him, and his thumbs massaged the ball of her left foot.

"Mmmmm."

Had she just moaned? The involuntary sound hung in the air.

*   *   *

"Ticklish, darlin'?"

"I do not think so."

We're fixin' to find out.

He brushed his lips along her instep, and she jerked her leg away. Luke tamped down the urge to chuckle. So damned responsive. Wanting his kiss to linger, he moved to her right foot and massaged her instep with his thumbs. When he placed a kiss on this one, she jerked a little but quickly relaxed into his hands.

Man, he loved her dainty feet.

"Good girl." Her control of her responses told him she would have good discipline if they ever tried anything kinky. His cock stirred as he thought about restraining her with rope.

Slow down, Denton. You have a lot of ground to cover first.

Such a delicate foot. Yeah, he did have a thing for her feet. He grinned.

You're a goner, man.

They had the rest of their lives to explore each other's bodies, too. Although they'd been legally married for two months, he didn't think she considered herself truly married until today. This was the first time she'd surrendered herself to his ministrations.

The exhaustion from tonight's events ebbed away when he looked up a little while ago to see her standing in the doorway, her curves silhouetted by the hallway light. They wouldn't be sleeping much tonight.

Her level of trust had ramped up, too, during this trip. Maybe with the threat of those bastards behind her, some lasting healing could start. He flexed his hand. He never thought himself capable of killing another living thing, but tonight he would have killed Pedro—and the others, too, if need be.

When he pressed his thumbs into the ball of this foot, she moaned again.

That's my girl.

Emboldened, he laid her foot down and raked his fingers past her ankles and over her calves. Goose bumps sprang up. Her tiny gasp told him he'd surprised her. Well, he planned to spend the rest of his life bringing surprises like that into Cassie's life.

He kneaded her calves again on the way back up, but she was much less tense now. He spent a good fifteen minutes on one before doing the same with the other. Realizing he hadn't heard anything from her in a while, he glanced up. Her eyes were closed.

"Cassie? You doing okay, darlin'?"

No response. He placed one hand on either side of her body and leaned over her. Her chest rose and fell with her shallow, rhythmic breaths. *Asleep?* Was she kidding?

Luke sat back on his heels and shook his head before a wide grin spread across his face. That his bride trusted him enough to fall asleep while he touched her body spoke volumes. He stretched out on the bed beside her, lying on his back as he stared at the ceiling. It was going to be another long, frustrating night.

Oh, what the hell? He rolled onto his side and pulled Cassie toward him, half expecting her to wake up and acknowledge his presence. Instead, she sighed and the corners of her mouth curled slightly.

He bent down and placed a kiss on her lips before reaching for the covers. Tonight, he would have Cassie in his arms. Nothing else mattered but holding her as close to his body as he could. So he did.

"Goodnight, sweet bride of mine."

*   *   *

Cassie dreamt she was cocooned like a butterfly sprite and then emerged into the light of a new day, her wings fluttering as she tested them for the first time. The steady beat of a drum encouraged her to break free of the bonds of earth and fly.

Free.

As the fog of sleep lifted, she found her cheek resting against Luke's chest. Their legs were entangled in a suggestive way, and her gown had ridden high on her thighs. She pulled away to adjust it, but Luke protested in his sleep and tightened his arm around her body, holding her closer.

An instant of panic melted away as she reminded herself this was her husband. *I trust him.* Luke had never done anything to take advantage of that trust. Rather than returning to her cocoon, she decided to relish the euphoria she had experienced in the dream.

Had she finally broken free of the past? Reclaimed her power?

Goddess, please make it so.

Cassie was abundantly tired of having to be on guard every moment of the day. Five years of living that way had exhausted her and turned her into a person even she did not want to spend time with. Why had Luke put up with her months of constantly pushing him away and distancing herself from him?

Such a patient man.

He must see something in her that he wanted, unless he was merely the type of person always rescuing the lost. Luke's empathy for wounded creatures whose spirits had been shattered was one of the first things that endeared him to her. She had seen it in how he treated his horses. Even the dog and puppies they found at the cabin. She couldn't wait to check on them when they returned home.

But she had also experienced it in the way he nurtured and cared for her.

Last night, his touch had been so innocent, and yet her mind and body twisted it into something carnal. Parts of her body she did not know existed throbbed, ached for his touch. Even now, hours later. She wanted a man's touch for the first time since…

Don't think of that time. Live in the moment.

Wanting to show she was ready to try harder to do just that, her hand brushed across Luke's T-shirt. His muscular chest—honed by hard work rather than barbells in a weight room—might be hard as steel, but her subconscious had led her to use it as her pillow while she slept.

Raising herself onto her elbow, she traced her fingertip down the center of his chest, avoiding his pecs and nipples. She paused just above his navel and retraced her path. Above his heart, the steady beat made her realize this had been the drumbeat heard in her dream.

Solid, strong, steady.

Luke.

How long had she slept with her ear over his beating heart? She leaned over and placed a kiss on the spot, feeling the beat reverberate against her tingling lips.

"Mornin', darlin'."

She pulled away and stared into Luke's sleepy eyes. Is this what was meant by bedroom eyes? Her heart fluttered as the smoke returned to his smoky-gray eyes. "How long have you been awake?"

He grinned. "Long enough. Don't stop on my account."

She drew her hand away from him. "I...I think I was finished."

"You sure?"

She was not sure of anything anymore.

"I think so."

"Well, ain't that a shame?"

"I am sor—"

His fingers pressed over her lips, cutting off her apology. "Don't apologize for everything all the time, or I'll take you over my knee." Her eyes widened, and she started to pull away until he grinned and she realized he must be teasing her again.

He moved his hand up to brush a strand of her hair away from her cheek. "You allowed me to touch you last night. Waking up to find you touching me, well, do you have any idea how incredibly happy that makes me feel?" He did not wait for a response. "But I don't want to hear you ever regret anything that happens between us."

"I am—" She almost did it again, but caught herself. "I am going to work on it."

"Good girl. And for future reference, the best way to wake me up that

I can think of—well, at this point in our relationship—is with a kiss wherever you want to leave one." He framed her face and leaned toward her to place three chaste kisses on her mouth. When he released his hold on her, she retreated to a more comfortable distance, bringing her fingers to her tingling lips. Her heart pounded, but she knew this to be the result of arousal, not fear.

"We're just going to keep taking baby steps." He touched the tip of her nose and grinned. "This is going to be a nice, leisurely trail ride, darlin', not the Kentucky Derby. We have the rest of our lives to wake up in each other's arms, to explore what each of us enjoys, to deepen our relationship in ways we can't even imagine right now."

Her heart swelled at his words. How had she found a man so...? She kept coming back to the word "patient." That he was joyful about every little crumb she meted out, even though he had to be incredibly frustrated, enchanted her even more.

Cassie leaned over and placed a lingering kiss on his lips, breathless when she put some distance between them again. "Thank you, Luke. Now I think we should go see what our last day in my homeland holds for us."

*   *   *

When they ventured out of the bedroom, Cassie was surprised to find the house filled with children's voices and the smells of wonderful foods wafting through the front room. How long had she and Luke been in bed?

She started toward the kitchen when Luke steered her toward the living room. Perhaps he wanted to visit with Eduardo's children first. Cassie came to a standstill when she saw the portrait she had given her parents at last night's reception hanging over their mantle.

"Your dad asked me to help him hang it last night while you were in the bathroom. He is proud of his daughter's talent and wants to be sure every visitor to his home sees it."

She blinked back the tears. Would they never stop? "Thank you."

"*Tía* Casandra, why do you cry?" Eduardo had instructed his oldest son to speak English around Luke as a show of hospitality.

"Lalo, it is because I am so very happy." He shook his head and went back to playing a game with the others.

Luke took her hand. "Now, I need coffee, and you need breakfast." They entered the kitchen where *Mamá* set down the soup ladle and crossed the room to give them both hugs. After pouring two mugs of strong, black coffee, they decided to share a seat at the opposite end from where Susana nursed Quenti so *Mamá* could sit when ready. No one seemed to want to move to the larger dining room table. The kitchen was cozy.

Quenti must have been feeding for a while because now he only sporadically chomped on Susana's nipple to squeeze out a little more. Cassie smiled, thinking of Kitty and her three babies all demanding her milk at the same time. Well, only two could suckle at their *mamá's* breasts at a time, but she pumped in between to always have some on hand.

Cassie looked up to see Luke wearing a sappy smile, and although he was not looking at Susana and Quenti, she just knew that was why. Susana had not covered herself in front of him as American women might. But he didn't seem embarrassed or horrified at the natural sight, either.

What would it be like…

Don't think about a baby, Cassie.

Only baby *steps*, as Luke had said.

Like sitting on Luke's lap now. She found herself wanting to touch him, be held by him, just be closer together physically. Intimacy. He played with her hair and rubbed her back, innocent touches that just melted more of the ice away from her heart.

Eduardo entered the room and placed a kiss first on Susana's smiling upturned face and then on the crown of her newest nephew's head. Only then did he look across the room at Luke and Cassie.

"How are you two doing this morning?"

Eduardo relaxed visibly when she smiled at him. "Wonderful. I hope you are not suffering any ill effects from the excitement last night."

"I would do it all again to protect my family." Cassie noticed bandages on his knuckles, but when asked, he assured her Susana was just overreacting.

Luke had refused to let her treat his hands, but now she wished she had insisted, too. She met his gaze. "Next time, you will listen to me and let me take care of you, too."

"Yes, ma'am." He grinned, and she was not sure if he was serious or not. She hoped there would be no next time. The thought of seeing him or Eduardo hurt again made her ill.

"Lucas, you showed me last night I have nothing to worry about with you watching over my little sister."

"You did not seem so worried when you let me marry him in May. When were you going to tell me you were worried about him?"

Eduardo smiled. "I did not worry he would hurt you. Just that he might be too…gentle to be able to stand up against a threat." Funny, but Eduardo's fighting had surprised her more so than Luke's. While a nonviolent man, Luke had a protective streak as tall as the mountain peaks outside her home.

"You first encountered Luke at a time when he was physically healing." She smiled up at her husband. "But he played American football in college. I never doubted he would be able to tackle someone who threatened me."

He kissed her on the bridge of her nose. "Thanks, but I'm afraid I played quarterback, Sweet Pea. My job was to call the plays, throw passes, run the ball—basically take the lead on offense. The defensive-line guys were bigger. They did all the tackling."

Eduardo said, "Well, you called the play last night to perfection. Even found a way to alert Cassie to prepare for our barging in to rescue her. Pretty impressive, if you want my opinion."

Luke's eyes narrowed. "Cassie deserves some credit, too. She might have had her own playbook, but if not for her quick thinking, she could've been seriously injured."

Cassie shuddered, remembering Pedro's knife at her throat. "Let us speak about something more pleasant on this morning after my wedding." She turned to *Mamá*. "How is *Papá*? He landed a few blows himself."

Mamá grinned, pride in her man evident. "A little stiff, but he insisted on going with Eduardo to talk with the authorities."

"Pedro and Luis, the bastards, will rot in jail." Cassie glanced up to see *Papá* in the doorway. Until *Mamá* spoke, she had assumed he was still in bed recovering from the ordeal. "Diego will join them, *if* he survives his wounds. Already another woman has come forward to file charges against them. I am sure if they show their faces on Lima news reports, others will as well."

That any other woman had suffered at the hands of these monsters broke Cassie's heart. Slipping off Luke's lap, Cassie reached for her husband's hand, but he was already rising to give up their seat for *Papá*. "Here. Sit."

Watching how gingerly he walked, Cassie's heart broke. She met him halfway and let him lean on her arm. Despite his stiffness, though, a spark of renewed life and purpose stirred within his spirit today.

She had been estranged from him for so many years without being able to tell him why. Last night, after they had returned home, she was able to share with her family for the first time what Pedro and his friends had done to her. Having told Kitty, then Luke, made it easier to repeat the words, as did knowing the attackers no longer held any power over her.

Seeing *Papá* kicking Pedro in the kidneys showed her that, in his own way, he had come after her and defended her, despite his age and weakened state.

Once settled into the seat, he continued to hold onto her hand. When his cloudy green eyes met hers, she detected a shimmer of tears. "I am sorry, *mi hija*, to have promised you to a *bastardo* like Pedro. He…"

Tears shimmered in her eyes, too, as she bent to kiss him and hug his neck. Luke's hand rested on the small of her back. "Pedro is a monster, *Papá*. He hid his evilness from everyone, even me. Do not blame yourself. I do not blame you." She truly had forgiven her father already, knowing in her heart that he could not have known what Pedro was really like. Now she also knew that *Papá* and Eduardo would have defended her back then, if only she had told them. Pedro's privileged upbringing had made him into a coldhearted beast.

Papá turned to Luke, who leaned against the sink. "Casandra, you have chosen a better man than any I would have found for you here in Peru."

"Thank you, sir. I sure am glad she found me, too."

Cassie did not think he meant finding him in the snow after the avalanche, either. She grinned at him and went to his side, welcoming his arms around her, holding her tight.

Papá broke into their moment. "Thank you for returning home so that I could see you once more, Casandra."

She cast her gaze on her *papá*. She hoped this would not be the last time she would see him.

"Actually, sir, we're thinking about returning at Christmas. I want to see this place where my wife grew up when it's not so darned cold."

Everyone laughed, and she saw a light in *Papá*'s eyes at the thought she would be back in barely five months.

Luke turned to her. "I want my own private tour of Machu Picchu, too. Your spirituality intrigues me, and seeing the root of some of it should be fascinating."

"Christmas is definitely a more pleasant time to visit there, especially for someone who hates the cold as much as you do."

Luke bent to kiss her sweetly on the lips.

She no longer dreaded the thought of returning to her homeland, knowing the men who had tried to kill her spirit would no longer be a threat to her.

"Thank you for coming here with me. I do not think I could have done so without you by my side."

"Darlin', I plan to be by your side for the rest of our lives."

Chapter Twenty-Nine

A dam waited for Megan to answer his call. He checked the door to the hallway to make sure Karla couldn't overhear, but she was nursing the babies one more time before they left. Cassie was with her so he decided now was the best time to make the arrangements. Getting Karla to agree to go to dinner with Cassie had been a challenge, but he and Luke somehow managed to pull it off.

Luke was pretty resourceful. Karla probably agreed so she could hear how he managed to convince Cassie to marry him. Too damned many surprise weddings in this family. He grinned. His had been unexpected, too, but he *had* given people two weeks' notice to show up. Still couldn't believe how many of his Marines took him up on the invitation, especially so close to Christmas.

At the moment, Luke was behind him taking some measurements for what he'd need for the next round of renovations to convert this spare room into Karla's recording studio.

Megan answered, and he launched into his request without preamble. "Hey, if you have some time, Karla's heading out soon with Cassie, and I'd like to give her some new photos of the triplets to add to her scrapbook. Ones she doesn't expect. Something creative."

"I'd love to! I've done a number of baby shoots with new dads, so I know the perfect poses. Ryder and I will be there in thirty minutes. We just finished our hike at Mount Evans and were already headed your way."

"See you soon. Be safe, hon."

He hung up and watched Luke work a while. Ryder and Megan had moved in here until they could find a place of their own. All their possessions fit into one bay in the garage, not having accumulated as much stuff as Adam had over the years.

Ryder was working at Doc McKenzie's clinic hanging drywall and framing the doors in the extension. He told Adam that Savannah had been a big help to him when he became too overwhelmed by the noise and number of people around. If anyone understood dealing with PTSD, it was Savannah. She'd been through a hell that no child should ever be subjected to and still managed to survive. Sure put Adam's childhood issues in perspective.

Maybe Ryder should find a job somewhere smaller than Denver. No sense putting himself through hell every day if he didn't have to. He seemed to have any number of useful skills. Luke might need help with some jobs out his way. Adam grinned, wondering what Ryder would say if he knew about Luke's business making BDSM furniture. But he doubted Luke let anyone else work on those pieces. They were his artwork.

One thing was certain. Adam had no intention of inviting Ryder to the club with his little sister in tow, even if the man was into kink.

"Luke, I'm headed back to see if I can help Karla get ready to go to dinner with your wife."

"No problem. I'm going to need some time to get these measurements down right anyway."

Adam returned to their bedroom to find Karla seated with only one baby at her breast. Rori sometimes took feedings more leisurely than the other two did, so Karla must be almost finished. Cassie diapered Kate on the new changing table Marc and Angelina had given them.

"Paxton changed yet?"

Cassie looked up and smiled. "Not yet." Adam already saw a big change in her demeanor. Not as wary. She actually seemed happy for the first time since he'd met her.

Adam walked over to the baby bed and lifted up Paxton. "Hey, big boy. You're next. Don't you dare squirt me again, either. Hear me?" After two direct hits, he'd taken Karla's advice to cover the little guy with a spare cloth diaper until he finished changing him.

He sure had learned a lot about taking care of the babies, who had turned six weeks old last Friday. In some ways, time seemed to be crawling, and changes in the babies happened so slowly. In others, he just had to look at photos from when they were in the hospital to see how far each had come.

They loved sleeping next to each other in Luke's uniquely designed baby bed. He would hate it when they outgrew it.

"Adam, are you sure you and Luke can handle this? Savannah said she wouldn't mind coming over."

Adam gave her a stare he hoped would settle the discussion, but couldn't help but add, "I've been helping with the babies since you came home from the hospital the second time. Have a little faith. The only thing I can't handle is breastfeeding, and you took care of that. Besides, there's plenty of expressed milk in the fridge and freezer, so you girls take all the time you want."

Karla broke the suction Rori's mouth had on her tit, and Cassie took the sleeping baby. "Two hours max, Adam. I'm sure Cassie and I will be caught up on everything by then."

*   *   *

Cassie was glad Luke had agreed to spend the night at Kitty's last night, rather than drive home from the airport so late. Announcing their wedding upon arrival resulted in a mini-celebration. A shocked squeal from Kitty led to some intense grilling on how this had all come about, but Cassie had waited until they could be alone now to share her innermost thoughts. She didn't know Adam, Ryder, or Megan well enough to talk in front of them.

The men insisted they take this time alone. Kitty had not been away from the triplets since they were born. By the time she checked her phone for the fifth time in ten minutes to see if Adam had texted her about any problems, Cassie was not sure Kitty could ever really disconnect from worrying about them.

"Relax. Savannah promised to be on call if they need help." They had chosen their favorite fondue restaurant to catch up, because Adam didn't like this place. Thank goodness Luke was adventurous when it came to food.

"I know." Kitty turned the phone face down and slid it a foot away. She skewered mushrooms and chicken on separate sticks and set them in one of the simmering fondue pots between them. Cassie had her own for her veggie version. "I still can't believe you've been married since May and didn't tell any of us. Not even me!"

"Oh, Kitty. In my mind, the first wedding was not a real marriage. I always assumed Luke would come to his senses, or find someone who could love him the way he should be loved, and he would ask for an annulment. It was less complicated to ignore the whole thing than to have to explain it later."

"Annulment. So you didn't—"

Cassie shook her head, cutting off Kitty's words, and distracted herself a moment with her dinner. "Actually, Kitty, we still have not...done that."

"What? How could you not—oh, Cassie." She reached across the table to squeeze Cassie's hand. "I'm sorry. I didn't mean it that way. I know how hard it must be for you."

Cassie smiled and met her friend's gaze. "After our time in Peru and our marriage of the spirit, for the first time since the rape, I feel optimistic that the time will come when we are able to make love. Perhaps soon."

Kitty smiled. "You don't know how happy it makes me to hear those words. I have worried so much about you. Luke, too. You both need each other. I can't think of anyone more perfect for you."

Cassie could not hide her smile. "When he touches me, I just feel a...connection down to my soul. Does that make sense?"

Kitty nodded. "I have that with Adam. You can't even imagine being apart, even though you are in separate locations. Like now." Kitty glanced at the phone, but did not pick it up. "Then when you see him again...Ka-thunk!"

"Ka-thunk?"

Kitty smiled. "It's when your stomach drops after he stares at you a certain way. Or touches you just right. Or says something—"

"Sounds more like a physical attraction than a soul-level one."

"Well, there's that, too." Kitty smiled. "Come on. I mean, Luke Denton sure is easy on the eyes. He's also a take-charge man. Doesn't he sometimes just make your heart or stomach flutter when he grins at you?"

Cassie felt the heat rise in her cheeks. "Maybe." Is that what she meant by a Ka-thunk moment?

"Honey, just open your heart to him. He's the gentlest man I know. He would do anything to keep from hurting a person or an animal. I saw how he looked at you with such longing, even that night at Rico's before the avalanche. Trust him."

"I do. As much as I have trusted any man in my adult life. But I have not had one of those moments yet."

Kitty grinned. "You'll know when it happens. With Adam, it's usually when he goes all Dom on me."

"Oh, Kitty! We do not have a BDSM relationship!"

"It doesn't have to be in a Dom/sub relationship."

"Good, because Luke is too gentle to be like that."

Kitty shook her head. "Doms are the most gentle, sentimental people you'll ever meet."

Images of women tied up and being spanked or flogged flashed across her mind. No amount of argument would convince her BDSM was gentle. Luke would never do such things to her. He loved and respected her too much.

But Adam felt that way about Kitty—and Kitty certainly did not feel he disrespected or hurt her in any way. Maybe Cassie's libido—such as it was—had different wiring.

"I do not think that lifestyle is something either of us would be comfortable with. On our wedding night, he likened us to teenagers exploring each other's bodies with hesitant touches."

"Oh, that's so sweet! Sounds like Luke is taking things slowly. That's just what you need. But trust me. Luke has a dominant streak. I've seen it."

Cassie did not wish to talk about that side of Luke or his former activities in the club. When they married in May, Luke had promised that club stuff was behind him. He did not seem interested in it anymore, and she believed him.

The two friends spent the next course talking about the babies before moving on to Adam. "Is he sleeping with you again?"

Kitty shrugged, but a sadness came over her, and her chin trembled. "Sorry. Hormones are still out of whack." She dabbed at her eyes with the cloth napkin. "Some nights he'll stay with me part of the time, but I think he leaves before falling asleep."

Kitty blew out a breath in frustration. "Well, neither of us sleeps much with the babies. God, Cassie, I've never been so exhausted in my life! Honestly, even though Doctor Palmer will probably give the go-ahead for sex when I see her for my final postpartum visit in two weeks, it's the furthest thing from my mind at the moment."

Karla played with her fondue fork. "Adam has improved some since the baby shower. He and Ryder share a lot of experiences. Somehow, I think having Ryder around is helping both of them deal better with what they went through. Ryder and Megan are more open with each other about the war than Adam and I have been. I don't think he'll ever tell me most of what he went through, but at least he isn't shutting me out as much."

Cassie reached across the table and patted Kitty's hand. "Never give up. It took me a very long time to open up to Luke or my family about what happened to me. Just be patient. Give him time."

"Time. Patience." Kitty smiled. "I'll try, Cassie. But patience was never my strong suit."

The last thing Cassie thought she should ever dispense would be advice about intimacy, but she had been reading about something lately she planned to try with Luke one day soon.

"Have you ever thought about using tantric techniques to help you connect with Adam?"

"You mean tantra as in Sting's marathon sexcapades? I'm too exhausted for that."

Cassie rolled her eyes. "Stop paying attention to how Hollywood stars pervert sacred ways. Tantra is not about having sex so much as it is a way to establish, or in your case re-establish, intimacy between the two of you. You will connect in ways much deeper than the physical."

"Then I don't have a clue what it is. Tell me more."

How could Cassie explain something she only knew in theory from the many books she'd read on various mystical practices? "I have never actually tried it, but have studied the spirituality of the Kama Sutra."

"You mean the book with all the sexual positions?"

Cassie smiled indulgently. "Kitty, for someone so in tune with popular culture, you sometimes floor me that you never delve any deeper into a subject than what you hear on television."

"Don't forget YouTube!" Kitty grinned and shrugged without the least bit of remorse.

Cassie recalled the night while caring for the babies that Kitty and Savannah had reminisced about their foray into watching *educational* sex videos last spring to help Savannah reconnect with her sexuality. Cassie could never go that far. The video Savannah showed Cassie was lewd and left her feeling nauseated. When she and Luke finally had sex, it would be sensual, not pornographic or perverted.

"I am sure you will find videos of tantra there, too, if you would rather watch than read about it. But even if he refuses to spend the night in the same bed with you, the moments you spend connecting through tantra exercises could give you a level of intimacy that helps you feel fulfilled until things are back to normal."

"I'm willing to try anything."

Cassie squeezed her hand. "Trust me, Kitty, you and Adam will find ways to make the most of those precious moments you can steal away from the sleeping babies to keep your relationship...vibrant."

"Thanks. I hope so." They ate in silence a moment before Kitty started a new conversation. "I still can't believe you married him twice, and I missed both ceremonies."

"Maybe later this summer we can have everyone over for a belated *fiesta* at the ranch."

"We'll be there! You don't know how much I'd love to get away. I have spent so much time in our bedroom the past six weeks. Adam barely let me come down the stairs for meals until recently. He even carried me down to my baby shower, as you know. Just set the date, and we will pack up the Montague crew and be there in a heartbeat."

Excitement bubbled up in Cassie. She was certain Luke would want to share their joy with their friends, too. "Wonderful! Let me talk with Luke about it. And you can stay overnight. I can move into the studio with Luke."

"What do you mean? Aren't you two planning on sleeping together now?"

Oh, dear. How to explain? She glanced at the simmering fondue pot. "I am not sure. We did share a bed in Peru, not to mention the sofa bed at your place last night, so I am certain he plans for us to do so when we return home, too."

The heat rose into her cheeks, and she shook her head. Cassie met her friend's incredulous gaze. "I need to overcome my fears and aversions first, but this is why I know that touch and intimacy are so powerful. Even though we have not had intercourse, I feel a bond with Luke... And increased desire for him. It will happen when the time is right."

"Trust me, when you finally do, you are going to kick yourself for waiting so long. Sex with someone you love is *amazing*."

Memories of Luke's hands on her body, igniting embers that had nearly died, made her long to return to him. What would they do tonight when they arrived home? When would the time be right to...

Kitty patted her hand. "I'm sure being at Luke's place is a great relief after the fire, but how are you handling not having your place in the mountains?"

Tears stung the backs of her eyes. "Not living in the mountains hurts my soul, Kitty, but I have Luke, our animals, and we are surrounded by mountains that I can visit at any time."

"No chance the owner will rebuild so you can spend some time there again?"

Cassie shook her head. "Her memories were lost in the cabin that burned. She has no desire to rebuild. The only reason she kept the place was because of the sentimental reasons—or perhaps a tax write-off for supporting a starving artist." Cassie shrugged. "She was there when I needed her, though, for which I am grateful."

"That's so sad. I know you loved being up there. I think it reminded you of the good things you missed of home when you were unable to go to Peru." Kitty probably was right. "But, Cassie, if not for the fire, I'm afraid you might never have discovered your love for Luke."

"True on both counts. I hid away from the world while there—especially the men of the world. Now I am reconnecting with family and friends. I am sure in the long run this move will be good for me. Even if it hurts. I feel the Goddess has had a hand in this and will help me adapt to my new home."

"You and Luke love each other and have a whole lifetime to look forward to. It won't matter where you live as long as you're together. Everything else will fall into place."

"I hope so." She smiled. "I have missed our talks so much, Kitty. Thank you for coming out with me today."

Kitty stood and walked around the table to wrap Cassie in her arms. "I'm the one who needs to thank you. You and I have a long history together. We need to make sure we don't let so much time pass between visits. I'm sure the guys will hold down the fort once a month at least for us to do this."

She held on to her friend, so grateful to have someone like her in her life.

When the server returned to see if they wanted their check, Kitty broke away and insisted on an order of chocolate fondue for dessert. Cassie was not sure she could eat another bite, but while waiting, Kitty picked up her phone. "Oh my gosh! We've been here three hours already! Where did the time go?"

"See? Time flies when you are not focused on how much time it takes to achieve something you want."

"Point taken. I'll start living in the moment with Adam and quit wishing my life away trying to have what we did before I became pregnant." She glanced at her phone again. "Adam texted an hour ago that all is fine, but my breasts are so full they're like rocks. The babies will be ready for another go at me the minute I walk in the house." She smiled. "Now I need to quit thinking about them or I'm going to soak through these breast pads before I get home."

Kitty's mouth formed an O, and she reached for her purse on the booth seat beside her. "Oh, dear Lord, I almost forgot!" She pulled out a card in a white envelope and a small, ruby-red box with a white ribbon. "Happy Birthday, Cassie!"

"It is not for two more weeks."

"I know, but I can't wait."

"I cannot believe you had time to buy me something."

"I had to shop online, but when I saw it, I knew it was meant for you."

Intrigued, Cassie first read the card. The sentiment about friendships that never die throughout the sands of time brought tears to her eyes. "We are old souls, Kitty. I know we have been together many times, and I am sure our paths will cross many more times."

"If you say so. But I'm living in the moment, remember." Kitty grew serious. "You know, Cassie, how close I came to crossing over before I should have. I'm convinced you helped guide me back to Adam and my babies." She squeezed Cassie's hand. "Thank you."

Cassie did not wish to think about ever losing her friend in this lifetime. She nodded and opened the box. Pushing the tissue aside revealed a necklace with a rustic brass chain and three decorative pieces depicting angel trumpet flowers spaced between eight blue-quartz faceted stones.

"When you told me about losing your *abuela's* special wedding shawl and how she grew angel trumpets at her house in your village, I thought this would be something you could wear to remember her by."

A tear splashed onto the black napkin in her lap. "Oh, Kitty. I have no words to express my feelings—in either language. It is so beautiful. And blue quartz. That is perfect for me at this place in my life's journey."

"What do you mean?"

"Blue quartz assuages fear, calms the mind, and inspires hope."

"Wow. I just thought it was pretty." Kitty shrugged and grinned.

Cassie knew Kitty was not interested in esoteric things, but wanted to convey how perfect this gift was. "It also is a peace and tranquility stone that can promote understanding of one's spiritual nature. I have been reconnecting with the Goddess this summer for the first time in a long time. She even spoke to me during a meditation in Peru."

"Wow, Cassie, it's as if the Universe led me to the perfect gift. That's…incredible! Who needs Google? I'm so happy I chose this one."

"All stones represent many things, much more than their surface-level beauty." She thought of Luke and how he delved deeply beneath the surface to find something he found beautiful in her. "People have so much more to offer when you dig a little deeper."

"Like you, Cassie. I still remember finding you sophomore year on Columbia's roommate opportunities board. We hit it off immediately over lunch that first day when checking each other out to decide if we were compatible. Now look how much you have added to my life."

"Oh, Kitty, it is you who have enriched my life. Not only by being my friend, but without your network of friends, I never would have met Luke."

Kitty dabbed at the tears in her eyes with her napkin. "I hope you two find much happiness together. No doubt, you both have a lot to learn about each other. Just keep digging away at those layers. And talk. Let him know what you need, what you want, how you feel."

"I will try, although it is not always easy for me to express my feelings. But I am going to try."

*   *   *

"Adam, we need the quintessential daddy/baby pic. Remove your shirt."

He glared at Megan while continuing to rock Paxton to keep him quiet. Pax hadn't liked having his solo pics taken any more than the girls had. But they calmed down when all were cuddled together in their bed.

"What do you have in mind?" He didn't like going shirtless, except around Karla.

"I want a photo of you in bed with all three babies sleeping on your bare chest. Looks like you're broad enough that they'll fit."

He groaned inside. He'd let himself go since leaving the Corps. Not nearly as broad as he once was. But he had more important things to do than work out in the gym at the club since moving in here.

She turned to Ryder and Luke and barked more orders. "Guys, be ready to remove their clothes for this one." The men each held one of the girls like a pro considering neither had kids. Better than Adam had done his first time holding one.

"Here, let me take Pax while you strip for me." Megan grinned.

"Don't push your luck." He handed the now-sleeping baby over and pulled his USMC T-shirt over his head. So far, his favorite shot was when he'd worn his desert digitals, one girl in each cargo pocket with her arms wrapped around her daddy's thighs and his hands supporting their still-wobbly heads, while Paxton was facing the camera in the baby sling across Adam's chest. Damn, Karla was going to love these photos of their babies.

Just as he started to stretch out on the bed, Luke announced, "Whoa. I think this one needs a diaper change before that photo is shot."

Not wanting to inflict a messy diaper on the man his first time out, Adam reached for the baby and headed to the changing table.

The room grew silent behind him as he worked, but soon Megan was clicking away, recording for posterity that Adam Montague actually changed a poopy diaper. Whoa! The smell! If the kid ate the same thing all the time, how could one be different from another?

"Just leave the diapers on until we're ready." Megan's voice sounded strange, and he turned around to find all three of them staring at him with varying degrees of horror on their faces.

Shit. "No shots of my messed-up back."

Ryder looked like he was shell-shocked, but asked, "Did that happen in Afghanistan?"

"Most of it."

The man's face paled. Would Ryder continue to blame himself for not being there during the ambush? What the fuck did he think he could have done differently?

Megan crossed the room, Paxton still in her arms, and Ryder turned his focus to her. She said something quietly to him, and after a minute, Adam watched him visibly relax. He nodded and gave her a kiss. Thank God, Megan understood the unseen wounds warriors like Ryder tried to hide from the world. Good thing they'd found each other.

Also good that Ryder hadn't gone into a panic attack while holding

Rori. Adam had been ready to snatch her away, but if anything, when he seemed to be losing it, he'd held her even tighter as though afraid to drop her.

"Let's get this done. The girls could be home any time." They'd just passed the two-hour mark, although Adam didn't think Karla and Cassie would truly catch up that fast. He remembered how Karla lost all track of time when she was with Cassie. He shuddered. The disastrous effect one of his orders had had on her when she hadn't been able to tear herself away from Cassie's cabin to make it home in the time Adam had—

Fuck. He reached for his phone. "Luke, hold Kate again. I need to send a message to Karla." With both hands free, he texted, *"Everyone's fine on the home front. Take all the time you need."* He didn't want her having another accident.

Pocketing the phone again, he headed for the bed. "Okay, let's do this." Adam stretched out, and Megan positioned the three babies on his bare chest. Paxton woke up and started rooting around. "Sorry, buddy. Wrong parent." He wondered if his dad had ever held him like this when he was little, but pushed the thought aside. He wasn't going to be like his father with his own kids.

More than half an hour later, he realized Megan had been busy shooting the photos of him ever since the babies had been placed on his chest. She really was professional about this photography business. Unobtrusive, efficient. No wonder, since she'd gone to graduate school to perfect her skills. He couldn't wait to start another photo album after things settled down a little.

Megan pulled away yet continued to rally the troops. "Ryder and Luke, on the count of three, take off their diapers."

"Whoa!" Adam could just imagine how badly this could go. "You sure about that?"

"Trust me." She smiled sweetly and set up her camera on a tripod. "I'm going to go with natural light, so I need to be sure I don't move the camera. You try to stay still, too, Adam. Hopefully the babies will remain laid back until we're finished."

The time came for the babies to be stripped, and Adam was instructed to feign sleep. Karla had been asking to take a photo like this while he napped with all three, but damned if he trusted himself to fall asleep with them.

This would have to do.

Finally, realizing he wasn't going to get anything from Daddy, Paxton nodded off again. All three of his little angels were snuggled together, arms around each other. His arms covered most of their bare butts. No need to embarrass them later. Adam blinked away the sting in his eyes.

Megan fiddled with her camera, testing it with a few clicks probably. "I think we're ready."

On cue, Adam closed his eyes, glad that the photos wouldn't show his tears. He heard the shutter's rapid-fire clicks and stayed as still as he could. He'd never expected to be given the chance to be a father to his own little babies—not even one, much less three.

In his musings over how blessed he was, he lost track of time until something warm ran down his left side. *Fuck*. His first thought was Paxton, but it was on Rori's side. "Shoot's over. Somebody grab me a towel."

When he started handing the babies to the waiting hands, his agitation woke Kate and Paxton, who both started screaming. He accepted the towel from a laughing Megan and dried himself off. At least it was only pee.

Surprisingly, Rori joined in the bawl-fest this time. Sweetest sound in the world because she was always so quiet. He stood and reached for her. "Come on. It's not so bad. Daddy forgives you. When you gotta go, you gotta go."

She cried louder, and he finally figured out all three probably were hungry. When the hell was Karla going to come home? You'd think she'd be leaking milk by now, breast pads or not.

No sooner had the thought formed than he looked up and there she stood, two wet spots on her shirt. She crossed the room while unbuttoning her blouse, giving the tripod a sideways glance but not asking. *Good thing.*

He let her settle into the chair while Cassie took Rori and diapered her. Luke and Ryder, unable to suppress their grins, diapered the other two.

"What have you all been doing? Adam, where's your shirt?"

"Rori peed on me." That much was true. She could draw her own conclusions. Megan quickly rid the room of her camera and tripod, still laughing that he'd been peed on. He wondered if she'd show *that* shot to Karla. Probably. They seemed to hit it off and shared things he didn't even want to know about. But he'd better oversee which ones went into the family photo album. God, had he cussed around the babies? He couldn't remember.

Karla had Rori and Paxton cuddled on her nursing pillow when Cassie announced on her way out of the room, "I'll warm up a bottle for Kate. I'm sure she's hungry, too." He realized Ryder must have helped Megan hide the equipment.

He should have thought of the bottles, but had been too busy with the photos. Where'd the time go? He sure hoped Karla liked the surprise pictures.

When he glanced down at Karla, she had tears in her eyes. What now? He couldn't take much more today.

She met his gaze. "Thank you for giving me some time with Cassie. I didn't know how much I needed some girl time."

"You can thank Luke, too. It was his idea."

She turned to Luke. "Thank you. And, Luke, even more important, thank you for loving Cassie, too."

"Darlin', it's no chore to love someone as sweet as Cassie. Now, I think I'll go help her out in the kitchen."

Chapter Thirty

Cassie watched Luke working with Picasso in the pasture a week later as she tried to capture the image on the canvas she had set up just outside the corral. His parents had returned home to Texas two days ago, leaving Luke spending long hours working with the horses during the day and on some project in the studio at night.

She could not help but think part of what drove him was that they had yet to had sex, even though they shared a bed. He had even replaced the bed she had been sleeping in when she first came here after the fire with one that included a headboard with an elaborately carved scene depicting the two of them soon after Milagrosa's birth. The memory brought tears to her eyes. He was so talented—and sentimental.

Ryder and Megan had come to the ranch for the day yesterday, and the two men had holed up in the studio for hours while she and Megan went down to the stream on horseback to swim nude. Megan was a lot of fun to be with. Definitely a free spirit and someone who knew what she wanted in life. Cassie noticed some surgical scars on the woman's abdomen, but did not pry.

During their time together, Megan had taken a number of photos of Cassie. The one of her nude body silhouetted by the sun, while not revealing anything to the eye, was very sensual. Next week, she would give a framed print to Luke at their party to celebrate their wedding and her birthday.

She also had begun a sketchbook of her sensual drawings of Luke. She began by drawing his face or hands, but recently had started sketching nudes of Luke while alone as he worked in his studio. Memories of their first nights in the cabin when she had removed everything but his boxers helped her fill in most of the details. She blushed. Drawing him in that pose excited her, even though she had no clue how to share those feelings—or even the sketches—with him.

Perhaps someday soon. In bed last night, they had cuddled and talked about the horses, the alpacas—not to mention how much they enjoyed Ryder and Megan's frequent visits—while Luke idly touched her in nonsexual, but increasingly bold, ways. He avoided her breasts and groin, but left her aching for more. She understood his frustration, too, now. What was he waiting for?

You, little one.

The wind seemed to whisper a message from *Mama Quilla* to her.

At times, she thought she was ready to ask Luke to caress her the way she knew he wished to touch her. However, she feared the triggers more than his touch. Would he kick himself for causing one or be upset that she could not separate his touch from that of her rapists?

What if she would never be ready to make love?

Cassie's paintbrush stroked the canvas. Unlike in her sketchpad, here she showed a fully-clothed Luke as he put Picasso through his paces. She wondered what exercise they were doing. Apparently, he left a trail for Picasso to follow, but the horse seemed confused. Should she interrupt and see if she could find out what Picasso was thinking?

No. If Luke needed her, he would ask. But she could not help but notice that these latest exercises seemed more intense than those he had worked on before the trip to Peru. Perhaps it was just that Luke was more driven. She and Luke did not talk about the abduction or subsequent rescue, but she could well imagine the helplessness and fear he had experienced that night when he realized she had been taken.

Luke was a 'take-charge guy,' as Kitty put it. Like Adam, he probably wrongly thought he could control every circumstance in his life. Keeping those he loved safe from harm, both humans and animals, was of tantamount importance, even though people generally have little control over their lives. She certainly had come to understand that.

Luke removed his Stetson and raked his fingers through his hair. Was he frustrated with himself or with Picasso? Most likely himself. Luke had infinite patience with animals—and his wife. He was being too hard on himself. Perhaps she could help Luke relax tonight by doing something fun.

Feeling Luke's arm around her each night this past week had kept the monsters at bay. Surprisingly, she had only had one nightmare since

Peru—one in which Luke had been knifed by Pedro.

When he awakened her and she heard his name reverberating in her ears from her scream of warning, she immediately knew he was safe. She had curled up against him, needing to feel the beat of his heart against her cheek. Luke kissed her head and stroked her hair until she fell asleep again.

A nudge to her shoulder nearly sent her hurtling over the easel. She turned to see it was O'Keeffe leaning her head over the fence rail. "Hello, girl. You scared me."

Cassie telepathically interpreted the messages the horse conveyed. *"Not my intention."*

She turned to nuzzle the horse and whisper in her ear. "I know. I'm just hypersensitive sometimes to unexpected movements." She reached up and patted the mare on her cheek. "Now, if you'll excuse me, I want to try and capture your master and Picasso in this painting before they catch me."

"Freeing."

Freeing? Did O'Keeffe sense Cassie's new state of being as she painted Luke? The savvy horse had noticed a difference in Cassie almost the minute she went to see her after they returned from Peru. Cassie had even shared her own story of abuse with the horse.

Cassie dipped her brush in the water and chose another color. She had been dabbling more with watercolors this summer. She loved exploring different ways of expressing herself through art. Perhaps someday she would focus on one, but until then, she wanted to try everything.

Watching the water bleed into the paper, taking on unexpected designs and shapes, she remained lost in the creative process until O'Keeffe nudged her again.

"My turn."

"You want to try your hand at painting?" She only realized later that the words that used to send her into a tailspin did not even faze her. Perhaps she had put one of her triggers to rest.

O'Keeffe nodded, her mane flying with the enthusiasm she showed.

Cassie laughed. "Okay, girl. Let me set up a new paper for you to work on. I will need some fresh water from the barn. Be right back."

She had heard about animals who expressed their creative nature. Excitement bubbled up inside her to see what O'Keeffe would do with a paintbrush. She could barely contain her giggle. A quarter hour later, she had moved the easel to inside O'Keeffe's corral. The horse stood with water and paints at the ready. She glanced from the horse to the paper and decided a large brush might be best for this first attempt.

Smiling, she dipped the brush into the water and turned to the mare. "Which color would you like to start with?"

"Earth."

"Brown?" She pointed to the color, and O'Keeffe nodded. Cassie filled the brush with the desired color before placing the handle between the horse's teeth. "Here you go."

O'Keeffe bent her head toward the paper and nearly toppled the easel. Cassie grabbed and steadied it. "Takes a while to judge distance, I guess. Just experiment at first with how the brush feels touching the paper."

Undeterred, the horse took a step back and tried again, but this time the brush made contact with the lower part of the paper and smeared a patch of brown paint. "Very nice!"

"More."

O'Keeffe extended the brush to her, and Cassie applied more brown paint to it and watched the horse add another streak on the paper. Quite abstract, but for a first attempt, a good effort.

"You have the idea, girl. Good job! The impressionists would envy your talent." She grinned, anxious to show Luke.

After three more strokes with the brown, O'Keeffe whinnied as she extended the brush again.

"Grass."

Dipping the brush into the water, Cassie cleaned it and applied the green. She'd never been an artist's assistant before, but that O'Keeffe trusted her enough to explore this talent with her pleased Cassie.

The painting now had the appearance of a brown blob with a head sticking up—a horse's head perhaps?

The green was splashed in three strokes around the brown. Definitely grass.

The image of a crow flashed in her mind. "Black," she whispered under her breath as she prepared the brush.

In angry strokes, the horse slashed paint across the top of the canvas. The horse's ears went back as if she were the victim rather than the attacker. Cassie's eyes stung. She refilled the brush quickly several times hoping O'Keeffe would be able to release this dark emotion. The top of the paper filled with more disjointed black streaks.

Dismal.

Depressing

The image of steel shackles embedded in her mind's eye.

"Broken." The word screamed in Cassie's head, loud and clear.

The paintbrush fell from O'Keeffe's mouth to the dirt below. Cassie reached up to stroke the mare's neck before burying her head and letting the tears flow. "It's in the past, baby. No one is ever going to try and break your spirit again." Sweat mingled with Cassie's tears, drenching the horse's skin. Memories of Cassie's own experience with being restrained as her monsters tried to break her led to more tears spilling from her eyes. But they did not succeed in breaking her.

"Jeezus. She was sacked out old style."

Cassie turned to find Luke staring at the picture O'Keeffe had painted. She brushed the wetness from her cheeks.

"Sacked out?" How could he tell from this abstract painting?

"It's a downright abusive way to train a horse to humans, if you ask me. Wouldn't think anyone would still use it these days when much more humane methods are known. But they broke her. The old style of sacking out a horse involved restraining it in some manner—usually they tied its head to a pole or hobbled it by the legs. Looks like the latter for O'Keeffe. Then they would have terrorized her with objects that scared her plus make loud sounds to frighten her further."

No wonder she had such an affinity for this horse. "She did convey the image of shackles to me. Poor baby." One on each side, Cassie and Luke spent some time loving on the horse who seemed so much more relaxed now that she had released that horrific memory.

A little while later, Luke reached out toward the painting. "You captured the hobbling here. See how her front legs are bent, and her head is rearing back in defiance? Usually these horses wind up fearing people worse than ever afterward."

"Oh, I did not paint that. O'Keeffe did." He turned toward her with doubt in his eyes. "No, really! She conveyed feelings of being shackled and broken, just as you said, but I did not understand what the painting meant until you interpreted it."

He looked from the painting to the horse a couple of more times. "Jeezus. Never saw anything like it. Maybe that's what she's been trying to let out all this time." He patted the other side of O'Keeffe's neck and shook his head in wonder.

O'Keeffe lowered her head to nudge the paintbrush lying on the ground.

Cassie picked it up and cleaned it in the jar of water.

"Want to do another, girl?" Cassie asked.

O'Keeffe nodded. Cassie removed the original painting and pinned a new sheet of watercolor paper to the easel.

"Sky."

Cassie confirmed she wanted blue. "You got it." She filled the brush and placed it between O'Keeffe's teeth. She laid a swatch of blue across the top of the paper.

"I'll be damned. She really *did* do it herself."

Cassie wondered why he doubted her, but soon became too engrossed in refilling the brush to remark. Soon another streak of what she supposed was sky lay on the paper.

"Crow."

Oh, no. What was O'Keeffe going to convey to them this time? More abuse and hurt? With some reluctance, she cleaned the brush and loaded it with black. This time, though, the downward stroke was higher on the paper. She reloaded it several times and watched the horse make more slashes across the page. A vee formed with the two black strokes against the blue sky. She did not know what it meant, but could feel the horse's peace of mind without O'Keeffe conveying anything telepathically at all.

Luke's voice sounded hoarse when he broke the silence. "She's free now."

Cassie turned to him and saw tears in his eyes as he stared at the painting. He buried his face in the horse's neck and stroked her back. O'Keeffe didn't shy away from him.

Trust. O'Keeffe trusted him, too.

Cassie turned back to the painting and this time saw blackbirds soaring high in the sky.

Free.

The word echoed through Cassie's mind, but did not come from O'Keeffe. She had been slowly coming to the realization that she could trust Luke even more than she had so far. No man had ever made her feel so free.

Trust him.

Tears blurred her vision. One hand on the horse's back, she reached around to Luke and stroked the soft hairs on his forearm. A tingle of awareness moved through her fingers, up her arm, and into her heart.

Then deeper. Lower.

She pulled away as if burned.

Trust him.

His patience and gentle touch had led O'Keeffe to feel free again. But would Luke be as successful with her? They were married, but he would never force her to do anything. She had protested having sex for so long, he might even be afraid to broach the subject for fear of yet another rejection. However, the feelings he stirred in her when he held her reawakened places deep inside her.

No, Luke awakened those places—for the first time ever.

"I am not sure if I am ready to make love," she said aloud before she realized she'd spoken.

Luke walked around O'Keeffe and cupped Cassie's chin, a furrow between his eyebrows. "I know, Sweet Pea. Remember what we said in Peru? Baby steps." He searched her face. "What's going on?"

"I want…"

She had never been able to express her wishes with a man, not since she had asked Pedro to dance with her in the cantina. The longing for Luke's touch nearly overcame her fear.

Nearly.

She took a step back. "Never mind."

He reached out to stroke her arm, halting her retreat. "Be honest with me. Tell me what you want?"

His gentle hand made non-threatening motions up and down her arm, strokes much like the ones he used to calm O'Keeffe's fear of the blanket or saddle.

Trust him.

"Will you…"

How can I ask him this?

"Go on. You can ask me anything you want, Sweet Pea."

Trust him.

"Will you…dance with me?"

*   *   *

Of all the questions he expected to hear, this wasn't even in the running. Not after what happened the last time she asked a man to dance with her.

I'm one lucky man.

Hell, if the lady wanted to dance, he was all in. Luke grinned.

"Love to, darlin'. Any particular dance you have in mind?" He could handle a Texas two-step, but would prefer something a little more intimate.

"The tango."

Aw, have mercy, baby girl.

All he knew about the tango were images of a hot Latin lover and a woman with a long-stemmed rose clenched between her teeth. He'd never taken dance lessons and didn't have the foggiest idea how to dance a tango.

Talk about a quarterback sack.

Not that he didn't plan to gain back the lost yards. She hadn't asked him to compete for MVP in the Super Bowl, after all, just to hold her and dance. "You'll have to teach me. Not much call for the tango in the road houses I hung out in during college."

She seemed hesitant for a moment then nodded. "Let me clean up this stuff, take care of the alpacas, and we can get started."

The determined expression on her face—as if she were about to face a four-man firing squad—didn't give him a lot of hope she would be able to relax in his arms, but if dancing the tango could help her overcome one of her internal hurdles, then he'd dance the damned tango. He watched as she packed up the art supplies in her canvas bag.

Luke folded up the easel. "I'll bring this in and rub O'Keeffe down."

She nodded and practically ran toward the barn. He'd better not leave her alone too long, or she would let the fear take over again. Too bad they couldn't start his lesson in the corral, but he needed to take care of something first.

"Thank you, girl," he said as he took a cloth from his pocket and wiped the remaining sweat from O'Keeffe's neck. "I'll give you a proper brushing down tonight, but whatever you did or said to help Cassie, I'm forever in your debt."

O'Keeffe laid a sloppy lick on his cheek, and Luke laughed.

"Don't you get too fresh with me, girl. I'm a one-woman man—and

I'm taken."

Thirty minutes later, after checking on the horses, he entered the cool house. The sun had been beating down on him all morning, but he hadn't noticed how hot his body was until he walked inside. The bedroom door was closed. Damn. Had she gone to ground already?

Should he push her limits a little? Maybe. If she couldn't get past this hurdle, she'd never tackle the rest of the ones still ahead.

First, though, he walked into the kitchen, filled two glasses with ice, and poured them both a tall sweet tea. The creaking of the bedroom door made him turn toward the kitchen doorway, and seconds later, there stood a new Cassie. The transformation surprised him. She'd pulled her hair back in a sleek ponytail and wore a colorful, long-sleeved top and calf-length pants—both skin-tight. He rarely saw her in form-fitting clothing. This outfit highlighted her slim waist and curvy hips. And those shoes. Sexy, black, with at least a three-inch heel. Much higher than the flats she usually wore.

Luke whistled. "Hot damn, darlin'! Gorgeous!"

She cast her gaze to the floor. "Please say nothing more. I am nervous already." She took several deep breaths before squaring her shoulders and meeting his gaze. Again, he saw the mix of fear and determination on her face.

"Trust me, Cassie."

"I do."

No, you don't.

Not completely, anyway. Despite the headway they'd made in Peru, he knew she wasn't ready for him to make love with her. But something had happened out there with O'Keeffe to help her remove a few more of the bricks from her fortress walls. He'd continue to go easy with her. He had the rest of his life to earn her trust.

Jesus, don't let me screw this up.

She started to move the coffee table out of the way, and he joined her to help. Soon they had cleared a dance floor of sorts.

She approached him slowly, the natural sway of her hips nearly causing him to lose his cool. "The tango has only a few basic steps to learn."

Breathe, man.

"Sweet Pea, you just show me what to do."

"I found a YouTube video we can watch first. You are visual, as am I, and I think this will help you understand what I am trying to convey before we begin." She picked up her smartphone from the mantle, and they watched a couple do the tango in slow motion. She pointed to the screen and paused the video. "We will begin with this embrace. See it?"

He wrapped his arm around her. "Uh-huh." So soft. The rest of the video passed by in a blur. All he could focus on was having her in his arms, her body pressed against his.

"Okay, do you understand the general concept?"

"Think so."

She laid the phone on the mantle again and wiped her palms on her pants before holding up her hands. He mirrored her arm movements, and she walked into his embrace as the couple in the video had done.

Don't you dare get a hard-on, Denton.

How he was supposed to avoid one stumped him, though. He forced his brain to ignore the sweet scent of her hair.

"Place your right hand behind my back."

He did so, resting his pinky finger at the top of the waistband of her pants. She stiffened.

"No, no, no!" She put some distance between them. He thought she'd retreat, but apparently, this "no" didn't mean they were finished. "Your hand must be in the center of my back. Just below the shoulder blades." Her accent had grown stronger. "If your hand is on my hips, I won't have the freedom to move as I need to do."

He wanted nothing more than to watch and feel her move, so he raised his hand to where he guessed was about right.

"Shouldn't we turn on some music?"

"Not yet. I need to walk you through the basic positions and steps first." Her breathing grew more ragged. Couldn't be their exertions because they hadn't really started. Maybe she was as turned on as he was. He grinned as she took his left hand in her right one. Luke wasn't sure whose palms were sweatier.

"Now, we hold our elbows out and open. If we were on a dance floor, this would keep others from intruding into our space."

"Can't have that." *Nope.* He didn't want any interference right now. When her breathing became labored, and she seemed to be fighting to keep her composure, he prompted, "What next, darlin'?"

"Um, I place my hand across your shoulders." She reached up with her free hand. "You are taller than..." She broke off, and he wondered who else she'd danced the tango with then didn't want to think about that anymore. This was between them.

"The man ultimately leads the lady in the dance, but let me show you the three options you have for where your legs can go."

She spent several tries without success to move his legs in the right direction before grabbing him by the hips in frustration. "No, sway. More like this." She maneuvered him so that his hips did as she wanted, before she released him with an expression of horror on her face.

When she pulled away, he let her go.

* * *

What was I thinking?

Cassie drew in a few forced breaths as she tried to regain her composure. Why did she propose the tango? The dance was too suggestive. Should she continue?

Trust him.

I am trying! But this is too hard!

"If you want to take a break, we can try again later. Sorry I'm two left feet here, but I've never tried to dance anything this precise before."

The disappointment on his face charmed her even more. He did want to learn. She would not stop now.

"No, let us continue." She walked into his embrace again, and they adjusted their bodies. He was so much taller than her ballroom dancing classmate at Columbia. She described what she wanted him to do with his leg, moving it to the outside of hers as he guided her in the dance.

"That was perfect, Luke!"

"Thanks, darlin'. I have a patient teacher."

Luke was the patient one. She continued to start and stop, fighting down the panic that arose at certain movements. The tango hadn't been a part of what led to the attack, and yet she'd not allowed herself to express her love of dance since that night, not even to dance with her husband at their own wedding celebration.

I want my freedom back.

Time passed as they continued to move through the dance steps. Luke was a fast learner, and soon they were moving around the space between the sofa and mantel with ease. "Now let's take it from the beginning with you leading me."

He executed the first step perfectly. "Excellent! Let your leg guide mine, like so."

As he gained confidence in his steps, she embellished her movements with a few *ocho* moves, carving the figure eight in a teasing manner before him on the floor. Undeterred, he responded perfectly to her steps. When Luke's leg stepped out, blocking her as she had taught him to do, she instinctively slid hers slowly over his thigh as she enticed him with a dip of her upper body.

Free your spirit.

He blocked her leg again, and she smiled, pulling away to trace another figure eight on the floor with the toe of her shoe.

"Damn, that's hot."

Cassie froze. Before she could escape his arms, Luke pulled her closer and forced her to gaze into his eyes. The pounding in her chest nearly drowned out his words.

"I'm not gonna hurt you, Sweet Pea. You're safe. We're just dancing."

Trust him.

"I know." Her voice came out in a whisper.

"You're doing great, baby girl. Don't stop now. I'm just getting the hang of it." She did not wish to disappoint him. "Your passion for dance and movement is obvious."

"It has been so long since I have expressed myself this way. I believed for so long that my dancing led to..." Why had she brought up that night?

Because she had been triggered yet again. Why could she not keep the past in the past?

A sadness came over his face, and he pulled her close against his chest. "Stop worrying about it, darlin'. We took care of all three of them, remember? You're safe here with me in our home."

"I know. What I do not know is why thoughts of that night in the cantina keep interrupting my progress."

"Sweet Pea, those bad memories will fade over time. Try to rid yourself of any guilt over that shit popping into your head, though. That night was a watershed moment in your life. Those thoughts are going to come up, especially now that you're introducing activities into your life you had walled off after the rape—like dancing. By feeling guilty about it, you're just giving them power over you again."

She relaxed. Perhaps he was right. "How did you become so smart?"

She thought he might be flippant because of his modesty, but he surprised her. "I read a lot of how-to books on grieving and letting go of the hurts from the past. That piece of advice stuck in my head while I was trying to find a way to do the same over my own watershed moment." He rubbed her cheek with his thumb. "I can tell you it takes a while to recognize that guilt in your thoughts, but I'll try and help point it out if I know what you're thinking. Just know this. *Any* time you want to dance, you just cut loose. I'm ready whenever you want—or here to encourage you to dance alone or with the animals if you'd like."

She smiled as another weight was taken off her shoulders. "I do sometimes dance with O'Keeffe and the alpacas."

"I'd like to see that sometime."

"O'Keeffe really gets into it. Her head and tail move along with me as she lets the music sink into her bones, too. Now shall we continue with this dance, cowboy?"

"Thought you'd never ask, my lady. I think I'm starting to catch on. Maybe later you can show me one of your native dances, too."

Was she ready to dance the *marinera* and *huayno* again?

With Luke? *Yes.* "I would like that. Let us try with music this time." She retrieved her smartphone and cued up a song from her playlist.

Luke grew serious as he took her into his arms again. He placed his hand perfectly across her upper back. Even in her heels, he towered over her, but she did not fear him.

Keeping their gazes locked, she allowed Luke's legs and lower body to guide her in several steps before she became playful and surprised him with some of the lady steps intended to express her sensuality. She closed her eyes as the music filled an emptiness deep inside her.

Cassie danced with abandon as Luke guided her. His arms and hands cradled her at times and let her go at others. But she always returned to his embrace. A longing built up inside her. She did not know what it meant until she recognized the feelings as arousal.

Asking for anything remotely sexual scared her to death. But as terrifying as it seemed, she wanted to experience what it was like to make love with this man. Her heart knew she could trust him. Actually, her mind did, too.

She came to a standstill and stared into his eyes. *I can do this.* "Will you kiss me, Luke? Like a man kisses his wife?"

He tucked his finger under her chin and stared into her eyes. "You want to tell me how you think a husband kisses his wife that's different than how *your* husband's been kissing you already?"

"Oh, you have been a very good kisser. I know you hold back, though. I want you to kiss me more deeply. With…your tongue. As if we were…not going to stop with a kiss." Would the invasion of his tongue trigger her? She needed to find out.

He cupped her cheeks, and she thought he was about to kiss her, but he did not. "Some of my friends use code words and gestures to indicate when they want to slow down or stop certain activities." He must have sensed her fear.

"Safewords like pickle or red?"

He nodded and grinned. "You remember our earlier talks."

"Yes."

Luke smiled. "You can also use yellow to tell me to slow down. But since I'll have your mouth otherwise occupied, we need a gesture. How about you pinch my side if you need to stop?"

"Okay." Was that her voice sounding so breathless?

"Now, darlin', be warned that I'm going to kiss your socks off until you use that signal."

Without giving her time to prepare, he lowered his mouth to hers and wrapped his arm around her back to keep her from escaping. The pressure of the embrace wasn't tight enough to make her feel trapped, so she forced the initial panic back down.

This is Luke. He would never hurt me.

He placed nibbling kisses at the corners of her mouth and pulled playfully on her lower lip before tracing the crease between her lips. Involuntarily, she opened for him, and his tongue entered her mouth. She moaned, and he pulled back to tease her lips again. Realizing she was more excited than panicked, she tentatively stroked his lower lip with her own tongue. His arm tightened around her as he drew her closer.

More. I want more.

I need more!

Her fingers entwined in the hair at the nape of his neck, and she gave herself to him. His free hand reached between them, accidentally brushing the side of her breast briefly before pulling away again. She had placed them on her list of limits. Oddly, his innocent touch did not cause revulsion, unlike the hands of those monsters from her past.

This was Luke.

No comparison.

In his arms, she felt cherished. Loved. Safe.

Stop analyzing everything, Cassie. Stay in the moment. Let yourself go!

Later she would tell him she liked him touching her breast. Or perhaps she should show him.

As he continued to kiss her, his hand stroked her back through her shirt. Another moan escaped her, this time one of passion. Her nipples hardened. She wanted him to touch her there—but could not ask.

She worried what he would do when she finally shoved him away, as she undoubtedly would. Not yet, though.

Kiss him back.

Emboldened, she thrust her tongue into his mouth and playfully tangoed with his tongue. Her sex throbbed. She wanted…

What was she doing? Her traitorous body was responding faster than she was ready. She pushed him away. His breathing sounded as if he had just chased down one of his horses. Her breathing was equally fast.

He held his hands at his sides in a show that he would not touch her again unless she asked him to. "You're in charge, Sweet Pea."

Tears formed in her eyes. "I am sor—" *Stop apologizing.*

"Darlin', that was the hottest kiss we've shared yet. I sure as hell am not one bit sorry." Her cheeks flamed hot. "Baby steps, darlin'. Okay, nothing babyish about the way you kiss. Hot damn, Sweet Pea."

"You are making me blush."

"Then I reckon my work here is done." He pivoted and headed for the bedroom door. "If you'll excuse me, I need a shower."

How could he think about a shower at a time like this? Her body screamed for more, even though her mind tried to silence its cravings.

No, he was right. Distance. Space. If they continued like this …

The image of hers and Luke's legs entangled in the sheets flashed across her mind. She could not wait until they went to bed together tonight.

All this because of a dance?

And a kiss.

But oh, what a kiss!

I did not want to stop.

Cassie followed him toward the bedroom. Why wait until tonight? Her body had burst into flames and melted away most of the ice she had encased herself in all these years. Enough baby steps.

I am ready to take a giant leap.

Chapter Thirty-One

Luke was cocky enough to think he could have talked her out of her fears, but backed off even though she hadn't used the safe gesture he'd given her. When he saw the fear in her eyes, he needed to give her some space.

He'd learned when to back off while working with his horses. This all started outside with O'Keeffe, who unleashed something inside Cassie.

Something that Luke's body responded to, heating him to the melting point. Nothing was going to cool him off except a shower. An extremely cold one. He stripped off his shirt and sat on the bed to remove his boots and socks.

While she'd been moved to learn O'Keeffe had been sacked out, it was the second painting that probably spoke best to her. *Free*. She had danced with a passion and abandon he knew simmered beneath the surface.

Shucking his jeans, he thanked God she'd finally let herself experience a sense of freedom. A niggling thought crossed his mind. Would Cassie's increasing freedom take her away from him the way Maggie's did? He'd encouraged Maggie to express herself, too, and she'd spent less and less time with him those last few months they were together. The trip to Colorado to track down her rare plant had been the first time they'd shared anything in a long time.

He shuddered despite the heat in the room. God help him if anything ever happened to take Cassie away. But seeing the joy on her face today, like a flower blooming in the desert, he wouldn't do anything to hold her back.

He removed the leather wristband and laid it on the nightstand. But he did plan to work on improving his piss-poor tracking abilities. Cassie had made it easy for him to find her, but what if he'd had to rely only on the physical clues she'd left? What if he had to find someone who didn't know to leave him clues? He couldn't rely on Pic in every situation. But he did spend a fair amount of time today trying to improve the horse's tracking abilities for future SAR missions. Luke had signed them both up for a class next month to help.

He entered the bathroom and turned on the water, starting at warm. Inside the shower stall, he lathered his hair and washed away the sweat from his session with Picasso.

He lowered the hot-water temperature and rinsed. A draft came over him when the door opened. Maybe she needed to use the john. He tried not to think about her looking at his naked body, even if only in a silhouette through the opaque shower glass.

When the stall door opened and she entered, he turned his back toward her and grabbed for the towel hanging over the top of the stall. "What the...?" Luke scrubbed at his face to remove the rest of the suds from his eyes.

"This water is freezing even by my standards!" Cassie reached around him to adjust the faucet, and the water soon turned warm.

Did she have no empathy for him at all?

Maybe this was a test of his self-control. He hoped to hell he passed.

Luke groaned and wrapped the now-soaked towel around his waist, tucking it in place before facing her again. Her dark-chocolate eyes were the personification of innocence, but her wet clothes plastered to her body left nothing to the imagination.

She wasn't wearing a bra.

He drew in a breath and let it out slowly. In her mind, she probably thought her clothing hid her body from him, but he saw more of her than she realized. Forcing his gaze not to linger on her near-bare breasts, he tried to rein in his libido. Too late. He was growing harder by the minute. His self-control had already been stretched to the breaking point these past few weeks. Did she have no clue what being in here did to him?

"Cassie, you sure this is where you belong?"

He had to keep reminding himself that, for all intents and purposes, his wife was a virgin. A very sensual, passionate one, but he needed to take this slow and easy.

She blinked then smiled enigmatically. "I am with my husband. Yes, this is where I belong." She reached out and picked up the bar of soap from the dish. "You are always taking care of me. Now I wish to bathe you and see to your…needs. Let me start with your back."

His needs?

She wants to bathe you, Denton. That's it. Don't get your hopes up along with your cock.

Clearly, the girl had no clue what she did to him. Expelling a lungful of air, he turned around and soon felt her hands soaping every inch of his back.

She kneaded the tenseness out of his shoulders and continued to work her way down his spine. Damned if he didn't feel himself shedding some of the rigid tension he'd held on to for so long. He closed his eyes. "Your hands are magic, darlin'."

"You are so hard."

His eyes opened. "What's that?" No way could she see his cock.

"All of your wood chopping and working with the horses has made your muscles as hard as marble."

Oh, those *muscles!*

"I hated having to spend time in the weight room in college, so I much prefer to stay in shape with hard work. I'll try to stay hard for you as long as I can, Sweet Pea." He grinned, unable to resist the double meaning of his words.

"I am glad you are not vain about your body or good looks."

She thought he was good looking, too? *Hot damn!*

"Now let me wash your front."

Knowing she couldn't see anything with the towel firmly in place, he turned. Her gaze moved lower almost immediately. So she was curious. *Good.* His erect cock jutted against the towel, giving her an idea at least of the effect she had on him. Would she be triggered by his erection? Her only point of reference had been when three cocks had been used as weapons against her body. He fisted his hand.

Don't let thoughts of those fucking bastards ruin this moment.

Hoping to strike a non-threatening pose, he moved his hands to behind his head and laced his fingers. "I'm all yours, darlin'."

Cassie nodded, meeting his gaze again. Suddenly, she smiled. "Yes, you are."

He wasn't sure how she meant it, but when she lathered her hands again and ran them over his chest and pecs, his mind went blank. Her reference to marble led him to think she might be picturing herself sculpting his body, making him less of a threat.

Whatever she needed to do in order to touch him like this, he didn't care.

She trailed her hands down to his abdomen, raising goose bumps along her path. Jeezus, his abs tensed, and his cock became harder.

God, help me survive this sweet torture.

"What happened here?" She traced one of the scars.

"Cleat injury."

"That must have been extremely painful."

"When you're caught up in the moment during the game, you hardly notice."

She met his gaze before rolling her eyes. "Spare me the *machismo*."

He chuckled. "Okay then. Yeah, it hurt like a sonuvabitch after the adrenaline rush was over. Took eight stitches to patch me up, and I missed the bowl game while recovering."

"I would have thought you'd have been happy to be on the sidelines, as much as you disliked playing football."

He shook his head. "Nope. If I'm gonna do something, I give it my all. When I played, I didn't hold anything back."

She rinsed off the soap and reached for the towel.

He brought down his hand and halted her. "Don't." The command sounded lame to his ears, as if he didn't really want to stop her, but his cock felt hotter than a firecracker and ready to explode.

She stared at him, a hurt look in her eyes. "Luke, I know your body better than you think. I'm not going to run screaming from the room at the sight of your...penis."

Hell, she could hardly say the word without cringing. He cupped her cheeks in his hands. "Cassie, we're going to take this intimacy dance in baby steps, just the way you taught me to tango. You being in here with me is a helluva giant leap. I love you for it, but I don't want you having regrets because I misread a cue or we went too far, too fast."

She rinsed her hands under the spray and reached up to pull his face toward hers. Just before their lips met in the tame kiss he had planned, she said, "Kiss me. Hard."

Damn it, Cassie. What are you trying to do to me?

He needed her to get out of here and give him a little time to...cool off. Wouldn't be the first time he'd taken matters in hand to relieve his ache for her.

But if she was ready to ramp things up a bit, he wouldn't deny her. The lady asked to be kissed—hard. Choosing to do things his way, he slowly pushed his body against hers until his lower body pinned her against the wall. Her eyes widened, no doubt at the feel of his erection. Was this a trigger? Or had she come to her senses? Would she tell him to get the hell out of here? He prepared himself to back off when she closed her eyes, relaxed her body, and pursed her lips.

Jeezus.

He leaned in. Her breasts pressed against his chest as her breathing became more rapid. *Shit.* She was as turned on as he was.

"Cassie, open your eyes." She did so, blinking in confusion. "Tell me what you want." He needed to hear her say the words before he jumped to the wrong conclusions.

She nibbled her lower lip, making him even harder. "I said it already. I want you to…kiss me. To take my breath away."

Good thing he'd checked in with her. Just a kiss. A *hard* kiss. He'd almost let his mind run away from him. But he planned to give his little lady what she wanted.

"If you need me to stop, push my hands away."

She seemed confused until he took one of her wrists in each hand and pinned her hands to the wall above her head. Her pupils dilated. *Dayum.* With a groan, he ground his lips against hers, unable to start out sweetly like all the other times they'd kissed.

She asked for hard.

He needed to enter her mouth as fast as possible, before she put the brakes on the kiss. When he reached out with his tongue, her mouth opened for him.

Sweet Jesus, take me now.

*   *   *

Her stomach did a weird drop when he held her hands above her head and pressed her to the wall with his body. Was that the Ka-thunk Kitty mentioned?

Cassie did not think her body could ache for him any more than it did, but when he took control and began kissing her, she melted. Asking for what she wanted made her uncomfortable, but she decided to show him with her acquiescence she wanted this—and more.

His tongue slipped between her lips and teeth, tangoing with hers again, only this time the movements were much more deliberate, forceful. How could he turn her on by being forceful? And yet letting him take control gave her a sense of freedom.

She moaned and ground her lower body against his erection. She pulled away instantly, not wanting to give him the wrong impression, but his kiss set her pelvis grinding against his of its own volition. Her sex ached to be touched, and she rubbed herself against him as best she could. Would he understand her need?

More. She wanted more.

Do not stop, Luke!

Her lungs felt as if they would explode, and she turned her head to break contact and gasp for air. His kisses moved down the column of her neck, not featherlike but hard. At the juncture of her neck and shoulder, he sucked on her skin, bringing her nerve endings to the boiling point.

She wanted him.

But what if she failed him in bed? She pushed against his hands. He pulled away immediately, breathing as fast as she did. Unable to meet his gaze, she reached for the door.

"Wait. Tell me what you're thinking."

Her face flushed hot. "I cannot."

"Yes, you can." His breathing became more regulated.

Refusing to look at him, she answered in a whisper. "If I stopped there, would you be disappointed in me?"

He grinned and lifted her hand to kiss her palm, igniting the fire once more. "Sweet Pea, you never disappoint me. Surprise the hell out of me sometimes, like asking me to dance with you or coming in here looking for a hard kiss. But you have never disappointed me." He reached out to turn off the faucets. "Why don't we dry off and go snuggle in bed a while? We need to slow things down some."

She nibbled at her lower lip before a firm sense of purpose came over her. "No, Luke. I came in here because I want to return a small portion of the love and affection you have shown me."

Luke traced his finger down her cheek to her lips. "Darlin', you make me feel loved every time you sigh, lean into me at night, or prepare a feast for supper."

"That is not what I mean. You must be so frustrated after all the times you've had to pull away. Including now."

She glanced down and saw his penis was no longer erect. As nervous as she was about touching him, the shower seemed a safer place to explore than in a bed.

She met his gaze. "I want to finish washing you."

"You did a fine job already, darlin'."

She reached out quickly before he could stop her this time and yanked away the towel. Not looking at him, she reached to turn the spray on and picked up the soap.

"Lock your hands behind your head again."

He followed her instruction, and she soaped her hands, finally becoming bold enough to look at him. His penis had already begun to stiffen when she reached for it, but continued to grow in her soapy hands as she washed and massaged him.

Her hands reached under him to wash his testicles.

"Careful, there. Not too hard."

She grinned up at him. "Sorry. I will try to be gentle with you, Luke."

He groaned. "You know you're driving me a little crazy, don't you?"

His words empowered her. "I hope so. That is what a wife should do, no?"

"My wife can do whatever the hell she wants with my body." He grinned, and she went back to work.

She probably washed him long after he was clean, but rather than stop, she began to explore his penis further. When she flicked her thumb across the notch at the head, his penis jerked toward her as if seeking her out. Surprised, she did it again with the same reaction.

With his hands out of the way and no chance of him grabbing her head, she rinsed off his privates under the spray. "Now, I wish to explore you with my mouth."

"What?"

He looked a mixture of confused and aroused. "Oh, not there!" How could he think her ready for that? She must be becoming more used to him touching her because the thought did not seem as abhorrent as it might have yesterday, or even this morning.

She leaned toward him and placed her tongue against his nipple before tracing circles around the areola. When she sucked the nipple into her mouth, it was as hard as stone. A heaviness in her lower parts made her tingle as she placed her hands on his sides and took his other nipple between her teeth and nipped him.

"Jeezus, Cassie!"

She pulled away, horrified. "I did not mean to hurt you!"

His quick grin told her she had not hurt him at all. "You keep exploring like that, and I just might explode all over you."

When his meaning became clear, she decided he might be right. They should wait and continue this in bed. She crouched down to place a quick peck on the notch of his penis, just to watch it jerk again.

Standing, she kissed his lips and opened the door. Before she exited, she turned and smiled what she hoped was an alluring smile. "I will be waiting for you in bed."

She grabbed a dry towel to take with her, wanting to put some distance between them while she prepared herself for him.

When he left the bathroom, Luke crossed the bedroom with a dry towel around his waist. She wondered why, because she had already seen and touched him. Probably afraid she would freak out otherwise. He walked over to the window and pulled the drapes closed, darkening the room.

"No, I think I would prefer some light." *Monsters lurk in the dark.* She wanted to be able to look at his beautiful body and stay in the moment. She hoped he would find her body sexy, as well.

After reopening the drapes, he crawled between the sheets. She automatically turned onto her side with her back to him, as she had every night since they had married. Her heart thumped loudly in her ears.

Wait. This is Luke. He will not hurt me.

Was her body's response fear? No. Definitely arousal. If she intended for tonight to be different from the nights they had lain chastely next to each other in the cabin and in Peru, she needed to open herself to him. Dancing and showering with him had lowered some major intimacy barriers. Time for another step.

Was she moving too quickly? Probably not by Luke's standards, the poor, frustrated man. Taking a deep, relaxing breath, she tried to calm any lingering fears. When he curled his hard, warm body against her back, he glided his hand along her exposed arm. His calluses seared her skin causing her nipples to pebble.

"Relax for me, Sweet Pea."

She nodded rapidly, but the lump in her throat kept her from speaking. She held her body rigidly until the strain began to hurt muscles she did not know she had.

"Deep breath, baby girl."

She did so and forced herself to relax.

"That's it. You're safe now." His voice was calm and reassuring.

She truly did feel safe. Luke made no move to touch her breasts or genitals, allowing her to relax a little more. "Thank you, Luke, for taking such good care of me."

"That's what I'm here for, darlin'."

"No, you are more honorable than most men would be."

Don't think about other men now and ruin this sweet moment.

Not wanting to shut him out any longer, she maneuvered onto her back and stared into his smoldering gray eyes, but she kept the sheet over her breasts. "You always have had a gentle way with me. I appreciate that…"

"Do I hear a 'but' in there?"

She shook her head. "No, not really. I do not think I would like you to be forceful, although Kitty described it as a wonderful release to let Adam take over like that."

He chuckled. "You girls telling tales about your men?"

She grinned. "We are just trying to figure you guys out."

"Ah, I see." He took his index finger and raised it to her face, tracing an imaginary line from her temple, down her cheek, and to her lips. Her skin tingled where he touched, and her lower abdomen grew heavy as if her womb had tightened. She had not been aware her body still had sexual wiring, but she had learned since their first night in Peru that the rape had not severed all feeling in that area.

Now her body ached for her husband. With Luke, it would be the first time. In truth, this was her first time making love with anyone. She needed to separate the past from this special moment.

"Will you touch me?"

"I am."

"I mean, lower."

He grinned. "Tell me what places are off limits."

Were there any? "I will not know until you try." She did not want there to be places off limits any longer, though.

"Why don't I start by giving you a massage?"

Luke gave wonderful massages. "I would like that." Perhaps it would help relax her tense body.

"Be right back." The mattress moved as he crawled off and returned to the bathroom. Cassie closed her eyes and tried to focus on her breathing. *Relax.* Moments later, the sound of soothing spa music came from the phone near the bed. Luke probably didn't have any New Age music in his playlists so he must have found one on a design-your-own station app. She smiled at his resourcefulness. This would help her to relax more quickly.

"First, I want you to lie crossways on the bed with your head near me and the edge of the bed. On your tummy. We're going to start with your head, neck, and shoulders."

Standing at the side of the bed, he placed a pillow near the edge of the mattress and directed her where he wanted her. Tamping down any lingering reluctance, she maneuvered herself into the position he wanted, keeping the sheet over most of her body. His penis was hidden by the towel, thankfully. Why was she still so shy about seeing him naked after their time in the shower earlier? She glanced up at him, and he smiled down at her.

"Lift up on your elbows and move closer to me." She did so, hanging slightly over the edge. "Lift again." He gathered her hair and then let it cascade over the edge of the mattress. For a moment, his hands simply played with the long strands. Her scalp tingled in anticipation.

Oh, how he made her feel beautiful. The soothing music filled the air, and she closed her eyes, sinking into the pillow as she let go of any remaining defenses.

Luke's fingers began massaging her scalp. She melted. "You have no idea how good that feels, Luke."

"Glad you're enjoying it, but no more talking. Just feel."

"Yes, sir."

He chuckled, and she realized she sounded like Kitty responding to one of Adam's commands. "Not sir like that. You know what I mean."

"Shhh. I'm from the South, remember? I know what you meant. Either way is nice, though." He bent over and kissed her cheek, surprising her but ending the peck before she could turn and kiss him back.

Kitty said he had a dominant streak. He had even said so. Did he want to dominate her at some point? Would she ever be interested in something like that?

To be honest, when he held her hands over her head in the shower, he freed her of her inhibitions. Of course, at the slightest pressure, he had released her. Perhaps if she could not let herself go otherwise, she would ask him to—

His hands massaged her temples. "Stop thinking. Feel."

She tried to empty her mind of thoughts and to enter into a meditative state. To float.

The pressure of his hands was the only sensation she allowed inside her consciousness. His fingers returned to the top of her scalp, and she sighed. Tension flowed out of her as she sank into the mattress. His hands worked down to her shoulders, and he spent a fair amount of time releasing the stiffness she had stored there.

Without speaking or breaking the mood, his hands focused on the nape of her neck, and she soon relaxed again. Cassie moaned, a mixture of pain and pleasure as he worked on her stress knots. She had no idea she had become so stiff.

Time to let go. She was safe with Luke. Her body floated again as if drifting on a cloud. She never wanted this moment to end. She kept her head down and opened her eyes. Her hair covered his bare feet. She closed them again, and the scent of lavender massage oil perfumed the air. The friction of his hands rubbing together made her realize he was warming the oil before applying it to her skin.

Always so considerate.

When his hands touched her shoulder blades, she flinched, but the oil and the soothing way he massaged her back soon had her moaning in pleasure again.

"You, too, have magic hands."

"Don't you forget it, darlin'. Now hush."

"Just feel."

"That's right."

She heard the smile in his voice and had to grin herself. His lack of seriousness helped her relax even more, and for the next half hour or so, she simply let him knead the tension out of her back, slowly working his way down her spine.

He pushed the sheet down to her thighs exposing her backside…

…cantina music assailed her…

Hands pulled at her skirt and blouse. The sound of a knife cutting through the material made her stop fighting for fear she would be cut as well.

Run!

She stiffened and started to rise.

"Relax, darlin'. I'm just massaging you. Helping you relax."

Luke. I am with Luke

He removed his hands, but soon she heard him warming more massage oil between them and knew he was about to touch her lower body.

Despite that brief flashback, she wanted him to do just that. Since the shower, she had desired for him to touch her more intimately, but had no clue how to make that happen. Asking outright to be touched a certain way made her extremely uncomfortable.

Luke's hands firmly stroked her lower back. His fingers pressed into the skin on either side of her spine and moved closer to the curve of her buttocks. She clenched her thighs together, both dreading and anticipating his touch in more intimate places, but he surprised her by walking around to the other side of the bed and lightly tracing a fingertip down the sole of her foot.

Her leg involuntarily bolted up at being tickled. Using mind over matter, she relaxed her leg again and let him continue.

"Good girl. I love your self-control. But I also want to see you totally lose control for me before the night is over."

Cassie tensed again. Could she do this? Before she could worry too much, he elicited a moan from her as he rubbed the ball of her foot.

"That's my girl."

"That feels heavenly." The man definitely knew how to give a great full-body massage.

"Happy to hear my lady is pleased."

His lady. Her cowboy.

She let the romantic image envelop her. She did believe in romance now.

Luke seemed in no hurry to move to a new area, and she relaxed farther into the mattress as her muscles melted like butter. He massaged her calf before crawling onto the bed beside her and removing the sheet. He focused on the back of her knee and thigh.

When had she unclenched her thighs? She started to close them again, but fought back the urge.

Be brave.

Instead, she forced her body to remain relaxed. Mind over matter.

Wait! Did she just open her legs a little bit wider? Why? What would happen if he touched her there? Would she shut down, run away—or enjoy it?

Perhaps she was inviting him to do more. Her sex tingled, aching to be touched. What was he doing to her? Her heart pounded. *Arousal, not fear.* She trusted him, so why was her body trying to rebel at his touch? How could she clamp down on her excitement?

Dirty.

"Relax, Sweet Pea. You're tensing up again. Stop worrying about what's coming next. Just enjoy the moment."

"How did you know I was worrying?"

He chuckled, and she heard him rubbing more oil into his hands. "It's my job to pay attention to your body and read the signs, especially when you won't come right out and tell me what you want or need."

Ah. Body language. He had paid attention to her pulse point the time she had told him about the rape. Very observant, indeed. Good, because asking for what she wanted was impossible.

She smiled and loosened up again as his hands surrounded her left thigh, working the oil into her skin. She spread her legs wider to allow him access to her full thigh.

Touch me.

As if he had heard her thoughts, the side of his hand brushed against her sex, and she gasped in surprise but did not close her thighs. It must have been accidental.

Then he touched her there again.

Her sex throbbed, but he pulled away again. Did she just groan in frustration? One minute she was afraid he would touch her more intimately and the next she regretted he did not.

"Like that, baby girl?"

"Oh, yes."

She liked being his baby girl, too, but by tonight, she wanted to become Luke's woman in every sense.

He played her body like an instrument, eliciting responses she never expected as he caressed her other thigh before applying more pressure. This time, when he came into contact with the juncture of her legs, she lifted her hips seeking more.

"I think we'd better stop now before things go too far. I love touching your body like this, though. We'll have to do it again tonight." His hands stopped moving and left her body.

No! He was stopping? *Now?*

"Please, Luke."

"What, darlin'?"

"Please…keep doing what you're doing. It feels so good." There, she had spoken the words. Had asked for what she wanted. No, *needed.* Her heart pounded as she waited for him to respond.

"That's my good girl."

He chuckled. Had he been testing her? He warmed more oil in his hands, and she expelled the breath she had been holding. Where would his magic hands roam next?

Anticipation caused her to hold her breath again, and she gasped in surprise when they came down with one hand high on each thigh, his thumbs *so* close. Without being asked, she opened her legs wider for him, inviting him to explore farther.

His hands kneaded the back of her thigh. Strong, firm motions left her inner thighs tingling at his touch.

"Mmmm." She could not form a coherent sentence now if he commanded her to, but simply gave in to the feel of his hands. Her sex pulsed as though her heart was beating there. The ache to be touched became a raging need.

"Please. More."

Cassie's frustration increased when his hands ignored her and moved lower on her thigh again. She spread her legs even wider, but his hands left her again altogether. She growled. Why did he not take the hint?

Oil. Rubbing his hands. *At least he wasn't finished!* Where would he touch her next?

Anticipation engulfed her.

Facing away from her as best she could tell from the position of his hands, he straddled her lower back, rocking the mattress.

Pressure. Fearing the images from the cantina would bombard her again, Cassie twisted to her side and threw him onto the bed. "Stop! Pickle!"

She gasped for air as Luke stretched out beside her and met her gaze, his hand stroking her face. "Shhh. You're safe. It's Luke. Tell me what's going on."

Her face flamed with embarrassment. "I am sorry."

"Don't apologize. Let's just figure out what triggered you so I won't do it again."

"I am not sure it was really a trigger, but when you pressed your body against my lower back, it felt like…" She sucked air into her chest. "I did not really experience a flashback. It was more like the panic that I might, if that makes sense."

"Sounds like you're saying you were anticipating a trigger because you thought there should be one."

"Perhaps. I think the pressure is what scared me."

"Would you like me to try again but from another position?"

"No."

The disappointment in his eyes was evident. "It's okay. We don't have to. We can cuddle and talk instead."

"No!"

Clearly, she was not expressing herself well. "What I mean is that I do *not* want to stop. I do *not* want you to try another position. I *do* want to try and control my body from reacting like this." Tears filled her eyes. "Oh, Luke, I want to do this. To please you. I just want to be normal!"

Luke grinned. "Well, that would make one normal person in this bed. Hell, I don't even know what the standard is for normal. All I know is that whatever *we* do or *want* to do is normal for us today, and if tomorrow we redefine what we want, then that will be our new normal."

She smiled and leaned toward him to press her lips against his before pulling back again. "Thank you for not making me feel like a freak."

He brushed the hair away from her eyes. "Darlin', I'm telling you, based on thirty-three years of experience, even freaks set their own normal."

"I love you, Luke."

"Love you, too, baby girl." He leaned up and propped his head in the palm of his hand as he traced a finger down her arm. "Tell me what you want me to do next."

Tell him. Speak the words.

Gathering her hair in one hand, she resumed the position. "Touch me the way you were touching me before."

He bent over her and kissed her cheek. "Thanks for using your safe-word, Sweet Pea. Helps me relax knowing you will if you need to."

She did not realize he was nervous, too. He seemed so self-assured and in control.

He straddled her facing away from her head, but she noticed he did not put his weight on her right away. Heat from his feet and legs warmed the sides of her breasts. His hands focused first on her upper thighs and then her bottom. She remained in the moment and allowed no more worries from the past to interfere with her enjoyment of this time with her husband.

She had enjoyed his massages before, but none had made her feel so alive. He awakened parts of her body long dormant. Using indirect touches, he made her genitals tingle in anticipation of more. Would he ever shift his focus there more directly?

Goddess, I hope so.

Cassie felt something stiff pressing between her butt cheeks, and it took a moment before she realized he was erect again. The prospect of Luke making love to her tonight became very real, very fast. She smiled.

I can do this.

Abruptly again, he stopped and crawled off her. She heard the cap snap closed on the bottle of oil. "Why don't we cuddle awhile?" Her smile faded. That was it? He intended to stop with only the massage?

No! That is not what I want!

She rolled onto her back and covered herself with the sheet. Underneath, her nipples bunched. If he would only touch her there, he could see how excited she was without her saying a word.

Becoming aroused in front of a man once scared her to death, but this was Luke. She loved and trusted him. She wanted to please him with her body.

Do it!

She drew the sheet down as he placed the bottle of oil on the nightstand. When he turned to look at her, he zeroed in on her breasts.

Yes, look at what you have done to me, Luke.

Instead of appearing to be excited, a pained expression flashed across his face. Slowly, he met her gaze. He swallowed hard. "Maybe we can take a nap before we get to our chores later on?"

"Nap?" Luke never slept in the middle of the day. He slept only a few hours each night. How could he expect her to sleep when her body was on fire?

He removed the towel that had been around his waist, and she saw his own state of arousal. How could he just ignore that, as well? He helped maneuver her body lengthwise on the mattress, stretched out, and placed the sheet over them. He did not spoon her as he did at night. Did not allow his erection to touch her as it had moments ago. She wanted to beg him to touch her there. The man had cast some kind of spell over her.

And now he wanted to nap?

Luke draped his hand over her, and it came to rest on her side. She tilted her body toward him until his fingers brushed her breast, but he pulled away. Did he not realize she wanted him to touch her breasts?

She ached to be stroked, touched, put out of her state of misery. Parts of her anatomy she did not know existed burned now. Literally *burned.*

For Luke.

Kitty said he was a take-charge man. Why did he not take charge of her now? She wanted him to release this unbearable tension from her body. She wanted to have him give her what she needed…without making her ask for it.

Putas *ask for it.*

No! This is right. This is my husband. He loves me, honors me, cherishes me. He would never do anything to make me feel dirty and used.

Why could she not just tell him what she wanted…no, *needed?*

How could he bring her to the brink and stop abruptly?

Had her body turned him off? Was she too unresponsive for him?

Well, she had certainly sent him enough messages these past few months about how touching her sexually was off limits. How could she expect him to know that now she welcomed more intimacy?

"Luke?" she whispered.

"Is there something you need, Sweet Pea?"

Yes, you.

But asking him to make love to her was out of the question. If he could not tell she was ready…

"Never mind." She rolled to her side, losing contact with his hand, and clenched her thighs together as she drew them up. But that movement only created friction in the very place she was trying to ignore. She groaned.

"What did you want to ask me?"

"Nothing."

His body shook as if he tried to smother a laugh. If only he knew the seriousness of the predicament she was in.

Chapter Thirty-Two

H is little lady was horny—and he'd made her that way.
Hot damn!

Even though he knew what she needed, he planned to wait for her to ask him. Yeah, he was testing her limits a little, but he didn't want her to regret anything he did with her. He'd waited this long. She wasn't going to be able to hold out much longer before she begged him for more.

She wasn't the only sexually frustrated one in this bed.

"Naptime, darlin'." He placed a kiss between her shoulder blades, and she pressed against his lips, rather than move away. *That's my girl.* "Now, curl up against me." He placed his arm around her, hoping his aim was right so he could brush the side of her breast again. Damn. When he drew her toward him, though, she resisted.

"I am fine over here."

Don't run from me now, darlin'. "We're just going to snuggle."

"But I…" Apparently unable to explain her wants or needs or to tell him why spooning naked against him was a problem for her, she had no recourse but to scoot toward him and curl her back against his chest and thighs. This time he let her feel his hard-on. She clenched her ass cheeks and pulled away to keep from touching him, but he held her more tightly. Her body had to be screaming for more, even though her mind cautioned that she needed to maintain her distance.

He moved her hair aside and placed a kiss on the top of her shoulder this time. Soft. Sweet smelling. "Nice dreams, darlin'."

With all the willpower he could muster, he closed his eyes and feigned sleep. Her body remained rigid as she fought sleep and sexual longing, no doubt. How long would it take her to break down and ask him to touch her where she wanted to be touched?

No, *needed* to be touched.

However long it took, he'd be here when she was ready…

Luke awakened with a start. What the… Damn, he never fell asleep in the daytime. Between the trip to Peru and burning the midnight oil while he prepared to surprise the hell out of Cassie, he must be behind on his sleep.

He glanced at the window. Still daylight. The clock on the nightstand indicated they had hours before they needed to take care of the animals.

Good.

The weight of Cassie's head on his chest and her leg sandwiched between his thighs made chores the last thing he wanted to think about.

Stubborn girl.

She hadn't begged him for more as he'd hoped, but she had sought to get even closer to his body in her sleep. All hope wasn't lost. He stroked her back lightly, wanting her to know he was there but hoped she wouldn't fully awaken. She moaned, which was all the encouragement he needed. His cock grew hard as his hand trailed down her back to the curve of her ass. When he touched her there, she ground her pelvis against his leg as if seeking relief. Yeah, he could give her that.

But he wouldn't.

Not yet.

He continued to explore her satiny-soft skin, drawing closer to the cleft between her ass cheeks. When his finger slid lightly over her butt crack, he elicited another moan from her.

Cassie rolled onto her back. "Do not stop."

Her eyes remained closed. Was she still sleeping? Did she know what she was asking?

"Please, Luke. Touch me."

He grinned. Yeah, she knew. Her breasts beckoned, but first, he wanted to tease her a little more. He took the tip of his index finger and skimmed it lightly across one collarbone then the other before trailing it down between her breasts. She moaned as her chest rose. Her skin broke out in goose bumps.

That's not all that rose. Besides his cock, he watched her nipples swell, leaving him wanting so badly to take one into his mouth.

Not yet.

Anticipation would be good for both of them. And sheer torture.

When his finger continued its exploration down to her belly button, she giggled.

"Ticklish?"

"A little. But do not stop. I like it when you touch me."

Progress. He wondered why she kept her eyes closed, but she knew who was with her. Maybe it helped her in some way, so he wouldn't insist on her opening them—yet. So should he head farther south or come back up and tease her breasts a little more? She hadn't placed any limits on where he could touch this time.

"Use your safeword again if you need to."

"I will."

He'd still listen for a "no" or "stop," too, in case she panicked.

His hand reached for her right breast and cupped it, avoiding the nipple. God, she had the most beautiful bare breasts he'd never touched. Before she'd always had clothes on as a barrier.

High. Firm. Her dusty-rose areolas just begged to be kissed.

Testing the waters first, he grazed her nipple with his knuckles and her chest heaved upward again.

"Yes! There!"

He smiled. "You sure about this, darlin'?"

"Mm-hmmm. Touch me, Luke."

She was getting better at asking.

"Love to."

He took the nipple between thumb and index finger and squeezed lightly at first. With a little tug, he watched it double in size. A frown came over her face. Too much—or too little. He lifted himself and leaned on one elbow before bending down to take her left nipple into his mouth.

"Oh, yes, Luke!"

He sucked, gently at first, but when her pelvis tilted upward, he knew she was ready for more. Drawing her engorged peak between his teeth, he suckled harder. When he pulled his head away, he didn't release her nipple.

"Oh, Goddess! That feels so good. More!"

He sure as hell hoped she knew her goddess wasn't responsible for what she was feeling. Just to be sure, his hand roamed down to stroke her thigh. She opened to him.

He let her nipple go with a plop. "Tell me what you need, Cassie."

Her brows furrowed. She blinked her eyes open, but closed them again quickly.

"Please…"

"Look at me and tell me what you need."

She groaned but opened her eyes. "Why do you make me speak the words? You know what I want."

He traced a finger down her nose. "No, darlin'. I know what *I* want. I'm not a mind reader. I don't want you upset because I misinterpreted what I thought you meant. Until you're more comfortable with intimacy, I need for you to put into words what you want. What you *need* from me."

While he waited for her response, he rolled her nipple lightly between his fingers, as if twirling a dandelion stem.

"I need…you…to touch me. There."

"Where specifically?"

"Luke, why are you torturing me like this? You know what I want! Must you force me to speak the words aloud?"

"Yes. Tell me."

She grabbed his hand. He expected her to fling it aside and escape from the bed. Instead, she stared at him before coming to some kind of decision. "I need you to touch me *here!*" Without hesitation, she moved his hand lower until he cupped her mound.

He grinned. "Good girl."

His fingers ruffled the curls covering her precious triangle. He liked that she wasn't shaved. Somehow, that made her more innocent. Not that he wouldn't like to shave her sometime—but that would be different because he would be the first—and only—one to do so.

He pulled gently at the hairs before sliding his middle finger down the slit. She brought her knees up and opened wider for him.

Anxious, Sweet Pea?

He slipped inside her folds, avoiding her clit, and found her wet for him. He teased the sides of her clit hood until she began panting. *That's it, baby girl.* He continued to explore and tease her as she rocked her pelvis against his hand. *So responsive.* When she finally allowed herself to let go, he'd better be ready.

Without letting up on what his hand was doing, Luke bent his head over her again and took her nipple into his mouth, flicking the peak until it became hard.

"Oh, yes, Luke! Faster."

Hearing her excitement, he sucked hard until her thighs squeezed his hand. His finger slid down toward her opening, but he didn't enter her.

Not yet.

Knowing Cassie's history, he needed to hear her words. What her body wanted and what her mind was ready for could be two wildly different things.

But he hoped like hell she'd let him make her come before calling an end to this session.

Luke removed his mouth and hand and leaned away. "Sweet Pea, open your eyes for me."

A frown creased her forehead. "Do I have to?"

"Yes, you do. We need to talk."

"Now? Can it not wait? We were in the middle of something wonderful."

"Tell me where you want this to go so neither one of us is on the wrong page in our ever-changing playbook."

She blinked. "You are finally going to touch me *there*. And...I want you to."

What did she mean *finally*? He'd wanted to for...

Wait! "What did you say?"

"Yes, I want you to touch my private areas, Luke." She smiled. Jeezus, hearing her say those words made him harder than ever.

She was ready for more.

Now.

The girl continually surprised him.

*   *   *

"Whatever the lady wants." Luke reached for a pillow and tossed it to the foot of the bed. Without another word, he lowered his mouth to her nipple again. Electricity shot up to her jaw and down to...

She placed her hand on the back of his head, not wanting this to end by letting him get away. The intense emotions roiled through her like a storm through the mountains. She wanted to be loved in every way by Luke.

He moved away from her breast only to take her other nipple between his teeth.

Ay-eee. Her nipples burned while her body screamed for some kind of release. Would he give her what she wanted? Needed?

He let go and trailed kisses down her tummy. Why was he taking so long to move to her sex? He was so slow it was nerve-racking!

He crawled to the bottom of the bed and stared at her, not saying a word. Did he wish for her to do something? What? His penis was erect, jutting out from a nest of hair. She blushed and met his gaze again.

Perhaps he wanted her to give him the go-ahead again—to reassure him. But she had not used their safeword. She was not ready for him to enter her, but she needed some kind of release. "Touch me, Luke." She clenched her fists as she held on to the sheet and prepared herself.

"Lift your hips."

She quirked her eyebrow and met his gaze again at his command. Her take-charge guy was in control now. Thank the Goddess, because she had no clue what to ask for or what to do.

She tented her knees and lifted up so he could slide the pillow under her bottom. When he looked at her again, she fought the urge to close her knees, but the desire to open herself to him was stronger.

He trailed his hands down the insides of her thighs, closer and closer to her core. Her womb contracted under his intense scrutiny.

When he began to lower his head to her, she did fight to close her legs, but his hands blocked her from doing so. "What are y-you doing?"

"My bride asked me to touch her. I'm about to do so." He grinned at her. "My way."

She tried to squirm away. "No, not like that! I meant the normal way!"

He pulled back. "Sweetheart, what did I just say about normal?"

"We are going to define our own idea of normal."

"Good girl. Now, unless I hear you say 'pickle' to stop or 'yellow' to slow down, I want you to lie there and enjoy the ride."

She had the power to end this if she wanted to.

She did not want to do that.

Yet, after giving her time to speak her safeword, he hooked his arms under her thighs, placed his hands over her hips, and lowered his head once more.

She squeezed her eyes shut, and heat infused her face as Luke's tongue touched her most private place. She held herself so rigidly her muscles soon began to ache. Why was he doing it this way?

He pulled away. "Relax, Sweet Pea. It will be a helluva lot more fun that way."

She took a deep breath and let it out slowly, the air making a whoosh-ing sound between her lips. He returned to what he had been doing, and she reminded herself to breathe deeply as she attempted to relax her body. His tongue pressed inside her vagina. He held it there, as if waiting for her to scream her safeword. She tensed. No triggers. She relaxed.

What did she taste like? Her face burned. No, her entire body did. She would not worry about that now, especially when he slid his tongue along the bundle of nerves that had been begging for his touch for so long.

But she wanted more. What other surprises were in store for her?

When his lips surrounded her hood as if to kiss it, her hips jerked up. The movement intensified the effect of his mouth on her. He chuckled as though he had been anticipating this response. Then he sucked on her hood.

"Oh!"

Tension built inside her belly. She could no longer relax no matter how intentionally she breathed. What was he doing to her? She reached down to grab his head, intending to push him away, only to have him start flicking the little button.

"Yes! There!" She latched onto his hair. *More!*

Oh, Goddess! Her heart pounded as the tension rose. She could no longer breathe. Her chest ached as the pressure continued to build.

His finger entered her and began pumping in and out of her wetness. No resistance. He pulled his finger out, but quickly filled her with two. The feeling of fullness made her close her eyes and imagine it was his penis. She was ready for him.

"Yes. Oh, Luke. Come inside me!"

What had she just asked? No matter, because he ignored her and continued to use his fingers and mouth to elicit such exquisite responses from her. But what was he waiting for? She was on the brink of…something wonderful.

When he flicked his tongue rapidly against her sex, the world exploded into thousands of shards of light.

"¡*Sí!* Do not stop!"

Unable to hold back, she shattered as the waves rolled through her body.

She rode a wave of ecstasy that went on forever. But all too soon she began to float back to earth, noticing her rapid breathing and heartbeat.

His tongue became painful as he continued stroking her sensitive bundle of nerve endings. "Stop! I cannot take anymore!"

He lessened the pressure, removed his fingers from inside her, and stretched out to cover her body with his, careful not to allow his entire weight to crush her. Still, she felt the monsters looming. He sensed her rising panic and rolled onto his side.

"You okay, Sweet Pea?"

"Yes." She did not want to talk about the near-panic. "That was amazing! I had no idea!"

He smiled and kissed her. She turned away again, embarrassed at smelling her scent on his lips.

"What are you thinking now?"

Her face flushed. "That it is strange to smell my...myself on your lips."

He chuckled. "You taste as sweet as honey. I just might have to have another nibble before the day's over."

His penis throbbed, reminding her they were not finished yet. Why had he stopped? She did not want to deprive him of that euphoric experience. No wonder Kitty was so frustrated with Adam all these months when he held back.

She reached up and brushed her fingertip across his lower lip. Her face grew warm thinking about his lips on her so intimately, but she did not intend to shy away from going all the way with her husband any longer. "Make love to me, Luke. Now." She was ready. She hoped. All she knew was that she wanted to feel him inside her.

He grinned. "Bossy little thing. You sure? There are other ways I can come without being inside you."

"I am sure." *As sure as I will ever be.*

"First, I want to make you come."

"I just did." Did she do it wrong? How could he not tell?

He chuckled. "You ladies are luckier than us men. You can come again and again in no time. Takes us a little longer to build up to another erection. Then it's over. So I plan to take my time and enjoy you as long as I can."

She had so much to learn about how to have sex. No, to make love. Thankfully, Luke was a patient man and would guide her along the way.

He kissed her again, and she ran her hands over his broad shoulders.

So strong.

Mine.

Thank you, Mama Quilla, for entrusting him to my care.

His erect penis throbbed against her thigh as he kissed her again. She opened her mouth to his, but when he placed his hands on either side of her head to deepen the kiss, her body stiffened.

Triggers. *Damn it, not now!*

Frustrated with her body, Cassie pushed him away but did not surrender. Instead, she guided him onto his back. "Please avoid holding my head that way. It makes me freeze up—and I want to stay hot for you." His lopsided grin told her she had said it wrong, but that he understood her meaning. "Let us try me being the one on top."

He opened his eyes wide in surprise. "Hell, yeah. You're in charge, Sweet Pea. Have your way with me." He was teasing, but she had no clue what to do next. "Why don't you start by straddling my waist?" he suggested.

Thankful for the direction, she nodded and placed her leg over him until she was kneeling on the mattress, with his torso between her knees. If she sat back, she would be on his...

Not ready for that yet, she remained upright. Her hair would soon be in the way so she wound it around her fist to try and tame the mass, but it had a mind of its own. "Let me get something to get my hair out of the way."

When she would have moved off him, he placed one hand on each of her hips and stopped her. "No way." He reached up and loosened her hair again, letting it cascade over her breasts. "I love your hair loose like this."

She had no idea. He had never asked her to wear it down. What else did she not know about this man's likes and dislikes? At least they had a lifetime to learn it.

*   *   *

Jeezus, Cassie is every man's wet dream.

And she's all mine.

"I also love looking at you like this, darlin'. You can be on top anytime you want."

She smiled and bent over to kiss him. The rasp of her lips against his five-o'clock shadow made his cock throb even more. When she broke the kiss and sat up again, her breasts bounced. She smiled in triumph.

Cassie Denton sitting on top of him, with her hair shielding her bare breasts from view, just made him ache to bury himself inside her. Her long curls didn't completely hide one nipple this time.

He reached up to pinch the protruding nipple. Her tiny gasp excited him even more. When a look of concern came over her face, she stretched out over his chest. Damn. Another trigger?

Her words were barely a whisper. "Teach me what to do next."

At least she didn't apologize for a lack of carnal knowledge, because nothing excited him more than to instruct his virgin bride in her first experience with making love.

He placed his hands lightly on her back, waiting to see if her body rejected his touch, but she relaxed into his chest as if in surrender. Having her pressed against him like this did amazing things to his ego. She trusted him.

He wondered how long he could hold out. His hands swept up and down her bare back, keeping her in the moment. So soft. "Hope I'm not scratching you with my calluses, darlin'."

"Hmmm? Oh, no! Do not stop. I like the sensation." She lifted herself up, placing her hands on his shoulders before leaning down to kiss him again. Her hair curtained them in their own private world.

He moved his hands lower and placed them over her butt cheeks. She moaned rather than try to escape. He broke the kiss. "Lift up your hips." Reaching between her legs to take his cock, he rubbed it along her slick cleft. She closed her eyes when he touched her clit and leaned back, her mouth open. So full of passion.

Take me now.

His blushing bride was hotter than a firecracker. He reached up to tuck the strands behind her ears, careful not to touch the sides of her head, although he suspected the trigger came from using firm pressure. *Fucking bastards.* He tried not to let thoughts of them violating her body ruin this moment.

He'd let her set the pace and give her free rein.

Her breasts thrilled him, and he reached up with his hand to give in to the temptation to cup and squeeze them. His thumb and index finger rolled her nipple, and she clamped her thighs against his sides.

God help him survive this girl because he wasn't sure he was going to be able to keep up with her now that she'd decided to explore her sexuality with him.

Once again, he marveled that he had to be the luckiest man alive. What he'd ever done to deserve this girl in his life, he didn't know. He just hoped he didn't ever screw things up with her.

She stared down at him with a puzzled expression on her face. "I'm not sure what to do."

"I'm pretty sure anywhere you want to touch me would be right, dar-lin'."

She reached out and ran her hands over his pecs before letting her fingernails trail down his rib cage. He hissed, not expecting her touch to be so lethal.

When she bent over and took his nip between her teeth, his hips bucked, and her teeth bit into his skin. She pulled away in horror.

"I am sorry! I did not mean to do that!"

"A little pain never hurt anyone—not when it's part and parcel of such a pleasurable act."

Cassie smiled. "Still, I will try to be gentle with you. I am not one for giving—or receiving—pain." She bent over his chest again and nibbled this time. He splayed his hands over the cheeks of her ass, kneading them and wishing he could touch her clit, but he didn't want to have her move from where her sweet mound was pressed against his hard-on.

That she didn't seem bothered having him so close to her made him want to bury himself inside her even more. He would wait until she was screaming for him to take that step first. Now all he had to do was take her to that point. Although she was well on her way.

Her lips surrounded his nip in a gentle kiss. When her tongue licked over his tender peak, he bucked again. *Sweet Jesus.* He might be the one screaming for release soon if she kept this up.

Scooting down his thighs, she let her tongue trail toward his abs, and he clenched in anticipation of where she might go next. He wanted more.

Her chin bumped against his erection, and she pulled away. Her eyes opened wider before she smiled, and he wondered what she planned to do next.

"I cannot believe how quickly you become so…hard."

"Darlin', being naked with the most beautiful, sexy woman in the world has that effect on me."

She glanced back at his hard-on and then up at him, insecurity show-ing in her eyes. "I do not know if…"

He held up his hands to halt her before she let fear or doubt take over. "Come here."

She crawled up his body again, and he pulled her onto his chest where he let her rest her head on his chest. "Why don't we start by talking about what we *do* want to have happen next? In explicit language, darlin'."

"I am not sure. I know what I feel…" Her hand reached out to stroke his pec. "However, I am not sure how to…."

"Tell me what you feel." *Come on, baby girl. Say the words.*

She idly flicked at his hard nip, driving him a little more crazy for her, before continuing. "Like my body is ready to explode. I am ready for you to…come inside me." The remaining words came out in a rush. "I am afraid having you on top of me will be a trigger, but I do not know how to…do it with me on top."

His cock jerked in anticipation. *Easy now. Don't scare her away, Denton.*

Knowing how serious she was, he fought back the urge to laugh. Okay, probably a little nervous energy on his part. "Sweet Pea, you're assuming there are only two options here. We can do this in any number of ways. Heck, think of the Kama Sutra and all the positions that are possible."

She leaned up and met his gaze, her eyes opening wide. "I never thought about the more advanced positions for making love."

He stroked her cheek. "One's not more advanced than another. Just different." He lowered his hand to her shoulder and slowly pressed her onto her back. Careful not to put too much pressure on her chest, he positioned himself so he could take her nipple into his mouth. The responsive peak hardened and grew as he sucked, and her hips jerked up when he gave her a nip similar to one she'd given him. Her breathing grew more labored, but she wasn't where he wanted her yet. His hand reached out to her other breast, and he plucked at the nipple there until it equaled the size of the one in his mouth.

"Oh, Luke! That feels so good!"

He pulled at her nipple, stretching it until it plopped out of his mouth. She hissed.

"That's it, baby girl. Just feel." Without waiting for further response, he maneuvered onto all fours. "Raise your knees and spread your legs. It's my turn."

While her brows furrowed in confusion, she did as he'd instructed her. He straddled her in a sixty-nine position, keeping his body off her except for his knees brushing her sides, and lowered his head to her lower lips. When she reached up and grabbed his cock, he nearly lost it.

"Go easy there, darlin'. You come first." He grinned at the double meaning of his words. Her body relaxed into the mattress. "That's my girl." He wanted her to be able to look at his cock dangling before her eyes to desensitize her for the future, but needed no distractions.

Using his thumbs, he spread open her folds. When he lowered his face to her clit, he gloried in her swollen nubbin just waiting for him to give her release. Not just yet, though. They had all evening—well, up to a point. The horses would be whinnying in a couple of hours if neglected too long.

Right now, his wife was the one most in need of his attention.

Luke stroked her button in another lick, and she bucked upward, nearly dislocating his jaw. He smiled and let his tongue tease the sides of her hood, avoiding direct contact with her tiny erection. Hearing her panting nearly made him turn around and bury himself inside her right then, but it would be much more enjoyable for her if he kept increasing her level of arousal. Even better if he let her come first.

His finger traced down her wet slit to her opening, and he dipped the tip inside to lubricate his finger. She clenched around his finger before he moved back toward her clit hood. With his tongue on one side, he applied pressure to the other.

"Oh, Luke! What are you doing to me?"

The excitement and wonder in her voice again left him aching for her, but he'd only just started. She wasn't going to need a vibrator or anything other than him when he decided it was time for her to come.

Not yet, though.

He flicked his tongue against her exposed clit and held her hips in place so she wouldn't jump up off the bed. He didn't want his lady coming again just yet.

Despite the angle, he managed to work his finger a little farther into her opening. Feeling her clench around him again only made his balls tighten in anticipation, but he was determined to continue this slow build up. Dipping his middle finger more deeply inside her, he continued to lick at the side of her hood and then slipped two fingers inside her.

"Oh!" She squeezed him with her pussy muscles, and he imagined what it would feel like when she did that to his cock.

Time to slow down his own libido. He thought about an intricate rigging lesson Adam had been teaching him before the avalanche. They hadn't had time to delve into further lessons because their lives had exploded after that, but remembering the loops and knots required to suspend a girl safely helped keep his mind focused—until the image of Cassie's naked body suspended in ropes with a beautiful Shibari design flashed before his eyes.

One thing's for sure, he wasn't going to be able to give her the pleasure-filled release she enjoyed earlier in this position. He pulled up and swung his leg over her body. When he glanced down at her, the expression of shock and awe on her face made him feel about ten feet tall. He hadn't even given her another orgasm yet, but already she was riding a wave of bliss.

Damn, he was going to have fun in the next hour or so.

He reached for a pillow from the top of the bed. "Lift your hips." She did, and he slipped it underneath and then went for another. "Again." Once he had her bottom elevated to where he wanted her, he crawled down the bed. "Spread your legs again for me."

Within seconds, his arms were bracing themselves around and over her thighs to open her dewy flower. So wet, she glistened. He lowered his face to her mound and reached out with his tongue, lapping at her sweet honey. Her hiss told him she loved this as much as he did, so he gave her another long, slow lick from her opening to her clit. She grabbed onto his hair, clamped her legs around the sides of his head in a vise grip, and screamed, "Please, Luke! Do not torture me like this!"

Closer.

But not there yet.

He continued to *torture* her by slipping his finger deep into her, and then he added his second finger. When he curled them toward her G-spot, her legs began to tremble.

Okay, here we go, darlin'.

He flicked his tongue against her clit while continuing to massage her G-spot. The pained moans coming from her made him wonder if this was too much for her, and he paused a moment to search her face and make sure she was okay.

Pain mingled with ecstasy.

Cassie met his gaze. "Please, do not stop now!"

Hot damn!

"Don't worry, baby girl. I won't leave you hanging."

He lowered his face to her and continued where he'd left off. Soon she was moaning again, from excitement not pain. She needed to experience another orgasm without him taking anything for himself to show her a real man took care of his lady first. Others had taken pleasure from her. He could wait until…

"*¡Sí, sí, sí!*"

Hearing her revert to her native Spanish pleased him even more. Her tight rein of control gone, she was merely feeling now. Time to take her home again.

He increased the pressure on her G-spot and sucked her clit into his mouth.

"Oh! Oh!"

With the knuckle of his pinkie, he pressed against her anus, but didn't attempt to enter her. Just wanted to overload her senses. Letting her clit go, he brushed the tip of his tongue rapidly back and forth over her swollen button until her thighs shook harder and her screams became incoherent. She clamped her thighs against his ears again, and he kept flicking his tongue against her clit.

"Yes! Oh, yes!"

Spasms coursed through her, and Luke grinned until she scooted her body away from his mouth. "Stop! I cannot take anymore!"

Perspiration bathed her face. Her nipples were distended and hard. The wonder and exhaustion on her face left him grinning ear to ear. She tried to raise herself to her elbows but collapsed against the pillows, gasping for breath. Watching the rise and fall of her breasts made him hornier than a longhorn bull, but he'd have to wait and hope there would be more opportunities for them tonight after their chores were done.

Then Cassie wrapped her arms around her chest and began to cry. No, sob.

Aw, damn. What happened?

Chapter Thirty-Three

Cassie crashed off the roller coaster ride of a lifetime, not understanding why she was crying after something so beautiful.

"Come here, darlin'."

When Luke crawled up to lie beside her on the bed, he encouraged her to curl up against his shoulder as he stroked her hair. "Shhh, baby girl. That was intense—and long overdue, I'd say. When's the last time you came before a little while ago?"

How could she answer that? She'd never even masturbated since she was raped, not wanting any connection to her sexual self. But the orgasms she'd given herself before had been nothing compared to what Luke had just given her.

"That was...incredible. I do not know why I am crying. Each one was more intense than the last."

He relaxed a little. Had she worried him? She hated being overly emotional like this or making him think he had hurt her in some way. "Each orgasm was beautiful. Thank you."

"The horses and alpacas can wait a little longer for us. We're just going to lie here and enjoy the afterglow."

She glanced up at him and blinked away the tears. "But you did not come. I wanted to please you, too."

He grinned. "Oh, Sweet Pea, hearing and seeing you come like that was all I needed at the moment. I could just about float off this bed if I didn't have you to hold on to." He pulled her closer.

How could he be so selfless?

And yet, in this moment, she just wanted to be held, to be close to him without having to do a thing. She rested her head in the crook of his shoulder and chest and splayed her right hand across his bare chest, playing with his hard nipple. "You not only have magic hands, but a magic tongue as well." Her face grew warm at her bold comment, but he just chuckled. The vibration of his laughter through his chest tickled her nose.

"I love you so much." She didn't want him to think all she loved about him was that he could give her an incredible orgasm. Luke meant so much more than that to her. "Not just because of what you just did, though." He chuckled, puzzling her. How to convey what she felt? "I mean I loved *that*, too, but I love *you* for making sure I reached such ecstasy." Tears pricked her eyes again, and she held on to him more tightly.

"Shhh. No need to explain, Sweet Pea. You said it all in the way you opened yourself up to trust me enough that we could share *that*."

She wanted to stay with him like this forever, sheltered in his strong, protective arms. Nothing could intrude on their love, not after they fought so hard together to keep the evil ones away from destroying what they have.

Her eyelids grew heavy, and her hand stilled.

Cassie startled awake. Muted evening light streamed through the opening in the drapes. "How long did I sleep?"

"Not quite an hour."

She leaned up on her elbow and looked down at him. "Did your arm fall asleep?"

He grinned. "It's okay. I wouldn't have moved you for anything." He reached up and brushed her cheek with the pad of his thumb. "You make me feel like some kind of hero just holding you in my arms."

"You *are* my hero, Luke Denton." The words were out, but she had no regrets or desire to pull them back. "I do not know how anyone can have as much patience as you do, but thank you for staying with me no matter what."

"I honor my commitments, darlin'."

Was she just a commitment?

"Hold on there, baby girl. Before getting your panties in a twist, I want you to know I didn't marry you for any reason other than I want you to be my wife. I want to hear you call me your hero. I want to wake with you in my arms."

"But I am the one who awoke."

"Oh, I dozed a little myself. Wanted to be sure I had enough stamina to keep up with you today—and tonight."

Would there be more tonight? Her lady bits throbbed in response. She smiled, but made no promises. If she was going to do anything tonight, she didn't want the pressure of his expectations on her.

Cassie tossed the sheet away and swung her legs over the edge of the mattress. "Do you think Graciela, O'Keeffe, Picasso, and the others have broken down their stall doors for leaving them waiting so long for their dinner? They are used to you being in there by six o'clock."

"They'll be fine a little while longer." Luke stood and walked around the bed to stand in front of her. Her face grew warm, and she averted her gaze. Would she ever be able to peer at his naked body without becoming embarrassed?

"Are you hungry?"

"I already ate."

He had? When had... She turned to ask when she saw his grin. *Oh!* Cassie's cheeks flooded with heat, and she swatted his thigh. "Must you tease me so?"

"What? I just answered the question."

"I think the animals *are* hungry, though."

He reached for her hand and helped her to her feet. She didn't realize her legs would be so wobbly and grabbed for his arms to steady herself.

"Whoa, there." He scooped her into his arms. "Let me carry you until you have your legs functioning again." He started for the living room.

"But I am not dressed!"

"Neither am I, Sweet Pea. No one is going to give a rat's ass that we're walking around naked in our own house."

True. Out here on the ranch, they would certainly hear an approaching vehicle. She wanted to become more comfortable in her own skin—and under his gaze—so she did not argue any further. He lowered her to her feet in the kitchen and bent to take her lips in a kiss that promised more pleasure to come later.

Her nipples responded to the kiss, and when his tongue entered her mouth, her toes curled. She tasted herself on his lips and tongue again.

She broke the kiss and tried to catch her breath. "I think we must stop doing this, or we will not make it to the barn anytime soon."

He swatted her backside and walked away. The sting surprised her and lingered.

Before he reached the bedroom door, he turned around. His gaze swept over her body, not missing an inch, and her entire body grew warm under his slow appraisal. That he approved of what he saw was evident by his erection.

"That will have to last me until our chores are done. Let's get dressed."

Oh, this was going to be a long night as she waited to see what else Luke had in mind for her.

*   *   *

Luke and Cassie worked alongside each other to complete their chores double time. His lady was anxious to get back to bed—and so was he.

"Excuse me." Cassie left Cassatt's stall in a hurry.

Was she okay? The slamming of the screen door told him she'd gone in the house. He grabbed the brushes and stored them in the tack room before following her. Inside, he found no sign of her in the living room or kitchen and went to the bedroom.

The bathroom door was closed. Ah, she just needed a nature break. He relaxed and went to the kitchen to pour them each a glass of fresh-brewed sweet tea. His was half gone when he realized she'd been in there an awfully long time.

Returning to the bedroom, he knocked gently on the door. "You okay, Sweet Pea?"

Silence.

Dread ripped through him. "Cassie, open the door."

"I need a few minutes, *por favor.*" Her voice was thick from crying.

"I'll give you one. Then I'm coming in to check on you if you don't come out."

What the hell happened? They'd had a good day, hell, the best of days. He waited for what seemed forever, but was probably barely a minute, and the door opened. A red-eyed Cassie greeted him, and he opened his arms.

She walked into them, thank God. At least she wasn't shutting him out again.

"What's the matter, baby girl?"

"I do not wish to say."

He stroked her back, hoping to calm her concerns. "Why don't we go sit on the bed?"

She sniffled loudly, and he stepped back, taking her hand as he led her across the room. After he sat on the bed, he pulled her onto his lap. She didn't resist.

"Tell me what's going on." Maybe if he made it a statement rather than a question, he'd get a response. "Did something trigger you?"

She shook her head and laid it against his chest. He wrapped his arms around her and waited. Sure enough, the silence prompted her to fill the space.

"I cannot make love with you tonight."

"That's okay. But I need you to tell me what happened between the time we were enjoying each other's bodies here in bed this afternoon and when you ran out of the barn a little while ago."

"Must I? I am not comfortable talking about such matters with you."

"I'm your husband. If you can't tell me, who can you tell?"

"Not this time. Please understand."

He was more curious than ever and sensed he needed to push her on this, even if he had no clue what *this* was.

"Why don't we get out of these clothes and take a shower together? That might relax you before we go to bed."

She vehemently shook her head. He wasn't sure if she was opposing the idea of the shower—or of going to bed with him.

"Are you hungry?"

"No, thank you."

"How about a glass of wine? Might make you feel better?"

She shook her head again. He sighed. This conversation was going nowhere fast.

"If I did or said something that upset you—"

Cassie sat up straight and pulled away. "No! It was not you, Luke! I just…hate disappointing you because of my traitorous body."

Now we're getting somewhere.

"Just what did your body do, darlin'?"

Her face grew ruddy, and she glanced away.

Oh, no, Sweet Pea. You aren't shutting me out that easily. "Look at me."

"Oh!" Her hand went to her belly.

"What's wrong? You feelin' sick?"

"No." She met his gaze. "My stomach did that weird thing again that Kitty said… Never mind. It is nothing."

"Well, something's going on. We aren't going to bed until you tell me what it is."

She crinkled her brow. "I am sorry. I cannot make love with you after all."

"Because…?" he prompted.

"Because…it is my time of the month."

"You got your period?" When she would have turned away, he cupped her chin and held her gaze.

"Please, Lucas. *Luke*. This is not something men and women should discuss with one another."

"Why not? It's a normal function of a woman's body. Besides, I want to know what's going on with your body. If we decide to try for babies, it'll be good for me to know when you're having your period."

"You want children?"

"Someday. God—and you—willing, of course. But if we aren't blessed with kids, we have our furbabies and our friends' kids to dote over."

She nodded. "I have never given any thought to being a mother. Except…"

"Except?"

"There was that one time while we were in Peru when *Mamá* was hinting at wanting grandchildren that I imagined a little brown-skinned Luke."

Damn. He'd never given kids much thought after Maggie died. "Making babies with you is something I look forward to someday. But getting your period tonight could be God's way of reminding us that, if we don't take precautions, there's a chance we'll have little Dentons running round sooner than expected."

"In my culture, the use of contraception is not accepted unless it is with traditional family planning."

He reached up and tweaked her nose. "You're living in the United States now, Sweet Pea. No one controls decisions about your body but you."

"I suppose we can try to use the calendar to postpone the unexpected arrival of babies, but once we are settled into our lives together, we could try for babies."

Luke grinned. "My guess is that Eduardo and Susana are using that method. With four kids in about five or six years, I think we'd better be prepared." She smiled, but he grew more serious since this was something they needed to agree upon. "How do you feel about being a momma?" She tended to blend her beliefs based on what worked for her.

"I would rather not inhibit what is meant to be if a child chose us as his or her parents, but I also do not think I would want to have that many children that quickly. Susana has chosen motherhood for her career, and that is the right choice for her. But I will always need to pursue my art. It is what sets my spirit free and helps me to process things." She smiled again. "Until I met you, anyway. You have a way of forcing me—in the nicest of ways—to face things I might otherwise avoid. Such as talking about menstruation." She blushed again, and he allowed her to break eye contact.

Jeezus, she was cute when she blushed.

Suddenly, she faced him again. The smile spread slowly, and he couldn't help but see the mischief in her expression. "At least you have shown me that full intercourse is not always necessary in order to enjoy each other's bodies."

Lordy mercy. I'm a rich man.

"Damned right. But we are going to take a break while your body is preparing itself for whatever God and the universe have in store for us."

"Thank you. I would not be comfortable having you touch me at this time."

"Oh, darlin'. I intend to touch you, all right. In any number of ways. We just won't be having intercourse during your period. Not my kink."

"Kink? People actually do that as a kink?"

"People can do pretty much anything as a kink. Maybe I'd try it in the shower, but I—"

She reached up and cut off his words with her hand. "I think we will agree that this is not our kink—or desire—and move on. As you said, there are other things we can do. I might even learn to find ways of pleasing you more during those times."

"Now that's something I'd be open to trying."

*   *   *

A week later, Cassie pulled into the lane and drove to the house. She did not know how to break the news to Luke that the mama dog and her puppies they had rescued up on her mountain had been claimed by their owner. She had hoped to surprise him today by bringing them to their new home, only to find every one of them gone. After all the visits she and Luke had made over the past two weeks since returning from Peru, when the new receptionist told her the owner had taken them this morning, she wanted to cry. She hoped they would keep a better eye on them than they had before. Of course, the mama dog might have been one of the many pets that wandered away from their homes during the wildfires.

Cassie blinked away the tears, feeling the loss as keenly as if she had just lost someone she loved. Now she had to tell Luke. Her phone buzzed seconds later.

Luke. "Meet me in the barn, Sweet Pea."

She sighed as she opened the door and left the vehicle, a heavy weight on her shoulders. He would have to be told, but what a lousy birthday present for her today. When everything else in their lives had been going so well, too.

"We're in the stall after Pic's."

We? She hadn't noticed any other vehicles. Luke enjoyed surprising her—shocking her sometimes. No doubt he had something sexual planned for her now, but her heart was so distraught about the dogs that she did not think even her handsome husband would be able to coax her body to respond today.

The blood rushed through her ears as she thought about how to tell Luke. When she walked into the dark barn, it took her eyes a moment to adjust from the bright sunlight. Wanting to get it over with—and perhaps have Luke console her as he so often did when she was sad and hurting—she rushed down the barn aisle to the last stall, slid the bolt, and shoved the door aside.

"Happy Birthday, darlin'." He was not naked, so lovemaking was not to be her surprise—yet, anyway. Then he stepped aside to reveal the mama dog. She had a big green bow around her neck and five plump puppies vying for position to nurse.

"It was you!" Tears coursed down her face by the time she crossed the stall. She punched him. "I thought someone else had stolen them from us!"

"Hey, I asked Doctor Lewis to keep it on the down-low so I could surprise you. No need to go beating on me for that."

She knelt down and ran her fingers through the scruff of the mama's neck as she petted her. "We truly will be keeping them?"

"Yep. Doctor Lewis said most likely someone abandoned her because she was pregnant."

"How could anyone do such a thing?" The mama dog stared back with such soul-filled eyes. "You poor thing. No one here would ever dream of doing that to you. You are safe now. Home."

"Unfortunately, happens all too often. But this time, their loss is our gain."

Luke hunkered down next to Cassie and placed an arm around her, enveloping her in love. "I couldn't believe it when she called this morning to tell me they were ready to be discharged."

"You told me your squad had a meeting when you left."

"Well, we did, but then I ran over to the clinic to pick up this crew and snuck them inside the barn, hoping you wouldn't peek."

She turned to Luke and launched herself fully into his arms, burying her face in his neck. Soap and leather. Her favorite combination of scents.

"Thank you. It is the best birthday present I have ever received."

He ruffled the mama dog's hair. "Actually, this is just part of your present. The rest is waiting inside."

Cassie smiled and picked up one of the puppies. As if the mama understood her puppies were safe with Cassie, the dog relaxed and closed her eyes, and she petted her again. "Rest now, little mama."

Each of the five puppies had gained at least another pound or two each since they had rescued them. "I feel like a new mama myself." She picked up another one that had fallen asleep and nuzzled her nose in its fur. "New puppy—my second favorite smell."

"What's first?"

She met his gaze and felt the heat rising in her cheeks. She still felt shy about telling him some of her musings. She smiled. "Luke." Let him draw his own conclusions.

"I'm going to take that as a compliment."

"Oh, yes. Very much so!"

As the puppies she held began squirming and looking for their mama, she placed them inside the padded bed and watched them latch on again. "What on earth will we do with all of them?"

"Love 'em, I suppose."

She met Luke's gaze over the puppy's back. "I think we can manage that." She walked over to him, and he wrapped her in his embrace. "You have such a big heart."

"Hate to see anything suffer." He broke away. "Next job will be naming them all."

"Do you have any suggestions?"

"Only one. Since we live here at Fairchance and this is a place for second chances, I think Chance would be a good name for the momma."

"Chance. Yes, I think that is perfect!"

"Great. Now we just have five more to come up with."

She glanced down at them. "Let us wait and get to know them better. Perhaps their personalities will suggest the perfect names." She could stay here and watch them all day. "How long before they are weaned?"

"Any time in the next couple weeks, Doctor Lewis said. I bought some puppy chow to start them on. Think we can coax Chance to come inside the house?"

"You have tried already?"

"Yeah, she wanted nothing to do with it."

"Let her rest now. I will have a talk with her later."

Luke wrapped his arm around her back and started out of the stall. "What if some of our friends want a dog?"

"I would not want to give them to anyone we did not know, but if someone wants to raise one of the puppies, I think it would be a good idea to share the love. We should wait and see how they are around them first and whether they bond."

*　　*　　*

At dinner, Luke tamped down his anxiety. He'd tried to prepare a vegetarian meal for her, but between the dried out baked potatoes and putting too much vinegar in the cucumber and onion salad, he was embarrassed to serve it to her. At least the penne pasta bake and corn on the cob came out unscathed. In retrospect, this meal was a little heavy on the starches.

"Next year, I'm taking you out for your birthday dinner. At Angel's new restaurant."

She giggled. "Oh, stop apologizing. I loved every bite!"

They had both dressed up for dinner. She wore several layered skirts in bold colors and an off-the-shoulder blouse. He had donned the clothes he'd worn on both their wedding days. On the table was a vase of pink Peruvian lilies he'd given her earlier. He'd even found some candles and a bottle of Chardonnay to set the mood.

Now it was time to give her the presents he'd made. Hell, he'd not been this nervous when unveiling some of his most intricate pieces of furniture. He hoped she liked them. He'd never carved anything so tiny before.

"Happy Birthday, Sweet Pea."

Cassie smiled and accepted the flat rectangular box. "I have been wondering what it could be since you told me about it in the barn."

"Just a little something I thought you might like."

She tugged at the ribbon and lifted the lid. He waited, holding his breath until she reacted. "They are beautiful!" She pulled out the hair sticks first. "Peruvian lilies!" The seven-inch long sticks each had unique lilies carved into the ends. "It must have taken you forever to make these."

"Not too long. I started soon after we returned from Peru."

"The detail is amazing. You do such intricate work. Let me put them in." She took her hair, twirled it behind her into a ponytail, and poked in the first stick, twisting it to hold the top of the knot in place. She then tucked and twisted the other one in the middle of the bun. "How does it look?"

All he noticed was the column of her neck as he leaned over to kiss her, placing little love bites on her skin. Her hand held him in place as if she wanted him to continue. "Keep that up and I will think I am on your menu as dessert."

"I can't think of anything sweeter." He pulled away. "There's one more thing in the box."

"Oh, you distracted me!" She reached in and pulled out the matching *tupu*. She grew silent, and when he searched her face, there were tears in her eyes. "I will be right back." She left the table and ran into the bedroom. What was wrong?

Minutes later, she returned wearing her shoulder cloth, the same one she had worn at their wedding, only this time the *tupu* holding the front closure together was the one he had made her. He stood and crossed the room to meet her.

"Luke, thank you for honoring me with such heartfelt gifts reflecting my heritage."

"I've been doing a lot of reading about Peru lately. Fascinating culture."

She smiled, and he realized she was no longer at odds with her heritage. Even so, her next words surprised the hell out of him.

"I wish to dance the *marinera* for you, Luke."

"You sure, darlin'?" This would be her first time since the night in the cantina five years ago.

Despite tears staining her cheeks, she struck a flirtatious pose and produced a lacy handkerchief that had been hiding within the folds of her skirt. He bowed and encouraged her to cut loose.

She walked over to her phone, and the Spanish music began to play. Crossing the room to the doorway, she retrieved his Stetson and handed it to him. "Let me do the work, but I find your hat much sexier than the ones the men carry during the dance in my homeland." She winked, and he grinned.

She thinks my hat is sexy.

As the music played, she struck a dramatic pose and then began to twirl around him, swishing her skirts, showing her tantalizing legs. He grew hard and couldn't wait to get her into bed tonight.

She danced with abandon. Once she regained her power on their wedding night in Peru, her natural sensuality had exploded. Tonight, though, she was downright seductive as she teased and flirted with her hanky and the lift of her skirt.

Whoa! That last flounce revealed she wore no panties.

Hot damn!

Luke donned his hat and moved toward her, but she evaded him and continued to dance with abandon around the living room. At one point, she came close enough for Luke to reach out and grab her by the waist. Her smile faded. Well, hell. He'd triggered her.

Breathing heavily, she came to a standstill before him. Figuring the night's entertainment had come to an end, he reached for the phone to turn off the music. When he faced her again, she was pulling the *tupu* from its hold and opened her shoulder cloth to reveal she had removed her blouse—and bra.

Her nipples protruded, begging for his hands, his mouth. She began to sway again, and the smile returned to her face. When she danced within his reach, he wrapped his arm around her lower back and pulled her against his chest.

His hand reached up to cup her breast. "You're so beautiful. And you're mine."

"All yours."

He lowered his face and captured her lips in a searing kiss. He would never grow tired of this woman or her many surprises.

When she broke away, she grabbed the pockets of his shirt and sashayed as she pulled him toward the bedroom door behind her. The expression on her face told him tonight would be another turning point for them.

Hot damn!

Maybe he would get to claim her in a way she hadn't surrendered herself completely yet.

Inside the bedroom, she stopped and began to unbutton his shirt. He reached for his belt, and she stilled his hands and shook her head.

"You're in charge." Instinct told him he needed to surrender and let her take the lead. She smiled, promising all kinds of carnal delights.

Chapter Thirty-Four

Cassie's heart soared. Luke giving her control over their time in bed unleashed a vixen in her she did not know existed. *I will not hold back tonight.* While they had enjoyed intense moments together, including many orgasms for each of them, she had not allowed him to "go all the way," as Americans called it. Tonight, she wanted to show him how much she loved him by going all the way this time.

Dancing for him her beloved *marinera* had shattered another barrier on the road to reclaiming and owning her sensuality. At last she was ready to lay claim to her sexy husband's body. She had a lot of lost time to make up for.

Sliding his shirt down his arms, she discarded it on a nearby chair and reached for his silver longhorn belt buckle. When she had commented on it earlier, he told her it was from his days playing football in college.

Luke also seemed more at peace with his past after the events of this summer. They were healing together.

Sliding the belt from its loop, she gave in to the urge to wrap his belt around the back of his neck and draw his head toward her breast until he captured her peak. A thrill rushed through her at her boldness. She threw her head back and swayed to music only she could hear. When he nibbled at her tender peak, she gasped.

"Yes, Luke!"

He let go but cupped her other breast and then moved to take that nipple between his teeth. She swayed and danced, causing slight pain when she strayed too far from his mouth, and he did not let go. She felt herself grow wet in anticipation—and preparation. Burrowing her fingers in his hair, she held him close, but his height made this an uncomfortable position for him.

Better to be horizontal.

She nudged him away. "Strip off your jeans, cowboy." She wanted to see him naked again. He obliged, taking his boxers, too, leaving her staring at his erection.

Mine.

Taking his penis in her hand, she smiled and lured him toward the bed. She reached for the waistbands of her layered skirts, but he stilled her hands. "Leave 'em on."

Confused, she asked, "But I want you to make love to me."

A spark lit his eyes. "Darlin', I can do that just fine with you wearing those skirts."

Her face grew warm as the image of him taking her while partially clothed flashed across her mind.

Pedro stood between her legs and lifted her skirt.

As if doused with cold water, she fought her way back before letting the memory ruin their time together.

"Where are you, darlin'?"

She blinked and saw Luke standing before her. "With you, Luke. I am sorry, but..." *Tell him what you need.* She nibbled at her lower lip, and then gathered the courage to speak, letting the words out in a rush. "I would prefer not to wear the skirts, if you do not mind."

A look of frustration crossed his face, making her regret saying anything.

"Jeezus, I wasn't thinking." He wrapped his arms around her, and the beat of his heart against her cheek reassured her. At least she learned something that he enjoyed that she could try to work on sometime.

"You give me so much. I want to be able to do this, but I'm afraid of triggers."

He pulled away and framed her face gently between his hands. "Darlin', you turn me on no matter what you wear or don't wear. We're probably going to hit a few other bumps as we navigate this new road, but I'm proud of you for speaking up, baby girl."

"I am sorry I did not use my 'yellow' word."

He grinned. "You said what you needed to say to get my attention. Over time, the use of safewords might become second nature, but you just keep talking to me, and everything's going to work itself out." He paused a moment, then grew serious, and pointed to her skirts. "Now, take 'em off."

The pressure off, she felt giddy—and emboldened that Luke would welcome anything she would like to do. She reached out and pushed him gently toward the bed. "Lie on your back, cowboy."

A slow grin spread across his face as he complied. As if surrendering himself to her—or preparing for a show—he bent his elbows to tuck his hands behind the back of his head. "I'm all yours, darlin'."

Not sure what to do with him, she decided to postpone joining him in the bed again. If he enjoyed her skirts, why not dance for him in them? She wanted to create new memories when it came to dancing.

After returning to the living room to retrieve her phone, she chose a new song on her playlist and moved in the steps of the flirtatious and suggestive *huayno* as she entered the bedroom. He seemed captivated as she sashayed, twirled, and jiggled her bare breasts for him, all the while lifting her hems to give him brief glimpses of her naked private areas. No longer allowing thoughts of what happened the last time she performed this dance spoil her mood, defiance bubbled up inside her as she reclaimed this part of herself.

This is *my* husband.

This is *my* body.

This is *my* right!

"You're making me hotter than a firecracker when you dance like that, darlin'." Another pained looked crossed his face. "Damn, Cassie. I didn't mean to—"

Interrupting his apology, she threw her head back and laughed with abandon. Before he thought her totally insane, she met his gaze and smiled. "You do not know how it thrills me to know I excite you, Luke."

Before this bubble of exuberant sensuality burst, she brought the dance to an end, maneuvered the waistbands off her hips and down her legs in one move, and tossed them onto a chair. Realizing she was standing before him naked, she became momentarily shy and scooted onto the bed to stretch out beside him.

She reached for a sheet, but he stilled her hand and cupped her chin. "Kiss me, darlin'."

Happy to have something to do again, she obliged and leaned over him. Her breasts rested on his chest and rubbed against his skin as she closed the gap. She pressed a kiss against his lips. *Más.* Wanting more, she opened her lips and welcomed his tongue when it entered her mouth and mated with her own.

His hand traced light touches on her breasts before trailing down her waist.

Having him stretched out before her, she licked her lips before bending over him and taking his hard, but tiny, nipple between her lips. Were a man's nipples as sensitive as a woman's? She sucked the way he did hers and flicked her tongue over it rapidly.

"Jeezus! Keep doing that!"

Empowered at his response, she continued. Her hand stroked his chest seeking his other nipple, and she squeezed it between her thumb and index finger. His hips bucked up.

Was she only igniting the flame, rather than slowing things down?

But she did not wish to slow down. She stretched out on top of him and brushed the curls of her sex against his erection. He reached between their bodies and she froze again. "Hands behind your head. Let me set the pace."

He probably thought she meant the pace of his penis, but she merely wanted time to prepare herself. She did not want to freeze or stop him, but what would happen when—

"What are you worrying about, Sweet Pea?"

She closed her eyes. "I am afraid I will have to stop before you...finish."

"Tell you what. You focus on your body, and let me worry about when it's time to finish. Having you exploring like this is one helluva turn-on, by the way. If you continue to rub against me like that, well, I'll finish, as you put it, sooner than I'd like." He grinned.

"I do not know what to do next."

"Want me to take over again?"

Yes! She nodded.

"On your back, darlin'."

His words gave her the confidence she needed to let go and surrender to him. His fingers splayed open her lower lips, and she gave him better access by spreading her legs wider.

"Oh, darlin'. You're so wet for me." When he rammed his finger inside her without warning, her hips bucked upward.

"Yes!" More! She wanted more than his finger tonight. *"Por favor."*

"Please, what?"

Cassie groaned rather than say it out loud. She searched his face, hoping to telepathically convey what she wanted—no, *needed*—but he insisted on hearing the words.

"Please make love to me. I want you…to come inside me. Now!" She finished in a rush and waited. When a slow grin spread across his face, she relaxed into the mattress. He would take care of her needs.

"Love to."

He grew serious immediately and continued his assault on her senses by blazing a trail of kisses from her mouth to her neck to her… "Oh!" He took her nipple into his mouth at the same time he plunged two fingers deep inside her, and she screamed. His thumb began stroking the bundle of nerves… *Call it what it is, Cassie.* …her clitoris. *Oh, yes! There!*

He released her nipple. "Look at me, baby girl."

She gasped for a complete breath and failed, but looked at him. "Don't overthink it. Just feel. I'm going to bombard you, almost make you come before I enter you, make sure you're screaming your release at the same time I do. But try to shut your brain off. This is about what we're experiencing at the most elemental level."

She wanted this. "I will try."

He grinned. "Good girl." The assault began again, only this time he took her other nipple into his mouth, plucking it between his teeth until it became even more engorged. Pain. Teeth. Lips.

Fingers. Inside her. "*¡Oh, Santa Diosa!*" He pressed against a spot inside her that turned her legs to jelly and her body to molten lava. Once again, his thumb played with her clit, and the overload on her senses had her at the brink in seconds.

"*Por favor!*"

He released her nipple, removed his hand, and positioned himself over her, propping himself on one elbow as he reached between their bodies. Without being asked, she opened her legs as wide as possible for him, but when he pressed his penis against her opening, she closed her eyes and held her breath.

"Look at me."

She drew several breaths and opened her eyes. Luke communicated with his expression that she was with her husband, her lover. He only wanted to bring her pleasure.

"Keep your eyes on me. I want you to stay in the moment. Don't close them until you come."

She nodded, and he rubbed his penis against her clitoris, sending her back to the brink in seconds. "*¡Sí! ¡Sí!* Oh, yes!" Close, so close. Suddenly, Luke plunged himself inside her, closing the space that had separated them from being one. The friction of their bodies kept the delightful pressure on her clit as he pounded inside her again and again.

"Oh, baby. You feel so good." His breathing grew more rapid. "Squeeze the life out of me."

She tightened her vaginal muscles, trying to hold him inside her a little longer with each stroke. The pained expression on his face made her worry until he groaned in ecstasy.

"Jeezus, come with me, Sweet Pea! Now!" His fingers joined in the onslaught, and as his penis rammed deep inside her, her clit burned for more. She closed her eyes and opened her mouth to let in more air.

"*Sí! Sí! Sí!*" She was coming! No, she was about to have an orgasm with Luke inside her. Euphoric, she wrapped her ankles around his butt to make sure he didn't pull away before they both reached the heights they sought. He plunged even deeper inside her, touching that spot inside that made her shake with desire.

"Yes, baby girl!" He moaned as if in pain.

"*¡Másssss!*" Exquisite, beautiful pain.

She exploded at the same moment she heard him grunt his own release. "Oh, Cassie!" She waited for him to say more, but he continued to move against her, milking as much pleasure as possible.

When he collapsed on top of her, for the flash of a second, the weight of him took her back to the cantina. Then she opened her eyes and saw she was still with Luke, in their bed in Colorado, joined in the most primitive, beautiful way possible.

She reached up to run her fingers through his hair, grinning to herself, and he pulled himself up to rest on both elbows.

"Sweet Jeezus, darlin'. You sure didn't hold anything back. When you squeezed me like that..." He took a deep breath. "Have mercy."

The feeling of pressure as his lower body held her in place did not trigger a sense of panic in her as when she had been held against her will. Luke's body had not held her down, taking only his own pleasure, but had helped her soar to amazing heights.

"Thank you, Luke."

He quirked his brow. "I think I ought to be the one thanking you, darlin'."

"I cannot wait to do that again."

He chuckled, and she realized he was still inside her. She squeezed him again and smiled.

"Keep that up and you just might get what you wish for sooner than you think, baby girl." His smile faded as he brushed the dampened hair away from her forehead. She realized she was bathed in sweat from their exertions and her release. "You amaze me, Sweet Pea. And you honor me with the gift of your delightful treasure."

"Is it a gift when my body belongs to you, Luke?"

He closed his eyes, and she thought he might be in pain until he met her gaze once more and grinned. He lowered his face to hers and nibbled at her lips before plundering her mouth with his tongue. Her senses became heightened again, and she marveled that after such a beautiful orgasm she could even think about wanting more.

But she did.

*   *   *

Cassie set the covered bowl of corn-and-bean salad in the fridge and washed her hands. Saturday had arrived, and she grinned remembering how they had barely torn themselves apart from each other before the first guests arrived.

They had made love every night since her birthday—and several times during the day, too. Doing chores in the barn, he had started enticing her up to the hayloft for what he called "a roll in the hay." She had to pick scratchy hay out of her bra and panties the rest of the day, but each annoying piece had only reminded her how it had gotten there in the first place.

She blushed, remembering how yesterday he had taken her on this very table. She was convinced he was trying to shock her with his innovative ideas—but she was tired of being inhibited.

Actually, she truly was shocked sometimes still, but tried not to show it. She enjoyed the illicitness of making love in places other than the bedroom.

She turned to see Luke picking at the barbecued pulled-pork Angelina had just brought in and smacked his hand, shaking her head. "You are worse than a child. Go help Marc and Angelina bring in the rest of the food!"

"Marc said he had it under control." Luke wiped his hands on the dishtowel by the sink, and just when she thought he would be going out to do as she said, he wrapped his arms around her and pulled her to his hard body.

He lowered his face as she moved to meet him in a kiss that left her wanting more. She pulled away, gasping for breath. "Why did you do that?"

"Because I like having you on the brink and thinking about when the next time we'll make love will be."

She pressed her fingers to her tingling lips. "When will it be?" They had a houseful of guests ready to descend on them for the day, some planning to spend the night. How could he be so cruel?

"When the time is right, just be ready."

"I am ready now."

His gray eyes smoldered. "Damn, that'll teach me, huh?"

He drew her against him again and traced a finger from her forehead to the tip of her nose. "Have I told you lately how much I love you?"

"Oh, only two or three times today, but it's only nine o'clock. You are slacking off after only three weeks of marriage, cowboy." She pretended to pout and then wiggled out of his arms, but not before he landed a loud swat onto her backside.

She turned to find Marc and Angelina watching them, their hands filled with food, and her face heated with embarrassment. "Um, just put them on the counter."

"Sorry if we're interrupting anything, *cara*."

"No. Not at all." Cassie could not remember what she had been doing before Luke had distracted her.

The roar of a Harley caught everyone's attention. Ryder and Megan entered the house with her carrying a plastic storage container. "Ryder made his delicious fry bread if anyone wants to nibble on some since we won't eat for a few hours." The delicious bread was soon devoured.

"Do you know when Kitty and Adam will be here?"

No sooner were the words out than he walked in with a car seat in each hand followed by Kitty with the third. "We tried to keep up with Ryder on the way out." He glared at Ryder.

"Sorry, Top. I thought I was going slower than ever."

"See that you keep it at the speed limit on the way back. That's my sister you're hauling on the back of that bike." Adam smiled, although Cassie was not sure he meant it.

"Hey, Adam," Luke said. "When you get settled in, come out to the studio with me. Gunnar's stopping by later to pick up…" He glanced at Cassie and finished with "…something I made for his place." Curious, she wondered why he did not give the piece of furniture a name. Perhaps it was so original it did not have a name yet. Luke's drawings resulted in some amazing things. "Anyway, I think you might be interested in something similar someday soon, now that Karla's almost good as new."

Marc kissed Angelina. "I want to see this. Not my kink, but someday we may venture into Shibari."

Shibari? Oh, those beautiful rope bindings in Luke's art book. "I would like to see it, too, Luke!"

He turned to her, but did not seem to want to show it to her. He had never kept any of his work from her before. What was different about this piece?

She had been flipping through the book the other day, trying to find the nerve to ask him to try some of the bindings on her. One image in particular kept pulling her back for another glance—bright yellow rope tying a woman's lower legs and ankles together with rays of rope strung in a web-like effect between each of her toes. The artist had used only one piece of rope for the entire design. Luke certainly enjoyed her feet. It would make a stunning photograph.

"Megan, you should see this Shibari art. It is beautiful!"

Luke pulled her aside and whispered, "Darlin', what do you know about Shibari?"

"Give me a minute." She went into the living room and pulled the book off the shelf, finding it exactly where she had left it, and brought it over to him. "I saw it in your art book." Everyone in the room suddenly looked anywhere but at Cassie. Kitty's lips were twitching as if she could barely keep herself from laughing.

What was the matter with everyone? Had she said something wrong? "I just thought Megan might like to take some photographs of it for her collection. It is a classic art form dating back to the days of the Shogun in Japan."

When Megan tentatively reached out to look at the book, Cassie thought it best to warn her. "Do not take offense at the nudity in the book. I was a little taken aback at first, but the artistic beauty is stunning, and all the photos are tastefully done."

Megan nodded, but also seemed to be fighting back a grin. "I'd like to see it done myself sometime."

"Oh, I was going to ask Luke if he knew how to do this one." She flipped to the page she had been obsessed with and showed each person in the room as she slowly moved around the circle. Adam and Ryder cleared their throats at the same time, but avoided making eye contact with each other.

Kitty carried Kate to the sofa. "Cassie, come sit by me. We need to talk."

Thank the Goddess. She hoped her friend could shed some light on what was happening, but they suddenly took an interest in fawning over the other two babies.

After propping some pillows around Kitty to make her comfortable, Cassie sat with her foot tucked under her thigh.

"Cassie, you're right. Shibari is indeed an ancient art form from Japan, but it's also very popular in the kink community."

"What?" Oh dear Goddess, no wonder everyone was acting oddly. Knowing what they must be thinking, she was a little embarrassed herself.

"In fact, Shibari suspension is my absolute favorite kink in the whole world."

Cassie held up her hand. "I do not want to know any more about it, Kitty."

Kitty glanced over her shoulder and apparently gauged that the others were far enough away before leaning closer to Cassie. "Don't ask me how I know, but I think Luke would love to do some bindings with you."

"No, not like that, Kitty!"

She shrugged. "It is what you make it. If you want it to be classical Japanese rope binding, then call it that. Just give it a try. There is great freedom in being bound tightly in the rope. At the same time, it makes you feel as if your lover is embracing every inch of you that has been bound."

Cassie's face was on fire. "I do not wish to talk about this any further. I think I have made everyone uncomfortable, and that does not make me a very good hostess."

Kitty shook her head and smiled. "Oh, trust me, Marc and Angelina as well as Luke and Adam all know about Shibari. And judging from the looks on Megan and Ryder's faces as they look at that book, they are going to want to learn more about it soon, too. I'm just not sure if Adam is going to be comfortable teaching it to his brother-in-law."

*   *   *

Ryder became turned on looking at some of the images and picturing Megan in the ropes. Damn, he needed to get some training on how to do this. He looked up from the book and found Adam scrutinizing him too closely. Ryder took the book from Megan and closed it. Her breathing told him she was equally excited, though.

At least she kept her voice to a whisper around her brother. "Ryder, that looks so hot. We need to try that."

"We'll talk about it later, Red. Sounds like Luke may know someone in the area—Gunnar, did he say?—who may be able to instruct us."

"Thank God, but let's be discreet. I'd die if my brother found out what we enjoy doing in the bedroom. He's kind of a straight arrow. So's Patrick, for that matter."

Ryder would have to check into this man's dungeon, although he wouldn't have a minute to spare until next month. He and Luke had been working harder than ever to finish their project. As soon as that was done, he and Megan would be moving out of his master sergeant's house.

As it was, they had spent time camping out on the mountain near Iron Horse Pass while the weather was still mild. Being on site helped him get more work done. Should be finished with the crucial parts in a few weeks.

He loved it out here, away from the city. Up on the mountain or here at the ranch, nothing worse than a screeching hawk made him jump.

Sure was better working there than at that clinic in Denver. Being in the inner city those two weeks of renovations had been like working in a combat zone again. Every car that backfired or door that slammed had him thinking they were under attack.

He willed himself to breathe. Just thinking about it set his heart to racing. A cold, wet tongue licked his fingers, and he looked down to find a beautiful dog—one blue eye, one half blue, half brown—staring soulfully up at him. He smiled and crouched down beside it.

"Hey, beautiful! Where'd you come from?" The markings on the dog looked like a patchwork of browns around the eyes and silver and white throughout her body. A few black spots, to boot.

Luke answered. "We rescued her in the shed at Cassie's old place after the fire—her and five puppies. Her name is Chance."

"Hi there, Chance, you pretty girl." He felt a peace come over him as he stroked the dog's fur. Chance kept staring at him, as if trying to reassure him that everything was going to be okay.

He hadn't been around pets much in a long time.

Megan joined him in loving on her. "What kind of dog is she?"

"Blue merle Australian shepherd, predominantly," Luke answered. "Who knows what else, but she's got the classic coloring and markings of an Aussie. They're good herding dogs. She's been helping us round up the alpacas at night. Good for companionship, too. When you guys move down…"

He stopped himself and glanced over at the sofa where Karla and Cassie were seated and lowered his voice. "Well, you can have pick of the litter if you'd like to keep one. I don't think we need to keep all five of them."

Angelina, who had been stirring a pot on the stove, must have overheard him. "Luke, can Marc and I take a look at the puppies? We've wanted to get a dog. Do you think these would enjoy hiking?"

"Sure. They love being outside. It's all we can do to keep her in the house," he said, pointing to Chance. "But Cassie had a talk with her, and they reached some kind of agreement." Luke glanced over at his wife again. "I know Cassie's become attached to them all, but we already agreed that, as long as they go to the homes of our friends—and are spayed or neutered—we're okay with adopting them out. You just have to give us generous visitation rights." He grinned.

A dog. Ryder hadn't thought about having one before, but the way she put him at ease when he had been headed toward a mild panic attack just now made him wonder if having one might be a good companion for him.

Megan seemed to be on the same wavelength. "Where are the puppies?"

"In the bedroom. We're trying to wean them from Chance, so be sure to keep the door closed."

She took Ryder's hand. "Come on. Let's see if one speaks to us as strongly as this one has. I'm sure Chance is already taken."

"Better believe it," Luke said.

They walked into the bedroom and found two of the five puppies chewing on Luke's boot. Those two might be more than they could handle. The other three were curled up together in a large dog bed lined with fleece. When he and Megan drew closer, one with mostly chocolate brown and white coloring poked its head up. With a distinctive brown mask around its eyes along with a streak down its nose, it reminded him of a bird kachina doll's mask.

Seeing them, he or she stretched, yawned, and then gamboled over to them. Ryder picked it up, checked quickly underneath, and determined its sex.

"Female."

"Oh, Ryder, she wants us to adopt her!" Megan scratched the puppy on the back of her neck. "She's so soft." The dog looked from one to the other and began licking Megan's hand. She giggled. "I think she likes me."

Ryder handed the puppy to her. "What's not to love about you? Obviously, she has good taste in mommies."

Megan met his gaze as she nuzzled her chin back and forth against the puppy's fur. Her eyes welled with tears. "Our own little furbaby."

Ryder was struck by how peaceful this dog also made him feel, but clearly, having a tiny creature to look after would be good for Megan, too. "We're going to have to keep her out here until we move, though."

"It won't be long now. Can you believe how everything is working out for us here in Colorado?"

He really couldn't. "I think it's where we're supposed to be. And helping Luke with his woodworking projects will keep me busy enough I won't have time to worry about anything."

"I'm so proud of you. Even when you were stuck in downtown Denver, you didn't back down. But you shouldn't have to go through any more projects like that."

"Savannah helped a lot. She talked me down a few times."

"She really is amazing. I wonder when they'll get here." When the puppy yawned and curled against Megan's breast, he knew they had made the right decision about this one.

Megan's face broke into a grin, and she leaned forward to kiss him. "Congratulations, Daddy, it's a girl!" He couldn't help but smile back seeing his girl so happy. "What should we name her?"

Ryder looked at her face again. "How about Kachina?"

"I love that! Distinctive and exotic, just like her." She pressed her face against the sleeping baby and closed her eyes, like a madonna. Too bad his camera skills were nil, because that would have made an awesome photo. But he pulled his phone out anyway and snapped a few pics. Good thing the ringer was off and he didn't disturb the moment.

"Can we have one, *Maman*?"

Damián answered. "You sure Boots will want to share you with a puppy?"

Ryder looked up as the three Orlandos came into the bedroom. Marisol dove straight for one of the puppies chewing on a boot. *Good luck with that one, Damián.* The man probably prized his biker boots as much as Ryder did his.

The mostly silver puppy with black spots on its back quickly lost interest in the boot and jumped into the kneeling little girl's lap. Marisol's giggles were contagious.

"Is it a boy or girl, Daddy?"

Damián checked. "Looks like a girl. Runt of the litter, too, from what I can see, but she's feisty enough."

Marisol let the puppy play with the strands of her hair, teasing her. "I'm going to name her Chiquita. Isn't that the perfect name, *Maman*, for my little girl?"

Savannah didn't seem too thrilled with the name as she exchanged a horrified glance with Damián, but he just shrugged and grinned. Relaxing, she smiled and turned to her daughter. "Chiquita would be a fine name."

"Come on, Marc. They're going fast."

* * *

"*Tesoro mio*, don't worry. I'm sure there are still plenty to choose from."

Angelina dragged him into the bedroom in her exuberance to see the puppies. She hadn't been this excited since they had closed on a restaurant property in Breckenridge last month. He and Angelina had mentioned how it might be nice to have a dog—one that could watch over her when he was on a call or away—but he'd been thinking more along the lines of a full-grown, combat-trained Doberman or German shepherd. Not this little ball of fluff. Chance, the mother dog, seemed pretty laid back to him. Not exactly watchdog material.

One of the puppies bounded across the room to greet Angelina, and she was soon on her knees scooping it into her arms. He pretty much figured that would be the one they'd be taking home to Aspen Corners.

Cute little thing. Had the markings of a wolf with its silver-gray and white. He joined them on the floor, and the puppy fought to get to him for a little more loving. It probably didn't weigh four pounds. Its eyes were blue like a husky's.

When he held it to his face, it licked him. Not wanting to keep calling it "it," Marc sexed it and found it to be male. Maybe that would bring out the dog's protective nature.

Ah, shit. Nothing wrong with having a dog just for companionship. One like this that had been abandoned and nearly died would surely appreciate a good, loving home.

Did dogs have abandonment issues the way Marc did? At least he and Angelina were working things out when they came up. No more secrets. No more shutting her out. Sometimes he fought the urge to run to the mountains to be alone, but he only had to remember that day ice climbing last February when he'd nearly gotten himself killed to know he didn't need that kind of reckless behavior in his life. Sure, he'd still go ice climbing, but not alone.

Angelina had nurtured his soul back to life. He wanted nothing more than to spend the rest of his life with her.

Angelina smiled at him and cupped the puppy's face. "He looks like a wolf." He remembered the mask he had worn the night he met her and thought she was probably thinking the same thing.

Marisol interrupted their thoughts. "We read a book at school about a wolf named Lobo. That would be a good name."

Marc smiled and nodded. Angelina turned to the little girl. "That would be a fine name. Thank you for helping us find the perfect one, *bambolina.*"

"I like helping find baby names. *Maman,* are you going to let me name the new babies when they come?"

The wistful expression on Angelina's face told him he'd better be careful or she'd be walking down the aisle with a baby carriage at their wedding next June. He wasn't ready to share her yet, well, with anything but this puppy. He'd almost lost her because of his insecurities. Obviously, he still had work to do in that area, but at least she was willing to put up with him.

Angelina glanced at Savannah and then Damián. "Are these wish-list babies, Savannah, or is there another reason to celebrate today?" Marc followed her gaze. He had assumed the little girl was talking about babies in a wishful way, but the couple exchanged a look that gave him the answer, even without saying a word.

Savannah turned to Angelina and smiled. "We're due in late January. But there is only one anyone can find. Mari has it in her head she can just order up triplets like Grandpa's and Grammy Karla's."

Angelina abandoned the puppy and ran squealing across the room to give Savannah a hug. "I knew it! You've had a glow about you for weeks. Congratulations!"

Marc went over and picked up the lonely little Lobo as Luke and Cassie entered, hand in hand. He'd never seen his SAR partner happier. About time. The man deserved some happiness—and a second chance at love.

"What did we miss?" Luke asked.

Marc filled him in. "Three of your puppies have found new parents, and it looks like Damián and Savannah are going to add more than a new puppy to their family come January."

Cassie followed Angelina in hugging Savannah while Luke patted Damián on the back. Cassie would probably be the next one pregnant judging by the way she had let down her defenses.

Adam carried two of the baby car seats into the room. "Time for some diaper changes. Whose turn in the barrel?"

"Oh, Adam, no one is going to volunteer to change our babies' dirty diapers." Karla followed him with the diaper bag and the third baby, this one wearing the Navy-blue sailor outfit he and Angelina had given them. Paxton. Good thing they color coordinated these kids or Marc would never be able to tell them apart.

"Nonsense," Angelina said. "Let me have that precious little boy." She took Paxton and laid him on the bed, going to work on the diaper like a pro. She was going to be a wonderful mother—when they were ready to start a family.

In a few years, maybe. They had a lot going on in the next year. She'd soon be top chef in her own restaurant. Fortunately, she already had lined up two sous chefs from the culinary school she graduated from in Boulder.

The three had been busy creating menus, testing recipes, and preparing for an opening early this fall, in time for the beginning of the busy ski season.

Knowing he wasn't going to be seeing much of her anyway, he'd enrolled in a paramedic school. Being there to provide medical assistance to Savannah when she'd been kidnapped and taking care of her made him realize how badly he missed his Corpsman days. He'd start classes in a few weeks, both online and on-campus ones. Angelina's brother, Rafe, said he could work with his department in an EMT capacity, too.

He seemed to be winning her oldest brother over incrementally. Man, he couldn't screw up again with Angelina.

They were on the road to rebuilding trust and embarking on a life together. By the time their wedding rolled around, they would be more settled into their new lives and have more time for each other again. Still, they were making the most of every moment they had tucked away in her cozy bungalow in Aspen Corners.

If her restaurant was successful, maybe they could talk about building their dream home in the mountains closer to Breckenridge. And if anything intruded on their commitment to each other, they would talk it over and re-evaluate their goals. Bottom line, they would be together.

He looked down at the puppy fast asleep in his arms. Maybe this furbaby would slow down the ticking of her biological clock, too. She'd spent so much time helping Karla and Adam with the triplets that he was sure she'd want to start a family right away—with or without a marriage ceremony.

"Oh, Adam, look! One of the puppies has latched onto your pants leg. I think she likes you." Karla giggled and reached down to extricate the puppy, and in its exuberance, it whined and licked at her face.

Marc grinned. "Looks like you're only going to have one left, Luke and Cassie."

Cassie glanced around the room and saw which ones had been claimed. "That leaves Suyana."

Luke seemed surprised. "You named them already?"

"Not all of them. Just that one, oddly enough." She reached down to pick up the still-sleeping one. Her cheeks were brown with black spots under her eyes, brown streaks above her eyes looking like bushy brows, and gray everywhere except each of her brown paws. "I guess it was meant to be. Suyana means 'to hope' in Quechua." She met Luke's gaze and smiled.

"Chance and Hope, huh? Sounds like we got to keep the best of the bunch, darlin'." He kissed Cassie on her forehead before announcing, "Let's take the puppies outside before we take you out to the barn to show you all the horses and alpacas. After that, we can set up the picnic tables and enjoy that good food you all made."

"Sounds like I'm just in time." In the doorway stood Grant. He hadn't noticed her come in but had the feeling she'd been watching over the room for a while now. She'd long ago appointed herself as the guardian of the veterans in this room, anyway. But her protective net included their loved ones as well.

Cassie crossed the room to her, although not quite as enthusiastically as she had greeted some of the others. Did the Domme intimidate her? Did she know Grant's role in the Masters at Arms Club now?

"Grant, we have found homes for all the puppies, but if you want one, Luke and I could share Suyana."

Grant stared at the puppy a long moment, but didn't reach out to touch it. She finally shook her head. "No, that's okay. With my travel schedule and running the club now, I wouldn't be able to give the little fella enough attention."

Dark circles under her eyes made Marc wonder if taking on running the club was more than she could juggle. He hadn't been to the club in over a month—although each of the owners tried to stop by at least that often. Distance, children, and other priorities made it difficult, but they wouldn't abandon the place. Grant had found a number of kinksters to help with the programming, and the community in Denver needed a safe place to play. It also had become a hangout for other military men and women, who apparently had been drawn to it because the owners were all veterans.

But he had run into her at Gunnar's dungeon, which was closer to Aspen Corners than was the club in Denver. Angelina's little cottage didn't have any place they could set up a playroom. Not that he didn't find ways to explore kink with her. Her kitchen alone had a treasure trove of pervertibles.

Grant and Gunnar had been working together on something covert that had involved a number of flights to Pakistan this summer. Patrick seemed to be involved on a regular basis now, as well. Marc had never asked Gunnar and Patrick for details about their trip to Pakistan last May. He had been too focused on winning Angelina back and uncovering what he hoped was the last piece of the puzzle that was his elusive past.

As Marc surveyed the room, he thanked God for these people. His family of choice. No matter what, they had each other's backs and could pretty much handle anything life threw at them, as long as they stuck together.

Before they went outside, there was one bit of unfinished business. "Adam and Karla, you haven't named your puppy yet."

Karla glanced over at Adam, who was changing Kate's diaper. Without looking her way, he asked, "Boy or girl?"

Karla started to look at the puppy in her hands. "Oh, I just assumed a girl, but it's a boy."

They shared a look that told Marc they were remembering when Paxton had been born. Adam cleared his throat. "Kitten, you have any ideas?"

"I'm tapped out after naming all of *our* babies." She grinned.

Adam then turned to his granddaughter. "Marisol, what do you think?"

She placed her puppy in Savannah's arms and, with a serious face, crossed the room to inspect the dog. After a moment, she turned to Adam and pronounced him, "Hero. Because he's yours, Grandpa, and you're an American hero like my daddy."

To say Adam was poleaxed was an understatement. When he finally spoke, his voice was gravelly with emotion. "Thanks, pun'kin. Hero, it is."

What an honor. And fitting. Adam had seen this ragtag bunch through the bowels of hell and brought them home. Not just in Fallujah, either. Both before and after. Adam had nearly died trying to save Marc's brother, Gino. The man had been there for every single one of the people in this room at one time or another, and probably a dozen times for Marc.

Despite suffering great losses in his life, Adam never became bitter or lost his compassion for others. Sometimes, he could be a little clueless, like when he let Karla get away last year. But, hell, the man soon figured out how much he needed her—and a lot faster than Marc had with Angelina.

Marc cleared his throat. "I'll second that. Perfect name for the puppy."

He heard several sniffles in the room, not sure if all of them were from the girls. Damián cleared his throat. "Marisol, we have a few other heroes in this room. Wilson, Grant, and Marc all saved my life in Fallujah."

With a trembling lip, the little girl turned to each of them. "I want to be like you when I grow up. I want to be a Marine."

Damián had to be proud of his little warrior, and scared shitless at the same time. Remembering how Marc had had to help Damián keep Marisol from going out to save her *Maman* left a lump in his throat too big to allow him to speak. She would do the Marine Corps proud.

But the only woman Marine in the room did respond. Grant entered the room, joining the group she often stayed aloof from. She walked over to Marisol before dropping down to one knee and meeting her eye to eye.

"You can be anything you want to be, Marisol. If you decide to be a Marine, you come to me any time you have a question or concern. Just be true to who you are, and give it your best, no matter what."

*   *   *

Several hours later, Luke leaned over at the table to whisper in Cassie's ear. "Darlin', if you really want me to try some Shibari ties on you, we can start tonight out at the studio after everyone either goes home or to bed."

She grew serious. "Kitty explained to me why everyone was so surprised at my wanting to try it."

Darn. If she knew it had anything to do with BDSM, she probably wouldn't want to give it a chance.

Cassie smiled. "She also told me how free she felt when bound. So I would like to try it, if you will start slow. I really like that photo of the woman with her toes, feet, and ankles bound."

Was that arousal in her dilated pupils? *Hot damn!* This party might go on for hours, but as soon as they could be alone, he intended to follow through.

"My little lady continues to be full of surprises."

"I do not wish for you to become bored with me." She smiled, but he noticed some anxiety.

Luke leaned over to kiss her cheek and whispered, "I could never tire of you, Cassie Denton."

"How about a toast to the newlyweds?" Luke turned as Marc stood. They had set up some planks over sawhorses in the front yard for a table big enough to hold their entire extended family. The blue-checked tablecloth reminded him of the many times Momma had prepared picnics for him and Dad, sometimes at parks and other times right in the backyard.

Marc held out his glass of sweet tea in front of him before addressing those gathered around the table. "Luke and Cassie, I hope I'm quoting Lao Tzu correctly here. 'To love someone deeply gives you strength. Being loved by someone deeply gives you courage.' I have watched the two of you grow strong in each other's love this summer, and I know that as you go through life you will have the courage and conviction to face anything life throws at you."

Everyone at the table raised a glass and shouted, "Hear, hear!"

He hoped they didn't expect him to make a speech because getting up in front of people to convey such heartfelt emotions would be damned-near impossible no matter how much he loved and trusted them. Then Cassie stood.

"I wish to thank you all for enfolding me into your family—and for loving and supporting my husband over the years."

Tears stung his eyes, and he reached for her hand to give it a squeeze.

"I have learned that, with Luke by my side, anything is possible because his patience and love will see us through."

Tears shimmered in her eyes, too, and she bent to kiss him. *Damn.* He couldn't sit here and stay quiet another minute.

He stood and held up his glass, as well. He had to clear the frog from his throat before he could speak. He looked at her, and her alone. "Cassie, darlin', our lives collided in many unexpected ways, but I think we both know there have been a number of forces—seen and unseen—at work to help us reach this point." He didn't care how she came into his life; he was just thankful she had. "Thank you for letting me be the man you put your faith and trust in. If I ever do anything to shatter either, well, there is a table full of D—" *Hell, don't call them Doms!* "—men here who will kick my ass six ways from Sunday." He felt the tears roll down his face, but didn't give a shit. One thing he'd learned was that life didn't always go as planned. "They not only have my back, but they have yours, too. If anything ever happens to separate me from you in this life, you just know they are going to be there for you. You can trust every one of them." *Aw, hell.* Why'd he go maudlin like that on their wedding celebration day?

Cassie wrapped her arms around him and sniffled. "Nothing can break this bond we share, not even death. You and I will be together forever. But Goddess has shared with me images of us on this plane old and gray with many great-grandchildren surrounding us. She might not have the location right—I definitely envisioned us up on the mountain where my cabin once stood—but I know She plans to let us make up for the many sorrows in our lives by allowing us many years to be together.

He cupped her chin and held her as he lowered his mouth to hers for the first of at least a gazillion more kisses he planned to share in this lifetime. When they ended the kiss, their friends broke out in cheers and applause.

"I'll love you forever, Sweet Pea."

*   *   *

By the time the party guests left and the chores were finished, it was nearly eight o'clock. Cassie visited with Adam and Kitty a while in the house, but Luke had gone ahead of her to the studio. Chance was curled on the floor at Adam's feet while Hero chewed at the leg of his jeans. They might want to try to break that habit. Perhaps Cassie could have a talk with the little guy and see what they might use as a substitute for Adam's pants legs.

Anxious to join Luke, after helping to prepare the babies for bed while Kitty pumped her breasts, Cassie jumped at Kitty's first yawn. "I will leave you all alone now, Kitty. Help yourself to anything you two need. Luke and I will be back in the morning to have breakfast with you."

Kitty reached out and took her hand. "This has been the most fun we've had in months. Thanks for having us out here. This is such a wonderful place."

Cassie nodded. "It *is* very special."

"You and Luke make it that way. I can't tell you how happy I am that you two found each other. Seeing you today was proof of how right you are for each other. I'm so happy for you, Cassie."

She smiled. "Kitty, I did not think love was possible for me, but he did not give up. Now I think he has a surprise for me, so I should join him."

"Oh, I like the sound of that! Go! We'll be fine!"

After kissing Kitty on the cheek and saying goodnight to Adam, she left the house, nearly dancing down the lane to the studio. Her heart was filled with both anticipation and excitement.

Inside, she found the only light shining on a worktable, spotlighting a bundle of bright yellow rope. Her heart skipped a beat. She remembered the photo in the book and hoped he was going to use that rope on her.

"I missed you." She jumped at his voice and turned to find him standing shirtless near the bed. Shadows and light played off his pectorals, and she could not resist walking over to him and placing a kiss to one, while playfully flicking her tongue against the hard peak.

He wrapped his arms around her waist. "Keep that up, and you're not going to get tied up tonight."

She smiled and met his gaze. "I was hoping that rope was for me. I am ready when you are!"

Luke took her hand and led her toward the table. "Remove your clothes. Everything."

Her heart beat in double time. "I thought you were going to just bind my feet."

"I am. But I like looking at you naked." He grinned and winked.

She removed everything quickly, rather than doing a slow tease. She wanted to try this as soon as possible. Without warning, he placed his hands around her waist and lifted her to the table. "Sit there."

The table was cold against her bottom, but she did as instructed and watched him return to the bed to retrieve several pillows. Laying them on the end of the table, he cupped the back of her head and neck, lowering her to them. "Now, tent your knees."

She followed his instructions, placing her hand on her belly when it erupted in butterflies. Nerves. She did not know why she was nervous. Maybe excited was a more accurate term.

He lifted the bundle of rope and loosened it. It looked soft. He left her with no doubts as he rubbed the rope over her chest, her thighs, and stopped at her upturned knees before repeating the motions. She relaxed, feeling the silkiness of the rope on her skin. Goose bumps broke out over her entire body, even her scalp.

"Mmmm."

She could let him do this all night. She closed her eyes and let him work his magic over her.

Magic fingers.

Magic hands.

Magic rope.

On his third pass over her body, he took the rope beyond her knees to her calves and then down to her ankles. He wrapped it loosely around her ankles and picked up her left foot. He kissed the instep, and she shivered in anticipation. She loved when he played with her feet—and he seemed to enjoy it, too.

He kissed the back of each toe and then spread each open and closed with his fingers several times, as if preparing her to accept the rope she knew would be threaded between them from the photo she had seen. Good thing she could control her body's ticklish responses.

He rested that foot on his upper chest and picked up the other to perform the same tender motions. "Mmmm. That feels so good."

He didn't say anything, but placed another kiss on her instep before he put this foot on his shoulder and adjusted the other one to a similar height. She opened her eyes and found him staring at her sex. The spotlight must have revealed everything. She fought the urge to close herself off to him.

"Beautiful."

"Thank you." Her voice sounded breathless, not surprisingly. How else should she respond? She had never been so exposed to him before. Usually they played with each other or made love in dim lighting.

He reached out, spread her lips open, and her clitoris tingled as if he had touched her with more than his gaze.

"You just clenched. Made my cock throb remembering when you squeeze me inside you."

She wanted him inside her. "Make love to me, Luke."

He grinned. "I am."

"No, I mean, I want you inside me again. I am now insatiable, I think." She smiled.

"I sure can see how wet you are, but my lady asked me to tie her up." He released her, closed her knees, and lowered her feet to the table. She felt disappointed until he picked up the rope again. She did want to feel the rope on her, too. *Then* they could make love.

She never wanted this night to end.

* * *

Tearing his gaze away from her fascinating core took self-control he didn't know he possessed. That she had opened herself up to him and didn't try to hide when he drank his fill told him she was comfortable in her own skin. Seeing how wet she was just from the feel of the rope and the way he had played with her feet promised a delightful session with her tonight.

"Keep your eyes closed, darlin'."

Stroking her body with the linen rope had given him an erection that actually ached at the moment, but he wouldn't be burying himself inside her just yet.

With everything going on today, he hadn't had a chance to ask Adam about the rope tie she requested from his book on Shibari and macramé, but it looked more like the latter. Not that Luke cared. He just liked playing with rope. He'd try to replicate the tie as best he could from memory, but regardless, he would make sure she enjoyed the hell out of her first rope session. First of many, he hoped. Man, did he ever like to play with rope.

Who would have thought only four months ago that they would be doing this now? Grinning, he caressed her thighs to her ankles before picking up the rope again. She hadn't balked or squirmed when he spread her toes or ran his fingers between them a few minutes ago, so he figured she would be able to take having the rope there, too.

Fashioning a loop, he lassoed her pinky toe, and she flexed her toes on both feet as if trying to give him better access.

"Lovely. Thank you."

She giggled. Unable to prolong this any longer, he made quick work of lassoing each of her toes before doing a basket-weave pattern over the tops of her feet.

"How are you doing, baby girl?"

No response. He set her feet on the table and walked up to lean over her face. "Darlin'? Still with me?"

She opened her eyes and blinked in confusion. "I think I zoned out." Her voice was husky and her pupils dilated.

He smiled. She must really be getting into it. At least she hadn't been triggered. He bent and placed a kiss on her lips.

"Almost done," he promised and went back to the end of the table.

"Do not rush on my account. I love the feel of the rope on my feet. I hope you have your camera out here. I want photos."

"Don't you worry." Given how fascinated she was with his book, they might have to start their own private collection of photos.

He took the ends of the rope and finished pulling them through as he continued to weave a pattern over her joined feet. When finished, he wrapped the ends around her ankles similar to how he would do a hogtie.

But he didn't plan to use that one tonight.

Luke ran his hands up her legs, over her knees, and down her thighs. Silky soft. He took a step back and surveyed the tie. Not exactly like the photo, but beautiful nonetheless. The lighting seemed perfect to enable him to take photos without flash. He wanted the warm tone of her skin not to be washed out.

"I'm just going to snap a few shots to show you before we proceed."

"Proceed? I thought you were finished."

He chuckled. "Well, I'm finished with the tie, if that's what you mean. But I have plans for other parts of your body tonight, too."

"Oh." The expectant tone in her voice made him anxious to move on, but first, he would preserve the rope design.

The first few shots were taken from above her looking down then one looking straight on, the curve of her ass framing either side of her bound ankles. Hot, but tasteful. He put the camera down, not wanting to turn this into a porn shoot. But, damn, he needed to see her body.

"Draw your knees up to your chest, darlin'. The camera's gone now. This is just for me to see." She hadn't even waited for him to explain his intent before lifting her legs.

She trusts me.

"I like when you look, *amor*. It excites me."

He reached out and opened her to his gaze. "I can see that." So wet. So ready.

"Having you playing with my feet and binding my ankles together excited me, too."

Who was he kidding? Why stop at just looking? He needed to touch her, fill her. Luke came around to the side of the table and scooped her into his arms. She giggled.

As he carried her across the room, he asked, "What's so funny."

"I like my take-charge man."

Jeezus.

"Good because we're going to try a new position."

"Another one?" She smiled.

"Remember the Kama Sutra. I don't think we'll run out of ideas for a long time."

"Good."

He laid her on the futon and went back to grab the pillows from the worktable. She raised herself up on her elbows to let him place them under her head.

"I hope you took lots of photos, but I would like to see what it looks like before you take off the rope."

"Who said anything about taking it off?"

Her mouth formed the cutest little O as she processed that information. But he remembered the mirror he had bought to back her artwork. "Stay put."

"I am not going anywhere." She lifted her bound feet over her hips and took a look. The lighting wasn't the best in the corner, but she could still get the idea.

He returned with the four-by-two foot mirror and positioned it at the bottom of the bed. "Now, tent your knees again." She did so. "Lift your head and look down at your feet's reflection in the mirror."

When she did, she scrutinized the design, and he wondered if she liked what she saw. "I had to make some chang—"

"That is very erotic looking. While everything is hidden, seeing the sides of my hips and the beautiful rope work… I cannot wait to see the photos."

Luke relaxed, as if worried she might not be pleased. "Me, too, but I think the image is already seared on my brain." He set the mirror against the wall and unhooked his belt buckle. Her gaze on his crotch made him harder as he slowly unzipped his jeans and worked them, along with his boxers, off his hips. Her appreciative smile was all he needed as an invite, and he joined her in the bed. "Roll onto your left side, and pull your knees to your chest again."

He ran his hands over her side, hip, and thigh several times. Her moan told him she was ready for him, but he wanted to work her up to a frenzy. His hand slid to her butt and then around to the downy curls covering her treasure. So wet. His first finger went in so easily he didn't hesitate to drive a second one home. He curled them to stroke her G-spot.

"Oh, yes!" He brought her to the edge of the bed and rolled her onto her back.

Kneeling near the foot of the bed, he placed her bound feet against his chest, keeping her butt lifted off the mattress. After dipping himself inside her and hearing her groan of frustration and need, he pumped his cock deeper inside her.

"¡*Siiiii!*"

Sounded like he hit the right spot so he withdrew before pounding into her again and again. She grabbed onto his thighs as if not wanting to let him go.

No worries, darlin'. I'm not going anywhere.

As her mewling cries reached a fever pitch, he was ready to explode and reached between them to stroke her clit and send her screaming over the edge as they both came. He didn't think he would ever stop pumping his seed inside her.

Mine.

His broken heart had finally found a home.

Epilogue

Cassie's sight remained obstructed by the blindfold Luke had placed over her eyes before they drove off the ranch with Picasso and O'Keeffe in the trailer behind them. He had promised her a picnic and trail ride. She remembered him telling her once that their romance would be a slow trail ride, not a race. She certainly had been enjoying the pace and the view, but did not understand why he wanted to keep her literally in the dark today.

"Don't you peek now, darlin'." He sounded as if it was Christmas morning, and he was filled with excitement for her to open his gift, but not wanting to spoil the surprise.

She shook her head and grinned. "I will not, but how much longer before we reach our destination?"

"Not your worry. A little anticipation is good for you. Just sit back, and enjoy the ride."

His hand squeezed her thigh to reassure her. He had asked her to wear her flouncy skirt—and no bra or panties. Her face flamed, wondering who might be aware of her slightly indecent lack of apparel. But she did not care what anyone thought. He would not put her in a compromising or embarrassing situation.

Without being asked, she spread her legs for him. His hand remained on her thigh for the next few minutes before he slowly inched upward. She held her breath, waiting, anticipating his touch—

Her face grew warm. They had made love this morning, only a few hours ago, and they had come at the same time. How could she be ready for more already? She could not wait to return to the house because he promised to try a new Kama Sutra position soon.

His truck hit a rut, and her mound pressed against his hand. She groaned, aching to have him inside her.

"Hold on, Sweet Pea."

She reached for his hand and pressed it firmly against her. "Only if you hold on *here*, cowboy." He laughed at her nickname, but since they had brought Picasso and O'Keeffe with them, it seemed appropriate.

Where in the world was he taking her?

Luke placed his hand over hers and gave her a squeeze. "You aren't peeking, are you?" His teasing brought a smile to her face.

"No, I am being a good girl."

He chuckled, and she laid her head against his shoulder until another bump caused him to rub against her slit. Only he did not stop. His finger entered her.

"*¡Sí!* There!" She tingled with awareness and need.

She could not believe how comfortable she was with Luke's touching her all the time. Sure, there were times when his touch caught her off guard and triggered a bad memory, but he was so good at noticing them and quickly centering her in the moment.

"*Te amo*, Luke Denton." Her love for him had grown so much since she first told him she loved him that *te quiero* no longer expressed the depth of her love for him.

"I love you, too, Cassie Denton."

She still wasn't used to her married name, but looked forward to growing accustomed to hearing it often.

The truck came to a halt. She thought perhaps they were at a stop sign or something, but when he cut the engine, she knew they had arrived at their destination.

"Wait right there."

"*Sí, amor.*"

He exited the truck and slammed the door shut. She heard him unloading the horses, and then her door opened. "Scoot toward me. I'm going to carry you to the horses."

"I can walk if you remove this blindfold."

"Cassie, I said scoot toward me." His tone sent a shiver down her spine. She secretly liked when he became forceful with her, but did not want to let him think he could always boss her around.

She lowered her skirt, uncertain if anyone could see them, and started scooting when he reached in and lifted her into his arms. She squealed and grabbed for what she hoped was his neck and held on tightly.

The smell of spruce and the roar of the wind told her they were high in the mountains. *Home.*

No, her home was with her husband. One day, she would come to accept the ranch as a true home for as long as she was with Luke. Her heart had found its home with Luke.

"Follow my instructions. I don't want you to get hurt, but I also don't want to spoil the surprise. Hear me?"

"*Sí.*" She could barely speak past the lump in her throat.

"Now, lift your left leg, and I'll put it in the stirrup." He positioned her foot inside and guided her hands onto the pommel before telling her to pull herself onto the horse. His hands under her backside helped lift her into the saddle. She felt a tingling where his hands had touched her, and her mound pressed against the saddle sent more tingles throughout her.

Erotic horseback riding lessons—blindfolded and without panties? She giggled.

Luke patted her thigh. "Thank you for your trust, darlin'." She heard the squeak of the leather on his saddle as he mounted. "Ready?"

"But I can see nothing."

"Don't you worry; I'm going to be holding O'Keeffe's reins. We'll take care of you."

They rode for a while. Besides the wind, she heard the crunch of gravel beneath the horses' hooves, but that disappeared quickly, and she was left with only the wind against her face and neck. Her hair sticks pulled her hair off her neck, allowing the sun's warm rays to beat down on her. Her arms were covered by her *lliclla.* She loved wearing it, along with the *tupu* he had made for her to keep it closed. She might be a little over-dressed for a picnic, but liked being feminine around Luke.

No people sounds. She wondered if they were riding at a national or state park, but chose not to analyze it. He had promised her frequent visits to the nearby mountains and truly did take care of her emotional needs.

Cherished.

Protected.

Loved.

She took a deep breath of mountain air. There was a pungent odor—cinders, perhaps—mixed with grass. The way her body leaned backward for balance, she could tell they were going downhill and wished she could see where they were riding. It must be beautiful. When would they—

Did she detect the scent of angel's trumpet blossoms? Her mind instantly returned to *Abuela's* garden. Was she sending a sign that she was here with Cassie? She blinked her eyes behind the silk blindfold, feeling it grow damp from her tears.

"Here we are."

"Where is here?"

"You'll see when I'm ready. This is actually just our first stop. Hang on while I do a little prep work."

Was he going to keep her blindfolded all day? She heard him dismount and several sounds she could not make out.

"Now I'm going to help you down first. Swing your right leg over the pommel." He placed his hands on either side of her waist and lowered her to the ground. She arranged her skirt and felt a wet spot in the back. Would he notice the effect he and the horseback ride had on her?

She did not think she could wait until they returned home to have him touching her, filling her again.

Luke's hands behind her head unknotted the blindfold. "Keep your eyes closed until I tell you to open them."

"Yes, sir." She didn't know why, but when he gave her commands, she responded much like Kitty might. Of course, Kitty would totally jump to the wrong conclusion if she overheard her. She giggled at the thought of being a submissive like Kitty.

"What's so funny?"

"Nothing. I was just thinking about Kitty." A sharp swat to her backside sobered her quickly. "What was that for?"

"To bring you back to the moment—and me. Plus, I like the feel of my hand on your butt." His hand cupped and squeezed her backside. The blindfold fell away from her eyes and upper cheeks, but she kept her eyes closed as instructed. She wanted to please him however she could, even when not making love.

Luke wrapped his arms around her and pulled her against the length of his body. Warm. Hard. Inviting.

"Okay, darlin', open your eyes."

She almost was afraid to do so, but opened them slowly. The vastness of the mountain vista lay like a carpet before her stretching to the far horizon. It looked so much like the view from... She blinked several times to remove the fuzziness before realizing tears were keeping her from seeing clearly, not the residual effect of the blindfold.

"I did not realize how much I missed being in the mountains." She tried not to notice the scorched patches of earth on the side of the mountain they stood on, focusing on the horizon instead. She turned to him. "Thank you for bringing me—"

Spread out on the ground was a horse blanket covered with fresh fruit, cheese and crackers, and a bottle of wine and two glasses. "What is this?"

"Dinner—just a little something to tide us over until supper."

He reached for his shirt and pulled it from his jeans. When he began unbuttoning it, she glanced around to make sure they were alone. Not a soul around but them. Yet another illicit place to make love. Was this private property, though?

"Remove your blouse."

"What?" She surveyed the area again.

"I'm hornier than a jackrabbit. I need to see you, touch you... Remove your blouse."

With shaking fingers, she removed the shoulder cloth and tucked the *tupu* safely inside before laying it on the blanket. Next she began unbuttoning the blouse, her gaze on her husband who watched with interest as she revealed more flesh with the unfastening of each button. Her nipples bunched as she felt his scrutiny. What did he have in mind? When she removed it and let it fall to the ground with her shoulder cloth, he smiled his appreciation.

"I've missed the view."

She swallowed hard, her heartbeat causing her throat to close. "But you just saw them a few hours ago." Her voice sounded breathless.

He closed the gap and seized her by the hair sticks, pulling her head back until her mouth opened. She enjoyed how he used the hair sticks to control the movement of her head. Unlike holding her directly, which still sometimes triggered her, hair pulling was something she connected with Luke and only Luke.

His tongue, hot and urgent, entered her and danced a tango of desire with her own. He eased her onto the blanket, and they made love slowly.

In the afterglow, he fed her grapes and cubes of cheese, alternating with sips of wine. The deep blue sky blanketed them with only the occasional hawk to disturb their cocoon of love.

All too soon, they had to dress and pack up their picnic. "Will we be able to ride here again sometime?" The word ride took on added meaning, and her face grew warm.

"Anytime you want."

"Oh, that would be nice. I love it up here."

"I know you do, darlin'." Of course he knew. Luke was attuned to all her needs. "Why don't we ride a little farther?"

"Are we trespassing?"

"No. It's public land."

"Public!" She glanced around, expecting to find a family of campers watching them in their sexual afterglow.

He chuckled. "No worries. It's a newly acquired nature preserve the tourists don't know about yet."

She relaxed, and they mounted to set off. The area they rode through had been burned, probably in the June wildfires. So sad. She tried not to think about her own cabin, although her mind saw a few things that reminded her of her own mountain. The ruins of an old mine entrance. The line of trees. Even Iron Horse Falls in the distance.

Wait! How could the falls be there if she was anywhere *but* on her mountain?

She dismounted and ran toward the ridge, exuberance filling her before she crested the rise and saw the studio that had been part of her home for four years. The sight brought on more tears. She walked closer to the edge until what she saw broke her heart. She literally felt as if it split in two.

A two-story cabin had already been built to replace the burned-out one she had lived in. Much more elaborate than the original, it must be someone's new vacation home.

How sad that this incredible view would only be enjoyed by someone for perhaps a few weeks of the year. Americans had more money than they had sense.

"Are you sure we are not trespassing?"

"I have permission from one of the owners."

When she heard him standing so near and was too overwhelmed to look any longer, she turned to bury her face in Luke's chest.

"Why the tears, Sweet Pea?"

"I guess I will always think of this as my mountain, even though I was only a tenant for a short while."

"I think you can consider most of it yours." He pushed her away, dried her eyes, and pointed to a spot a few hundred yards away. "From about that ridge over there, on down the mountain is a public preserve. No one will ever be able to build on it. Your landlady wanted to make sure the mountain she and her husband had enjoyed for many years would never be overdeveloped."

Public land. Perhaps she could at least visit as they were doing today. "She loved this place. I am sure it broke her heart to have to sell it, but I can imagine it would be too expensive for anyone to afford the whole side of the mountain. When I asked if she would rebuild, she told me her heart would rather remember the cabin that last summer she and her husband lived here."

Cassie glanced up at the new house. "I think she would approve of the new cabin, though. So beautiful." She tried to tamp down her jealousy at not being able to live there. A generous number of windows and skylights made it possible to bring the outdoors in, and the front entrance seemed to be wrapped around one of the trees that had survived the fire. One of the skylights was octagonal. She would love to look at the moon through that one while cuddled in...

Stop thinking of the impossible. Cassie nodded. "Mrs. Wickersham was a good steward of the land."

"She said the same about you."

"I tried." She focused on the slightly singed, but still standing, studio to the left. No sense peeking inside. She and Luke had removed everything that had been hers. The burned out shed had been razed, but she had what was important from there—her alpacas and Chance and her puppies.

If not for the fire, though, she would still be hiding away up here. In retrospect, she realized the cabin had not provided her much happiness. Cassie had used it as a place to escape from the world.

Until Luke, in an attempt to make sure she was safe, had collided with a falling snowpack. "I am okay not living up here anymore. The time had come for me to come off the mountain and rejoin the world." She reached up, placed her hand at the nape of Luke's neck, and pulled him toward her for a kiss. "Thank you for being a soft place to land when I needed one, Luke, and for bringing me back to life so gently and patiently."

"Do you miss the mountain with us living down in the valley?"

Cassie reached up and placed her hand over his heart. "Luke, I love being with you. Chance, Suyana, and the alpacas love it there, too, judging by how they are thriving."

"How about you, though?"

"I will thrive wherever you are. You have opened up so many new possibilities for me in my life that I thought would never be possible."

He pinched her bottom. "Like making love?"

She could not keep the telltale warmth from rising in her cheeks. Would she ever become able to speak or think about making love without blushing? "No, I meant things like horseback riding and shearing alpacas and skinny-dipping together in the stream—" Practice might help. She glanced away and grinned. "And, yes, making love."

Luke lifted her chin and bent to press a quick kiss on her lips. "Love you, darlin'." He pecked her on the cheek and took her hand. "Grab O'Keefe's reins. Let's go down and take a look. Doesn't appear that anyone's home."

"Luke, we really should not be snooping around." But her argument was half-hearted. She wanted to see her former home just once more. "But if you are sure we will not be caught." She grinned and took her horse's reins as she led the way down the familiar hillock.

They explored around the exteriors of the two buildings, and she drank her fill one last time of the place that had salved her battered soul, preparing it for further healing at Luke's hands.

When he walked onto the porch, she followed, stroking the spruce tree that now was embraced by the cabin's porch. With so many trees lost to the fire, she was happy that the new owners hadn't chopped it down. As she cupped her hand over her eyes and peered inside, Luke opened the door.

"Luke! What are you doing! We cannot go inside!" He grinned at her, unperturbed. "Can we? I *would* love to see the inside of this beautiful place."

She closed the gap between them and would have entered the house if Luke hadn't swept her into his arms. Luckily, one of them was thinking clearly and stopped before they broke the law.

He grinned at her, and she removed his Stetson, not wanting any of his face hidden from her view. She tossed his hat to the twig chair on the porch and ruffled her fingers through his hair. The house was forgotten as she stared into his eyes. A twinkle of mischief caught her by surprise, and she feared he would decide they should make love right here on someone else's porch. Maybe someday they could rent this place for a getaway.

Luke grinned and took a step inside. *Good!* Perhaps just a quick peek. She took in the massive stone fireplace—Goddess, the stones looked as if they flowed like water in a stream! "Look at the fireplace, Luke!"

"If you've seen one, you've seen 'em all. I'd rather look at you."

She met his gaze again and pulled his mouth to hers for a lingering kiss. When she could speak again, she said, "Put me down."

"Only if you kiss me again. I like holding you—and carrying you over the threshold."

But he hadn't carried her over the threshold when they returned from Peru. Now she wondered why a traditional man like Luke would have forgotten something like that, but she had not given it a thought back then. It was not a custom in her country.

Something niggled at the back of her mind.

"I'm waiting."

Distracted, she held the side of his neck and pressed her lips to his. He ignited the flames again, but she broke away realizing what had been nagging at her a moment ago. "Why were you talking to Mrs. Wicker-sham?"

Rather than answer, he set her on her feet and crossed the room to a roll-top desk. He opened the center drawer. "Luke! What has gotten into you?"

He reached for a packet of legal-looking papers and handed the sheaf to her.

"A belated wedding gift to my bride."

Her heart pounded as she accepted the papers and began to unfold them. Was he saying what she thought...the word DEED jumped out at her immediately. Confused, she met his gaze. He seemed serious, awaiting her response. She furrowed her brows. "We cannot afford a place like this."

He grinned. "Turned out, Mrs. Wickersham wanted to make sure it went to someone who would keep the land from being overdeveloped. Without any heirs, she chose to sell this parcel to us. Honestly, I think she sees you as a daughter."

She glanced at the paper, but couldn't decipher the words. Too many tears in her eyes, not to mention racing thoughts scrambling her mind.

"We only own the ten acres right around the house, though."

"How could you afford this?"

"I said she gave us a good deal."

"It still had to be a fortune, not to mention the taxes and upkeep on a place like this—" He silenced her with his finger on her lips.

"We can afford what she asked in part because of the money your family gave us at our wedding reception. They were more than generous. I had no idea when they kept stuffing envelopes in my pocket what was in them until I opened them up the next day. Good thing I didn't put them in our suitcase with all that cash."

The gifts were a tradition in her country, but she had no idea how generous they had been, either. Luke had shown her the cards, and she had told him how she was related to or acquainted with each person. She knew there would be money in them, but left it to Luke to put it in the bank.

"That money more than paid what she asked. She really did practically give us the land. Then I took the money from the sale of the ranch house—"

"You sold your ranch? Luke, no! You love that place! How will you continue to work with the horses without—" He silenced her with a warm finger to her lips.

"I sold the *house* to Ryder and Megan Wilson. She said her father would have liked her spending his inheritance that way. They'll be overseeing the ranch and helping me with the horses. Ryder will also be helping me with some of my carpentry jobs. He did most of the work on this place this past month."

"So that is what you two have been so busy doing when you left Megan and me to our own devices. Oh, but I like being with her so much. Now we are going to get to spend even more time together."

Cassie had sensed her life would be entwined with Megan's as soon as they had met. She was like a sister to her already. Well, not as close as Cassie's relationship to Kitty. No one could replace her dearest sister-friend in the world. Still, she looked forward to getting to know Megan, whose spirit was so brave and free.

"But how did you keep all this from me? I had no idea any of this was happening."

"Megan was a big help, distracting you when we needed to go over plans or paperwork from the attorneys. Darlin', I hated deceiving you like that and promise it won't ever happen again, but I hope you don't mind now that you know I did it to surprise you." Luke smiled reassuringly. "Of course, I'll be down at the ranch every day I can be, barring any more avalanches. The horses are still my responsibility, and I want to oversee their training. But Ryder's going to help me take the operation to the next level. He wants to try some things that have worked for him that might help other wounded warriors. It will be a sanctuary where the wounded or abused can find peace and hope."

"But it already is for your horses."

He ran his finger down her nose and tapped it. "Not just for animals, but people. Watching your transformation while there makes me certain it will be a special place for healing all types of hurts. Ryder and I have been talking about building a bunkhouse and a group of cabins for guests and hiring professional staff to give veterans, first responders, sexual-abuse and rape survivors, and others a sanctuary to come to and heal with the animals."

Tears pricked the backs of her eyelids. She reached up to stroke his cheek. "Oh, Luke, that sounds amazing. But you know you were as much a part of my healing as the horses were. No, much more."

He bent to place a kiss on her lips. "Thanks, Sweet Pea. That means a lot to me. But those animals will provide much-needed peace and healing to anyone who needs it. I saw it happen with Ryder the few times he was with O'Keeffe. And he told me Chance helped him avoid a panic attack when we all gathered at the ranch to celebrate our wedding a few weeks ago. Look at how we've spread her puppies around to others who will benefit from them. Karla already plans to send Hero to be trained as a service dog after hearing how Chance helped Ryder. Maybe we can get Chance some formal training, too, as well as Suyana. The horses also understand and help people in the healing process."

He paused, but he sizzled with energy and excitement. "Cassie, it's going to be an amazing thing to be a part of. I doubt I'd have ever figured it out if not for you."

When he leaned toward her and she was certain he would have kissed her, another thought sprang to mind, and she pulled away. "Wait! Luke, you hate the cold winters up here." He would not survive the first month.

He grinned. "I'll never get used to cold, true, but I'm sure there's a hot-blooded Peruvian lady willing to have mercy on me and sacrifice some of her warmth on those cold nights."

"At twelve thousand feet, that will be every night."

"Damn straight."

Thoughts of being snuggled with him in their bed, staring up at the moon and stars through the skylights, brought a smile to her face. He wrapped his arms around her and drew her near, crushing the deed between their bodies. When they separated, she checked out the fireplace again and noticed it had a modern insert that probably would provide them with efficient heat. No doubt he had back-up heat plans, too. Luke was good at providing for their needs and thinking of all contingencies.

"Luke, a dance floor!" The inlaid wood covered a good-sized area in front of the fireplace. She could not wait to dance there with Luke.

"I'm counting on more lessons—and might even want to just watch you cut loose every now and then."

"I would much rather dance *with* you."

His eyes twinkled. "Sounds good. Here, let me give you the ten-cent tour." He showed her the downstairs, including the kitchen, one and a half baths, and two small bedrooms for visitors—or children perhaps. He even included a small area to serve as a second altar, perhaps on days she did not wish to go out to the studio, even though she looked forward to meditating in her studio again.

"I'm going to take down your ideas and make you an altar for in here this winter. Oh, that reminds me. Ryder and I will be working on a shed for the girls, but didn't have time, yet. I know your alpacas like the cold up here as much as you do."

"We are mountain born. It's in our blood."

"I saw how invigorated you were in Peru. But from the time we spent up here, I knew you needed to be on the top of this mountain."

"Oh, Luke, I was happy with you in the basin. The ranch is surround-ed by mountains so I could get my fix anytime."

"No regrets. Seeing the way your face lights up with everything I show you up here, I know I made the right decision. Now, let's see what's upstairs." He guided her to the open staircase leading up to the loft.

As she neared the top of the stairs, she noticed the octagonal skylight she had seen while outside looking down on the cabin. "Oh, I already thought how wonderful it would be to look out that window at night!" When she lowered her eyes to the bedroom, the bed from the ranch he had given her when they returned from Peru was here, assembled and made up as if waiting for them.

"How did…we just slept in that bed this morning!"

"Ryder and Marc delivered and set it up while we were on our trail ride and picnic."

Her face flamed. "You do not think they saw us without our clothes, do you?"

He chuckled. "No, Sweet Pea. We were nowhere near the road. They also had strict orders to set it up and get off the mountain as quickly as possible."

She relaxed and began surveying the room where apparently she would sleep tonight. Her gaze went to the framed artwork above the bed. "My *quipu* piece!" She saw the two of them reflected in the mirrored backing, just as she had envisioned it would be if she had completed it for the gallery event. "It is not even finished. I was blocked after the fire, and then so much happened."

"You said it represented your life story. It will always be a work in progress, and anytime you need me to remove the mirror backing, I can, so you can add to it."

"Oh, that would be perfect because I want to add the scrap of *Abuela's* shoulder cloth that I retrieved from the burned-out cabin. This would be a wonderful way to preserve it and her memory."

He wrapped his arms around her and pulled her back against his chest. "Sounds good. I don't want you to ever be finished adding to that one, darlin'." He bent to kiss the side of her neck, and she shivered.

Her heart melted even more, if possible, for this man who intended to spend eternity with her. "That is perfect. So sweet. Thank you for understanding my artist's soul."

Facing them from the wall to the left of the bed was an elaborate shadowbox, Luke's signature carvings including sweet peas, Peruvian lilies, and a representation of their simple but meaningful wedding bands. She walked closer to peek inside.

"Our *lazo!*" She found not only the rope rosary he had made for their wedding ceremony, but other mementos from the occasion including the bag of *Arras*, with some of the coins spilling out. Opened up for all to read was the paper with their hand-written vows from their two wedding ceremonies.

She blinked back more tears. She was sentimental, perhaps, but she loved that her husband was, too. "Thank you for preserving our wedding memories so beautifully."

"Well, I have a bit of an artist's soul myself, darlin'."

She spun toward him and returned to his arms. "Yes, you do. One of the first things that endeared you to me was talking about art at Karla's while Adam was recovering."

He grasped her arms and gently pushed her away until he met her gaze. "What? I didn't think you even noticed I existed."

She smiled. "Oh, I noticed. I did not know what to do about you, but I definitely noticed. At the time, I thought my body's response was its usual fear, but at some point since the avalanche, it became clear that it was not fear at all."

He bent down and kissed her lips, taking her breath away. When he stood again, she surveyed the room to see what other surprises it held.

On the nightstand, she saw another framed piece. Breaking away from him, she crossed the room to pick it up. It was the photograph Megan had taken of her at the stream, silhouetted by the sun. "I was going to surprise you with that!"

"Well now, my seeing it was accidental. Megan was editing photos one day up here when I stopped by to check on the progress with construction—she and Ryder camped out a lot during the project and sometimes stayed in the studio if the weather was bad. Anyway, when I saw it on her laptop, I knew it had to be framed and displayed in our bedroom—but for my eyes only."

Honored.

He smiled nervously when she did not say anything. "Welcome home, Cassie."

She launched herself at him and wrapped her arms around his neck. "Oh, Luke, really? I love you so much!" He grabbed her around the waist and swung her in a circle a few times.

"I feel an unbreakable connection to Iron Horse Peak."

Luke's thumb brushed her cheek. "Why's that?"

"Because this mountain brought you to me."

Glossary of Terms
for *Nobody's Dream*

4-H—Though typically thought of as an agriculturally focused organization because of its history, 4-H today focuses on citizenship, healthy living, science, engineering, and technology programs. Its goal is to develop citizenship, leadership, responsibility, and life skills of youth through experiential learning programs and a positive youth development approach. The name represents four personal development areas of focus for the organization: head, heart, hands, and health. Luke was a member of 4-H as a boy.

Abuelos—grandparents, in Spanish

Aji Panca peppers—The Panca chili (or *Ají Panca* as it's known in South America), is a deep red to burgundy pepper, measuring 3-5 inches. It is the second most common pepper in Peru, and is grown near the coast. It has a rather sweet, berry-like, and slightly smoky flavor. The *Ají Panca* can be made into a paste or dried and minced to be used as a condiment. They can be found for sale on the internet in either form. Used in Peruvian cooking, the Panca is great for stews, sauces and fish dishes. See **Puca Picante** below for a link to a recipe Cassie makes for Luke.

Amor—love, in Spanish

Astral projection—(also known as **astral travel**) is an interpretation of out-of-body experience (OBE) that assumes the existence of an "astral body" separate from the physical body and capable of travelling outside it.

Bambina—female child, in Italian (Marc's nickname for Marisol)

Blocking sled—a heavy piece of American football practice equipment, usually a padded angular frame on metal skids, used for developing strength and blocking techniques.

Boarding a horse—where a stable or farm provides the service of feeding and caring for one or more horses in exchange for money or barter. Also known as agistment in Australia/New Zealand

BP—blood pressure

Braxton-Hicks contractions—intermittent weak contractions of the uterus occurring during pregnancy (over the months prior to active labor)

Caldo de gallina—In the highlands, soups like *"caldo de gallina"* made with a hen broth are part of the regular breakfast. Traditionally, Andean highlanders need meals that support them in the cold weather and with their high level of activity.

Camerera—barmaid, in Spanish

Cara—dear, in Italian

Casarse—to marry me, in Spanish (rather than directed at someone being asked to marry, which would be casarme)

Chica—girl, in Spanish

Chicha morada—a sweet, fruity punch popular in Peru that is made from purple corn

Cria—baby alpaca

Déjà vu—a feeling of having already experienced the present situation, in French.

Desert Digitals—digital camouflage uniform worn by Marines, also referred to as MARPAT (Marine Pattern), Digitals, or digis/diggis

Dom/sub or D/s Dynamic in BDSM—a relationship in which the Dominant(s) is given control by consent of the submissive(s) or bottom(s) to make most, if not all, of the decisions in a play scene or in relationships with the submissive(s) or bottom(s).

"¡Ella no está!"—"She is gone!" in Spanish

"Es mi turno."—"It's my turn." in Spanish

"¡Eso es tan hermoso!"—"It is beautiful!" in Spanish. I chose the masculine because it is ambiguous whether Cassie is referring to the design (masculine) or the shoulder cloth (feminine), in which cases masculine is dominant.

Graciela—"grace," in Spanish

Gringo—derogatory term for American or white man, in Spanish

Head—bathroom (Navy/Marine jargon)

Huayno—a flirtatious Peruvian courting dance

In utero—in the uterus

IPA—India Pale Ale

IV—intravenous needle and tubing for delivering liquids, medicines to patients

Ka-thunk!®—the way Karla describes the feeling of her stomach dropping when a Dominant gives her a "Dom" stare, command, or praise; the word has been trademarked by Kallypso Masters LLC

K'eperina—a large, rectangular carrying cloth worn over the back and knotted in front. Children and goods are securely held inside.

Karma—the sum of a person's actions in this and previous states of existence, viewed as deciding their fate in future existences

Killa—"moon," in Quechua (spelled *Quilla* in Spanish)

Lliclla—a small, rectangular, hand-woven shoulder cloth fastened at the front using a *tupu*, a decorated pin.

Madrinas—godmothers, in Spanish

Mama Quilla—a goddess revered by the indigenous people of the Andes. Quilla is Spanish for moon; can also be spelled Mama Killa (in Quechua). She is a guardian of women and for marriage unions.

Maman—mother or mama, in French. NOTE: Savannah's mother was born in France and responded to Maman, as does Savannah with her daughter

Mamina—nickname for grandmother, in Spanish

Marinera—a Peruvian dance

Mi hija—my daughter, in South American Spanish (not spelled the same as the Mexican version, *mija or m'ija*)

Milagrosa—means "miracle," in Spanish; name for one of the alpacas

Mohena—a tropical hardwood very similar to but stronger or sturdier than Mahogany

Montera—hat, in Spanish. Hats vary tremendously throughout the communities in the Andes. Often it is possible to identify the village from which a woman comes from just by the type of hat she wears. Hats are secured with delicately woven *sanq'apa* straps adorned with white beads.

Narthex—vestibule of the church

NICU—Neonatal Intensive Care Unit where premature and high-risk newborns are treated

No es nada—it is nothing, in Spanish

¡Nunca màs!—never again, in Spanish

Ocho—a figure eight traced on the floor in a tango by the follower's feet.

Old Maid—a single woman regarded as too old for marriage.

Pachamama—a goddess revered by the indigenous people of the Andes. She is also known as the earth/time mother.

Padrinos—godfathers, in Spanish

Polleras—a colorful skirt, in Spanish. Made from hand-woven wool cloth called *bayeta*. Women may wear 3 or 4 skirts in a graduated layered effect. On special occasions such as festivals women may wear up to 15 polleras tied around the waist. Often the trim of each skirt is lined with a colorful *puyto* which is usually handmade. In some areas polleras are also referred to as *melkkhay* (Quechua)

Puerco—pig, in Spanish (Latin American)

Puca Picante—literally, Red (puca—Quechua) and Hot (picante—Spanish). This is a Peruvian dish (can be vegetarian) made primarily from beets and potatoes; see photo and recipe at perude-lights.com/meatlessmondays-puca-picante-spicy-red

Punulla Waway—a Quechua lullaby

Qhawa—"one who watches, one who monitors," in Quechua

Quaking Aspens—a poplar tree with rounded, long-stalked, and typically coarsely toothed leaves that tremble in even a slight breeze

Que Bueno—very good, in Spanish.

Quipu—an ancient Inca device for recording information, consisting of variously colored threads knotted in different ways.

Safeword—a word agreed upon prior to a BDSM scene that can be used to end (temporarily or completely) a play scene

SAR—Search and Rescue

Sat Phone—satellite phone that has coverage in remote areas where cell phones are not as useful

Scree Slope—scree is a mass of naturally occurring small loose stones that form or cover a slope on a mountain

Shibari—also known as Kinbaku, a Japanese style of bondage popular in the BDSM lifestyle that involves tying up the bottom/submissive using simple yet visually intricate, sometimes artistic, patterns.

Shibori—Japanese word for a variety of ways of embellishing textiles by shaping cloth and securing it before dyeing. The word comes from the verb root shiboru, "to wring, squeeze, press."

Sí—yes, in Spanish (or Italian)

SNAFU (snafu)—Situation Normal, All Fucked Up (a Marine Corps expression)

Sous chef—the culinary chef located just below the executive or head chef in a kitchen's chain of command; a vital role in any commercial kitchen.

Starter—a general term used to describe sourdough before it is added to bread dough. Starter needs to be "fed" with flour or other suitable foods (e.g. sprouts, soaked grain) to keep it active and make it strong enough to raise bread dough. The starter can be shared with others so they can "start" their own for breadmaking.

Suyana—"hope," in Quechua

Tarukaq mosqoyning—Quechua song meaning "Dreams of a Deer"

"¡Te ves hermosa!"—"You look beautiful!" in Spanish

Tía—aunt, in Spanish

Tika—"flower," in Quechua

"Todo va a estar bein, estamos seguros aqui."—"Everything's going to be okay. We're safe here." in Spanish

Tupu—the decorative pin, often made of precious metals like gold or silver, used to pin together the shoulder cloth, or k'eperina, worn traditionally by Peruvian women.

UT—University of Texas

Vamoose—to depart quickly

"Whose turn in the barrel?"—Kally asked her Marine subject expert, Top Griz, how Adam might ask for volunteers in Marine speak. He said: "He could just let them know it was their turn in the barrel."

Zia—aunt, in Italian

About the Author

USA Today bestseller author Kallypso Masters writes emotional, realistic Romance novels with an emphasis on healing using sometimes unconventional methods. Her alpha males are dominant and attracted to strong women who can bring them to their knees. Kally also has brought many readers to their knees—having them experience the stories along with her characters in the Rescue Me Saga. Kally knows that Happily Ever After takes maintenance, so her couples don't solve all their problems and disappear at "the end" of "their" novel, but will continue to work on real problems in their relationships in later books in the Saga.

Kally has been writing full-time since May 2011. She lives in rural Kentucky and has been married almost 32 years to the man who provided her own Happily Ever After. They have two adult children, one adorable grandson, and a rescued dog and cat.

Kally enjoys meeting readers. Check out the Appearances page on her web site to see if she'll be near you!

To contact or interact with Kally,

go to Facebook,

her Facebook Author page,

or Twitter (@kallypsomasters),

or her Web site (KallypsoMasters.com).

To join the secret Facebook group Rescue Me Saga Discussion Group, please send a friend request to Karla Paxton and she will open the door for you. (Please give her a few days!) Must be 18 to join.

For more timely updates and a chance to win great prizes, get sneak peeks at unedited excerpts, and more, sign up for her newsletter (sent out via e-mail) and/or for text alerts (used ONLY for new releases of e-books or print books) at her Web site (http://kallypsomasters.com). And feel free to e-mail her at kallypsomasters@gmail.com, or write to her at

Kallypso Masters

PO Box 1183

Richmond, KY 40476-1183

Get your Kally Swag!

Looking for your own Ka-thunk! shirt, a culinary bondage tee or apron, even an evil stick handmade by Toymaker and eirocawakening? How about signed paperbacks of any available books in the Rescue Me Saga? With each order, you will receive a bag filled with other swag items, as well, including pens, bookmarks, trading cards (with the original covers of the early books), and whatever is available and fits in the swag bag. Kally ships internationally. To shop, go to kallypsomasters.com/kally_swag.

Excerpt from
Nobody's Lost
by
Kallypso Masters

(Fifth in the *Rescue Me Saga*)

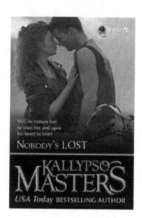

Prologue

Fallujah, Iraq, 15 November 2004

Ryder Wilson enjoyed talking with Lance Corporal Grant. She was young, but sure as hell knew her shit when it came to advanced satellite communications.

His recon Marine unit had been on this rooftop in Fallujah for hours, waiting for something to break and to go after the insurgents who had terrorized this part of the city for the last few days.

Too damned quiet. Sergeant Miller suggested they eat in shifts while they could. He was informing Damián Orlando of the SITREP while Ryder spent time getting to know the Marine newly attached to their unit.

Didn't usually find women Marines assigned to combat units, although the cease-fire they were under meant they probably wouldn't have any direct engagement. He hoped not anyway.

"So where are you from?" Grant asked.

"Born and raised in New Mexico. Albuquerque. How about you?"

"Army brat. I've lived all over and then some."

"That why you enlisted?"

Silence dragged out before she responded. "I guess so. Pissed my dad off that I didn't choose the Army, but I had something to prove to myself. I just hope I'm still in when women Marines are allowed to serve in combat."

"Not so sure that's a good idea."

She sat up straighter and glared at him. "Why not? I can perform just as—"

"Grenade!"

Orlando's voice jarred them from the conversation. He and Sergeant Miller were hurtling across the rooftop in their direction when the sound of an explosion threw Ryder against the wall he'd been leaning on. His ears rang from the blast. They were under fire.

Momentarily dazed, Ryder tried to remember what he had been doing, but his focus shifted to protecting Lance Corporal Grant. She was his responsibility and shouldn't be in the middle of this shit.

"Get behind me," he said, picking up his rifle.

"Sergeant Miller and Orlando have been hit." Ignoring him, she moved toward the two fallen Marines, and he followed.

"*Madre de Dios*! No! Sergeant, don't you fucking die!"

Orlando was lying under the body of Sergeant Miller. *Holy fuck!* Ryder and Grant reached the body at about the same time and lifted their Sergeant off Orlando with reverence and speed combined.

"Corpsman up!" Ryder called. Once they had set Sergeant's body down, they returned to check on Orlando.

Jesus, no. His foot dangled by what looked like some skin and meat alone. Where was Doc? Grant grabbed Orlando's hand and spoke to him. Ryder had never seen so much carnage in all his years serving in the Marines.

Ryder moved so Doc could assess the situation and keep Orlando alive.

"Keep his head down!" Doc ordered, and Ryder moved to his head where he placed one hand on the young private's forehead and another on his shoulder. Ryder filled Doc in on what had happened, but the mention of Sergeant's name had him glancing over at the man's head.

So much blood.

The hiss of an RPG made it clear the attack was still under way. Ryder realized he hadn't done his damned job. He radioed their immediate need for artillery and air support with their preplanned fire coordinates.

Doc shouted, "Let's get him off the roof!"

"Sure thing, Doc!" With Doc's help, he and Grant lifted an unconscious Orlando onto a litter...

* * *

Just after midnight

Ryder rolled over in bed, drenched in sweat. His heart pounding, he gasped for breath. Fucking nightmares. He laid his arm over his eyes, but the images came back in living color. Vivid, but different than the one the other night.

Blast.

Brains.

Blood.

Sergeant Miller's lifeless body. Damián Orlando's foot blown off. Doc D'Alessio nearly killed.

Jesus, I fucked up that mission. While he was shooting the shit with Grant, all hell broke out for his unit.

His cell phone buzzed. *Not now.* He didn't want to speak to anyone until he had time to regroup. Tossing the sheet aside, he sat up. A beer. That ought to take the edge off.

Before he could open the door to the fridge, his landline phone rang. Whoever it was could leave a message. He wasn't talking to anyone tonight. Even if it was Marcia. He could call his sister back in an hour or however long it took to regain control of himself.

The answering machine kicked in, and he waited for his sister's voice.

"Wilson. Pick up the phone. Adam Montague here."

How the fuck did Top have his phone number? He must have been the one calling on the cell, too.

Had Orlando mentioned to his former master sergeant that they had run into each other a couple of months ago on a Patriot Guard ride in southern Colorado? He had known it was a bad idea to go, but the man being buried had served with him in Kosovo. To lay low during his funeral would have been disrespectful, and he damn well wouldn't let any asshole activist protester disrupt his buddy finally being laid to rest.

Another brave and hurting hero's fucking suicide.

Other than the Patriot Guard Riders, Ryder had severed all ties to those who survived the past and had hoped Orlando would respect his request not to say anything to the others. He wanted to put all that behind him.

The nightmare from the mayhem on the rooftop in Fallujah told him he wasn't doing a very good job of that, though. He reached for the phone.

"Yes, Top. Sorry. I was…in the head."

"Glad I waited. How're you doing?"

"Great. Got myself a nice place in the Jemez Mountains. Nice and quiet."

Nobody bothers me, and I sure as hell don't bother anyone else.

"Sounds good." Top paused a moment. "Listen, Wilson, my sister is staying at our brother's place in Albuquerque. I have no fucking clue what's wrong, but when I called a little while ago, she said the police were there. Also said she'd call me back when they left, but I haven't heard a thing. Patrick's out of the country, and I'm worried about her."

"Sorry to bother you this late, but would you mind running over to make sure she's okay? It would mean a lot to me knowing someone I trust has taken a look around."

Go into the city? All those people? Adrenaline kicked in, and Ryder's heart began pounding.

A mission. His master sergeant hadn't given him orders in nearly eight years.

Someone I trust.

The desire to live up to those words and help the man who had brought him and nearly every man home from their deployments outweighed Ryder's penchant for drowning in his own shit.

"Sure, Top." He reached for a pen and pad of paper. "What's the address?" The neighborhood was more familiar than he liked. Ryder also jotted down her name—Megan Gallagher. Must be married since they didn't have the same last names. Why wasn't her husband looking in on her?

But Ryder would help where he could. She was Top's sister. That's all that mattered.

After also taking down a couple of phone numbers where he could reach Top, he said goodbye and tucked the paper inside his jeans pocket before returning to the bedroom to grab a long-sleeved flannel shirt and his leather jacket. It got colder than a witch's tit when the sun went down here in the high desert. Riding a Harley without a windscreen didn't help.

But he preferred to detach it when he rode alone. He couldn't stand being cooped up in a car or truck either. Needed to be able to breathe—and have an unobstructed view of any potential threat. Usually, his treks were on mountain roads and small highways, limiting the danger.

Not like tonight. The lights of the Albuquerque valley spread out before him as he headed south on I-25. He couldn't avoid the city this time.

Still, he wished he was alone back at Carlos's house in the mountains. Being around people wore him down quicker than the road.

Only because you asked, Top.

A man didn't turn his back on his Marine family, ever—no matter how fucked up he was. He hadn't been in a real city in nearly two years. If he needed anything he couldn't acquire for himself, his friend Carlos usually took care of it. But Ryder prided himself on being self-sufficient. He might be totally useless as far as holding a job went, but he didn't take handouts.

If he'd truly gone off the grid, Master Sergeant Montague never would have found him. But he kept a phone because of his sister Marcia in Santa Fe. Maybe he'd tracked him through phone records. But didn't he say he'd just heard from his sister about some trouble? Had he already known Ryder's number? No answers came as the lights of the valley grew brighter.

Fucking city. God, he hated being around that many people.

Just let me keep it together in front of Top's sister.

The last thing he wanted was for his unit to find out how badly he was handling the aftermath of his years in service. He'd tried going to the VA, but they were too far away—in miles and philosophy—to be of much help.

Hell, why was *he* so screwed up? He'd come home. In one piece, even. Look at Orlando. He'd adjusted well to his amputation, at least from what Ryder could tell from their brief meeting during the Alamosa PGR procession. If he hadn't seen the man's foot blown off by that damned grenade with his own eyes, Ryder would never have guessed Orlando wore a prosthesis.

Why couldn't Ryder put the past behind him like everyone else in his unit had done?

Chapter One

Megan Gallagher surveyed the makeshift studio she'd set up in her brother's condo only a couple of weeks ago. She balled her hands into fists. How dare someone break in and steal her property?

Some welcome to New Mexico.

Her brother had invited her to stay with him this summer after she graduated from USC in Los Angeles. She wanted to build a strong portfolio before deciding what to do next with her MFA. Well, looked like she'd be going computer shopping tomorrow. She couldn't postpone it because she needed to finish editing the photos she'd shot this past week for some clients who answered her local ad.

Two of Albuquerque's finest had left ten minutes ago after taking her report. As soon as she came home from dinner and saw the garage door open when she'd most definitely left it closed, she'd called 911 and waited for them to check the premises before going inside. They'd asked her to see what was missing. As far as she could tell, nothing but her computer, but she'd told them her brother would have to take inventory of his possessions after he returned Sunday or Monday.

Her studio props and lighting equipment stood where she'd left them. No street value on those, she supposed.

Brother dear needed to improve his security system, although breaking into Fort Knox might be simpler considering all the numbers she had to push to open the garage door.

Why hadn't the alarm gone off during the break-in?

She doubted anyone would be arrested and brought to justice, but felt better for reporting the crime. At least Patrick's fireproof safe was secure. It held her more expensive cameras and the external memory drive where she stored photos not still in her online cloud backup. Patrick's weapons were in there, too.

Thankfully, she took her digital SLR wherever she went. The heavier cameras in the safe were used more often for her studio work. She'd just leave them there.

No sense trying to call Patrick about this. He said he'd only be in Italy briefly before flying to Pakistan with someone he was co-piloting for. The man went to great extremes to build up his flight hours.

The thought of staying here tonight didn't hold as much appeal as it once had. Her sense of security had been shattered by the thieves. What if they returned for more? Suddenly afraid, she went to the bedroom and retrieved her own pistol, prepared to take on any intruders.

In the kitchen again, she opened the garage door from the box on the kitchen wall, but her cell phone buzzed before she could go into the garage. She glanced down at the caller ID.

Adam again?

Oh, crap! She'd forgotten all about him.

She'd met her long-lost half-brother for the first time last Thanksgiving. He'd called her while the police were here, and she'd forgotten to call him back to let him know what had happened. Did Marines come with internal radar or something? Or had he been calling to let her know how his wife Karla was doing?

He'd worry more if she didn't answer, so she returned to the kitchen and dead-bolted the interior door before accepting the call.

"Megan, is everything all right? What happened?" The concern in his voice was palpable.

She cleared her throat, knowing her silence would only stress him out more. "I'm fine. Some asshats broke into Patrick's place and stole my computer."

"Well, f—." She smiled hearing him reroute his mouth around the expletive she knew had almost spewed out. "You need to get out of there, but stay put a little longer. I've sent someone to check on you."

Without even knowing what the problem was? The man didn't let any moss grow under his boots.

"Are you armed?"

She smiled again. "Patrick made sure I knew how to use a weapon before I went to college."

"You didn't get too rusty while on campus?"

"No. Went to the firing range regularly."

"Good for you. I'm going to stay on the phone with you until Wilson shows up."

She guessed she ought to be thankful he hadn't sent in a platoon of Marines. Still, knowing someone was on the way did make her feel a little less scared.

"How's Karla doing?"

"She's fine. Tired mostly. We just took four days to drive back from a Memorial Day weekend wedding in San Diego County. Remember Damián Orlando?"

"Yes." Adam treated him like a son. One of his beloved Marines.

"Anyway, Karla's trying to get some shut-eye. It's not easy these days."

"I can imagine. Give her a hug and kiss from me. I hate to take you away from her tonight."

"Oh…well, she'll sleep better if I'm not in the bed with her." His voice sounded funny, but she smiled as she remembered taking some special photos of Karla a few months ago when the family came together in Denver for a weekend. He was in for one heck of a surprise, but they had turned out beautifully. Still, Megan regretted she would never—

"How's mom doing?" Adam interrupted her thoughts, thankfully. He had only just found their shared mother again after spending decades on his own from the age of sixteen.

"Going as strong as ever. She's glad the weather's improving so she won't be cooped up inside as much." Being wheelchair-bound kept her mother from traversing Chicago's snowy streets, but her attendants made sure she had regular outings. Megan had never known her mom to feel sorry for herself. And, having been paralyzed long before Megan had been born, she had never thought anything odd about having her mother confined to a wheelchair.

While Adam talked about the wedding he'd just attended, Megan looked around to see what else she should pack in her SUV. The safe provided more security for her equipment than she would have inside her SUV or a hotel room. The thieves hadn't tried to break into the safe, either, according to the police. No, she didn't really see much of anything she needed to take with her. Just the overnight bag.

But would she really only be away from the condo one night?

She sighed. "Uh-huh." She should be listening to the phone conversation, but her mind was too rattled to focus.

How long would she have to wait around for Adam's Marine to show up so she could send him on his way? No doubt in her mind that he would come, though. At Adam's wedding, she'd witnessed how much the men and women who served with him adored the retired master sergeant. Any of them would move heaven and earth to please him.

With any luck, the Marine would quickly see she could take care of her own problems and leave.

*   *   *

The roar of the hog's engine lulled him away from giving in to the anxiety nipping at his heels like a rabid dog. He had memorized the woman's address and merged onto I-40 as he headed toward the Sandias. She lived in one of the older neighborhoods in the foothills there. Couple of miles farther.

The sound of a long-range rifle split the air. *Sniper!*

Ryder ducked and tried to take evasive maneuvers into another lane. No, wait. That wasn't a rifle. A fucking car must have backfired. Thank God the highway was nearly deserted at this hour. He could have gotten himself or someone else killed.

Maintain control. You're okay. No one is gunning for you.

He repeated those phrases for the duration of the fifteen-minute drive to her exit. The quiet residential streets helped him relax somewhat, but there were too many fucking places for insurgents to hide with all these houses and condos.

No one is aiming for you. Get a fucking grip.

Barely two o'clock in the morning. No doubt he'd piss off some of the older residents in this wealthy neighborhood. Easing off the throttle, he slowed and rounded the corner onto the street where he'd once lived. Impossible to keep a hog quiet, so he gave up.

The houses began to look familiar. Not much had changed since he lived here as a teenager. He passed by the place his mom had owned and tried not to stare. He'd lived there with her and his sister until she lost the place. Ryder married Sherry at nineteen, and his mom moved into an apartment about the same time Marcia relocated to Santa Fe. Like him, his sister preferred the beat of her own drum.

A few years later, unable to find steady work, he joined the Marine Corps. Maybe he'd just wanted to escape from family problems.

How'd that work out for you?

His mom died while he was in the Corps. No chance to reconcile.

He loved his Marine family, but, man, he'd sure gotten himself fucked up over there. Big-ass wuss. Couldn't be around people more than a few hours now without shutting down or running away.

Just keep your focus on Top's sister—then get your ass home.

Three blocks later, he pulled into a cul-de-sac and parked in the driveway beside a luxury townhouse. Why was the garage wide open? The BMW motorcycle parked in the corner sure didn't fit the mental image he had of Adam's sister. Must be her brother's.

Ryder eased his helmet off and retrieved the knife from his boot. A month in the psych ward at the VA hospital and he'd voluntarily surrendered his sidearm and shotgun to Carlos. Last thing he wanted was to have one of those night terrors lead to him blowing his brains out. So many veterans had lost that battle…

Not that he couldn't use other means, but if he was going to do it, he'd make sure he succeeded with one try.

Even without a sidearm, he could cause a lot of damage to an insurg— no, intruder—with his Bowie. Carlos's people had taught him well.

He heard a woman's voice coming from inside the house. He relaxed a bit. Probably Adam's sister. Her voice sounded younger than her forty- or fifty-something age.

"Megan Gallagher? Ryder Wilson out here. Your brother Adam sent me to check on you."

She said something he couldn't hear and then yelled, "Speak loudly. Adam's on the phone and wants you to confirm you are who you say you are."

"No worries." At least she didn't let just anyone inside.

She spoke into the phone and listened before relaying the message to Ryder. "Adam asked me to ask you where the two of you first met."

"Kosovo. I was a replacement for one of his recon Marines."

Apparently, Adam gave her the go-ahead to let him inside. "Okay. Talk to you later. Love you, too."

The still night air was split by the sound of a deadbolt unlocking, and the door opened slowly.

"Sorry. My brother taught me to be careful."

"Megan Gallagher?"

She nodded and extended her hand in greeting.

Holy fuck. The woman standing before him was years younger than Ryder had expected. How much younger was she than Top?

Her dark auburn hair spilled over her shoulders, long and thick. A man's hands could get lost in those curls. She didn't look anything like Top, who had dark hair and Lakota blood. She looked more Irish or maybe Scottish.

He couldn't make out the color of her eyes in the dim light, but imagined they sparkled with life and humor. A tiny nose sprinkled with freckles and full, red lips adorned the most beautiful face he'd ever seen.

Man, what would it be like to kiss her? He hadn't kissed a woman since his ex walked out on him five years ago.

Shit. What was he doing thinking about kissing her? This was Top's sister. Top's *little* sister! His master sergeant would have his hide if he did anything inappropriate with her.

God, he hoped he didn't fuck up this mission. He needed to redeem himself in Top's eyes.

"Close the garage door before anyone gets in."

The *Rescue Me Saga*

Masters at Arms & Nobody's Angel (Combined Volume)

(First in the *Rescue Me Saga*)

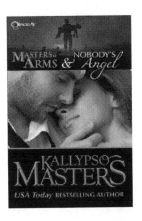

Masters at Arms is an introduction to the *Rescue Me Saga*, which needs to be read first. The book begins the journey of three men, each on a quest for honor, acceptance, and to ease his unspoken pain. Their paths cross at one of the darkest points in their lives. As they try to come to terms with the aftermath of Iraq—forging an unbreakable bond—they band together to start their own BDSM club. But will they ever truly become masters of their own fates? Or would fate become master of them?

Nobody's Angel: Marc d'Alessio might own a BDSM club with his fellow military veterans, Adam and Damián, but he keeps all women at a distance. However, when Marc rescues beautiful Angelina Giardano from a disastrous first BDSM experience at the club, an uncharacteristic attraction leaves him torn between his safe, but lonely world, and a possible future with his angel.

Angelina leaves BDSM behind, only to have her dreams plagued by the Italian angel who rescued her at the club. When she meets Marc at a bar in her hometown, she can't shake the feeling she knows him—but has no idea why he reminds her of her angel.

Nobody's Hero

(Second in the *Rescue Me Saga*)

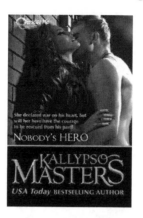

Retired Marine Master Sergeant Adam Montague has battled through four combat zones, but now finds himself retreating from Karla Paxton, who has declared war on his heart. With a significant age difference, he feels he should be her guardian and protector, not her lover. But Karla's knack for turning up in his bed at inopportune times is killing his resolve to do the right thing. Karla isn't the young girl he rescued nine years earlier—something his body reminds him of every chance it gets.

Their age difference is only part of the problem. Fifty-year-old Adam has been a collector of lost and vulnerable souls most of his life, but a secret he has run from for more than three decades has kept him emotionally unable to admit love for anyone. Will Karla be able to break through the defenses around his heart and help him put the ghosts from his past to rest? In her all-out war to get Adam to surrender his heart, will the strong-willed Goth singer offer herself as his submissive and, if so, at what cost to herself?

Nobody's Perfect

(Third in the *Rescue Me Saga*)

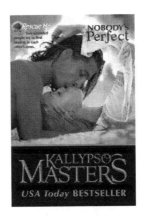

Savannah/Savi escaped eleven years of abuse at the hands of her father and finally made a safe life for herself and her daughter. But when her father once again threatens her peace of mind—and her daughter's safety—Savi runs to Damian Orlando for protection. Eight years earlier as Savannah, she shared one perfect day with Damian that changed both their young lives and resulted in a secret she no longer can hide. But being with Damian reawakens repressed memories and feelings she wants to keep buried. After witnessing a scene with Damian on Savi's first night at his private club, however, she begins to wonder if he could help her regain control of her life and reclaim her sexuality and identity.

Damian, a wounded warrior, has had his own dragons to fight in life, but has never forgotten Savannah. He will lay down his life to protect her and her daughter, but doesn't believe he can offer more than that. She deserves a whole man, something he can never be after a firefight in Iraq. Damian has turned to SM to regain control of his life and emotions and fulfills the role of Service Top to "bottoms" at the club. However, he could never deliver those services to Savi, who needs someone gentle and loving, not the man he has become.

Will two wounded survivors find love and healing in each other's arms?

Somebody's Angel

(Fourth in the *Rescue Me Saga*)

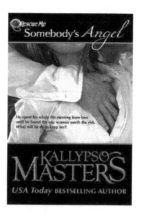

When Marc d'Alessio first rescued the curvaceous and spirited Italian Angelina Giardano at the Masters at Arms Club, he never expected her to turn his safe, controlled life upside down and pull at his long-broken heartstrings. Months later, the intense fire of their attraction still rages, but something holds him back from committing to her completely. Worse, secrets and memories from his past join forces to further complicate his relationships with family, friends, and his beautiful angel.

Angelina cannot give all of herself to someone who hides himself from her. She loves Marc, the BDSM world he brought her into, and the way their bodies respond to one another, but she needs more. Though she destroyed the wolf mask he once wore, only he can remove the mask he dons daily to hide his emotions. In a desperate attempt to break through his defenses and reclaim her connection to the man she loves, she attempts a full frontal assault that sends him into a fast retreat, leaving her nobody's angel once again.

Marc finds that running to the mountains no longer gives him solace but instead leaves him empty and alone. Angelina is the one woman worth the risk of opening his heart. Will he risk everything to become the man she deserves and the man he wants to be?

Nobody's Lost

(Fifth in the *Rescue Me Saga*)

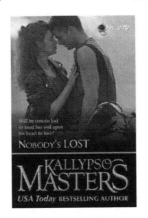

Ryder Wilson returned from serving multiple deployments, but can't leave the hell of combat behind him. Frustrated and ashamed of his inability to function in the world, unlike the veterans he had served with, Ryder retreated. When sent on a mission to protect the sister of retired Master Sergeant Adam Montague, Ryder's days of hiding out may be over. Can he fulfill his mission without failing again?

Megan Gallagher has two big-brother Marines bent on protecting her from the evils of the world, but she's tougher than they think. When her older brother sends Ryder, one of his recon Marines, to her doorstep in the wee hours one night following a break-in, she realizes he needs rescuing more than she does. A friendship forms quickly, but unexpected passions run hot and complicate her resolve never to have a romantic relationship, much less marriage. So why are her body and her heart betraying her every time he comes near?

Can these two wounded people lower their defenses long enough to allow love to grow?

Nobody's Dream

(Sixth in the *Rescue Me Saga*)

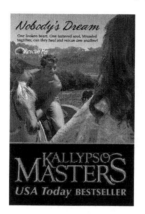

One broken heart.

One battered soul.

No one said life would be fair or easy. Quiet, Peruvian-born artist Cassie Lopez learned this the hard way. Betrayed by the man she planned to marry, she shut herself off as far away from all but her closest friend from college...

Until the night Luke Denton came crashing into her Colorado mountain sanctuary with a vengeance. Confused by her heart's response to this kind and gentle man, Cassie pushes herself to help the cowboy recover quickly so she can send him on his way. But Luke's patience and understanding threaten to break down the very defenses she needs to survive in this world after he's gone.

Search-and-Rescue worker Luke, who lost his wife and unborn child in a tragic accident, also knows firsthand of the unfairness of life. He keeps his own nightmares at bay by focusing on his rescue activities, most recently adopting and working with abused and neglected horses.

Can two wounded people find trust and love together? Do nightmares end where dreams come true?